THE TRAITOR'S WIFE

THE TRAITOR'S WIFE

A Novel of the Reign of Edward II

Susan Higginbotham

iUniverse, Inc.
New York Lincoln Shanghai

The Traitor's Wife

A Novel of the Reign of Edward II

iUniverse books may be ordered through booksellers or by contacting:

iUniverse
2021 Pine Lake Road, Suite 100
Lincoln, NE 68512
www.iuniverse.com
1-800-Authors (1-800-288-4677)

ISBN-13: 978-0-595-35959-2 (pbk)
ISBN-13: 978-0-595-80409-2 (ebk)
ISBN-10: 0-595-35959-0 (pbk)
ISBN-10: 0-595-80409-8 (ebk)

Printed in the United States of America

To my family

Acknowledgments

In researching this novel, I was fortunate to have access, as a member of the public, to the libraries at the University of North Carolina at Chapel Hill. Without its facilities I would have been greatly hampered in my ability to complete this novel. I also benefited from the use of the Wake County public library system, the Duke University library, and the North Carolina State University library. I thank these institutions, and in the appropriate cases the taxpayers of North Carolina, for making these invaluable resources available.

I found two online resources extremely useful. Through reading the postings at Gen-Medieval-L, I obtained valuable information about the genealogy of the Clare and Despenser families, including new findings. Many of these findings are mentioned at www.medievalgenealogy.org.uk. I would like in particular to thank Brad Verity, a poster on Gen-Medieval-L, who shared his findings about Eleanor de Clare's children both with the group as a whole and with me personally. Any errors, genealogical and otherwise, that I have stumbled into are, of course, my own.

My most heartfelt thanks goes to my family. My parents, Charles and Barbara Higginbotham, have encouraged me and aided me in every way possible. My husband, Don Coomes, has encouraged me, humored me, and put up patiently with my Mrs. Jellyby–like abstraction. I can think of no luckier wife than myself. Finally, my children, Thad and Bethany, endured many tedious hours at the library, bore with my hogging the family computer, and have given me indescribable joy.

Characters

Noble families in fourteenth-century England generally named their children after the royal family and after their own close relations, which militated severely against variety and in this novel resulted in a plethora of real-life Edwards, Hughs, Eleanors, Joans, and the like. In keeping with my personal preferences, I have not changed the names of any of the historical characters in this novel, with the single exception of Eleanor's damsel Gladys, who is actually named "Joan" in the record in which she appears.

Married women or widows, when referred to separately from their husbands, were not necessarily known by their last husband's surname or by their maiden name. The thrice-married Elizabeth de Clare is referred to in records as Elizabeth de Burgh, from her first husband's name, while Isabel le Despenser, also married three times, is referred to as Isabel de Hastings, from the name of her second husband.

The following, and my policy of trying never to have more than two people with the same first name speaking at once, may be of use to the reader. It does not purport to be a genealogical table; children and spouses who played no part in the events here are generally omitted. Major characters are all listed here; minor characters are listed when I thought their inclusion would aid the reader. Titles are those that individuals bore when they are mentioned in this novel.

The Royal Family

Edward I, King of England, married to Eleanor of Castile and Margaret of France.
Edward II, Prince of Wales and later King of England, son of Edward I and Eleanor. Married to Isabella of France.

Joan of Acre, daughter of Edward I and Eleanor. Wife to Gilbert de Clare and Ralph de Monthermer. Countess of Gloucester.

Mary, daughter of Edward I and Eleanor. Nun of Amesbury.

Elizabeth, daughter of Edward I and Eleanor. Wife to Humphrey de Bohun. Countess of Hereford.

Edmund, son of Edward I and Margaret. Earl of Kent.

Thomas, son of Edward I and Margaret. Earl of Norfolk.

Edward III, later King of England, son of Edward II and Isabella. Also known as the Earl of Chester and the Duke of Aquitaine. Married to Philippa of Hainault.

John of Eltham, son of Edward II and Isabella. Made Earl of Cornwall in 1328.

Eleanor, daughter of Edward II and Isabella. Later married to the Count of Guelders.

Joan, daughter of Edward II and Isabella. Later married to David of Scotland, later King of Scotland.

Adam, out-of-wedlock son of Edward II by Lucy, a peasant girl.

The Church

Robert Winchelsey, Archbishop of Canterbury (1294).

Walter Reynolds, Archbishop of Canterbury (1313).

Simon de Mepham, Archbishop of Canterbury (1328).

William Melton, Archbishop of York.

Walter Langton, Bishop of Coventry and Lichfield (1296).

Roger de Northburgh, Bishop of Coventry and Lichfield (1322).

John de Hothum, Bishop of Ely.

Walter Stapeldon, Bishop of Exeter.

Adam de Orleton, Bishop of Hereford, later Bishop of Worcester (1328) and Bishop of Winchester (1333).

Henry Burghersh, Bishop of Lincoln.

Stephen Gravesend, Bishop of London.

John Salmon, Bishop of Norwich (1299).

William Ayrminne, Bishop of Norwich (1325).

Hamo de Hethe, Bishop of Rochester.

John Stratford, Bishop of Winchester.

The Clares

Joan of Acre, Countess of Gloucester. Daughter to Edward I and widow of Gilbert de Clare, late Earl of Gloucester.

Gilbert de Clare, son of Joan and Gilbert. Earl of Gloucester.

Eleanor de Clare (Eleanor le Despenser), daughter of Joan and Gilbert. Married to Hugh le Despenser the younger and William la Zouche.

Margaret de Clare (Margaret d'Audley), daughter of Joan and Gilbert. Countess of Cornwall. Married to Piers Gaveston and Hugh d'Audley.

Elizabeth de Clare (Elizabeth de Burgh), daughter of Joan and Gilbert. Married to John de Burgh, Theobald de Verdon, and Roger Damory.

The Despensers

Hugh le Despenser ("the elder"). Later Earl of Winchester. Married to Isabel Beauchamp.

Hugh le Despenser ("the younger"), son of Hugh and Isabel. Married to Eleanor de Clare.

Hugh, Edward, Gilbert, John, Isabel, Joan, Eleanor (Nora), Margaret, and Elizabeth, children of Hugh and Eleanor.

Aline Burnell, daughter of Hugh and Isabel. Widowed from Edward Burnell.

Isabel de Hastings, daughter of Hugh and Isabel. Married to John de Hastings, her second husband, and Ralph de Monthermer, her third husband.

Thomas, Hugh, and Margaret, her children by John de Hastings.

Margaret de St. Amand, daughter to Hugh and Isabel. Married to John de St. Amand.

Philip le Despenser, son to Hugh and Isabel.

Nicholas de Litlyngton. Out-of-wedlock son of Hugh le Despenser the elder.

Earls and Their Kin

Edmund Fitz Alan, Earl of Arundel. Married to Alice, Countess of Arundel.

Richard Fitz Alan, later Earl of Arundel. Married to Isabel le Despenser, daughter to Hugh le Despenser the younger.

Edmund Arundel, son to Richard and Isabel.

Andrew Harclay, Earl of Carlisle.

Piers Gaveston, Earl of Cornwall. Married to Margaret de Clare.

Joan, daughter of Piers and Margaret.

Amie, out-of-wedlock daughter of Piers.

Gilbert de Clare, Earl of Gloucester. Married to Maud de Burgh.

Humphrey de Bohun, Earl of Hereford. Married to Elizabeth, daughter of Edward I.

Edward de Bohun, their son.

Thomas, Earl of Lancaster.

Henry of Lancaster, Earl of Leicester. Later Earl of Lancaster. Brother to Thomas, Earl of Lancaster.

Henry de Lacy, Earl of Lincoln.

Roger Mortimer of Wigmore, Earl of March.

Aymer de Valence, Earl of Pembroke. Married to Beatrice and to Marie de St. Pol.

Jean Bretagne, Earl of Richmond.

John Warenne, Earl of Surrey. Married to Joan of Bar, granddaughter to Edward I.

Richard de Burgh, Earl of Ulster.

Maud de Burgh, his daughter. Wife to Gilbert de Clare.

William de Burgh, his grandson, later Earl of Ulster. Son of John de Burgh and Elizabeth de Burgh.

Guy de Beauchamp, Earl of Warwick. Married to Alice, Countess of Warwick.

Thomas de Beauchamp, their son, later Earl of Warwick.

The French Royal Family

Philip IV, King of France (1285 to 1314).

Louis X, his son, King of France (1314 to 1316).

Philip V, his son, King of France (1316 to 1322).

Charles IV, his son, King of France (1322 to 1328).

Isabella, his daughter, Queen of England.

Philip VI, his nephew, King of France (1328 to1350).

The Scottish Royal Family

Robert Bruce, King of Scotland (1306 to 1329).

David Bruce, his son, King of Scotland (1329 to1371).

Donald, Earl of Mar, Robert Bruce's nephew.

Others

Hugh d'Audley, friend of Edward II, husband of Margaret de Clare.

Bartholomew Badlesmere, steward to Edward II.

Robert Baldock, Chancellor of England.

Henry de Beaumont, lord.

Simon de Bereford, associate of Roger Mortimer of Wigmore.

Thomas de Berkeley, keeper of Edward II.

Maurice de Berkeley, his son.

Ingelram Berenger, knight to Hugh le Despenser the elder.

Roger Damory, friend of Edward II, husband of Elizabeth de Burgh.

Benedict de Fulsham, pepper merchant.

Gladys, damsel to Eleanor le Despenser.

John de Grey of Rotherfield, knight.

Thomas Gurney, associate of Roger Mortimer of Wigmore.

Gwenllian, nun of Sempringham and daughter to Llywelyn ap Gruffydd, Prince of Wales.

Joan of Bar, granddaughter to Edward I, wife to Earl of Surrey, and friend to Queen Isabella.

Alice de Leygrave, former nurse to Edward II and damsel to Queen Isabella.

John Maltravers, associate of Roger Mortimer of Wigmore.

William de Montacute, friend of Edward II.

William de Montacute, his son, friend of Edward III.

Ralph de Monthermer. Married to Joan of Acre, daughter of Edward I, later to Isabel de Hastings, daughter of Hugh le Despenser the elder.

Thomas, Edward, and Joan de Monthermer, children of Ralph and Joan of Acre.

Roger Mortimer of Chirk, uncle to Roger Mortimer of Wigmore.

William Ogle, associate of Roger Mortimer of Wigmore.

Simon of Reading, knight to Hugh le Despenser the younger.

John de Ros, lord.

Thomas Wake, son-in-law of Henry, Earl of Leicester.

Isabella de Vescy, sister to Henry de Beaumont and lady to Queen Isabella.

William la Zouche. Married to Alice, Countess of Warwick, and Eleanor de Clare.

Alan, son to William la Zouche and Alice.

William, son to William la Zouche and Eleanor.

PART I

▼

MAY 1306 TO
NOVEMBER 24, 1326

CHAPTER 1

▼

MAY 1306

Prince Edward and Piers Gaveston had slept together and too late, neither of which was at all unusual. Edward was the first to awake. "Up, Perrot."

"No." His beautiful friend yawned and rolled to his side.

"You must. We have a wedding to attend. And what if my father finds you here?"

Piers considered. "Apoplexy?"

"At the least." But his friend made no move to leave the bed, and Edward did not press the matter.

"So it is your niece who is getting married. It occurs to me that I have hardly seen the girl."

"Eleanor is but thirteen. She has spent some time lately in my stepmother's household, and then she stayed at Amesbury priory with my sister Mary for a time too. She has just lately returned for her marriage."

"I cannot for the life of me understand why girls go to convents before they are married. One thinks that the company of elderly virgins would be dampening to marital ardor. Now if they went to brothels at least it would be educational and practical."

Edward swatted his friend with a pillow. He said a bit wistfully, "When Eleanor was younger I used to row her and her brother in my boat. Her sisters felt it was too unladylike, so they would never go along. But she loved it. She and Gilbert used to stick their noses in the air and pretend I was their boatman and shout orders at me." He stroked his friend's hair. "I am sorry my father gave her to Hugh le Despenser. I would have liked her to be your wife."

"I want no wife."

"Nor do I. But I must have one, and you really must yourself, you know. When I am king you shall have titles and lands and that means you must get heirs. And Eleanor would have been a fine wife for you. Sweet and shy, but with a sly wit once you get to know her."

"And now I won't have the opportunity. I shall throw myself in the Thames forthwith."

"There's her sister Margaret. A good-natured girl, not as much so as Eleanor, but a definite possibility. Elizabeth is by far the prettiest but has too much of the grande dame about her even at her young age. Yes, I would pick Margaret."

"Before I have recovered from the loss of Eleanor? For shame! Is my rival Hugh pleased with the match?"

"He ought to be, getting a Clare for a wife; I would have thought my father would have insisted on an earl for Eleanor. But who knows what young Hugh thinks of anything? He keeps his own counsel. It is disconcerting in a youth of his age." He bestowed a tender kiss on Piers. "I prefer the more open temperament."

"And so do I." Piers returned the kiss, with compound interest, and for some time afterward no talking was done.

Eleanor de Clare, some chambers away from her uncle and his friend in Westminster Palace, had been passing the morning less pleasantly, though more decorously. Though in her naiveté she was quite content with the drape of her wedding dress, the styling of her hair, and the placement of her jewels, her mother, aunts, sisters, and attendant ladies were not, and each was discontent in a different way. As her hair was debated over and rearranged for the seventh time, she snapped, "Enough, Mama! I know Hugh is not being plagued in this manner. He must take me as I am."

Gladys, a widow who had long served Eleanor's mother as a damsel and who had agreed to go into Eleanor's household, grinned. "Aye, my lady, and he won't much care what you are wearing. It will be what is underneath that will count." She patted Eleanor's rump with approval. "And he will be pleased."

Elizabeth gasped. Margaret tittered. Eleanor, however, giggled. "Do you truly think so, Gladys?"

"Of course. You're well developed for your age, and men love that. And you will be a good breeder of children, too, mark me. You will have a fine brood."

"You can tell me, Gladys. What will it be like? Tonight?"

Eleanor's mother, Joan, the Countess of Gloucester, had been sniffling sentimentally at the prospect of her first daughter's marriage. Now she raised an eyebrow. "Your little sisters, Eleanor—"

"They shall be married soon, too, won't they? They might as well know."

"We might as well," Margaret agreed.

"Each man will go about his business in his own way, my lady. But I'll wager that he will be gentle about the matter."

"Will I be expected to—help at all?" At thirteen Eleanor was not quite as naive as she pretended, having heard enough courtiers and servant girls whispering to piece together what happened on a wedding night, but it had occurred to her that no one was fussing over her hair now.

Gladys had been left entirely on her own by the gaggle of women, who were plainly finding this entertaining. When Gladys paused before answering, Mary, Eleanor's aunt the nun, piped up, "Well, answer, my dear, because I certainly can't."

"I've no doubt that once you get interested in him, my lady, you shall want to help."

Eleanor nodded and considered this in silence.

Margaret, sitting on a window seat, sighed. "I wish I was getting married," she explained.

"I'm sure you will be soon."

"And better." Elizabeth sniffed.

"Elizabeth! What mean you?" Her mother glared.

"I only repeat what I overheard you say the other day." Elizabeth was only ten, but she had the dignity of a woman twice that age. "Nelly is an earl's daughter, and Hugh is only a mere knight. He has no land to speak of. And he's not even truly handsome, like my uncle's friend Piers Gaveston."

"As though we need more of that!" Joan went over and patted her oldest daughter on the shoulder. "I did think you could have done better," she said gently, "but it was your grandfather's match, and he has always thought highly of Hugh's father, who has served him well for years. There is no reason why his fortunes should not grow in years to come." She frowned at a tangle in Eleanor's waist-length red hair—it was difficult at times to determine what was tangle and what was curl—and began to brush it out.

Eleanor glared at her youngest sister.

"Tell me," she said, submitting ungraciously to having some color put on her naturally pale cheeks, "who is this Piers to my uncle? I have never seen my uncle out of his company since we came to Westminster. And why does his being around him vex my grandfather the king so?"

Gladys became deeply interested in a discarded bracelet lying on a table. The other women stared absorbedly at Eleanor's robes. Only her little sisters looked at Eleanor, and their faces were as curious as hers.

"We must get to the abbey," Joan said. "Come, ladies."

Eleanor's husband-to-be was only nineteen, a fact that had gratified her, as she had long worried about being married to an ancient knight in his thirties or even older. He was not a stranger to her, having been brought over to meet Eleanor a few days after the contract was entered into by his father and the king, but they had exchanged only a few words and had never been alone in each other's company. It startled her as they exchanged their vows in Westminster Abbey to find that his dark, unreadable eyes were searching her face as closely as she was searching his own.

The wedding feast and the bedding ceremony that followed were subdued affairs. The elderly but still intimidating king, even though accompanied by his second queen, Margaret, more than forty years his junior, lent an air of dampening dignity to the occasion. The prince and Piers, who might have otherwise enlivened matters, behaved themselves with tedious decorum in his presence, and the other young men—all of whom had been knighted only days before in a splendid ceremony meant to provide recruits for the never-ending Scottish wars—followed suit. Only Eleanor's fourteen-year-old brother, heir to one of the greatest fortunes in England and with only his good-natured stepfather to hold him in check, felt free to overindulge in wine and to make ribald jokes so feeble that no one but his young sisters tittered at them.

Eleanor's bridal nerves, meanwhile, were beginning to show. She openly fidgeted as the priest blessed the marriage bed. She submitted to the king's toast, to the prince's toast, to her stepfather's toast, to her father-in-law's toast. When her brother began his own meandering toast, however, she snapped, "Gilbert, you fool, go to bed! All of you! Leave me alone!" To her utter mortification, she burst into tears. She yanked the covers over her head.

There was a stir among the onlookers, and then she heard Hugh's pleasant voice. "You heard my wife, good people. Let her alone." From under the covers, she heard some laughter, then the sound of feet filing out of the room. Her husband, however, had not moved. Without budging from underneath the covers, she commanded, "You, too."

"Me?"

"Especially you! I don't want to be married."

"But you have been." Hugh lifted the covers from his own end and revealed Eleanor. She had been put to bed naked by the other ladies before Hugh arrived clad only in his robe, and the expression of tolerant amusement on his face changed to admiration as he saw her body. "You're lovely, Eleanor."

"Go away!" She flounced away from him.

"You're as lovely from the back as from the front."

"Stop it!"

"You're nervous, I know. It's natural for girls getting married."

"How would you know?"

"I've sisters."

"I've a brother. But I've never set myself up as an expert on men."

He took off his robe and wrapped his arms around her, and she lay against him grudgingly as he talked into her hair. "My sister Isabel, the mildest creature in the world, threw a comb at my mother on her wedding day. Then she threw a bracelet at her servant. By the time her husband appeared she'd run out of missiles, which was fortunate for him." Hugh saw a glimmer of a smile on Eleanor's face. He began scratching her back, very slowly. "I'm nervous too, you know."

"You? Why?"

"I've only been with whores, who are paid to act delighted. So now I have a beautiful girl in my bed, to live with for the rest of our lives. What if I can't please her?"

She said confidently, "I am not beautiful."

"Who told you that?"

"My sisters, for one."

"They are silly chits." His hands were browsing. With Hugh's encouragement, Eleanor's were doing the same, rather to her surprise. "All my family, all your family, have let me know that you are too good for me. And looking at you now, I think they're right."

"They say that to you?"

Hugh's voice held a trace of bitterness. "You are the eldest daughter of a great earl, the granddaughter of the king, while I am the landless son of one of many advisors of the king. They have let me know the difference between us, believe me."

"But Hugh, I don't think that at all." She pulled back and looked at him in the candlelight. He did not have the overwhelming good looks of Gaveston, which demanded the full attention of man and woman alike, but his sharp features were agreeable and regular, and were much improved by an expression of alertness and intelligence. She had been proud to see him standing beside her at the altar, no matter what her sister had said.

"No?"

"Truly, no." She put a hand on his bare shoulder and looked imploringly at him.

"Good." He looked her in the eyes solemnly. "But someday I will make you proud of me, I swear to it. I will be the man your father was."

"Hugh."

"Yes."

"Stop *talking.*"

He laughed and kissed her, and it was much, much later when he spoke again. "Do you still want me to leave?"

Eleanor shook her head. "No." She settled herself against the body she had just learned so much about and looked up at Hugh wonderingly. "I don't ever want you to go."

CHAPTER 2

▼

FEBRUARY 1308 TO MARCH 1308

In the chill of a February morning, Dover Castle sparkled in the sunshine as though scrubbed for the occasion. It had indeed had some freshening done to it, for it was in a state of high hospitality, with flags flying and the drawbridge lowered as noble after noble rode over it. Eleanor saw none of this, however, for she was dozing in Gladys's lap in the litter that both ladies rode in.

"Nelly, is that you? Wake up!"

Eleanor stirred and opened her eyes as a young couple on horseback—her sister Margaret and her new brother-in-law, Piers Gaveston—drew beside her. "Are we near Dover?"

"We're *in* Dover, Nelly dear. Now why are you riding in that litter like a matron—I beg your pardon, my good lady—why are you riding in the litter on a fine morning like this when you could be on that fine palfrey Hugh gave you when you married?" Piers patted his steed emphatically.

Eleanor blushed. "Hugh has forbidden it."

Margaret looked puzzled, but Piers laughed. "Your modest sister is trying not to tell us that there is a young Despenser in the offing. Am I not right, sister?" Eleanor nodded. "How far along are you?"

"Three months, Gladys and I think. I did not want to tell the family until I was more sure."

"We shall keep it quiet," Margaret said. "Won't we, Piers?"

"Death itself would not drag it from me. So where is the proud father?"

"Hugh stayed behind to attend to some business of his father's. He will arrive later this morning."

"Hard-working men, your husband and your father-in-law. They can't stand to be out of harness, can they? As for me, I shall gladly shake mine off when the king arrives." He helped Eleanor out of the litter, then Gladys.

"Have you enjoyed being regent, Piers?"

"Lord, no! It's a dreary task of the sort your husband might enjoy. My only satisfaction in it has been in goading the barons. I force them to kneel before me, you know. It drives them mad."

"Piers, don't you think of the consequences of that?"

"Now, Nelly, don't you turn all dreary on me. Did they think of the consequences when they prevailed upon the old king to exile me?"

"They certainly did not," put in Piers's new bride.

Piers smiled at his fourteen-year-old wife, nearly ten years his junior. "Indeed, they did not."

It had been a year before when the king had ordered Piers's exile. Eleanor had learned it from her father-in-law, the elder Hugh. She and her husband had been lounging in the great hall of Loughborough, one of the elder Despenser's best manors. Gilbert, her older brother, was with them, having dropped in for a several days' visit as was his wont. The elder Hugh, who had been attending Parliament, entered the room, dripping wet. Eleanor had hastened to remove his things, although there was a servant close at hand attempting to do the same thing, somewhat more efficiently. "Thank you, ladybird," he said. "Hugh, have I told you that you have a fine wife?"

"Indeed you have, and you're right, Father. How was Parliament?"

"Miserable, in a word. Carlisle's a dreary place at the best of times, and the king and the prince made it drearier with one of their quarrels." He looked apologetically at Eleanor. "The king has exiled Gaveston."

"Why?"

"The prince had the temerity to ask for Ponthieu for him—for services rendered. It must have seemed a trifling gift to young Edward, but the king fell into a fury. He called Edward a baseborn whoreson, asked why he who had never won any lands wanted to give them away. Then he actually fell upon his son and pulled out chunks of his hair. You can see the bald spots here and there." The elder Hugh grimaced. "After that his rage cooled through sheer exhaustion, but the next morning he saw his council and the order went out—Gaveston must be gone."

"But it's natural to reward one's friends with land," said Eleanor. "Gaveston has been a loyal friend to my uncle for years. And he excels in the joust and in military matters, I'm told, which is why the king brought him into Edward's household to begin with. As a soldiery example. So why would the king oppose such a reasonable request?"

The younger Hugh and Gilbert smiled. The elder Hugh looked at his daughter-in-law in some distress. "It is not a thing to be discussed before a young lady," he said finally.

Hugh the son laughed. "Come, Father. Eleanor is a hardened married woman now, and we're all family." He waited for a servant to leave the room, though. "The truth is, Eleanor, the king believes that his son and Piers have an unnatural relationship."

"I do not understand."

Hugh the elder looked stricken, so Hugh whispered a single word into his wife's ear. She gasped. "Hugh, is he right?"

Hugh shrugged. "Who knows? They're often alone together at Langley; anything could go on there. No doubt they're discreet when the king's around. I sure as hell would be."

"The prince calls Piers his brother," added Gilbert. "You've heard him do so yourself, haven't you, Eleanor? But it seems more than a brotherly relation to me."

"Brothers don't gaze into each other's eyes like that," said Hugh. "Speaking from experience as one." He yawned and stretched his legs. "So has he started packing yet?"

"No," said his father. "The king has given him quite a bit of time to prepare—until after Easter."

"With his wardrobe he'll need every day of it," Hugh said dryly.

Hugh was not far wrong. Caring not a whit that his father would see his household accounts, Edward bought tunics and tapestries for his friend and accompanied him to Dover himself, along with Gaveston's household and two minstrels. Even the king was unwilling to make life too harsh for the exile, for Piers had been given an annuity of a hundred marks. "*I* should get myself exiled," said Hugh, upon hearing the details. "Money from the king, gifts and money from the prince. And minstrels! What's an exile without minstrels?" He threw his head back and sang in an unmelodious voice, much to the distress of two dogs sitting by the fireplace, "Piers, sweet Piers, my life will be a vacancy without you…"

"Don't be so cynical, Hugh. My uncle is deeply grieved." Her voice caught as she added, "Grieved about my mother, too."

Joan, Edward's favorite sister and Eleanor's mother, had died just days before. Eleanor had not been much with her as a child, but their relations were affectionate. She was rather in awe of her mother, in fact, for her mother had done what few had done—stood up to the king. Eleanor's nurses had told her the story often enough. Joan had been ordered by the king to marry a man twice her age, Gilbert de Clare. Having done so, she had persuaded her husband to take her from court after their marriage so that they could enjoy their first days of married life by themselves. Irked at this show of independence, the king had had his daughter's valuable wedding clothes seized. Then when Gilbert died after just a few years of marriage, Joan had taken charge of her future. The king had lost no time in looking for a second husband for his daughter, and soon announced her betrothal to the Count of Savoy, only to find that Joan had married a nobody in Gilbert's household named Ralph de Monthermer, a squire who had been knighted only weeks before at Joan's own request. Edward tossed Ralph into prison. Joan had bided her time. She had sent Eleanor and her two other little girls by Gilbert to visit the king; then, trusting that her father had been put in a grandfatherly mood, had asked to appear before him. There, visibly pregnant, she had not quaked or cried, but had coolly explained that a widow should be allowed to choose for herself and that there was no shame in a great lady's raising the status of a poor knight. Whatever reply to this philosophy the king had made, he had gradually been brought round, and Ralph had been released and given the title of Earl of Gloucester. Would Eleanor have been able to defy the king so? She often wondered. She'd been a timid child, except among those she knew well. Her uncle Edward was one of the few persons she'd felt totally at ease with, probably because he was naturally shy himself. He too had loved her mother. When he'd fallen afoul of the king the previous year and had to stay out of his presence, with most of his funds cut off, Joan had lent him her seal so that he could borrow money and had offered to let him stay with her.

She turned away from the window where she and Hugh had been standing and began to cry. Hugh's sardonic expression vanished, and he instantly came to her and pulled her against him. She settled into his arms comfortably. "She died only as I was coming to truly know her, Hugh. And she was still so young. Why couldn't it have been later?"

"I don't know, my sweet."

"I could not bear it if anything like that happened to you."

"Don't be silly."

She crossed back to the window. "And whatever people say about my uncle and Piers, I know it must be breaking his heart to part with him, however you might scoff at him, Hugh."

"I don't scoff to be cruel. The king is an old man in failing health, Eleanor, and however sad your uncle and Piers may be today, it won't last long. They must be aware of that as anyone else. All Gaveston has to do is bide his time, and soon he'll be back in England."

"His ship could sink! All sorts of things could keep them apart."

"Gaveston would swim to shore. He loves to thumb his nose at those who consider him an upstart Gascon; he'd never give them the satisfaction of not returning. Trust me."

Gaveston's ship did not sink. Though he had been exiled to Gascony, he went no farther than Ponthieu, and the king, perhaps because of his preoccupation with military matters, perhaps because even he had a certain liking for the lively Piers, did not press the issue. The rich possessions Gaveston entered his exile with were soon added to by the prince, who purchased more clothing just so his friend could make a fine showing of himself at the French tournaments, then, for good measure, several horses, a gift that caused Hugh to wonder to Eleanor whether the prince would soon be sending his friend a supply of hay. There was scarcely time for Piers to attend the tournaments, however, for his exile ended abruptly when the old king, having made one last Scottish expedition, took ill and died in early July. The old man had told his son not to recall Gaveston, to lead one hundred men on a crusade each year, and to boil his bones down and carry them before the army on each subsequent incursion into Scotland. Edward, hearing the news, found the first order as absurd as the last two. Within minutes, a messenger was heading toward Dover with a simple message to Gaveston: to return home to England and his dearest friend.

The new king soon proved himself to be different from his father. Though he was no coward, he had neither an interest in nor an aptitude for warfare and spent his days in Scotland not plotting strategy but figuring out how best to reward his loyal friend. Ponthieu had been acceptable when the prince was in the position of a meek suppliant before his father, but hardly worth the giving when Edward himself was king. The earldom of Cornwall was eminently more suitable. Next, the Earl of Cornwall deserved a proper countess, and who better than Edward's own niece Margaret de Clare? It was only a pity that Edward's one unmarried sister was a nun. Settling for this next closest female relation, and certain that his friend would be delighted with the match, the king had the charter proclaiming Piers as the new earl decorated with the Clare arms as well as Gaveston's own.

Eleanor and Margaret's brother, Gilbert, had sanctioned the marriage, rather to Eleanor's surprise. "Gilbert, what about the—brotherhood—between Gaveston and the king?"

"What about it, sister?"

"What of Margaret? Have her wishes been consulted?"

Gilbert shrugged. "He's a handsome and agreeable man, and now that the king has made him Earl of Cornwall, a rich one as well. How can she complain?"

"But she will be sharing her husband with the king."

"Those may be just idle rumors, Nelly. I've never noticed anything so very much amiss. In any event, the king is king now and must act up to the role. He will be married soon himself, you know."

"Hugh does not believe they are just idle rumors."

"Your husband is a cynic, Nelly, always has been."

"He is older than you, Gilbert, and more observant."

"Maybe. But I have promised Margaret to Gaveston, and told her of the match as well. She didn't threaten to take the veil, or faint, or refuse dinner. In fact, you'll find her very engrossed by the subject of her wedding dress, I believe. So don't concern yourself with the matter." Gilbert's voice was sharper than he meant it to be, for he himself had had doubts about the marriage, not so much because of whose bed Gaveston would share but because of his awareness that Gaveston had never been a popular man at court. Even when he first came to Edward's household, the son of a loyal but financially strapped Gascon knight, he had carried himself as proudly as any great landholder's son and spared none his insolent wit. Any humility he might have possessed had vanished when the prince, almost from the moment of looking upon the handsome young man, found him to have every quality he had ever wanted in a brother, a friend, and even a lover. Humility was in short supply in the new king's court, as it had been in the old king's, and Gilbert knew that the barons would not tolerate any missteps by the new earl or his royal patron. He had wondered about catching his sister in such machinations. But no man who could aspire to the hand of the king's granddaughter was likely to live a life of quiet obscurity free from such intrigue, and Gilbert as his father's heir did not feel that he could deprive his middle sister of the chance of being a wealthy countess. Nor had he been truly inclined to offer any opposition to the uncle the king, who after Joan's death had granted the sixteen-year-old Gilbert the right to enjoy his estates immediately. Gilbert otherwise

might have had to fritter several more years away while someone else managed—
or mismanaged—their hefty revenues for him.

He looked at his sister, who still looked concerned. Talk about quiet obscurity! Poor Hugh might have to wait years before he got his hands on any of his
own father's land, though there was the possibility that the king might give him
and Eleanor a manor or two, especially as he had always been fond of Eleanor.
Perhaps this concern about Margaret was due to a little jealousy? He smiled tolerantly. If Gilbert's plans with the Earl of Ulster worked out, little Elizabeth would
be on the way to being a countess too. That would leave Eleanor the lowest ranking of the three sisters, perhaps a mortifying situation for the eldest Clare girl. He
patted his sister on the head kindly but a little patronizingly. "Don't worry," he
said again. "All will be well."

Eleanor and Hugh's wedding had been a dignified affair, thanks to the old
king; Margaret and Piers's wedding was a merry one, thanks to the new king. All
of the males, even the temperate Hugh and his father, even Edward's little
half-brothers, were at least tipsy. Eleanor, called on as the bride's closest married
relation to give a wedding toast, herself found that her cup had been refilled more
often than she thought. She had to be steadied by the ever-alert Gladys when she
raised her cup, and her toast, very simple and practiced for a good hour the night
before, reduced her to giggles before she was halfway through.

"Did I do badly?" she whispered to Hugh when she finished, unaware that her
whisper was not much of one and that no one else was speaking.

Hugh laughed and embraced her. "You did fine, my sweet."

She threw her arms around his neck and kissed him, long and slow, wishing
nothing so much as that he would take her out of the room and to bed then and
there. Someone applauded, and she blushed, recalling herself, and pulled away
from Hugh. He squeezed her hand, stepped forward, and raised his cup. "Piers
and Margaret," he said, with a tender expression on his face that Eleanor would
never forget, "I wish you as much joy in your marriage as I've had in mine."

Some years before, the first Edward, widowed from Eleanor of Castile, had
agreed with King Philip of France that he would marry Philip's sister and that his
son Edward, the Prince of Wales, would marry Philip's daughter, Isabella. The
king had made his marriage shortly thereafter, in 1299, but the prince's marriage
had waited, as Isabella was but a child. By 1308, however, Isabella was twelve,
fully marriageable in the eyes of the Church, and Philip was ready for his prospective son-in-law, now king himself, to fulfill his father's bargain. Leaving

Gaveston in charge of the kingdom as regent, much to the disgust of the barons, and to the particular disgust of Thomas of Lancaster, the richest earl in the country, he went to France to marry and bring back his young bride.

Now he was on his way home, and Piers, in his last act as regent, had summoned the nobility to Dover to greet their new queen.

"What is she like, Piers?" asked Margaret, watching as the royal ships finally appeared in the distance. "You must know."

Gaveston shrugged. "Can't say that I do. I don't think she and the king had exchanged so much as a letter or a gift before he went to France. She is called Isabella the Fair, because of her beauty, and that is all I have heard of the girl."

"I am to be one of her ladies if it pleases her, have you heard, Piers?"

Piers grinned at his sister-in-law. "Quite a few times, Nelly."

"Well," said Eleanor, reflecting. "I am excited."

The time dragged on before the ships finally reached the harbor. Trumpets sounded as the king and his new queen were rowed to shore. Finally, the queen's face became visible, and the crowd gasped.

Eleanor had never seen a more beautiful girl. Isabella was not yet thirteen, but she was tall for her age. Her height and her figure, which was slender but not so much so as to be unwomanly, could have allowed her to pass for a girl of fifteen or sixteen. The wind catching at her headdress revealed blond hair, more silver than yellow. She would have to get closer for the onlookers to see that she had dark blue eyes, the color of sapphires, but everyone was sufficiently near to appreciate her red lips, curled in a smile at something the king was saying, her fair, unblemished skin, and her white teeth. Her nose was perfectly straight; her neck long and slender; her cheekbones well-defined. Eleanor, short and freckled, her red hair tangled by the sea breeze that had been whipping it around despite its covering, her waist already beginning to disappear in pregnancy, felt positively dumpy next to her new queen, and even her sister Elizabeth, blond and elegant like her mother, experienced a sense of diminishment.

Someone squeezed her hand and she started. "Hugh?"

"Arrived just in time, sweetheart. So here is our queen."

"Isn't she lovely?"

He shrugged. "If you like perfection."

Edward and Isabella stepped ashore. Though Edward was holding her hand, it was clear that his attention was no longer focused on her. He looked around him, more and more anxiously, until Piers Gaveston stepped out of the mist that must have been obscuring him. With a cry of relief and joy, Edward hurried forward, all but dragging his bride behind, and clasped Gaveston in his arms, then kissed him on both cheeks. "Brother!"

"My dear lord."

"I have been away too long." Between the arrivals from France and the greeters from England a hundred people must have been present, but Edward had forgotten them all. He stepped back and gazed at his friend raptly. "Too, too long."

Isabella, standing beside the two men with admirable composure, spoke. Her clear voice, like the rest of her, was more womanly than might have been expected. "Who is your friend, Edward dear?"

Gaveston dropped to his knees as the king replied, "My dear! I forgot my manners in my happiness at being home. This is my dear friend Piers Gaveston, sweet wife. He and I have been inseparable since youth."

Piers kissed the hand she proffered. "Your servant, your grace."

"You may rise." She gave Gaveston a glance and then turned to the king, who had been cheerfully oblivious to the stir his embrace of his friend had caused in the crowd, especially among his new French relations. "Introduce me to the others, dear Edward."

Chivalry had returned to Edward in full force. "I shall do so in the castle. You must not stay here in the cold."

He led his new wife inside the castle and was soon seated by her as his men brought group after group of nobles to pay their respects. Having finished introducing his sisters and half-brothers, then a group of cousins, Edward reached his nephews and nieces. "These are my sister Joan's girls, dear Isabella. Poor Joan is dead but she has left three beautiful daughters. Margaret the Countess of Cornwall is scarcely less newly wedded than we. She is married to my dear brother Gaveston, whom you just met."

The blue eyes were not happy, but the queen managed a civil commonplace or two.

"This is Eleanor, Lady Despenser, my eldest niece. She hopes to have the honor of waiting upon you."

Eleanor executed a curtsey, for the first time flawlessly.

"I am sure she will please me," said Isabella absently.

"You have met Hugh le Despenser the elder in France, of course, and here is the reason it is necessary to call him that in company, his son Hugh. They are a fine family."

"Delighted," said the queen as Hugh bowed before her.

"Elizabeth has come all the way from Amesbury, where she is living in my sister's convent, to see you, my dear. She shall be married soon herself, I believe."

Elizabeth's curtsey far excelled her older sisters'.

"She is almost exactly your age," the king added, as if offering the queen a playmate.

"Are you sure it won't hurt the baby?"

"The midwife says it is fine. *Please*, Hugh."

"Lord, you are a hot little vixen." He needed no more persuasion, though, and thrust into her as she stifled cries of pleasure. As the king's relations, they had been given a room in the crowded castle to themselves, but their servants were well within earshot. Somehow this gave their encounter an added zest, though Eleanor was not yet at the stage where she would admit this to herself.

"A vixen," Hugh gasped some time later. "And I am happily married to her."

She drowsily wrapped herself around him. "It has been so long since we have been together."

"A week."

"It feels longer."

"I know. I love you so much."

"And I love you."

He stroked her hair and she was beginning to fall asleep when she was roused by the sound of his wry laugh. "Hugh?"

"Go back to sleep, my dear. I was only wondering."

"Wondering what?"

He lowered his voice. "Which Gaul our poor king is sleeping with tonight, his Gascon playmate or his Parisian bride. He has so much choice now!"

Eleanor yawned. "What a rude thought, Hugh." She drifted off again and soon was very comfortably asleep on Hugh's chest.

Edward lay in his bed, feeling the rocking sensation that one had sometimes after spending a long time on a boat, even hours after getting off. He had plenty of room to stretch, for his lovely young bride was in a sumptuously decorated chamber a respectable distance off. A pretty girl, but how young she was! He'd said goodnight to her with his usual affection and courtesy before going to his own chamber. Affection and courtesy were all he could manage for now. There was something almost indecent about lovemaking with a girl that young. Surely she must feel the same way.

He was tired, but he would not fall asleep. Soon his door would be slipped open, surely, and it was. He all but sobbed with relief when the familiar body climbed in beside him. "How long has it been?"

"Only two weeks," said Piers.

"It felt like forever," said the king.

At Westminster, there was a never-ending supply of the queen's trunks to be unpacked, each containing garments that were richer and more beautifully worked than the last. Isabella's French attendants, having seen the clothing go into the trunks, were quite indifferent to its unloading, but Eleanor and the other English ladies, none of them strangers to fine garments themselves, were rapt as each delved into a different trunk. "You must wear this to your coronation, your grace!"

"No, this!"

"Too light. This!"

Isabella, who had already planned her *tout ensemble* for the coronation and certainly needed no help from these dowdy Englishwomen, none of whom appeared to have any idea of the difference *cut* could make to a garment, watched them indulgently. "They are fine, aren't they? My father would settle for no less." Her expression changed. "But I had no idea when they were ordered that I would appear shabby next to my lord's *brother* Gaveston."

Eleanor laughed. "Your grace, you could appear shabby next to no one." She stroked a mantle lined with the softest fur she had ever felt.

"Do you like it, my lady? You may have it. It suits your coloring more so than mine."

Isabella had been displaying this generosity to all her ladies. "I have already taken so many gifts from you— that fine material, and the headdress, and this beautiful ring." Eleanor glanced at her finger. "I can take no more."

"You are no Gaveston, I see. Would he have shown your restraint!"

Very soon after the royal party had arrived in Westminster, Gaveston had appeared for dinner in a robe fastened with a magnificent clasp of gold and emeralds, a crucifix studded with sapphires and pearls, and a splendid ruby ring. Isabella had no sooner caught sight of these when she gasped to her ladies, "The upstart! He is wearing my father's wedding presents!"

Eleanor herself had been taken aback, but she replied, "The king regards Gaveston as his brother, your grace. What comes to the king, comes to Gav—"

"Brother! I don't see those two little boys who are the king's real brothers dripping in my father's jewels, just that creature. I shall write to my father about this impudence." She had taken her place beside the king and sat fuming during the duration of the meal and the entertainment afterward, heedless of the fact that the minstrels had been chosen especially to suit her taste.

Gaveston had continued to wear the jewels, however, and if the queen had more to say on the subject, she had not said it to her ladies, though since then she had not missed an opportunity to disparage the handsome Gascon. Now having satisfied herself with this latest dig, she settled back in her chair, and a thoughtful look came upon your face. "You may all leave me now except Lady Despenser. I wish to speak to her in private."

Had she offended her queen so soon? Eleanor wondered. Isabella had not shown any ill temper thus far, but Eleanor had sensed the need to remain on guard. And it was true that she was somewhat lax in matters of court etiquette. Neither her grandfather, who cared not how a man addressed him as long as he was fighting on his side, nor her uncle, who would as soon keep company with a brick mason as with his barons, had demanded the strict decorum that was probably de rigueur in the French court, and her rebellious mother had not been a shining example herself. The dowager queen Margaret, Isabella's aunt, had been kind enough to give her some hints, but Margaret was far less formidable than her young niece. She waited for her dressing-down, thinking it was kind of Isabella to give to her in private.

"I know I met your husband, but I cannot recall his face. Is he handsome?"

"He is thin and dark, with a beautiful smile. To me he is the handsomest man in the world—but others might say different."

"You are deeply in love with him, I see. How sweet!" She smiled as Eleanor, blushing, looked down. "Is your sister Margaret so enamored of her husband?"

"She is very much in love with him, and he is very kind to her."

"Whenever I discuss Gaveston with Edward, it ends in a quarrel. Tell me about him, Lady Despenser."

Eleanor hid her blushes behind an embroidery hoop. "Edward's father brought Gaveston to his household, your grace, some years ago. They say that my uncle took a single look at him and regarded him as his brother from that day forward. Piers's father was a Gascon knight, a brave man who had served the king faithfully but who had lost most of his goods and lands. Piers was an able soldier and my grandfather wished to reward him, both for his own sake and for his father's. So he placed Gaveston in the prince's household with the sons of the great barons of the land. They were furious that the prince preferred Gaveston, with so little to call his own, over them, with all their prospects of riches and titles. And so it has been ever since."

"And what did the king—the late king—think of all this?"

"Little enough at first, your grace. He was always preoccupied with his wars and his differences with the barons—my own father among them. When my uncle and Piers were in his company, they were usually in Scotland, and Piers always pleased my grandfather as a soldier. But then something displeased him, and my grandfather banished my uncle from court."

"Banished! By his own father? Why, what did Edward do?"

"I have heard that he and Gaveston were poaching deer in the Bishop of Coventry's park, your grace. It was a trivial thing to them, but when the bishop found out he confronted them, and they spoke mockingly to the bishop. The bishop was furious, and he complained to the king. So my grandfather cut off my uncle's funds, and removed his household. He was forced to ask help from my mother and his other sisters. My mother was glad to help; she even offered to have the prince live with her. But my uncle thought it would be better to follow the court at a distance until my grandfather relented, which he did after a few months."

"And then I know Gaveston was banished not so long after. After the king asked for Ponthieu. Which I understand is to be mine now, if the king ever gets around to assigning me it."

Isabella fell silent for a while, then looked straight at Eleanor. "You may find this question impertinent, but I shall ask it anyway. Do you lie with your husband?"

Eleanor, though shocked, saw no way to avoid the queen's question. "Certainly, your grace." The opportunity to share her good news was irresistible. "Indeed, I am with child."

"That's not here or there at the moment. When did you start lying with him?"

"On our wedding night, your grace."

"My husband has yet to lie with me—in the full sense of the word."

"Each man is different," Eleanor ventured. "I was as close to fourteen as to thirteen when I married, and my husband was young himself. The king is a man of four-and-twenty, twice your age. It may be that he is—squeamish—about lying with a wife so young."

"Is Gaveston so squeamish about his wife? He is Edward's age, even a bit older I think, and Margaret is between your age and mine."

Eleanor knew that he was not squeamish, having been given a full description of the couple's wedding night—fuller than Eleanor in truth had cared for—by the enthusiastic bride. Forthcoming as Margaret might be with her elder sister, however, Eleanor doubted that she would be so much so with the queen, so she said simply, "I know not, your grace."

"You do, but you don't tell. He must sleep with her." She scowled. "I might be young, but I am as womanly as either of you two Clare girls. Am I not?" Isabella stood up and studied herself in a glass with considerable satisfaction. "My hips and bosom are not as developed as yours, I admit, but what does it matter? I am already taller than either of you."

"I very much doubt that the king is dissatisfied with you or your person, your grace. It is your age, and nothing more. What does not bother Gaveston with Margaret may bother the king with you. In a few months the king will incline to you." Eleanor laughed. "And recline with you."

"This is not a joking matter, Lady Despenser!"

"I beg your pardon." Eleanor let the queen simmer for a moment before asking, "Your grace, does he give you a reason?"

"He says that if I were to get with child so early it might injure my health."

"There's sense to that, your grace."

"I don't see it being an objection in your case."

"But it was considered. Before I married Hugh, my mother sent for a midwife and had me strip stark naked in front of her. She looked me up and down like some sort of great heifer at the fair—it was mortifying. If she had not thought it would be safe for me to carry children I would have had to live apart from Hugh after we were married, or at least in different quarters, until I turned fifteen or even sixteen. And my brother insisted that the same be done when Margaret married Gaveston." How cruel it would have been had she not passed the midwife's test! Eleanor thought. She could not have borne the idea of not sleeping with Hugh.

"I wonder that my father did not do the same for me."

"He must have trusted that the king would be careful."

"He certainly is that!" Isabella snorted, albeit in a manner befitting royalty. She said with some bitterness, "I've seen him with you, you know. You are his little pet. Sometimes I think I will become just another—at best."

"That will never be the case, your grace. You will make yourself indispensable to him, you'll see. And when you are ready for him in that other way, he will be ready for you."

"And this Gaveston? Do you truly believe he and the king are nothing more than brothers to each other?"

"I don't know, your grace, and it would be presumptuous of me to guess, I think. I can only tell you this: the king loves Gaveston more than anyone in the world. And Gaveston for all of his ways loves the king too, I think."

"And I should accept this?"

"Now you are asking me to be presumptuous again, your grace. I can only say that I think you would be happier if you did."

"You're not stupid, Lady Despenser. Perhaps I will try then."

To be told by the queen that one was not stupid was a high honor indeed. Eleanor smiled and, seeing that the queen was lost in her own thoughts, worked quietly until Isabella came out of her reverie. "Now, tell me about this Tower of London we must go to before the coronation."

"It is a royal palace, your grace, a fine one, but it is also a storehouse for the king's jewels and records, and a prison—a state prison for traitors and the like."

"And what do you do to traitors in your kingdom?"

Eleanor shuddered. "It is horrible, your grace. They are hung, but cut down while still alive, and then they are cut open and their insides are burnt before their eyes—unless they have been so fortunate as to lose consciousness or die beforehand. Then they cut their heads off and cut or tear their bodies into quarters. Their heads are put on display, and sometimes their quarters too."

"How grotesque!"

"It is so cruel, your grace. My grandfather used several men that way, and I wish he had not. If a man is to die, why can't he simply be beheaded? He's dead either way. But men seem to think it is necessary to make a great show of it. I think men can be fools sometimes." Eleanor felt the need to move to a happier topic. "But the Tower's royal apartments are beautiful; I have visited my grandfather and uncle there many a time. There is even a menagerie there, with lions and tigers. They are fascinating to watch; you must have the king take you there. And has he told you about the camel?"

"A camel! I was not certain such beasts actually existed."

"There is a camel at Langley, his favorite retreat. It's ill-tempered, though, and hates to have anyone ride on his humps. I tried when I was little. He shook me off and ruined my robes—spitting at me—but I finally got on and held on for dear life. My nurse scolded me for so long she lost her voice. She told me that such a hoyden would never find a husband."

The queen laughed, and for the moment appeared no more than twelve years old. "As I have found a husband, I would like to try someday. Perhaps you can show me how to ride him."

"It would be amusing, your grace."

"I am glad you are here, Lady Despenser. My ladies from France are so proper and matronly, and my English ladies so dull—except for you. I am glad there is someone I can talk to freely."

"I am pleased that *you* are pleased with me, your grace." And indeed she was. To be in favor with the queen, and carrying Hugh's child—there was nothing more that she could ask for.

Edward and Isabella were crowned king and queen of England on February 25. Edward, blond and tall like his ancestors, was magnificent in his royal robes, and Isabella's gown would have been talked of for years had not Gaveston turned up in a robe of purple that made the royal couple's garments look to be almost everyday apparel in comparison. He only wanted a crown, and he did the next best thing by bearing the king's for him.

Gaveston had organized many an entertainment for the young prince's household, and it was thought even by those who disliked him most that the coronation and the ensuing banquet would go smoothly. They did not. Either Gaveston in his glee at having yet another chance to irk the barons had overlooked key details, or servants took pleasure in making him look a fool, for the rooms were overcrowded and the food poorly prepared and late. The young queen's uncles departed for France in a huff, and the queen herself, who had been neglected in favor of Gaveston at the banquet, was snappish with her ladies, even Eleanor, for two days afterward. Even Hugh's father, who had taken part in the ceremony and who was one of the few men in England who supported Gaveston, was embarrassed for his king's behavior. Only Margaret, who wrote to her old friends at Amesbury that her husband had been the handsomest man in England that night, had no complaints.

A couple of weeks later, at Westminster, the queen, who was fond of music and had learned that her new English attendant had a lovely voice, bade one of her chamber ladies to find Edward and see if he would lend her his crwth player to accompany Eleanor as she sang. One of the damsels would have happily gone, but Eleanor, slightly nauseated with her pregnancy and eager to walk in the fresh air in search of the king, offered to go herself.

Edward was with his gardener when Eleanor found him. After he gave the man very precise instructions about some rose bushes—for Edward had very definite ideas about what the royal gardens should look like and would not have found life at all amiss if he had been born a gardener instead of a king—he turned to his young niece with his usual sweet smile. "What can I do for you, Nelly?"

Eleanor gave her Isabella's message, and the king readily agreed. "So the queen is fond of the crwth? I did not know that."

"She is fond of many of the things you are, your grace."

"When will you learn not to your-grace me? Such as?"

"She loves to hunt, she has told me. She is an excellent horsewoman; I've watched her ride."

"I'll take her tomorrow when Gaveston and I go, then."

Eleanor wondered if Gaveston could be left at home, but said nothing. The king continued, "Now tell me about the queen. Does she task you and the other ladies too much? I know that she has a trying temper. Even Queen Margaret has admitted as much."

"She is usually quite good-humored with me, your—Uncle." After a moment or two of silence, she added, "She truly is beautiful. I was bedazzled when I saw her step off the ship."

Edward nodded. "Everyone tells me how beautiful she is. I can see it. But beauty is like a tapestry. What hangs well in one room may simply not in another." He threw a stone in an ornamental pond. "Sometimes I wonder if she was not hung in the wrong room."

"Uncle, I really should not be hearing this."

"You're right." Edward threw another stone. "Certain choices are made for us, and we must adapt ourselves to them, must we not? You are right to keep me from indulging in self-pity."

"Someday you will have a child, and that will give you a common interest and purpose."

"You are a wise as well as a beautiful young woman." He smiled. "Speaking of which, Gaveston was not discreet, as usual, and told me what he probably should not have told me yet. You are with child."

"He can keep nothing to himself. I was waiting until I was further along to tell others."

"He knew it would please me, that's all. Don't be angry with him." He bent and kissed her on the cheek. "Congratulations."

She smiled her thanks.

"They want to send him away, you know."

"Gaveston?" But she should have known better than to ask; no other "him" could be in her uncle's mind. "Why?"

"To spite me, I think." He scowled. "There seems to be a new reason, every day. His title is too high; Cornwall should have been given to one of my half-brothers. When he is closer to me than any brother. I consult him before I consult the barons; why not? He has my interest at heart; they do not. I give him jewels and land. They are mine to give, are they not? He insults the barons. My God, the pompous fools need a little insulting!" He smiled suddenly. "Have you heard the nicknames he has invented for the earls?"

"Warwick is the Black Dog of Arden, I believe."

"That's his best, I think. He's always reminded me of a dog guarding his territory against an intruder, barking and snapping with as much show as possible.

Burst-Belly—Lincoln—was a bit obvious. Joseph the Jew—Pembroke—was another inspired one, I thought, with that dark visage of his."

"Lancaster is the Fiddler."

"Yes, he's always looking for someone to dance to his tune!" He frowned as he remembered the nickname his friend had coined for Eleanor's brother, the Cuckold's Bird. Edward had been rather hurt to hear it, directed as it was to Gilbert's mother, his favorite sister, who certainly had made a clandestine second marriage but who hardly deserved the epithet. Gaveston, seeing this, had quickly explained that cuckoldry was the only likely fate of a man married to a woman as young and lovely as Joan. Still, Eleanor was even less likely to appreciate the remark than Edward had, so he fell silent.

"Does he have one for my father-in-law?"

"Dear Hugh? No. Hugh's done nothing but be loyal to me. He's the only one who hasn't slighted Gaveston in any way. He understands what he means to me." He smiled. "I'll never forget those little gifts he sent to me when I was estranged from my father, raisins and wine. Small things, but they cheered me."

"I am certain things will right themselves."

"We can only hope." Edward gazed ahead moodily, then pointed a finger. "What do you think of having a fish pond put in there? I want the queen to like it here at Westminster."

"I think it would be lovely." Eleanor paused and said gently, "But why not ask the queen herself?"

CHAPTER 3

▼

June 1308 to July 1308

The barons had won. Gaveston was to be exiled. The barons had been relentless about his removal since the coronation, and Edward, to avoid a civil war he was not entirely sure he could win, and knowing that his French father-in-law might not be at all unwilling to intervene against him, finally agreed to his removal. As had happened when his father exiled the Gascon, there was time to prepare, and the friends went to Langley, Edward's favorite manor. Isabella went also, accompanied by Eleanor and her other ladies.

If the queen was satisfied with Gaveston's removal, she kept it to herself. The king, working toward his friend's recall even before he left England, had finally granted her Ponthieu, and even as he sought to enjoy his last few days with Piers, he was careful not to neglect his wife. Eleanor wondered if he had finally consummated his marriage, but Isabella said no more on the subject. She was looking more womanly with each passing day, however, and the days when Edward could validly complain that his wife was but a child were quickly becoming numbered.

The day was fine, and Isabella, having been given a hunting pack by her husband, had gone with some of her ladies and knights to try the hounds out, the king having stayed behind to attend to some documents before quickly giving up his duties for the day and heading outside with Gaveston. Eleanor, too far gone in pregnancy to wish to sit a horse, even if Hugh would have let her, stayed behind too, but soon found sitting by a tapestry rack insupportable with the birds chirping cheerfully outside and a light breeze rustling the curtains at the window.

She heaved herself to her feet and went outside, where she walked by the river gathering wildflowers as her son—all the older ladies had declared she was having a son, and Eleanor saw no reason to gainsay them—kicked her vigorously as if himself eager to be outdoors.

Soon the king and Gaveston rowed into view. If they had been doing anything besides sitting decorously on opposite sides of the boat before they saw Eleanor, it was not apparent.

"Niece!"

"Sister!"

"Had we known you were around we would have had you join us," said Edward.

Eleanor laughed. "I'd sink any boat you put me into now. I am enormous!"

"Nonsense, you look beautiful. But all women look beautiful when they are with child."

Gaveston hopped out of the boat while Edward tied it up and said, "But you of course look more beautiful when you are with child than other women do when they are with child."

"Oh, stop it. Save your compliments for Margaret."

Gaveston bowed. "I shall do so." He glanced at the considerable bulge under Eleanor's gown. "May I, sister?"

"You may as well. Everyone else in the family does."

Piers put out his hand and touched Eleanor's belly, with a gentleness that surprised her.

The king shyly touched it too. Then he asked, "Is the queen still hunting?"

"Yes."

"Good. I wish to speak to you privately for a moment."

"He is sending my brother Hugh on crusade, Nelly. Go, Hugh, with our blessing! Fight the infidels."

"Leave us be for a while, Piers," Edward said patiently.

"Oh, very well." Gaveston again patted Eleanor's belly, gently as before. "Keep young Hugh safe, now. As opposed to Hugh the younger."

"*Piers!*"

"I'm going. Good-bye."

Edward looked after him fondly. "He's irrepressible, isn't he? I can't tell you how sweet life has been since he returned. It was so bleak without him. And now he must go away again." He gave a sigh, then forced a smile. "But let's have our chat now." He paused awkwardly. "On second thought, let's go inside."

She followed her uncle indoors. Langley had been Edward's favorite residence as a boy, and he had lovingly improved it since so that almost every room in it bore some stamp of his individuality. The room he led her to, however, had scarcely been altered in twenty years, when Edward had slept in it with his nursemaid. Now a new nursemaid sat in the room, and a child, little more than a year old, slept in a little bed. "Uncle, he is an angel! Who is he? Who are his parents?"

"His name is Adam, and he is mine. He was born eleven months ago."

"He is the most beautiful little boy I have ever seen." She knelt beside his bed and stroked his hair, which was still sparse and whitish but seemed to be acquiring a reddish tint.

"Aye, he is a pretty little fellow. Bastards always are, for some reason." He shook his head sadly and led her away. "Let's go into the next room so we don't interrupt his nap."

She sat in a window seat in the adjoining room, which was well supplied with toys. "If I may ask, sir, where is his mother?"

"In the next world, poor thing." Edward stood next to her, staring out the window. "I met Lucy while rowing. She had no idea who I was and I didn't tell her at first."

"She must have been very pretty."

"A handsome peasant girl, no more and no less. But that's what I liked about her, no false airs or graces, all natural. Rather like y—" he glanced at Eleanor and broke off. "Just a sweet-tempered village girl. She was doing laundry on the bank when I rowed by, and I stopped to talk. She was no wanton, poor thing; it was I who seduced her. Not that I'd planned it; I started kissing her and couldn't stop myself from taking it further."

Eleanor said sadly, "She died in childbirth."

"No, she died but four weeks ago. I told her who I was—rather to her surprise—and told her that if anything happened to her she was to leave word at Langley that she needed to see me and I would take care of her. Fortunately she took me at my word, and I found her a nice manor to live upon. She and Adam lived there together and I saw her from time to time, though I never lay with her again. I didn't want to put her in the position of being a royal mistress; she was too innocent for that. I was keeping an eye out for a man in my household who would be a good husband for her. But a bad fever came through the area and killed her and half a dozen others. It nearly killed my son too, but you can see he recovered nicely. So I had him brought here—her parents are dead—and here he shall remain."

"Does the queen know?"

"No. Only Gaveston, and a few servants, and now you." Edward flushed. "The truth is, Eleanor dear, I wish you would tell the queen about him."

"Me!"

"I know it sounds absurd, but it's awkward for me." He winced. "I've—how shall I say it—done my duty by the queen, quite often, but I can't seem to get her with child. I think it is because she is little more than a child herself, but she of course thinks it is that I am—distracted, shall I say." He looked at Eleanor, whose cheeks were as bright as her hair. "This is really a conversation I would prefer not to have with you, Eleanor."

"I agree, Uncle. Emphatically."

"In any case, knowing that I have fathered Adam might set her off into one of her rages. Not against you, of course, otherwise I wouldn't ask. I would just like her to have calmed down a little before I see her. For with Gaveston going, I'm not sure how I would react if she were in a fury. She doesn't say so but I know she'll be glad to see him gone. I suppose it's to her credit that she says nothing. If I must lose him I at least want things to be pleasant between her and me."

His voice was so wistful that Eleanor, who had been dismayed at his weakness and who had been trying to think of a diplomatic way to avoid this odd commission, said, "Very well, Uncle. I will tell her."

"You are a good girl."

The rather patronizing tone irritated her. "But if you have any other commissions for me to the queen, Uncle, now is the time to tell me. I will soon be leaving court to prepare for the birth of my child. Her grace has given me leave."

"No others." Edward smiled. "This is quite enough, and I thank you." He paused. "You know that my old nurse, Alice de Leygrave, is one of the queen's damsels. I love her like a mother—better, in fact, because I hardly knew my mother. I could have asked her to broach this with the queen. But I asked you first, because there's no woman I trust more than you. Except, perhaps, for your late mother."

"I am honored, sir." She was so deeply moved that she curtsied. Then she hurried away in search of Isabella.

"Have you been much about Langley, your grace?"

Isabella frowned at this odd question. "My duties have hardly given me time to explore, if that is what you mean. Am I missing something?"

"I was wondering if you might have seen an infant boy."

"I've heard a brat squalling in the distance from time to time, yes. The keeper's, I supposed."

"His name is Adam, your grace. He is the king's natural son." Eleanor added hastily, "Conceived before your marriage to him."

Isabella's face registered surprise only for an instant before she smiled broadly. "A bastard? Then there's hope."

"You are not angry?"

Isabella shrugged. "At least it shows he's a proper man. Who is the mother?"

"A peasant girl, your grace. She died some weeks ago."

"Leave it to Edward to father a child by a peasant when he might have had a lady of the court." Isabella laughed mirthlessly; she was descended from royalty on both sides, and her husband's liking for chatting familiarly with masons and gardeners and the like was nearly as distressing as his fondness for Gaveston. Her voice turned sharp. "You do tell the truth, don't you? She is not someone of consequence, someone who frequents the court?"

"I tell you only what the king told me, your grace, and there is no reason for him to tell me false."

"He isn't yours, is it?"

Eleanor sprang up, forgetful of all propriety. "How dare you?"

Isabella gave her indulged child's shrug. "Don't make such a fuss. It's not such an unlikely idea. He is very fond of you, always giving you little presents"—she glanced at Eleanor's bracelet, which indeed had come from the king just days before—"and you're attractive enough in your style. Perhaps—"

"No 'perhaps,' your majesty. I am carrying my first child, and it is Hugh's and no other man's. If you please, I will leave you now."

"Come now, Lady Despenser. I meant no harm; I know you are as prim as any Englishwoman. But what made you take it upon yourself to tell me this?"

"It was my uncle's request." Eleanor was suddenly very weary of being attendant upon the queen, of the need to be constantly cheerful and obliging and sensitive to her mistress's capricious moods. As her lying-in grew close and she began to fret more about the ordeal of childbirth, she found herself missing her own mother more than ever, and instead of waiting on the queen, she longed to be comforted and cosseted by her own damsel, Gladys. More than anything, she missed Hugh. Soon, she told herself, she would be on her way to him. They could not make love now, but they could at least share a bed, and he would scratch her back in exactly the right spot as she dozed against him. "He was afraid you would be angry since he has not begotten a child on you—yet."

"How little he knows me!" Isabella too sounded weary. "I understand that many girls don't conceive until they are fifteen or sixteen even. He always thinks the worst of me, as if I were a child liable to have a tantrum over the smallest thing."

"He is sorrowful over Gaveston's leaving. It is hard for him to think good of anyone now." But the king thought well of her, she remembered. Would he and the queen ever be a happy couple? She pondered this, then roused herself from her reverie. "Should you like to see the little boy, your grace? He is the prettiest child, truly." Eleanor added with some wickedness, "He looks nothing like me, you shall see."

"I should not have insulted you so, even in jest. But it does pique me, having him use a go-between for a message such as this."

"He has known me since birth, your grace, and he was very fond of my mother. Shall we go see Adam?"

This time, Adam was awake and playing when Eleanor arrived in the nursery. He had begun wobbling about upright, and he made his way to his elegant visitors with alacrity. Isabella, by far the prettier, caught his eye first. He grabbed her skirts, and she admitted him to her lap, where he pulled at a few strands of the silver-blond hair before becoming squirmy and having to be put down. Eleanor, kneeling on the floor with difficulty, pushed a ball toward him and made silly faces at him, making him giggle wildly before he lurched off in pursuit of some object that he found more interesting than either of the ladies.

"He is a pretty lad," said Isabella. "Edward could hardly fail to have handsome children, though. Was his father good-looking?"

"They say he was as a young man, but of course I never saw him except as an older man. I never thought of him as being handsome or otherwise, just intimidating, although he was always kind enough to my sisters and me in a stern sort of way. He had a fierce temper, though. He once threw my aunt's coronet in the fire after some quarrel with her, although he later replaced the gemstones that were damaged."

"They must have been frightened of him."

"No, actually they were all women of spirit, particularly my mother. He probably respected them for it. I must have been a disappointment to him, because I was so timid as a child. But then, he didn't see much of me and my sisters."

"Was Edward a disappointment to him?"

"I hope not, your grace. But they did not suit each other, that's for certain. My grandfather was a great warrior; he wanted Edward to be just like him. And he was so concerned with Scotland! My uncle is not so single-minded." Eleanor hesitated, then decided it was safe to say what had long been in her mind. "To tell the truth, your grace, I often wonder why we can't leave the Scots alone, and they us. All this warfare costs a great deal of money—and lives—and what do we have to show for it?" Adam swaggered over to Eleanor again, and Eleanor took him up and smiled. "But what do I know?"

"Your opinions would probably best be kept to yourself," said Isabella, dryly but not unsympathetically. "I imagine they are not to the liking of the barons."

"Indeed no," said Eleanor, stroking Adam's fuzzy head. "But you won't tell anyone, will you, Adam? That's a good boy."

Eleanor's mother had willed Eleanor her chariot and all of its trappings, and it sat ready to receive Eleanor when she left the king and queen a few days later to prepare for the birth of her child. The royal couple was there to bid her good-bye, as were her sister and Gaveston, soon to leave England themselves. Edward had sweetened Gaveston's exile by making him governor of Ireland. Rather to Eleanor's surprise, Gaveston was taking his new role seriously and had had several conversations with the king about the Irish situation that Eleanor and Margaret, neither of whom were much interested in politics, had found excruciatingly dull. She suspected the king had not enjoyed them much himself. When the king's fool had entered the hall, with a great deal of uncomplimentary things to say about the barons who had exiled Gaveston, they had all been much relieved.

As she was helped into the chariot, followed by Gladys, Eleanor was touched to see that someone had contrived to make her ride most comfortable. The chariot cushions had been augmented by much thicker, softer ones, and baskets of fruit sat in a corner. Even the sumpter horses that pulled the chariot had been given fresh harnesses, and their cloths, bearing the shields of the Clares and the Despensers, appeared to have been made but recently.

"We wished you to leave us in high style," said the king cheerfully as Eleanor thanked him and Isabella. "But credit must go solely to my lady the queen for the food. She did not want you going without sustenance for long in your condition."

Eleanor felt tears come to her eyes. "That is so sweet of you, your grace."

"You must send us word the moment your child comes," said Isabella cheerfully. In planning for the comfortable departure of Lady Despenser, Isabella and Edward had become oddly companionable, even now standing side by side beaming at each other like a prosperous merchant couple. Margaret and Gaveston stood beside them looking equally well-matched and cheerful. All four, even Isabella, kissed her goodbye, and Edward looked over the sumpter horses and pronounced them perfectly adequate to the task of carrying her to Loughborough.

"Piers, do take care of my little sister in Ireland," Eleanor said, leaning out of the litter to kiss Margaret once again. "It is quite wild there, I hear."

"We'll slay the dragons straightaway," promised Gaveston. "Then we'll start on the tigers, and then on the lions, and then on the sea demons, and then—"

"If your list grows longer, I'll never get to leave!" Eleanor settled back and waved as the litter moved forward. The two couples were still waving as the litter pulled out of sight, and their cheerful expressions had not faltered.

Hugh's mother had died shortly before Eleanor had married him, and it was her old chamber, freshly painted, that Eleanor was given to await the birth of her child. There she received all the cosseting that she had wistfully longed for when she was with the queen, and more.

She had brought back a couple of tapestries given to her by the queen, and spent so much time deciding where to hang them and then changing her mind that Hugh teased her, "Shouldn't you be moving this one again? It's been hanging in the same place for the entire morning."

"I may be moving it soon, but I like the way the light catches at it. Of course the sun will fade it, so perhaps I should move it after all. Doesn't Isabella have wonderful taste, Hugh?"

"Exquisite." They had been lying in bed together, Hugh with his hand on her belly feeling the baby's gyrations back and forth, but at Isabella's name he drew his hand back for an instant. "What is it, Hugh?"

"Nothing, my love. Here's an elbow, I'll wager."

"You dislike it when I speak of the queen. And I don't see why. She has been very kind to me."

"I know, my love."

"And you needn't agree with everything I say."

Eleanor was eight months with child now and growing rather fractious. Fortunately, Hugh was not unprepared for this, for shortly after Eleanor's arrival back at Loughborough Hugh's father had taken him aside and explained some things to him. "Your mother when she was with child was hell on earth during the last few weeks, son. Hell on earth. Be patient, Hugh."

"My mother was not of the easiest temperament at any time, Father." Hugh smiled complacently. "Eleanor is of a much sweeter nature."

"True," Hugh admitted rather wistfully, for he had loved his high-strung wife, Warwick's sister Isabel Beauchamp, and had married her without royal license after remaining a bachelor until he was well into his twenties. He could have obtained the king's permission, he supposed, but so eager had he been to marry her that he had not bothered to wait. "But they can turn on you when they're with child, son, and no one warned me of it as I am warning you. Trust me. Something happens to women in that condition." He shook his head. "Right before you were born I would have welcomed being sent off to fight the Scots single-handedly."

And now, inexplicably, Eleanor was crying. Hugh reviewed the events of the last few minutes and could not think of anything amiss. "Darling?"

"I look like hell, don't I? You'll never touch me again, will you?"

"I *am* touching you," Hugh said reasonably.

"I'll never have a pretty figure like the queen. I'll be fat."

"The queen is too thin."

"There you go! Always criticizing her."

Hugh, realizing he was beaten, took a deep breath and stood up. "I'm going hunting, my sweet."

"Why did I ever let him touch me, Gladys? I'll never let him touch me again. Never!"

Gladys, rubbing her lady's temples with ice, nodded sympathetically, but Janet the midwife, standing patiently by Eleanor's feet, suppressed a grin. Fifteen years ago at Caerphilly Castle in South Wales she had stood by in awe, holding supplies, as her own mother, midwife to the Clares for many years, had brought the young lady she now attended into the world. Since then many babies had come to that place under Janet's own auspices, and this birth, for all of Eleanor's complaining, was proving to be easy and quick, for a first child. The girl was built for childbearing, and if she broke her vow never to let her husband touch her again, as fortunately her charges invariably did, there would be many more Despensers to come. "Push, my lady. Harder."

"I am pushing, damn you."

Oh, things were going nicely indeed. "Look at your fine boy, my lady. What a big fellow he is!"

Eleanor, smiling and crying, took little Hugh, who was holding forth indignantly on the subject of being hustled out of his womb into Loughborough. He was indeed bigger than most newborn babies, but no less red and wrinkled, and no one but the woman holding him could have found out a resemblance between him and any adult human being. "Look at him, Gladys. Doesn't he look just like Hugh?"

"Most like, my lady," Gladys said loyally.

She would have had Hugh—Hugh her husband, that was—brought to her immediately, but the ladies—Gladys and Hugh's sisters—insisted on tidying her up first, while the wet nurse bathed little Hugh and swaddled him. At last, however, she and her baby lay side by side on fresh linen, and Hugh came into the chamber. As Eleanor lay in a newly made bed with her freshly brushed hair flowing prettily over her shoulders, and little Hugh after expressing more indignation about being bathed had fallen asleep, the new father could perhaps be forgiven for thinking that the travails of childbirth were somewhat overrated. He stared at the baby as if his being there was a surprise to him, and then he bent and kissed his wife on the forehead. "He is beautiful, Eleanor. Absolutely beautiful. I am so proud of you."

"Won't you hold him?"

"What if I drop him?"

"You won't drop him, silly! Sit beside me and I'll show you how."

He obeyed, and Eleanor eased Hugh into his father's arms. Hugh held his son gingerly at first, then daringly moved an arm sufficiently so as to put a finger between the baby's. "My God, Eleanor. He is *perfect*."

Eleanor laughed. "I think so too."

They sat smiling at their new son and each other until Eleanor yawned. Hugh carefully passed the baby back to the wet nurse, who had timely appeared in the background. "I will let you rest now, sweetheart. Gladys told me you need it, and I obey Gladys in all matters."

"Hugh, I have been horrid to you lately. Scolding and crying and arguing. I wonder how you have borne with me, my love."

"You have made me the happiest man in the world."

"You don't wish you had married a great heiress?" It was a thought she had from time to time; she could not say why.

"What nonsense! You are all I want in this world—you and our fine new son and the other children you shall give me. There is nothing else I desire, my love."

And on that day, he meant it.

CHAPTER 4

▼

FEBRUARY 1309 TO
FEBRUARY 1310

To the barons' utter disgust, Gaveston was doing well in Ireland. His qualities as a soldier had won him the notice of the first Edward, and Ireland gave him ample opportunity to exercise his abilities.

Edward, still working assiduously to end his friend's exile, was delighted as reports came in of Piers, each more favorable than the last. "How can they not allow him to come back now?" he asked any confidant who happened to be around him—Hugh le Despenser the elder, or Gilbert de Clare, or even Isabella. "He'll be back soon, I warrant." And then he would call for a clerk and dictate yet another letter, either to his friend or to someone on his behalf.

Eleanor herself knew of Edward's efforts only secondhand, for she had not been at court since Hugh's birth. Though Hugh of course had a wet nurse, Eleanor spent much time with her son herself. He was a thriving baby, seldom succumbing even to routine ailments, and was regarded by his parents and grandfather as precocious in all things.

She was not entirely happy, though. Hugh her husband was a concern to her. Always restless, he had been more so after his son was born. With Eleanor reluctant to leave Loughborough because of the baby, Hugh would set out on horseback by himself and not return for weeks at a time, then return just as unexpectedly. Within minutes of his return he would contrive to get Eleanor alone somehow, and soon they would be carrying on together in a manner that made Eleanor blush sometimes to think of afterward. So he could not possibly have a mistress, could he? She was too proud to question him closely about his comings and goings, though, and he volunteered little information beyond the fact that he had been traveling.

Philip, Hugh's younger brother, and Isabel, Hugh's younger sister, could be questioned, however. Philip was still in his teens and had not yet married. Isabel had already been widowed—her first husband had been a Clare, a cousin to Eleanor—and married again, to Lord John de Hastings, not long before. She was a pretty, delicate-looking girl of eighteen with thick dark hair that fell almost to her knees when loosened. Her husband, a man in his late forties with children older than his second wife, doted on her, and when she announced her first pregnancy he had readily agreed to let her stay at Loughborough to await the birth.

"Do you know what Hugh does when he leaves here?" she asked Isabel one day as they sat in her chamber. "Do you think he has a mistress?"

Isabel laughed. "I doubt it, Nelly. He gets bored, that is all. Life here has never suited him. He might be going abroad, for all I know."

"Without the king's license!"

"Hugh never was one to stand much upon formalities."

"He would like to have a place at court." Philip, whose health had always been delicate, had been standing by the fire warming himself, though the February day was mild and the women saw no need to be near the fire. "A high place, though; he would prefer to go elsewhere rather than just to be another face in a crowd of courtiers."

"It is true," agreed Isabel. She hesitated. "As you and my father are in favor with the king, Nelly, I have often wondered why he has not risen at court. He has brains and could serve Edward well."

"No need to wonder about that!" Philip laughed. "Forgive me for speaking frankly, but Gaveston crowds out all others. Even while he is in Ireland."

"I should hardly want Hugh to rise in *that* manner," said Eleanor primly.

"In any case, our father has not won himself any friends for staying by the king and Gaveston," said Philip. "Hugh is wise to stay detached from all of this. A hornet's nest it is." He could not keep from sounding a bit wistful, however, for he longed himself to be of service to the king. But even after a few miles' riding, he felt tired, although he tried to hide it.

A messenger approached Eleanor and handed her a letter. "From the hornet's nest itself!" said Eleanor, seeing the royal seal.

"How important we are," said Philip cheerfully.

The short letter did nothing more than inform Eleanor that the queen would very much like to see her back at court soon. Though not worded as a command, it was certainly one, and a similar note from the king underscored it. "The queen asks me to join her at Langley," said Eleanor. "I must get ready. But if only I knew where Hugh was!"

"How well you look, Niece! Motherhood suits you. How is little Hugh?"

"Thriving, sir."

"We will not keep you here for so very long, but we have missed you so. Did your husband come with you?"

"No."

"Occupied with his father's affairs, I suppose."

"I don't know what he is doing, Uncle."

Edward frowned. "I do not like this, Nelly. Surely you are not estranged from him?"

"No, sir, but he goes his own way at times."

"He will find his own way unpleasant if he slights you. But let us go to the queen now."

Isabella was dictating letters to a clerk when Eleanor followed her uncle into her chamber. "Lady Despenser! How is your babe?"

"Growing well, your grace."

"When he is older you must bring him here to visit," put in the king. "He will be good company for Adam."

Eleanor wondered how the queen, whose belly was as flat as ever, would receive this suggestion, but she said only, "An excellent idea, Edward. The boy will want young companions." Isabella turned back to the clerk and dictated several more lines; evidently she had been asked to aid a poor priory. Then she dismissed the clerk. "And how fares the Countess of Cornwall?"

Even though Piers and Margaret had been married well over a year now, Eleanor still could not adjust to her sister's new title. It did not fit her as it would have the dignified Elizabeth. "She sent me a ring for New Year's, your grace, and at that time she was doing very well. She finds Ireland very pretty, but she is a little homesick, I think."

"We will bring her home soon," said Edward firmly. "Soon she and my brother will be back among us." He forestalled Eleanor's next question. "Yes, things are going well. We are holding profitable discussions with the Pope and the barons."

"And my father," said the queen magnificently.

"And the King of France," agreed Edward. "Next month I shall send an envoy to the Pope to have his excommunication reversed, and then this waiting shall soon be over, I hope." He reached for Eleanor's hand and kissed it. "I must meet with my council now, but I am glad to see you safely here. I know you ladies are eager to gossip now, anyway."

He went away whistling.

"What may I do for you, your grace?" Eleanor asked the queen. "Shall I tell you the latest news from Loughborough?"

Isabella laughed. "That would take too long!" She glanced at Eleanor's robes. "You seem to have gotten your figure back, Lady Despenser. Are you with child again?"

"Not that I know of." Eleanor hesitated, then confided, "Truth be told, your grace, I hardly see Hugh anymore, it seems. He comes to Loughborough and stays for a few days, and then he is off again."

"Are you tiring of each other?"

"I hope not, your grace, because I love him dearly."

"I would not let a man treat me that way."

"He treats me well when he is with me." Eleanor began to brush the queen's hair. Unlike her own hair, which pretty much went its own way and would barely consent even to hold a braid, the queen's was a pleasure to style. "I shall braid your hair and coil it about your ears. Won't that be pretty?"

"You digress, my lady."

"I don't wish to speak ill of Hugh, your grace. He has a restless spirit and no real outlet for it."

"He should visit Gaveston in Ireland if he is so restless."

"For all I know, he might have done so." Eleanor finished a braid and started to coil it. "Shall he be there long, do you think?"

Isabella held a glass mirror up to her face to admire her lady's handiwork. "The king insists on telling me how things are progressing, and he seems to feel they are progressing well, as you yourself heard. I don't know why he confides this to me."

"He confides in you, your grace, because he is fond of you and trusts your judgment," Eleanor said a bit reproachfully.

"Well, then, he must trust my judgment a great deal, because I am at no loss for news of that upstart Gascon."

The days went by pleasantly at Langley as the weather grew milder. Eleanor had shyly requested several favors of her uncle. Her damsel, Gladys, was having difficulty with her dower lands. Would the king put a word in with the chancellor? A word was put in, and Gladys's problems were soon over. A knight wished for a hundred. Would the king…? It was granted. The king also hinted at granting Eleanor and Hugh a manor, in honor of their fine new son, but Hugh was still in parts unknown.

At last, word came from Hugh that he was back from wherever he had gone to and was preparing to attend a tournament at Dunstable, along with Eleanor's brother Gilbert, most of the other earls, and a great quantity of knights. Eleanor would have liked to have seen it, to give Hugh her favor to wear and watch him joust, but her uncle was so put out by news of the well-attended tournament that she did not dare ask leave to travel there. "You know what the earls are doing," he told her and Isabella. "Plotting to keep Gaveston away! Preparing some absurd demands for the upcoming Parliament. If they don't take him back, I'll be damned if I'll allow them any more tournaments in the future."

The tournament over, its attendees began to straggle back; some to their homes, some to Westminster to await Parliament, some few to Langley where the king and queen remained. Early one fine morning in late April, Eleanor sat outside in the garden, playing with Adam and wishing her own son was nearby. She was bent on all fours looking for a ball that he had thrown into a bush when she heard a whistle, followed by, "Upon my word, wench! You have a fine arse!"

The speaker had used English, a language the nobility spoke only with those whose French was too poor for communication. Eleanor turned to glare.

"Fooled you, didn't I? But it's true."

"Hugh!" She ran into his arms. "I have missed you so."

"And I you, my love."

"Where have you been besides the tournament?" He was dressed plainly, like any respectable but common traveler might, and was deeply suntanned.

"Traveling." He pressed her against a tree and began to kiss her, moving from her lips to her bosom as Adam, fascinated by these unusual goings-on, stared raptly. Only when he started to undo the buttons on her gown did Eleanor recall herself and whisper, "The child, Hugh."

"The— Oh, hello." Hugh smiled down. "And who is this fine young man? Adam, I'll wager."

"Yes." Eleanor drew back a little. "And Hugh, I am sorry, but I told the queen I would be back presently. She bade me leave her while she wrote to her father."

"The queen!" Hugh pulled her back to him. "You are my wife, and I'm mad for you just now. The queen will have to wait."

"The queen? Wait? How?"

"Easily." Hugh turned as Adam's nurse hove into view. "Miss! Tell her grace, if you please, that Lady Despenser is ill and has gone to lie down."

The nurse glanced at Lady Despenser, who with her gown opened, her cheeks flushed, and her hair tumbling free over her shoulders looked anything but ill. "Yes, sir." She nodded at Adam. "Come along, young man."

"Now," said Hugh. "Back to it." He put his arms back around her.

It took all of Eleanor's self-control to push him back. "Hugh. Not here!"

"Why not?"

"Anyone looking from a window could see us."

"Oh, very well," said Hugh grudgingly. "We'll take a walk by the river."

By the river, they lay in some tall grass, both gasping for breath, only partly dressed. "Was that worth standing up the queen for?"

"Oh, yes," She rolled off him and lay on his shoulder, staring up at the perfectly blue sky. Shyly, she asked, "Hugh, why do you dislike her? I only am curious."

Hugh yawned. "Just a natural antipathy, I suppose. No good reason, really. Some people do that for one. I suppose I do dislike sharing you with her."

"I would be sorry to do so, but I could leave her household if you pleased."

"No, it is an honor for you, and for our family too. I should not have mentioned it."

"I am sure there would be a place for you at court if you wished it, Hugh."

"But I don't wish it." He tickled her with a blade of grass. "Chilly, my love?"

"A bit. And I am still afraid someone might see us."

"And a man who saw us would go mad with jealousy of me. Let's go to my inn, then. I have gifts for you in my saddlebags."

There were rooms at Langley in which Hugh could have stayed, but Eleanor asked no questions. They made themselves decent and walked to Hugh's inn, the proprietor staring at Eleanor. Hugh laughed when they came to his room, a quarter of the size Eleanor was used to. "He must recognize you from the queen's household, my love, and wonders at my skill in getting such a prize to my room. I will have to disabuse him of that notion later, I suppose. Now let me show you your gifts."

He opened the saddlebags and pulled out jewel after jewel, of a workmanship Eleanor had never seen in England. "I have never seen anything like them. They look as if they must be from Italy."

"They are from Italy."

"Hugh, where—"

"This garnet necklace would look pretty on your chest, but your clothes get in the way. Take them off."

She obeyed.

Much later they walked to the king's residence, Eleanor utterly drained yet not wanting to part. How could she sit quietly with the queen after those hours with Hugh? "Tonight while the queen sleeps I'll slip out and meet you in your inn," she whispered as they entered the great hall.

"You are an insatiable little harlot, but I can't have you wandering around after nightfall by yourself. I'll meet you in the garden. Or perhaps I'll make the supreme sacrifice and ask for a chamber here."

"It would be much more comfortable for us than that horrid room at the inn."

"Spoilt earl's daughter."

"Yes."

They were kissing again when they heard footsteps approaching. "My lady. Son."

Eleanor pulled away from Hugh as his father came to stand beside them. "My lady, the queen has wondered where you were. She sent me to find you, as a matter of fact."

"I am sorry, sir, to have troubled you. I will go to her immediately."

"No. Come to my chamber for a moment, the two of you."

In Hugh's chamber, he waved his daughter-in-law to a chair and turned to face his son. "Hugh, what kind of fool behavior is this? You come here without a word of warning, steal your wife away —"

"Steal my wife away? She is my wife, Father."

"She is attendant upon the queen. You cannot snatch her away at a moment's notice, for your pl—" He looked at his flushing daughter-in-law with her grass-stained clothing and finished awkwardly, "At your whim. You must have her ask the queen for leave."

Eleanor, tired of being spoken of as an inanimate object in the room, said calmly, "We meant no harm, sir. But it will not happen again, and I am sure the queen does not mind."

"You are wrong, my dear, for she does mind, very much. She comes from a court that stands very much on ceremony, and she took this as a sign of disrespect."

"She told you this, Father?"

"No, Hugh, not in so many words. But it was obvious when she asked me where Eleanor was that she was displeased."

"My wife's first duty is to me. The silly French piece has other ladies and damsels to serve her whims."

"The silly French piece is the Queen of England! Are you trying to lose both of our heads?" Hugh paced around the room, trying to calm himself, and succeeded. His voice was at its normal level when he resumed. "I speak too strongly, for this is hardly a matter of treason, only a minor impropriety. Let us say no more about it. How long do you stay here, Hugh?"

"For a few days, but I have rooms at the inn where I can go my own way. I might even have my wife there if her grace allows."

"Hugh, I have served the king and his father faithfully since I was of your age, and it has paid me well. It would you too, if you would only bend to convention a little. Let me find you a place at court where you can show your talents. You have them, by Jove, and the king will soon find them out. In time."

"While I serve time like you."

"Have you forgotten what our family owes the king and his father? When I was but a child my father was killed in Montfort's rebellion. Yet when I reached manhood the first Edward welcomed me at his court, when I might have been relegated to obscurity. He was gracious to me and I do not forget that. If you call that time-serving you may." Hugh was pacing again. "Your brother would be happy for such opportunities. I've a mind to bring him here instead."

"That weakling!"

Hugh's blow knocked his son off his feet. Eleanor gasped but remained where she was standing, too frightened to come to his side. Hugh, however, appeared to have forgotten her existence. He stared down at his son and said calmly, "The Lord has blessed me with healthy daughters and one healthy son. Your brother is not a weakling; he is dying. Slowly but inexorably. Up until today I had not admitted it to myself."

"Father, I know. I am sorry."

If Hugh heard his son he paid him no attention. "I suppose I should be grateful for my lot; all but he are healthy. But by God there are days when I look at him and wish it were you with all of your arrogance and impertinence in his place."

He strode out of the room, shutting the door behind him as softly as he and his son had been having the most amicable of conversations. Only then did Eleanor run to Hugh's side. "My love, he did not mean it. He is grieved about your brother and you probed the wound, that is all."

"Leave me, Eleanor."

"You must go to him, Hugh. You have hurt him dreadfully. Your brother—*I knew he was sickly but I never thought he was dying*—go to him, Hugh, please!"

"Leave me, you silly girl!"

Eleanor, not knowing how she did so, left. As though sleepwalking, she made her way to the queen's chambers, curtseyed, picked up her embroidery where she had left it, and sat quietly stitching with the other ladies. Isabella sat stitching herself, smiling sardonically for a while. Then she spoke. "You are feeling better?"

"Yes, your grace."

"Then endeavor to look less wretched."

"Yes, your grace."

For an hour or so Eleanor worked, listening to the conversation around her and trying to hold back her tears. Then they began to trickle down her face. Isabella de Vescy, one of the older ladies, said kindly, without her usual brusqueness, "Child, what ails you?" The queen only sighed. "Leave me, Lady Despenser, and don't come back until your face is less sour. It is like having a funeral mute attending me."

"Yes, your grace."

She ran outside the manor house into the park and walked by the spot where she and Hugh had made love that morning. She kept going, and soon the king's orderly park had turned into simple woods, completely unfamiliar to her.

A silly girl. It was all she was to him. A plaything, perhaps, on occasion. How could she have been so stupid as to think he cared for her?

Farther and farther she went into the woods, paying no attention where she was going and losing all sense of time and distance. A deer leapt past her and she gasped, as scared of it as it was of her, and then pushed her way on resolutely. But what was her resolution? Only to get as far away from Langley and Hugh as possible.

Suddenly she heard male voices, speaking in English, and froze in terror. What danger had she put herself into? Brigands traveled through the forests, robbing those who they encountered. Usually they were after horses, money, or jewelry, but Eleanor had no horse or money and wore only her wedding ring and the jewel Hugh had put on her that afternoon. What would they do to her if they were disappointed? She flattened herself against a tree, praying silently, desperately, to the Virgin, and all but fainted with relief when the men went by her, passing not three feet away but not turning their heads in her direction. She looked at them as hard as she dared; they were certainly no one she recognized from Langley.

She had to get out of the forest. But how? It was growing dark, and she had no idea where she had come from.

Walking in the opposite direction from the men, and praying that there were none to follow them, she caught sight of a stream. It would certainly lead her to the river. Sobbing with relief, she hurried to the stream, not seeing in the growing darkness the root that caught her foot and sent her headlong down the bank and into the water. Soaked to the skin, her hands scraped on the pebbles she had grabbed in a vain effort to stop her fall, she emerged coughing and sputtering from the water, only to find that her throbbing ankle would not bear her weight. She crawled out of the stream and pulled herself upon a large rock, utterly defeated.

Then she heard dogs barking, then running toward her. She tried to move again but could not. Was this what a deer felt like? Good God, if she made it out of the forest alive she would never hunt one again. They were all on her now, but they were doing nothing more than sniffing her, eight cold noses against her at once, tickling her. Then they began barking triumphantly, and the huntsman arrived. "Eleanor! Thank God you are safe!"

"Uncle!"

Edward bade the dogs to sit. He sat too and put his arm around her, raising his eyebrows at her soaked gown. "My dear, you have given us a fright. What on earth made you wander here by yourself? You must have heard of the sort of men who can pass through the forest."

"I am sorry, Uncle." In her relief at being safe she snuggled against him, taking in his familiar woodsy smell.

"But what brought you here?"

"Everyone is angry at me, Uncle, and I am so miserable."

"Angry at you, my dear? There is not a soul at Langley who is not worried half to death about you. My men, and the queen's men, and your father-in-law and your husband are all out searching for you this instant."

"Hugh is looking for me?"

"Did you not think he would be?"

She shook her head. "He thinks me a silly girl."

"And you are." Hugh, followed by his father, stepped through the brush, panting but smiling. "Silly to think I would not be looking for you." He reached for her, but she shrank against her uncle. Hugh looked helplessly toward his father.

"Eleanor, it was Hugh who discovered you gone," said the elder Hugh. "When he saw you were not in the hall tonight and could find no one who knew where you were, he begged the king to send out his dogs in search of you."

Edward smiled. "Not that he had to beg, for I could not have borne it had something happened to you."

He stood and moved discreetly away, along with Eleanor's father-in-law, leaving only the dogs standing near them, thumping their tails complacently. Hugh took the king's place and said quietly, "I was distressed at the scene with my father, my love—which was entirely my fault, and I made it up with him upon your advice—and lost my temper with you. I should not have spoken hastily to you. Will you forgive me?"

"You think me a silly fool."

"I think I have been blessed with you, and that I was the fool to speak as I did. If anything had happened to you in this forest I would have been in agony. Please, Eleanor?"

She was silent. Suddenly she became aware of the absurdity of the entire situation—the waiting pack, all gazing patiently at her, and the even more patiently waiting king, carving a likely-looking stick at a distance with his back turned toward Hugh and Eleanor as if there was nothing else in the world to command his attention than the quarrel between his niece and her husband. In spite of herself, she began to laugh. She took Hugh's hand. "Does that mean I am forgiven?"

"No, it means I want you to help me out of here."

"And then you will forgive me?"

"I will consider it."

By the time she arrived back at Langley, her ankle was swollen and aching and she was shivering in her soaked clothes. But Hugh ordered a hot bath and a good deal of wine to warm her and ease the pain, and after the bath he wrapped her in a blanket and put her by the fire, stroking her hair as she chattered on in his lap, happily tipsy. "Hugh, I was so frightened in the forest. But you came and found me."

"Yes, my love."

"You and the king. But not the queen." His wife looked momentarily sad.

The queen had in fact taken Eleanor's disappearance with an equanimity that had infuriated Hugh—"She couldn't have gone far, I'm sure"—but Hugh could not bear to see his young wife downcast. "She was concerned as we, but she could hardly go wandering around the forest like the rest of us, my love."

"That is true." She drained her cup and held it out shakily. "Might I have some more wine, Hugh?"

"No, my love. You will be sick."

"Oh, all right." She began kissing him instead, languorously. Then she giggled. "This is so strange. I'm floating away, Hugh."

"I'll anchor you." He lowered her to the rug by the fire, letting the blanket fall off her, and had her, moving very slowly so as not to hurt her ankle inadvertently. Never had he had so much pleasure in lovemaking, and as for her—"Hush, love. You'll scare the horses."

She laughed and pressed fiercely up against him, and then his cry put hers to shame. He gasped, "Forgive me?"

She hugged him close to her. "Yes."

After lying quietly in his arms for a time, she propped herself with some difficulty on her elbow and looked him full in the face. He had never seen her green eyes look so serious, or so green for that matter. "Hugh, please tell me. What do you do when you travel? I don't want to pry, but I miss you so much when you are gone. But I suppose I *am* prying."

"I will be better in the future, I promise."

"But won't you tell me?"

Her voice was becoming dreamy, and he knew that in minutes she would be asleep. He looked at her—sixteen years old, the sweetest, most innocent creature he knew. What would it be like to dream the dreams of the guiltless every night? There were times when he wondered if the kindest thing he could do for her was to leave her, to free her for a man who had no dark thoughts in his mind. He sighed. "If you must know, my love, I know men with ships—pirate ships. I join them, and I share in some of the spoils. You are wearing one around your neck."

As he had expected, she giggled. "I may have had a *little* too much wine, Hugh le Despenser, but I am no fool. But if you won't tell me"—she yawned—"I won't...press...further."

She was fast asleep. He carried her to bed, blew out the candles, and slipped in bed beside her, holding her as she slept.

At least, he thought, it could not be said that he had not told her.

"Margaret! How well you look!"

It had taken longer than Edward had anticipated, but Gaveston was back in England, the Pope having issued a bull of absolution that Edward would soon wave in front of Parliament when it met later in that July of 1309. The king had traveled to Chester with a small entourage to greet his friend and his niece. Now they were at Langley, with the queen, and Eleanor, who had left Isabella for a visit to her baby, was back there too. Even Hugh had left his affairs at the manor in Sutton the king had granted them to greet his brother-in-law.

The sisters embraced while their brother Gilbert, then Hugh, did the same with Gaveston. Beside him, the king beamed. "It is so pleasant to have *all* of my family nearby again."

"But less of Nelly," said Gaveston. He nodded at Eleanor's belly. "How is your boy?"

"He is here, as a matter of fact. The queen was kind enough to ask me to bring him while the weather was so fine he could travel."

"I thought I was with child last month," said Margaret. "But then my monthly course started, just like that."

"Meg!"

"Well, Nelly, don't look so shocked. We are family, are we not?" She turned to the king, who was smiling indulgently. "Now Uncle, tell us. Are these stupid earls and barons of yours appeased for good? Because I do not care to be taking another trip abroad."

"Meg was seasick," said Piers.

"Seasick isn't the word. I was at the point of death. I am just now recovered. Don't roll your eyes at me, Hugh le Despenser!"

"My apologies." Hugh shrugged.

Gilbert said briskly, "As for the earls, Richmond is well-enough disposed to you, Piers, as is Lincoln. Warenne is too much occupied with his latest mistress to care either way. Pembroke is wary. Arundel is still sulking because you defeated him at that tournament following your marriage. Lancaster and Warwick would see you hanged if they could. Not to be unpleasant about it."

"Gilbert's summing up is all too accurate," admitted the king. "But they'll come round. We'll not let them ruin our time here, will we?"

For a time it appeared that all would go well. Gaveston had been given all of his Cornwall lands back, and Margaret made it her business to enjoy them, hostessing great feasts to which she invited the duly admiring Eleanor and Gilbert. With Eleanor came Hugh, sometimes, and with Gilbert came his bride of about a year: Maud, the daughter of Richard de Burgh, Earl of Ulster. Their sister Elizabeth had married also, to Maud's brother John, and moved to Ireland to live with him in October 1309. "The poor girl," said Margaret complacently. "It is green and pretty there, but how I missed England! I do hope Piers never has to return there."

Hugh waited until Margaret had left the room. "I'd be looking to getting my sea legs again if I were her."

"It has started again?"

"It has started."

"Gaveston has made an effort to get along with some of the barons," Hugh the elder said some days later to Eleanor. "But most despise him, and he does nothing to help the situation. If they want an audience with the king, he is there in the room. And those nicknames! Childish, but they seem to gall the earls as much as anything. And they stick in one's mind, too. Warwick is my brother-in-law, you know, and I cannot think of him at all now but as the Black Dog of Arden. I have to make a great effort to not address him as that."

The king was irked. "Ever since my father died, they have chided me for ignoring the Scottish problem. And now that I am trying to discuss the Scottish problem with them, as surely they expect, they refuse to come to Parliament if Gaveston is there. And he an earl as much as they!"

"They, Uncle?"

"Arundel, Pembroke, even Lincoln, and the Black D—that is, Warwick. And a new ally. Lancaster."

The Earl of Lancaster was Edward's first cousin, like him a grandson of Henry III. Eleanor recalled the gossip she had heard in the queen's chamber. "Isabella de Vescy says that not even his own wife cares for him."

"A sensible woman, his wife."

The king, Gaveston, and their wives spent Christmas at Langley, but Eleanor and Hugh did not join them. Nearly a year and a half had passed since little Hugh was born, and Eleanor was worried. Had she become barren? Hugh was a fine boy, a chatty fellow who looked more like his father every day. He was perfectly healthy so far, but one never knew... She had consulted the midwife, who had sternly told her that she had to be on her back at all times when she lay with Hugh. Eleanor had obeyed, at least most of the time, but despite this she had had no success, though once or twice her monthly course had been late enough to give her hope for a week or so. It was time to try something else. "I would like to go on pilgrimage," she told Hugh.

They were at Loughborough again, the king having taken only the smallest possible group of attendants with him to Langley and Eleanor having been given leave to spend Christmas with her husband and child. Hugh the elder was there, of course, along with Philip and the youngest of the Despenser children, Margaret. Dinner was over, and they were lazing in their chamber, having seen little Hugh to bed. "Where?" asked Hugh.

"Canterbury, I think."

"So it shall be."

She was delighted. Hardly ever had she and Hugh traveled together, save from one family manor to the other, followed by men and baggage.

So to Canterbury they went. Never before had she spent so much time alone with Hugh, whose comings and goings, though still frequent, were less noticeable now that Eleanor herself had resumed her own travels with the queen. Together, they traveled with only a squire, and moved much more quickly than Eleanor, used to the cumbersome progress of the court, was accustomed to. It was with real sadness that she reached the shrine at Canterbury and offered up her prayers and coins, for now there was nothing to do but to turn back home. She said as much to Hugh as they sat at supper at one of the hole-in-the-wall inns Hugh had a knack for finding and for which Eleanor had developed a certain affection.

"Actually, my love, I was thinking of going to Dover."

"Dover? What is at Dover?"

"The Channel, what else? I thought we would go to France."

"France!"

"Aside from being full of Frenchmen, it's a pleasant place."

"We must get the king's permission."

"The king has other things on his mind," said Hugh offhandedly. "And why would he care? You have leave from the queen to be away from court until February, so her pert little nose won't be out of joint."

"Hugh!" Eleanor swatted him.

"So will you go?"

"I would love to."

In her worst moments years later, Eleanor could tip her head back and remember their trip to France that winter of 1310: the salt water spraying her face as she stood on the deck with Hugh's arm around her; her wobbly legs as he handed her off the boat; the sleet storm that blew in from the shore just as they reached their inn; the day when it was too cold and miserable outside to do anything but stay in their warm bed and make love (breaking the midwife's rule without shame) and talk to each other.

"Hugh, what was your mother like?"

They had undressed for the night, and Hugh had had other plans in mind, but he answered obligingly, "Beautiful. You know her brother, Gaveston's Black

Dog of Arden, of course. He is a handsome man, and she was better looking than he. Beautiful, and she could sit a horse better than most men." He smiled sheepishly. "She put me in mind of the goddess Diana."

"She must have been lovely. Was she delicate-looking like your sister Isabel?"

"Lord, no. Isabel gets her name from my mother but nothing else. Mother loved hunting more than anything in the world—Diana again—and she was good at it. As a matter of fact, she took five deer on one occasion and had the hue and cry raised against her. I was only about ten when it happened, and I still remember when she came galloping home, in a fury. I don't know what made her angrier, having the hue and cry raised against her or leaving her five bucks behind. Father was with the king at the time, or she probably would have made him slay the gamekeeper. If I'd been a trifle older she probably would have had me do so."

"Do you miss her?"

He shrugged. "In a way. But she never saw much of us children; it was our nurses or Father we went to when we were troubled. It is his loss that I would take to heart." Hugh crossed himself and looked at the sleet beating against their window. "A gloomy topic for a gloomy night."

"I am sorry, Hugh. But I enjoy talking to you so much. There is so much I don't know about you even yet."

"Aye, you women must talk. But now I am done with words."

He gathered her to him and began kissing and fondling her, and she responded with her usual eagerness. It was therefore with great disappointment that she suddenly felt him arise from the bed. "Hugh?"

"I am getting some wine."

"*Now?*"

"Now."

He went to the table where the remnants of their supper sat and returned with a cup of wine, smiling. She shrugged and lay back, naked and irritated. It was not like Hugh to arouse her and then to leave her unsatisfied, but as she had said, there was much she did not know about him. Then she jerked back as wine splashed in the hollow of her throat and began to trickle downward.

"How clumsy of me, my love. But I shall clean it up."

And he did, in a manner that so shocked and pleased Eleanor that she expected lightning to strike them dead at any minute. As none did, she settled against Hugh for the night and reminded herself that after all, they were in France.

Her father-in-law, meanwhile, had returned to court and was paying his respects to the king. Edward had spent a very pleasant Christmas at Langley with Gaveston and the queen, and was in good spirits. "And how is your family, Hugh? How is Philip?"

In the case of those he liked, Edward could remember all manner of minutiae. Philip had never been to court; Hugh had probably never mentioned his name more than once or twice to the king. Yet Edward had never forgotten him. "He is a cause of concern to me, sir, as you may recall. He is not at all strong, and the winters are always bad for him. Would that he had a tenth of Hugh's good health." Hugh stopped awkwardly, for he had not intended to mention his eldest son.

"Aye, Hugh. And how are he and my little niece Eleanor?"

"Quite well."

"They are still at Loughborough?"

Hugh had a policy of never lying to his king. "No, your grace. They are—"

Edward saw his advisor's discomfiture. "Abroad."

"Yes, I am afraid so. Abroad."

Edward shook his head. "Without license and against my orders. Hugh, you know I cannot let this pass unnoticed. If your wild son flouts my authority in this manner, what will the barons who hate me do? I must seize his lands."

"You must do what you must do." Hugh grimaced. "He is my beloved son, but he has always been lacking in a sense of propriety. It is that Warwick streak, I think."

"What does he do on these jaunts of his?"

Hugh could answer truthfully. "I don't know, your grace. He is a grown man, and minds my own affairs splendidly when I am unable to attend to them because of my duties here. I ask no questions, and he tells me nothing."

"Piracy."

Hugh and Edward turned to look at Gaveston, who had been bent over a table spread with maps during the whole of their conversation. Hugh was well used to Gaveston's constant presence, but there were times when he had to acknowledge that it might irritate others. Though in all fairness, he reminded himself, Gaveston had always willingly left the room on the one or two occasions that Hugh had requested privacy. Did he do so for others? Perhaps not. Gaveston looked up and smiled dazzlingly. "He disappears for long stretches; he never seems to be in want of money when he returns, does he? So his wife says to my wife anyway—women do talk. I don't think with luscious little Eleanor there would be a wench he stays with, and such cost money anyway. He'd be coming home poorer if that were the case."

"That is utter nonsense. My son is not a pirate," said Hugh loftily. "And my young daughter-in-law is not luscious." He stopped, aghast at the trap he had wandered into.

Gaveston, for once, declined to spring it. "In any case, you said they were together, so I would guess they are merely on pilgrimage on this occasion."

Hugh relaxed. "That is what he wrote." He dropped to a seat by the fire. "And now, may I ask, is there to be a Parliament in February or is there not?"

"Not with me there, it appears," Gaveston said cheerfully.

"I have scheduled it for Westminster," said Edward. "But the barons are refusing to attend if my brother is there."

"It is my understanding from Gilbert that they have parchment after parchment of grievances to put forth," said Gaveston. "So they'll have to attend to let them be heard, I suppose." He kicked at the fire. "I suppose you are aware of their grievances, Despenser?"

Hugh shook his head. "No. I have not their confidence, being older than most of the earls and not of their rank. And—"

"And they dislike you because you have been steadfastly loyal to me," finished Edward. "Someday, good friend, you shall have your reward."

Margaret was annoyed. "My husband to leave the court just so the barons can complain to the king!"

"The king tried everything to avoid him having to leave," said Eleanor. "But Hugh said that the earls threatened to come in arms, and even when the king promised that our brother and others would keep the peace, they would not relent."

"And what are these grievances anyway?"

"Hugh says they are angry about the conduct of the Scottish problem, among other duller things I didn't quite understand."

"With you it is Hugh says, Hugh says, Hugh says!" Margaret scowled.

"We had much time to talk over the past few weeks," said Eleanor mildly. She smiled at the thought of their sojourn in France. Even having Hugh's lands seized had not diminished the joy she had taken in his company, although to her dismay her monthly course had started only a few days ago. "I am sure he will not be gone for long, and you will be together, after all."

"Where shall you stay, Countess?" asked the queen, who had been listening to the sisters' conversation with undisguised interest, as she had a perfect right to since it was taking place in her chamber. Margaret had stomped there to bid Eleanor farewell.

The countess shrugged, then remembered herself. "I beg your pardon, your grace. We shall be staying in Knaresborough for the time being, I suppose. I am not certain. It depends on the stupid earls."

"The earls may have valid grievances," said Isabella. "Perhaps some good will come out of this."

"None that I can imagine, your grace," said Margaret. "Now if you will give me leave, your grace, I will go and decide what to pack."

CHAPTER 5

▼

MARCH 1310 TO JUNE 1312

Edward's opponents had presented their grievances to the king, who had most reluctantly agreed to allow them to elect of group of earls, bishops, and barons called the Ordainers. Till Michaelmas of 1311 they planned to work, drafting a series of what they called reforms and what the king called a number of other things, all of which made Eleanor blush.

Gilbert de Clare was the youngest of the Ordainers. Though loyal to the king, he was rather proud to be part of what he considered to be a worthy object. With an almost paternal air he brought Eleanor a parchment containing the first products of the Ordainers' handiwork. "Very reasonable, you see, sister. We are to protect the franchises of our Holy Church. We are to sit in London so that we might have all the necessary records at our disposal. We are to maintain Magna Carta."

All this sounded reasonable enough to Eleanor. But were there not other Ordinances? She leaned over her brother's shoulder. "No gifts are to be made by the king without the assent of the Ordainers— Gilbert! You know full well this means Gaveston here. The king will never agree."

"But he has no choice, you see."

Edward's reaction to the preliminary Ordinances was to ignore them. Instead, he and Gaveston planned a Scottish campaign and went north to Berwick, while the Ordainers remained in London. Shortly after the preliminary Ordinances took effect, Edward tweaked the Ordainers' noses by making Gaveston a justice of the forest north of Trent and keeper of Nottingham Castle.

Aside from these snubs, the king was making little progress in Scotland, though Gilbert, Gaveston, and the Earl of Surrey, who had married Eleanor's cousin Joan on the same day she had married Hugh, had brought troops with them and at least could take credit for keeping Robert Bruce, the Scottish leader, from complacency. Lancaster, meanwhile, made great progress in February 1311 when his father-in-law, the Earl of Lincoln, died, giving Lancaster more earldoms. His income of eleven thousand pounds a year dwarfed even that of Gilbert, and he quickly showed his hand by refusing to cross the Tweed to swear fealty to the king. For weeks the king remained north of the Tweed, Lancaster south of it, until finally the king gave in and crossed the river to take Lancaster's fealty. Lancaster enjoyed himself still more by refusing to acknowledge Gaveston's presence.

The completed Ordinances arrived in the king's hands in August 1311 as the court, dispirited from what had ultimately proven to be no more than a change of scene, made its way back to London. Edward went off to read them and returned livid. "Look at this, Isabella! Look, Niece! They have charged my brother with providing me with evil counsel. Evil counsel, from my one true friend! With draining the royal treasury and sending it abroad. With—"

"No doubt the charges are excessive," said Isabella coolly. "But they cannot come as a surprise to you. They are only what the Ordainers have been saying all along."

"Aye, but this will be a surprise to you, Isabella. Gaveston is not the only one they proscribe. They have targeted one of your ladies. Isabella de Vescy." He picked up the parchment that he had thrown upon a table and read, "It is determined by the investigations of the prelates, earls, and barons that the Lady Vescy petitioned the king to give to her brother, Sir Henry de Beaumont, and others, lands and franchises to the damage and dishonor of the king and the disinheritance of the crown. Moreover, she had procured letters of privilege contrary to the law and the intentions of the king."

"What utter nonsense!"

"They demand her departure by Michaelmas and require that she relinquish her wardship of Bamburgh Castle," said Edward almost complacently. "Of course it is nonsense. It was my father who gave her custody of that castle, after she served for years as one of my mother's ladies in waiting. Her late husband was my father's good friend. I only renewed her wardship, and for good reason; she has been loyal and carried out her duties well."

"The impertinence!"

"They call for her brother Beaumont's dismissal as well." Seeing Isabella's indignation had almost cooled Edward's. He glanced at the parchment again. "The rest of these are what one might expect. Magna Carta is to be fully kept. Royal revenues are to be paid in the exchequer. Escheators are to be appointed in Parliament. My right to issue pardons is restricted. Prises are to be abolished." He tossed the parchment aside. "Fine words from the Fiddler, but can he play? And can the Black Dog bite as well as bark?"

"Do they want Gaveston gone too?" the queen asked.

"He is to depart from Dover by the first of November." Edward's mood sank again. He walked to a window and stared out of it.

Eleanor had been sitting in silence listening to the royal couple's conversation. Now she burst out, "Uncle, they cannot send him away! Margaret is with child."

Edward started. "I have heard nothing of this, Niece."

"I heard of it from Margaret only yesterday. She said she would wait a couple of weeks more before telling Piers." Margaret and Piers had not followed the king south, but had stayed in the north.

"Is she certain?"

"She feels ill all the time, and she says she is losing her waist."

"Then she must be with child," said the king. "What splendid news! Gaveston to have a heir! We shall give him—that is, Margaret—a churching as has never been seen."

"Not if he is in exile, Uncle."

"Those damned Ordainers," said the king. "I'll fight them."

The king did fight the Ordinances, but it was of no use. In the end, fearing civil war, he grudgingly acceded to all of the Ordinances but the one concerning Gaveston, and eventually he was forced to accede to that one too. Though Gaveston left from London, not Dover, and on the fourth of November, not the first of November—the minor discrepancy a source of some small satisfaction to the king—he still left, with his pregnant bride remaining in England.

Isabella de Vescy had left the court before Gaveston, though only for her lands in Yorkshire. "Don't fear, your grace, I'll soon be back," she promised the queen. "Fool barons!"

The king, Margaret, and Eleanor had gone to the side of the Thames to see Gaveston off. Eleanor had never learned whether the rumors about Gaveston and the king were true, but as the years had passed by, she had ceased to wonder about them. Margaret and Piers seemed as happy as most couples she knew, and it was not like Margaret to keep her complaints to herself if she had any. She'd wanted to join Gaveston in his exile, but he had not wanted her to travel by sea in her condition.

Edward was making no effort to control his emotions as he embraced his friend to say goodbye, and Eleanor tactfully took a great interest in the unloading of a nearby merchant ship. Then Gaveston turned his attention to Margaret, whose bulk prevented him from holding her as close as he had the king. "I know I can trust you to take care of my wife, Nelly," he said at last, tapping her on the shoulder to unfix her gaze from the merchant ship.

"I will do everything possible for her, Piers. But where shall you go?"

"Where life takes me, as has always been the case."

"But you cannot be so careless once you have had your child, you know."

He laughed. "Your earnestness delights and instructs me as always." He drew her into a hug. "Good-bye, Nelly. Where is Hugh? Traveling as ever?"

"No. He is back at court for the moment." She frowned, for Hugh had greatly irritated her that fall by borrowing her carts and sumpter horses without warning, forcing Eleanor's elderly chamberlain to scramble about to hire some for her own travels with the queen. Isabella had had a great deal to say about Hugh's presumption, and Eleanor had found herself agreeing with much of it. Even after the horses and carts had arrived back in their designated place in the royal stables, and Hugh had apologized, Eleanor still remained a little piqued.

"Someday, my dear, you and I will have a chat about Hugh's travels, but not today. If I run into him abroad I shall tell him you have taken a French lover and have no need of him."

"Piers!"

"Very well. A plain old Englishman." He turned to embrace Margaret again, then the king, and turned to board his ship. Only when its sails went out of sight did the three of them turn away. Eleanor could see from the king's and Margaret's slumped shoulders that they were both dejected; what surprised her was how dejected she was herself.

Immediately after Christmas, Eleanor and her father-in-law were summoned to attend the king in York. Eleanor was disappointed, for life at Loughborough had been extremely agreeable. Philip's health had improved so much that he had married, and he and his new bride had come for the holiday festivities. Isabel de Hastings, whose second son had been born a few months earlier, did not visit, but sent good reports of her family; she and her husband had just returned from Gascony. Margaret came home from some great house where she had been improving her manners and conversation, as was the custom among girls her age, and all at Loughborough agreed that she was duly improved. Hugh the elder had his eye out for a match for her.

Hugh her husband was there too, of course. It had snowed a few days before Christmas, and he and Eleanor and their three-year-old son had had a delightful time throwing snowballs at each other. Even Margaret had temporarily abandoned her fine manners to join in, ganging up with little Hugh and his nurse against his parents. Eleanor had been freezing cold afterward, and Hugh had taken her inside and helpfully removed her sodden clothes, which had led to an even more delightful time. She'd then forgiven him entirely for so high-handedly taking her sumpter horses.

"York!" she asked now. "Why York, this time of year?"

Hugh the elder said, "It can mean only thing, my dear. He is bringing Gaveston back to England."

"York! This time of year! We just came from York. I do not intend to go back there." Isabella looked around her at the comforts of Westminster, where she and the king were spending Christmas. "I will not go there."

"Then you may stay. I go to York."

"Edward. You cannot be contemplating having that Gaveston return."

"I am not contemplating it. My messenger has already given Piers his instructions. He is to make his way to York immediately."

"Edward, are you mad?"

"Certainly not. Only a madman would consent to be treated the way I have been treated, being told whom I can have around my own court. Do you think for an instant my father would have tolerated this? I did a short while, but 'tis past." He glanced at his seething young wife. "But there is no need for you to hurry, as you may join us at York at your leisure. We shall travel slowly too, for we must stop at Wallingford and bring my niece Margaret with us. Traveling with a pregnant woman will slow us down, but Piers will like to see his child, and Margaret is of hardy stock. Piers's old nurse, Agnes, and Lady Despenser shall go with her."

"You take my own lady now, without informing me?"

"I am informing you now, Isabella, and is it not natural that Eleanor should attend her younger sister in childbirth? When the child is born Eleanor shall return to her duties with you. In the meantime your household will not much feel the diminution by one, I imagine."

"You forget that my lady Isabella de Vescy has also been forced from me."

"By those Ordainers you find so irritatingly sensible at times, my lady, not by me. They seek to control you as much as me. Shall I read you the Ordinances again?"

"You need not. I am having them transcribed for me."

He laughed and said, with genuine approbation, "I have always admired your inquisitive mind, Isabella." He glanced at Isabella's figure, now entirely that of a woman, and smiled. "Shall Piers be alone in his fatherhood, my queen, or shall we give him a rival? We have not made any efforts in that regard lately, I think. I must leave in the morning."

She nodded and dutifully let him lead her toward her bed.

Eleanor, having had a fairly easy time in childbirth herself, had hoped that Margaret would be similarly blessed, but hours had gone by with Margaret no closer to giving birth than she had been when a boy awoke Eleanor from a deep sleep to bid her to attend her sister.

"Did he say he would come?" Margaret whimpered between spasms.

Eleanor said gently, "I know only what the king told me, and the king says he will soon be here."

"I want him, Nelly. I miss him."

"I know you do, Meg."

"I don't care what they say about him and the king. He loves me, and I love him. I am so scared, Nelly. What if I die before he comes?"

"You will not die," said Eleanor. Though women did every day, of course. Yet their mother had borne four babes from Gilbert de Clare and four more from their stepfather, and their grandmother Queen Eleanor had borne even more. Neither had died from childbearing. "You are a Clare, and we are from strong stock." She cast her mind back on what her own midwife had told her. "Breathe. Like this."

Margaret was in between pains. She said loftily, "I know well how to breathe, sister."

Three more hours had passed, and Margaret had at last gone into hard labor. Only then did she remember that she had packed a relic to clutch at as she gave birth. Eleanor, relieved to be out of the room and away from Margaret's yelps for a short while, went to find her trunks to unpack it.

Exhausted and dizzy from bending over her sister, she scarcely noticed the men sauntering toward her. Then she started. "Uncle! Piers!"

"Nelly. How fares Meg?"

"Well as can be expected, but Piers, she is in the worst stage, and it would help her so much if she could see you. You must go to her."

"Go to her? In childbed? But Nelly, no man goes there."

"This is special." She tugged at Piers. "Get you there now!"

"Nelly! What a fierce little creature you are. Quit yanking at me, and I will follow you to wherever you wish. But what if I collapse?"

"If you can stand battle," said Eleanor, "you can surely stand this."

Gaveston followed her back to the birthing chamber, where the midwife—a local woman who had said no more than a dozen words in so many hours—stared at him in horror. "Sir! No man comes in here."

"It is all right," said Eleanor, pushing him forward. "I asked him to come. Meg, look who is here."

Margaret was in such intense pain that her face was contorted, but her eyes lit up when she saw her husband. "I am so glad to see you," she panted when she could speak. "Now get out!"

"Women," said Gaveston as Eleanor escorted him briskly out of the room. "Where shall you drag me now, Nelly? To a nunnery?"

"I knew she would be happy to see you," Eleanor said softly. "Wait nearby. It won't be long now."

A half hour later, Margaret was delivered safely of a daughter, and Eleanor dispatched her sister's youngest, gawkiest page to give the message to Piers and to the king, knowing that the lad would get a handsome reward for his short walk. The midwife cleaned the baby, while Agnes and Eleanor made Margaret pretty to see Piers, who was regaling the unenthusiastic king with his very brief glimpse of a childbed.

"How shall you name her?" asked Eleanor.

"After our mother."

"Not after Piers's?"

"Claramunde? Too French." She smiled apologetically at Agnes. "Piers himself suggested Joan if the baby was a girl. Anyway"—she lowered her voice—"I suppose you have heard the rumors about his mother."

"Rumors?"

"Really, Nelly! How do you stay so naive? Have you never heard the talk that Piers's mother was burned as a witch?"

"No! I have never heard such a horrible thing. Surely—"

"There's no truth to it," said Agnes coolly. "I was with the poor lady when she died. She had a fever, and it carried her away in a few hours, her dying in her bed just as any other lady might. There wasn't much out of the ordinary about her but her beauty, though Lord knows she stood out enough for that. Piers takes after her in that respect. But it suits the barons to say that she was a witch, and that she passed her powers on to my lord."

"They are vile men," said Eleanor. "My uncle was right to bring Piers back in defiance of them. They and their Ordinances deserve no respect." She patted Margaret on the hand. "But let me bring in Piers and show him what a beautiful daughter you have given him."

During the hurried, cold trip to York, Eleanor had not presumed to ask the king his intentions regarding Gaveston; she and Margaret knew only that he was to return to see his child born. Perhaps, Eleanor had thought, Gaveston planned to take Margaret with him after she went through with her churching, which would take place about forty days after the birth of her child.

Now, however, Edward's plans became clear. The household, and more important, the chancery clerks, were all making their way to York, men and cartloads of documents moving from south to north. No sooner were the clerks ensconced in their new headquarters at St. Mary's Abbey did Edward sit them down and begin issuing orders, each calculated to infuriate the Ordainers, who had not joined the move to York. In writs issued to all of the sheriffs of the land, he declared Gaveston's exile to be contrary to law and reason. He granted Gaveston all of the lands that had been forfeited with his exile. He declared that he would not abide by the Ordinances, though later he softened his approach by stating he would not abide by those harmful to him. The Ordainers stayed away from the court, planning strategy.

Meanwhile, the small court enjoyed itself. Margaret was churched in the grand style Edward had promised; Edward's minstrels provided the entertainment. Eleanor herself did not enjoy the churching much, however; she had been tired for days, no matter how well she had slept the night before, and wanted nothing more than to fling herself on her bed and sleep. Only when she lay in bed that night did it occur to her that the last time she had been so bone-weary was when— She started up and frantically began to prod her sleeping husband, who had joined the court for the churching ceremony. Hugh, like all of the other men, had been somewhat fuddled by the churching and the vinous entertainments that had followed. It took Eleanor several shakes to awake him. "Hugh!"

"Mmm."

"I believe I am with child again!"

"Mmmm!"

The queen herself, complete with household, arrived a few days after Margaret's churching, by which time the court was fully sober and Eleanor was feeling thoroughly queasy. Edward seemed genuinely pleased at his bride's arrival, and Isabella, who liked Margaret well enough, admired little Joan and often took the infant on the royal lap.

As the Ordainers plotted in the south, Isabella's ladies and damsels plotted in the north. "Who shall take the king this year?" asked Ida de Clinton, one of the ladies.

"I shall only watch," said Eleanor, who had discovered the whereabouts of every garderobe in York Castle. She smiled at the oldest of the queen's damsels, Alice de Leygrave. "You should lead the effort, Alice."

"Very well," said Alice, who had been the king's nurse. She looked over the women sternly. "We meet at dawn."

At dawn, the women, trailed by a giggling Isabella and a yawning Eleanor, met in the deserted great hall at York Castle and made their way to the king's chamber, unopposed by the guards they met along the way. Finally, they entered the chamber and tiptoed to the bed, surrounded by heavy curtains. There the king slept soundly, decorously clad in drawers, for he knew well of the plans against him. Alice threw back the curtains. "Your grace! We have caught you abed on Easter Monday, and you must pay the price."

Edward stirred. "I must protest, good ladies."

"No excuses, your grace. Come, ladies. Bring him to be ransomed."

It took all of the women, most who were on the diminutive side, to haul the king out of his bed and down to the great hall. Eleanor was feeling hale enough to help by grabbing hold of her uncle's ankle, and Isabella cheered them on as they proceeded from whence they had came. There stood the king's steward, who watched as the women lowered the king to the floor triumphantly. "Aye, your grace," he said, shaking his head solemnly. "The ladies have taken you once again."

"Good man, set me free."

The steward opened a purse and gave each of the damsels several sparkling coins. By now all the members of the miniature court had gathered in the great hall, dressed in whatever robes they had found near at hand, and they cheered as Alice bade the king to rise.

But there were no light hearts in the south of England, where the Earls of Warwick, Lancaster, Pembroke, Hereford, and Arundel, outraged over Gaveston's return and the flouting of the Ordinances, were meeting and planning. They had even assigned themselves and their followers duty over different parts of the kingdom: to Eleanor's dismay, the Earl of Gloucester was in charge of the south. The Archbishop of Canterbury, Robert Winchelsey, had excommunicated Gaveston. "No need to bother with indulgences now," was Gaveston's comment.

Isabella, at the king's request, wrote to Gloucester, Hereford, Warenne, Lancaster, and Pembroke, begging them charmingly to desist from taking any action that would divide the realm, but received only polite, tolerant, meaningless, and rather patronizing responses, the equivalent of a pat on the head. The weaker sex, the womanizing Warenne explained, simply did not have to or wish to be involved in national affairs. An emissary met with a similar reception, save for the remark about the weaker sex.

"This is not a safe place for your grace to be," said Hugh le Despenser the elder one evening in late March, shortly after the king had been ransomed from the queen's ladies. "Rumor—from what my son has heard—has it that the Ordainers will be heading north. They are setting up tournaments, but they are nothing but shams to disguise the moving of troops."

"So where to?" asked the king. He did not wonder if Hugh's information was correct; it always was.

"Scarborough, I would suggest."

"I shall order it fortified immediately."

Several days later, the king and his household prepared to head north, Margaret and the baby and their attendants remaining in the comfort and safety of the abbey. The queen's household lagged behind the king's a few days; Isabella was not feeling well.

"I have borne these removals with remarkable patience," she said to Eleanor in mid-April. "But I am nearing the end of it. All for an upstart Gascon who could not even sire a male heir!"

"The king's brother, in all but birth, your grace."

"Brother!"

"I think it beautiful that their loyalty is so strong that the king is willing to risk all for Gaveston."

"You take a rosy view of life, my lady."

"Better than the opposite, surely." Isabella said nothing, and Eleanor went on dreamily, "I sometimes wish Hugh had such a bond; someone he loved better than himself, and vice versa. Then if he ever had to go to battle I would know that he was being looked after. But of course he and his father are devoted to each other; most men's fathers are dead." She frowned. Though she had been chattering to keep Isabella's spirits up, it was true she did worry that Hugh had no close friends, at least that she knew of. She supposed it was partly to do with his cool self-possession, which some could mistake for arrogance.

"You wish Hugh had a sordid relationship with another man, to expose you to gossip and calumny and neglect?"

"Of course not, I am thinking of a brotherhood in arms. If men must fight, and I suppose they must because they always have, it seems good that they should form such bonds. And in any case, there is more at stake than Gaveston, is there not? The Ordainers seek to impose their will upon the king in all matters, great and small. He is right to resist."

In reply Isabella merely shook her head and gazed bleakly out the window. "You are feeling no better, your grace?"

"No. I feel as if I want to vomit, and I am deadly tired."

Eleanor stared at the queen. "Tell me, your grace. Is your monthly course late?"

Isabella stared at Eleanor. "Several weeks, in fact."

"Do you miss months?"

"Not since I was fourteen. Lady Despenser! Could it be?"

"I can think of nothing else, your grace." She started as Isabella's embrace nearly knocked her off her feet. "Your grace!"

Isabella gave Edward the good news as soon as she stepped into the hall at Newcastle. Edward's delight was tempered by his concern over Gaveston, who, quite unusually for him, had fallen ill, seriously so. "I have had the best physician here attending him, Isabella, but to no avail. My God, what shall I do if I lose him?"

Had Isabella answered the question as she longed to, her life and the king's might have turned out quite differently. Instead, she said serenely, "I am sure he will recover, Edward. People who are never sick are always frightening when they become ill, because of the contrast."

"There may be truth in that," said Edward with a sigh.

Eleanor said, "Uncle, are others here ill? Because if they are, surely you will not want the queen and your future child here."

"Only Gaveston has been affected, but by God, you have a point! Who knows who else might become ill? You must not stay here, Isabella, and you neither, Eleanor." He glanced at Eleanor's belly, which by now was showing itself. "I wish you to move on."

"To where?"

"Tynemouth Priory is a good place for you, quite comfortable."

Move on Isabella did, but without much good grace. As they were sharing a litter, both having been forbidden by their husbands to sit a horse, Eleanor could not fall behind her, as she sometimes allowed her palfrey to do on the days when the queen was out of temper. "Barely a word about our child! Barely a word!"

"But your grace, we are where we are because of your child."

"He is totally preoccupied with that Gascon. You know, I sometimes believe the rumors that he is a witch's son."

"His nurse says they are nonsense."

"Well, she would, wouldn't she?"

Once at Tynemouth and out of her jouncing chariot, which Eleanor blamed for the queen's ill temper entirely, Isabella busied herself with charitable works and became quite good-natured. She put her almoner to work in the surrounding neighborhood, wrote to London to see how a little orphan boy whom she had provided for fared, and gave the priory church a splendid cloth of gold.

Nearly two weeks had passed quietly for the queen and her household when late one evening as the queen and her ladies were on the verge of retiring, a commotion was heard outside the priory, where the only noises were usually the chanting of the monks and the lapping of the waves at a distance. "My God! 'Tis the king and Gaveston!"

The king and Gaveston had been riding hard. They were followed by a few men, including Hugh the elder, but no baggage train and no sumpter horses. The women ran out to meet them as they pulled in front of the abbey. "Edward! What is happening?" asked Isabella.

"Lancaster was within an hour or so of Newcastle, so our spies told us. We have brought almost nothing with us—only ourselves."

"So the Ordainers are not bluffing, Uncle? They do truly intend to be at war with you?"

"It certainly seems so," said the king. He appeared a little dazed.

Gaveston said dryly. "We left so much at Newcastle it should keep them busy for a few hours or so, though, fighting over the booty."

"So what shall happen now?" asked Isabella.

"Gaveston and I will take ship for Scarborough."

"And I?"

"The queen should not take ship," said Hugh the elder. He bowed apologetically. "Your grace was ill on that crossing from France to Dover, with the seas quite calm. A severe bout of seasickness now might injure your babe."

"But she should not stay here," said Gaveston dispassionately.

"Lancaster would surely not harm the queen!" said Eleanor.

"No, Nelly, but he might hold her—and yourself—as a hostage of sorts, and he will soon be on our heels. The queen should go—back to York, I think."

Isabella stared at her husband, who thus far had remained silent. "You let these persons speak of me as though I were a pawn in a chess game, Edward! An object! And it is all due to you!" She glared at Gaveston. "Why should we all submit to being chased about the north of England for your sake? Why don't you leave us?"

"I have suggested it to the king, your grace," said Gaveston quietly.

"And it is out of the question," said Edward. "My brother will not be sacrificed to Lancaster." Edward could look magnificent when he chose, and he chose to now. "Isabella, you will go to York by land tomorrow morning. Take only necessities, as we have. And now we must go to bed. Gaveston and I go at first light."

Five months pregnant, Eleanor struggled to find a comfortable position on the pallet she slept on in what had become the queen's chamber, vacated for her by the abbot himself. Failing, she decided to spend her sleepless hours in prayer. Never had she dreamed that the Ordainers—her own brother among them— would turn so wholly against Edward. She had expected sulks, petitions, not the hundreds of men now being amassed against her uncle.

She pulled on a robe and went to a chapel she knew would not be used by the monks for their next round of prayers. But a figure already sat praying there, turning his head when Eleanor pushed the heavy door open. "Nelly?"

"Piers? I did not expect to find you here."

"No doubt you expected me to be communing with my familiar. A cat, or a toad, perhaps."

"No, Piers, I never believed that rumor."

"I am glad, Nelly. For some reason I wish you to think well of me. I shall leave this place if you want to pray alone."

"It was you I was going to pray for, Piers."

"Nelly. How did that Hugh deserve you? If that is all you were going to do, then perhaps you would not mind walking outside with me. I daresay your prayers for me will keep."

She nodded and let him guide her over the uneven floors of the priory into a little garden outside it, where a bench stood. There was but a touch of a chill in the night air, and he draped his cloak over her shoulders. "Thank you."

"How are Meg and Joan?"

"Very well. Joan is thriving, a big healthy girl."

"I wonder if I shall see her again. Or Margaret."

His voice was matter-of-fact. Eleanor turned to look at him in horror. "In case, of course, I must go back into exile."

"Of course."

He was silent for a time. "You heard the queen earlier this evening. Before I came into the chapel, I had every intention of acting on her advice, you know. Of finding myself a boat and disappearing. It might be the best thing for all."

"But it would break my uncle's heart."

"Yes. Mine too. That is why I went to the chapel instead."

The moon was full, and it reflected in the fish pond in front of them, allowing each to see the other's face. "How well did you know that rascal grandfather of yours, Nelly? The king, of course."

"Not that well. He was kind to me when he saw me, and gave me pretty things, but his mind was on other matters."

"I remember the first day he brought me to live in Ned's household. You won't believe it, but I was frightened—I didn't know if he would care for me being there. My father was a brave, loyal knight, not the nonentity some say he was, but he was in debt and he needed all the wages he got from the old king to live upon. It was a far cry from what the other young men in the household were like, with their fine manors and castles, and I knew it. Anyway, old Edward could tell I was uneasy, so he said, 'Boy, don't worry, if the young puppy doesn't like you in his household, there'll always be a place for you in mine.' We were on good terms then, you see. Pity it didn't continue. I admired the old man; still do. Edward could stand to emulate him in points."

"And did my uncle like you?"

"Instantly, and I him. It was as if we had known each other long ago and were meeting again. I know that sounds foolish."

"No." She picked up a stone and threw it into the water. Piers tried one too. It made a satisfying splash, but not as satisfying as the one Eleanor's had made. "Piers, forgive me for being impertinent, but is there nothing you could do to conciliate the barons? Surely it need not have come to this."

He shrugged. "What have I done, Nelly? Edward has been overgenerous to me, and I should not have accepted so much, perhaps, but I have taken no man's lands or goods. I've married above myself, but have not others? I've jested overmuch, I suppose, but how much pomposity can a man stand and stay sane? Perhaps I've made some people less influential at court than they thought their right, but has any good man really gone unheard? Loyal and faithful men like your father-in-law and Joseph the Jew—I mean, the Earl of Pembroke—have been given their due. The Fiddler and the Black Dog of Arden lie to themselves if they think they would have influence over Edward if it were not for me."

He looked away from her. "Nelly, I am speaking to you now as your brother. You are a grown woman, and you must know the other complaint against me—the one that is only whispered—that I give my body to the king."

Eleanor gulped, "Yes."

"It has not been true for some time now. It was up until the barons exiled me after the king's marriage, but since then Edward and I have been chaste with each other. Sweet Nelly, it has not been easy."

"I suppose not."

"We took a vow for our children's sake. More for mine than his, for whatever rumors swirled the king's children would be the king's children, who would never go a-begging for a match, but we knew it would be different for mine. We wanted them to be able to marry as befitted their station. And I am fond of your sister too, and did not want her to be miserable among the great ladies of the land."

"You have acted rightly, Piers. I am sorry it has brought you no profit."

He laughed, "Oh, we were wild enough beforehand! I could tell you stories—" He shook his head. "Not for your sweet little ears. But I have had one lapse, though not in the direction you might think. Joan is not my oldest daughter. She is the youngest, though the only legitimate one."

"*You* have a bastard?"

"Amie is her name. She is at Shaftesbury Abbey, to be raised by the nuns there until she comes of age. Margaret and the king know naught of her."

"Do you wish them to know?"

Piers shrugged. "Not now; it would only cause them grief and anger. For all I am speaking rationally to you now, I was angry at Edward after we exchanged our vow—it was his idea, you see—and I took a woman lover to spite him. It probably wouldn't have. Your uncle is a man of staggering loyalty, Nelly. All I did was betray poor Margaret and Edward."

"And the woman?"

"I was not her first paramour, and will not be her last. Amie is best off in the convent, poor child, until some suitable match can be arranged for her. I wish her to stay innocent."

He stood up and stretched. "How grim we have become! What do the women say about your child? Girl or boy?"

"They are undecided, but I hope for a girl." She stood up too. "I am going to try to sleep now."

"Yes, we must all be up early to evade the Fiddler."

"Piers, you speak of them as though they were characters in a mummers' play, but they are hard men, I fear. Pray be careful of yourself."

"You are sweet to worry about me, but all will be well." He gave her a peck on the cheek. "Give this to Margaret for me, with feeling. And commend me to your pirate husband."

"Pirate?"

"Only a matter of speaking, Nelly."

The king and Gaveston left sooner than they had planned, after a spy arrived to tell them that Lancaster was a short distance away. The queen's household was still slumbering when the friends and a handful of men set sail for Scarborough.

Once arisen, the queen and her household were not laggards. Packing only necessaries, they had mounted their horses and were all but leaving when Lancaster and his men rode up. The queen's knights tensed, but Lancaster motioned his men to put down their weapons. He slid off his horse and bowed. "Your grace. Where is the king?"

"He is not here."

Eleanor watched as Lancaster mentally debated whether to accept the queen's word. Evidently, he decided in her favor. "The Gascon?"

"My brother-in-law is not here," said Eleanor herself. She was half afraid the queen might reveal his whereabouts.

The compunction Lancaster had about questioning the queen's veracity did not hold for her lady. "You tell the truth, Lady Despenser?"

"Of course. But why believe me when you may search the priory? Do check everywhere. I believe there is a hollow window seat in which a man might fit."

Lancaster scowled. "You do know that your brother works with us, do you not, my lady?"

"To his shame. Yes, I do."

The earl tried a different approach. "Do you know where he has gone?"

"Pregnant women are forgetful creatures, sir. I do not remember." Eleanor yawned and settled into her chariot more comfortably. "And now I must rest, sir."

Lancaster looked to the queen again, but Isabella's own sense of mischief was upon her. "I suffer from the same malady as Lady Despenser, sir."

This not having been known to Lancaster or his followers, there were gasps from Lancaster's men. Lancaster, however, hid his surprise. "Damn this nonsense! I came here to offer the queen my support against that insolent Gascon, who bleeds the treasury dry and casts a spell over our king and flouts our Ordinances as if they were no more than hand cloths. It appears, however, that the queen does not wish to be delivered from him. So I shall—"

A horseman was galloping toward them. Eleanor squealed with delight when she recognized her husband; Lancaster scowled even deeper. Hugh slowed to a trot and took in the scene before him, the queen's household with its handful of knights facing Lancaster's troops. His lip curled. "Lancaster, I am no strategist, but I must say the odds appear in your favor, though that is a vicious-looking headdress my wife is wearing."

"We seek the Gascon, Despenser, and do not seek to harm the queen or her household. Where is your father?"

"With the king, no doubt. Do you seek him?" Hugh's brown eyes were as innocent as a puppy's.

Lancaster released a string of expletives. Eleanor frowned. "For shame, sir!"

"Let us start on our way," said Isabella. "The sun already grows high."

"Do take care of our things, Lord Lancaster," said Eleanor. "Would you be so good?"

Toward York they rode at a leisurely pace, unhindered by Lancaster's men. Hugh, riding beside Eleanor's chariot, laughed as Eleanor recounted the morning's events for him. "What a spitfire you can be, my love! I did not know I was married to such a shrew."

"Perhaps I was rude to him, Hugh, but he has caused my uncle and Margaret and Piers such grief. And I do believe that beneath all his talk of principles lies nothing more than his desire for power."

"Probably, and as Lancaster has always borne my father enmity—I think for no reason than that my father has always been loyal to the king—I am glad you spoke to him as you did."

"What brings you here?"

"Why, you, of course. This business worries me, Eleanor. I saw my uncle Warwick several days before I set off to find you, and he looked even more sour than is usual with him. When I asked him if he planned to go north with the other Ordainers I thought he would take his whip to me."

"And the others? Where are they?"

"Pembroke and Warenne are in pursuit of the king and Gaveston. Poor Warenne! He has changed sides so often, I doubt he knows from day to day who he is trying to seize—Gaveston, Lancaster, or himself. Your brother stays behind in the south, and Hereford is in the east. Frankly, Eleanor, that is where I wish you were, far away from all this. That is why I rode here, to take you back to Loughborough." He nodded in Isabella's direction. "With her grace's permission, of course."

She shook her head. "I cannot leave my uncle—or the queen. He needs every friend he has, and the queen is nervous with her baby as it is. It would distress them both were I to leave."

"Very well. Then I shall stay with you."

Eleanor smiled. "That I like. But how dare you insult my headdress?"

"It kept Lancaster off, did it not?"

Soon they were settled into York as though, Isabella said a tad sourly, they had never left it. They were a comfortable lot there. Margaret was delighted to see her sister and the queen because, as she said, one could talk about babies with the monks for only so long. Eleanor in consideration of her pregnancy was given a chamber with her husband and no longer had to sleep in the queen's chamber at night. Hugh hunted by day and diced with the ladies at night; sometimes, though, he and Eleanor slipped off by day and went for aimless walks, enjoying what Eleanor thought was the loveliest May she had ever seen.

The king himself soon arrived in York, minus Gaveston, who had stayed in Scarborough. Edward had been confident that Gaveston would be safe there while Edward himself traveled south to muster more troops, but no sooner had the king entered York Castle than word arrived that Scarborough Castle was under siege.

Eleanor had never seen a man as distracted as her uncle during the next few days. Edward ate little and slept less. His efforts toward raising troops went for naught. Finally, a messenger brought word to the king that Gaveston had come to terms with Pembroke and Warenne. He would soon be at St. Mary's Abbey in York, where he had come but a few months before for the birth of his daughter, and there the agreement would be put before the king.

"I like this not," said Edward unhappily, gazing at the message after having read it a dozen times or so. "Why couldn't he have held out longer?"

"There was little time to bring ample provisions in," Hugh the elder reminded him.

"And while it might have been well stocked with weapons, they are useless with no one to wield them," Hugh the younger said tartly. "How many men did Gaveston have there?"

"Few," said Edward dazedly. "Very few."

When Gaveston and his captors arrived at the abbey several days later, however, all were in good spirits, even the captive. Negotiations were to remain open until the first of August, during which time Gaveston's safety would be guaranteed by Pembroke, Warenne, and Henry Percy, a great baron who had been present at the siege. If a final concord could not be reached by August 1, Gaveston would return to Scarborough—"Of which I have such fond memories," he said sweetly—with a garrison.

Gaveston had agreed not to attempt to persuade Edward to change anything in the agreement, and kept his promise as Pembroke sonorously explained its terms. "I see no reason why we cannot reach an agreement by August," he concluded. "We all want what is best for the realm, do we not?"

Edward was too relieved by the agreement's terms, which were more favorable to Gaveston than he had hoped, to chafe at Pembroke's patronizing tone. "Indeed we do."

"Perhaps," said Hugh the elder, "Parliament should be summoned. If it took place in July there would be ample time to finish discussions before August."

"An excellent idea," agreed Pembroke.

Margaret had rushed to see her husband when he entered the castle and still sat clinging to him. "In the meantime, can't he stay here?"

"I do not think that best under the circumstances," said Pembroke. He was a thin, dark man in his early forties, and the siege and the hasty journey to York appeared to have tired him more than his captive. "Here there might be—difficulties."

"He means that I might break my part of the agreement," said Gaveston dryly. "Pembroke, I am dead tired, as are you. Let me retire with my wife—put a guard by my door if you wish—and we may discuss this more tomorrow, shall we?"

Pembroke, who had been taken aback to see the countess so affectionate toward her husband, nodded slowly. "Very well."

After a couple of days more of discussion, it was agreed that Gaveston would be taken to Wallingford, where he could live on his own lands while the Ordainers were near enough to keep an eye on him. Pembroke and Warenne pledged to forfeit all of their land and goods if they did not keep their end of the bargain. Parliament was to be summoned to meet in Lincoln on July 8.

Soon after this date was set, Pembroke and Gaveston departed York, Gaveston looking nothing like a prisoner in fine clothes and mounted on the best steed the king's stables could provide. Days passed, and several letters arrived from Piers, letters that made Edward smile. "Piers is planning his defense in front of Parliament," he told the Despensers. "What a lawyer he would have made! The points he makes here are brilliant."

"So the earls plan to let him speak there?" asked Eleanor.

"Pembroke says they will, and Pembroke is an upright man, for all that he consorts with the Ordainers." Edward yawned. "A pity he must go all the way to Wallingford, and then back to Lincoln, but I daresay he will prefer riding back and forth to sitting at Wallingford without company. He tells me that he and Pembroke are getting on well now, for all that Pembroke is entirely lacking in a sense of humor. Who knows, Gaveston may develop one in him."

The king and queen, meantime, began preparing to leave York for Lincoln. All was ready, and Eleanor was taking one last walk in the coolness of an evening in late June, when she saw a messenger approaching the castle in great haste. Curious, she hastened to the great hall of the castle. It was empty. Somewhat hampered by her growing bulk, she hurried to chamber after chamber, finding the same lifeless air over all of them, until she saw a knot of people standing near an outer room that led to Edward's bedchamber. Her husband was there. "Hugh? What is wrong?"

"A messenger has brought news about Gaveston. My father is in there with the king now."

"News? What news? Have the Ordainers have not honored their part of the agreement?"

A cry came from the king's bedchamber. Never had Eleanor heard a sound like it. It was animal-like, otherworldly, yet it had to have come from a man, for it was followed by sobs. Eleanor could not have believed that a man could feel such anguish, and survive. There was no need for Hugh to say the next words; she knew what had happened.

"They have killed Gaveston, Eleanor. 'Tis the work of Lancaster and my uncle Warwick."

CHAPTER 6

▼

JUNE 1312

Pembroke's wife, Beatrice, was French and fair, and none but a churl would have argued when Pembroke, having stopped for the night with Gaveston at the rectory at Deddington in Oxfordshire, decided to ride the few miles to Bampton to pay her a visit. He thought of taking his captive with him, but Gaveston, still feeling the effects of his illness a month before, was not as strong as he used to be, and did not look up to the ride. Moreover, turning up at Bampton with his charge might spur his wife, a proper hostess to the bone, to pull out the stops of hospitality for the Gascon, and Pembroke had been parted long enough from his bride to wish her attentions to be given to no one but himself. Shaking his minimal misgivings from his mind, he hired a fresh horse for the journey and galloped happily away, grateful for the extra hours of light the June days were affording him.

Gaveston himself ate a simple but delicious meal and retired early, pleased to see that he had been provided with a comfortable bed in a pleasant, airy room. He was dreaming a dream to match his cheerful surroundings when he heard his name called, again and again, followed by, "Arise, traitor! You are taken."

Mother of God! it was the Black Dog of Arden, with dozens of men. Pembroke's few men, taken unawares, were themselves under guard, save for a couple who had been gravely wounded and needed none. Gaveston opened the window. "Don't bark so loud, Warwick. You disturb the neighborhood."

"Aye, I bark. And I bite too, you fool. Dress yourself and come down."

"Where is Pembroke? What about his oath?"

"I care little where he is, and I care naught about his oath. Come down, or you will be dragged down."

A voice from outside the door—the rector's—said, "My lord, all is lost. Pembroke's men have been captured—one killed already—and there is a guard all around the rectory."

"Very well," Gaveston said, "I'll come down."

Pembroke, having passed a very pleasant evening with Beatrice, was on the road to Deddington when he heard the news from one of his men, who after having been disarmed by Warwick's men had been left behind at the rectory. Gaveston had been stripped of his shoes and jewels and had been made to walk, wearing nothing but his shirt and hose, through the town. Only when Warwick's men tired of the slow pace this necessitated had a horse been produced for him, although the horse was such a nag the change did little to speed the procession.

Aymer de Valence, Earl of Pembroke, had worked with Warwick long enough to know that approaching him would be futile. Instead, he galloped off to Tewkesbury, where the Earl of Gloucester was staying. Gloucester was a moderate man, and second only to Lancaster in riches; if any man could save Pembroke's honor and Gaveston, it was Gilbert de Clare. But young Gilbert was not in an accommodating mood. He felt affronted, having not been consulted about Pembroke's arrangement, and through his association with the Ordainers he had grown over the years rather to dislike Piers Gaveston. It did not help matters that Gaveston was a father, while Gilbert's wife had suffered several miscarriages.

He heard Pembroke out, but barely. Then he lifted his red head and said coolly, "We all agreed to capture him, did we not? The wrong done to you is not to be imputed to Warwick alone."

"He was captured, Gloucester, and in my custody. And now that he has been taken out of my custody my goods and lands will be forfeit."

"Then you must negotiate more carefully in the future."

"The future! There is no future for me, nor for Gaveston I fear. Can nothing move you to pity? For God's sake, man, Gaveston is married to your sister!"

"It is that marriage that prevents me from going to Warwick now, and only that marriage. The man is bad for England, and it and my sister will be better off without him."

Pembroke stared at Gloucester, who looked back at him with all of the arrogance of his twenty-one, largely untroubled years. "Then I curse you, you arrogant brat."

Almost weeping, Pembroke rode away from Tewkesbury in a daze. Reaching Oxfordshire again, he decided to appeal to the clerks and burgesses of the town and university of Oxford. At the very least, he would be able to clear his name, he hoped, for he was beginning to realize that his foolishness in leaving Gaveston at Deddington might be regarded as treachery.

He was met with inaction at best, derision at worst. Did he expect the scholars at Oxford to raise an army? What made him think anyone would stir to help the sorcerer Piers Gaveston? And what would be the displeasure of the king to that of the mighty Lancaster?

Utterly dispirited, Pembroke returned to see his wife once more, this time as the one person in the world he knew would give him comfort and understanding. Then he would rejoin the king in the north and offer him his undivided allegiance. It was all he could do now.

Meanwhile, the Earls of Lancaster, Arundel, and Hereford journeyed to Warwick Castle, where the Earl of Cornwall was being held in chains. Warwick, having taken the bold step of seizing Gaveston, was beginning to have some doubts, but Lancaster silenced them. "With Gaveston alive, there will be no peace in England!"

"And there will be peace with him dead?" said Hereford glumly.

"Yes, there will. Why, the queen is with child, did you know that? That cannot but help matters. An heir may be what it takes to force the king to act as one."

"If the king acts as one we shall all die a traitor's death for this."

"He will be in no position to act as one," said Lancaster, illogically but with great force. He nodded toward a clerk, sitting glumly in a corner. "In any case, he is not a match for all of us acting in concert. We shall draw up letters patent in which each of us swears to save and defend the others from any loss they might incur from this."

"Should he have a trial before he dies?" asked Arundel. He himself had no compunction about executing Gaveston, who had humiliated him several years before by trouncing him at a tournament, and he was tired of listening to Lancaster and Hereford debate over what was plainly a foregone conclusion.

"It would be best," assented Lancaster. "We'll find suitable justices."

The justices examined the evidence presented to them—an easy task as Gaveston himself had no chance to speak or call anyone to speak in his behalf—and sentenced the Gascon to death. Here Gilbert de Clare, though unwittingly, came to Gaveston's aid, for the earls deemed it unseemly that the brother-in-law of the Earl of Gloucester should die a traitor's death. Instead, he was granted the nobleman's death of beheading.

"They finally took him out of the dungeon, on June 19 it was," said the Countess of Pembroke's laundress. She cleared her throat; it was not usual for her to speak in front of so many people, and certainly not in front of a group of people like this—the king, the queen, her lord Pembroke, the king's nieces, the Earl of Surrey, Lord Despenser and his son. Gaveston's young widow was in full mourning; most of the others were in black or at least in their drabbest robes. "Poor man, he was filthy and looked in need of a good meal—he'd been in there nine days—but still he bore himself proudly, like the fine knight that I had heard he was. The Earls of Lancaster, Arundel, and Hereford came to Kenilworth to watch it be done."

"Only the three?" asked Hugh the elder. "Where was Warwick?"

"He was not there, sir, I'll swear it. They say he stayed in his castle at Warwick the whole day."

"Then he is not only a scoundrel, but a coward," said the king's niece Eleanor. It was odd, the laundress thought, that it was she, not the queen, who had reached over and clasped the king's hand while the tale was being told, but the ways of the royal were inscrutable and the girl after all was the king's near relation.

"Aye, my lady, they say he wanted no part of the business once he started it. So they brought him to Kenilworth, as I said, to the Earl of Lancaster's land, I think. Then they took him to a place called Blacklow Hill—many a day I rolled down it as a girl, and no longer will anyone want to play there—"

"Was he shriven?" asked the king. "Do you know?"

"There was no priest there, but he prayed before he died, and many of the bystanders did too—although others laughed."

The king was weeping, and so were his nieces. Strange, the laundress thought, the queen—the closest thing to an angel in looks she had ever seen—was dry-eyed. But if the rumors about the king and Gaveston had been true...

The second Edward wiped his eyes. "Go on."

"There's little left to tell, your grace. They bade him to kneel down, and he did, as graceful as though he was here in court. He had just time to commend his spirit to God. Then one man—a Welshman he was—ran him through the heart, then another Welshman cut off his head. Oh, but he did ask before, joking-like, that they leave him his head so as not to spoil his beauty so much."

The younger Despenser's mouth twitched upward.

"The Earl of Lancaster did not go up the hill for some reason, so they had to bring the head down to him, to show him that the deed had been done. Some friars came and got the body later, as you now know, your grace, and took him to Oxford." She paused awkwardly, then remembered that she had been asked to tell everything she knew. "I heard—but do not know for sure—that his head was sewn back on."

"God bless the friars," said Edward. "They shall be well rewarded. And so shall you." He nodded at his steward, standing nearby, who approached the laundress with a purse.

"It was the countess's doing, your grace. She sent me to visit my family near Warwick Castle, knowing that I would keep my ears and eyes open and report on what had happened."

"And it was you, Pembroke, who asked the countess to provide those eyes and ears. Thank you."

"It was the least I could do, your grace."

CHAPTER 7

▼

SEPTEMBER 1312 TO
APRIL 1314

In September 1312, Eleanor gave birth to a daughter, named after either Hugh's mother or the queen, depending on which parent one asked. Either way, Eleanor adored little Isabel, who within a few weeks showed every sign that her hair would be as flaming as that of Eleanor's father, who had not been called Gilbert the Red for naught.

She was grateful to be away from court; it had become too sad there. Edward went through the motions of daily life, hearing petitions, issuing orders, meeting with his council, but something of him had died at Blacklow Hill. Not infrequently, he would stop whatever he was doing and leave the room, and every person around him knew that he was going to his chamber to weep for Gaveston anew.

For a time that summer, the country in fact had seemed on the verge of civil war. Days after Gaveston's death, his killers—including Warwick, who had ventured out of his castle at last—gathered at Worcester, while the king and his council traveled to Westminster, having summoned Parliament to meet there in August. Both were debating what to do next; both were preparing for war. When Lancaster, Warwick, and Hereford arrived in London, days after Parliament had begun, they were accompanied by hundreds of men.

Gloucester had become a mediator between the factions. His encounter with Pembroke had left him shaken, for all that he hid it at the time, and he had felt more than a little guilt upon seeing the grief of his uncle, who had always treated him well and kindly. Worse was the anger of his sisters. Margaret, meeting him for the first time since her husband's death, had simply slammed him across the face and run out of the room. Eleanor he had not seen, as she had gone from York to Loughborough to await her child's birth, but she had sent him a letter so uncharacteristically contemptuous that Gilbert shuddered when he remembered it, even though he'd read it only once before putting the fire to it. She didn't accuse him of bringing about Gaveston's death, and neither did Margaret; they suspected, as did Gilbert himself, that there was nothing he could have done to prevent it. But at least he could have tried, for the name of Clare was not one without power in the realm, and he had done nothing.

So in some small attempt to expiate his sins he set about the tedious business of negotiating between the king and the group of men of whom Lancaster had become the leader. He was not without help, for the Earl of Richmond shared in his efforts, as did papal envoys and Isabella's uncle Louis d'Evreux.

The accusations went back and forth. The goods Gaveston had left behind at Newcastle—jewels, horses, and robes—were rich, and they were in the hands of Lancaster, whom the king accused of being little more than a common thief. Lancaster protested that he had seized the goods for the crown and had even inventoried them with that noble purpose in mind, but he made no move to return them.

Edward said that the earls had killed a peer of the realm and would depose the king himself if they could. The earls protested that Gaveston was an outlaw under the Ordinances and that he had been punished accordingly. They wanted to brand Gaveston as a traitor; Edward would accept many of the demands made upon him, would even pardon the earls, but never would he declare the person he had loved best in the world to be a traitor.

London, never far from ferment, was also tense; when Pembroke, Hugh le Despenser the elder, and several others met with city officials to discuss the Londoners' own grievances, they ended up running for their lives.

In the midst of all of this anxiety, Isabella lay comfortably ensconced at Windsor in November 1312, awaiting the birth of her first child. Eleanor, churched only a month before, joined her there, for who would want to miss such an occasion? On November 13, Isabella gave birth to a boy, who was soon created Earl of Chester.

The pleasure Eleanor took in seeing the queen's happiness was trebled by seeing that of the king. The look of brooding misery at last left Edward's face; he spent hours in the nursery with young Edward and heaped presents upon Isabella. For the first time in months, he was heard to make a joke. The birth of the third Edward did much to ease the nation's tension, for a short time anyway. If few loved the king, the birth of a healthy heir at least made him less disliked, and the absence of Gaveston removed a vital source of dissatisfaction. Even the Londoners turned their thoughts to a happier direction, preparing a grand ceremony to welcome the heir. A treaty was made in December 1312, and Gaveston's valuables were finally turned over to the crown several months later, but Lancaster and Warwick refused to confirm it.

To the barons' dismay, Edward had drawn closer to his French father-in-law, and in the spring of 1313, as the glow of the birth of an heir was beginning to wear off, he accepted the French king's invitation to visit him in Paris, where Isabella's brothers were to be knighted. The trip was hardly a jaunt for Edward—there was diplomatic work to be done as well as feasting—but the barons grumbled nonetheless.

Back in England, the peace efforts resumed, complete with Gloucester, Richmond, and papal envoys, and in October 1313, they at last bore fruit. More worn down with time than anything else, the king and the earls entered into a treaty.

"The king cannot but be pleased with it," said Hugh the elder. "Nothing branding poor Gaveston the king's enemy; no one removed from court—not even me as Lancaster has wished—and Henry de Beaumont and Lady Vescy are no longer outlawed by the Ordinances. Lancaster and the others must kneel before the king and accept his forgiveness, and that cannot be something they are stomaching well."

There was no satisfaction in Hugh's voice, though. After a brief improvement, his son Philip's health had rapidly declined, and just weeks before, he had succumbed to consumption. Hugh had reached his deathbed just in time to be recognized by his son; shortly after Philip's burial at the house of the Augustinian friars in London, he and his elder son and daughter-in-law had returned to Westminster, where Parliament was in session, though it was clear from Hugh's bearing that his heart was not in his duties as a peer. He continued tiredly, "There will be a banquet, of course, to mark their reconciliation. There always is."

The banquet, hosted by the king, took place several weeks later. The entire court was present. From their table a distance from the dais where the king and the earls sat, Eleanor and her husband watched as the king embraced and kissed earl after earl. Warwick and Lancaster more or less submitted to their embraces, and the king's was hardly heartfelt either, but all were more gallant when it came time to approach the queen. With each embrace, Hugh's lip curled more and more perceptibly.

"It'll not last long," he said, yawning.

"Really, Lady Despenser! You must be half fish."

Isabella de Vescy, restored to the queen's household, looked none too happy about it at the moment, for the crossing from Dover to France on the last day of February 1314 was proving to be a rough one. Joan of Bar, the Earl of Surrey's wife, also looked queasy, but Eleanor turned back to the ladder and the boy waiting to assist her up to the deck. "If none of you wish to go up, then I will go by myself. It is wonderful—the waves just high enough to give you a bounce, and the salt on your cheek."

"Why not take service as a cabin boy, Eleanor?" asked Joan, Eleanor's first cousin, humorlessly. Joan had cause for her grumpiness, Eleanor reflected, because her husband had recently set up open housekeeping with his mistress, who had already borne him a fine bastard. Rumor had it that he was trying to get his marriage annulled, although as he had received a papal dispensation to be married in the first place, his chances appeared somewhat dubious. Eleanor, therefore, only laughed and ascended the ladder.

Up on deck was her brother, who along with Henry de Beaumont and others was there to accompany the queen on her second visit to France in less than a year. Although the English royal couple's visit to Philip the previous year had been a cordial one, issues remained to be worked out, and Edward, having concluded his peace with his barons, had come to France briefly in December to meet with the French king. His stay had been but a brief one, and with the Scottish situation growing ever more alarming, it was decided to send the queen to France to intercede with her father while her husband and most of the English nobility stayed at home.

Gilbert turned as Eleanor's head emerged from the hold. "Is that you, sister? Shouldn't you be holding a basin for the queen or something?"

"She has her damsels to do that, and in any case she is bearing up well this time. It is Lady Vescy and the Countess of Surrey who are seasick today."

"Well, I am glad, because it is good to have some privy conversation with you." He smiled awkwardly, for their breach over Gaveston had been slow to heal. Margaret, who had been granted dower lands by the king and was living very comfortably, had still not forgiven her brother, despite Eleanor's efforts. "I feel as if I am somehow shirking a duty, coming here with the queen, for we are heading to war with the Scots, you know."

"I hope it will not come to that."

"How can it not, Nelly? The king has summoned us earls and the barons to be in Berwick in June. We will be the superior force, but Bruce is wily, and even our grandfather the first Edward could not subdue him. I just hope our uncle is a match for him."

"He is no coward."

"But he has never led a large campaign before, and he hasn't that single-minded quality our grandfather had."

"Perhaps you underestimate him, but I know nothing about these matters." She shrugged in a pretty manner that she had learned from the queen.

"You should care, because your husband and father-in-law will certainly join in whatever takes place. But enough of this talk. How are your children?"

Eleanor knew it cost Gilbert pain to ask this question, for his one child—a boy—had died soon after birth. "Hugh sits a horse beautifully, but I wish he had more interest in his lessons! It is all his tutor can do to get him to sit still for five minutes. Isabel prattles and prattles now—to think I was worried that she was slow to talk! I hope after this I can go and stay with them a while." To talk of her children before her brother seemed almost like gloating, so she changed the subject. "Have you heard from Elizabeth? Does she mean to stay in Ireland?"

Elizabeth's twenty-three-year-old husband, son of the Earl of Ulster, had died suddenly the previous June, leaving her with a boy, William. Gilbert shrugged. "The Earl of Ulster looks after her well, and I daresay scares off any suitors who might have an eye on her dower. As long as she is happy there I shall not press for her to come home."

"How is Maud?"

Gilbert's face changed. "She sorely feels that we have had no living child, and it affects her temper. Young as she is, sometimes she reminds me of a bitter old woman."

"I am sorry, Gilbert. But there is hope; you know you can have children together, and you are but young."

"I envy your marriage, Eleanor. You and Hugh seem happy together."

"I am lucky, for there is no one to me so dear as he."

"And he seems very fond of you. How unlike our poor cousin downstairs! I'll swear, the day she was married to him, Surrey already had his eye on another woman! But this is gloomy talk once more. Let us walk to the ship's railing where we can look at the water better. You like that, I know."

Philip of France had spent the last seven years suppressing the Knights Templar, a group of monastic knights that had gained fame, wealth, and enemies over the years. Seeing a chance to line his coffers, Philip had arrested every Templar in France in 1307 on trumped-up charges of heresy, idolatry, and even sodomy; through torture, he gained a number of confessions, which in turn led to a papal inquiry and the eventual dissolution of the order. The inquiry in many countries, including England, had been a halfhearted one; the Templars in England had been allowed to confess and do penance, after which most returned to secular life with small pensions. In France, however, thirty-six men died, apart from those tortured. The wealth of the Templars passed to the French crown.

Among those who had confessed was Jacques de Molay, the grand master of the Templars. Having done so, he was awaiting his sentence in front of Notre Dame when he recanted his confession and declared himself ready to face death. It came on March 19, 1314, at Philip's order, in front of the royal palace. Rumor had it that as the flames engulfed him, Molay cursed the Pope and the French king.

Isabella and her party were not witnesses to this event, Isabella having stayed only a short time in Paris before departing on pilgrimage to Chartres the day before Molay's death. The court was still talking of little else, though in whispers, when Isabella and her household returned to Paris at the end of March. If the queen was shaken by the curse laid upon her father, or if she felt any moral revulsion at her father's conduct, she did not reveal it to her horrified ladies, who in turn did not dare discuss the subject with Isabella.

Philip went about his business—it was probably not the first time a dying man had cursed him, as Philip had also persecuted the Lollards and the Jews—suavely, and graciously welcomed his daughter and her ladies to his court. Eleanor trembled as the queen presented her and the others to her father, who had countenanced such wickedness and brought a curse upon himself; yet Philip the Fair received the ladies with perfect courtesy, even remembering enough about their backgrounds to inquire about their relatives by name.

The Pope would be dead within a month. The French king himself would be dead within eight months, and all of his sons would be dead without male issue by 1328, leading to the Hundred Years' War, but no shadow of those events hung over the French court during the next couple of weeks as the court welcomed Isabella back among its midst. Nearly the whole family was together, Philip noted cheerfully: Isabella, her three brothers, Louis, Philip, and Charles, and their wives, Marguerite, Jeanne, and Blanche.

As she had been the year before, Isabella was much admired by all, her face being lovely as ever and childbirth having given her figure a nice rounding it lacked before. Rather to her own surprise, Lady Despenser also attracted a certain amount of admiration, which Eleanor attributed partly to the beautiful robes that Hugh had allowed her to have made for her trip to France and partly to the lack of any other redheaded woman at the French court at the time. The men of the court would not have completely contradicted either of these theories, but they would have also noted Lady Despenser's full bosom, sweet speaking voice, and appealing countenance. Beyond this, Eleanor had the fascination that came from unattainability, for even when dancing with another man she was very much the wife of Hugh le Despenser, notwithstanding the fact that he was across the English Channel.

Two of the most charming of the knights were Philippe and Gautier d'Aunay, brothers. They had a younger companion, Jean, and it was he who always seemed to be at Eleanor's side when it was time to dance.

Eleanor was no flirt—she had been married before she had developed any expertise in this area, and once married, she had found no reason to look at any other man beside her husband. Yet she had improved her social graces since joining Isabella's court, and she found no difficulty in bantering with Jean, even if the meaning of some of the glances he sent her way escaped her entirely.

"You have made quite a conquest, Eleanor," said Joan of Bar one morning as Isabella, her sisters-in-law, and their ladies sat at their needlework, the men having gone hunting.

"What on earth do you mean?"

"How can you ask? That knight Jean was at your side all evening."

Eleanor pondered this and found it to be true. "I suppose he was, but there was nothing improper in his conduct. If there had been I would have had my brother deal with it immediately."

"What did he talk of?"

"Truly, Joan, I think it no concern of yours," snapped Eleanor. They had in fact mainly discussed the recent business in England, during which Eleanor had become very heated in defense of her late brother-in-law Gaveston, but she saw no need to mention this with the queen within earshot.

"Then you must have spoken of love," said Marguerite, and her cousin Blanche giggled.

Marguerite spoke only to tease Eleanor, she had heard enough of Eleanor's wistful references to Hugh, whom she was desperately missing, to realize that Eleanor was indeed a faithful wife. Eleanor herself recognized the jest for what it was, and snorted. She thought nothing of it, then, until late that evening, after a long evening of dancing during which Jean had appeared at her side only a few times, Blanche tapped her on the shoulder. "If you wish to see Jean alone, my lady, you know it can be arranged."

Eleanor saw to her shock that Blanche was a bit tipsy. "There is nothing I desire less, madam."

"But my lady! It can be done so easily. No one shall ever be the wiser, and you will have much pleasure. Trust me, Eleanor dear."

"You have misconstrued the situation, absolutely. Pray excuse me."

She turned and hastily made her way back over to the queen, watching with a frown from a distance as Blanche downed another cup of wine before being led out of the room by one of her ladies.

Isabella followed her glance. "Why is it you look at Blanche so, Lady Despenser?"

"Was I? I did not mean to do so. She is dressed very strikingly tonight."

"Yes, she had a beautiful purse with her when she came in. I presented it to her when I was here the year before. Who do you think has it now?"

Isabella had never entirely forgiven her husband for giving her father's wedding presents to Gaveston, and for a few moments Eleanor thought confusedly that this might be more of the same. "I know not, your grace. I did not notice a purse at all."

"Let us leave this place, Lady Despenser. Come with me to my chamber."

Puzzled, Eleanor obeyed, following Isabella with the other ladies after Isabella made her farewell to her father. When all were in Isabella's chamber, the queen raised her hand for silence. "My brothers are being made fools of, and this must stop."

Isabella de Vescy, the only one of the ladies who could be brusque to the queen, said gruffly, "Explain yourself, your grace."

"Those whores Blanche and Marguerite, is not it obvious? They are cuckolding my brothers, with those Aunays. Do you remember the purses I gave them last year? Those knights are clutching them like favors!"

"Purses prove nothing," said Lady Vescy.

"Aye, but look at Lady Despenser's face! Tell us what you know, my dear."

"N—Nothing, my lady."

"You fool! Your face shows it all. That Blanche said something to you tonight, and you will tell us."

Eleanor said shakily, "She told me that if I wished to meet a man privately, it could be arranged, and it would give me much pleasure. But I am sure it meant nothing; it was only her French way of talking."

Joan of Bar laughed nervously at this gaffe, but the queen paid no attention to it. "You see, she knows how to meet a man on the sly, and she is willing to counsel others to do so. The whore! I must inform my father of this."

"Good God, your grace! You cannot do that!"

The queen gasped in rage, but Eleanor paid her no mind. "Your grace, it will be a death sentence if your father finds out about this! You saw what he did to Jacques de Molay, that brave man; what will he do to those girls and their knights? You cannot tell! If you must tell anyone, tell Blanche and Marguerite what you know! They will not dare to continue in their ways when they know that you suspect them."

Isabella said crisply, "Do you have any more orders to give me, Lady Despenser? Or do you care to insult my father further?"

"Your grace, you must not tell."

Lady Vescy said dryly, "Lady Despenser overreaches herself, but what proof do you have, your grace? It would indeed be a pity to tell your father and have it turn out that these stupid girls are guilty of nothing more than flirtation and folly."

"I assure you I have no intent of hurting the innocent. I shall tell my father my suspicions, and ask that a watch be put on them. If they are guilty of nothing but indiscretion, it will end there." She glanced at Eleanor, who was white as chalk beneath her freckles. "And Lady Despenser, if you are thinking of warning them in the interim, do think again. I will have my eyes on you too."

"For pity's sake, your grace! Have some mercy on them. Their adultery is between them and their husbands—and God. It is not an affair of state."

"You have odd ideas, Lady Despenser. My brother Louis will be king of France by-and-by, the Lord's anointed; shall I sit quietly and see him cuckolded? My family's honor is too precious to me. Get you gone."

King Philip's spies quickly went to work and found Marguerite and one of the young men in a room together. They, Blanche, and the other brother were arrested; even the third daughter-in-law, Jeanne, was detained, as she was Blanche's older sister and was presumed to have concealed her knowledge of the younger woman's activities. On April 19, 1314, the two young knights were flayed to death and beheaded. News of their fate reached the queen's party as it headed toward the coast of France.

"You see, they were guilty after all, and they have received their just punishment," said the queen matter-of-factly. She was not even put out with Eleanor any longer. "Mind you, I pity my brothers, but they will find worthy wives soon, I hope."

Eleanor spent the return journey to England by her brother's side, silent and listless. Only when she landed at Dover and saw a familiar face did she brighten. Forgetting all protocol, as soon as she could get to shore, she rushed into her husband's arms.

"My love, you look ill and tired. What is it? Look at the offering someone has brought the queen: a porcupine!"

Eleanor buried her head on Hugh's shoulder as he tried in vain to turn her attention to the bristly little animal, which was quite sated with apples. "Please," she whispered, "take me from court."

CHAPTER 8

▼

JUNE 1314 TO JULY 1314

While the queen's party was in France, Robert the Bruce had invaded two castles, Roxborough and Edinburgh. Roxborough Castle had fallen on February 27 to the terrifying James Douglas, who had dressed his men in black surcoats and ordered them to crawl on their hands and knees so that they resembled a herd of black cattle straying toward the castle. When the cattle arrived at the castle, they had produced collapsible ladders carried beneath their bodies, scaled the castle walls, and overcome the garrison, the members of which were vigorously celebrating a feast day. The next month, Thomas Randolph, aided by one of his men who had been accustomed to using rope ladders to get in and out of the castle to meet his lover, led a group of experienced mountain climbers into Edinburgh Castle.

The year before, Robert the Bruce's brother, Edward, had besieged Stirling Castle. He had no siege weapons; his only strategy was to starve out the garrison, a tactic that was tedious as it was sound. Sir Philip Mowbray, the castle's commander, had recognized his besieger's frustration and had offered in June 1313 to yield the castle a year hence if he were not rescued by battle. Robert the Bruce, whom Edward had not thought to consult before entering into this treaty, was furious at his brother, but the King of England, heartened by the peace with the barons, the cordiality of his relationship with his French father-in-law, and the quiet prevailing in Ireland and Wales, took up the challenge. As Gloucester had told his sister, the king had begun making plans to bring troops north, and as the queen's household traveled in France, he was mobilizing his troops.

Gilbert, of course, had responded, as had Pembroke and Hereford. The Earls of Lancaster, Warwick, Arundel, and Surrey, however, did no more than send the required numbers of cavalry and footmen; they did not set foot outside England. Edward scarcely missed them, for his army was of a size not seen even in his father's day: twenty thousand men. In his confidence he granted some men Scottish land; to the son of his trusted advisor Hugh le Despenser the elder he granted the lands of the Earl of Moray. Hugh the younger, like many others expecting to move into his new castle shortly, brought tapestries, plate, and other furnishings with him; the wagon train groaned with such baggage of the confident.

"Who is that?" asked Eleanor as she watched the army, finally assembled in Berwick, prepare to depart.

She and the queen, both being about to send their husbands to war, had recovered something of their friendly relationship, although Eleanor would never dare to mention their visit to France. It had been a modest success from an English point of view: Philip, perhaps contrasting his daughter's behavior with that of his faithless daughters-in-law, had granted some of the concessions she sought. Isabella smiled as Eleanor pointed to a tonsured figure sitting in a wagon. "That is the poet."

"Poet?"

"He is Friar Baston, a monk who is proficient in Latin verse. He is to sing England's triumphs when the Scots are defeated. Rumor has it that he has written much of his material already."

"Isn't that premature?" asked Margaret dryly. Although Gaveston's lands had been forfeit to the crown after his death, Edward had arranged for Margaret to have a dower worthy of her husband's riches, and she had been left very well off. Nonetheless, she frequently traveled with the queen's household now, Edward liking to keep her safe from fortune hunters and Margaret preferring the company of her sister and the other ladies to the solitude of her manors. She caught the queen's disapproving look and added, "I mean, shouldn't he wait so he can write an account of the actual battle?"

"I suppose some of what he wrote could serve for any battle," said Isabella. "The clash of armed men on horseback, the agony of the wounded, the grief of the widowed and orphaned... He can fill in the details later."

"And he need not wait to write about our magnificent army," said Eleanor. She almost pitied the Scots, but wisely said nothing.

Indeed, the tail end of the procession as it left Berwick was almost as impressive as its beginning. A hundred and six carts, each drawn by four horses, and a hundred and ten wagons, drawn by eight oxen, bore the army's supplies: corn and barley, portable mills, wine in jars and casks, gold and silver, gold and silver vessels, Hugh's plate and furnishings and those of many others. Herds of cattle, sheep, and pigs followed the wagons and carts, and more was coming by water. Two thousand knights, each attended by at least one squire and mounted on the finest pieces of horseflesh to be found in England, had answered the call to battle, and the king's best Welsh archers were there. Even the lowly foot soldiers looked somehow grand and glorious. Those churlish earls, thought Eleanor, would be sorry to have stayed away.

Berwick Castle was a sad place, though, one that Eleanor did not like to wander alone after her husband had departed from it. Nailed to the castle walls, as one of Eleanor's young pages had gleefully noted to his companion when he thought his lady could not hear, was the left arm of William Wallace, who had been hung, drawn, and quartered in 1305 on the orders of the first Edward. It was mostly gone now, but enough was visible to provide the page boys with some satisfaction and to make the ladies shudder. Worse, though, in Eleanor's mind, had been the fate of the Countess of Buchan, who had crowned Robert the Bruce King of Scotland in the absence of her brother, the Earl of Fife. She had been seized and sent to Eleanor's grandfather the English king in 1306, not long after Eleanor's wedding, and had been ordered to be confined in a cage hung from Berwick Castle; other female relations of the Scottish king had been similarly caged or, if they were lucky, sent to nunneries. For years the Countess of Buchan had remained in her open cage, visible to passersby; her only comfort was a privy, to which she could at least retreat in the worst weather. The second Edward had released her from the cage in 1312 and sent her to a nearby convent. She had died only months before, aged about twenty-seven. Eleanor, gazing at the spot where her cage had hung, had said a prayer for her soul; that night, praying for her family dead, she had for the first time purposely omitted the name of her grandfather.

Much to the exasperation of its staff, Berwick Castle was full of noblewomen, either attendant upon the queen, awaiting someone's return from battle, or both: the Countess of Pembroke, the Countess of Hereford, the Countess of Cornwall, the Countess of Surrey, the Lady Vescy, the Lady Despenser. Given an emergency, all could have undergone any manner of inconvenience; none were fools or faint of heart. But no emergency being present, all expected their accustomed comfort and had brought retainers with them, as well as greyhounds (the queen), lapdogs (most of the countesses), birds (the Lady Despenser), and even a cat (the Lady Vescy). The animals did not all get along, and neither did all the noble-women. The acerbic Lady Vescy, being somewhat older than the rest and not at all in awe of a superior title, felt free to give her opinion on any subject, no matter how irritating to the rest. The Countess of Cornwall was quick to take offense regarding her late husband, Gaveston, even when none was intended. The Countess of Surrey was quick to take offense regarding her very alive husband, John Warenne, even when none was intended. The Lady Despenser might be granddaughter to the first Edward and daughter to an earl, but she was married to almost a nobody and tended, the countesses thought, to get above her place. The Countess of Pembroke, who had yet to produce a child, even a girl child, disliked hearing about all matters maternal, which was one of the great unifying subjects among the women. The Countess of Hereford could not be around a lapdog without sneezing, and none of the lapdogs were inclined to stay away from the Countess of Hereford.

On the other hand, the staff speculated philosophically, there were certain advantages to having a castle full of women; no one had too much wine and called her neighbor a misbegotten whoreson, no one who lost at dice challenged the winner to a fight, and no one spent the evening at a brothel and then insisted on being admitted to the castle in the dead of the night. It was a boon, too, that the weather was proving unusually pleasant and dry, so complaints about fires and drafty rooms were kept to a minimum. Still, everyone agreed, it would be a good thing when the Scots were defeated and the noblewomen were claimed by their menfolk and either taken home to England or to the Scottish castles so many had been granted or expected to be granted.

Then, just as everyone in the castle was itching for news, a traveling merchant, delivering goods to the castle, told the queen's steward news so odd the steward could not believe it. Several hours later, another merchant told the steward the same news. When a bedraggled man came to the castle to beg admission a little later, telling the same incredible story, the steward had no choice but to take his news to the queen.

"Lost! Are you mad, churl? The English could not have lost the battle!" The queen was normally not a harsh mistress, but on this occasion, she rose and smacked her steward across the face, either to reprove him or bring him to his senses.

"Madam, I have heard no less than three independent accounts, the last from a foot soldier, and there is no reason to think them false! God hope that they may be proven wrong, but I could not in all good conscience keep their reports from you. They are all consistent in the larger details."

The queen was silent. Backing off a bit, the steward continued, "From what I hear, no harm has befallen the king. I know naught about any of your ladyships' husbands. But there are some of you with brothers or nephews…"

His eye had fallen on the Earl of Gloucester's sisters. Eleanor said, with as much firmness as she could muster, "Tell us."

"The main part of the battle was fought on the second day after the troops met. The Earl of Gloucester was killed early on the second day, charging bravely into the Bruce's men."

He turned to the Countess of Hereford. "Your husband's nephew Henry, my lady, died on the first day, in single combat with the Bruce. Others were killed, of course—the king's steward, Sir Edmund de Mauley, Sir John Comyn, Sir Pain de Tiptoft, Sir Robert de Clifford, Sir Giles d'Argentan—"

"Not Sir Giles!" said the Countess of Pembroke. "He is reputed to be the third greatest knight in England."

"He died bravely," said the queen's steward. He looked at the ladies before him. "Shall I tell you what I have heard?"

The ladies, even the Clare sisters, nodded, but the queen said bitterly, "Why bother, sir? The king's poet shall return and sing of it to us!"

The steward was not noted for his sense of humor. "No, your grace. He is a captive of the Scots, or so I hear."

"Then we had best hear it in prose," said Isabella de Vescy with a sigh.

To reach Stirling Castle by June 24, the army had proceeded at a punishing pace, but by June 23, they had reached the forest of Torwood, near the stream of the Bannock Burn. There they had consulted with Sir Philip Mowbray, the constable of the castle, who told Edward that as he had arrived within three leagues of the castle within the proper time, there was no need for a battle now. No one heeded this suggestion; the English army had not pushed this far to glance at Stirling Castle in the distance and then turn back home.

As the vanguard, led by the Earls of Gloucester and Hereford, emerged from the forest, watched by Scots standing to arms in the New Park, Hereford's young nephew, Henry de Bohun, saw a horseman inspecting the Scottish troops. No unusual sight that, save that the horseman wore a crown. The Bruce himself! Bohun saw the chance to bring things to a swift conclusion. Allowing himself only a brief moment to contemplate the fame and riches that would be his, he let out a yelp and charged at the Bruce, lance pointed straight at him. The Scottish king, not budging an inch, was on the verge of being impaled when he pulled away, just far enough to avoid the lance and to sink his axe into Bohun's helmet and down into his skull.

The Scots, delighted by this promising start, charged the stunned English cavalry, which as it attempted to resist had discovered the existence of many small pits camouflaged with twigs and grass, just enough to trip a horse. Bohun's squire rushed to stand by his master's body and was promptly killed; Gilbert de Clare fell off his stumbling horse and had to be rescued by his squires. The English retreated, while the Scottish king recalled his troops. Reproached by his commanders for putting his life at risk by the unfortunate Bohun, the Bruce said only that he was sorry he had broken his good axe.

Meanwhile, Sir Robert de Clifford and Sir Henry de Beaumont were heading toward Stirling Castle, where they might have evaded notice had not the Bruce spotted them and reproached the Earl of Moray, who should have been in a position to see them earlier, with his neglect. Moray hurriedly went to make good his mistake. Soon the English found themselves facing a veritable wall of spearmen. Charging them was in vain. When an opening appeared, it was in the ranks of the English, who fled in two directions, charged by the Earl of Moray, honor fully restored. His men, exhausted and delighted, fanned themselves with their helmets, then accepted the congratulations of their fellows. Both sides had done fighting for the day.

The English foot soldiers, encamped to the south of the Bannock Burn, had not seen the knights' defeat, but they had heard rumors, and Edward's heralds, sent to boost their morale by reminding them that victory was certain, singularly failed at their task. Their newfound pessimism was shared by one Sir Alexander Seton, who deserted in the night to the Scots and advised them that this was an opportune time to regain Scotland.

Gilbert de Clare, seeing the exhaustion of the English troops and the difficulty they were having in finding somewhere to bed down for the night in the marshy area, urged the king to rest his troops for twenty-four hours. For such sensible advice he had been called disloyal; worse, a coward. Gilbert's first impulse had been to strike the king, but with difficulty he controlled himself and instead wheeled around and left the king's tent without another word.

His troops had had little chance to sleep, for dawn on June 24, 1314, came at three forty-five. The king gave the order for his men to arm themselves. As they were doing so, he started. In the distance, Scottish foot soldiers were advancing, silently and deliberately. "What!" he said. "Will these Scotsmen fight?"

Sir Ingram de Umfraville, standing beside him, shook his head. "It is the strangest sight I ever saw, your grace. To take on the might of England—"

"And look now! They kneel for mercy."

Umfraville shook his head. "They are asking God for forgiveness, not entreating you. These men will win all or die."

"So be it then. Sound the trumpet!"

As their squires made haste to dress them in their armor, Gilbert de Clare and Humphrey de Bohun were arguing over who should command the vanguard. Hereford said that the duty was lawfully his because he was the constable of England; Gilbert contended that his forbears had always led the van. "And," said Gilbert, looking toward the king, "I shall tarry here no more, for this day I shall prove that I am no coward!"

He had not waited to put on his surcoat with the chevrons of Clare, the garment that would have identified him as one of the richest men in England, worth a fortune in ransom money to any man lucky enough to take him alive. Instead, he charged straight toward the Scots, an anonymous young knight, and was promptly knocked off his horse and killed by enemy spears.

The stage had been set. More knights charged the Scots; more were killed against their spears. Wounded horses, their riders dead, trampled English foot soldiers. The English archers, with no clear line of fire, desperately tried to shoot at the Scottish spearmen, but their arrows reached more English backs than Scottish chests. At last, a group of the archers succeeded in crossing the Pelstream Burn and shooting at the Scots, with deadly results. The Bruce ordered his light cavalry to charge the archers. Few withstood the charge, and the Scots moved even farther forward.

The Scots leader sent in a fresh schiltron, his last. Coming in behind the men already in front of them, the new spearmen pushed their fellows forward, so that a wave of spears pushed the English back. The English, Edward no less than his army, continued to fight ferociously, but they were so close together they could scarcely move, and those who slipped in the pools of blood underneath them were trampled to death. "On them!" shouted the Scots. "On them, they fall!"

A fresh group of Scots had now arrived: the "small folk," screaming "Slay!" Untrained or unequipped soldiers, laborers, even camp followers, even women, they had heard the battle was turning in their favor and were eager to join in; some for the prospect of plunder, some out of loyalty to their king, some out of a desire to tell their sons that they had fought alongside the Bruce. For many English, the appearance of this motley group, through eyes that were obscured by blood and sweat, was the breaking factor. Another cursed army! Some turned and ran.

King Edward had already been unhorsed once, but had found a mount from among those running loose, and he had not ceased to fight since entering the battle. Fiercely as he was fighting, he was in imminent danger of being captured, for Scottish knights were grasping at his horse's trappings and would have had the king if Edward had not struck them off with his mace. The Earl of Pembroke, seeing no hope of victory left, determined to get the king off the field. With the aid of Giles d'Argentan, reckoned one of England's finest knights, he turned the bridle of Edward's horse and dragged him away toward Stirling Castle, followed by five hundred knights. When the king was within a safe distance of the castle, Sir Giles looked back.

It was pandemonium. With the departure of the king and his knights, most of the men who remained had nothing left on their minds but escape. The few men who still were attempting to put up a fight were being slaughtered. Sir Giles looked at the safety of the castle and the certainty of death on the battlefield, and quickly made up his mind. "I have never left a fight," he said, and galloped away toward the waiting Scots. Within minutes he had been killed.

Men attempting to cross over the Bannock Burn were drowning; so many that after a point those who lagged behind were able to cross to safety over the bodies of dead men and horses. The Earl of Hereford and his men made their way without much difficulty to Bothwell Castle, where the constable, upon learning of the Bruce's victory, took the earl and fifty others captive and handed them over to Edward Bruce as prisoners. The king and his party, meanwhile, were denied entry to Stirling Castle by Sir Mowbray, who told them that if they came inside they would certainly be taken prisoner by the Scots.

The king and his men did not wait to argue, but set off toward Linlithgow, pursued by Douglas, and then toward Dunbar. So close was Douglas in pursuit that it was said that no Englishman dared stopped long enough to make water. Any man who checked his speed was killed or captured, even with Pembroke's men desperately fighting off their pursuers. Finally, the party reached Dunbar Castle, where the king was admitted by the Earl of Dunbar. From there he and a few others sailed in an open boat to Berwick, to an England bowed down with shame.

Not an hour after the steward told his story, a mean fishing boat docked at Berwick Castle. As the queen and the ladies wound slowly down the narrow walk to the Tweed, the king, with no fanfare, stepped on shore. His face was nearly as grim and sad as it had been in the days after Gaveston's death. Following were the Earl of Pembroke and Henry de Beaumont—the cries of relief from the Countess of Pembroke and Isabella de Vescy echoed off the water—and a dozen or so knights. At the very end of the grim procession coming off the boat was Eleanor's father-in-law, staggering under a great weight—Mother of God! The weight was her husband!

Stepping off the path and all but tumbling down to the riverside, Eleanor rushed to her father-in-law. At any other time she would have marveled at his strength, for Hugh the elder was not a large man, and the man he carried was fully his equal in height and weight. "Sir! Is he dead?"

Hugh shook his head. "He lives—barely." His voice was choked. "He was badly wounded—though he fought like a tiger—but I was able to bring him off with the others safely. He kept up with us with my help but developed a high fever on the boat. He has been delirious ever since."

He lowered his son to the ground, unable to carry him farther. Eleanor bent over him, sobbing. "Hugh! My love. My poor love."

He opened his eyes at the sound of her voice, but there was no recognition in them. After staring blankly for a moment or two he closed them again. Hugh the elder gently touched her shoulder. "Come, child. Let them take him inside."

Two men lifted Hugh and carried him into the castle. Eleanor rose and tried to walk, but she could not move forward for her blinding tears. Then someone lifted her in his arms too. Who it was she did not know until she heard the king murmur, "It will be all right, my dear niece. He will recover."

All of the men had suffered some wounds, and the ladies, all of whom had been trained since childhood to tend the sick and injured, were soon busy bandaging and binding and cleaning, including Eleanor, though her attentions were devoted almost entirely to Hugh. The queen herself dressed the king's wounds and soon was seen, to the astonishment of her ladies and damsels, cleaning his armor. The anger she had shown when the steward broke the news to her was not at all displayed toward Edward; she was all sympathy and understanding. Upon learning that his seal had been seized, along with the knight who carried it, she promptly lent him her own so that the administrative work of the kingdom could go on as usual.

From her station by Hugh's bedside Eleanor gathered bits of news. Word had gotten out that the Earl of Hereford had been taken prisoner, and as he was the most illustrious captive, wagers were being made as to how much ransom the Bruce would require. Eleanor's stepfather, Ralph de Monthermer, had also been captured. Years before, it was rumored, the first Edward, when Robert the Bruce was dining with him as his guest, had planned to take the Bruce prisoner when the dinner was over. Ralph, who had formed a sort of friendship with Bruce, was said to have foiled the plan by sending a servant to Robert with money and a pair of spurs. The Bruce had taken the hint and disappeared into the night. Eleanor doubted her grandfather had known of the warning, otherwise Ralph would not have survived to the year 1314, but she had once overheard her mother and Ralph talking in a manner that made her suspect the rumor was true. If it was, she hoped the Bruce remembered it.

She was too concerned with Hugh, however, to fret over her stepfather or to properly mourn her brother, though she and Margaret had sent a letter to Gilbert's countess gently informing her of his death, and Margaret, accompanied by her own men and several of Gilbert's who had come straggling back, had gone to see how the widow fared. Hugh had gotten neither better nor worse since the day his father had borne him off the boat. The surgeon had cut at the cause of his fever, a minor wound that had nonetheless festered, and he was bled periodically, but he continued to burn with fever and to turn and toss. He did at least seem to be able to distinguish Eleanor and his father from the others around him, for when one or the other was seated at his side, he was noticeably calmer.

Eleanor had heard that the delirious often revealed deep secrets as they ranted and raved, but Hugh, self-contained in health, was no less so in sickness. He appeared to be reliving the battle at times, and he fretted a great deal about a horse that Hugh the elder said had died when his son was but a boy of nine, but he otherwise showed nothing of himself.

On the fifth day of nursing Hugh, Eleanor herself looked so tired and ill that her father-in-law ordered her out of his chamber, gently but in a manner that brooked no opposition. He had been watching his daughter-in-law closely and had discovered what Eleanor was still keeping to herself. Eleanor was too exhausted to argue anyway. She went to the chamber that had been made ready for her and stretched on the bed fully clothed, intending to nap only a bit. It must have been twelve hours later when Gladys gently shook her awake. "My lady, there is good news. Hugh is better, and has been asking for you."

She drew the bed curtains aside and saw that Hugh was asleep. He had been shaven, and with his head on his arm and his dark hair falling over his cheek he looked vulnerable, younger than his twenty-seven years. She touched his face and found that for the first time in days it was cool. So comfortable did he look that she almost hesitated to wake him, but she wanted so badly to hear his voice, his rational voice. "Hugh, my love."

He stirred, and she repeated her words. Then he fully opened his eyes, and smiled in recognition of her. "Eleanor. My little redheaded angel."

"Oh, Hugh. I thought—never mind what I thought. I am so glad..." She ducked her head and let her tears fall, until at last she got her voice under command. "You have frightened me most shamefully, sir."

"I apologize. Lean over and let me kiss you."

She did so, and he lay quietly for a while, holding her hand against his chest. Finally, he met her eyes and said, "I suppose you know about your brother. I saw him fall. I am sorry, Eleanor."

"He is with God now."

"Yes. Eleanor, it was a rout—a total humiliation. All of us a pack of cocky fools, and I as much as the rest." He grimaced. "I suppose someone else is furnishing his lodgings with the goods I brought, so you can't say it was a total waste. What a fool! I could supplant Rob Withstaff from his position if there weren't so many other contenders."

"You could not have known, Hugh, that things would turn out so dreadfully."

"We were slaughtered, Eleanor, and none came out with much credit."

"I am sure that is not true. I know that you fought bravely."

"The dolts tell us that jousting in front of an audience of ladies and old men prepares us for battle. They are wrong, Eleanor. What happened at the Bannock Burn was a horror, Eleanor. I just want to forget it."

He shivered and turned his face away from her, obviously doing everything but forgetting. Eleanor waited a while, then put a hand on his. "Hugh. I do have some good news for you. I suspected before you left, but I wanted to make certain. I am with child again. I must have conceived shortly before I went to France."

Hugh's face brightened. "My love. We shall have a fine brood, won't we?" He pressed her hand. "Eleanor, with every horror I saw, I tried to remember your sweet face. It brought me here—it and my beloved father—when I could hardly put one foot in front of the other. Even in my nightmares it appeared to me and gave me hope and strength."

His face was drawn. "Hugh, you don't know how proud those words make me, but you must rest now."

"I will if you will lie down beside me. Here. This is my good side."

She stripped down to her shift and lay down on Hugh's right, where his wounds had been minor. She guided his hand to her swelling belly and stroked his hair as he drifted off to sleep. Soon she was asleep too. So Hugh the elder found them some few minutes later. He drew the bed curtains around them and softly slipped out of the room.

Hugh was still convalescing when Eleanor, sitting by his bed as usual, was summoned to the king. There he sat in the great hall, along with the queen, Hugh the elder, and two men.

She uttered a cry of delight and ran forward when she recognized the older of the men, for he was her stepfather. As she stepped from his embrace, she saw that the second man was a stranger to her. He was broad-shouldered, with dark hair. His rugged, rather overbearing handsomeness did little to appeal to Eleanor, who preferred Hugh's wiry body and sharply etched features, but she could see where other women might find him attractive.

"Lord Monthermer and Lord Roger Mortimer have been sent home by the Bruce without ransom," said the king.

Mortimer. Eleanor stole a glance at her father-in-law. A Mortimer had slain his father at Evesham, when Hugh was but a child of three, and had grossly dishonored the body of Simon de Montfort. Hugh had been left with only the faintest memories of his father, but his mother had taught him to emulate him, and though he was too sensible to hold the Mortimer in front of him responsible for a killing committed many years before his time and almost before Hugh's own, he would gladly have excused himself from the young man's company were it not for what Mortimer had brought with him. Hugh said quietly, "He also released your brother's body, Eleanor. Here it is."

For the first time, she saw the plain coffin. Without thinking, she started as if to lift the lid, but Ralph stopped her. "It is not a sight for your eyes, Eleanor. I have seen him. He is your brother, though. Trust me."

Eleanor turned her head away. After a few minutes, she said quietly, "I shall write Maud. I am certain she will want to have him buried with our ancestors at Tewkesbury." She managed to smile at her stepfather. "Lord Monthermer, I am grateful the Lord has returned you to us." She paused. "And you, Lord Mortimer. Lord Monthermer is my stepfather, so I naturally spoke to him first, but I am glad he spared both of you."

"Oh, of course," said Mortimer carelessly.

"Were you treated badly?" Eleanor asked.

"To the contrary, I was feasted," said Ralph. He shrugged apologetically. "Once I saved the Bruce's skin from the first Edward, by warning him so that he could flee, and the Bruce did not forget that, it appears."

"Had you not done so, things would be quite different now," muttered Mortimer.

"True," said Ralph coolly. "But this was a fair fight. What happened years before was a trap, and I do not like traps." He turned away from Mortimer and said, "He treated Gilbert's body with great respect, sitting vigil with it all night in the church to which it was carried. He mourned your brother, as a matter of fact. You should know that."

The Clares were relations of Robert Bruce, as was Mortimer. "It comforts me, sir, and I will make certain that my sisters and the Countess of Gloucester know it too."

"In addition to sending us the body, he has sent the Great Seal, which the king lost in retreating, and the king's shield." Mortimer held it up almost in triumph. Eleanor saw Edward flinch. *Retreat* was not a word with which the first Edward would have expected someone to use in conjunction with the word *king*.

"It is magnanimous of him," said the king with a sigh.

For some minutes the men traded news of the battle: who had returned, who had died, who would be ransomed, and who was as yet unaccounted for, while Eleanor, unnoticed, went to Gilbert's coffin and knelt beside it.

Mortimer said abruptly, "So what of the Countess of Gloucester? Is she with child?"

He was looking at Eleanor. "I do not know, Lord Mortimer."

"Aye? I think it would be a subject of the greatest interest to you."

"I do not take your meaning."

"Come now, Lady Despenser! Surely the thought has entered your mind. If Gloucester left no heir, you and your sisters will be rich women, even with the Clare inheritance divided into thirds."

The thought had not entered Eleanor's mind, in truth. She blushed as all those present stared at her. Her father-in-law came to her rescue. "My son has been gravely ill from his wounds these past few days, my lord. It was thought until recently that he might not recover. My daughter-in-law has scarcely had time to consider the future between her grief over her brother and nursing her husband."

"Aye? A devoted wife as well as a potentially rich one. Sir Hugh is a lucky man."

"He is indeed," said Ralph coldly. He put his arm around Eleanor. "There will be time to consider this later. My stepdaughter's grief is still fresh."

Mortimer turned away from Eleanor and began a conversation about the situation in Ireland, where he had been stationed up until this foray into Scotland.

Eleanor paid no attention to it. She had spoken truthfully about not thinking of Gilbert's inheritance, so all-consuming had been her fears for Hugh. But now she remembered odd looks she had been given over the last few days when she had emerged from Hugh's chamber, remarks she had not fully understood. She had even heard someone whisper, "If Sir Hugh dies there will be *three* wealthy widows for the king to parcel out," and so horrified had she been by the first four words that she had paid no attention to the ones that followed. Of course, she and Elizabeth and Margaret would inherit their brother's estates if Gilbert had left no heir—and the only child Maud had produced previously had been short-lived. Was she indeed a rich woman now?

She wondered if Hugh had thought of it. But she was certain of one thing: it had been inexcusably gauche of Mortimer to mention it, with poor Gilbert lying feet away in his coffin. She heartily wished him back in Ireland.

In his bed, Hugh started awake. *If Gilbert de Clare died without an heir, I could be Lord of Glamorgan.*

It was the first time the thought had occurred to him, for in the midst of battle and flight not even Hugh was capable of reviewing his landed status, and he had been too sick and weak after the escape to concern himself with the Clare inheritance. But now the words ran though his brain again and again. *Lord of Glamorgan.* And then, *Earl of Gloucester.*

He sat bolt upright in bed for the first time since he'd been carried there and gestured to a page. "Fetch me my father."

"He is an odious man!" Eleanor jabbed her needle fiercely into her embroidery hoop. Joan of Bar, who had made the mistake of telling the other ladies that she thought Mortimer handsome, started.

"He is outspoken," said the queen thoughtfully.

"If such rudeness and effrontery can be called that! Not a word of condolence for my dear brother, who was a greater man at twenty-three than that nasty creature could hope to be at forty. And to insinuate that I should see his death as a boon!"

"He only pointed out the obvious, Lady Despenser. You cannot blame the man for that."

"And what is my inheritance—if I have one—to him?"

"Glamorgan," said Lady Vescy. "Do you not know the importance of Glamorgan, girl? As the eldest, you are bound to get that as your portion, and Mortimer, though he has hitherto been serving in Ireland, is one of the most powerful lords in the Welsh march. It is everything to him who gets Glamorgan."

"Yes," said Eleanor thoughtfully, "I seem to remember that my father and the Mortimers were in a dispute over Wales."

"The Mortimers have been in disputes with everyone over Wales, English and Welsh alike. It's no marvel that they should wonder which of you sisters will have the lordship of Glamorgan, if at all."

"If I have to have Roger Mortimer as a neighbor, I hope I don't get a single acre of it."

"Somehow," said Lady Vescy, "I doubt your husband would share your opinion."

Hugh was all but on his feet when his father arrived in the sickroom. "Father! Have you heard whether the Countess of Gloucester is with child?"

"I have not. Strangely, Lord Mortimer asked your wife the same question a few minutes hence. It seems you are thinking on the same lines, which has surely never happened before when our family and the Mortimers are concerned. Lie down. You are still not strong."

Hugh obeyed, but caught at his father's hand. "Do you not understand what it means? Eleanor as the eldest will get the best lands, and that is Glamorgan. Glamorgan!"

"I understand full well what it means. Danger."

"Not in the hands of the right man." Hugh settled back on his pillows, with a tired but visionary look on his face.

Hugh looked at his son thoughtfully. From a very young age his son had been wont to go his own way, and no amount of discipline, even the occasional caning, had stopped him. Hugh, in truth, had not tried all that hard. Perhaps his own lack of a father had something to do with that; though he'd had a loving grandfather and his stepfather had been pleasant enough to him, he'd remembered and heard enough about his father to miss him deeply, and his death had left a void in Hugh's heart that nothing had completely filled until his own children had been born. He loved them all, but perhaps inevitably, his deepest love had been bestowed on his eldest son, and Hugh, for all the rows they'd had over the years, had fully reciprocated. As a small boy, he would wander away from his nurse and seek out his father for no better reason that that he wanted to be near him; many a council meeting had Hugh spent with his little son on his lap, the boy sometimes watching the proceedings alertly, other times sleeping soundly against his father's chest. When he was older and had become an expert hunter—and, Hugh knew, an expert poacher—he had proudly had plates of venison brought to his father's table; it seemed churlish to inquire too closely about its provenance.

Eldest sons and their fathers were often in an uneasy relationship; many a father who'd reached his fifties, as had Hugh, was conscious of a feeling, not always well hidden, that it was time to make a graceful exit and get land into younger, more capable hands. Not so his son; he'd taken the manors that Hugh had granted him gratefully, never asked for more. Was it because he'd found other ways of getting money? Once, in a rare unguarded moment, Hugh had mentioned the Bardi, the great Italian bankers, and his father had started: what the hell did a man with an income of only two hundred pounds a year need or want to do with the Bardi? And then there were Gaveston's ridiculous accusations of piracy. Sheer nonsense, as so much of poor Gaveston's remarks had been, but Hugh had not been able to shake them off. He'd looked more carefully at the necklace his daughter-in-law wore every day: not of English workmanship, not of French either. Something that might have come on a ship from Italy, one that had been plundered...

He was relieved from thinking more about the matter by a knock on the door. He smiled as his daughter-in-law entered the room. "Eleanor?"

"The king has heard from the Countess of Gloucester, sir. She is much grieved by her husband's death, and she is inquiring about when she can expect her dower to be set aside."

Hugh the younger smiled. "That's the Maud I know!"

"And she writes that she is in good health but that she is a little tired, for she is expecting a child."

CHAPTER 9

▼

OCTOBER 1314 TO
APRIL 1317

"Forgive me, Nelly, for missing your lying-in! But these rains have been so horrid, I thought I would never get here."

Hugh's sister Isabel, still damp, bent by the bed where Eleanor lay and kissed her on the cheek. Eleanor laughed. "Edward was no laggard, so I have no cause for complaint, Bella. And it is so good to see you, dear, especially without that horrid black on."

Isabel's face changed, and Eleanor instantly regretted her words. Her sister-in-law's husband had died suddenly in the spring of 1313 at age fifty-one, leaving her with two sons, Thomas and Hugh, and a daughter, Margaret. "I put off my mourning only because I was told it was time to, Nelly. I miss him so much."

"I know you do, Bella. I am sorry. But you do look so pretty in that saffron you are wearing, with your dark hair."

"He was so kind to me, so loving. I will never look at another, whatever I wear." Isabel's face brightened. "But where is your boy?"

On cue, the wet nurse entered and put two-day-old Edward in Eleanor's arms. "He came so quickly, Bella! The midwife barely had time to get here; Gladys and I thought she would have to deliver him herself. But everything went fine."

"He looks like Hugh, I think. He must be delighted."

"He is; he loves Isabel, but a boy is different somehow; men can never have enough, as you well know. He and your father are talking about purchasing a reversion of land for him."

"How is your sister-in-law Maud? Do you hear from her?"

Eleanor snorted. "Margaret and I went to Tewkesbury Abbey—a most gloomy place, someone ought to put in some stained glass—to see Gilbert buried there, and she treated us as little more than spies, checking on her pregnancy. She certainly wasn't showing it then; chest and bosom flat as a board. I loved Gilbert; once I learned Hugh would be all right, I cried every night over my brother. I am still angry with the king for speaking so hastily to him, although I understand it was a tense time for all. And for Maud to act as if my sisters and I would want to see something befall his heir, so that we can come into his land! It is just too sad. So I do not write to her, and I don't think Margaret does either. Elizabeth might hear from her, seeing as she was married to Maud's brother, but Elizabeth is still in Ireland."

"Do you plan to return to court after you are churched?"

"Not if I can help it, Bella. I have seen so little of my son Hugh, though my uncle has kindly told me he can stay at court with me if I wish, but with Isabel and now Edward, I do not want to be such a stranger. And I do not enjoy being there much now that Lancaster is there. He makes me uneasy, Bella."

Isabel nodded, "As well he should. I despise him for the hurt he has caused my father."

Thomas of Lancaster had publicly attributed the ignominious defeat at the Bannock Burn to the king's failure to observe the Ordinances. At the York Parliament held in September 1314, Edward, in no position to bargain, had capitulated to virtually all of his cousin's demands. He had sworn to abide by the Ordinances, and many of his household officials and most of his sheriffs had been replaced by others. Hugh le Despenser the elder was among those whose removal Lancaster sought. Just days before the birth of his latest grandchild in October 1314, he had returned to Loughborough from that Parliament, looking grim and not a little bit sad. He had served Edward and his father for over thirty years, and though he knew that Lancaster had always wanted to see him gone from court, the moment of dismissal had rankled.

"Whom do you despise, dear?"

Isabel looked up at her father, who had noiselessly entered Eleanor's chamber. "Lancaster, Papa, for making you leave court."

"Don't trouble yourself, child. Lancaster will give himself plenty of rope, and one day he will hang himself with it." He kissed Isabel on her cheek. "I was meeting with my council when you arrived. My absence from court does have its advantages; I'm getting much more done here."

"You shall soon be back, sir," said Eleanor.

"Indeed I shall. In the meantime, it has stopped raining for a moment or two. I thought I would take your boys riding." He nodded toward Edward, sleeping in Eleanor's arms. "Present company excepted, of course."

After his death, Gaveston had been embalmed, but he had not been properly laid to rest. Aside from his dying excommunicate, Edward had vowed not to see him underground until his death had been avenged. By January 1315, however, Edward had at least gotten the sentence of excommunication reversed, and although Piers's death had by no means been avenged, the king had healed enough to bear his friend's funeral. He was buried at Langley, the king's and Gaveston's favorite retreat.

Lancaster and Warwick, needless to say, did not attend, but Pembroke and Hereford did, along with Henry de Beaumont, the Despensers, and many other dignitaries. The king made no attempt to hide his emotion, and as for the cost— Lancaster be damned! He'd not give the dearest person in the world a mean burial just to appease cousin Thomas's miserly little soul.

March arrived, still rainy, and every day, Eleanor awaited word of Gilbert's heir. March departed, still rainy, and no word was heard from Maud at all. "Surely she would tell us, would she not, Hugh?"

"To gloat if nothing else. Eleanor, I've held my tongue, for I was sorry to see Gilbert fall. But now I must tell you that I think this whole pregnancy is a fraud."

"Hugh?"

"Nine months have passed, Eleanor, and that's assuming she became pregnant just before the Bannock Burn, although from what Gilbert let slip one night when he'd had too much wine, I don't think they'd had relations in a while, so shrewish had she become."

"But you don't know; they might have made it up, especially with Gilbert facing battle." Eleanor thought this most likely, for she had been careful to send Hugh off to Scotland with the happiest of marital memories. "And babies can be late, Hugh."

"True."

"And why, Hugh le Despenser, would Maud do such a silly thing? For shame, Hugh! You are so cynical."

Hugh shrugged. "So I am, always will be. But if you're making clothes for this one, I wouldn't bother." He strolled out, shaking his head, as Eleanor frowned at her work basket, which indeed contained a beautiful swaddling blanket for her latest niece or nephew, embroidered with the Clare arms. She picked it up, finishing the last of the stitching defiantly.

After Parliament met in the spring of 1315, Lancaster, much to Edward's relief, returned to his estates for a while, having first forced the king to void all royal gifts made in the past few years, but Warwick, now on Edward's council, remained at Edward's side, an ever-present reminder of what Edward could not bear to think about: Gaveston's last days in the dungeons of Warwick Castle.

Warwick's snarling Black Dog days were behind him, however. He was scrupulously polite to the king now, with none of the insolence that surfaced from time to time on Lancaster's part. He was too polite, thought Edward; had he not been it would have been the king's obligation and pleasure to knock him flat. Instead, he had to sit patiently on a rainy day in late May while Warwick droned on and on in his respectful monotone about problems in Scotland, problems in Ireland, problems in Wales, problems in Bristol, famine caused by the never-ending rain, food prices, Warwick's fool nephew seizing Tonbridge Castle in Kent—

The king started. "Your nephew?"

"The younger Despenser." Warwick was politely apologetic. "Your grace recalls he is my late sister's son. I was rather fond of the lad when he was a pup, but we haven't had much contact lately."

"Why in God's name has he seized Tonbridge Castle? Who would even want to seize Tonbridge Castle?"

"He refuses to speak of the matter to anyone but you and your council, your grace."

Edward was on the verge of turning to the seat to his left and asking the elder Despenser what his son was up to, when he remembered that Despenser had been dismissed from his council. He sighed sharply. "Have him brought here, then."

"Your grace, here are the keys to Tonbridge Castle. Easy come, easy go."

Edward stared at the young man in front of him. "Hugh, what is the meaning of this fool stunt of yours?"

"To make a point, your grace."

"You seized a castle just to make a point?"

Hugh shrugged. "It got me here, did it not?" His lighthearted tone turned cold. "Were my lord father here on your council, as he deserves to be from his long years of service, there would no need to resort to such stratagems, but with him rusticating as he is, there seemed no other way for a Despenser to get before your council."

"I deeply regret your father's absence; you know that, Hugh. But what point is it you wish to make?"

"This one, your grace: the Countess of Gloucester has been claiming her pregnancy for well over eleven months now. How long can this farce continue?"

"You are impugning the Countess of Gloucester's honor, Sir Hugh. Were she a man—"

"Were she a man, she would not be claiming this pregnancy, now would she?" Hugh smiled. "Your grace, I spoke in haste. It is right that I should give her the benefit of the doubt. Perhaps she did feel the stirrings of life at some point; perhaps she miscarried. Perhaps it is one of those odd cases where a woman's belly swells but she is not with child. But I cannot think of a case where a woman has taken eleven months to bear a child, and I believe the law presumes against such a happenstance."

"Your attorneys will have a chance to make such an argument in chancery, where this matter belongs. I shall take care that it is reached there promptly."

"I thank your grace." Hugh paused. Though his seizure of the castle had been bloodless, really quite a lark, he was not at all certain he had not earned himself a sojourn in the Tower. "I am free to go?"

The king did not answer immediately. To seize a castle to make a point! He looked at Hugh as if seeing him for the first time. His features were too sharp for real handsomeness, his leanness bordered on skinniness, and at some point he'd broken his nose, or had it broken for him, for it was slightly askew. Not a beauty like Gaveston, not even close.

So why did Edward suddenly long to take this man into his bed?

No! He'd never lose his heart again in that manner; he'd concentrate on his beautiful queen, who could be loved with absolute safety and who had many excellent qualities, all of which Edward reminded himself of daily. He'd keep this unsettling young man far from him, even if he was husband to his sweet little niece, whom Edward could prefer to his wife if he thought about it, which he certainly would not. "Yes. You may go." The next two words came unbidden. "For now."

Long before Eleanor's father, Gilbert the Red, had married her mother, Joan, Gilbert had been married, quite miserably, to Alice de Lusignan. With the connivance of the first Edward, who wished to see the sometimes troublesome Gilbert safely married to his daughter Joan, the marriage had at last been annulled, and Alice's children had been barred from receiving any of the Clare inheritance. One of these children was a woman by the name of Isabel, and her name had been confused with that of Eleanor's sister Elizabeth in the postmortem inquisitions held regarding the disposition of young Gilbert's estates. County by county, each jury that had named the hapless Isabel as a coheir of Eleanor, Margaret, and Elizabeth was finding out its mistake, but at a slow pace. Meanwhile, Maud, staying in Caerphilly Castle in Glamorgan, doggedly continued to claim she was pregnant. By this time, Eleanor herself had lost patience. She had yanked out the Clare embroidery on the baby blanket in her work basket and put it aside in hopes that she would soon have use of it for a fourth Despenser child.

"*I* could have told them that Elizabeth and Isabel were two different people, and that Isabel is only a sister of my half blood," she complained to Hugh. "Why, I've only seen her three or four times in my life, I think. She's years older than I am, much less Elizabeth. Why did they have to put the question to the jury?"

"Patience, my dear, patience. Is that not what you were telling me?"

"At least I have never seized a castle over this, Hugh." Though Eleanor had tried to be affronted at her husband's actions in the spring, she had not been able to muster up any true indignation, and Hugh knew it. He grinned.

"Give Maud another year, and then you will, so practice your swordsmanship, sweetheart. But I've a petition to take to the king at Lincoln. As Maud is in her fifteenth month, perhaps he'll see reason. But I wonder why she hasn't had any vassal of hers do her a small favor in between the sheets? Either the fool woman is barren or entirely lacking in imagination and initiative."

The Black Dog of Arden had ceased to bark. Warwick, having taken ill in July of 1315, had left the court in hopes of recuperating and had died a month later at Warwick Castle. Edward wrote what was proper to Warwick's widow, Alice—he had been married to her for only five years, but the marriage had been fruitful and had produced a handful of young Beauchamps—but privately felt nothing but intense satisfaction, for Warwick had been only in his fourth decade of life. If Gaveston had been cheated of so much life by Warwick, at least the Almighty had done nearly the same to his killer.

To his new friends, Roger Damory, Hugh d'Audley, and William de Montacute, Edward ridiculed Warwick's desire to be buried simply. "What, did he think I was going to bear him to Westminster, with the Archbishop of Canterbury himself officiating? I'd see him buried a deal more simply if I could: throw him into the moat at Warwick Castle for the fish to snack on."

Damory and Audley laughed, but Montacute, who was of a somewhat more thoughtful temperament, said, "Perhaps he felt remorse, your grace?"

"If he did, it's too late." The king snorted. "I have even heard rumors that I am said to have poisoned him! If I had, trust me, I would have done it sooner."

The men were dicing in Edward's private chamber at Lincoln Castle, where Edward had summoned his council and other great men of the realm to discuss the Scots, who since the battle of the Bannock Burn had not lain idle, but had made frequent raids into England. Now Montacute, staring out the window, started, "If my eyes don't fail me, young Despenser is riding up. Has he business with your grace?"

"He makes it his business to remind me regularly that the Countess of Gloucester has not yet given birth, and that my niece Eleanor waits patiently for her share of the late earl's lands." Edward stood. "And as he is married to my dear niece, I will see him in the presence of my council."

"Strange case, that," said Damory, after the king had left the chamber. "Do you really think the wench is with child?"

"I don't in the least," said Montacute. "I suspect the king simply wants to keep the lands in his hands as long as possible, to keep them out of the wrong hands and the revenues flowing into the royal coffers, and she's making it easy for him with this preposterous story of hers."

"Aye," said Audley. "And Lancaster is in no hurry to see young Hugh get his share. There's been bad blood between him and the older one since the old king died and old Hugh stood fast with the king on the Gaveston matter."

"Pity that the other sisters have to wait. The Countess of Cornwall has turned into a fine woman. And little Elizabeth, tucked away in Ireland, is pretty, I've heard."

"Aspiring, Damory?"

"Why not? Two rich young widows, already broken in, if you can count Gaveston as breaking in. And as he left a brat behind, I suppose we can count him." Damory yawned, then grinned at William. "Sorry, Montacute, that as a married man, you won't get to pluck any of those flowers."

"I'm pleased with my lot, thank you." Montacute had bored of the dicing and had resumed his station at the window seat. "And you should be for a while too, for young Hugh's coming out of the castle, and he doesn't look like a man who's just been awarded the lordship of Glamorgan."

"The council told the king that the case was novel and hitherto unseen in the realm and that they would do nothing without the consent of Parliament. Of course it's novel! It's novel because no damn fool woman has ever been mad enough to claim she is fifteen months pregnant before. God, if the first Edward was alive he'd have cut her belly open by now, just to check."

Eleanor shuddered, but Hugh, having vented his anger, shut himself up with his lawyers and after a number of conferences emerged with another petition, which he presented to the king in October. The king duly sent it on to his council in London. The council, having consulted with the chancellor, sent back a beautifully sealed reply stating that they dared do nothing without the assent of the great men of the realm because of the strangeness of the case. There being nothing to be done until Parliament met, as it was scheduled to do in Lincoln in January, Hugh took this latest disappointment graciously and contented himself with remarking to his father that in the time it took Maud to produce one child, his Eleanor could produce two, for by the time the council made its decision in October 1315, Eleanor was once again pregnant.

In late January 1316, as her husband and father-in-law were preparing to depart for Lincoln—Hugh the younger had received his first summons to Parliament in 1314—Eleanor received some welcome news. "Hugh! My uncle is recalling Elizabeth from Ireland. She shall soon be in England. I have worried so, with the Bruces invading Ireland."

"Worried for her, or for the Bruces, darling?"

"Hugh! But it is true she is rather a formidable character."

Robert Bruce had lately turned his attentions to Ireland, which his brother Edward had invaded the previous May. Elizabeth's father-in-law, the Earl of Ulster, one of whose daughters was married to the King of Scots, had been forced to flee from his son-in-law in September, an inglorious episode that gave rise to hints of treason on the earl's part, and Roger Mortimer had suffered a humiliating defeat in December after being deserted by his English vassals. He too was on his way to Parliament, having come to England to report on the disastrous situation in Ireland. It needed no Roger Mortimer to report that it was a dangerous place for a widow of twenty-one, however, and Eleanor was heartily glad to hear that the king had decided to bring Elizabeth to England, forceful character or no. As she had not seen her sister in six years, she determined to meet her at Bristol Castle, where Elizabeth would be staying for the time being.

She made the trip with some trepidation, for although Elizabeth was three years her junior, she slightly intimidated Eleanor, who was much more comfortable with Margaret or with her sisters-in-law. When the girls had been together at Amesbury, Elizabeth was the Clare sister whom the nuns had never had to nag about neatness or punctuality. She'd baptized all of her dolls (though without the sin of using real Holy Water) at age seven. After she learned to write, she had started off each day by listing what she needed to do in a handwriting that was as perfect as a clerk's. Gaveston had aptly nicknamed her the Prioress.

Still, Eleanor was pleased to see her, and she was hurt, therefore, when Elizabeth did not appear to be quite as happy in return when Eleanor arrived after dusk on the fourth of February, having traveled rather slowly by chariot, as she always did when she was with child. Perhaps it was because Eleanor had arrived without warning, having had no time to send a messenger, and Elizabeth was not one to like the unexpected. She quickly recovered her good manners, however, especially after seeing that Eleanor was accompanied only by Gladys and a few attendants, and soon the sisters were sitting cozily by a fire together, sipping wine. Eleanor's condition, which was visible once she removed her heavy cloak, provided a natural topic of conversation, and from then they could move on smoothly to discussing their children. William, nearly four, had been left behind in Ireland in the care of his uncles, and Eleanor's three children were at Loughborough. Next, Eleanor was careful to ask Elizabeth about her charitable work, for good works had always been a feature of her sister's daily lists. She listened meekly, feeling completely frivolous, as Elizabeth modestly spoke of the friary she had founded in thanksgiving for William's birth. Eleanor gave the small priory of Wix, on one of her husband's estates, money and goods from time to time, but she could hardly match Elizabeth in this respect.

"This is where our grandfather imprisoned Ralph Monthermer after he married our mother, you know," said Eleanor finally as the sisters' conversation lagged.

"Eleanor! What a depressing thought."

"I am sorry; it just occurred to me. But Lord Monthermer doesn't find it depressing anymore, so you shouldn't. He regards the whole escapade as quite humorous now."

"He was always rather light-minded."

"Oh, I think he just makes the best of things. He was a great comfort to me when Gilbert died. And speaking of Gilbert, have you heard from Maud?"

Elizabeth shook her head. "She might have written to her father from time to time"—Maud was a daughter of the Earl of Ulster—"but he did not mention it to me. With his troubles in Ireland he scarcely has time to care whether she is pregnant or not. I understand your husband is pressing for a partition."

"Yes, Hugh is working very hard to see that we get our shares soon. We will all owe him our gratitude when it is taken care of, for he has been very conscientious in pursuing this matter."

"Of course, he wants to be Lord of Glamorgan."

"Well, yes, what man would not?" Feeling rather guilty that as the eldest sister, she would surely get the best lands, Eleanor hastened to change the subject. "Tell me, how long does the king plan to have you stay here?"

"Not long, I hope."

"Perhaps you can come back with me to Loughborough. There is no particular need for you to remain here, is there? I am sure our uncle will not mind. Or perhaps until things are settled in Ireland again you can travel with the queen's household, as Margaret does now. Or—"

"Eleanor! So many plans you are making for me in one breath! I should like to rest here a few days before I do anything, thank you; the crossing was a rough one." Elizabeth half-suppressed a yawn.

Eleanor took the hint. "It *is* late, isn't it? I will leave you, then, to rest."

She kissed Elizabeth on the cheek, and Elizabeth reciprocated in a friendly enough manner. Then Eleanor followed her page to the chamber that had been prepared for her, where Gladys sat yawning over a prayer book. As it was indeed late, within minutes after climbing into bed, she was fast asleep.

It was very early in the morning when she heard frantic voices outside her bed curtains. "Lady Despenser! Is Lady Burgh here with you?"

Dazed with sleep, Eleanor looked around her several times before replying, "No, why do you ask?"

"She's gone, my lady! No one has seen her since last night."

"She is probably in the chapel, have you checked there? My sister is very punctilious in her religious observance."

"'Twas the first place we looked, my lady."

"I know! She has probably gone to the cathedral to pray. She has been cooped up in Ireland so long, and it is most beautiful."

"My lady, that has been thought of also. She is not there, and no one there has seen any sign of her."

"Good Lord! Then where can she be?"

Search parties were promptly sent out in all directions, but their mission was a short one, for by late afternoon, a squire had arrived at Bristol Castle, where he asked particularly for Eleanor. "My lady, I come from your sister. She begs your pardon if you and the others here have been worried, and she asks that she be pursued no longer."

"What in the world has happened to her? Is she safe?"

"Quite safe, and with a protector. You see, she was married this morning to my lord, Theobald de Verdon."

At Lincoln, Roger Damory and Hugh d'Audley gave each other sour looks, for with only one single Clare almost-heiress remaining, who would be the lucky man?

Theobald de Verdon, facing the possibility of abduction charges, journeyed from Alton to Lincoln, where he maintained in front of the king's council that he had been betrothed to Lady Burgh, whom he had met during his own recent stay in Ireland. The lady would have waited for the king's license, he explained gallantly, but being uncertain of her future in England, had reluctantly agreed to walk outside Bristol Castle late at night, where Theobald was waiting with a snow-white palfrey and a wedding ring, and elope with him. As nothing indicated that Lady Burgh had been taken by force or violence, the king let the matter drop, settling for collecting the usual fine imposed on the impetuous who wed without license. Theobald, a widower with three little girls, went back to his bride and daughters in the best of spirits.

There were other matters, in any case, bedeviling those at Lincoln. Though as the leading adherent of the Ordinances, Lancaster might have been expected to be at Parliament, nearly half of February had come and gone before he put in an appearance there. Trouble, however, had not waited for the Earl's arrival. In late January, under the leadership of one Llywelyn Bren, the Welsh in Glamorgan, upset at the actions of the royal administrator who had been given custody of the land after Gilbert de Clare's death, had surprised the sheriff of Glamorgan while he was holding a lordship court at the gates of Caerphilly Castle. They had killed a number of the officials attending the court. Though they could penetrate no farther into the castle, the surrounding area had been devastated, and the Countess of Gloucester, who had been living in the castle, was trapped there. "With a midwife, I trust," Hugh had said when he heard the news.

Had the countess not been playing her tricks, Glamorgan would have been his. And the countess was winning for now. Hugh had gone before Parliament and pointed out, in his politest voice, that Maud had been claiming pregnancy for over a year and a half, twice the time any other woman took to bear a child; that any child born eleven months after his father's death would be presumed illegitimate; that Maud had not been seen in public in months. Surely she could not be with child?

He was met with the response that the countess's pregnancy was well known in the parts where she was living. (By a bunch of mad Welshmen, Hugh thought, but did not utter aloud.) That he should have obtained a writ from chancery to have the countess's belly inspected by discreet knights and matrons to see if she were indeed with child, and that Hugh's negligence in this regard should redound to his loss and prejudice. That the king had nominated certain men, well versed in civil and canon law, to advise him on the matter, and that they could not reach a final decision because of the case's difficulty and rarity. Because of this, no action would be taken now, but Hugh and Eleanor could bring the matter again before the king and his council at the Easter term.

"I will have a man examine the woman's belly if Parliament wishes," said Hugh testily. "Llywelyn Bren!"

As Parliament dragged on, Hugh grew tenser and more irritable each day, alarming his father, for however many Hugh's faults were, ill temper was generally not one of them. These days, however, he brooded over the situation in Glamorgan and muttered dark threats about what he would like to do with Llywelyn Bren, and darker ones about what he would like to do with the Countess of Gloucester. "Hugh!" his father reproved him after a particularly scabrous tirade. "Your mother would turn in her grave to hear a son of hers speak so."

Hugh snorted as father and son made their way from their lodgings to Lincoln Cathedral, where Parliament had been holding its meetings. "Mother would have scratched the bitch's eyes out by now, Father."

"That may be so, but can you at least hold your tongue as we approach the cathedral? It is a house of the Lord."

"I'm fed up with this nonsense! Most of all, I'm fed up with this king of ours. How can he let this drag on like this? He's well content enough, I suppose, with those pretty boys Damory and Audley to keep him happy—"

"Hugh, for God's sake curb your tongue!"

"Let the king curb his!"

"Hugh!" The elder Despenser decided, desperately, that it was time to change the subject. "Did I tell what happened to Berenger?"

Ingelram Berenger was one of Hugh the elder's closest friends. The younger Hugh looked at him as something of a father. He softened when his name was mentioned. "No, what?"

"John de Ros tried to have him arrested." Hugh chuckled; he had not taken the episode very seriously. "Some land dispute. Ingelram sent his men packing, I'll tell you. He said— Hugh?"

Hugh had stormed ahead of him and entered the cathedral, where the king was standing chatting affably with Montacute, Damory, and Audley. (The King's Three Lapdogs, Hugh privately called them.) Edward smiled at him, but Hugh ignored him, looking around until he found the man he sought. "Lord Ros. Might I have a word with you?"

"Certainly."

"What do you mean, arresting my father's man Ingelram Berenger? What gives you the right?"

"It is my dispute with him, Despenser, and none of your concern."

"It is precisely my concern, when you meddle with my father or his men. Now tell me. What makes you fancy you have the right to arrest him?"

Hugh the elder caught up. "Hugh—"

"Leave me, please, Father. I intend to have this blackguard talk to me. Tell me!"

Ros snorted. "Despenser, just because your marriage to that little redhead of yours hasn't brought you the land you hoped for gives you no right to manage my affairs. She must be good in bed, with that hair. Let that be some consolation to you."

Hugh struck Ros across the face, drawing blood. Though the men were closely matched in terms of height, weight, and age, Hugh was by far the better fighter on his feet, having had practice in his pirate days, and he was taking months of frustrations out on his opponent besides. Ros was at last able to knock Hugh to the ground, but Hugh quickly got to his feet and began to lunge toward Ros again. The better jouster of the two, Ros pulled his sword and rushed toward Hugh, who had no time to draw his own. It seemed that Hugh was doomed; then, at the last possible minute, he leapt aside. As Ros's sword swished at the empty air, the king's sergeants at arms ran forward and put both young men under arrest.

"Learned that from the Bruce himself," Hugh said as his father, who had been all but dead with fear for his son's life seconds ago, hurried forward to Hugh's side.

If the king had intended to give Hugh a part in the reclaiming of lands that even the most stubborn defenders of the Countess of Gloucester had to admit would someday be his own, his unseemly fight with John de Ros in Lincoln

Cathedral changed his mind. Instead, the Earl of Hereford was appointed to subdue the Welsh rebellion, along with William de Montacute; the Earl of Lancaster's younger, better-natured brother, Henry; Bartholomew Badlesmere; Roger Mortimer of Wigmore, the man whom Eleanor thought of as the odious Mortimer; and Mortimer's uncle, Roger Mortimer of Chirk. By March, Llywelyn Bren, facing certain defeat and not wishing to be the reason for a slaughter of his followers, gave himself up and was sent a prisoner to the Tower. The Countess of Gloucester, wrapped in a voluminous cloak, had been freed from Caerphilly Castle and sent safely to Cardiff.

Meanwhile, in March a charmingly written letter arrived for Eleanor, from the queen. It had been so long since Eleanor had been at court. Wouldn't she like to pay a visit to her queen for Easter? Recognizing a sugared command when she saw one, Eleanor set her servants to packing.

Hugh, who like John de Ros had been jailed for a short time and fined ten thousand pounds for his parliamentary antics, had prudently decided to stay away from court for a time, but Eleanor's children had been invited to join her. Little Edward was too young to make the trip in Eleanor's opinion and would stay in Loughborough with his nurse. He bid her goodbye with the utmost gravity, for he was the most serious child Eleanor had ever seen, the opposite of his elder brother, who was finding it hard to contain his excitement about visiting the court and his old friend Adam. Since daybreak he had been in the stables, pestering Eleanor's men with questions about when the chariot in which they were to travel would be ready. Isabel's governess, upon hearing that her three-year-old charge was to meet the queen, had been frantically trying to teach Isabel to execute a perfect curtsey, and Isabel proudly showed her grandfather her new skill over and over again before their departure.

Seven months pregnant, Eleanor settled back in the chariot cushions, feeling not for the first time a twinge of guilt as she contemplated the contrast between herself and her children, warm in their furs and lap robes, and the ragged passersby she saw as they slowly made their way toward Langley and the king. The year 1315 with its constant rains had been a miserable one for England, bringing famine in its wake as crops were ruined, and 1316 had thus far been more of the same. People were dying on the roads, yet Eleanor had noticed little change in her own standard of living, nothing that could not be dealt with by a bit more frugality on the part of her husband's and her father-in-law's stewards. Were she one of the pathetic wenches she saw standing along the road, clutching whimpering babies, what would she have thought of the cosseted lady in her chariot, who had never wanted for anything in her life? Envy? Hatred? Eleanor sighed. At least her almoner had come along on the journey, and he was staying busy.

Eleanor had not seen the king or the queen for some time, and when she arrived at Langley and was conducted to the royal couple, she was struck anew by the queen's loveliness. At age twenty, Isabella was prettier than she ever had been, and her outer radiance was matched by inner satisfaction, for as Eleanor soon learned, she was expecting another child in August. This news had had a visible effect on the king, whose usual optimism had been much taxed by the dreadful battle of the Bannock Burn and the famine that had come in the following year. He had wondered if Gaveston's death had not brought England under some sort of curse, which extended to the queen's womb, for he had visited the queen regularly since the birth of Edward, the Earl of Chester, with no results until now. His good humor was much augmented by the departure from Langley by Lancaster, who had visited for a day or so to report on the activities of the council and then taken himself off to spend Easter on his own estates, where Edward liked him best.

With the queen, and receiving the beautiful green, miniver-trimmed and–lined robes issued to a select few that Easter, were not only Eleanor, but the Countess of Hereford (Edward's slightly older sister Elizabeth), the Countess of Warwick, and the Countess of Cornwall. Eleanor thought this group a singularly ill-assorted one, as the first two countesses' husbands had destroyed the husband of the third countess, but the ladies were being perfectly polite and gracious to each other, though they seemed relieved at the arrival of Eleanor, whose husband had played no role in the Gaveston business. They all admired sturdy young Hugh, who spent only a few minutes in the grasp of the ladies before bolting to search out Adam, and Isabel, who curtseyed a full seven times before being taken off by her nurse to play with the Earl of Chester.

Once the children had left the room, Elizabeth de Burgh's runaway match to Theobald de Verdon became the chief topic of conversation among the ladies, who were working on baby clothes for the expected royal arrival, clothes that would be embroidered so beautifully that it seemed almost a pity to expose them to the depredations of a baby. "Surely she could have done better," said the Countess of Hereford. "Who is this Theobald de Verdon?"

"He was justiciar of Ireland for a time," said Eleanor. "He is not a mere nobody; he has lands in six counties here in England and also interests in Ireland. And I believe he is also associated with the Earl of Lancaster."

"Hardly a recommendation," said Margaret tartly.

"She has written me, did she not write you, Margaret? She said that she was quite happy and that she was enjoying being stepmother to Theobald's little girls."

"Yes, she wrote me. Someone to manage, of course Elizabeth would be happy." Margaret glanced at the queen. "Was the king upset by the match, your grace?"

"Upset, aside from the loss of the license fee? Should he have been?"

"I would think so, because he surely planned to marry my sister and me to Roger Damory and Hugh d'Audley, or I am sadly mistaken."

"I have heard nothing of any plans to marry you to anyone, Countess."

"Oh, he is probably waiting until he decides to partition the lands, which I think will never happen as long as that blockheaded woman continues to claim she is pregnant."

"Hugh is doing all he can to speed it," put in Eleanor loyally.

"Is that what you call his antics at Lincoln?"

"He was sorely provoked," said Eleanor in an injured tone.

"Well, I give notice that I will not mind if the king does choose to marry me to one of those men. I am tired of being a widow, especially of a man no one will name in front of me." She glanced at the Countesses of Warwick and Hereford, who each took great interest in the work in their hands. "I am wasting my youth here."

Eleanor was rather shocked by this speech, but the queen was not, Margaret having been in the habit of making similar ones every few days. Instead, she said, "Well, now that you have two to choose from, which would you prefer?"

"Audley," said Margaret with the air of one who had thought about the question minutely. "He is more handsome, and I think rather more agreeable."

"I shall put in a word with the king," said the queen dryly.

Margaret looked rather maliciously at the Countess of Warwick, who was no longer a girl, being in her thirties. "And perhaps you may marry Damory, Countess, now that you are free. I daresay the king would make it worth your while."

To everyone's shock, Alice burst into tears and fled from the room. Eleanor gasped. "Margaret! How could you be so cruel? Whatever a scoundrel Warwick might have been, he was her husband, and she has been widowed but eight months. How dare you?"

Margaret only shrugged, but the Countess of Hereford laughed. "It is not what you think, Lady Despenser. Lady Alice is not mourning for Warwick. She is very much in love with the knight who escorted her here, Sir William la Zouche, but she cannot let him know it, of course, so she is frightened that he will marry someone else." She glanced at Margaret. "Perhaps you, Countess."

"I! I know of no Sir Zouche."

"He is a younger son of a branch of the Mortimer family. He acquired land from his uncle Zouche, and so he assumed the name. He was in Warwick's household, I believe."

The queen was frowning at her sister-in-law. "Elizabeth, how do you know of all this?"

"Oh, I was in the great hall when Zouche brought her here, and any ninny could see that she was in love with him, the way her eyes filled with tears when he bid her good-bye. She and I are friends, so I asked her. She has been in love with him some time, all quite chaste though, I assure you. Why, I don't know. He's not what you would call handsome, he's quite taciturn, and he has the charisma of a sumpter horse. But there you have it."

The queen beckoned to a page. "Fetch the Countess of Warwick here immediately."

The countess returned promptly, her cheeks pink and her eyelashes damp. She curtseyed deeply. "Your grace, I do beg your pardon."

"Countess, my sister-in-law tells me that you are in love with a knight in your husband's household, that indeed, you have been love with him for some time, and that you wish to marry him."

"Your grace, my own mother was in the same situation! It can happen even to a lady of the greatest virtue—"

"Hush, Lady Despenser," the queen said, not unkindly. "Countess, I am told that he is unaware of the feelings you have for him."

"Indeed he is, your grace! Sir Zouche did nothing to encourage me. He is the kindest, bravest, most chivalrous kn—"

"I gather," said the queen. "Now take this glass, and look at yourself. Do you really think he would not care to be your husband, would that he could?"

Alice dutifully looked in the mirror, as the ladies studied her in turn. Alice's hair was still gold, and with some help, it could have been even more so. Her eyes were the color of cornflowers, and the several children she had borne Warwick had not adversely affected her figure. Whenever an artist illustrated a romance, he drew a heroine who looked much like Alice, and Alice knew this as well as anyone else. "I—hope he would, your grace."

"How could he not? Now, Countess, instead of bursting into tears whenever someone mentions marriage, you must let your Sir What-his-name—"

"*Zouche*," said Alice firmly.

"You must let him know you care for him. When he comes to fetch you, as I will make sure he does, you must smile at him like this." The queen demonstrated. "You must send for him as often as possible, with questions about your estates."

"Indeed, your grace, I have many questions about my estates. I am not sure my steward is as able as he used to be."

"Then you must ask Sir Zouche to set him straight. And each time he comes, you must smile at him as I have demonstrated. Just enough to remind him that he is a man and you are a woman, in case he needs reminding. And then you must ask him about himself, for men love to talk about themselves. Even Edward does."

"He was in the Scottish wars with the first Edward. I will ask him about that."

"Indeed, you must. Now. In August you will have been widowed for a full year, and then you must take off that dreary black dress of yours immediately and wear light blue, say, to match your eyes. And you will wear that whenever you send for Sir Zouche, which by then should be quite often. And I tell you, it work."

"You think so, your grace?"

"I am certain of it."

Back at Loughborough, Eleanor waddled from room to room, feeling rather sorry for herself. One of the last items of business at Lincoln had been the appointment of Lancaster to head the king's council, a duty the earl had graciously accepted. Nonetheless, when the king's council resumed business after Easter, Lancaster, for reasons that were unclear, had not joined it, but had stayed on his own lands, deigning to reply to letters from the king but otherwise showing little interest in performing the role he had been assigned at the Lincoln Parliament. It was not lack of business in the summer of 1316 that kept Lancaster away: although Wales had been subdued, the citizens of Bristol, angry over an infringement of the city's liberties, had begun to riot, and Edward was still trying to raise cash to fund a Scottish campaign. With Lancaster playing truant schoolboy, Edward had placed his reliance mainly upon the Earl of Pembroke, who had not swerved from his role of faithful subject since Warwick's treachery in regard to Gaveston. Yet an older and even more faithful friend than Pembroke had not been forgotten either. In May, Hugh le Despenser the elder had been invited back to court, albeit in a rather indefinite capacity, and his son had joined him. So Eleanor was facing a lying-in without Hugh, and it did not help her spirits to recall that just a month after her Easter visit to court, the Countess of Hereford, who had given birth time after time without incident, had died in childbirth.

"Eleanor?"

Eleanor started, then sniffled. "Elizabeth! What a sight you are to my eyes! I have been here feeling lonely and sorry for myself, as you can see, but no more. I am so glad to see you."

"I am glad to hear it. But why are you feeling sorry for yourself?"

"Pure foolishness, Elizabeth. Hugh is at court, and he may not come in time to be with me when my child is born. But I am in the best hands, and it is merely me being a fool. I should be glad he and my father-in-law are no longer unwelcome at court. Now, tell me. Can you stay a while? Or are you merely passing through?"

"We are passing through, but I hope you will let us stay the night. I wanted to break our travel here, because I think I was rude to you when you visited me in Bristol."

"You were preoccupied," said Eleanor cheerfully. "An elopement scheduled, and your elder sister arrives unexpectedly! What a nuisance I must have been." She paused. "Elizabeth, it was an elopement, wasn't it? You were not—er—forced into this marriage, were you?"

"No, Eleanor. Theobald and I became acquainted not long after John died, and we had talked over marriage for some time. We were planning to ask for a license. But when the king recalled me from Ireland, I was fearful that he would marry me to one of his friends, and I did not want to be parceled out in that manner. So I got word to Theobald, and he arranged to take me from Bristol Castle. You know the rest."

"And I thought you were over at Bristol Cathedral praying!"

"We did stop to admire it," admitted Elizabeth.

"So you have not become completely impious." Eleanor smiled. "I hope you are happy in your marriage, Elizabeth?"

"Very."

"Then let me meet your husband, immediately."

Theobald soon joined the sisters. Despite his association with Lancaster, he was very much unlike the dour earl, and they spent a pleasant evening together. Eleanor and Elizabeth were both musical, and Eleanor being the better singer and Elizabeth the better lute player, they sang and played several duets for Theobald, who was a most enthusiastic audience. When the newlyweds left the next morning, Eleanor watched them go with regret, for it was the most relaxed evening she had ever spent with her younger sister, one that she hoped might lead to more such.

Eleanor gave birth to a girl, Joan, several weeks later, and soon after, in August, the queen, lying in at Eltham, gave birth to a boy, John. The latter birth had the effect of coaxing the Earl of Lancaster off his estates, for he at the queen's request stood as one of the sponsors to the new prince. But before the good news from the queen reached Eleanor, before Hugh had written her a loving letter and ordered that she receive a handsome sum to buy new robes for her churching, another letter had arrived. She read it, unbelieving, and crossed herself, and then she whispered, "Poor Elizabeth," and began to cry.

"Nelly?" her sister-in-law asked.

"Oh, Bella, it is so sad. Theobald de Verdon is dead. He died from a fever he caught while traveling."

"Gentlemen! Look about you! Are your ladies accounted for? Good! Then let us dance!"

Rob Withstaff's jest might have fallen flat had the wedding guests been more sober, but as large amounts of wine had flowed since Hugh d'Audley and the Countess of Cornwall were married in the chapel of Windsor Castle that day of April 28, 1317, everyone laughed most heartily, Hugh le Despenser the younger as hard as anyone. He then ran his hand down Eleanor's robe, inspecting her contours so minutely and publicly that she swatted him. "Hugh! You are drunk."

"Merely following the fool's orders, m'dear. And you are not precisely a model of sobriety yourself either, sweetheart."

Hugh had good reason to celebrate. On April 17, the king and his council, which these days included both Hugh and his father, had at last ordered that the Clare inheritance was to be divided between the late earl's three sisters, the Countess of Gloucester's claim of pregnancy having finally been rejected. It would be months before clerks determined which sister was to have which land, and what was to be held by the widow in dower, but for all intents and purposes, Eleanor, Margaret, and Elizabeth were rich women now. Eleanor herself had received the news of the partition nearly as joyfully as her husband had, for if she had not asked to be given a fortune, God had willed otherwise, and it was high time that Maud stopped interfering with this divine edict. She had not been in the mood to pay heed as her wine cup was filled again and again, and now she laughed and let Hugh's hands rove where they would.

There were several significant absences at the wedding—or weddings, since a much younger couple, William de Montacute's son John and one of Theobald de Verdon's daughters, had also been married that day. The Countess of Gloucester, needless to say, had not been invited. More of interest to the guests, and the cause for much of the fool's jests, had been the absence of the Earl of Lancaster, whose wife had been abducted by the Earl of Surrey only days before. As the Earl of Surrey was securely ensconced with his mistress, everyone believed that the abduction was intended only to harass the Earl of Lancaster. There were even rumors that at a meeting held in February, Warenne and the king, and perhaps Audley, Damory, and the Despensers, had plotted the escapade. The Countess of Lancaster, whose relations with the earl had been barren in all senses of the word, settled down quite happily on one of the Warenne estates.

Damory was at the wedding, but his bride-to-be, Elizabeth de Burgh, lately widowed of Theobald de Verdon, was not. Despite the wine she had ingested, Eleanor winced when she thought of her sister. Soon after Theobald's death, Elizabeth had found that she was pregnant. Unable to return to Ireland safely, and as yet not assigned her Verdon dower, she had elected to spend her confinement at Amesbury priory, where her aunt Mary, the king's older sister, lived a very uncloistered existence. There she had been visited by the king, who urged her to marry Damory. When Elizabeth proved unwilling, the king had enlisted the aid of both the queen and Mary. At last, Elizabeth, shortly after giving birth to a daughter, had agreed to the match. As a sweetener, the king had offered to pay for Elizabeth to take a pilgrimage of thanksgiving for the safe birth of her child. She was accompanied by Mary, a most seasoned traveler, and was to wed Damory after her return.

Finding that a bench had appeared behind her, Eleanor sank down on it and smiled as she saw the Countess of Warwick, now wife to William la Zouche of Mortimer, pass by. It had taken the countess only a little more than a year after the death of Warwick to bring Zouche into a marrying frame of mind, and after duly obtaining the license of the king, the couple had wed earlier that year. Eleanor had not met this epitome of knightly virtue, but she could tell from Alice's spry walk, never seen during her years with the stern Warwick, that her new marriage was agreeing with her. And was it her imagination, or did Alice look a little thick around the waist?

The king and queen had also attended the wedding. Isabella had joined in the earliest dances, but along with the other sober and relatively sober wedding guests had yielded the floor to the rowdy. She sat at the dais speaking with the Countess of Pembroke and the Countess of Surrey, whose marital woes with Warenne were now so famous that she had not even frowned at the fool's jests about her husband and the Countess of Lancaster. The king, however, was very much part of the party. As Eleanor watched, he gave Audley an avuncular pat on the shoulder and Margaret a smacking kiss that resounded in the great hall, noisy as it was.

Eleanor wondered what was going on in her uncle's mind. It was not so long ago, after all, that he had wedded this same bride to Gaveston at Berkhamstead Castle, not so long ago that he had watched as his friend set off on the journey that would end at Blacklow Hill. Now only one trace of Gaveston could be found in the hall, the very tired little five-year-old girl nodding off in a corner, and she favored her mother, Margaret, not the dark Gascon. It was as if the brother-in-law whom Eleanor had grown very fond of had never existed. As if to reinforce her thoughts, Joan's nurse pushed through the crowd and bore her exhausted little charge away.

"Nelly, what are you thinking, sitting there looking so pensive? Or are you merely low on wine?"

The king made as if to slosh some of the contents of his own cup into hers, but Eleanor shook her head. "I have had quite enough, Uncle. I was thinking about Gaveston."

His smile faded and he nodded slowly. "I knew you if no one else would be. Come outside with me, Niece. Now."

"Uncle! Are you sure we should be doing this?"

The king had handed Eleanor into the rowboat deftly enough, but he was having more difficulty getting in himself. "Nelly, I could row a boat with a raging fever. I could row a boat with one arm. I could row a boat if I were blind. I could row a boat—"

"I take your meaning, sir."

He took the oars and did indeed seem to get more sober with that very gesture. After rowing out a ways, he put the oars aside, stretched out at full length, and beckoned Eleanor to lie beside him. She obeyed, for she trusted him utterly, and let her head rest on his arm as a cushion. "Look at those stars, Nelly. What do you see?"

"They are very beautiful, Uncle."

"Aye. But what do you see?"

"Well—stars."

"So do I, now. But I used to be able to see Piers's face in every one of them. Now I can't unless I am blind drunk."

"I was looking for it tonight in his little girl, Joan. In Margaret."

"Joan was too little when he died; she never knew him. Margaret—I used to see it in Margaret's. But she no longer cares for him, does she, Nelly?"

"No, Uncle."

"I knew it."

"Do you see his face in Damory's? Audley's? Montacute's?"

"No. I have tried so hard to see it there, Nelly. So hard." He absently stroked her hair. "These marriages had to take place; if your sisters were not married to men I could trust, like your Hugh, there would be sure disaster. And Audley and Damory deserve your sisters; they have been loyal to me. But I wish to God I had not come to this wedding."

"I know, Uncle. But you have not forgotten him, and that is all that counts."

He lay beside her so quietly for a while that she thought he had drifted off. Then he said, "But this was our favorite thing to do as boys, and as men. What you and I are doing now, rowing a boat at night with the moon sparkling on the water. And tonight I think I can see his face in yours—a little bit. Thank you, Nelly."

They lay there in silence, and Eleanor shut her eyes, listening to the water sounds around them. Finally, the king stirred, gently moving his arm from beneath Eleanor, and found that his niece was fast asleep. He took off his cloak, draped it over her, and rowed back to whence he came, but when he came by the castle, he kept rowing. He would not be a witness to the dreaded bedding ceremony where another man took possession of the woman who had once been Piers's.

Only after a hour or so more had passed did he return to the mooring spot by Windsor Castle. Hearing no more sounds of revelry in the distance, he secured the rowboat and looked down at his sleeping niece. *Nelly*, he thought, *I lied to you. There is one face in which I can see Piers's, and it is driving me mad. How much longer can I resist?*

And there the face was, waiting at the dock. Fear and worry had sobered Hugh le Despenser. "Your grace! 'Tis my Eleanor. She was last seen heading in this direction with you. Have you seen her?"

The king pointed toward the bottom of the boat. "My apologies, Hugh. She wished to go for a ride in my rowboat—and so did I." He stepped out of the boat, making room for his nephew by marriage to climb inside.

Hugh gently nudged the sleeping figure. "Sweetheart?"

Eleanor opened her eyes and stared at him in some confusion. "Hugh? The king—" Her eyes opened wide with horror. "Hugh, you must not think—"

Hugh laughed. "My dear, with any other man or any other woman I would be livid—but with you and the king I have no doubt that the two of you did nothing more than ride in this boat together. Perhaps at Elizabeth's wedding, he'll have you thatch a roof with him." Too late, he looked around, but the king was fortunately nowhere in sight. He helped her alight. "The brides and grooms have been safely bedded, my dear. Shall we lie down ourselves?"

For an answer, she kissed him.

They would be making love very shortly, Edward knew, either somewhere on the grounds or in their chamber. And it was the greatest source of misery to the king that morning as he made his solitary way to Windsor Castle that he could not decide which pained him most: the thought of her making love to him, or the thought of him making love to her.

CHAPTER 10

▼

NOVEMBER 1317 TO
DECEMBER 1318

The Lord and Lady of Glamorgan were on their way to their new home. Despite a series of catastrophes besetting the kingdom—relations between the king and the Earl of Lancaster had broken down completely, and Lancaster had seized lands belonging to the Earl of Surrey and Roger Damory—the Clare lands had at last been partitioned. Eleanor and Hugh had received lands in Glamorgan, Somerset, Surrey, and Ireland, with other lands in Berkshire, Buckingham, Gloucestershire, Oxford, and Worcester to come to them upon the death of the Countess of Gloucester. Retainers had been dispatched to Somerset, Surrey, and Ireland to take possession, but Glamorgan was the jewel of the Clare estates, and no sooner had the order been signed by the harried king than the Despensers were packing for the trip to Wales.

Her three youngest children, Isabel, Edward, and even little Joan, heaped with furs, were riding in two chariots with their nurses, and Gladys was riding in considerable state in a chariot by herself, being a very ample lady and of an age where she needed to stretch her legs. Hugh's sister Bella, of whom Hugh had always been fond, had been invited along, accompanied by *her* ladies, though unlike Gladys they were mounted on horseback. Her little girl, Margaret, joined Eleanor's youngest children in the chariots. The Hastings boys, Thomas and Hugh, rode alongside Eleanor's own Hugh. All three boys were well beyond riding in the baby carts, as they dubbed them, and when not comparing the merits of their horses, they were casting derisory looks at Isabel and Edward, who were old enough to feel the insult.

Hugh the elder had come, needless to say. Of the travelers on the last leg of the trip to Caerphilly Castle, he alone looked perturbed, for Hugh the younger had been confiding in him during the journey to Wales. "The king has given me not only the Clare estates, but Dryslwyn and Cantrefmawr for life," Hugh had said cheerfully. "I think it was a mark of affection for my lovely Eleanor, and perhaps a bone for making us wait so long for the partition. But there's one drawback. The lordships of Wentloog and Machen are to be fully separate from Glamorgan; they're to go to that puppy Audley. But they've always been part of Glamorgan! The tenants won't stand for that."

"The tenants, Hugh?"

"They will want to retain the liberties and privileges that the rest of the men of Glamorgan have. I shall have to discuss the matter with them."

"Hugh!"

But his son had trotted over to the three boys, leaving Hugh the elder with nothing but his sense of unease for company. Fortunately, his daughter and daughter-in-law were riding up behind him, and as neither of these ladies had ever given Hugh cause for concern, he was soon laughing as Eleanor and Bella tried to teach each other the smattering of Welsh they each knew. Hugh shook his head at Bella's attempt. "So far, child, if you were a man, you would have only succeeded in getting yourself challenged to mortal combat. You've just called Eleanor there a horse thief and a scoundrel."

"But I meant to tell her what a beautiful robe she was wearing. And Thomas taught me that, he said he had it straight from my stepson John—" Bella whirled. "Thomas de Hastings! You saucy creature! If I could get this horse near you, I would—"

Hugh the younger, guessing what his nephews had been up to, called, "Best stick to French, sister dear."

Eleanor laughed, thinking as she did that it was strange she knew so little of a land where she, after all, had been born, in the great castle of Caerphilly where they now were headed. It was another bond with her uncle, who had been born in Caernarfon. Perhaps, she thought, the Despensers would get on well with their tenants. But in her heart she knew that such a hope was tenuous. The Llywelyn Bren revolt was still fresh in men's minds, and the very building of Caerphilly Castle by her father a half century before had been a source of anger to the Welsh. However fine the red-and-gold Despenser banners and horse trappings and chariot hangings might look to Eleanor and her companions, to the Welsh they were the marks of yet another English intruder.

Power in Wales, however, lay not with the Welsh people but with the Marcher lords, one of which Hugh had just become. Eleanor's stepfather, Ralph de Monthermer, who had been styled Earl of Gloucester after his marriage to Joan until her death and who had assisted Joan in managing her lands, had told Eleanor, "Your husband had best conduct himself circumspectly in Wales. The Marcher lords are used to fighting for their rights, and they'll not take kindly to any intrusions upon them."

"Why would you think he would not conduct himself circumspectly, Lord Monthermer?"

Ralph had shrugged and resumed the game of chess he had been playing with Lady Hastings.

As the Despenser party, red and gold banners flying, neared the castle, the three boys drew their reins abruptly and stopped, awe-stricken. "Papa! Is this ours?"

Hugh ruffled his eldest son's hair. "Ours indeed, and yours when I meet my maker. Quite a sight, isn't it?"

It was indeed. Gilbert de Clare, Eleanor's father, had built his castle to serve notice on the Welsh and anyone other comers that he was not to be trifled with, and few approaching Caerphilly Castle would be so inclined. Gilbert had cut ditches so as to put the central part of the castle on an island, which was surrounded by lakes, also manmade. To get to this inner island, one had to go through a daunting series of walls, dams, gatehouses, islands, drawbridges, moats, and lakes, and the inner island had its own gatehouses to keep out intruders.

Hugh and his Hastings cousins were bouncing in their saddles as they observed all these features. "We can sleep *here* tonight!"

"And *here* tomorrow night!"

"No, *there*!"

Hugh took Eleanor's hand as her horse trotted up beside his. "We're home, sweetheart."

Every member of the party, even Hugh the elder, was secretly longing to explore the castle, but the adults at least were denied this luxury, for their more important tenants had lined up to greet them, and they of course had to be fed in the great hall, along with the staff Hugh had brought, the staff the king had left, and the staff that had hurried up ahead of the rest of the Despenser party to smooth the transition. Sitting in her place of honor, Eleanor could only watch with envy as her eldest son and the Hastings boys took off for parts unknown, followed, to their great dismay, by Isabel, whose nurse then had to follow as well to make sure nothing untoward happened to her charge. Edward and Joan had already been taken to the rooms that had been assigned to them. At long last, however, the meal ended, and Eleanor and Hugh, trailed by Hugh the elder and Bella, were able to begin their tour. It was as much a tour for Eleanor as it was for the others, for she had been but a babe when her parents had occupied the castle, and she and her sisters had stayed in England when Joan and Ralph de Monthermer made their visits to it.

"Your chamber, my lord and lady."

Bella and Hugh the elder had tactfully retreated to the rooms assigned to them by the time the exhausted chamberlain unlocked the door. Hugh smiled as the man started to push it open. "Thank you," he said. "You are excused."

He lifted Eleanor in his arms and carried her over the threshold. All was ready, Eleanor saw—their bed with all its trappings, a fire glowing in a fireplace, wine and two gold cups sitting on a table, even her birds hanging in their cages. But it was only the bed that mattered to the couple.

"What was that absurd vow the king made back when we were knighted?" Hugh mused as they lay tangled together some time later. "That he would never sleep in the same place two nights in a row until Scotland was conquered? Eleanor, I vow that I will never rest until I have had you in every castle and manor we own."

"Even the Irish ones, Hugh?"

"A vow's a vow, my lady."

The administrative center of Glamorgan was not Caerphilly Castle, but Cardiff Castle, not far off, and it was there that Hugh, his father, and Eleanor traveled a couple of days later, the children and Bella staying behind at Caerphilly.

Hugh was much busier at Cardiff than he had been at Glamorgan, meeting with someone almost constantly, and Eleanor herself, as the lady of the household, was almost as beleaguered by petitioners wanting her to exert her influence over Hugh on her behalf. So occupied were they both that there were days when neither saw each other except in the great hall for meals and at bedtime, and sometimes Hugh barely had time to eat before ushering in yet another group of men. It was to her father-in-law, then, whom Eleanor spoke when she noticed Hugh speaking to some men she had seen him with several times already. "Who are those men, sir? Hugh seems uncommonly interested in them."

Her father-in-law shifted in his chair uneasily. "They are from Wentloog."

"Wentloog," Eleanor echoed, wondering what on earth the name looked like on paper. "But sir, didn't my sister Margaret's husband get Wentloog?"

"Yes, but my son has his own ideas about the matter." Hugh sighed. "You'd best get him to explain to you."

She did not have to ask, however, for it was just several hours later when Hugh, beaming and carrying a parchment, strode into their chamber. "My dear! Guess who shall be giving us their fealty?"

"The men of Wentloog, Hugh?"

"Yes, the men of Wentloog, and Machen as well. But my love, how did you guess?"

"Your father told me. Hugh, this is not right. That land is Margaret's—and Hugh d'Audley's."

"But the men of Wentloog do not wish to be separate from Glamorgan, my love. Wentloog has always been administered with Glamorgan—or at least since your father's time, which is as good an 'always' as need be." Hugh looked for a smile and got none.

"How did you get them to agree, Hugh?"

"They are to have the same privileges as the men of Glamorgan. I shall show this indenture to the king"—he held up the parchment—"and if the king does not approve, a new indenture shall be drawn up."

"What if Margaret and Audley do not approve?"

Hugh shrugged. "Can I help it if the Welshmen would prefer my lordship to theirs? I think not!"

He sauntered out of the room, ending the conversation.

The king did not receive the news about Wentloog as docilely as Hugh had expected. He promptly ordered the men of Wentloog to pay homage to Hugh d'Audley.

Meanwhile, the Despensers returned to Caerphilly Castle for Christmas. They were still there as January wore on, and were undressing for bed one evening when a messenger arrived, with a note for Hugh. Hugh read it and tossed it into the fire. "Seems I must go to Cardiff tomorrow, my dear."

"The weather has been so sunny the last few days. Perhaps I shall go there with you." She liked Cardiff Castle, with its view of the river.

"Not tomorrow, my love." He said this so quickly and urgently that Eleanor started.

"Why not, Hugh?"

"I didn't like Joan's looks tonight, Eleanor. She looks as if she might be catching another cold. If she does, she'll want you."

Eleanor was a most solicitous mother, but she had noticed nothing amiss with Joan or the other children, nor had Hugh seen fit to mention his concerns before. As it was plain, however, that Hugh did not want her going with him, she said, "Very well, I will stay here."

Hugh's relief was almost palpable. "Next time, my love, you shall go."

"Yes."

Nothing more was said, and they rolled on their respective sides to go to sleep. But Hugh was up and gone very early the next morning, as if he did not want another chance for Eleanor to question him.

The atmosphere in the castle was very odd that day, too. There were much fewer petitioners than usual, and conversations stopped when Eleanor came within earshot. Eleanor had little leisure to contemplate this in the morning, as her chamberlain, her almoner, and her children's tutors, governesses, and nurses all had business to transact with her, but after a very quiet meal in the great hall, she excused herself to her chamber and dismissed everyone but her damsel Gladys. Having come from Gilbert de Clare's Welsh estates, Gladys spoke excellent Welsh, and her English was good as well. She was an invertebrate receiver of gossip, although she was much more guarded in what passed her own lips. "Gladys, what is happening here?"

Gladys shifted in her seat uncomfortably. "You remember the rebel Llywelyn Bren?"

"The man who caused so much uproar here two years ago? Yes, I remember. He is in the Tower, is he not? The Earl of Hereford and that dreadful Mortimer urged the king to spare his life."

"And the king agreed. But he was taken from the Tower some days ago, my lady, and arrived in Cardiff yesterday. On Lord Despenser's orders. He was to be executed today. I suppose it has happened by now."

Eleanor's stomach churned. "On Hugh's orders?"

"Yes, on his orders." Gladys crossed herself. "He was to die a traitor's death, my lady."

Hugh arrived back from Cardiff the next morning. He made his way immediately to his chamber, where Eleanor sat in a window seat. She had seen him and his men approaching, but had made no effort to hurry and greet him as she usually did, nor did she turn to greet him now. "My love?"

No answer. Hugh sighed. "I see you have heard."

"Yes. I have heard." Her lips were barely moving.

Hugh put his hands on her shoulders, and she wriggled away. "Do not touch me."

"Eleanor—"

"Do not touch me, did you hear me? I cannot bear it!"

He looked at her, and the expression of hurt puzzlement in his eyes almost made her relent. But before she could, he sighed and dropped his hands. "Very well. I'll have a bed made elsewhere tonight. As our Hugh has pointed out many times, there's more than ample room for all of us here."

Eleanor resumed her gaze out the window. Hugh turned to go. "It was what your grandfather the first Edward would have done, Eleanor. You know that."

For the next two days they lived the most formal of married lives, eating together in the great hall, talking over what business needed to be talked over, even saying goodnight to their children together. For the latter they made some show of affability, for the children adored Hugh and had greeted him after his one-night absence as if he had been gone on crusade. Hugh to his credit was a loving father who saw no loss of dignity in letting Edward and Joan ride him like a horse, in pretending that Isabel was nowhere to be found until she at last emerged from underneath her bedclothes, and in promising Hugh that they would go for a ride tomorrow, all by themselves. It was a promise Eleanor knew would be kept. But when the children were at last put to bed, she and Hugh went into different bedchambers, for the first time in their twelve years of marriage.

On the third night, however, she was despondently letting Gladys braid her hair for bed when Hugh appeared in the room. He waited until Gladys had excused herself. Then he said, "Llywelyn Bren surprised the people here while they were holding manor court and slew five of them. No warning, no time for them to fight him like men. Do you remember that?"

"Yes."

"No one in Caerphilly but the Countess of Gloucester and one of her ladies. For weeks they were penned up there, under siege, with only a small garrison to defend them. Do you remember that?"

She nodded.

"Others were killed too, many of them innocent Welsh who just happened to get in the way. Buildings and livestock were destroyed, crops ruined. The town of Cardiff still shows the effects, as do some of our castles. Do you remember that?"

"Yes. Hugh—I don't say Llywelyn Bren was a saint by any means. Perhaps he earned himself the death he suffered. But he was promised imprisonment."

"At the instigation of Mortimer and Hereford, neither of whose lands—or tenants—were harmed. Do you really think they would have showed him any mercy had it been Ludlow or Brecon that was attacked?"

"But he was in prison, Hugh. What harm could he do there?"

"A prisoner can escape."

"From the Tower?"

He shrugged. "It's been done. And if it was done while I was away, and you and the children here if he made his way back—that's not something I was prepared to face."

"Yet it was a noble thing he did, surrendering so that his men would not suffer."

"Or so they would not turn on him. But maybe he did have a higher motive, albeit rather late in the game. And I'll spare you the trouble of telling me that among his confiscated goods was a copy of the *Romance of the Rose.* Would it make you hate me less if I had a copy made for myself?"

"Hugh! You know I could never hate you." Her eyes were streaming tears. "But it seemed so unworthy of you, and such a terrible death."

"It was vile; I'll grant you that, though if it's any consolation, he died bravely. I was impressed."

"You watched?"

"I had to, my love. One shouldn't give an order like that and then shirk from seeing it carried out, as Warwick did."

She shuddered, and Hugh touched her hand. "But this was not a Gaveston, a man who did little more than make the wrong people angry and enjoy the royal largesse. Llywelyn Bren was an enemy of the king, whatever his motives."

"Yes. I suppose he was."

Hugh was silent, watching the moonlight play on the manmade lakes that surrounded Caerphilly Castle. "Tomorrow I go to the king, to give him much the same explanation I gave you just now. I was hoping to depart knowing that when I came home, I might share a bed with you again."

"Yes, Hugh."

"Tonight?"

"Just to sleep. I am bone-tired, Hugh. I have not slept well these past few nights." She sighed. "I never sleep well without you."

He kissed her on the cheek. "Nor I without you, my love. But now I am here, so let us rest."

At Westminster his father was waiting for him with a lecture, albeit a half-hearted one, for Hugh the elder also had to tell Hugh that his younger sister Margaret, married to John de St. Amand, was ailing. "John thinks she will not last until spring. Consumption, just as poor Philip had."

"Poor thing. I will try to see her on my way back to Wales."

"If the king doesn't toss you in the Tower. Hugh, have you lost your mind? First this business of Wentloog, and now Llywelyn Bren, all without a word of warning to the king."

"Well, he can't say I've had things all my own way in the March. Those whoresons in Dryslwyn and Cantrefmawr won't let me near the lands, and they were a grant for life by the king himself!"

"I hope you don't expect sympathy from him. When he got word about Llywelyn Bren, he all but burst a blood vessel."

"I shall deal with him. My Eleanor has forgiven me, and that is far more important to me."

Hugh scowled. "You don't deserve that woman, Hugh, you truly don't."

He turned on his heel and Hugh, having sent in word that he would await the pleasure of the king, was left with nothing to do but await it. His brothers-in-law Audley and Damory had noticed his arrival and were pointedly ignoring him, Audley being angry about his Welsh lands and Damory siding with Audley. William de Montacute was friendly enough with Hugh and would have probably talked to him, but as he had been one of the captors of Llywelyn Bren, his execution would likely be his chief topic of conversation, and Hugh was in no mood to discuss the Welsh rebel further than what would soon have to be discussed with the king. So he stayed in an obscure corner, waiting.

Hugh's feelings toward the king were somewhat confused. Like most men, he had feared and respected the first Edward in equal measure. The second Edward had dared to cross his father on several occasions, and this took no small amount of courage, Hugh knew. Yet few feared the current king, and a distressing number did not respect him. Hugh did not fear Edward, that was for certain, and he did not much respect him, although Hugh was honest enough to admit to himself that fear and respect were areas in which he was somewhat lacking anyway. But he did like the king; to Hugh's mind he was impossible to dislike, rather like a big friendly hound dog. If the king saw reason and let him have his way in Wales, there'd be nothing Hugh would not do for him, for if disloyalty was not one of the king's vices, it was not one of Hugh's either.

"Lord Despenser, the king will see you now."

"What is the meaning of this, Hugh?"

The king and Hugh were alone in the room. The king was not shouting; in fact, his voice was very soft, his face composed. It was a tactic the first Edward had used on occasion too, Hugh now remembered. For the first time he felt a twinge of fear. Might the king really send him to the Tower?

The king's question had been purely rhetorical. He was going on, "I shrugged off your fool stunt with Tonbridge Castle. I've never tried to collect your fine for your assault on John de Ros. I've been extraordinarily patient with your escapades regarding Wentloog. But now you take a man out of my own Tower and execute him, without seeking my permission! You've presumed too long on my good nature, Hugh."

"That was not my intent, your grace. I've my reasons—"

"Oh, I'm sure you do, sir."

"Will you not let me explain myself?"

Edward shrugged. "Explain away."

Hugh did, justifying his execution of Llywelyn Bren much as he had in his conversation with Eleanor. Then for good measure, baffled by the king's stony silence, he explained why the men of Wentloog would clearly be happier and better for staying in Hugh's lordship of Glamorgan. The king seemed scarcely to listen, and his face had taken on a peculiar, far-off look. He interrupted Hugh in mid-sentence and said in the same quiet voice, "The truth is, Hugh, you sought to make a fool of me."

"No! Nothing of the sort."

"You lie." The king was even quieter, and he had moved so close that Hugh felt compelled to step back.

"Your grace, this serves for naught. I meant no such thing. But I was rash and thoughtless, and I humbly beg your pardon. Tell me what my punishment shall be, and I shall abide by— Christ!"

The king had knocked Hugh to the floor, and when Hugh struggled to rise, he hit him again. Hugh, dazed, fell back, and the king rolled him over on his belly. "You have sought to master me, Hugh, and you miscalculated. It is I who shall master you."

Hugh, his face pressed into the rushes on the floor, felt his drawers being tugged down. He struggled, but the king was tall and muscular, and he was like a man possessed besides. He heaved against Hugh, groaning and muttering unintelligibly.

Then his movements abruptly stopped. Hugh felt the weight lift off him, then heard the king give a great sigh. "I can't force you, Hugh. Forgive me." The king pulled him to a sitting position and gently touched his face. "I've hurt you, I see. Let me get you some wine."

He guided Hugh to a seat and poured some nearby wine into a gold cup, from which Hugh sipped slowly as the king made encouraging sounds. Finally he recovered his breath and gasped, in as cool a tone as he could muster, "Is this your new method of bringing your barons into line, Edward? If so, you'll find it inefficient, and perhaps disagreeable when some like Lancaster are concerned. Perhaps you should consider delegating this task."

Edward looked more closely at his forehead. "There'll be a bruise, but I don't think it will be a very bad one. Do you wish to leave? You may now."

Hugh stood up gingerly, and the world began sliding around. Only the king's arm stopped him from falling. "I can't be seen like this."

"Then lie on my bed and rest."

Obediently, Hugh let the king help him onto his great bed and lay down. The dizziness eased when he closed his eyes, so he shut them and felt himself drift off. Then he woke to find a cool cloth on his forehead. His boots had been taken off, and someone sat next to him, stroking his hand. The room was dim. "How long have I been here?"

"Hours; it is quite late. I gave word out that you had taken ill and would be resting in my chambers."

Hugh snorted. "That's one way to put it." He sat up, relieved to find that doing so caused him no difficulty. "With your grace's permission, I will retire now. I trust I look fit to be seen?"

"You do, and you may retire if you wish. But I wish you would stay. I love you, Hugh."

"*Love* me?"

"I have loved you for years."

Hugh gestured toward the gold cup. The king let him take a gulp, then continued, "I've kept it hidden well, haven't I? I've fought this for so long, because I knew it could bring me no good. But the years went on and the angrier you made me, the more I loved you. Finally there was the business of Wentloog, and Llywelyn Bren, and I could stand it no more. That's why I brought you here, to master you for once and for all, as I've said. But you see, it didn't work. I love you too much for that." He shook his head. "I want you willing, Hugh."

Hugh drained the cup, and the king poured him another one. "Damory? Audley? Montacute?"

"Dear friends, Hugh, no more. I've been with but one man in my life, and you know full well who that was. If you were to be the second it would give me indescribable joy, and there would be nothing in this world I would not do for you."

"Have you forgotten I am married to your niece? Your favorite niece?"

"No, Hugh. I have thought of my niece, and that thought has stopped me in what I am asking you now many, many a time. I would not hurt Eleanor for the world. Neither would you. But she cannot be hurt if she does not know, and I assure you I have no intentions of letting her know. I can be discreet, as you can."

"There is the small matter of the Church."

"The Church! Fine words from a pirate. Gaveston guessed the truth about those trips of yours long ago."

"I haven't done that in years."

"Once a pirate, always a pirate, Hugh. Don't turn righteous on me now."

"The queen…"

"*You* to worry over the queen! Leave that to me."

Edward was laughing now; Hugh's protests had begun to take on an encouragingly formalistic turn. "I won't know what to do, how to please you."

"I shall teach you, as Gaveston and I taught each other." He stroked Hugh's hair. "But we were naught but two clumsy boys at first, and it will be different for you and me." He shuddered. "Not as it was earlier, I promise you that. That was unforgivable of me. It shall be beautiful."

Hugh sighed. "Might I at least have some more wine to fortify myself?"

Edward smiled. "All the wine you want, and the cup too."

The sun woke Edward, and he turned to look for Hugh beside him. He was still there, sleeping soundly. Edward smiled. From the copious amount of wine Hugh had consumed the night before, it was unlikely that he would wake soon. Edward reached out and stroked Hugh's hair, too gently to wake him, noticing for the first time that its darkness was relieved by reddish tints, almost as if he had absorbed some of Eleanor's bright red tresses. So much he had learned about his lover, but there was still so much to find out… He trembled with the very joy he was feeling. Not since a morning in his sixteenth year of life, the morning after he and Gaveston, drunk and laughing, had fumbled each other's clothes off and discovered, to their astonishment, that they could be so much more than brothers to one another, had Edward felt so utterly happy.

He was fond of Audley, Damory, and Montacute, the more so because he knew his fondness for them irritated Lancaster, but theirs had never been a physical relationship; it had never occurred to him to take one of them to bed, and if one of them had offered, the king probably would have refused. There had been no one, man or woman, who could arouse in the king the depth of the love he had borne for Gaveston. No one, until now.

He kissed the head that he had been stroking and smiled again, thinking of the game he had played last night with Hugh, making him remove one item of clothing each time he finished a cup of wine. Hugh had gotten down to his shirt before the king, able to bear no more, had called the game to a halt and begun undressing him himself. With enough wine in him, Hugh had not needed as much guidance as the king had anticipated, nor had the enjoyment of the pair been one-sided. The cries of pleasure that had emanated from behind the bed curtains had not all been Edward's, and they had not been pretended. Edward had been sleeping with Isabella long enough to recognize a sham when he saw one.

He pulled Hugh against his chest and listened to his heart thumping against his. Hugh slept on, and the king did not care that his arm was growing numb under the pressure of his companion's weight. He could have stayed there forever, cherishing his new love.

At last Hugh awoke. He started to find his head resting on the shoulder of the king, then flushed as he remembered why he was there. His embarrassment only endeared him more to Edward. "Did you sleep well, Hugh?"

"Yes, but my head is killing me, and my body aches like a maiden's after her wedding night."

"There will not be pain next time," Edward promised. He paused. "Hugh, there will be a next time, won't there?"

"Yes, Edward."

Edward's eyes filled with tears of gratitude. "Thank God." He pulled Hugh closer and spoke into his hair. "You won't regret having my love, Hugh. You shall be as my brother, shall share all with me. Nor shall your family suffer. I will love my sweet niece Eleanor all the more for knowing that we both love you. And per-haps"—a certain wistfulness had crept into the king's voice—"you will come to love me too."

"Perhaps."

"And now, dear one, get dressed before I call my men in. I shall order us something to break our fast"—Hugh shook his head vigorously—"to break my fast then, and some ale for you to help your poor head. And we shall discuss Wentloog."

Hugh the elder did not understand it, but his son and the king had emerged from their conference on the best of terms. Hugh the younger appeared before the king and his council and swore that he had withdrawn from Wentloog and released all of those whose oaths he had taken, and the lands were taken into the king's hands, pending future discussion of their disposition. The matter of Llywelyn Bren seemed to have been forgotten altogether, at least by those present at Westminster. What had his boy and the king said to each other? Hugh the elder wondered. He was somewhat hurt by his son's failure to confide in him, but as he had browbeaten Hugh so much about the matter, perhaps it was only to be expected that Hugh would be so closemouthed. At any case, the worst he had expected had not come to pass, so he was not wont to complain.

In Wales, Eleanor felt similarly relieved when a messenger arrived to let her know that her husband was well and would soon be on his way back to Wales, after he stopped to visit his ailing younger sister. Before Hugh arrived, however, she was much puzzled over the unexpected arrival of a cart groaning with gifts from the king: tuns of wine, fine cloth, even a barrel of sturgeon. This was an excessive outburst of avuncular affection even from the king, Eleanor thought, and then she smiled. The king was obviously anxious to let her know that Hugh had not offended him.

Meanwhile, efforts had been underway to mend the breach between the king and Thomas of Lancaster. Lancaster, ostensibly dismayed by the prominent role Damory, Audley, Montacute, and the Despensers had assumed at court, the non-observance of the Ordinances, and the king's gift-giving, had remained intransigent, but at last in April 1318, a preliminary agreement, to which the king was not privy, was reached. It was extremely favorable to Lancaster—royal gifts were to be taken back into the hands of the crown, "evil counselors" would be removed, Lancaster would be pardoned for his aggressions of the previous year, and the Despensers were to stay in Lancaster's retinue for their lives—and as such was satisfactory to few but Lancaster himself. Negotiations resumed.

Eleanor had been invited to attend the queen, who was expecting her third child in June. She was staying at Woodstock for her confinement, and Eleanor happily showed her Fair Rosamund's Bower and later sang a very sad ballad, accompanying herself on her lute, about how jealous Eleanor of Aquitaine had poisoned her husband's lovely young mistress.

"Do you believe that nonsense, Lady Despenser?"

"Oh! I don't know, your grace, but it is very romantic, and it makes a pretty song." Secretly, Eleanor was rather hurt, for she had a expressive singing voice and thought she had excelled herself in her ballad; two of the queen's damsels had even sniffled appreciatively.

It was a beautiful spring day, and the queen and her ladies were sitting out in the garden. Two men came into sight, the king and Hugh the younger. They kissed their wives, and Edward questioned Isabella as to how she felt, for she was expected to go into labor any day. Then they went inside the manor.

"Your husband has certainly become a confidant of mine lately," said the queen, watching as they went inside.

"Yes. I am glad of it, for he well deserves it. If only this business with Lancaster would get settled! Then he and his father and Pembroke and the others could do good work for the king, instead of wasting their time going back and forth with the earl."

She settled back in her seat rather complacently and smiled at little John of Eltham, who was toddling toward her with a flower. "Did you pick that for me, sir? It is lovely."

"Pretty," said John solemnly.

It was unclear whether John was referring to Eleanor or the flower, but both were undeniably pretty. Since the division of the Clare inheritance, Hugh had insisted that Eleanor have some new summer robes made and that she add to her jewels, and if there were women who would argue with such a mandate, Eleanor was not one of them. Her hair had been dressed most carefully by Gladys, and the light spring breeze had called a glow into her cheeks. "Wealth seems to agree with you, Lady Despenser," said the queen.

"I am happy, your grace, but I hope it is not only the wealth. I am content, and it seems that most around me are too." She thought of Hugh's younger sister Margaret, who had died around Easter, and her grieving father-in-law, and said softly, "Almost." She crossed herself.

The queen did not reply. She winced, and Eleanor dropped John's flower and went to her. "Is it time, your grace?"

The queen nodded.

The queen's labor was long and hard, but at last the midwife held up a wailing baby. "A beautiful little girl, your grace."

The king was delighted. Edward and John were in excellent health, so he had not been unduly concerned to have a third son. He found the business of teaching his eldest son kingship as dreary as kingship itself; it would be much more pleasant to have a girl to make much of and to have taught to sing all of his favorite songs. Of course, the girl would have to marry suitably, but as he held her in his arms, this moment seemed very far away. He kissed Isabella. "She is beautiful, my dear. Thank you."

He looked over toward Eleanor, who was tying ribbons on the royal cradle. "Niece, I can think of none better than you to stand godmother to her."

"I am honored, sir."

"And my dear nephew Hugh shall stand as godfather. She shall be named Eleanor, after my beloved mother, of course." But his eyes met Eleanor's, and she knew that the little girl had been named for her, not for the mother Edward had hardly known.

Soon after little Eleanor's birth and christening, the king departed for Northampton, it having been planned that Lancaster would meet the king there. He left orders that over three hundred pounds be allotted for Isabella's churching.

Despite the difficulty in achieving a settlement with Lancaster, the king had not been happier since the days of Gaveston. On his travels, except when the royal party headquartered itself at a monastery or when the queen or his niece was in too close proximity, he shared his bed with Hugh, who no longer needed to fortify himself with wine before coming to the king. He had become, in fact, an energetic and imaginative lover, sometimes tender, sometimes rough depending on the king's mood, which he was adept at discerning. (That was Hugh for you, the king thought lovingly, a quick study.) He was almost as wonderful as Gaveston. Yet there was an intriguing difference between the men. While Gaveston's eyes had glazed over on the few occasions the king had discussed the affairs of the realm with him, save those that concerned himself, Hugh's were bright and eager; more often than not, the king thought, Hugh was better informed than he.

"Have you heard Lancaster's latest excuse for failing to come here?" asked Hugh one evening as he opened the bed curtains. "Now he is swearing that Damory and Montacute are plotting to kill him."

"I know, dear one. I am going to send you, Bartholomew Badlesmere, and the Earl of Pembroke to meet with him, along with the Bishops of Norwich and Ely. Some agreement must be reached with that tiresome man, so we can deal with the Scots."

The envoys did in fact return with an agreement. Save to attend Parliament and answer military summonses, the king's intimate friends were to be removed from court, and gifts contrary to the Ordinances were to be revoked. There was to be a standing council, some of whose members would stay with the king each year, some of whom would stay with the king each quarter. Though Hugh himself stood to lose from this agreement, he did not worry overmuch about it, for

Hugh doubted that the king would ever agree to it, much less the king's other particular friends and the many barons who would lose valuable lands, and he was quite correct. A second group of envoys, this time minus Hugh and with the Earl of Arundel and Roger Mortimer of Wigmore, was sent to Lancaster. By August, at Leake, the king and Lancaster had exchanged a kiss of peace, and a couple of days later, on August 9, what became known as the Treaty of Leake had been drawn up.

"Lancaster gave a great deal up," Hugh told Eleanor, who had remained in England with the queen over the summer. "Oh, he got his standing council, all right, but he's not on it—only a banneret of his! There's quite a few bishops on it, and the Earls of Pembroke, Richmond, Hereford, and Arundel. No Warenne, as you can well imagine. Hugh Courtenay, John de Segrave, and that Roger Mortimer you dislike so much. The membership of the council is to rotate, though. All the rest is quite vague. Nothing about royal gifts or the removal of us so-called evil counselors. We'll just have to see what happens when Parliament meets at York in October. But I do have an additional piece of news for you, my love, that won't be found in the Treaty of Leake."

"What is that, Hugh?"

"The king has appointed a new chamberlain."

"Oh? Who is it?"

"Me, my love. Come. Kiss the royal chamberlain."

After marrying Joan, Countess of Gloucester and daughter of the first Edward, Ralph de Monthermer had been made Earl of Gloucester, once the old king saw fit to let him out of prison. He had lost the title, of course, upon Joan's death, and he had accepted this graciously, knowing that the title by all right and justice now belonged to her young son, Gilbert. It was his lovely, spirited Joan he had mourned, not his lost earldom. In any case, though he was no longer a particularly important man in the realm, he was a busy one, for the second Edward had found much for him to do. He was the keeper of the forest south of Trent, he had a number of manors that had been granted to him by the king, and he had several lady friends who were pleased to have him stay the night.

And he had his chess games with Lady Hastings. Ralph enjoyed playing chess as much as he enjoyed riding and wenching, and these were things that he enjoyed very much indeed. In the chess aspect, he had found, some years ago, a kindred spirit in Lady Hastings, who had trounced him mercilessly the first time he'd idly suggested a game. When Ralph had recovered from the shock of losing to this doelike creature, Bella had explained that her father, no mean player himself, had taught her the game and that they still played together whenever they visited each other. Since then Ralph, whenever he found himself near one of Bella's manors when she was in residence, stopped in, and Bella's servants knew well to bring out the chessboard and men when he arrived.

But this game was far less interesting than usual. Bella's mind did not seem to be on it, and when he had captured the last of her men, she sighed. "It seems you and I will not be playing much together soon, Lord Monthermer."

"Not becoming a poor loser, are you, Lady Hastings? I don't beat you all that often, but it has happened enough that you should not be surprised."

He had spoken teasingly, but Bella's eyes welled up with tears. "No, Lord Monthermer. I always enjoy our games, whatever the result. But my brother writes that he wishes me to remarry, and I suppose I must."

"Remarry? Who?"

"One of his retainers, Peter de Ovedale. He has been loyal to Hugh, my brother writes, and he wishes to show him a mark of his favor by marrying him to me."

"And do you not like him?"

"I do not know him. Oh, Hugh has always been fond of me, and I know he would not choose a disagreeable man. And since I did not take a vow of chastity like my older sister Aline did after her husband died, I suppose I should have expected this. After all, I have been a widow for nigh on five years now."

Ralph frowned. He was of an age with Bella's father—fifty-five—and had first met Bella when she was quite a child, at about the time she had married into the Clare family via her first husband. It had never occurred to him to eye her the way he might eye a woman who was a stranger to him, and now that he did so, he was struck with several revelations. The first was that Bella was pretty and slender, with what surely must be small, firm, high breasts, and Ralph was a great admirer of small, firm, high breasts. The second was that although Bella's hair was bound and modestly covered, it would likely reach to her hips when loosened, and Ralph was suddenly overcome with an urge to see that hair loosened, preferably with the aforesaid breasts peeking out from beneath it. The third .was that he had been very foolish to confine his acquaintanceship with Lady Hastings to games of chess. Keeping his voice level, he said, "That's true, you never did take a vow of chastity. I suppose, then, you were never adverse to remarriage?"

Bella shrugged. "At first, but after a few years, it got rather lonely. Perhaps marriage to Sir Ovedale will not be so bad after all."

"Tell me, Lady Hastings, what qualities would you choose in a husband, if you were to pick one yourself?"

He thought the question might border on impertinence, but Lady Hastings answered readily enough. "Well, he would have to be good-natured, first and foremost. I cannot bear an ill-tempered man."

"Indeed, no."

"Handsome, but not so handsome that other women would always be throwing themselves at him. Intelligent, but not so much that he made me feel like a dolt. Brave, but not foolhardy. And above all, he must like to laugh."

"Those sound like fine qualities. And do you know what, Lady Hastings? I happen to possess all of them."

Bella's eyes widened. "But, of course, I am about twice your age. But you will find that I am young enough in other ways."

"Other ways?"

"Like this, Lady Hastings."

He kissed her, and it was a very long time before they drew apart, breathless. A servant came in, saw them together, and slipped out, entirely unnoticed. He kissed her again, and this time he pulled at her headdress with one hand, then at the fastenings of her hair. It was even longer than he had thought, and very soon it was entangling him and Lady Hastings as they lay naked in her bed.

The next morning, Ralph was all set to make love to Lady Hastings again when she pushed him away. "Not yet, Lord Monthermer. I am much troubled in my mind."

"Lord Monthermer? I thought we were well past the "my lord" and "my lady" stage myself." He caressed a breast, as high and firm as he had hoped. "Dearest, I promised last night that we would wed today, and I keep my promises. It will be a great pleasure to keep this one—in a couple of hours, please."

"You do not understand, Lord—Ralph. Hugh did write and ask me if I would marry Sir Ovedale. But I would never have agreed to marry him—or anyone—without first trying to get you to marry me."

"Bella. You are telling me that when I came into your chamber last evening you had every hope that I would ask you to be my wife, and that you have manipulated me shamelessly?"

"I could hardly ask you to marry me, could I?" She sighed. "For well-nigh on two years I have been hoping to wed you. You are so agreeable, so handsome, so kind. Every time you came to play chess, I thought it might end in an offer of marriage. I am no beauty, like your first wife, but I am not ugly either, and we do get on well."

"Ugly! I think not!"

"So when I got my brother's letter, I knew that if I ever had a hope of marrying you, it was now. And you reacted exactly as I hoped you would, Ralph. It was much like our games of chess, but—rather more pleasant. But I am feeling a little guilty now."

Ralph laughed. "So you beat me after all, you little minx." He kissed her, and they settled back among the pillows together. "I have always been a good loser, Bella. You know that."

"Have you had a letter from Bella, Eleanor?"

Eleanor shook her head. "No, Hugh, didn't you?"

"For this I thought she might have written you too. It appears that our little Bella has gotten married, without the king's license and without a word of warning."

"*Bella?*"

"Aye, here's her letter. She graciously informs me that she is honored to have been in my thoughts, and she is certain that Peter de Ovedale is a fine man, but not for her, as she has only just made a marriage to a man she has long esteemed and admired, who will do the family credit." Hugh paused. "Naturally, one wonders who the man is, but Bella being Bella, she apologizes for several more lines before we finally learn his identity. Well, who do you think he is, my dear?"

"I have no idea, Hugh. Bella seemed inclined to remain unmarried."

"Your stepfather."

Eleanor gasped, and then she started giggling. Hugh said a little testily, "Really, my dear, it is rather embarrassing, you know. I all but promised her to Peter. But who could have guessed about this long esteeming and admiring?"

"I know it is embarrassing for you, Hugh, but think how lonely she has been for these past few years. She is not like Aline, able to devote herself only to God. She needs a companion, and Ralph will be one for her. Now that I look back on it, they have always seemed quite friendly." She laughed again. "My stepfather's wife. Does that make her my stepmother now?"

"Well, it cannot be undone. Of course, the king's standing council will want to seize their lands, as a salutary lesson for this rash marriage, but I daresay my father will make sure his darling wants for nothing. But poor Ovedale! I wonder if I can persuade Aline to abandon her vow of chastity."

Soon afterward, in late October of 1318, Ralph dutifully obeyed the king's summons to the Parliament to be held at York. There, his marriage having slowly become known around the court, he was subject to the jokes a man married to a much younger wife could expect. Ralph bore them all good-naturedly, for he was as happy as he had not been since Joan was alive.

Though the jesters had to be careful to hold their tongues when Bella's brother came into earshot, there was no need to look for Bella's father. Hugh the elder had not been included in the peace made with Lancaster; he had gone on pilgrimage to Santiago and was unaware of his new son-in-law. Warenne likewise avoided the Parliament of York.

The lords, however, soon stopped twitting Ralph about his bride and got to work. Hugh was confirmed as the king's chamberlain. Bartholomew Badlesmere became the king's steward, replacing Montacute, who was promoted to Seneschal of Gascony, Lancaster, who spent an entire month at Parliament, rather a novelty for him, forced Montacute, Damory, and Audley to pay him large sums in order to settle their differences with Lancaster. Despite this addition to his coffers, he was unhappy. He had not wanted Badlesmere to be steward, having recently conceived the notion that as hereditary steward of England, he had the right to appoint the steward of the king's household, and Edward seemed entirely too pleased with his new chamberlain for Lancaster's liking.

Hugh the younger was considerably more satisfied with the parliamentary proceedings. As chamberlain, he, along with Badlesmere, the Earl of Hereford, Roger Mortimer, and sundry other barons, bishops, and royal officials, had been appointed to reform the king's household. Hugh, whose head was already swimming with ideas of how the office of chamberlain might be refined and improved, set to this new task with alacrity—and, to his credit, no mean ability.

His Welsh business was proceeding nicely also. Edward, with the approval of Parliament, regranted him the lands of Dryslwyn and Cantrefmawr, which Hugh had not yet been able to enter; with Parliament's backing, his possession seemed more assured. Better yet, Edward had decreed that he would enjoy as full privileges over Glamorgan as Gilbert the Red had ever enjoyed, Gilbert himself having forfeited some of these during his disputes with the first Edward.

And there was the matter of Wentloog.

Although Hugh had officially resigned his claim to Wentloog, which had been taken into the king's hands, Audley's attempts to persuade its men to give him their homage and fealty had proven fruitless, and in December, he and Margaret conceded defeat and signed Newport, Wentloog, and Machen over to Hugh and Eleanor. The Audleys were not impoverished by any means—Audley had been granted two thousand marks in lieu of his claim to the earldom of Cornwall, which he had been coveting since his marriage, and Eleanor and Hugh had agreed to grant some of their English lands to the Audleys in exchange for the

Welsh estates. Yet Eleanor was uncomfortable as she watched Hugh d'Audley and Margaret sign the necessary documents. Margaret signed her name so fiercely that she nearly tore a hole in the parchment, and when she had signed the first set of indentures, she turned on Eleanor. "Are you satisfied now, sister? Your beloved husband has another piece of Wales."

"My lady, Eleanor had nothing to do with this," said Hugh calmly. "She is signing in accordance with my wishes, as befits a wife. If you have any complaints, make them to me."

"Margaret, love, this has been settled," said Audley. "We have discussed this."

"Oh, we have discussed it, all right. But I need not like it."

She resumed signing. The room was silent but for the scratching of pens on parchment, the shuffling of paper, and the suppressed yawns of the clerk who was directing the proceedings. Eleanor sat with downcast eyes. In a moment or two, it was over. Hugh le Despenser was Lord of Newport, Wentloog, and Machen, and Eleanor was for all intents and purposes minus one sister.

CHAPTER 11

▼

JULY 1319 TO JANUARY 1321

Hugh draped an arm around Eleanor's shoulder as they lay in bed. "Did you know that William de Braose has the reversion of Gower up for sale?"

Eleanor shook her head no.

The Despensers were at York, where the court had been since the spring. With the king and Lancaster no longer at loggerheads, the long-threatened Scottish campaign was at last under way, to Eleanor's secret terror. She snuggled closer to Hugh. "For sale? Why?"

"That wastrel Braose needs the money, that's why. He's squandered all he has, they say. He's been negotiating with Hereford and with your friend Roger Mortimer of Wigmore."

"My friend! Ugh."

"Then you won't mind if I put a bid in?"

"I suppose not." Although there were still hard feelings regarding Wentloog, Eleanor knew, surely no one could complain if Hugh simply bought the reversion of Gower.

"I shall mention the matter to Inge, then." John Inge was the sheriff of Glamorgan. With Hugh having left Glamorgan to reside at court, seldom a day went by without him dictating a letter to or receiving a letter from Inge. For a few minutes Hugh settled back, obviously composing a letter in his head. Then, the letter mentally written, he gently touched Eleanor's belly. "How are we doing down here, my love?"

"Oh, it is still too early for any movement."

"I wish you would go back to one of our manors, sweetheart. Rotherfield, maybe, or even into Wales. Or visit one of my sisters or your sister Elizabeth the Prioress." Hugh paused almost guiltily, for he knew that Margaret and Eleanor were estranged, and knew that it was his doing mostly. But when Eleanor was Countess of Gloucester, as Hugh had every intent of making her, Margaret would no doubt come calling. "I don't like you staying this far north, with this business in Scotland."

"I promised the queen I would keep her company while the king is away. But we are even, for I wish you would not go to Scotland."

"Has to be done, my love. Bruce has had his way with us long enough. He took advantage of our infighting last year to seize Berwick, and he'll be unpacking his carts at Westminster if he's not stopped. So to Scotland we go."

Once the men had departed, Isabella and her ladies remained at York, though not at the castle, which the queen found overly gloomy. It was, in any case, overrun with royal officials, for Edward had ordered the transfer of the Exchequer there. Instead, they stayed at a comfortable manor, near enough to York Castle for convenience but far enough away for there to be no demands upon the queen. Unfortunately, the manor was so tranquil that within a few weeks, Isabella had grown very bored.

"Really, Lady Eleanor, it seems you are always with child!" Eleanor had just refused the queen's invitation to ride.

"Only my fifth, your grace."

"Well, I don't understand why you cannot sit a horse. It is not as if that little mare of yours is a destrier. And you are an excellent horsewoman."

"I promised Hugh that I would not."

"Why? Did his mother have a riding accident?"

"Indeed, no." Eleanor smiled. "Hugh says she was a splendid horsewoman and a hunter, better than many men, and she certainly rode when she was with child—in fact, my father-in-law swears Hugh was almost born in the saddle. But nonetheless, he has asked that I not ride while I am carrying a child. It is something he worries about."

"Who would know, my dear? What harm would ensue?"

"No one but your grace and the rest of the ladies, and probably no harm at all. But I would not deceive Hugh."

"You fear him?"

"No, your grace. I love him."

The queen gave an exasperated shrug. "Then you must stay here with the little ones, I suppose."

"Yes, your grace."

The queen turned away. Eleanor, who very much wanted to ride, watched from a bench in the garden as the horses were led out to the queen and the other ladies, along with a pony for seven-year-old Edward, Earl of Chester. She sighed, wishing she had stayed with her own children. She and Isabella had never regained the closeness that they had lost during their trip to France, and Eleanor knew that Isabella much preferred several of her other ladies, particularly Eleanor's cousin Joan of Bar, to herself. Yet the queen had expressly asked her to join her while the men were in Scotland. Was it the ordering more than Eleanor's company the queen enjoyed?

She did not dwell on this question, though, for the queen's younger children, John and Eleanor, had been sent outside with their nurses. As both were fond of Lady Despenser, they each had to be amused for an hour or so before their nurses disappeared inside with them again. Her charges gone, Eleanor being in the sleepy stage of pregnancy had begun dozing in the sunlight when she heard a horse coming to her, very quickly. For a confused moment she thought that this was a last effort by the queen to induce her to break her word to her husband, but then she saw the rider's frantic face. His garb indicated that he came not from the queen's household, but from the Archbishop of York, William Melton. "The queen! Where is she?"

"Out riding. Why, what is the matter?"

"Douglas plans to take her prisoner. There is no time to lose; he could be within a mile of us as we speak. Quick, where did she go?"

Douglas, who had pursued the king and his knights to Dunbar Castle so hotly that none could stop to make water. "It is easier for me to show than explain. Help me into your saddle."

The man needed no persuasion and within seconds Eleanor was seated behind him, holding on and crying "Left! There! At the lake!" and such until they had arrived at a clearing, where the queen and her ladies were spreading a picnic lunch. The ladies froze at the sight of the horseman, then his passenger. "And what on earth does this mean?" demanded the queen.

The rider made no effort to observe the formalities. "Your grace, you are in the gravest danger. Douglas of the Scots has gotten word that you are here, and there is a scheme afoot to capture you and take you hostage. We must get you back to York Castle, and from there to Nottingham."

"But—"

"There is no time for argument or questioning, I tell you! Your lady here was wise; she got astride my horse immediately and brought me to you. Follow her example, I beg of you. Do you wish to be hung in a cage for all to gawk at, as the first Edward did with Bruce's women?"

The queen did not. Without another word, she let her wide-eyed page help her to her horse, and in moments, the ladies were galloping away.

While the queen and her household were fleeing to Nottingham via water, the king and his men had been besieging Berwick Castle.

Edward had high hopes for this venture, and this time the support of Lancaster and his troops, along with those of Pembroke, Hereford, Hugh the younger, Audley, and Damory. The Scots put up a fierce resistance, but without James Douglas, who had elected to ignore Berwick in favor of pursuing the queen of England. Only the timely capture of a Scottish spy, who had confessed under threat of torture, had saved the queen from capture, but the Scots were very much in England still, and the Archbishop of York, having seen to the queen's escape, gamely set out to fight them. The best fighting men were in Berwick with the king; the archbishop, a man of humble birth, had no knightly training. His talents were administrative, for he had risen as a royal official in the first Edward's reign, and ecclesiastical, for he took his duties as archbishop seriously and had done much to help the poor in his diocese. Above all, he was a Yorkshireman, and even if the queen had not been placed in distress, he would have wanted to come to the aid of his countrymen, whose lands were being devastated by the Scots. He and the chancellor of England, the Bishop of Ely, gathered a thoroughly unmilitary force—monks, priests, clerks, friars, and any man who could handle a weapon, any sort of weapon—and, acting on the information they had been given by the spy, attempted to take the Scots by surprise. The Scots, seeing instantly as the ragtag group advanced what they were dealing with, set brush on fire and formed a schiltron, terrifying many into fleeing instantly. Most of those who stayed were killed or taken captive, though the archbishop and the bishop escaped.

This news, and the news of the attempt on the queen, reached the king at Berwick two days later. "It seems we have no choice but to raise the siege," Lancaster said coolly.

"Raise the siege!" The king turned to stare at his cousin. "After we have brought our best men here, our siege engines, our sappers? To turn tail and run?"

"Not an entirely unfamiliar scenario for you, your grace," Lancaster sneered.

"But one for you," put in Hugh the younger. "While the king was risking his life at the Bannock Burn, where were you, Lord Thomas? Safely tucked away on your estates."

"I sent my men."

"Oh yes, your men. They might not lack for courage, but do you, Lord Thomas?"

"Why I countenanced this creature as your chamberlain I have no idea," said Lancaster. "But I've an idea why he leaps to defend you; you promised him Berwick Castle, didn't you? And the town to Damory here. My God, Ned, when will you leave off bestowing gifts on these wastrels?"

Only Gaveston had had the privilege of calling the king "Ned" in public. Hugh, intimate that he had become, still used the name only in private, and seldom outside the king's bed curtains. The king returned, "What I give or do not give is not the issue, Lord Thomas, it is why you are so intent on abandoning this fight! Are you in league with the Scots?"

"That is a vile accusation. I'll stay for no more of this."

"Go, then; you are always odious to my sight." He added, "When this wretched business is over, we will turn our hands to other matters. For I have not yet forgotten the wrong that was done to my dear brother Piers."

Lancaster rose from the jointed table around which they had all been conferring and strode out of the tent. Soon, the sounds of his own troops readying to leave camp could be heard. "The treacherous snake," breathed Hugh, poking his head out of the tent. "He is actually leaving!"

"Leave him to be damned," said the king.

But the loss of Lancaster's men left a gap in the English ranks that could not be filled, and the king abandoned the siege. The Scots themselves withdrew into their own territory, despite the English army's efforts to prevent this. In the end, the king returned moodily to York, where Hugh wrote to John Inge, "The earl acted in such a way that the king took himself off with all his army, to the great shame and grievous damage of us all. Wherefore we very much doubt if matters will end so happily for our side as is necessary."

From Eleanor's point of view, however, things had ended happily indeed. Edward, now under pressure to perform homage to the French king, Isabella's brother Philip, elected to enter into a truce with the Scots, though not until after the latter had conducted harvest-time raids into several English counties that left them devastated. Hugh the younger was one of those appointed to negotiate with the Scots; while he was away in December 1319, Eleanor gave birth to a girl, whose name, Eleanor, was shortened to Nora by common consent. As for the queen, any fright she might have experienced at her near-capture by Douglas was compensated for generously by the king, who upon his return to York had presented her with jewels and other fine gifts in recognition of her ordeal.

With the Scots settled for the time being, and Lancaster once again avoiding the king, the court's attention turned to France. Queen Isabella's father, King Philip, had died in November 1314, a victim, it was thought, of the curse of Jacques de Molay. His eldest son, Louis, had reigned less than two years before dying of a fever. Louis's infant son—he had a daughter also, but a woman could not rule France—reigned for five days before dying himself. He was succeeded by Louis's brother Philip, who since that time had been pressing his English brother-in-law to do homage. Edward, beset by all of his other problems, and never caring for paying homage to begin with, had stalled, but in June 1320, he and most of the English court crossed the Channel into France.

Eleanor joined her uncle on the trip. Her initial reluctance to return had been much allayed by the reflection that Isabella's dreadful father was no more, and besides, Hugh was going also. His father was already in France, having been one of those sent ahead to negotiate with the French king.

As the English proceeded to Amiens, people and horses both gloriously bedecked, Eleanor watched as Hugh and the Earl of Arundel rode a little ahead of her, talking earnestly yet apparently amiably. She pursed her lips. Since Gaveston's death, Arundel had played little part in the disputes of the realm, but he had been loyal to the king. Lately, he had made a point of being cordial to the Despensers. Yet Eleanor could not quite like him, for she could never forget that he had been one of the men who decided that Gaveston had to die, or that the earl had stayed away from the Bannock Burn when Eleanor's brother had gone at such a cost.

There was no "not quite" about Eleanor's not liking Arundel's lady wife, however. Alice, the Countess of Arundel, was the sister of John de Warenne, and unless the Earl of Surrey begat a legitimate child, which seemed most unlikely given the fact that he and Joan of Bar were never seen together, it appeared that Alice would be his heir. The Earl of Surrey had a certain rakish charm, but Alice was haughty and cold, so much so that Eleanor found herself pitying the Earl of Arundel after all.

Hugh, in the meantime, had slowed his horse down and was looking behind him, obviously with the intent of letting Eleanor catch up to him. The earl had moved away toward his own wife. "The Earl of Arundel and I have been discussing a little business, my dear," said Hugh, smiling at Eleanor as their horses moved together. "What say you to a wedding?"

"A wedding, Hugh?"

"Between our Isabel and his eldest son."

Isabel was eight years old, and the earl's son, Richard, was probably about the same age. Although Eleanor knew perfectly well that children of that age often married each other, consummating their relationship years later, the thought of this happening to little Isabel nearly put Eleanor out of her saddle. Recovering, she said, "Hugh! Surely this could wait until they are older?"

"Why?" said Hugh practically. "It's not as though they will be setting up their own household any time soon. I didn't mention it, but I am sure the earl will be agreeable to Isabel staying with us for a few more years instead of going to live with them."

"Isabel is not ready for marriage. She is shy; you know that, Hugh."

"Not marriage, but a wedding; two very different things. And I daresay that the prospect of being a countess will make her a bit less shy. Who knows, she may then be trying to take precedence over you." He tweaked Eleanor's coiled hair. "Until, of course, I make you a countess." He saw Eleanor's downcast face and said, in a lower tone, "The truth is too, Eleanor, this alliance would be good for us, Arundel being a Marcher lord. The more allies we have in that area, the better."

"What do you know of this boy?"

"Richard? Nothing. I daresay he is a perfect horror; most boys that age are, my love. I certainly was; ask Father. But when he is fourteen or so, I've no doubt he will be quite presentable."

"Like his father? Hugh, you know I don't care much for Arundel. After Gaveston and the Bannock Burn—"

"Arundel's made his peace with the king on those scores, so you should too. After all, he could have sided with Lancaster in all of this recent business. He didn't."

Eleanor sighed. "When shall this wedding take place, Hugh?"

"We were thinking early next year, perhaps February."

Up ahead, the Arundels were talking too. Eleanor could glimpse the countess's face; she looked even more unhappy than Eleanor. Hugh laughed. "I daresay Arundel is having a hard time making his lady accept a match with the upstart Despensers. He did say that she was hoping to marry the boy off to an heiress."

"Upstart! Your family is as good as theirs, and as for mine— How dare that woman oppose the match?"

Hugh grinned, having guessed accurately as to how Eleanor could be worked round. "So will you agree to the wedding, sweetheart?"

Eleanor looked at the Countess of Arundel, who even from a distance was visibly fuming. "Certainly, Hugh." She thought of Isabel, still sleeping each night with her doll, and amended this. "If she continues to live with us until she reaches a suitable age."

"So it shall be, my love. Now what shall you wear?"

"Mowbray? Gower? So many *ow* sounds. Slow down, Hugh dear. You are confusing me."

Parliament was in session that fall of 1320, and the king and Hugh were at Burgoyne, a retreat that the king had built for himself, much to the dismay of the monks, in the precincts of Westminster Abbey. On the outside, it resembled a peasant's cottage, albeit that of a very comfortably off peasant, with a roof thatched by the king himself. On the inside, it was as comfortable as any of the royal manors, with fireplaces, garderobes, a well-equipped kitchen, and several chambers, the best of which the king and Hugh were in.

Edward had started constructing Burgoyne shortly after his departure from York. The work, on which Edward had often lent a hand, had helped solace him after this latest Scottish fiasco, and its completion had much raised his spirits. It was only after he had seen the last of its furnishings moved into place that it had occurred to him that this would be a perfect place to meet Hugh, who for all of his ardor in private was the most discreet of souls in public. Instead of padding through Westminster Palace, dogged by the eyes of servants, petitioners, courtiers, and relations, Hugh could slip on the monk's habit he had though it prudent to acquire, walk over to the abbey, and let himself into the cottage. There, in the weeks after the court's return from France, he and the king had spent many happy hours, sometimes making love, sometimes playing chess, sometimes laughing over one of Hugh's anecdotes. He had a boundless supply—about the other barons, about his pirate days, even about his children—and the king loved to listen to them.

On this occasion, however, Hugh had arrived at the cottage tense and irritable. "Mowbray has moved into Gower!" he had said as he took off his habit.

The king had clucked his tongue. "Lie down, dear one, and let me knead your back for you. And you will tell me all about it."

Only two other people in the world—Gaveston and the queen—had enjoyed one of the king's back rubs, and not even the queen had ever refused one, not because of the king's royalty but because of his technique. Hugh lay down and closed his eyes as the king positioned his hands on his back and began to knead expertly. Despite his annoyance, Hugh was all but purring when he said, "Mowbray, of course, is William de Braose's son-in-law. Braose put Gower up for sale some time ago, as you will recall."

"Yes, you seemed intent on purchasing it."

"And so I was. But now this Mowbray has taken it upon himself to enter upon Gower and claim it for himself, on the basis of a grant Braose made to him, with a remainder to the Earl of Hereford! Lower, please. Thank you. Ned, it would have been perfect to have Gower!"

"What if I took it into my hands?"

Hugh started up. "On the grounds that it was alienated without a royal license? That'll not sit well in the March; the Marcher lords claim there is no need for such a license there."

"I know that, my love. I am king, you recall; I am forced to know such things, though I don't dwell on them. But what if I took Gower into my hands regardless?"

"You would do that for me?"

"I would do anything for you," Edward said quietly.

Though Hugh had become the king's lover mostly out of expediency, partly out of curiosity, he had found himself, as the months passed, becoming more and more attached to Edward. With those words of the king's, signaling his willingness to alienate every other Marcher lord for Hugh's sake alone, Hugh's last defense crumbled. He had often wondered why Gaveston, against all reason, had come back from that last exile of his to stay, and now he understood fully. "I love you, Ned," he said, amazed to find his voice trembling. "I'd do anything for you, too."

"You have done all you ever can for me, by saying those first four words and meaning them."

They lay embracing each other by the fire for a long time, too joyous to speak.

Rob Withstaff, the king's fool, had arranged the Christmas fare on his plate in the shape of southern Wales. "Glamorgan," he indicated, taking a large bite. "It went down well enough. Dryslwyn and Cantrefmawr. A little harder to digest. Wentloog—stuck in the throat. Gower—why that the Marcher lords just couldn't swallow!" He made a series of dreadful choking noises and ran from the great hall, to titters of nervous laughter. When he returned, it wisely was to juggle.

Eleanor watched him from her seat at the high table, with the king, the queen, the Earl of Chester, the king's half-brothers, the king's sister Mary the nun, both Hugh le Despensers, an unescorted Joan of Bar (the Earl of Surrey, a devoted family man, spent Christmases with his family, albeit not his legitimate one), the Earl of Arundel and his countess, and Ralph de Monthermer and Bella. Nearby sat a host of other minor barons and their ladies. At a table prudently placed some distance away sat the king's younger two children and their attendants, flanked by other noble children, including those from the Despenser family.

The Earl of Pembroke would certainly have joined the rest at the high table, but he was in France, having been widowed in September. He was there not only to take care of some of his late wife's affairs, but to look for another bride, for the earl had lived for nearly half a century without producing a child, but still had hopes. The Countess of Gloucester had died that year also, taking her reasons for claiming pregnancy for three years with her to her resting place at Tewkesbury Abbey. The abbey was in Despenser country now, for it had been part of the countess's dower lands. It had now reverted, along with many other English manors, to Eleanor and her husband.

Hugh d'Audley, furious over the seizure of Gower, had left the court in December. Roger Damory had elected to spend Christmas elsewhere. Lancaster had not come to Parliament and would certainly not come to the Christmas court. William de Montacute had died the previous year during his service in Gascony, leaving behind him a son of the same name. All in all, it was a depleted court, though a determinedly cheerful one, that celebrated Twelfth Night in 1321.

Eleanor shifted in her high-backed chair, grateful that she was sitting there instead of on a bench, for she and Hugh had done more in France besides plan the wedding of their daughter, and she was near her seventh month of pregnancy. Her back ached fiercely, but she had been sitting a long time.

"Well, Eleanor, what do you say to this Gower business?"

Joan of Bar had been indulging a bit too freely in her wassail, and she winked at Eleanor in a way that would have been comical had Eleanor not been so tired of hearing about Gower. The fool was right, though; Gower had stuck in many Marcher throats. "I say nothing, Joan. It is between the king, Hugh, and the Marcher lords."

"Oh, what a dutiful wife you are!"

Eleanor was saved by the fool. "A dutiful wife!" he screeched, scanning the room like a sailor looking out for land. "Where? Does anyone know where I can find one?"

While the fool ambled away to search the room ostentatiously, Eleanor pretended to watch his antics with great absorption, hoping to stave off further conversation. After initial resistance, the king had finally succeeded into taking Gower into his hands just a few days before, and since then Eleanor had heard nothing but Gower, day and night. The queen had been downright insulting. "Mark my words, Lady Despenser, your husband has been a fool. Does he think the Marcher lords will take this without a fight?"

Bella had been puzzled. "Eleanor, what on earth has gotten into Hugh? Is he mad?"

Mary had been inquisitive. "My dear niece, I miss so much shut up in Amesbury. Now tell me, what exactly is this Gower business? We nuns hear only half of it."

Her eldest daughter had asked, "Mama, may we see Gower soon? Papa talks of it so often."

Yes, Eleanor was very tired of hearing about Gower. Hugh had sat her down and explained it to her. It was all quite reasonable. And yet—so many people were so angry at Hugh now. Hugh had made enemies when he had Llywelyn Bren executed, Eleanor knew, and enemies when he took over Audley's land. Moreover, Eleanor had heard whispers that since Hugh had become chamberlain, it was nearly impossible for anyone to get an audience with the king, unless Hugh was bribed handsomely.

It was a great relief to her when the servants started clearing the tables and pushing them away for dancing. It being Twelfth Night, the dances were quick and lively, and when the pains started, she thought at first she had simply overexerted herself. She twisted her way out of the carol and braced herself against a wall, waiting for the pains to ease. Instead, they grew more intense.

With so many people dancing and milling around, no one had paid any attention to Eleanor. Then Hugh saw her against the wall, her face contorted. "Eleanor! What is the matter?"

"I am in labor."

"But it is far too early!"

"Yes, Hugh. It—is!"

She let out a cry, and Hugh asked no more questions. He whistled, and the room went still for an instant. "Someone get a midwife here, now! And help me get her to her chamber." He hugged Eleanor against him. "Don't worry, my love. It will be all right."

Not even her firstborn's birth had been so hard, so long. It was an all-female ordeal, as ever, with Gladys and Bella on either side of her, the midwife standing grimly by her legs, but beyond the inner chamber in which Eleanor labored, she could hear anxious male voices. Someone mentioned getting a priest: for the babe, for herself, or for both? she wondered.

Nearly twelve hours had passed when at last she heard Bella murmur, "It is over, dear." She heard no baby's cry, and she had not expected to hear one. Yet there turned out to be enough life in the poor little boy she had borne for the priest to baptize him, enough time for her to hold him and whisper loving words to him as he slipped out of the world he had entered so prematurely. Then she let Bella take him from her and wrap him up in a dainty cloth.

Hugh walked slowly into the room, and Bella lifted the cloth as he stared wordlessly at what was beneath it. Tears ran down his face; he had always been an affectionate father. Finally, when Bella had left to take her sad little bundle to the chapel, he said quietly, "Philip. An unlucky name."

"Hugh, I am so, so sorry."

He came to her bed then and gently pulled her against him. "'Twas not your fault, my love. It was God's will."

Eleanor nodded. "Yes, Hugh, it is. Don't you understand? We are being punished. All healthy children—until now. We have overreached ourselves."

"Punished?"

He looked genuinely puzzled. Eleanor did not dare to look him in the face. She continued, her eyes on the bedclothes, "Yes, Hugh, punished. For all that has happened in the last few years. Llywelyn Bren–"

"A traitor, my love."

"Wentloog and the rest, then. Gower. Why could not we have just been satisfied with what we had? It was plenty, more than anyone could ever want or need. Let us give back the rest, Hugh. Then God will surely forgive us."

Hugh smiled tolerantly. "Give it back? And then we would lose all, bit by bit. You do not understand these things, my love. It is eat or be eaten. And—"

He was setting off on his Gower speech, in which he would patiently explain why every step he had taken was absolutely necessary and just, the ends justifying the means. Eleanor had heard it often. It was convincing; he had probably come to believe it himself. But this time Eleanor cut him short. "Justify it to yourself however you must, Hugh. I only know that our beautiful little son is dead, and that somehow we have displeased God."

Hugh was silent for a while. Finally he said, "You say 'we,' but what part have you taken in any of these things? God may want to punish me, but there is nothing He would want to punish you for, my love."

For acquiescing, He can, Eleanor thought. But she was suddenly too tired to argue with him. Hugh saw the exhaustion in her face and said gently, "All parents lose children, and we have been luckier than most to have so many alive and thriving. In due time we will have another child, I'll warrant, and that will put your fancies to rest."

"But I am so frightened, Hugh, of all that might come. I don't think you realize what you have wrought." She began sobbing.

He held her as she cried. Finally, she quieted and he said, "You need sleep, my love. The midwife sent this in with me. I want you to take a good sip of it for me. It will help you rest."

She nodded and let him bring a goblet to her lips. Then she settled herself on his shoulder and waited for sleep. Mercifully soon, it came.

CHAPTER 12

▼

FEBRUARY 1321 TO AUGUST 1321

On February 9, 1321, Eleanor stood in the chapel at the royal manor of Havering-atte-Bower, fighting a temptation to box her new son-in-law on the ears. Richard Fitz Alan, son to the Earl of Arundel, had come to his wedding with all the enthusiasm of one about to have a back tooth drawn, and as the young couple knelt before the altar, a fine cloth paid for by the king being held over their heads, he was making no effort not to squirm. Once again, Eleanor thanked the Lord that her daughter would be staying with her own parents for the time being.

The wedding was a worrisome event in what was proving to be a worrisome year. Lancaster continued to stay away from court, claiming illness. In January, the king had ordered the Earl of Hereford and numerous other lords not to join armed assemblies or make secret treaties, while Hugh had ordered his sheriff in Glamorgan to guard his castles well. Roger Mortimer of Wigmore had left the court in a fury and had been replaced as justice of Ireland by one of Hugh's own men.

The object of all of this anger, Hugh, bore it coolly. At the celebration that followed the wedding, he was in fine form, treating the little bride, who otherwise might not have thought much of her wedding day, like a veritable queen. He danced with her, paid her courtly compliments that made her giggle, and kept a weather eye on all of the entertainments during the feast to make sure they were to her liking. With Eleanor, who at his insistence had worn so much jewelry that she twinkled from a distance, he flirted so shamelessly that it was difficult to believe that the couple had been married for nearly fifteen years. His other little daughters looked charming in their brand-new robes, as did Bella. Even his older sister, Aline Burnell, who had taken a vow of chastity, had been coaxed out of her russet robes and into velvet for the occasion. Hugh the elder's nature was less sanguine than his son's, but he had managed to cast his cares aside for his granddaughter's wedding. Partnered with the queen in one of the dances, he led her around with the gallantry of a man half his age.

"You are looking lovely tonight, Eleanor dear."

"Thank you, Uncle." Eleanor smiled up at the king.

"I have worried about you. I am glad to see you looking your old self."

The king was utterly sincere, for he had indeed worried about Eleanor in the days following the loss of her child, when she had been so wan and quiet. It would have grieved him immeasurably if she had followed her child to the grave. But she was very much alive now, in a rich gown the king himself had paid for. Only when Edward stepped close to her could he see the dark shadows under her eyes. She shook her head and said, "I do not feel much like my old self, Uncle."

"I know you don't, my dear, but it will come in time."

"Uncle—"

"What, dear?"

Save Hugh from what is sure to overtake him, Uncle. Stop him. She bit the words back. She was still bleeding from her recent childbirth, still sorrowful and overwrought. She was merely being fanciful, as Hugh had gently told her. The worst was over, surely; all would work out. She stood on her tiptoes and kissed her uncle on the cheek. "You have given Isabel a lovely wedding, Uncle. Thank you."

Hugh too had seen the dark circles under his wife's eyes, and being worried that her health was in a decline, suggested that she go to Hanley Castle, which had just come into Hugh's hands, having been one of the dower lands of the deceased Countess of Gloucester. Save for her eldest son, who now was a squire serving in the king's household, Eleanor and her children, including the newly-wed Isabel, dutifully traveled to Worcestershire.

Built by King John as a royal castle and given to the Clare family in the last century, Hanley Castle was more domestic than defensive, and Eleanor soon came to love it. Weather permitting, she rode out daily with the older children, ambitiously began making a tapestry for her chamber wall, played her lute for the children in the evening. The letters Hugh sent were cheerful and loving.

They were also utterly uninformative. Happily isolated in Worcestershire, Eleanor did not know that later that February, news had reached the king that Lancaster had met in Pontefract with others, whose identities were unknown to the king's spy, and plotted to attack Hugh's estates in Wales. She did not know that Hugh was ordering that his Welsh castles be armed and victualed, or that the king and Hugh had traveled near the Welsh marches to appraise the situation. Hugh reserved his news for the sheriff of Glamorgan, whom he was sending letter after letter.

The Earl of Hereford had also received a letter, an order by the king to appear at Gloucester to discuss the assemblies that were being held in the Marches. His reply arrived in the person of the Abbot of Dore, who clearly wished himself back in Dore after he delivered his message to the king, privately. The king returned to his chamber to report to Hugh. "They propose, dear one, that you be put in the custody of Lancaster—Lancaster!—until a Parliament can be summoned, where you and Hereford can put forward your complaints. Lancaster! My God, Hugh, do they think me an utter fool? After what happened to Gaveston—"

He broke off, shuddering, and Hugh, who was alone with him, put his arms around him and kissed him on the cheek. "Does the good abbot await a reply?"

"Yes."

"Then let's give him one. I'll answer whatever I am asked in Parliament, but I have been charged with no crime, have I? Then to commit me to Lancaster's custody would be groundless and contrary to Magna Carta, common law—"

"And my coronation oath," said the king, taking heart.

"And the Ordinances. Let us not forget the Ordinances. That'll irk Hereford and Lancaster—you know full well Lancaster is behind this—to no end, to be accused of violating their own Ordinances."

Edward laughed. "You think of everything, dear one. Find a clerk and dictate our reply."

"Hugh! Uncle!"

Eleanor leapt from her window seat in her chamber to greet the two men coming toward her. Hugh embraced her, then stepped back to look at her. "How healthy you look now, love."

"It is beautiful here, and I have been able to go riding every day for weeks now that the weather is so pleasant. But what a lovely surprise!"

"We are on our way back to Westminster, and thought we would stay a night. What of it, my lady? Can you manage to entertain us?"

Eleanor laughed. "I shall endeavor to do my best, your grace. Now tell me. What am I missing at court?"

Hugh paused for only a second or so before replying smoothly, "Have I told you Pembroke is back? No? Well, he is, and he has chosen himself a new French wife, Marie de Saint-Pol, a count's daughter. They are only waiting for the Pope's dispensation, as they are related within the fourth degree."

"That is good; he was so fond of his first wife. What do you know of her?"

"Only that she is young and fair, and being virtuous, time will have to tell if she is fertile."

"And the queen?"

The queen was expecting a fourth child in July. Edward said, "Doing well. She plans to have this one in the Tower, of all places."

The children having gotten wind of their father's appearance, they soon straggled into the chamber, and for the next hour or so they dominated the conversation, Edward enviously speculating on the life his brother Hugh must be leading as the king's squire, Isabel bringing her new puppy, Joan wanting to know when *she* could have a wedding, and Nora evincing the greatest of interest in pulling the king's beard. When Eleanor could get a word in edgewise, she idly asked whether things had quieted down in Wales, and Hugh assured her that they seemed quiet enough. Then Eleanor remembered that Hugh had never seen the castle, and the children had to take him on a tour, Eleanor and the king following behind. At last, all the children were stowed in bed, and the king took himself off to the fine chamber and steaming bath that had been made ready for him. "Would you like a bath too, Hugh?" Eleanor asked as they entered their own chamber. "I can order one."

"No." Hugh tipped her face up to his. "Remember the vow I made at Caerphilly? I haven't kept it."

It had been months since they had made love. Among Eleanor's fears since Philip's death had been one, pushed to the back of her mind, that she might no longer be able to respond to Hugh as she had in the past, or worse, that he might no longer find her desirable. Now with his wiry body pressing against hers, she found she had been wrong on both counts. She had also feared that she would be unable to conceive a child. On that point she would turn out to be wrong also, for when she and Hugh finally went to sleep, she was pregnant once more.

It was early May. She was to join Hugh at Westminster in a few weeks. Worcestershire was obviously agreeing with her, Hugh said, and it would be a pity to send her to sweltering London too soon when the fresh country air was having such a beneficial effect. It and her as yet undiscovered pregnancy certainly made her sleep more soundly, for she was deep in slumber late one night when she was shaken roughly awake. "Lady Despenser! Get up. There is no time to lose."

"Up?" Eleanor stared groggily at her chamberlain as he yanked the bed curtains back and pulled her to a sitting position.

"We have to get out of here, all of us. Have you got her clothes? Good. I will get the children up." The chamberlain sped away.

"Gladys, what is it?" She shrugged her way into the gown that her damsel was pushing onto her head.

Gladys stood her up and began lacing her gown with unprecedented roughness. "Your lands in Wales are being laid waste. Several men have been killed, and many more have been captured. One of your men from there escaped and reached here a few minutes ago. He thinks they are headed this way, or that more may be coming from another direction, and if those whoresons found you here alone—"

"Good God, no! Hugh thought—"

"Hugh was dead wrong," Gladys said heavily. "They say they have hundreds of men at arms and thousands of foot soldiers, all of them looting what they can carry off and burning what they can't."

Eleanor was surprised to hear her own voice so flat. "Who are they?"

Gladys put her arm around Eleanor. "Your brothers-in-law, Audley and Damory. Roger Mortimer of Wigmore and his old uncle. Hereford. Mowbray. Lord Berkeley. Sir John Maltravers. Many others whose names I don't know."

From a distance the chamberlain's voice called, "Lady Despenser! The children are in the carts, ready to go. Are you?"

Eleanor stared at the fastenings of the cloak Gladys threw over her as if she had never seen them before. "Yes," she said dazedly.

Several days later, dirty, exhausted, and aching all over, Eleanor and her household arrived at Westminster. Though no one appeared to have been pursuing them, they had not dared to go east at a more leisurely pace, their progress already being slowed by the children's needs. Save to feed them and to rest for a few hours at nightfall, they had not stopped.

"Eleanor! Thank God you are safe." Hugh held her tightly, then pulled back to survey the children, covered with dust from the road. He kissed them one by one. "What poor little ragamuffins. Are they all right?"

"They are fine. They are merely bewildered, like I am. How did it come to this, Hugh?"

Hugh shook his head. "We underestimated the whoresons, didn't we? But let us go to the king now, love. He has much to say to us."

In his chamber, the king sat with Hugh the elder, Pembroke, and Arundel. Eleanor was shocked at her father-in-law's appearance. Though he had long since lost most of the hair on his head, he had otherwise escaped the ravages of age—he was close to sixty—and could have passed for a man ten years younger. No more. He looked weary and stooped and chilled as he sat by the fire, but he managed a smile when Eleanor entered the room. "Daughter."

Edward said quietly, "Seeing as you have no home at the moment, Niece, this shall be your home now."

"No home?"

"They are still ravaging our lands," said Hugh the elder, looking out the window. "Killing our men, imprisoning others, burning, looting. We cannot possibly return to them at this time." He looked at Hugh. "This is your doing, boy. Are you satisfied?"

"Father, I have said—"

"You have expressed your regret, very well indeed. But what of my lands, that my grandfather saved from forfeiture in King Henry's time to give to my mother?"

"Good God, Father, we shall get them back! The damage can be fixed! New livestock can be bought, new crops planted—"

"And what good will that do us in exile?"

Pembroke coughed. "One hopes it will not come to that." He turned away from the Despensers to the king. "Your grace, I know you and the Lords Despenser want revenge. Pray forbear. Your grace has not the men at present to fight, and a full-scale war would devastate England. We are only now beginning to recover from the famine, the Scottish wars."

"Then what is your advice?"

"Summon Parliament, let the barons' grievances be aired in the manner of civilized men. At worst, it will buy you time."

"There is sense in what you say," admitted Edward. He looked toward the window seat where Eleanor sat. "I will summon my council and discuss the matter further. Hugh, look to my niece. The poor lass is crying her heart out."

Eleanor swatted a fly as the queen grimaced her way through a contraction. The pain passing, she grumbled, "Really, Lady Despenser! Cannot something be done about this leak?"

With singularly ill timing, the queen's labor had coincided with a heavy rainstorm and with the roof in her chamber springing a leak. "Not without bringing some men in here, your grace, and I am not sure who would find that more disagreeable, you or they. But we could certainly move you to a more suitable chamber, and it seems as if there would be plenty of time to do so." She swatted again. "Maybe one with less flies."

The queen shook her head. "I intend to give birth in my own chamber, not in borrowed lodgings. Really, Eleanor, this is your husband's fault, you know. If he were not so stingy with the king's money, save when his own self is concerned, this leak would not have sprung."

Eleanor counted to ten, then to twenty. "The king is well pleased with my husband's work as his chamberlain, your grace, and it seems we are quite comfortable here except for the leak. They will occur in a building this old. But what if we moved your bed a foot or two? Then this bucket would catch the leak, and you would be well out of harm's way."

"Very well."

Eleanor had not wanted to attend the queen in her childbirth, but as the alternative was sitting in her chamber worrying, she had agreed to accompany her to the Tower, where Isabella regularly held forth on the shortcomings of Eleanor's husband. The king, following the advice of Pembroke, had summoned Parliament to meet on July 15, but the opposition—all carrying royal standards—had continued to devastate the Despensers' estates throughout May and June. Soon they would be on their way to London, and rumor had it—as the elder Despenser had predicted—that the king's opponents would be content with nothing less than the Despensers' exile.

Leaky ceiling and all, a few hours after this exchange between Eleanor and the queen, on July 5, 1321, the queen gave birth to another girl. Edward gave Isabella the usual gift and pronounced the child's name—Joan, after both Isabella's mother and Edward's favorite sister—but the poor infant girl went otherwise quite unheralded in the weeks that followed.

Lancaster and a group of barons and knights had held a meeting at Dunstable at the end of June. The king had sent his steward, Bartholomew Badlesmere, to the assembly to urge that the destruction of the Despensers' lands cease and that the lords present their grievances before Parliament in the manner of civilized men, but Badlesmere instead had joined the king's opponents. After that meeting, the attendees had gone on to loot more Despenser lands, including Hugh the elder's beloved Loughborough. Eleanor had never seen her father-in-law so dejected as when the news came to him. Immediately afterward he departed the court to go to Canterbury, where he planned to pay a pilgrimage visit to Becket's shrine and await developments in the royal castle nearby.

Hugh the younger, cast down at his father's lingering anger at him, had stayed in London with the king, but with the opening of Parliament had deemed it prudent to reside on a boat, where he cruised up and down the Thames by day and visited the king and Eleanor at night when feasible.

With the king preoccupied, the queen ensconced in her (now dry) chamber following the birth of Joan, and the two Hughs absent, Eleanor, having been replaced in the queen's chamber by Joan of Bar, found herself relying on her son Hugh and the king's bastard son, Adam, for news. Hugh, now thirteen, and Adam, now fifteen, were the best of friends. Adam had spent most of his childhood at Langley, with a tutor, while Edward pondered his future. He had been inclined to have the boy enter the Church, where other royal bastards had flourished in the past, but Adam's own inclinations tended toward knighthood. For several years, he, like Hugh, had been a squire in the king's household. In a few years, Edward would find him a suitable wife.

When their duties were over, Hugh and Adam liked nothing better than to roam the city, dressed nondescriptly so as not to attract the attention of robbers. It was to their wanderings that Eleanor owed the news that came to her at the end of July.

"My uncles Audley and Damory have finally come to London," said Hugh in his mother's chamber at Westminster, where Eleanor spent most of her time these days. She had thought it wise not to show herself much in the great hall. "So have Roger Mortimer and the Earl of Hereford."

"Lord Mortimer is lodging at Clerkenwell," said Adam. "The Earl of Hereford is at Holborn. Lord Damory is at the New Temple, and Lord Audley is at Smithfield. They entered the town today, all wearing green tunics with yellow quarters on the right arm with my father's insignia on them. To pretend that they are loyal to him, Father says."

Adam's voice swelled with pride when he said, "Father," and Eleanor once again thought it a great pity that the king's eldest son should have been born a bastard. As the king himself had derived so little pleasure from his role, however, perhaps Adam was better off for it. Her mind was too much on this news, though, to consider Adam further. "So they have come at last to London. Are they armed?"

"To the hilt," said Hugh.

"Good God, Hugh! I hope they did not recognize you boys."

"Not in what we were wearing." Adam grinned. "We sat in a tavern with a bunch of them for two hours, and they paid us no mind." He paused. "Lady Despenser, we heard that they want the exile of Lord Despenser and his father. Do you think that could happen?"

"I pray not, Adam."

"But it happened earlier with my father's friend Gaveston."

Hugh's usually cheerful face turned somber. He was growing up, Eleanor reflected sadly. Just yesterday, she had caught him eying the king's laundress as if the rather blowsy woman were Venus herself, and he was itching, he'd informed Adam the day before, to go fight the Scots. Eleanor prayed nightly that the truce stayed in effect. "Gaveston died, Mama. Didn't he?"

"Yes. But the situation is much different. The king and Gaveston relied on the earls' word that Gaveston would be safe with them. They broke that word, and he had been left with no means of resistance. Knowing that, your father is staying well away from his enemies, and he has soldiers on that boat with him."

"If he goes into exile, will we go with him?"

Eleanor had asked Hugh that very question, but Hugh had only shrugged. "We'll deal with that when it become necessary, and I hope it will not," he had said. Now Eleanor echoed her husband. "There is no point in worrying about this now, Hugh. Now that they are here for Parliament, some just agreement will surely be reached."

Pembroke had enjoyed a few weeks with his new bride in France, which was fortunate, for as soon as the newlyweds arrived in England, Pembroke was summoned to court to negotiate between the king and his opponents. As the barons were threatening to burn London from Charing Cross to Westminster, and were even threatening the king with deposition, Pembroke's services seemed sorely needed. The Archbishop of Canterbury, and a host of bishops, had already tried to break the stalemate, and might as well have been talking to two sets of walls.

"This must end, your grace." Pembroke took a deep breath. Although his sympathies edged closer to the side of the king's opponents than to that of the king and the Despensers, his own father and uncles, half-brothers to Henry III, had been deeply unpopular in England themselves at times, and he could understand the king's stubborn refusal to give way to the barons. Yet this could not go on. Nothing was getting accomplished; already in May a delegation from Gascony had gone home, unheard, after spending three weeks seeking an audience with the king, Hugh the younger, or himself, all of whom were too preoccupied with this crisis to see them. "You will lose your kingdom at this rate. Have you the money to fight these men now? You know you don't, not the money or the men."

"Hugh has been the epitome of loyalty to me." Pembroke shifted uneasily. During the barons' meetings, Bartholomew Badlesmere, with a convert's enthusiasm, had produced a document in which he claimed that Hugh had declared that homage was owed to the crown but not necessarily to the person who wore it. The Bishop of Rochester had denounced the document as a forgery, and Pembroke suspected he was correct. Yet the charge had stuck. "He has never wavered from my side, neither he nor his father. Why should I send them off to please these men?"

"It is for the common good, your grace. With them gone England can yet be united and strong, and you will reign in power and glory."

"And without the man I hold dearest in the world." The king looked out upon the Thames. "There he sails as we speak, Pembroke."

"For God's sake, man, consider! They have threatened you with deposition. They may have the numbers and the men to do it. Think of your successor, a mere boy of nine. You will be handing the government over to Lancaster, you know. He would be worse than Des— Your grace, you must not for any living soul lose your kingdom. He perishes on the rocks who loves another more than himself! I can say no more, your grace. If you are not convinced, you never will be, and you will suffer the consequences." He added deferentially, "I fear."

From a corner in the room, skirts rustled. Both the king and Pembroke had forgotten about the queen, who with the infant Joan had arrived at Westminster from the Tower only a day or so before. She stood and walked a few paces over to the king, only to drop at his feet. "Your grace, I beg that you listen to the good Earl of Pembroke. Would you risk your crown, your child's crown, for this man who is so unworthy of you? Your grace, I have been your faithful queen and consort, borne you four thriving children, supported you in all. And now I am asking you only one thing. Banish them! 'Tis for the good of the realm, my lord. I have come to love this England of yours. If you cannot do it for my sake, do it for hers." The queen bent her head and kissed the king's robe.

Pembroke, astonished at this impassioned speech, sank to his knees also. Looking at their downturned heads, the king felt a strange mixture of annoyance, admiration, and weariness. Weariness predominated. He raised them to their feet. "Pembroke, have the Archbishop of Canterbury summon the barons here forthwith."

As a squire in the king's household, on August 14, 1321, Adam had every right to be in the great hall at Westminster where the leaders of the Church, the earls, and the barons had assembled, although his friend Hugh le Despenser had been advised to keep distant of the proceedings.

The group dropped collectively to its knees as the king entered, flanked by Pembroke and the Earl of Richmond. In response to an impatient gesture by the king, the magnates arose and waited for the king to speak. They did not have to wait long. In a cold, clipped voice, the king said, "Out of necessity, and at the urging of the great men of the realm and my beloved queen, I have agreed to the exile of the Hugh le Despensers, father and son."

He turned and walked out of the room. After a few minutes Adam slipped out also. Someone, he thought, should tell his cousin Lady Despenser of the news.

"You wished to speak with me, my lady?"

Though Adam had hastened to Eleanor with his news, he had been forestalled by the king himself, who had told Eleanor in the gentlest possible manner. "Yes, your grace. Why did you urge the king to exile my husband and his father?"

The queen stared at Eleanor coolly. "You are rather presumptuous, particularly in light of your husband's position. It is not for me to justify my actions to you. But to satisfy your curiosity, I believed it was for the good of the realm."

"My husband and my father-in-law have always been loyal to the king. Who has been more loyal than they? How will the realm be served by exiling them?"

"You seem to have forgotten, my lady, that your husband brought this on himself. His greed has made him many enemies in the March."

"That was between him and them. That is no cause to exile him, to take him away from the land of his birth! Where will he go?"

"That is his concern, isn't it?" The queen lifted her hand in dismissal. "Under the circumstances, it would not be mutually beneficial for you to continue to attend me, I gather, but you and your children may certainly stay at court if you choose."

"With all respect, your grace, it is my uncle who shall determine whether we may stay at court, not you." She curtseyed and backed out of the room.

Parliament dispersed on August 22, having drawn up an enormously long indictment against Hugh in which he was charged with some things that were true, such as taking Hugh d'Audley's lands and having Llywelyn Bren executed, some things that were false, such as having declared that allegiance was not due to a king who did not guide himself by reason, and some things that were debatable, such as having guided and counseled the king evilly. The Despensers had until August 29 to leave England from the port of Dover. Those who had attacked their lands and the people on and near them were given full pardons.

The day after Parliament disbanded, the king and Eleanor walked to his cottage of Burgoyne, where a man dressed in seaman's garb awaited them. "Hugh!"

The king, who longed to embrace Hugh as much as Eleanor did, tactfully stepped into another chamber. At last husband and wife drew apart, and Eleanor asked, "Hugh, where shall we go? I understand that your father left for France as soon as the messenger brought him the news. Shall we join him?"

"Let the king come in here again, my love, and we shall discuss our plans."

Edward entered the room on cue. "My dear niece, we have been thinking about this matter, and we think it best that you and the children stay in England for now."

"Not here, without Hugh!"

"It is only for a short time, my love."

"A short time? You have been exiled! Good God, Hugh, you are not thinking of coming back like Gaveston, are you? They killed him!"

"Which I have not forgotten for a moment," Edward said, staring out a window. "My brother Piers came back ill-advisedly. We had no plans; we trusted in the honor of men who had none. With Hugh it shall be different. He will not come back until it is safe to come back, and when it is, it will be a black day for our enemies."

"Until that day comes to pass," Hugh said, "You and our children are safest here. Don't fear, my love. We shall be reunited soon, forever, and in England."

Eleanor shook her head. "I understand none of this and like none of it, but you must know best. But Hugh, where shall you go?"

Hugh smiled. "Ned—the king, that is—intends to put me under the protection of the men of the Cinque Ports. I have developed a taste for this seafaring life."

CHAPTER 13

▼

OCTOBER 1321 TO
MARCH 1322

"Edward, are you going to let this go on? The man has turned pirate! He is a menace to England's sea trade, and you know it."

The king, riding away from Canterbury with his queen and Eleanor on a fine day in October, shrugged. "You forget, my dear, that Hugh is an exile. He is not within England's borders, and I have no control over him."

"Lady Despenser, are you pleased to be the wife of such an illustrious pirate?"

Edward started to defend his niece, but Eleanor from her litter said coolly, "I do not approve of Hugh's actions, but as he was turned out of his own country with nothing to live upon but his own wits, I cannot blame him overmuch."

"In any case, he has been most successful at it," said the king cheerfully. "Two ships seized already, with cargoes worth thousands of pounds! Hugh never was one to do things by halves."

Edward had been unusually cheerful lately, and unusually busy. He had suddenly ordered Bartholomew Badlesmere, his faithless steward, to give up custody of Tonbridge Castle—the same castle that Hugh had seized in his pique over the Countess of Gloucester's false pregnancy—and Badlesmere had refused. Badlesmere had also gone into Kent, against royal orders, and after a trip to Canterbury himself had traveled to Oxford. There the Marcher lords had assembled, ostensibly to attend a tournament, in reality to be within striking distance of the king should he foolishly try to recall the Despensers. Edward had responded to Badlesmere's acts by sending knights to secure Dover Castle. Now he had suddenly got it into his head to go to Canterbury, and with him had come the queen and Eleanor.

Eleanor had been invited by each of Hugh's sisters to spend his exile with them, but the king had wanted her to stay with him at court. In her anger over Hugh's banishment, she took a certain pleasure in sitting at the high table beside her uncle each night, knowing that her very presence there, big with Hugh's child, was irksome to Hugh's enemies. This state of mind, as well as the news that had been circulating about Hugh's new career, had made her feel very much of a sinner as she knelt beside Becket's tomb. She said abruptly, "But it is very wrong of Hugh. He must make amends somehow."

"You can tell that to his face, my dear niece."

Eleanor started up in her litter, where she had been stretching out as languidly as one could in the jouncing vehicle. "We are to see Hugh?"

"We are?" asked the queen.

"I have arranged to meet Hugh on Thanet Island. Eleanor, naturally, will want to go with me." Eleanor nodded vigorously. "Isabella, I think it best that you return to London. I doubt that Hugh will be able to receive you on Thanet in the manner in which you are accustomed."

"Very well," said Isabella. "I should not like to be entertained by Hugh's accomplices in piracy."

"I would like you to break your journey at Leeds Castle. You miss nothing, and will be able to tell me how well Badlesmere has it fortified."

Isabella nodded graciously.

Hugh had found a large, comfortable house near the village of St. Peter's, so close to the sea that by walking only a few feet to a waiting boat, he could be out of England and therefore not in violation of his terms of exile. He came to the door himself to greet the royal party, and as soon as Eleanor saw him, her dismay about his new livelihood melted. She flung her arms around his neck as he bent to help her from the chariot, and he pulled her as close as he could to him, her belly being in the way.

"Did you enjoy the pilgrimage, my love?"

"Very much," said Eleanor. She thought of that earlier pilgrimage she and Hugh had made there, at a time when they had had so little to concern them, and fell silent.

Hugh, however, had turned to the king and was giving him a manly embrace. "How is the queen?"

"She is well," said Edward. "She is headed to London, and will be stopping at Leeds Castle." He gave Hugh a knowing look that puzzled Eleanor.

The weather being fine, and the king having never lost his scandalous predilection for swimming, he proposed that he and Hugh go into the water. Hugh most reluctantly agreed, and after a few minutes of paddling about arrived cloaked and shivering in the house's modest hall, where Eleanor, Hugh's cook, and the king's cook were consulting as to the evening's menu. Edward came in about a half hour later, glowing. "That was splendid! Hugh, if you had stayed longer, you would have warmed up beautifully."

Hugh grinned. "That's what a fire is for, your grace."

After a meal of fish, combined with a wine so exotically delicious that Eleanor suspected that it must have come from the spoils of Hugh's piracy, the trio of Edward, Hugh, and Eleanor retreated to the room Hugh had designated as the king's chamber. The night having turned crisp, they lounged by the fire, Eleanor leaning cozily on Hugh, the king with an avuncular arm draped around his nephew by marriage. It was not a setting conducive to worry, but one concern nagged at Eleanor. "I do not understand. Bartholomew Badlesmere still has control over Leeds Castle, does he not? What if he refuses to admit the queen?"

"He won't be there; that shrewish wife of his and Walter Culpeper are holding it while he and the Marchers tilt and plot in Cambridge. But you are right; they may well refuse the queen, either on their lord's orders or just out of sheer contrariness. That is what we hope."

Eleanor stared. "Hugh? You want the queen to be refused entry?"

"Ingenious, isn't it?" The king beamed. "It's Hugh's idea. Isabella won't take such a refusal lightly—after all, Leeds is her castle by rights. She will be outraged. She will complain to me, and I will avenge this ill behavior by besieging Leeds Castle. All of England will be indignant on my queen's behalf. Badlesmere will be utterly isolated."

"Lancaster has long disliked Badlesmere; he thought that he had no right to be appointed steward without Lancaster's consent because Lancaster claimed to be the hereditary steward of England." Hugh chuckled. "So Lancaster is unlikely to come to his aid. And as for the Marcher lords, who among them will want to fight against the queen?"

Eleanor's head swam. "So with all the advantage on our side, we seize Badlesmere," the king concluded cheerfully.

It seemed a very unlikely outcome to Eleanor. Who would be fool enough to deny the queen entry to her own castle? The very next day, she had her answer: Lady Badlesmere.

After being turned away, Isabella had gone to the royal castle at Rochester, minus nine of her men, who had been killed in the clash with Badlesmere's garrison. Edward and Eleanor promptly joined her. Hugh, knowing that his presence would be ruinous to a scheme that was going to plan, put back out to sea.

In mid-October, the king sent Pembroke, the Earl of Richmond, and the Earl of Norfolk—the latter being his much younger brother Thomas—to begin besieging Leeds Castle. Badlesmere succeeded in persuading Hereford and the two Roger Mortimers, uncle and nephew, to aid him, but Lancaster not only refused his aid, as predicted by Hugh, but persuaded Hereford and the Mortimers to withdraw theirs. Pembroke, the Archbishop of Canterbury, and the Bishop of London had been sent to Kingston to negotiate with Hereford and the Mortimers, but their desertion of Badlesmere's cause left the king, now at Leeds, with no need to negotiate with his enemies. He was even able to send for his hunting dogs to pass the time as the siege progressed. There turned out to be little time for hunting, though. On October 31, 1321, soon after the king's arrival, Leeds Castle fell. Badlesmere's wife and children were sent to the Tower and a half-a-dozen members of the garrison were summarily hanged. Badlesmere himself, far from the castle, fled north.

Lady Hastings frowned at Eleanor's lying-in chamber in Canterbury Castle. "How cheerless, my dear!"

"I had to leave most of my goods behind me when I left Hanley, Bella, and it was too dangerous to send for anything afterward. And, of course, Hugh's enemies still have possession of many of our lands, even though they were to be taken into the king's hands."

"Well, I had suspected as much, and I have brought some lovely tapestries for you to hang."

"It is so sweet of you, Bella. Thank you."

"I hoped they would cheer you, for I know you must be frightened. With Hugh gone, and what happened the last time you were with child—"

Eleanor winced and nodded. "I must say that I am. After all that has happened in the past year... But things are looking brighter. You know, of course, that Hugh and your father have petitioned the king to annul their exiles? That means they must be in communication again with each other; it was so sad to have them estranged. The king showed me Hugh's petition before I came down here to stay; it was truly eloquent. So was your father's."

"I had not seen them, but I know the king's council—though not exactly a full council, since only four of the bishops on the council were there—have agreed to their return. But Lancaster has sent his own petition, along with the Earl of Lancaster and Roger Mortimer of Wigmore. They accused the king of maintaining my brother and aiding him in his piracy! Then—you will not believe the effrontery, Nelly—they set a deadline for the king to answer their grievances. As if he were their subject!"

"I had not heard of that, but I know the king is on his way to Cirencester now, with an army."

"I hope John de Hastings will join them. He did nothing to hinder the Marchers in Wales out of fear, but has told me he wishes to make his peace with the king over Christmas." John de Hastings, the Earl of Pembroke's nephew, was also Bella's stepson by her second husband, though stepmother and stepson were about the same age. She added wryly, "I can only hope he keeps his word. It is not as if I can send him to bed without supper if he disobeys."

Eleanor sighed. "I am sorry things have reached this pass, but I do think this exile was horribly unjust. I only hope that when Hugh is back, life will be more peaceful for everyone. But Bella, how I miss him! I should be angry with him that he turned pirate, I know, but I can only think of how much I miss him."

"Has he sneaked ashore lately?"

Eleanor shook her head wistfully. "I have not seen him since the business with Leeds Castle. That is why I asked the king to let me stay here in Canterbury, instead of in the Tower with the queen, for hopes that he might come. I wanted to go to Thanet Island, where it would be easier for him to do so, but the king and Hugh wanted me in one of the royal castles in case there was any trouble. But enough of me. Do you hear from your father?"

"I have had several letters. I am not sure he wants to come back from exile! He has grown spoiled by having the wines of Bordeaux so near at hand, he tells me. I just hope he doesn't come home with a little French bride half my age. Imagine having a stepmother at my time of life!"

Eleanor laughed more lightheartedly than she had in months. "You are a fine one to talk, Bella!"

"May I hold him, Mama?"

"If you are very careful, Isabel."

Isabel took Gilbert le Despenser from Eleanor's arms and cautiously cradled him in hers, while Edward, Joan, and Nora pressed closer to see. "He looks like a piglet," said Joan.

"All new babies do," said Edward in a bored voice, though he was itching to hold his brother himself.

"Well, *I* didn't," said Joan.

"Yes, you did!"

"Did not!"

Nora sucked her thumb, as she had been wont to do ever since Hugh went away. "Stop fighting," she said sternly.

"I'll second that."

"Papa!"

"Hugh!"

Hugh strode into the room, grinning. Tactfully, he greeted his daughters and Edward—his eldest son was still in the king's household—with hugs and kisses before he frowned as if just remembering something. "They told me at the gate-house you had a brother. Is that true?"

"Here he is, Papa!" Isabel thrust Gilbert in his father's arms.

"Oh?" Hugh eyed Gilbert critically. "Well, I guess he'll do."

"Papa!"

"Oh, he's handsome enough," Hugh conceded. He kissed Gilbert on the fore-head. "Now will you let me have a word with Mama? And then we will all sit together for a while before bedtime."

"Yes, Papa!"

Hugh admired his new son a bit longer, then gently laid him in the nearby cradle. He climbed into the bed next to Eleanor and wrapped his arms around her. "A fine boy. Didn't I tell you we would be blessed again with a healthy child?"

"Yes, you did, Hugh, and I am so happy and thankful."

"So am I, sweetheart."

They lay quietly together for a while. "I saw Bella on the way in here. She said that you had had an easy labor. Was she just sparing me?"

"No, Hugh. It was easy, and quite fast. Nothing like—" She crossed herself. "It was all that I had prayed for, and now that you are here, all my prayers have been answered."

"I cannot stay long, sweetheart, as much as I would like to. The king has given me a safe conduct, I hear, but that's not worth a great deal when ruffians like the Mortimers and Lancaster are still about. But I did want to see you and the children—and I have some money for the king. It came from a source we need not discuss."

"Hugh, I hope there is to be no more money from that source."

"No, I am quite ready to settle down to the straight and narrow. I think I shall go to my father in France, and make a complete peace with him. Soon the time will be right for us to rejoin the king, and we need to be working together when that time comes."

"Will that be a long time, you think, Hugh? I have missed you so, and worried so much about you."

"I think it will be very soon. The king is planning a surprise for the Marchers; he wasn't the Prince of Wales for naught. But no more about this now. Let's call the children back and have a pleasant evening, shall we?"

Hugh had visited Eleanor in late December of 1321. By the end of the year, the royal forces and those of the Marcher lords were clashing along the Severn. Hereford and the Mortimers, determined to prevent the king from crossing the river into Wales, burned the town of Bridgnorth, where a royal force led by Fulk FitzWarren was attempting to repair the bridge there. Undaunted, the king's forces crossed at Shrewsbury. Meanwhile, the surprise Hugh had spoken of took place. Welsh troops, led by Sir Gruffydd Llwyd, began attacking the Mortimers' lands in the north of Wales, including Chirk, along with lands belonging to Hereford and Lancaster. The Mortimers' troops, many of whom had been coerced into serving, began deserting, while Hereford took his men to Glouces-ter, sacking the Despenser castles of Elmley and Hanley on the way. Lancaster, occupied with besieging Tickhill Castle in the north of England, refused to send any aid to the Mortimers, ostensibly on the ground that Badlesmere was with them. Isolated, the Mortimers surrendered to the king on January 22, 1322. In the middle of February, they were imprisoned in the Tower. The queen, watch-ing from a window as they arrived, barely glanced at the elder Mortimer, a man well into his sixties, but her gaze lingered for a long time on Roger Mortimer of Wigmore. He was, she thought, an undeniably handsome man.

Before the Mortimers' arrival in London, however, the king had moved to Gloucester, where he received two more surrenders, those of Audley's father and Maurice de Berkeley, and encouraged others to follow their example. Hereford and the king's former friends, Audley and Damory, hastened north to join Lan-caster. Theirs were not the only troops moving around the north. As Edward sat in the great hall at Gloucester Castle, cheerful from having received the surren-ders, Sir Andrew de Harclay, a lord from Carlisle, hurried in. Dropping to one knee, he exclaimed, "Your grace! You must know that the Scots are afoot again in the north. They are back to their old tricks, looting, pillaging, and burning."

"Aye," said Edward dispassionately. "The treaty has expired; I would have expected as much."

"Your grace, cannot we march against them immediately?"

Edward shook his head. "By-and-by, but not now."

"But sir—"

"Lord Harclay, you have done well in bringing this news to me, and I thank you. I wish all of the other barons were loyal and faithful like you. But they are not, and I must deal with that first. If Robert Bruce threatened me from behind, and those of my own men who have committed such enormities against me should appear in front, I would attack the traitors and leave Bruce alone. I shall pursue these traitors, and I shall not turn back until they are brought to naught!" He added, "Go back to your lands. I shall have important work for you to do soon."

Harclay obeyed. Edward, having ordered Lancaster not to receive the rebel Marcher lords, and having received an unsatisfactory reply, ordered that troops be raised to join him at Coventry. Among those who received the orders were the Despensers. By early March, in Lichfield, the Despensers were sitting in the king's tent. With them, setting up camp outside, were the Despensers' own ample troops, raised with the help of their allies in the Midlands and Wales. Eleanor, from her station at Canterbury, had sent some of the necessary messages, just as the queen from her station in the Tower had sent messages on behalf of the king.

Hugh had not found it as difficult to win his father back to his side as he had thought. Though the older man still held the younger responsible for their joint exile, and had been angry—and not a little chagrined—to learn that his son was making his living by piracy, he, like Eleanor, had a hard time staying angry at Hugh, particularly when his son was braving the winter gales in the English Channel. "Never mind," he'd told Hugh when he arrived at the chateau in Bordeaux that the elder Hugh had rented for his own comfortable exile. The younger man had gone so far as to bend his knee to his father and ask him for his forgiveness. "Never mind," he'd repeated, impatiently pulling him up and embracing him. "We'll work together, from now and evermore."

"There is much news to tell you," Edward said, his fond gaze wandering from father to son, but especially on the son. Tonight, after dark, Hugh could at last visit him alone... He shook his mind back to the present.

"I heard a rumor that Kenilworth had surrendered," said the elder Hugh. Kenilworth was one of the Earl of Lancaster's grandest castles.

"Just a few days before," said the king. "And just look what was found in it, dear friends. Look."

He pulled out a few parchments. Several were safe conducts, allowing Lancaster's followers to go unmolested into Scotland. The first had been issued the previous December, the last less than three weeks before. Two were from the dreaded James Douglas; one of them was addressed to "King Arthur." The last informed an unidentified correspondent that Hereford, Damory, Audley, Badlesmere, and several others had come to Pontefract and were ready to make surety with the Scots if the latter would come to their aid in England and Wales.

"Good Lord," breathed Hugh the younger. "Lancaster has been treating with the Scots!" He turned delighted eyes in the king's direction. "Edward, did not I mention long ago, that after the siege at Berwick, Lancaster's lands were never touched by the Scots, while all the surrounding ones were despoiled? Now, you see, he has only continued what he was doing long ago."

"You were right, Hugh."

"And can he really be signing himself 'King Arthur'! I'm not sure which is worse, the treason or the delusion."

"We have him," said Hugh the elder. "Your grace, do you intend to make this public?"

Edward grinned. "For once, Hugh, you've not anticipated me. I forwarded these to the Archbishops of Canterbury and York, and to all of the sheriffs of England, to be read and published. Soon all of England will recognize Lancaster for the traitor he is."

By March 7, the two forces were facing each near Burton, one on each side of the Trent. Lancaster's forces burned the bridge and the nearby town, but after three days of fighting, Pembroke and Richmond discovered a ford upstream, over which most of the royal army crossed. Lancaster had unfurled his banners and wanted to meet the king in battle, but the five hundred men he had expected one of his retainers, Robert Holland, to bring, did not materialize, nor did Holland, who later gave himself up to the king. Meanwhile, Hugh the younger had stopped the king from unfurling his own banners as the army crossed the Trent. "Sire, no! They should never be able to claim that you made war against them!"

"It is war as far as I am concerned," snapped the king. But he kept the banners rolled up.

Lancaster and Hereford abandoned the castle of Tutbury, Hereford privately making plans to escape abroad to Hainault, where he had relations. They fled to Pontefract.

As the king's men were feasting on the provisions left behind at Tutbury, a servant of the king's approached him and whispered something. The king winced and without explanation followed the man to Tutbury Priory, hard by the castle. There in the infirmary lay Roger Damory, a blood-soaked bandage wrapped around his belly. "Roger."

"Your grace."

"Roger, why? I trusted you, gave you land, honors, even my niece—all because I was your friend. I would have pardoned you at any time, even yesterday, if you'd left Lancaster. Why didn't you?"

Roger shrugged. He was too weak to do much talking, and even if he had not been, what use was it to explain to this fool of a king what anyone else could have seen, that his had always been an eye for the main chance? He watched with no emotion but contempt as the king walked toward a window and began to sob for his dying former friend.

Damory died on March 12. The day before, the king had officially pronounced him, Lancaster, Audley, Hereford, and the rest to be traitors, but Damory did not suffer the horrid traitor's death, or any execution at all. He died of his wounds in the priory and was given an honorable burial by the king.

At Pontefract, Lancaster balked at going to his own castle at Dunstanburgh, belatedly worrying that a flight north would be seen as an attempt to seek aid from the Scots. Better sit and wait for Edward's forgiveness, he advised; after all, the king was his first cousin. Only under threat of death from one of his followers, Roger Clifford, did Lancaster relent. Meanwhile, Sir Andrew Harclay, having been given his promised orders by the king, came south from Carlisle and met Lancaster and his small army at the town of Boroughbridge. Lancaster first tried in vain to bribe him, promising him five earldoms if Harclay would join his forces. Harclay would have none of it. His experiences fighting the Scots had not been wasted on him, and Robert Bruce himself would have approved of the close-packed formations of pikemen that greeted Hereford's men as they attempted to cross the bridge. Pushed together, much like the king's forces had been at the Bannock Burn, Hereford's men could see little but the masses of arrows flying from the archers beyond the schiltron. Nor could they see the men hidden under the bridge, one of whose spear, thrust upward, skewered Hereford himself as he led the way across it. With Hereford's death, Lancaster halted the attack. He agreed to either do battle the next morning or surrender.

But in the end, he did neither. Overnight, scores of his men deserted him, abandoning their armor and dressing themselves in whatever rags they could find in order to be taken for common beggars as they made their way out of Borough-bridge. Harclay, seeing this, decided there was no point in waiting. He captured Lancaster, and virtually everyone of importance with him, the next morning, March 17.

"So this is where Lancaster planned to keep me?"

Edward and Hugh the younger were standing in one of Pontefract Castle's towers. This one was visibly newer than the rest. Hugh nodded. "So they say. He intended to shut you up for life in it."

"Well, I can't do the same for him, but we'll let him spend the night here, shan't we?" He shook his head. "What I would like to do," he said softly, "is to shut him up in one of his dungeons for nine days, as was my brother Piers. But no, let's get it over with."

Lancaster was tried the next morning before a tribunal that included the Earls of Kent, Warenne, Richmond, Pembroke, and Arundel, the two Despensers, and the king. The charges included negotiating with the Scots, further proof of which had been found on Hereford's body in the form of an agreement under which Robert Bruce and two other Scottish leaders would come with all of their forces to Lancaster, where they would make war against all those whom the earl and his allies wished to come to harm. As with Gaveston, the earl was not permitted to reply to the charges against him. He was ordered to be hanged, drawn, and beheaded, but in consideration of his royal blood—and as with Gaveston—his sentence was commuted to beheading alone. It was to be carried out that same day, March 22, 1322.

A late-season snow was falling as Lancaster, mounted on a unprepossess-ing-looking mule, was led from the castle to the place of execution a short dis-tance away. Enough had fallen already for some of Lancaster's own tenants to pelt him with snowballs; he had not been a popular landlord. As Lancaster, not with-out dignity, knelt before the executioner, the king watched as one last snowball hit his cousin, his mind not on the present winter's day but on a perfect midsum-mer's day nearly ten years before.

"Perrot," he whispered, "the Fiddler has played his last tune."

CHAPTER 14

▼

OCTOBER 1322 TO
MARCH 1325

With the king's enemies defeated, the king once again turned his attention to the Scots. The result was yet another disaster. The English had moved into Scotland to find that all around them had been stripped of crops and livestock. Starving and sick, the English army had retreated to England, only to find that Bruce had moved into Yorkshire and was planning to capture the king himself. Edward, who had sent most of his troops away, heard the news while he and Hugh were dining at Rievaulx Abbey. Leaving their valuables behind, he and Hugh had fled to York with the Scots at their heels.

Eleanor had remained at York, while the queen had stayed at Tynemouth. The day after the king and Hugh arrived, exhausted by their flight from Bruce and disheartened at the ruin into which the Scottish campaign had fallen, yet oddly exhilarated by their shared ordeal, the queen joined them. Though the king had not forgotten her safety, sending troops to protect her, they themselves had encountered the Scots, leaving Isabella to escape Tynemouth by boat with the help of her household squires. Even with their heroism, the Scots and their arrows had caught up with the boat just as it sailed, fatally wounding one of her ladies and causing another to go into premature labor.

Eleanor had wept for the fate of the queen's unfortunate women, while the king had thanked the Lord (aloud) for the queen's preservation and Hugh had thanked the Lord (silently) that Eleanor had not been with her. The queen, however, was neither tearful nor thankful. She stared straight at the king's chamberlain. "This was your doing, Lord Hugh."

"My doing?"

"That I was put in this danger."

"Your grace, perhaps you are unaware that the king himself was in danger? He came within a hair's breadth of being captured, along with myself for that matter. Many of our own men were killed; many captured, among them the Earl of Richmond and Henry Sully, who was to protect you. All of us were in grave danger."

"Except your lady wife. How prudent to keep her out of harm's way."

"Your grace, that is nonsense! You know I would have gone with you if asked, and that the king and Hugh would have agreed to it. But you did not ask."

"This is nonsense, indeed," said Edward coldly. "Isabella, you are tired and overwrought. You have been through a terrible ordeal, of course. That is making you talk foolishly and to place blame where none lies. I will accept your apologies on behalf of Lord and Lady Despenser while you go to rest— What is it?"

"Your son Adam, my lord."

Adam had finally gotten his way and had been allowed to accompany his father on his expedition to Scotland. The king had armored him expensively and carefully for his first taste of battle, but no armor could protect the boy against the fever that had stricken so many of the king's men. For some weeks he had been lying ill at the nearby priory, but in the last few days, he had seemed to be recovering. "How fares he?"

"He is very ill, your grace. He is being shriven. You must hurry."

"You sent for me, Adam?"

Adam lay on a cot in the priory infirmary, one hand in his father's. "Yes, Lady Despenser. Is Hugh back from hunting?"

Hugh had wanted to go to Scotland too, but his parents deeming him too young to join the fighting, the king had ordered him, as a consolation, to hunt deer for his tables, expenses to be paid by the crown. Accompanied by the king's huntsmen and the best pack of hounds to be found in England, he had been traveling from county to county, having a fine time of it. His expenses to date had included several mysterious sums paid to such worthies as "Clarabelle" that had baffled Eleanor until her husband had said wryly, "Wenching, love, wenching. The boy has turned fourteen, after all. I daresay the king's huntsmen saw it as their duty to educate him."

And now Hugh would come back from this happy junket to find his best friend dead. "He is not back yet, dear. I have sent for him, though. He will come to see you as soon as he gets the message, I know."

"I want to give him my sword. Will you make sure he gets it?"

Eleanor's eyes filled with tears. "Yes, Adam. I will make sure of it, and I know he will treasure it always."

"Tell him I hope he is better in the saddle now. He will understand." The boy managed a grin.

"Imp." Eleanor smiled as best she could and kissed Adam on the forehead. "I will certainly *not* give him such a scandalous little message. What do you take me for?"

"I like having you here, Lady Despenser. Will you stay?"

"Of course, Adam."

"I used to wish you were my mother. Isn't that strange?"

Eleanor was about to manage a light-hearted reply when the king spoke. "Your mother, Lucy, was very much like Lady Despenser, Adam. I knew her for but a short time but I still miss her. If things had been different—"

He fell silent and Eleanor took the opportunity to get Adam to take some sips of wine and to lay a fresh, cool cloth on his forehead. Adam continued his rally, asking his father a few questions about the Scottish campaign, which Edward answered with brisk enthusiasm, and asking Eleanor if she remembered the time he had placed a mouse in her workbasket at Langley just to hear Eleanor's own squeak of horror. Then he too grew quiet and dozed off, Edward holding his hand and Eleanor stroking the bright hair that was so much like Edward's. By dusk, his breath had grown shallow and ragged, and before sunset the king's eldest son was dead.

Adam's death having pushed the queen's travails aside, nothing more was said about Tynemouth. But several days after the boy's body was sent to be buried at Langley, not far from Gaveston's tomb, Isabella announced her intention to go on pilgrimage to various sites around England, in thanksgiving, she said coolly, for her many blessings. She planned to be away from Christmas to Michaelmas. At York, where the court had remained for Christmas, the king bade her a cordial good-bye. "Good riddance," said the king to Hugh the younger later. "Let her nurse her imaginary grudge on the road."

The queen was not the only person on ill terms with the king. Shortly before Damory's death, his wife, Eleanor's sister Elizabeth, had been taken prisoner by the king and sent to Barking Abbey, where she had remained for six months. The king had then invited Lady Burgh, as she preferred to be styled, to York for Christmas, where she had been called to a private conference with the king and Hugh and stalked out of the castle in a rage. Her council members had been put under arrest; evidently they had threatened the king in some manner. Then Elizabeth, halfway home to Clare Castle, had been persuaded to return to York, where, as Hugh explained it, she had settled Damory's considerable debts to the king by exchanging Gower, now back in Hugh's hands, for Elizabeth's more lucrative property of Usk. Eleanor had not been pleased with this transaction, but as Elizabeth as a traitor's wife might have been imprisoned and left with no land at all, Eleanor had kept her feelings to herself and sent Elizabeth a barrel of sturgeon and some cloth for her children's robes. The gifts had been returned straightaway.

England's two newest earls, the Earl of Winchester and the Earl of Carlisle, girded as such during the York Parliament held the previous May, had also traveled to York. The Earl of Winchester—none other than Hugh the elder—had enjoyed the Christmas festivities well enough, but Andrew Harclay, created Earl of Carlisle owing to his victory at Boroughbridge, had left court in a fury, deciding that not enough was being done about the Scots, who had finally taken themselves out of England, having left a path of devastation behind. Concluding that the Scottish situation was intolerable, Harclay took it upon himself to negotiate with Bruce. They reached an agreement that was sound and sensible—and completely beyond Harclay's authority to enter into. Humiliated by Harclay's ad hoc efforts, and furious at the agreement's terms, which amounted to a recognition of Scottish independence, Edward had the Earl of Carlisle executed as a traitor in March 1323. Yet he himself had little choice but to seek a truce with the Scots now. Days after the unfortunate earl's execution, a temporary truce took effect. By the end of April, four English hostages—including Eleanor's son Hugh—had gone to stay at Tweedmouth while two Scots envoys journeyed to England for further negotiations with Hugh the younger, Pembroke, Robert Baldock, and the Bishop of Exeter. A month later, they had entered into a thirteen-year truce.

The Earl of Lancaster, meanwhile, had achieved a following in death that had eluded him in life. Edward had had him buried at Pontefract, where within six weeks, stories were being told of miracles being performed at his tomb there. His hat, it was discovered, could cure headaches, while his belt was protection against the dangers of childbirth. ("Well, yes, if the woman puts it around her privy parts so she can't get with child in the first place," Hugh said to Eleanor. "Maybe that was why Lancaster never begat children off of his countess.") Disgusted and worried, the king shut off the chapel to the public.

But it was not the queen's anger, or Elizabeth's lands, or Harclay's well-meant treason, or Lancaster's miracles on which Eleanor brooded as Hugh, fresh from a meeting with the king and humming over his latest plans for the Exchequer, parted the curtains and settled in bed beside her: It was her sister Margaret. Hugh d'Audley, her husband, had been spared his life because of Margaret's pleas to the king, but he remained a prisoner. Margaret herself had been sent to Sempringham Priory, albeit with a maid and two yeomen. In her incarceration, sadly, she was like dozens of other wives or widows of the men who had fought against the king. The nunneries and royal castles were bulging with them: Lady Badlesmere (now freed from the Tower, though her husband had been executed after Boroughbridge) at the Minorites without Aldgate and Lady Mortimer of Wigmore at Hampshire were just a couple. Some of their children had been sent to nunneries to live, some to royal castles; some stayed with their mothers; some had even been made royal wards and lived comfortably in the households of the king's children. But all were, in one form or fashion, prisoners.

"Hugh."

"What is it, sweetheart?"

"Can't you set Margaret free? She has been confined well over a year." It was August 1, 1323.

"*I* can't set people free, Eleanor. That is the king's prerogative."

These days the king's prerogative was also Hugh's. Eleanor shook her head impatiently. "You know full well you have the influence to do so, if you wished."

"Eleanor." Hugh's voice was even; Eleanor could not remember him ever raising it to her. "Have you forgotten that Audley devastated our lands—your lands? Killed and imprisoned our men? Where was Margaret in all this? Begging him to stop?"

"I know naught about what she said or did not say, Hugh, but neither then do you. For God's sake, Hugh! I am not asking that you make her rich again. Give her enough to live on comfortably and pleasantly, instead of being shut up in that nunnery—"

"Shut up? She has the run of the place, servants, plenty of company, her child by Audley." Margaret's daughter by Gaveston, Joan, remained at Amesbury with her aunt Mary, where she had spent almost of all of her life. "Interesting company, too. There's Princess Gwenllian."

Princess Gwenllian, daughter of the last Welsh ruler, had been sent to Sempringham as an infant and veiled a nun on the first Edward's orders after her father, Llywelyn ap Gruffydd, had been killed in battle and her uncle David, his brother, had been hanged, drawn, and quartered. A woman in her forties now, she had never left the convent. Eleanor shivered. Would Margaret grow old in Sempringham too? "Hugh, that is not amusing! Please, let her out!"

"No." Hugh's voice was quiet. "Not now. Perhaps at some point, yes, when she can be trusted. What is stopping her from sending messages or aid to Audley, if she goes free?"

Eleanor knew not what to answer. She sighed. Hugh, considering their conversation over and done with, kissed her and settled to sleep. Soon she heard him snoring faintly. He slept well at nights; it was Eleanor who had tossed and turned since Boroughbridge.

She slipped out of bed, as she was wont to do these nights when she had difficulty sleeping, and made her way to the nursery where her newest little girl, born a few months earlier, lay in her cradle at the king's manor at Cowick, where Hugh and Eleanor were staying. Unusually, Eleanor had been ill after her daughter's birth, and the king had paid his own physician to attend her. There was nothing, he had told her when she thanked him, that he would not do for her and Hugh and his dear father, and he did not appear to be exaggerating. Since Boroughbridge, Edward had let his favor for Hugh and his father be known in no uncertain terms. These days, the Despensers had so much land that Eleanor, at least, could barely keep track of it. Even little Gilbert had been the unknowing recipient of the reversions of several forfeited manors, with Eleanor as the life tenant.

The new baby herself had been sick more than her older brothers and sisters, and it had been decided to send her to live in a country priory. Soon she would be leaving for there in the grand style to which Hugh was quickly making them all become accustomed, with a nurse and a great household. Perhaps, Eleanor thought, that, not her sister's problems, was why she was melancholy tonight.

The baby stirred in her sleep when Eleanor bent over the cradle and kissed her. "Good night, Margaret," she whispered.

Eleanor and her baby were not the only restless ones that night. At the Tower of London, Roger Mortimer of Wigmore waited impatiently as his guards, drinking drugged wine to celebrate the feast day of St. Peter ad Vincula, the Tower's patron saint, sank one by one into stupors. His plan depended almost entirely on other people: the sublieutenant of the Tower, Gerald d'Alspaye, with his crowbar and rope ladder; the pepper merchant John de Gisors, with his boat and men waiting on the Thames to take him to Greenwich; four men waiting with horses at Greenwich; another merchant, Ralph de Bocton, who had made a boat ready at Porchester, then a ship at the Isle of Wright, bound for Normandy. If only one of them made the slightest misstep, he was done for, and he would undoubtedly be hung, drawn, and quartered. But if all went right...

Alspaye was digging with a crowbar now, and soon Roger could see a chink of light shining through his cell walls, then a larger one, then one large enough through which a man could fit. Sending one last prayer to St. Peter, he knelt and struggled out of his cell.

"That's Mortimer for you! With the Tower garrison dead drunk or drugged, does he give a thought to his old uncle in his cell? Not a bit. Leaves the old man to starve there."

"He's being fed well enough," said the king defensively. He and his chamberlain were supposedly hunting, but the huntsmen and the dogs had moved off in one direction, the king and Hugh in another. "I would not mistreat the old man."

"I daresay he could teach you a thing or two if he chose. Did you ever hear what happened in your father's time? Two little boys, set to inherit Powys, were put in his charge. They drowned, strangely enough, and to whom did your father grant the better part of their lands? Their guardian."

Edward nodded. "Yes, I remember hearing of that. I'm glad the nephew didn't take the uncle with him, in truth. One Mortimer on the loose is bad enough."

"We'll catch him," said Hugh soothingly. "Or the Irish will for us, and I'm sure there's some with grudges there."

"What shall we do with his wife?"

"Keep her where she is for now, in house arrest in Hampshire. From what I've heard, Mortimer isn't exactly uxorious, for all he's had a passel of children by the woman. Ten? Twelve? In any case, she breeds them well out of sight. I doubt that Mortimer's confided in her, if he even troubles himself to think of her."

Edward smiled. "Your wife troubled herself to think of her. She and the queen took the Exchequer to task for not paying her expenses promptly, did she ever tell you?"

"Ah, yes, my softhearted wife. When she heard that Mortimer had escaped, she said, 'Hugh, what about Lady Mortimer?'" Hugh shook his head tolerantly. "She told me about the letter; she said that she felt guilty going behind my back. God knows what she sneaks to the other traitors' widows and children."

"You've a sweet wife. I wish I were married to her, Hugh."

"Too late, Ned. She's mine, thanks to your father."

"And I have Isabella, thanks to my father."

"Shouldn't she be back from that pilgrimage of hers soon?"

"In the next few weeks. I'm not looking forward to it myself. I wonder if she still blames us for Tynemouth."

"Probably."

"I can never forget that she begged me to exile you, Hugh." Edward leaned over his horse and touched Hugh on the cheek. "After that it was all I could do to lie with her, and that only because I thought we should try for more sons." The king himself had been his father's fourth son, but the first two sons had predeceased Edward, while the third had died within months of Edward's birth. Edward sometimes wondered what life would have been like if one of his older brothers had lived to be king. "And I must keep on trying once she returns. But my heart just isn't in it."

"The issue here isn't your *heart*, Ned."

Edward laughed. Hugh, like Gaveston before him, could always make him do so. "Let's leave the hunt to the others, shall we, and go to my chamber."

"What is this latest I hear about France, Edward?" The queen was back with the king, who commented to Hugh later that pilgrimage had not improved her temper.

Edward sighed. "Come to my chamber, dear, and we shall discuss it. The Earl of Winchester and Lord Hugh and Lady Eleanor shall join us."

Isabella narrowed her eyes. "Lord Hugh is most familiar with this French business, my dear, and his presence will be most useful. So will that of the Earl of Winchester."

"And Lady Eleanor? Is her presence also necessary?"

Eleanor had herself been wondering about this, but Edward said coolly, "Lady Eleanor is my dear niece. Her presence is welcome to me anytime."

The queen shrugged elegantly and the five of them went to the king's chamber. "As you know, my dear, your brother has been asking me for some time to do homage to him—"

While the king had been battling his enemies in January 1322, death had dethroned yet another French king. Isabella's second brother, Philip, had been succeeded by her third brother, Charles. "Yes, and I must say, Edward, his patience has been tried sorely. He has been on the throne for nearly two years."

"There was that business with Lancaster, and then the business with Scotland, and—"

"Lancaster is dead, and the business with Scotland is settled. So what cause do you have for delay now?"

She was not looking at the king, however, but Hugh the younger. He, therefore, replied with a disarming smile, "You well know, your grace, that no English king relishes doing homage to France. Aside from it being disagreeable in itself, it is an expensive business, at a time the kingdom can ill afford it."

"You are very well versed in the feelings of English kings, my lord, almost as if you were one yourself. And your concern for the finances of England is commendable. I wonder that you can bring yourself to accept another forfeited estate, when each could be fattening the king's coffers."

"They have been somewhat the thinner lately for your grace's traveling about."

Eleanor sighed imperceptibly. Ever since the queen's return from pilgrimage about a month before, in October 1323, she and Hugh had been having these types of conversations, trading polite insults back and forth. The queen and Hugh could keep up these exchanges forever, except when someone intervened, as the Earl of Winchester did now.

"In any case," said the Earl of Winchester, "the king had every intention of fulfilling his obligation to your grace's brother. However, there have been complications since then. You know that Mortimer is being harbored in France."

"Yes, after so much time was wasted searching for him in Ireland."

Edward said stiffly, "My dear, most of his career has been based in Ireland, was it so unreasonable that we should have thought he would be there?"

"This is beside the point," the earl said. "He is in France now, and would be a danger to our king if the king were to go there. Indeed, he may have sent agents to procure the death of my son and myself."

Eleanor gasped.

"No need to worry, love," said Hugh. He walked over to Eleanor and kissed her quickly on the cheek. Isabella looked on balefully. Hugh straightened. "But I suppose what you are referring to, your grace, is this business in St. Sardos. Is that correct?"

"Yes."

"In Gascony?" asked Eleanor.

"In Gascony, my love. Fine wine country, as my lord father can testify from his enforced stay there." Hugh's eyes glittered at Isabella, but he continued, "There are plans to build a fortress there, which the French have no business building, but that's for another day. In any case, in the midst of construction, Raymond Bernard of Montpezat, one of the Gascon lords, led a group of armed men to the site and burned it down. In the process they hung a French official. Now Charles has hinted that our seneschal of Gascony, Ralph Basset, is implicated in this business."

"Was he?"

"He says not."

"I shall order an investigation," said Edward. "Surely that will satisfy your brother, Isabella?"

"Perhaps about the St. Sardos affair, but not about the homage."

"If Charles sends Roger Mortimer to me in chains, or without chains and without a head, then I will gladly pay him homage," said the king. "In the meantime, if he wishes to show him hospitality, he will have to do without my company."

Hugh frowned at a letter bearing the papal seal. "Well, this is all but useless."

"What is, dear one?"

Hugh read, "'In answer to your complaint that you are threatened by magical and secret dealings, it is recommended that you turn to God with your whole heart, and make a good confession and such satisfaction as shall be enjoined. No other remedies are necessary beyond a general indult.'" He tossed the letter aside. "One would expect more from the Pope."

"Are you still fretting about those men making wax images of us? Dear one, they will be dealt with."

Hugh sighed. Though he had cleverly managed to get William de Braose to bring a writ of novel disseisin against Elizabeth de Burgh for Gower, with the result that Gower had passed back to the hapless Braose, who had subsequently granted it to the Earl of Winchester, who had then granted it to Hugh himself, his pleasure in having even more of Wales in his hands had rather been diminished by the news that a group of men in Coventry had been making wax images of the king, Hugh, the Earl of Winchester, and several nobodies in an attempt to kill them by black magic. "But what if there are more of them?"

"Well, you hear the Pope. You must make your full confession."

"That would take a while," admitted Hugh. He shook his head, trying to erase from his mind the look in Eleanor's green eyes when she had heard that Elizabeth had lost Gower. Hugh managed to keep a good deal from his wife, but there inevitably were leaks. Still, she had seemed almost convinced when he explained to her that Braose had acted quite on his own and that much as Hugh would have liked to restore Gower to Elizabeth, it seemed best for the realm that it not be in hostile hands. After all, he had pointed out, Elizabeth might marry again.

"Marry! I think she is quite tired of marriage by now. After all, she never wanted to marry Damory, and what did that marriage bring her?"

"But she might be abducted, as she was by that fortune-hunter Theobald de Verdon."

"Theobald was no fortune-hunter. They were genuinely fond of each other."

They had bickered about this side issue for so long that Eleanor had forgotten all about Gower for the time being. He supposed once she remembered, he would have to satisfy her somehow. Perhaps he could rent Usk to the Prioress...

"Hugh?"

"I beg your pardon. I was distracted."

"See your confessor after you leave me. In the meantime, I think we have something more important to worry about. Do you think the queen is loyal to us in this business of France?"

Although Edward had, as promised, appointed commissioners to hold an inquiry into the St. Sardos affair, the French king had summoned several men, including Ralph Basset and Raymond Bernard, to appear before him. When they had failed to do so, they had been sentenced to have their possessions confiscated and they themselves banished from France. Edmund the Earl of Kent, the king's young brother, had been sent to France with others to try to ease the situation and through what seemed to be a natural aptitude for bungling things had succeeded only in making things worse. He was followed by the Earl of Pembroke. But in June 1324, as Pembroke was traveling toward Paris, news reached the English court that the aging earl had collapsed and died while on his way. Though negotiations went forward in his absence, the castle of Montpezat had been razed by the French, after which Edward in late July had ordered the arrest of all French subjects in England and the confiscation of their goods. Charles of Valois, the queen's uncle, had invaded Aquitaine, where the Earl of Kent had been appointed lieutenant.

Hugh mused. "She's done nothing to help our cause, that's for certain. But whether she'd hurt it, I don't know."

"I think we should confiscate her lands."

This sounded so much like something Hugh himself would have thought of that he started. Edward continued. "Confiscate her lands, at least for the time being, and give her an ample allowance in their stead. And I think an eye should be kept on what she writes, what goes in and out, and what she spends. And it is high time that the younger children were given their own households, away from her influence. It's not that she has much to do with them now; she hardly saw them during that endless pilgrimage of hers."

"In whose charge are they to be put?"

"What woman do I trust more than your wife? I will put the queen in her charge, and my son John. I was thinking of Ralph de Monthermer and your sister for the girls."

"It will anger her."

"What else can she expect? After all, she is French, and we are in a war with France. Perhaps it will give her some incentive to use her influence against Charles. And speaking of Charles, it will give him the idea that we are not to be trifled with."

"It does sound like a good idea," admitted Hugh, still a little vexed that he had not thought of it himself. But then, he and Edward had reached the point in their relationship that they could complete each other's sentences, so why wonder that they were thinking alike? "Shall I make the arrangements?"

"Yes, you and Bishop Stapeldon." Bishop Stapeldon, the Bishop of Exeter, was the royal treasurer. "But I suppose we also should consult your wife."

"You sent for me, Hugh?"

"Yes, sweetheart. Sit down while I finish this. It won't be long."

Eleanor sat on a window seat and listened to Hugh finish the letter he was dictating to a clerk. Never had she seen anyone thoroughly enjoy dictating a letter as much as Hugh did. He would settle back in his chair, feet upon a stool, and hold forth, measuring his words to the exact pace his clerk needed to keep up with him. He never fumbled for a word, never forgot what he had just said, never changed his mind and had his clerk cross something out. Eleanor loved to listen to him; so did the king.

As promised, it was not long before he finished. Dismissing the clerk with a breezy wave, he turned to Eleanor and smiled. "This is rather formal, my summoning you here, isn't it? But it is a matter that requires immediate attention. This French nonsense. It's an irritant, but I trust it shall soon be gotten over. The king and I, however, are concerned about the queen's role in all this. She has, after all, divided loyalties. Has she ever confided in you about this business?"

"She confides nothing to me, Hugh. We have had very little to say to each other since she begged for your exile. And there was not much intimacy between us for some time before that. But in truth, I do not think she would work against England, Hugh."

"Still, it would be well to ensure that nothing passes from her to France during this delicate situation. The king and I have a suggestion to put to you. How would you like to be her housekeeper?"

"Her housekeeper?"

"Look over her accounts, superintend her correspondence. Sit with her council at its meetings. Screen her visitors."

"Spy on her, you mean?"

"I doubt you could spy on her. As my wife, you are hardly likely to be a confidante of hers, and I doubt she would do anything to betray herself before you. But your presence would certainly hamper her ability to intrigue with her brother, if that's her game. It may not be. But she has done, after all, very little to help the situation with her brother."

"True."

"But now I suppose you will have scruples about doing what I have asked you to do. So this is all I can say: I do not think you would be acting merely to spite the queen, or to please the king and me. I think you would be acting for the good of England. And—"

"Hugh, there is no need for one of your speeches. I will do it."

"Eleanor?"

"I will do it because of what I mentioned just now. I cannot forget that the queen begged the king to send you and your father away, knowing what happened to Gaveston. I cannot forgive it. I should, and I have tried, but I cannot. And I remember that she blamed you and the king for Tynemouth, with no justification. So if there are to be sides taken, with you and the king on the one and the queen on the other, I will side with you and the king, and I will do what you and he feel needs to be done. To a point, of course."

"A point, my dear?"

"I will not act dishonorably to the queen. To that point."

"Well, of course not. The king and I would not ask you to do anything dishonorable. But there's more, my love. You are to be in charge of John of Eltham's household. Bella is to take charge of the girls. Young Edward, of course, will continue in his present arrangements."

Eleanor stared. "All this responsibility to me and Bella? Hugh, it is an honor, I suppose, but— The queen will despise all of us for it!"

"I don't see why she should. They are of an age to be in the own households anyway, being royal children. In any case, the queen will not be prevented from seeing them."

"Does Bella know of this?"

"I will write her straightaway. She will likely enjoy the company, poor thing, with Ralph de Monthermer's health failing."

Eleanor nodded sadly. Age was at last catching up with her debonair stepfather, whose gout sometimes kept him in bed for weeks at a time. Yes, the company of two lively little girls would indeed be welcome to Bella. "Does the queen know of this?"

"Her lands are to be confiscated," said Hugh dryly. "As I haven't heard shouts or heavy objects being thrown anywhere, probably not. The king and I will undertake that agreeable task shortly."

The queen, however, took the news with dignity, which should have been a warning to them all. "I am sorry you feel these measures are necessary, Edward, but I will abide by them."

"It is only until this business is over," said Edward, much relieved at her reasonableness. "And it is no slur upon you. I am merely anxious to protect against what your brother may try. Most of your lands are on the coast, and always vulnerable to attack."

"And without your knowledge, he may be using certain members of your household to gain information," put in Hugh. "Therefore, it is the wiser measure that my wife be your housekeeper."

"I can think of none better," said the queen. She gave Eleanor a smile so radiant that it must have hurt. "It will be like the old days, when Lady Despenser was one of my ladies in waiting."

"Indeed, your grace."

John of Eltham, who was now eight, seemed no less pleased with the new arrangements. He had always been fond of Lady Despenser, whom he considered a soft touch as far as sweetmeats were concerned.

Bella came to Porchester Castle in person to collect Joan and Eleanor, the king's young daughters, who were to go to Marlborough Castle in Wiltshire. She knelt to the king, whom she had seen but a few times, shyly. "Your grace."

"You need not be so formal, Lady Hastings. I shall be at Marlborough and the vicinity quite often to see my daughters, and you will soon be very used to my being around. Well, girls! Here is Lady Hastings. She is to superintend your household."

Eleanor and Joan, aged six and three, looked at Bella dubiously. "Papa says we are to move to Wiltshire with you," said Eleanor.

"Yes, my dear, you are. You are getting to be big, old enough to have a household of your own, because you are the eldest royal daughter, the greatest lady in the land save your mother. And your papa thought you and Joan would be happier together than apart, so she shall go with you."

"I will miss my papa and mama."

"Of course you will, sweet, but they will visit you very often, I warrant. And you will like my husband, Lord Monthermer. Did you know he can pull a shilling from his ear?"

"From his *ear*?" put in Joan.

"Lady Hastings is right," said Eleanor. "Lord Monthermer is my stepfather, Eleanor and Joan. He pulled many a shilling from his ear for my brother and sisters and me." Her eyes stung, as they did whenever she thought of her sisters, but she added, "I used to wonder that his head did not clank, so many were in there."

"Well, does it? Clank?"

"No," said Bella. "He walks very carefully so it will not."

Hugh, lounging in a window seat, said, "And there are more wonders in Wiltshire besides Lord Monthermer. My sister Lady Hastings will show you Stonehenge, I warrant. Have you heard of that? It's a wondrous strange place, these stones set side by side by no one knows who for no purpose that anyone can make out."

"Yes, we *will* go there."

Young Eleanor, however, was still thinking of Lord Monthermer. "I want to tell Mama about the shillings," she announced.

"Me, too!" Joan hurried off behind her younger sister.

Hugh laughed. "Well, Bella, you broke the ice with them fast enough! Speaking of Lord Monthermer, I hope he is better."

"No, Hugh, he is not. He grows worse every day."

"Ah, Bella, I am sorry."

"I know he is not a young man, but still it is hard to accept." Bella brushed her eyes. "But he can still pull a shilling from his ear, I am certain. He did it on our wedding night."

"On your wedding night, Bella?"

"He told me he wanted to show me he had yet another trick up his sleeve," said Bella with a smile and a blush.

The girls hurried in. "Lady Despenser, Mama wants you. She is getting ready to write some letters."

Eleanor suppressed a sigh. The queen's correspondence thus far had proven not to be treasonous, but very tedious. There did not appear to be a cleric in England who did not want some favor from the queen, and each had to be answered. She turned to a page. "Fetch me the queen's seal, please."

In January 1325 the court, stationed at Langley, received news of a death, though it was not, as it had anticipated, that of Ralph de Monthermer. It was

Joan, Margaret and Gaveston's thirteen-year-old daughter. A messenger had scarcely arrived from Edward's sister Mary at Amesbury, bearing news of the young girl's illness, when a second arrived bearing news of her death.

Professed as a nun as a child by her reluctant parents at the urging of the first Edward's strong-minded mother, who had wanted family to keep her company when she herself retired to Amesbury, Mary had managed to find an outlet for her thwarted maternal instincts nonetheless when her nieces and great-nieces had been sent to stay at the convent. First had come the Clare sisters, and later there had been Joan de Gaveston and Eleanor de Bohun, daughter of the king's sister Elizabeth. "I mourn her like a daughter," wrote Mary of Joan, and the king did not doubt her sincerity. Probably, the king thought, perhaps unfairly, the girl had received more love from her great-aunt Mary than she would have received had she stayed with Margaret.

The king himself had occasionally seen his great-niece. He had granted her and her cousin Eleanor a generous allowance and had arranged a marriage contract between Joan and John de Multon, a royal ward whose mother was a daughter of the Earl of Ulster and whose father had been the lord of Egremont. Edward had looked forward to having Piers's girl married in great style, as would have pleased her father, in a year or so. He had liked the idea, too, of watching England fill with Piers's grandchildren and their grandchildren, even if they would bear the name of Multon instead of Gaveston. But now this would never be, and his last link to Piers was gone forever.

He told this to Eleanor, for he felt a certain awkwardness about discussing Piers with Hugh, and if there had ever been a time where he could have confided his sorrows and joys to the queen, it had long since passed. Eleanor was silent for a long time, remembering her last long conversation with Piers Gaveston.

"Uncle, there is a secret I must tell you. I have kept it for a long, long time. It was Piers's. He had another child, a bastard, a girl named Amie. She is at Shaftesbury Abbey. I know she is still there, because I have written from time to time and sent money for little treats for her. Easter robes and such like."

"He asked you to do this?"

"No. He said nothing of the sort; it would have been admitting his fear. But he told me about Amie in confidence, not long before his death, and I knew later he did so in order that she might be looked after by someone just in case the worst happened. I thought of telling you at Margaret's wedding to Audley, but we were muddled in our heads a bit."

"But what do you know of this girl, Eleanor? Who is the mother?"

"I do not know, Uncle. Gaveston never said. He told me only that she was fathered while the two of you were—"

She blushed and turned away. The king said gently, "How old is she, Nelly?"

"Fourteen."

"Conceived in about 1310, then. Yes. Piers was acting a little oddly at times back then."

"He did not tell you because he thought it would grieve and anger you if you knew that he had been—unfaithful, I suppose—to you."

"Nothing he did ever angered me. I wish he had told me."

"Are you angry that I waited so long?"

"No. I am glad you told me now. Thank you, Nelly."

He embraced her. Because of the great difference in their heights, it was an awkward embrace, which was just as well. He pulled back and said, too briskly, "I think I shall send her to stay with Ralph and Bella, don't you think that would be a good idea? Bella would probably enjoy having a companion, and I daresay Shaftesbury Abbey will have educated her so that she will be most suitable to be around my little girls."

"I think that will be an excellent idea." Eleanor hesitated. "Sir, you will let my sister Margaret see Joan buried?"

"I don't see why not."

"And might you consider releasing her? She has been in Sempringham for nearly three years."

Edward shook his head. "No, Nelly. I cannot release her. There is too much mischief afoot, between the French and our enemies that they harbor, and she is a clever woman, with a grudge against me. God knows what use might be made of her." He looked at his niece's disappointed face. "But if you wish to visit her yourself I would have no objections."

"It would be of no use. She would not want to see me."

"I am sorry, Nelly."

She nodded and walked out of the king's chamber slowly. Only when she was halfway toward her own chamber did her tears begin to fall—for Margaret, for little Joan, or for herself, she did not know. Perhaps for all three.

In the queen's chamber at Westminster, where the court moved in February 1325, all was in its usual order—letters and petitions to be read in one pile, letters and petitions to be answered in another, letters and petitions to be shunted elsewhere in another. Hugh had shown Eleanor his own tidily efficient system, minus the coins that accompanied most petitions directed toward Hugh and went from thence into Hugh's purse. Despite this lack, Eleanor found the system a most satisfactory one.

Isabella arranged herself gracefully in front of a loom while Eleanor settled herself at her housekeeper's table. "Well, Lady Eleanor? As my allowance is only a pittance, most of these petitions should present no problem to you. You simply tell them no."

"Most do not ask for money."

"No, they ask for my good word with the king, which is quite useless these days, isn't it? Better they ask for yours."

Some, in fact, did, but Eleanor preferred not to let the queen know this. This did not prove as much of a problem as she had anticipated, however, for in Eleanor's early days as housekeeper, every attempt to involve Isabella in the work she was doing had been met with, "Dear, don't trouble yourself to consult me. You and the king and your husband are wise and just, I know, and you will treat each petition as it deserves, I am sure." Eleanor had even been left to select the fabric for the queen's New Year's livery on her own.

The first few petitions were from poor monasteries and nunneries. Eleanor would put them in a stack to be turned over to the queen's almoner. Next, several petitioners asked that their daughters, as good Englishwomen without a trace of French blood, be received into the queen's service. (Isabella's French attendants had been sent packing as part of the measures taken by Edward; evidently this was becoming common knowledge.) Eleanor would reply that the queen was amply attended but that the writers would be kept in mind should one of the queen's damsels marry or leave her service through some other means. One correspondent asked for nothing, but ranted that it was a pity that such a good lady as the queen had to be under the governance of the despicable Despenser family. Eleanor fed this parchment to the fire.

The next letter was rather more impressive than its predecessors. "Why, your grace, this is from Bishop Stratford. It is a fair copy of a letter he has written to the king. In it, he proposes that as the situation with France has reached a stalemate, the king consider sending you to France to negotiate with the French king your brother. He—"

"Let me read it for myself, Lady Despenser." Isabella snatched the letter out of Eleanor's unresisting hand, but there was nothing in it that Eleanor had not mentioned in her brief summary. She tossed it back in her housekeeper's general direction and studied her tapestry. "I shall await the decision of the king."

"So, Hugh? Shall we send her to France?"

"I don't know," said Hugh, moodily studying the companion letter to the one sitting on Eleanor's desk. "On the one hand, I'm not entirely certain that she would have our best interests at heart. On the other hand, she is Queen of England; all her prestige and power lies in that title. It's to her advantage to work for our own good. And she did do well enough when she went to France some years back."

"The year Jacques de Molay was burned to death. His curse has nearly come true, hasn't it? The king and two sons dead, and the third yet with no heir." Edward shook his head. "Interesting to see how that will work itself out."

"If we don't send her," said Hugh, "they are only going to pester us more about your going yourself."

"And that would not do," said the king. Hugh himself was persona non grata in France, and what might happen to Hugh, left alone in England, if the king went to France? He was too unpopular. Edward could see this, but seeing and caring were two different things entirely. He touched Hugh's hand. "Leave you here, dear one? Never." He frowned. "Hugh, you don't think Mortimer would harm the queen if she were to go to France, do you? I'll not have her dishonored, for all we've grown apart."

"I doubt it. He is living off the lands his son holds in France. It's not to his advantage to alienate Charles by harming his sister in any way."

"True," said Edward. "Well, shall we put this before the council?"

The council was agreeable, the king's envoys to France were agreeable, the Pope was agreeable, the queen was agreeable, Charles was agreeable. Only one man in England had misgivings over Isabella's departure: the prior of Christchurch, Canterbury, Henry Eastry. Isabella dined with him on her way to Dover in March 1325. "Do you hunt, Prior Eastry?"

"On occasion."

"I have been in a quandary about what to do with my dogs and huntsmen, Prior Eastry. My greyhounds are high-strung, and do not travel well. And I doubt I shall have time to hunt when I am in France. Might I leave them here with you for a time?"

"Your grace—"

"It shall be but a short time, I am sure. And"—Isabella smiled broadly—"I am certain that Edward and Lord Hugh le Despenser will take care of any unforeseen expense. Indeed, I would leave you money to provide for them in advance, but as you know I am in very reduced circumstances."

"That is a pity," said Prior Eastry. He frowned as Isabella lifted a hand to wipe a tear from her eye. "Of course, your grace, I will take the dogs."

"And the huntsmen. They are of no use to me without the dogs."

"Of course," said Prior Eastry gloomily. The next morning, after his royal guest had gone on her way, he dictated a letter to his friend Archbishop Reynolds, though it was hard to be heard over all of the yapping of the greyhounds. "It would be better in my opinion—do they never fall silent?—if the queen—wretched beasts!—were given back her lands and French servants before she departed England. Otherwise—surely they can't be hungry again—I fear that some misfortune may arise out of her natural resentment. Well, feed them!"

CHAPTER 15

▼

APRIL 1325 TO SEPTEMBER 1325

Margaret d'Audley said thoughtfully, "I might get spoiled by this traveling your sweet husband and uncle have allowed me, Eleanor. One trip for my daughter's death and another for my stepfather's. I wonder who shall be the lucky person who next gives me an occasion to leave Sempringham?"

"Margaret, I told you. I have tried to persuade the king to let you out, and I will keep doing everything in my power to get you out."

"Your power is rather laughable, isn't it, dear? And then the king had such a nice surprise for me when I came here. Gaveston's bastard brat, Amie!"

"She seems very pleasant," said Elizabeth quietly. Unlike Margaret, she had directed no venom toward Eleanor upon finding her at Marlborough Castle, where Bella had summoned them to attend their dying stepfather. Eleanor almost wished that Elizabeth would take a turn at insulting her. Her polite reserve was more unnerving than Margaret's open hostility.

Gaveston, however, had temporarily eclipsed Eleanor in Margaret's enmity. "To think that all that time he was pretending devotion to me, he was canoodling with some whore!"

"Ah, Margaret, it was not like that. You were very dear to Gaveston. He told me so, and that he felt guilty about his relations with Amie's mother. And all men are unfaithful at times, I think. It is their nature." Loyalty made Eleanor add, "Although I don't think Hugh has ever been."

Margaret stared. "You do not think Hugh has ever been unfaithful to you?"

"No—why should I? I have never seen the least sign of another woman."

Margaret turned her stare to Elizabeth. "Good God, Elizabeth, she is more of a fool than I ever thought possible. Can it truly be—"

"Ladies!" A servant ran into the chamber where the sisters were standing. "Hurry. It is the end."

"He was conscious just long enough to give you all his love, and to hope that you return to harmony with each other," said Bella. Eleanor smiled wanly, thinking of her stepfather's words when she and her sisters had entered the sickroom. "It is good to see the three of you together again," Ralph had said. "Though I would much rather not have been the cause of your reuniting."

Bella, making an obvious effort to keep her composure, continued. "He is to buried in Salisbury, at the Grey Friars' house."

"Not with our mother?" said Margaret suspiciously.

"He requested Salisbury and the Grey Friars in his will, my lady." Bella brushed at her eyes. "He always had a special fondness for that order. I hope you will be able to attend his funeral."

"No," said Margaret. "I must return back to my *home*."

"And my children will be missing me," said Elizabeth.

"As you wish," said Bella. She said, more to herself than anyone else, "It shall be a simple tomb and a simple funeral, anyway. Ralph never did like a lot of pomp."

She began to weep. Eleanor put an arm around her. "Come, Bella. You are exhausted. You need to rest. I will take you to your chamber."

Bella obeyed. Soon she was seated in a warm bath, where she sipped wine while Amie braided the hair that Ralph had enjoyed so much. "I suppose they are leaving because Hugh and Papa will be at the funeral. Am I right, Nelly?"

"Yes, Bella."

"I am sorry for it, but I want them there."

"Of course you do, Bella."

"Ralph did not entirely approve of Hugh, I think, but he would never hear him ill-spoken of in my presence."

She sighed and let Amie and Eleanor help her out of the washtub. They slipped a smock over her head and helped her into her bed, where the sleeping aid that Eleanor had judiciously laced the wine with soon took effect. "My poor lady," said Amie. "She loved him very much, didn't she?"

"Yes, Amie."

"Better than her other husbands?" Amie had inherited her father's dark hair and eyes, though she was merely pretty, not overwhelmingly good-looking as he had been. She had also inherited, Eleanor had found, her father's famed tactlessness. But there was no malice in her.

"I think Bella loved all three of her husbands, Amie. She has the gift of loving. But Ralph was her own choice, whereas the others were picked out for her by her father, so perhaps her love for him went a little deeper."

"Your husband was picked out for you by your mother, Lady Hastings told me, and by the former king. But she told me you love him very dearly too."

"I do, Amie."

"So does Lady Hastings, I know. But why do so many dislike him? I have heard that my father was disliked in the same way. It is why I ask."

"Your father was very close to the king, Amie, as my husband is now, and that always breeds jealousy. And the king is a generous man. He was generous to your father—he even made him an earl—and he has been most generous to my husband. That also has led to envy and malice."

"So that is why your sisters are so cool to you and Lady Hastings," said Amie thoughtfully.

Eleanor's innate honesty surfaced. "It is not only that, Amie. My sister Elizabeth and my husband had some land dealings that were not satisfactory to her, and there were disputes between my husband and Margaret's husband over their lands in Wales. And, of course, Margaret is still required to stay in Sempringham, and her husband is still a prisoner. It has not been easy for them. I'll hear of nothing against them."

"Of course, my lady." Amie hoped that Lady Despenser would say more about her rather scandalous husband, but Eleanor instead rose and headed toward the wardrobe. "Has Lady Hastings enough black robes from her last husband's death, Amie? If not, we must have more dyed or made for her."

"Thought about my proposals, Lady Comyn?"

"Your threats, you mean, Lord Despenser?"

Hugh shrugged. "Call them what you wish, it all ends with Goodrich Castle and Painswick." He settled into a window seat. "Option one is, you marry my eldest son."

"That puppy!" Elizabeth Comyn, niece of the late Earl of Pembroke, was a good eight or nine years older than Hugh's son. "I'll not marry a seventeen-year-old boy."

"Why not? He's a brave lad, very agreeable, and good-looking to boot, in my opinion. And he'll inherit my father's estates, my own, and my wife's Clare estates. But have it your way. Now let us reflect on option two. You sign over Goodrich and Painswick, see no more of me, and enjoy an inheritance which is still substantially more than it would have been had I not exerted myself on your behalf and that of little Laurence de Hastings. Really, I think of Goodrich and Painswick as a commission of sorts. You didn't complain, after all, when the division favored you and Laurence over Pembroke's other heirs."

"And what happens to my cousin Laurence de Hastings?"

"He will be contracted to my daughter Nora. They're alike in age, and my wife reports that they are already quite fond of each other. It should be a happy marriage. Still not too late to say yes to option one, Lady Comyn."

"Is there an option three?"

"Of course. You remain here, at my pleasure. It's a comfortable enough life."

Elizabeth looked around at her chamber in Pirbright manor, the Despenser property in which she had resided for some time after the death of Pembroke. Hugh indeed kept her there comfortably—she had servants, and ladies, and ample provisions and furnishings—but she was not free to leave, and she knew it. "I will make a decision shortly."

"I won't rush you," said Hugh, who was unfailingly polite to Elizabeth and those similarly situated ladies he visited in person. He never raised his voice, never used vulgar language, never menaced them sexually. He even brought gifts, usually venison or sturgeon, when he paid his calls. "There is plenty of time."

Lady Comyn watched Hugh as he bowed and headed toward the door of her chamber. "Just how much does your wife know of these options of yours, Lord Despenser?"

Hugh's eyes widened and his mouth tightened, and for a moment Lady Comyn feared something more than losing her land. Then his face relaxed.

"Very little," he said, turning on his heel. "If I were you, though, Lady Comyn, I wouldn't unburden yourself to her. I would strongly advise that."

While Elizabeth Comyn was mulling over her options—by late April, she had chosen option two and conveyed Goodrich Castle and Painswick to Hugh le Despenser and his father, with Hugh graciously sending a clerk to her to sign the necessary papers—the queen was residing in Paris at the palace of the Bois de

Vincentz, where, between her own funds and the gifts given to her by Charles, she lived as comfortably as one could during Lent, when each dinner featured a fish of some sort or another. Her pleasure in her new residence increased even further by the end of April, when she was joined by her good friend Joan of Bar, Countess of Surrey.

Unwanted by her husband, who had tried every legal means to get shed of her, Joan, after some initial bitterness, had accepted this situation graciously and had determined to enjoy herself thoroughly on the ample allowance the Earl of Surrey was forced by honor to give her. Untouched by the troubles that had plagued Edward's reign, she nonetheless found England a rather dreary place and had spent much of the last few years in France. She had been delighted to find her friend the queen there, *sans* Edward. Isabella, who did not trust most of the people in her household, all of whom had been screened most carefully by Edward and Hugh, dismissed her ladies and settled down for a pleasant gossip with Joan.

"I hear you have been hard at work, your grace. Have you and Charles reached an agreement?"

Isabella nodded. "Of sorts, but how it will go is anyone's guess. My brother still wants the king to perform homage."

"And will he?"

"Not if Nephew Hugh has his way." The queen was quite right; only days before, Hugh had informed the king's council that anyone who advised the king to go to France was a fool or a traitor. Not surprisingly, the council members had not been free with their opinions after that. "And he will, and all my trouble here will have been for nothing. Though I have had a pleasant time of it here at least." She glanced at the exquisite embroidery on her robes, paid for by her brother. "Charles keeps me most comfortably, unlike my husband and his dear nephew."

"I don't see how you have endured it, dear. Shall you be going back soon? For your sake, I hope not."

The queen shook her head. "My letter will have not yet reached the king, and once he gets it, he and dear Nephew Hugh will have to discuss it, and then Edward's council and Parliament will no doubt discuss it, and then Hugh will talk Edward out of anything that the council and Parliament have decided, and so forth. It could take months." She yawned. "Though I miss my children, it is good to be at home."

"Have you seen many of our countrymen here?"

"The Earl of Pembroke's wife—Hugh has been holding up her dower, needless to say. Fortunately, she has lands here on which she can stay. The Bishop of

Norwich and the Earl of Richmond. And Roger Mortimer has been pressing me to meet with him."

"Roger Mortimer! The escapee from the Tower? Surely you do not intend to see him. The king would be furious."

"I don't know if I will see him or not," said the queen. "In any case, he is not here; he is in Hainault, for Edward would not agree to send me here if he were at the court. But he writes to Charles regularly, and Charles tells me that he wishes to see me alone, outside Paris."

"He can only mean bad news for you. Don't see him, darling."

"I will make that decision myself," said Isabella loftily. She had seen Mortimer but twice that she could recall, after the Bannock Burn and from a distance when he had been hauled to the Tower, but his good looks, admixtured with a hint of menace, were the sort that appealed to her. "He has one merit; he is the enemy of the Despensers. Joan, do you know the half of what they have done? After Boroughbridge, they detained William de Braose's widowed daughter in prison until she signed over her reversion to the Earl of Winchester. Nephew Hugh imprisoned Lancaster's wife at York until she surrendered most of her inheritance. Mother of God, the poor woman was separated from Lancaster! She had nothing to do with his rebellion, if you may call it that. Lady Burgh has lost her Welsh lands to Despenser. Margaret d'Audley remains at Sempringham. The Countess of Pembroke I told you about just now. And these are just the noble ladies one hears about. God knows what has happened to those at a lower level. And he has even forced the Earl of Norfolk, the king's own brother Thomas, to sell him the lordship of Chepstow at a ridiculously low price!"

"Does the Earl of Winchester have no influence over his son? I always thought of him as a honorable enough man."

"The Earl of Winchester wouldn't stop him if he could; since the destruction of his lands and his exile, he has changed. And Hugh's no fool; much of what he does appears on paper to be quite legal. I knew not the half of it before I came here and heard from men such as the Bishop of Winchester what was going on."

"Surely the king must see the danger in all of this."

"The king! Hugh le Despenser helped him revenge himself on the men who killed Gaveston, and he has become Edward's lover. For those two reasons, the king will neither see the danger nor do anything about it if he did see it. Don't look so shocked, Joan. It has become common knowledge that the king and Nephew Hugh are sodomites. Pages do talk. Only one adult person in England seems unaware of it, and that is Hugh's fool of a wife."

"Your grace! Lady Despenser is my cousin."

"And my niece by marriage, and a fool. She has been besotted with Hugh since the day she married him, and always will be. No one would dream of telling her the truth about him, and she would not believe anyone if he did tell her. After all, she bears Despenser's brats regularly; in her last letter to me about my son John she mentioned that there is another on the way. As if I cared!"

"First Gaveston, and now Hugh le Despenser. You have borne this nobly, darling."

"Oh, don't mistake the situation, Joan. Edward has never shunned my bed, and at least his exploits out of it won't produce a string of bastards to be given lands and titles. I was willing enough to overlook his perversity. But when Hugh le Despenser seized my lands, dismissed my own servants..."

"But are not the lands in the king's hands?"

"Yes, and whatever goes to the king goes to Hugh, directly or indirectly. He is waxing fat now. But someday..."

She got up and gazed out the window. "Roger Mortimer has the right idea. He knows that there will be no good government in England until the Despensers are separated from the king. And he is willing to risk all to make that happen."

"Your grace, how do you know this?"

"Because, Joan dear, he has told me so. Through my brother."

"And how does he plan to separate them from the king?"

"That," said Isabella coolly, "he has not decided upon yet."

Seventeen-year-old Hugh le Despenser, his first cousin Hugh de Hastings, and his young uncle Edward de Monthermer watched the breakers from the ramparts of Dover Castle, to which they had taken their dice and their boredom on a hot August afternoon. "Think this will be the day?" asked Hastings.

The three young men, along with many others, were awaiting the king, with whom they were to sail for France, for Edward, rather to the surprise of Isabella, had agreed to pay homage to Charles. While his would-be entourage had gathered at Dover Castle, and an advance party had headed to France, the king had settled at the nearby monastery of Langdon.

"I hope so, because I can't afford to lose any more money at dicing," said Monthermer. "What do you think, Despenser? Will he go or back out? What does your father advise?"

Hugh le Despenser winced, for he was always uncomfortable when the subject turned to his father, even in sympathetic company like that of Hastings and Monthermer. He loved his father and enjoyed spending time with him, but he had been in the wider world too long not to know that his father was disliked and that there was some justification for it. How much Hugh did not know, for his father was no more forthcoming about his darker activities with his eldest son than he was with his wife. "I've no idea," he said a bit irritably. "Father doesn't discuss the king's business with me, nor should he."

Hastings, who as nephew to Hugh le Despenser the younger and grandson to Hugh le Despenser the elder also had ambivalent feelings toward his relations, understood his cousin's discomfiture. Quickly, he said, "I'm in no hurry to go to France anyway, for I've a bride to meet. Did I tell you, Hugh? My mother has arranged with the king to purchase the wardship of Margery Foliot. Edward here already knows; he stood surety for Mother. Margery's quite pretty, I hear, and will bring Elsing manor with her. She has been a ward of the crown and staying in the Tower, but soon she will be coming to live with my mother at Marlborough, and then I shall see her. But I can't marry her until next year. Mother says she needs time to develop."

"Or you do," said Edward amiably. "Get that tavern maid you are always going on about to show you some things before your wedding night, will you, please? Or otherwise it will be a sad occasion."

"I don't go on about that tavern maid!"

Despenser consulted an imaginary memoranda book. "First of August, 1325. Went to Black Chicken. Saw tavern maid; mentioned her to friends. Second of August, 1325. Spoke to tavern maid; mentioned her to friends. Third of August. Tavern maid talking to blacksmith. Greatly cast down; mentioned her to friends. Fourth of August. Tavern maid accepted hair ribbon. Elated; mentioned her to friends. Fifth of August—"

"Well," said Hastings mildly, "she is a natural blonde."

Despenser's page hurried toward them. "Beg pardon, sir, but a messenger just arrived downstairs. The king has changed his mind. He will not be going to France."

"Why?"

"He says he is ill, sir."

Not a person at court could ever remember having seen the king ill; he did not even have head colds. As the friends glanced at each other, the page added, "I hear that he will be sending his son Edward in his place."

"You wished to see me, sir, and I have agreed. But I am rather surprised at your coming to Paris, when you are not supposed to be in France at all."

Roger Mortimer smiled at the queen. "As some who are supposed to be in France are not in France, perhaps that is an excuse, your grace?"

"Perhaps. What is your business with me?"

"I shall get to that. Tell me, your grace, now that your son Edward will be coming to France as Duke of Aquitaine, what shall you do after he pays his homage?"

"Why, return to England, what else?"

"Yet you have tarried here long enough this summer."

"I have expected all of this time to be joined by my husband, sir. And I might have been needed for other negotiations."

Mortimer laughed. "The truth is, your grace, you've been in no hurry to return home. And who blames you? Not I. What, after all, have you to return to? A husband who can't win a war, who can't command the respect of his barons, who is fair game for any man willing to bed him."

"How dare you speak of these things to me?"

"I dare quite a bit of things, as you shall see. And I only speak the truth, and you know it. But the list goes on. Your estates have been seized, your servants banished, yourself put into the keeping of Hugh le Despenser's little wife. Is that what you wish to return to, your grace? If so, you are a fool."

"You have overstepped your bounds, sir. Leave me."

"No, I won't." Mortimer took the queen by the wrist and looked straight into her eyes. "I know you are not a fool, and that is why I am here now. To offer you the chance of your lifetime."

"I do not understand you."

"In a matter of days, your son will be here. With him here, why should you come back to the king like a little lapdog returning to her master? Put conditions on your return. I'm sure you can think of one."

"That the Despensers leave the king."

"Excellent."

"But he will never agree to that."

"Probably not. But you have the heir to his kingdom with you, don't you? One king can be put down, another brought up. It's that simple, your grace."

Isabella started. "You mean the king—an anointed of God—should be deposed?"

"Only as a last resort."

"Last resort, first resort—that is outrageous!"

"No," said Mortimer. "*This* is outrageous." He tilted the queen's chin upward and kissed her.

CHAPTER 16

▼

OCTOBER 1325 TO OCTOBER 1326

Gladys did not know whether to look up, down, or around first as she entered the chamber in Sheen Palace that had been allotted to Eleanor. Up, the ceiling was painted a brilliant blue that the English sky only occasionally attained. Down, the floor was covered in carpet so thick and soft that walking on it took a bit more effort than usual. Around, there were the goldfinches—forty-seven of them, Gladys later counted—singing a greeting to the ladies as they stepped into the chamber. "My lady, this is fit for a queen!"

Eleanor, though no stranger to luxury, was equally taken aback. "My uncle told me that there would be a pretty chamber for me, but I was hardly expecting this." She looked at the bed, where several bolts of cloth in Eleanor's favorite greens and blues lay, begging to be made into robes, and on a table, where a romance, fresh from the hands of the illuminator, rested.

"Well, if Isabella knew what quarters the king was giving you, she'd be home in a trice to boot you out," Gladys said dryly. "When is she returning home, anyway?"

Eleanor shook her head. "Young Edward did his homage several weeks ago, and the French king said he was satisfied. There is no reason for her to be tarrying there. But I suppose Edward might want to travel around there a bit. After all, he is half French, and has never seen the land."

"Why'd he want to see it, I don't know," said Gladys, like a good English-woman. "There's plenty of England for him to see."

"There is no accounting for tastes," Eleanor said dryly. She stretched out on the bed contentedly and smiled as the babe she carried within her, due in December, gave a sharp kick.

The king and Hugh came to visit Eleanor and her charge John of Eltham a few days at Sheen, then moved on to the royal manor at Cippenham, near Slough, in late October. It was there one chilly morning, as the men lay together in Edward's chamber, the bed curtains drawn tight against intruders, that the knocking came, a knocking that was insistent yet so light that neither man could have guessed the fate for each that it portended. Finally, Edward yawned, "Enter."

A scrawny page spoke into the bed curtains—gossip had advised him never to pull at them, for one never knew whom one might find inside them. "Beg pardon, your grace, it is Bishop Stapeldon. He craves a word with you immediately."

"*Stapeldon*?" the king echoed. "Why, he should be in France! What is he doing here?"

"I don't know," admitted the page. "But he is here."

This point being unanswerable, the king dismissed the page. Hugh having retreated to the antechamber where he nominally had a bed, the king's valet and Hugh's valet set to work, and the bishop was ushered in shortly thereafter.

It was the bishop who could have used the attention of a valet, however. Walter Stapeldon's hair was untidy, his clothes travel-splattered—and he was not, the king suddenly realized, even wearing his normal attire. He looked like a traveling peddler whose business had hit a dry spell. "Sir, what is the matter here? Why have you returned from France with no warning? Where are your men? Why are you dressed as you are? Do the queen and Edward follow you?"

The king could have strung several more questions on to his bow, but Stapeldon held up his hand. "I know not how to tell you what I am to tell, your grace. I have been thinking, ever since I crossed the Channel, how to tell you it. So I will tell you it straight out. The queen has openly, publicly refused to return to England unless Lord Despenser is removed from court." Stapeldon glanced at Hugh's face, which was impassive. "Her exact words—*her* words, I emphasize— are that someone has come between your grace and herself, trying to break the marriage bond, and that she will not return until this intruder has been removed. She has even said that she will dress in mourning until she is avenged of this Pharisee, as she puts it."

"Which would be me?" inquired Hugh.

"Yes, my lord. And she has donned mourning robes, or at least a semblance thereof."

"Very becoming ones, no doubt."

"Rather, sir."

Hugh let out an expressive whistle.

The bishop said hesitantly, "This brings me to my next point. Your grace, you sent me there to watch over your son, I and Henry de Beaumont, and I must tell you why I have returned home without him, and in this poor garb. There were plots against my life, plots by Roger Mortimer's allies, that I learnt of from a person at the French court sympathetic to me as a man of the cloth. I have every reason to believe that if I had not fled at night, disguised in these clothes, I would be a dead man today."

"Why you, Bishop?" asked Hugh.

"Because of the role I played in expediting the seizure of the queen's land. Because I was regarded as a spy when I accompanied the king's son there. And because—I regret having to say this, sir—because I am associated with you." Hugh flinched, barely perceptibly, and Stapeldon drew a breath. "Your grace, there is worse to tell, and I fear the telling will anger you. But it must be said. The queen is allying herself with your enemies in France, with all those who have exiled themselves there following your victory at Boroughbridge. They swarm about her like so many bees. But she has allied herself with one man in particular. Roger Mortimer. She dines with him at table, accompanies him on the hunt, dances with him. Those things I have seen myself. And there are rumors—ones that I can neither credit nor discredit—that he has found his way into her chamber."

"Good Lord!" said Edward. "You are not telling us that they are lovers!"

"That is the rumor."

"Damn her soul if this is true," said Edward quietly. He paced around the room a couple of times, then wheeled on Stapeldon. "What of my son? Has she seduced my son away from me?"

Stapeldon shook his head. "I know not what your son thinks of all this. He is unusually reserved for a boy of his age, I have always thought, and our conversations have always been on trivialities or historical matters—he has always enjoyed hearing stories about your distinguished ancestors, your grace. He has never spoken on matters that concern the here and now. He was glad to see his mother, I can tell you—she is, after all, a most charming lady—and she welcomed him warmly. If she were able to appeal to a sense of chivalry within him by this widow business of hers, to convince him that she has been grievously wronged..."

He fell silent. Hugh finished the thought. "He might turn against the king. And the French might use this as a pretext to invade England."

Stapeldon nodded bleakly. All three men were silent for a time. Then Edward said briskly, "Let them plot and cavort in bed! The English people won't stand for an invasion by Charles's troops, nor will they stand for one led by a whoring Frenchwoman and her lover. Isabella and her brother and Mortimer are sadly mistaken if they think otherwise."

"I trust they are, your grace," the bishop said.

"Nay," said Edward confidently. "I know they are."

Though Eleanor would never have said so to the king, she disliked her quarters at Kenilworth Castle, where she and John of Eltham progressed in April 1326. It was not that the king had spared expenses in refurbishing Eleanor's chamber—he had not—or that any convenience was wanting. It was that Kenilworth, seized from the late Earl of Lancaster, in itself gave her a feeling of unease. Here, Lancaster had plotted and schemed against the king and Gaveston, then the king and her husband. Lying in bed at night, even when Hugh was in her company, especially when he was in her company, Eleanor could fancy that the earl's indignant ghost roamed the halls.

Her internal state of mind was not helped by the external state of affairs. Soon after Bishop Stapeldon's return to England, Edward had begun to deluge the queen with letters demanding, first graciously and later stridently, her return. England's bishops were also commanded to write to the queen. Though in his initial letters, the king had avoided any reference to Mortimer, deeming it prudent to give the queen the benefit of the doubt while the rumors of her conduct were unproven, there was soon little ground to disbelieve them. The king having cut off Isabella's allowance, most of her disgruntled household had returned to England at the end of November, bearing tales. On several occasions, a tousled-looking Mortimer had been seen emerging from the queen's chamber at the crack of dawn, and one of Mortimer's pages had been heard to boast of his master's royal conquest.

Whether the letters were friendly or unfriendly, whether they addressed Isabella as a pious daughter of the Church or implied that she was no more than Mortimer's whore, whether they came from king or bishop, they produced no effect upon the queen, who would say nothing more than that she feared to return to England because of Hugh le Despenser's presence there and that she would not budge from France until he was removed. Her three children in England had long ceased to ask Eleanor and Lady Hastings when she would be coming back.

Young Edward had also received letters from his father, stern but affectionate letters that simultaneously ordered and begged him to return home, with no better results than from those sent to his mother. There were even rumors that the queen and Mortimer had been negotiating with the Count of Hainault, a wealthy man who was also the lord of Holland and Zealand, for the marriage of one of his four amiable daughters with the thirteen-year-old Duke of Aquitaine. The king's wife and son were not the only members of the royal family digging in their heels. King Edward's younger half-brother Edmund, the Earl of Kent, who had bungled the St. Sardos affair so miserably, had married Roger Mortimer's cousin, Margaret Wake, in France. He too refused to return to England.

"What do you think, Hugh? Will the queen—or her brother Charles—invade England?"

The year before, Hugh's response would have been a breezy, "Nonsense!" Now he glanced at Eleanor and his newest son, John, and said only, "We are trying our best to prevent that."

Eleanor looked at the baby's thatch of whitish hair. "Hugh, even the Pope has advised you to retire from the court. Have you considered doing that? We could live comfortably—very comfortably—on our own lands, you know, and the king could visit us often. Would it be that bad?"

"Are the king and I to have Isabella dictate who shall serve the king?"

"Not Isabella, the *Pope*!"

"It all comes to the same thing," said Hugh, who had not quite forgiven the Pope for his lack of sympathy with regard to the black arts practiced against him.

"But England herself is in jeopardy, Hugh. Your children are in jeopardy; what do you think would happen if an invasion succeeded?"

"Succeeded! Eleanor, don't be absurd."

"Hugh, I love my uncle. I would give my very life for him. But he has not won a war, save at Boroughbridge, and that was due mainly to Harclay. He is not a military leader, and you know it."

"The English won't stand to be invaded by the French," said Hugh. "It is a matter of preparation, and the king is preparing for the worst."

"But Hugh, we have gotten off the subject. Can't you placate the queen a little by leaving the court? At least until she sees that you mean her no harm?"

Hugh started to make a sharp reply, then experienced one of those fits of conscience that occasionally afflicted him. Just a few weeks before, in the throes of one, he had offered Eleanor's sister Elizabeth some lands in compensation for those he had taken from her, and now, looking at the woman he had been married to nearly twenty years, he found that he could not lie to her. "It's not that simple, Eleanor. I can't just go away like that. The king needs me." He paused a long time. "And I need him. We love each other, Eleanor."

"Like David and Jonathan?"

"No, Eleanor. Like the king and Gaveston."

"I see."

John, who had been cradled in Eleanor's arms, rooted around with his mouth hopefully. Finding no waiting nipple, he began to whimper. Hugh rang a bell and John's wet nurse appeared in seconds. She sometimes nursed her charge in the presence of his parents, but seeing the expressions on their faces, she bowed and hurried to the nursery. When she was safely gone, Eleanor said, "Margaret implied as much when we were at Marlborough Castle together. I thought she meant you had women lovers, and I took it for pure spite. I should have known better."

"There's no other woman in my life but you. There's no other man in my life but the king."

"How tidy. How long has this been going on, Hugh?"

"About eight years."

"Eight years?"

"We tried to be discreet."

"You were that."

"Sweetheart, neither of us wanted to hurt you."

"But you have, haven't you?" She snorted and headed toward the door.

Edward, preparing for a spot of hunting and believing Hugh to be doing the same, was puzzled to hear that Lady Despenser wanted to speak to him urgently about John of Eltham's knightly training. They had spoken about the very subject the afternoon before. But it was not like his niece to bother him with trivial matters, so he bade his attendant to show her in, then agreed to her strange request that they be left alone.

"So, Nelly. You were concerned about my John?"

"No, Uncle. I have found out just now that you and my husband are lovers."

"I see. Have some wine, Nelly."

Eleanor took the cup he poured for her and drained it. "Another, please."

He complied. "Eleanor, I didn't mean to hurt you. Neither did Hugh. You were a scruple we both had to overcome, and should not have. But, of course, we did, and we will have to answer for it someday."

"You will give each other up?"

Edward shook his head. "No, Nelly." He stared out the window. "You probably heard from Gaveston that he and I gave each other up. Did you?" She nodded. "And what was his reward? Nine days in a dudgeon and then Blacklow Hill. No. I won't give Hugh up, not for you or for any man or any woman or God Himself."

"So be it. But Hugh comes with strings attached."

"Strings, Nelly?"

"Me."

She yanked off her headdress, letting her red curls fall past her waist, and unclasped her cloak. Beneath it, the king saw, she wore only a shift, so sheer that it revealed every outline of her body. He was still gaping at the shift when Eleanor shrugged and sent it slithering to the floor. "Christ almighty," he whispered.

"Edward," she muttered drowsily a few hours later. She stroked the golden hair on his chest, burnished by the light of the setting sun. "Edward, are you awake?"

He stirred and smiled. "Ned," he yawned.

"May I tell you something, Ned?"

"Anything."

"You won't remember this, but when I was little and you only in your teens, Gilbert and my sisters and I came to visit you at Langley. You had your boat, and I wanted so badly to ride in it, I could have cried. But I was shy, so timid that Mama was even thinking of giving me to God, like my aunt Mary. She thought I would never be able to assume the duties of a great lady like herself. I wasn't supposed to have heard of her plans for me, but I had anyway, and that made me all the more shy, because I was scared of being sent away. And that is when we came to visit you.

"Gilbert, of course, asked to get into the boat; he was never shy a day of his life, poor boy. But I didn't dare to ask for myself, because I knew all the women around me would disapprove, and you intimidated me so, with your muscles and height. So you helped Gilbert in, and got in yourself and then you looked at me back on the shore. 'Nelly? Would you like to come?' I don't think you'd ever spoken to me directly before; I was always hanging back, or always with my governess. Gilbert answered before I could get any words out. 'Nelly would like to come,' he said. 'But she's too shy to ask you, and besides, it isn't ladylike.'

"And then you looked at me and laughed. 'I am shy too, Nelly,' you said. 'And as for it being unladylike, I have been told I am too unkinglike too often to care whether you are acting like a lady. Come, sweetheart.' And then you stepped out and helped me in, and on that long ride—it seemed to last forever—you talked to me, and made me laugh, and I felt like a queen. I never was as shy as I had been, after I got out of that boat, and there never was any more talk of making me a nun." She swallowed hard. "I think it was then that I fell in love with you, quietly, so quietly that I did not know myself until today how much I loved you. And when Hugh told me he and you were lovers, I was angry at both of you, but I was also so jealous, that you had chosen him and not me." She rested her head against his shoulder. "So that is why I came here today."

"I've always had the gift of loving the wrong people," said the king ruefully. "First, when I was fifteen, there was my stepmother—a woman only a few years older than me! Thank the Lord I kept my infatuation to myself before it passed, though I've often wondered if my father didn't guess, and if that wasn't one of the reasons he disliked me so. Then there was Lucy, a peasant girl. Piers and Hugh, of course. And another, Nelly."

"Another?"

"For years, whenever I've made love to Isabella, it's your face I've pictured." He kissed her.

"I never knew."

"Don't you remember that time on the boat, after Margaret's wedding? I wanted you that night."

"I didn't know."

"It seemed best to leave the matter lie, but you intervened. Thank you, Nelly."

She felt tears come to her eyes. "But you know this cannot last. It would shame my children, shame Hugh. I cannot do that to them, Ned. I have been foolish and impulsive and wrong, but I am not so bad that I can brazen this out, day after day, and feel no guilt. We must end it today, just as I started it."

"Yes," he said quietly. "I think you are right." He smiled. "Hugh loves you dearly, Nelly. What he and I do makes no difference there."

"I know, and I love him. And I have never had a secret from him in my life."

"Doesn't everyone deserve to have one secret?"

"Mine will be that for a few hours, I loved the King of England, and it was the most beautiful few hours of my life."

She kissed him and started to get out of bed, but he stopped her. "Once more, for old times' sake, Nelly?"

Eleanor hesitated. Then she smiled and rolled back into his arms.

"So, Kent. You said you had news from your brother Thomas."

The Earl of Kent nodded and looked at a letter, which bore a date of July 1326. "Edward's been planning against an invasion. Thomas is to be put in charge of Essex and Hertfordshire and East Anglia—"

"If only that fool Edward knew!"

"Archbishop Reynolds—"

"Edward's play-acting bishop, God help him. Go on."

"Archbishop Reynolds and Ralph Basset are in charge of Kent. The Earl of Arundel will have Lincolnshire. Bishop Stapeldon is to array troops in Devon and Cornwall—"

"Stapeldon!" said Isabella. "I could spit when I hear that name."

"Old Despenser and Henry of Lancaster are to supervise the Midlands."

"Henry of Lancaster," said Mortimer thoughtfully. "How well can he be disposed toward the king? After all, he's never inherited his brother's estates."

The Earl of Kent shrugged. "Edward let him have the earldom of Leicester, but there was unpleasantness between them when Henry put a cross up to the Earl of Lancaster's memory. Leicester claimed that he was only concerned for the welfare of Lancaster's soul and that the Church prayed for even heretics and Jews. Edward seems to have dropped the matter after that."

Isabella frowned. "Of course, Henry was married to Maud, Nephew Hugh's older half-sister. That might work against us, although fortunately she's been dead for a while now."

"We shall just have to wait and see." Mortimer pulled the list out of Edmund's hand to scan the other names, ignoring the Earl of Kent's frown. Since allying himself with the queen, Mortimer had a tendency to forget that he himself was not of royal blood, particularly around Edmund, who was only twenty-five and who still smarted from his humiliation in Gascony. But it had been Edmund's doing that had secretly brought his brother Thomas to the queen's side, not Mortimer's, and it had been Edmund's efforts that were now bearing fruit in the form of this letter from Thomas. He had to resist the urge to snatch it back from Mortimer, who in any case had started laughing too hard to notice Kent's irritation. "'And our lord the king himself will make his way to the March of Wales to rouse the good and loyal men of that land and will punish the traitors'! Oh, yes, he'll rouse them—to our side, particularly if he has Nephew Hugh at his side, as he must be planning to, as this charming battle plan doesn't mention him elsewhere. Why, all of South Wales would love to see Despenser hang."

"You yourself are not too popular with the Welsh," Edmund reminded him quietly.

"But it is our queen and the Duke of Aquitaine who the people will be rallying round," said Mortimer coolly. He stood and stretched. "Time we repaid all of this preparation with an invasion, don't you think?"

"So what next?"

"I go to Hainault and put a fleet together." He turned to Isabella. "I thought of taking young Edward with me, so that he could ogle that Philippa girl he seems so taken with, but perhaps he's better off with you in Ponthieu. We don't want your fool husband persuading him to come back while your back is turned."

"I can manage my son quite well," said Isabella. "I am to go to Ponthieu?"

"Yes, and exercise your fatal charm to get us more men and cash, my darling." He glanced at the Earl of Kent, moodily toying with his brother's now-restored letter. "I would like you to assist me in Hainault, my lord."

Mollified by the respect in his voice, the earl agreed.

In days to come, Mortimer and Isabella would agree: God was on their side, for how could He have sent better weather? Their fleet of ninety-five ships, half of them small fishing vessels, was simply skipping over the Channel toward the Suffolk coast.

In their ships was an army of fifteen hundred men, many of them mercenaries, and an array of English expatriates. All but two of them were in a festive mood.

Joan of Bar's misery was purely physical; though she crossed the Channel quite often, each journey made her as seasick as her first. Young Edward, on the other hand, though he had not inherited his father's despicable taste for rowing, was every bit as much at ease aboard ship as the king. His misery was one of the mind. First, there was the sweet Philippa of Hainault. An objective onlooker could not call the plump, dark maiden beautiful, but Edward had never met a person so utterly comfortable to be around. The misgivings he had begun to have about his prolonged stay on the Continent had been instantly dispelled by the joyous news that his mother had arranged a marriage between the two of them, in return for the Count of Hainault's military help. But the count was no fool; he was not about to send his daughter to England until the queen's position was secure; and in any case a papal dispensation would have to be obtained because Edward and Philippa were cousins of a sort. So Philippa had stayed behind in Hainault.

Second, there was the king. Edward knew all too well that his father did not measure up to the kingly ideal set by his own father, the first Edward, and his great-grandfather, the second Henry. He was a blunderer, like his grandfather the third Henry. Yet Edward I, so the story went, had been loyal to his father Henry III, and had saved the crown for him from Simon de Montfort. Wasn't that the role Edward should be playing, the loyal son?

His mother had told him repeatedly that their mission was to remove the Despensers from the king's side, nothing more. After that, if the king agreed to certain conditions, all would be well. Only when Edward became too persistent about learning what the conditions were had the queen, her nose wrinkling, told him the truth about the relationship between the king and Hugh le Despenser. So deeply disgusted had Edward been at that point that he had thrown his father's last letter to him in the fire unread. How could the king look real men in the face? And yet, after a few days, Edward's loathing had faded a bit. He'd always felt at ease, loved, in his father's presence. How could he dislike someone who cared for him so much?

Third, there was Mortimer. In his more recent letters, the king had hinted darkly at some impropriety between his mother and Mortimer. Edward, especially after being told of his father's perversities, had shrugged this off; it was common for a weak king to accuse his queen of adultery if there was no other fault he could justly find with her. (Look at Louis and Eleanor of Aquitaine, he reminded himself.) But the desire that Philippa had awakened in him had made him more sensitive to the signs of it in others, and he had seen the looks his mother cast at Mortimer when she thought no one was watching. Well, no wonder, married to his father with his loathsome tastes. He would have to watch her, to make sure Mortimer did not take advantage of her vulnerability. For though Mortimer had very admirable traits—how many had escaped from the Tower of London?—and was never anything but deferential to Edward, the boy was not quite sure of him.

The Suffolk coast was now visible. Edward shook his head. Earlier that September, his father, in another of his harebrained schemes, had actually sent English ships to attack the coast of Normandy, evidently with the idea that the expected invasion would come from there. Good God, had the man never heard of false intelligence? Could he do nothing right? Surely Despenser with all of his tricks should have known better. Needless to say, the invasion had failed mightily, and whatever had become of the ships that had been sent limping back to England, they were not here in Suffolk. Neither were any others. The queen and her men would land entirely unopposed. God was with them, as his mother had said time and time again.

But for a fleeting moment, Edward wished He might have been with his father.

The queen landed on September 24, 1326, and progressed toward Bury St. Edmunds as if on pilgrimage, her shabby widow's weeds attracting almost universal sympathy and, more to the point, more armed men. At the abbey, she received her first windfall: eight hundred marks deposited there by the king's chief justice, Hervey de Staunton. As the king's chief justice could not be a friend of the queen, she promptly seized the money.

Isabella had sent a letter to the people of London beseeching their support, and though she had received no reply, it was becoming clear that whoever the Londoners were supporting, it was not the king. When Edward, now headquartered at the Tower, met with the city leaders to garner their support—though he was attempting himself to raise an army of nearly fifty thousand men, only a handful had responded—he was told only that they would support Edward against foreigners and traitors, which the queen and her son were certainly not, and that they would fight only if they were able to return home by sunset the next day.

Hugh had had much to say about the Londoners in the past few days, but his invective had worn itself out by the afternoon of October 1, when he climbed the winding stairs to the chamber that he and Eleanor shared. "Sweetheart," he said quietly. "The king has made a decision. He and I and Arundel and Chancellor Baldock are to go to Wales. Father and Hugh will accompany us. There we shall raise an army. You shall stay here with our children"—all of them, save for Isabel, who had finally gone to live with Richard Fitz Alan as his wife, had been brought to the Tower—"and John of Eltham. It will be safer for you here. The Tower's well fortified; I've seen to that. And the Bishop of Exeter will be here to help advise you, too."

"When shall I join you, Hugh?"

"Why, when the bitch is imprisoned, of course, which shall be soon. In the meantime, the Tower is in your charge, yours and the constable's. I know you'll keep it safe."

He was speaking as a man sleepwalking, and Eleanor was hearing him as in a dream. Hugh continued, "I've left the Tower well provisioned, in case you are besieged, and I've left you plenty of gold should you need it. But I am sure we will be back before you do."

Eleanor said in her half-asleep voice, "I shall help you pack what you need."

For the rest of the day, she rushed about superintending the packing of the three Hughs' clothes and bedding, leaving the men to worry about the armor and weapons. That being done, she wandered to the king's chamber, not in the idea that her services would be required there but in the hope that movement would keep her from thinking. She was let inside immediately, as she always was. A half-filled trunk sat near the wardrobe, and she picked up the black cap, powdered with butterflies and other beasts in white pearls, that lay on top, as if put there on impulse. She smiled in spite of herself. Only Edward himself, wonderful, foolish Ned, fleeing London to face an army of invaders, could still have made certain that his favorite cap was packed.

"Hugh."

Their preparations for the morning being done with, they had gone to bed early. Eleanor was all but coiled about Hugh. She could not bear to move away from him this night, even an inch.

"What, sweetheart?"

"I must tell you something, just—just—" Eleanor could not go on. What she had to tell was hard enough to say, but the prefatory words *just in case we do not see each other again* were impossible.

"Eleanor, is it about the king? That afternoon you and he shut yourselves up together?"

"Yes," she whispered. "Hugh, I—"

"He told me about it months ago, love."

"Hugh, I swear, we have not been together since, in that manner. I was so foolish. I do love you, truly. I—"

"I know, sweetheart. Edward knew you would tell eventually, and he wanted to spare you my anger, so he told me himself after we left Kenilworth. And I was angry for the time—very. But I cannot blame you for loving where I have loved myself, or him for loving you when I love you so much. We're a muddled bunch, aren't we, my dear?"

A lump was forming in her throat. "Yes, we certainly are."

"And soon this nonsense will be over and we shall be safe, to muddle our way through the rest of our lives together. You'll see. Now come, sweetheart. Let's give me a proper sendoff."

Not since the earliest days of their marriage had Hugh made love to her so tenderly, yet so passionately. Eleanor, tense and frightened, was slow to warm to him, but his touch finally aroused her and she was able to give herself over to him completely, feeling no emotions but love and desire. Afterward, they fell asleep for a while; then, without anything being said, they woke and made love again. Twice more they made love and slept, made love and slept, until, exhausted, they fell asleep in each other's arms and lay like that until dawn.

"Hugh! Are you here? We must leave now!"

It was the king himself who had barged into their chamber and was tugging on the bed curtains. Eleanor, not wearing so much as a sheet over her, grabbed for a coverlet frantically, but Hugh said good-naturedly, "You might have knocked, Ned."

"I beg your pardon, but we must go now."

Hugh shrugged and emerged from behind the bed curtains. He reached for his garments on the floor, not bothering to call for a servant.

"Nelly, you should be preparing to see us off. We cannot delay."

"I can hardly dress with you standing here," Eleanor snapped.

"True," admitted Edward. He sighed. "Hurry, the two of you."

With the king out of the room, Eleanor climbed out of bed. "Hugh, don't go."

"I have to, Eleanor. I explained."

"I know."

"You're making it no easier for me standing there without a stitch on. Get dressed, my dear."

She dressed and made a pretense of combing her hair. "I fear that I will never see you again," she blurted out.

"Nonsense." Hugh took her in his arms, and she realized as he did so that he too was having difficulty controlling his emotions. He held her a few minutes, then said quietly, "It will all be well, sweetheart, I promise. Come. Let me say goodbye to the children."

The younger children, used to Hugh's comings and goings, woke from sleep only long enough to be kissed goodbye before yawning and rolling back over, but Edward sat bolt upright in his bed. "Let me go with you, Father."

"No, Edward." Hugh ruffled his son's hair. "I need you to stay here with your mother and fend her suitors off while I am away. Like Penelope."

Edward did not laugh. "I am old enough."

"Not quite, Edward."

"But I am too old to be here with my little brothers."

"No," said Hugh again. "I must go, Edward. Come downstairs with us and see us off."

Grumbling, Edward followed, to soon be joined by a sleepy-eyed John of Eltham. If Eleanor had any hopes that all would be well, they vanished when she went down to the Tower's courtyard and saw her father-in-law amid the waiting carts. Edward wore the same look of desperate cheerfulness as Hugh, but the Earl of Winchester looked more like a man of ninety than a man of sixty-four. His eyes were hopeless when he said quietly, "Good-bye, daughter."

"Good-bye, sir." She embraced him and he patted her on the back in the way that Eleanor had learned long ago denoted deep attachment from her reserved father-in-law.

"Give the children my love for me. We may be gone awhile."

She fought back tears. "Yes."

Winchester saw his grandson, who in days would be twelve years old, and managed a smile. "Edward, when I return you shall have shot up another two inches, I'll wager."

Edward scowled. "Father won't let me go with you. He says I am too young."

"And so you are today, but when I come back you shall go live with me and be one of my squires. Should you like that?"

"Truly, Grandfather?"

"Truly. Now go say good-bye to your father. He will be hurt if you do not."

Edward, mollified, sprinted off in his father's direction as the old earl watched Eleanor embrace the king, then her son, then her husband. Sixty-one years ago Winchester's own mother, holding his very small self by the hand, had seen his own father off as he departed the Tower, leaving her in charge. Hugh would grudgingly admit that his memory was not what it used to be, but he had never forgotten the fine August day not long afterward when his pretty young mother, red-eyed and trembling, had snatched him and his sisters up and ridden as fast as she could to her father's house. There he learned that his father had been killed, slaughtered with the great Simon de Montfort and the rest of his followers, having loyally ignored Montfort's plea that he flee to save himself while he still could. There he learned that his mother as the wife of a traitor had nothing to live on, only what she could beg from her father, who had stayed faithful to the king. Crying as he huddled on a pallet hastily made up for him in his grandfather's small London house, listening as his mother sobbed herself to sleep, he'd wondered if he or anyone around him would ever be happy again.

Yet the good times had come back. His grandfather had treated them kindly, and in a few years his mother had remarried, no less a personage than the Earl of Norfolk. He'd been able to inherit all of his father's forfeited lands, had become wealthy in the service of the first Edward, wealthier still in the service of the second. He'd married his high-spirited, high-strung Isabel and had sons and daughters to make a man proud.

But he'd never been able to forget that scared little boy on the pallet.

"Time to set off, Father." Winchester started, and Hugh looked at him with concern. "Father, you look pale. Are you sure you are up to this? Perhaps you should stay with Eleanor—"

Winchester scowled and mounted his horse without assistance. "I don't need coddling, Hugh, thank you."

As the king and his entourage—a few men at arms, but mainly royal officials, clerks, and servants—passed through the Tower gate, Eleanor and Edward and John of Eltham waved goodbye and shouted out farewells. The city was awakening, and knots of people stood and watched as the royal party made its way west. No one cheered.

CHAPTER 17

▼

OCTOBER 1326

At the priory of St. Mary in Southwark, Hamo Hethe, Bishop of Rochester, leaned back and looked at the parchment in his hand. Signed by Queen Isabella, it put a price of two thousand pounds on Hugh le Despenser's head, double the amount that the king had placed on Mortimer's a few days before. Copies of the queen's offer had been placed around London, whose citizens had become so boisterous in their enthusiasm for the queen since the king's departure that Hethe, having come to the city for a meeting with the archbishop on October 13, had refused to cross the Thames. Archbishop Reynolds had obliged by moving the meeting to Southwark. Though the conference had been called some time ago to discuss routine church matters, the topic of the day could be none other than the king and the queen.

"I don't know what is to be done," said Bishop Stapeldon. He gestured with the odd devices, called spectacles, that a friend in Italy had sent him and that the bishop had warmed to immediately. Why every man over forty did not own a pair was beyond him. "Mediation? The Pope himself has failed. Compromise? The queen wants Despenser dead, the king wants Mortimer dead. I don't see any middle way there." He shook his head. "And what has the queen to gain from making peace at this point? No one has rallied to the king. And the Earl of Leicester has abandoned him. Instead of defending with the Earl of Winchester, as planned, he ambushed Winchester's man at Leicester Abbey and captured the warhorses and valuables the man was bringing to Winchester. Then he presented his booty to the queen. How can men be so inconstant?"

"One thing is constant in the world, Bishop Stapeldon. The world is an inconstant place."

Not a little pleased at this aphorism, Hethe was settling back, perhaps to deliver himself of another, when a large black dog ambled into the room. The Bishop of Rochester looked at the Bishop of Exeter. "Yours?"

"No. I've no dog."

"Well, look at him."

The dog had stopped to sniff Hethe's outstretched hand, but this had only slightly delayed its progress toward Stapeldon. Reaching the Bishop of Exeter's feet, he settled down at them, head contentedly on paws. Hethe laughed. "It seems you have a friend."

"It looks that way, doesn't it?" Stapeldon bent to scratch the mutt's ears, then stopped when he caught sight of the faces of his squires, William Walle and John de Padington. "What ails you?"

"'Tis an omen of ill," whispered William Walle.

Stapeldon, a man in his sixties, had lived too long to be particularly suspicious. "'Tis my meat, which I have not touched. Here." He began throwing scraps to the dog, but even after the food was gone, the beast remained at the bishop's feet.

Meanwhile, the king's party had split, the Earl of Winchester heading toward Bristol Castle, where the king's daughters were also staying. The king, Hugh the younger, and Hugh's son continued into Wales. On October 15, 1326, they were at Tintern Abbey. That was the day London, and Eleanor's world, exploded.

Even from his chamber in the Tower, where Edward le Despenser was attempting to conjugate some tricky Latin verbs, he could tell that something was afoot outside. People were running in and out of the courtyard below, and in the streets beyond the Tower, there seemed to be an unusual hum of activity.

He stood at the window, considering. If he told his tutor or his mother that he was going out alone to see what was happening, he would certainly be told not to go, for Bishop Hethe was not the only person worried about London these days. On the other hand, his father had instructed him to take care of his mother, and shouldn't his duty, logically, extend to making sure she was well informed? Besides, he had yet to get a satisfactory explanation from any adult as to why the king and his father were at war with the queen, and if the commotion outside had anything to do with their quarrel, it would be a chance, perhaps, for enlightenment.

Edward wished his brother Hugh was here, for he was a fount of information. It was Hugh who had done much to explain the mysterious, fascinating topic of Woman to him, and surely he would be equally informative on the subject of the Queen's Little Tantrum, as his father called it. If only they'd had a chance to talk before Hugh went away! But Hugh had been too busy the night before they left.

Making up his mind, he wrote a note (in Latin, as a sort of penance), stating that he had gone to take a walk, and left the chamber. As he headed toward the Tower gate, he heard a guard muttering something unintelligible about Hamo de Chigwell, the mayor of London. He also heard his own name called, but feigned that he had not, and hurried on.

Once he was outside of the Tower grounds, he remembered what he had heard about the mayor and decided to turn his steps in his direction. Just as he reached the Guildhall, he saw the crowd outside it turn in unison and rush down the twisting streets to Walbrook. The crowd contained almost every description of Londoner—rich merchants, small tradesmen, lawyers, physicians, barbers, clerks, craftsmen, bakers, butchers, servants, tavern keepers, apprentices, beggars, thieves—and it was armed with almost every sort of implement imaginable, from swords to clubs to bread knives.

With a shock, Edward recognized the handsome house they stopped at, for he had been there the previous June. It had been one of the happiest mornings of his life, one of those rare and special occasions when he and his father went out together, just the two of them. Their first stop had been the Smithfield horse market, where Edward, having solemnly listened to all of his father's lessons in what to look for in a horse, had walked round and round, sizing up all of the mounts for sale, until he had finally settled on a handsome chestnut with three white feet that he named Arthur on the spot. Then he and his father had ridden Arthur and Hugh's horse to this very house in Walbrook to dine with John le Marshal, who handled much of Hugh's London property for him. The men had mostly talked business while Edward sat quietly by his father's side, but John had remarked toward the end of the meal, "Fine lad you have there, Hugh. You must be proud of him."

Hugh had draped an arm over his shoulder. "Yes," he said, with none of the usual mocking tone that edged his conversation when he spoke to almost anyone besides his own family and the king, "I am, very much. He'll be a fine knight someday."

And now, at this house where Edward had received this ultimate in compliments from his father, the crowd was not waiting at the door, but was shoving its way in. Then the nightmare began. Screams and shouts, the sound of breaking glass and objects being thrown, and suddenly John le Marshal, his face bloodied, was being dragged out of the house, fighting fiercely but to no avail. Instinctively, Edward tried to push his way to help this servant of his father, but as a slight twelve-year-old with no weapon, there was nothing he could do; so far back was he, and so wild the crowd, his futile efforts to break through were not even noticed.

"Where shall we take him, Despenser's spy?"

"Cheapside!"

Roaring its approval, drowning out Marshal's curses, the mob ran to Cheapside, pushing Edward with it, and stopped at the great cross on Cheap. "What do we do with Despenser's spy, mates?"

"Kill him! For the queen!" called a rough voice.

"Kill him!" agreed the mob. "For the queen!"

"God keep her, Isabella the Fair!"

"Our queen!"

The men who had been dragging Marshal pinned him to the ground, and a man wearing a butcher's apron pushed forward and set a knife to Marshal's neck. After an endless interval, his dripping head was lifted into the hair, to cries of ecstasy.

Edward retched, again and again. Two boys, older than he by a few years, looked at him with amusement. "Soft, are you?"

"Mama's boy? Don't get out much?"

"Come on, mate! There's more fun to be had!"

The cry was going again. "Where to, mates?"

"Stapeldon's house! Despenser's bishop!"

"The bishop who took the queen's land!"

"Spied on her!"

"Get him!"

To Temple Bar the crowd ran, Edward being dragged along by his new acquaintances. But the bishop's doors were barred. The crowd groaned; then someone produced a torch. The bishop's doors were flaming, and then the crowd was in the bishop's house, some running from room to room in search of the bishop, others running from room to room grabbing any valuable they could lay their hands on. "Where is the traitor?"

"Not here!"

Edward's companions, goggle-eyed at the sight of a quantity of plate, suddenly released him, and Edward, forgotten, pushed his way out. Someone had to warn the bishop, but how? He had several houses in and around London, he could be in any of them, or in someone else's house. Then he remembered his mother mentioning that morning that Bishop Stapeldon had promised to look in on them that afternoon. So he might be riding to the Tower! Panting, he ran in that direction, but the mob, having carried off everything in sight worth carrying and torched what was not, was right behind him. Then the mob saw its quarry: the Bishop of Exeter.

Stapeldon saw the mob and galloped off in the direction of St. Paul's, followed by his two squires. When all that lay between him and sanctuary was one door, one damned door, the mob pounced. Stapeldon and one of his squires were dragged off their horses, through the streets, to Cheapside, to the great cross. There the awful chant went up again:

"What shall we do with him, mates? With Despenser's tool?"

"Kill him!"

"For the queen!"

But the butcher, having collected so much booty that he deemed it prudent to carry it home, had left, and it was a baker's apprentice who produced a bread knife. Edward, shoved near the forefront of the crowd, could hear the bishop's dying words, commending his spirit into the Lord's hands. He saw the head being raised, saw Stapeldon's squire being beheaded with less fanfare, heard the crowd bay in glee as the second squire, who had managed to get as far as London Bridge before being captured, was brought back and killed in like fashion.

"Where to now, mates?"

"Despenser's money! The House of Bardi!"

The crowd pressed on toward the great Florentine bankers' house, but this time Edward was able to get free. Somehow he stumbled alone toward the Tower, retching and crying.

"It is all true, what the boy said, Lady Despenser. Four men dead within an hour, and God knows what will follow. But they are just looting now, it seems."

Eleanor crouched in the constable's hall at the Tower, cradling Edward in her lap. He had been given a potion by the Tower physician and had at last fallen asleep in her arms after sobbing out a barely coherent account of the morning's events. "The poor child," she whispered. "The poor, poor child. To see what he saw. And if they had found out whose son he was..." She shivered, then composed herself and looked at John de Weston, the Tower constable. "They will be here next. Will they not?"

"It is only a matter of time. And Lady Despenser—your husband left the Tower well fortified. But some of our men deserted today. That armed crowd will outnumber us ten to one." He shook his head gloomily. "It can only get worse until they wear themselves out. The mayor and the responsible men of the city are powerless to stop the whoresons. This morning, before the murders, the mayor was taken to the Guildhall by force and made to kneel and swear an oath that he would stand with the city against all of its enemies. Others were made to swear the same oath. Archbishop Reynolds has fled the city, using Bishop Hethe's horses, they say. Poor Bishop Hethe has followed on foot. Justice Geoffrey le Scrope has left the city too. No one knows for sure where Bishop Stratford has gone, but they think he has gone to join the queen."

Eleanor said, "They won't hurt John of Eltham, surely, for the queen's sake. But the rest of us…" She looked at Edward in her arms, imagining him lying in the dirt at Cheapside with the others. "Let me put him to bed. Then I shall think what to do."

The next morning, an offshoot of the mob killed Stapeldon's treasurer at Holywell. Overnight, however, the mob had acquired a rather more organized, military quality, and it assembled and armed at Cornhill. From there, it marched to the Tower.

Save for the drugged Edward and Eleanor's youngest children, no one in the Tower had slept. Eleanor had spent the night in thought. With six young children of her own in tow, plus John of Eltham, she could hardly escape on land without attracting notice. She had considered an escape by boat, but this would require help, more help than Eleanor dared to ask of any man now. With escape not an alternative, there were only two choices: to resist or to surrender.

At dawn, she changed into her simplest gown, not wearing any jewelry but her wedding ring and a crucifix. Into her shift, and those of her ladies and ten-year-old Joan, she had sewn knives, ready to hand; in case someone tried to rape her or any of them, he would get an unpleasant surprise first. These preparations made, she waited. At about ten, the knock came. "You are still determined to do this, my lady?" asked Weston.

"Yes. I will not have any more good men dying if I can help it."

Her nerve nearly failed her once when she arrived at the gate and saw the crowd without, separated from her by only a few bars. It nearly failed her again when she was recognized. "Why, would you look here! It's the Lady Despenser. Ain't it?'

From the back someone called, "Two thousand pounds for her head, mates!"

"That's her husband, you fool. The lady's worth nothing."

"Not bad looking, though. She ought to be worth a pound or two, eh?"

"Give her a tumble and let us know!"

Eleanor's anger revived her flagging courage. "If there is someone here who can speak rationally, without stupid threats or taunts, I will speak to him. If not, there are enough archers in the Tower to shorten life for more than a few of you. It is up to you."

After a long pause, a rotund, expensively dressed man pushed forward. Eleanor recognized him as Benedict de Fulsham, a rich pepper merchant who also supplied wine to the court. He was shaped not unlike a pepper himself, Eleanor had often thought, and looked rather incongruous carrying a sword. "You may speak with me, my lady."

"Very well. What do you want?"

"The prisoners here released."

The prisoners. There were nearly a score of them, Eleanor knew. Roger Mortimer's sons, transferred to the Tower the day before the king had left the city. Llywelyn Bren's widow and her sons. Young men, most of them, knights or with knightly training, who would all be of use to the queen. But their release could hardly make things worse for the king, Eleanor thought. "What else?"

"The queen's younger son is here. Is he not?"

"He is here, and if anything happens to him all of you will answer to it on Judgment Day. And I think you have quite a bit to answer for already."

Benedict coughed. "We intend no harm to the boy, my lady. He must swear an oath of loyalty to the city, that is all. And he will be named its guardian, pending the arrival of the queen."

"Or the king," said Eleanor coolly. "Is that all you want?" Benedict nodded. "Very well. I will tell you my conditions. John of Eltham is in my charge, and shall remain here until one of his parents sends for him. You must guarantee his safety. And that of everyone else in here. Including my children and myself. And there shall be no looting here. You take your prisoners and leave."

Benedict stepped back and conferred with a group of respectable-looking men. At last, he stepped forward. "Agreed, my lady."

"Very well." She turned to the guards standing nearby. "Release the prisoners."

Bit by bit the prisoners began appearing, to the delight of the crowd. As each was let out, he was made by Benedict and the others to swear, on a relict someone had produced, the same oath that the mayor had sworn. She watched as they milled around, basking in the congratulations of the crowd and planning God only knew what.

"Where is the duke, my lady?"

"I will get him. Pray excuse me."

Slowly she climbed the stairs to John of Eltham's chamber. She and her charge had already spoken earlier that morning, and she was not required to give him a long explanation. Still, he balked. "Lady Despenser, I do not want to swear the oath. They say your family are the king's enemies! I can't swear to hurt you, my lady!"

"No one shall ask you to hurt me, John. Swear it, and it should soon be done with. The Lord will know that you acted under duress, and understand."

John's eyes were full of worry, but he at last shrugged. "All right. I'll do it."

Eleanor watched as the ten-year-old boy, standing on a crate someone put up for him, swore to uphold the liberties of the city and to ally with it in its great mission to destroy the enemies of the queen. Only when the mob, stronger by the addition of the Tower's prisoners, had dispersed did she sink to the cobblestones, weeping.

In her chamber at Gloucester Castle, Queen Isabella was having a splendidly royal tantrum, and it was not because the castle was in rather poor repair. It was because of what sat near the entrance to the chamber: a basket containing the Bishop of Exeter's head, a present from the Londoners that had just arrived by a fast-riding messenger. "Those fools! Do they not know how they are jeopardizing our cause? All our work, all of our planning and now—this!"

"Now," said Adam de Orleton, Bishop of Hereford, suavely, "let's not panic. Really, your grace, I doubt that his death will be held against you. Rather, it will be said that it is the king's lamentable misgovernance that has brought our great city of London to this pass." Orleton paused and added rather smugly, "And it cannot be denied that he *was* unpopular as a tool of the Despensers, your grace."

Bishop Orleton himself had had a hard time of it in England since Borough-bridge, for Edward had suspected him of sympathizing with his leading parishioner, Roger Mortimer, and later at conniving at his escape. Brought to trial, he had claimed ecclesiastical privilege. Though much of his goods and lands had been seized, he had been allowed to exercise his episcopal office. Just weeks before the queen's invasion, he had performed a burial at Wigmore Abbey: that of Roger

Mortimer of Chirk, who had at last died in the Tower. Then, hearing of the queen's arrival, the bishop had hastened from Hereford to lend her his support.

Though Orleton had joined the queen's cause only days before, he had already proven invaluable. At Oxford, he had preached a wonderful sermon, taking for his text Genesis 3:15: "I will put enmity between thee and the woman, and between thy seed and her seed; it shall bruise thy head." No one, it was true, had quite followed the twistings and turnings of the bishop's exegesis of the text, under which the head was that of Hugh the younger, "her seed" young Edward, and "the woman" the queen, and some might have foolishly interpreted "thee and the woman" to mean that Orleton himself would put enmity between the king and the queen, but the point about the head being bruised had been understood perfectly and exceedingly well received.

Isabella, however, was not in the mood to be easily comforted, even by the helpful bishop. "And they said that—thing—was an offering to Diana! Such pagan drivel, when they know that I am a good daughter of the Church!"

"What counts," put in Mortimer, "is that we know now that the Londoners are on your side." He flipped open the lid of the basket, shook his head, and flipped the lid down again. "And I am very glad they are, that's for certain, for I would rather not have them against us. A bread knife?"

Isabella relaxed a little. "And my younger son is safe? Are you certain?"

"The messenger was quite emphatic. He has been named guardian of the city, and is remaining at his apartments at the Tower until you send for him. Nominally, John de Weston is the constable of the Tower still, but everyone who goes in and out is being very closely watched by my allies." Roger chuckled. "Including the king's little niece, Lady Despenser."

"Fool woman! I cannot believe she surrendered the Tower without putting up a fight. I always did take her for a ninny, but I would have thought Nephew Hugh would have coached her better."

"Which brings us back to where we should be. Now that we know how the wind is blowing in London, let us press on westward and do what we came here for in the first place. And when people see Hugh's head on London Bridge, they won't care a fig about this meddling bishop's." He jabbed a finger at the basket.

"True," said the queen, greatly cheered. Then she frowned. "Bishop Orleton, what *should* I do with that—thing?"

"Take it with us, in a pickle barrel, and when the time is right, send it to Exeter Cathedral to be buried with all honor," said Orleton. "I suppose the body's in London still; if so, it can be retrieved and sent there too."

"Excellent," said Isabella with a smile.

On October 18, the queen and her forces arrived at Bristol, where the citizens threw open the gates in welcome. Only Bristol Castle, under the control of the Earl of Winchester, resisted. On October 20, the king, the younger Hugh and his son, Baldock, and a handful of others boarded a small boat at Chepstow, hoping to reach Despenser's Lundy Island, from which they would set sail for Ireland. But the very elements of nature had turned against them, and despite fervent prayers to St. Anne from Hugh's confessor, the wind refused to change. On October 25, the king and his men, exhausted and famished, gave up and disembarked at Cardiff.

Lately, the king's daughters, eight-year-old Eleanor and five-year-old Joan, had had to put up a great deal with the vagaries of grown-ups. First they had been dragged from Marlborough Castle to Bristol Castle, with only the vaguest of explanations by Lady Hastings, who was usually most forthcoming. Then, after they had settled in comfortably into their sunny chamber at Bristol Castle, they had been moved into an interior room where they could not see so much as a seagull flapping by. They could hardly sit in the dark, of course, so they had to use candles, candles, candles, all day long and all night until they went to bed. And yet, up to a week ago, Lady Hastings, while by no means stingy about the matter, had been very careful not to use too many candles.

And then there was all the whispering, all the conferences between Lady Hastings and her papa the Earl of Winchester and Donald of Mar, all the messengers going back and forth, all the *mystery*. It could mean only one thing, Joan had decided: Papa had found a husband for Eleanor. "They moved you here so you could meet him," she explained. "The Earl of Winchester and Donald of Mar are seeing to it for Papa, you see, because he is so busy in Wales now."

"Silly, that wouldn't explain this awful room."

Joan glared at her embroidery hoop. "It is because," she finally said triumphantly, "you are going to be living in a dark place."

The girls were still debating this issue, mentally and with each other, on October 26, when Lady Hastings sat listening to them say their lessons to their governess. So lost was she in worry that she did not hear her father's voice at first. "Come with me, Bella," he repeated.

He took her into his chamber. "I have decided to surrender."

"Why?"

"It is hopeless, my child. The men will not fight; they have told me so. That leaves you and me and the king's girls and all the ladies here to hold the queen and Mortimer off with their army. I don't care for the odds."

"There is Donald of Mar."

Donald of Mar, a nephew of Robert Bruce, had been taken hostage as a youth by the first Edward and had been raised at court. After the Bannock Burn, it had been arranged that he would be returned to Scotland, along with Bruce's wife and other relatives, in exchange for the English hostages. At the last moment, he had flatly refused to go, having developed an unshakable loyalty to the second Edward.

The earl shook his head. "Papa! Surely you cannot mean that even Donald of Mar has deserted us."

"No. I sent him off. He may be able to persuade Robert Bruce to come to the king's aid, if all else fails."

For an Englishman to speak of getting assistance from the Bruce was desperation indeed. Hugh paced about the room. "Bella, I did think of holding out anyway, of fighting to the last gasp. Of making a grand gesture. But that would jeopardize my grandsons' lives, perhaps, and in any case I feel too old for grand gestures."

Bella said bitterly, "Hugh has brought you to this."

"Yes, he is at fault. So am I. I tolerated much that I should not have, and participated in things that I should not have. We are both to blame. Don't be bitter with him, Bella." He saw her unrelenting face and said urgently, "He needs your prayers desperately."

Bella was silent for a while. She looked at the rich gown and jewels she wore, some the gifts of her doting father, some the gifts of her doting husbands, but others the gifts of a brother she had always loved and who had always looked out for her. Finally, she said, "Of course I will pray for him, Papa."

He put a hand on her shoulder. "I sent a message out a little while ago. I made certain that your life would be spared, that you would not be shut up. They agreed. You will be kept under guard while they look for your brother, but after that you will go free. Caring for the queen's children isn't treason, after all."

"And your life?"

Hugh shrugged. "It's been a long one, my child."

Bella began sobbing. Her father went on calmly, "And now I have a secret to tell you. Are you hearing me?"

She nodded bleakly.

"You have a younger brother, a bastard. I sired him some years after your mother died."

Bella looked up, shocked out of her tears. "You?"

"I don't recall taking Holy Orders, my dear. His name is Nicholas, named after his mother's father. He lives with his mother in Litlyngton. She was not a young woman when I met her, but a widow of many years. I was rather surprised to hear of our child, having thought she was past her time, but there is no doubt that he is mine."

"All these years I would not have guessed. But Father, why didn't you tell the rest of us? I would have welcomed him as our brother, and I am sure Hugh would have too."

"Hugh knows. I should have told you girls, but in truth, I felt too much of an old rooster doing so."

"Papa! What silliness."

The earl blushed. "His mother wants him to be professed as a monk. I think that is fitting."

Bella asked, "Does he know you are his father?"

"Yes. I have seen him and Joan quite often. When I am gone I would like you to see them and say good-bye for me. I have left plenty of money for their support, but I want you to give them my love." He touched Bella's hand. "Your sister-in-law Eleanor will be in sore need of kindness from you too, if the worst happens."

"Do you think there is no hope for Hugh at all?"

"Things are different now than in '21 when our enemies were divided. It would take a miracle, and I think miracles are in short supply these days, save at the tomb of the Earl of Lancaster." He gazed out the window, where the tents of the queen's army were visible in all directions. "But perhaps the circumstances have made me overly pessimistic." Hugh pressed Bella's hand gently. "Your sons will grow to be fine men, I think, and so will your brothers' and sisters' sons. And you and your sisters and my granddaughters and Eleanor have been the lights of my life. Don't mourn overlong for me."

Bella put her head on her father's shoulder and wept as she had not wept since she was a child of five. When she had at last quieted, her father said gently, "Wash your face, and get ready to take the girls to the queen. I am going to find my confessor."

She obeyed, and a few minutes later was back in her charges' chamber, smiling at the little girls.

"Come," she said lightly. "I know someone who wants to see you very much, who is waiting outside for you. Can you guess?"

"Eleanor's husband-to-be!" said Joan triumphantly. But Lady Hastings looked so baffled by this reply that Eleanor ventured, "My brother John?"

"No! Your brother Edward. And your mama."

"What! They are back from France!"

"Yes."

"But no one told us! Why, Lady Hastings?"

Bella's tone grew lighter yet. "So it would be a big surprise for you, of course." She smiled. "I am afraid I may be losing you, though. Your mama will want you with her, so I must give you up."

Together they walked over the drawbridge, presenting a weirdly domestic scene: Eleanor and Joan running ahead trying to glimpse their mother, the Earl of Winchester and his daughter walking arm in arm, Bella's ladies and the girls' attendants trailing uncertainly behind. However much the queen might have liked to give her attention to Hugh le Despenser, kneeling and offering his sword in surrender, Eleanor and Joan's exuberant greetings prevented this, and when Edward hesitantly put his hand out for the sword, he too was overwhelmed by his little sisters. It was Henry, Earl of Leicester, who at last had to step forward and accept Winchester's surrender.

"Where shall we take him, your grace?"

Take him? Eleanor and Joan frowned, for suddenly everyone around them looked very grim.

"To a cell," said the queen. "We try him first thing tomorrow."

"It was not a mere manner of expediency, I assure you. I did wrestle with my conscience."

In the great hall of Bristol Castle, where Queen Isabella's leading men had assembled after the Earl of Winchester had been hustled away, Robert de Wateville was sitting next to William la Zouche of Ashby, Wateville's face gloomy because of his aforesaid conscience, Zouche's face gloomy because this was by no means the first such conversation he had had with Wateville.

Wateville had cause for guilt. Till the very moment of Isabella's landing, he had been trusted by both the king and Hugh the younger, and just months before, the king had paid part of the expenses of his wedding—to Lady Hastings' daughter. Discovering her son-in-law in the midst of the queen's men who had arrested her father, the mild and gentle Lady Hastings had spat on him, had called him a Judas, and had been about to attack his face with her elegantly man-icured nails when she was yanked away by one of the Hainaulters. "But what else could I do, Zouche? I sincerely think the queen is justified in her actions."

"I do too. Despenser has gone beyond all bounds in his greed for land and money. England will be better for the steps we are taking."

Wateville sighed. "Tell that to my mother-in-law."

Zouche, the very same man who had taken the Countess of Warwick's fancy after the death of her husband, himself had been loyal to the king. He had fought for Edward at Boroughbridge, yet since that date he had watched with dismay, and then disgust, as widows were despoiled of their dower rights, men were forced to buy their freedom by executing huge recognizances to Hugh le Despenser, and highborn ladies such as Margaret d'Audley languished in con-vents. He had seen, and still saw, the queen as the savior of her country, and he knelt reverently as she entered the great hall, looking fragile and vulnerable in her widow's weeds, and motioned for the Earl of Leicester to speak for her.

It was a pity, declared the earl, but the king had deserted the realm, led out of it by the wicked Hugh le Despenser the younger. This state of affairs could not continue, clearly, so the only alternative was to name a keeper of the realm in the king's absence. Who better to fill this role than the king's own son, Edward, the Duke of Aquitaine? As one, those assembled—including Zouche, Wateville, the Earls of Kent and Norfolk, the Bishops of Hereford, Winchester, Ely, Lincoln, and Norwich, and Henry de Beaumont—agreed.

Young Edward, at fourteen already tall and well built, then stood to acknowl-edge the bows of the assembled company. Looking at him, dignified and grave, yet with an appealing air of boyish shyness, Zouche was reassured that the right thing was being done. Even Wateville stopped justifying himself for the moment.

The next morning, however, Wateville was glum again as William Trussell, accompanied by the Earls of Leicester, Norfolk, and Kent, Roger Mortimer, and Thomas Wake, tried, or made a pretense of trying, the Earl of Winchester. The regent and his mother, along with the other nobility and prelates of the Church, sat as spectators. The Earl of Leicester, although he had not much liked his ill-tempered older brother, nonetheless felt obliged to avenge his death properly, and chief among the charges against Hugh was that he had put the Earl of Lan-caster to death without reason, the man's traitorous activities being conveniently forgotten. He had made a law that men (like the Earl of Lancaster) could be con-demned without right of reply. He had appropriated royal power to himself. He had counseled the king to persecute the prelates of the Church. He had been such a robber that the people demanded vengeance. Despite the fact that he himself had stolen property from Winchester's manors in 1323, Trussell managed to make his voice shake with outrage.

Winchester, like Lancaster, was not allowed to reply, and as any reply would have been worthless anyway, he listened to the charges without emotion, his eyes never leaving the faces of his accusers. Trussell rolled on, "For your treason you are to be drawn, for your robbery hung, and for your offenses against the Church beheaded. Your head will be taken to Winchester, of which you were earl, contrary against law and reason. Because you have dishonored chivalry and hung men with quartered coats, you are to be hung with your quartered coat and your arms destroyed for all time."

Zouche thought he saw Winchester flinch at these last words. But his voice was level and quiet as he said, uninvited, "Would that I have had an upright judge and a just sentence. But we will look for what is not given to us in this world, in the next."

No one replied to the old man. Zouche found himself and others looking appealingly at Isabella, silently hoping that she would intervene and spare the earl his life. Her face was impassive as the defendant's, however, and after a moment the Earl of Winchester, head still held high, was led away.

"If this is not the damnedest thing you have seen, Zouche. Look!"

At Wateville's urging, Zouche looked. Standing slightly apart from the rest of the crowd ringing Bristol's common gallows was Lady Hastings, a guard on either side of her. William winced. He had been friendly with both Lord Hastings and Lord Monthermer, and had sat at many a meal with each man as he had endured good-natured, predictable jokes about his marriage to a much younger, pretty wife. Lady Hastings herself he had seen only occasionally, as neither he nor she had frequented court much. Up until now, he'd thought of her only as someone's wife, not as the Earl of Winchester's daughter, Hugh le Despenser's sister.

"Do you think they are making her watch? I'll only anger her if I approach her."

"I will see."

He walked to Lady Hastings' side. "Surely, my lady, you have not been forced to watch this?"

Though in her thirties, Lady Hastings was still slender and youthful-looking, albeit with a worry line etched between her eyes, and her ladies had taken the trouble to dress her with care even today. She looked at him vaguely as if not quite understanding or recognizing him, then said dully, "No. I asked to be brought here."

"Insisted," offered the young guard next to her in a whisper.

"If he were dying in his bed I would be there. I did not see a reason to make an exception for this."

"You have my condolences, my lady."

She nodded and for the first time looked at the surcoat he wore. "Lord Zouche. I have heard that you will soon be searching for my brother and the king."

"It is necessary, my lady, as they have left the realm."

"May you never find them!"

A cloud of dust kicked up by the two horses dragging Winchester on a hurdle announced the earl's arrival. Dazed and bleeding over his bright surcoat, Hugh was untied from the hurdle and hoisted to his feet. Even as he wobbled upright, grimacing with pain, he kept something of his dignity about him. The hangman fastened the noose around Winchester's neck, and Lady Hastings knelt. Zouche, knowing there was nothing more he could say to her, started to move away. Yet it seemed hard to leave her there all alone with no one but her guards for company, so he stayed by her side.

Lady Hastings, not taking her eyes from the scaffold, was oblivious to whether he stayed or went. She prayed as her father was lifted aloft, suspended in the air until he was half-strangled, and then dropped. Her prayers continued as he was cut down, as he was dragged to a block, as the executioner raised his axe, and as the head fell. Only when Winchester's balding head was raised by the ears for the crowd to admire did she crumple to the ground. "Fool woman," one of the guards said, half-admiringly.

Zouche knelt beside her. To his surprise, Lady Hastings had either never lost consciousness or had done so very briefly, for she was crying as he lifted her head. "There is no need for you to remain here," he said gently. "Let me take you to the castle. You have women there to look after you?"

"Yes."

The crowd was dispersing, the fastening of a headless body back upon the gallows being of little interest to all but the most dedicated of execution-goers. William waited impatiently for his squire to bring his horse, then helped Lady Hastings to mount it. She sat up straight as he settled behind her and took the reins. When they arrived at the castle, she let him help her dismount and walked into the great hall with him, saying nothing but, "This way," when William, not wanting to leave her until she was deposited safely with her damsels, looked to see in which direction her chamber lay.

"Lady Hastings!" Eleanor and little Joan appeared in the hall, their eyes wide with terror. "We have seen something horrid! From our window—a man hanging a ways off."

"A thief, no doubt, Joan. Do not look anymore. Where is your governess?"

"She felt ill, and we had nothing else to do but look out the window, so we looked."

"But she first told Joan and me not to look, but Joan looked anyway, and then I had to look. That was wrong of Joan."

"Yes, but you should not have looked either. In any case, the best you can do now is not to look." Lady Hastings managed to twitch out a smile. "You should practice your music. Your mama will be very pleased to hear how you have improved, although she is very busy now and may not be able to hear you for a while."

"I practice. Eleanor does not."

"Only when Lady Hastings reminds you!"

An attendant came and took the girls, rescuing Lady Hastings from any further need to make light conversation. She had been moved the day before to a cramped chamber some distance off from the girls', and she resumed her silence as Zouche led her there. At last they reached her chamber. "You may leave me here. Thank you."

"Is there anything I can do for you, my lady?"

She shook her head and he pushed open the door. Two of Lady Hastings' damsels were waiting inside. Zouche had never seen either of them, but the younger one, a girl still in her teens, bore a startling resemblance to Piers Gaveston. As he puzzled over this, they took off Lady Hastings' cloak as she stood passively, staring at the floor. Seeing from the gentleness which they performed their task that she was in good hands, he turned to leave. "Lord Zouche?"

"My lady."

"Will you tell the king's daughters good-bye for me?"

"Of course."

"Tell them"—Lady Hastings' tears were at last flowing—"that I will miss them so much."

The next day, Isabella, in her son's name, confidently began issuing summons for Parliament. Meanwhile, the Earl of Leicester, who had decided it was high time he was called the Earl of Lancaster, was sent to Wales, along with Zouche, several other knights, and some of the Welshmen who had been freed from the Tower, in search of the king and Hugh le Despenser. The queen herself began traveling to Hereford, where she would lodge at the Bishop of Hereford's palace while awaiting word from Wales.

Zouche and the rest of the search party left Bristol at the same time an ashen-faced Lady Hastings and her small band of attendants left Bristol Castle, under guard, for her dower lands. The Earl of Winchester's body remained on the gallows. It would hang there in its cords for several more days, after which the gallows being needed for the usual miscreants, it would be cut down and served to the pack of wild dogs that had lingered nearby in hopes of receiving just such a treat.

CHAPTER 18

▼

OCTOBER 1326 TO NOVEMBER 1326

Edward and Hugh and their few followers had arrived at Caerphilly Castle on the same day, October 27, that the Earl of Winchester was executed. After the news came, Hugh went off by himself. When hours had passed with no sign of his friend, the king went in search of him.

He did not have far to look. Hugh sat in the castle's chapel, lit only by a single candle. "I killed him, Ned, with my folly. If I'd gone as the queen asked…"

"Hugh, no."

"It's not too late, Ned. I can give myself up, disappear. You can make terms, save yourself at least."

"Without you, Hugh? Never."

"It's hopeless, Ned."

"Hugh, when we are together, there is always hope." He lit a second candle. "I loved your father as I could never love my own, Hugh. I never met a more loyal, true man in my life. Would we honor his memory by parting now?"

Hugh said nothing, but began to weep silently, his head in his hands. It was dawn when he finally let the king lead him from the chapel.

On November 2, the king and Hugh left Caerphilly Castle, and fourteen thousand pounds, in the hands of John Felton, its constable, and Hugh's eighteen-year-old son. They went to Neath Abbey, from where they sent a delegation, led by the abbot and including Edward's nephew Edward de Bohun, to attempt to negotiate with the queen. It was a futile effort; the queen had no need to negotiate.

"Edward, Sir Weston wishes to speak to me. Would you like to come along?"

Eleanor looked over at her son Edward, hoping that this inclusion of him in a conference between adults might bring him out of the shell into which he had retreated. After the bishop's murder, Edward, already the most reserved of her children, had been especially quiet and self-contained, but when the news of the Earl of Winchester's execution had reached the Tower, he had become so withdrawn and silent that Eleanor despaired of ever pulling him back into the world.

"No."

Eleanor sighed. "Very well, Edward. I will talk to him by myself."

Weston, waiting in an outer chamber, was Eleanor's only source of news these days, for it had been weeks since any royal messenger had passed through the Tower gates. Eleanor herself had not ventured outside of the Tower grounds since Stapeldon's death. "My lady, there are some changes you must know about."

"Changes, Sir Weston?"

Weston nodded bleakly. "Today, the Bishop of Winchester came to London bearing orders signed by the Duke of Aquitaine. The bishop has been appointed deputy treasurer, since Archbishop Melton has remained in the north."

"And as he has always been loyal to my dear uncle, he would be murdered too if he tried to come to London."

"Probably. In any case, the bishop was greeted with great joy by the Londoners because he came from the queen. These are some of the orders he has been instructed to carry out: I am to be removed from my post here, and Hamo de Chigwell is to be removed from his position of mayor. John de Gisors and Richard de Betoyne will hold the Tower for the time being, and Gisors will be the mayor."

The names sounded familiar, but Eleanor could not place them.

"They are allies of Roger Mortimer. They helped him escape from the Tower. Naturally, such changes will affect your ladyship."

"Yes, I imagine so. What will happen to us, Sir Weston?"

"I do not know for certain, my lady. But it appears that you and your children will be held here as prisoners."

"We have been virtually prisoners here since the Bishop of Exeter's death, so I suppose I can face that."

Weston looked at her curiously; he had expected more than this almost nonchalant reaction. "I wish there is something I could do to help you, my lady."

"There is only one thing anyone can do to help me, and that is to return Hugh and my son and the king safely home. And I fear that will never happen, Sir Weston."

William la Zouche had experienced three revelations during his mission in Wales. The first was that there were more fat, woolly sheep in the world than he had ever dreamed. The second was that Henry of Lancaster's eyesight was so bad that if Hugh le Despenser had been dressed in a white fur and put next to one of them, Henry could not have told man from mutton. The third was that when offered a few shillings, the most solitary of shepherds instantly evidenced the keenest of familiarity with the features of the king, Hugh le Despenser, and Robert Baldock and had, in fact, seen them only an hour ago, or a few miles back.

With all these false leads, on November 15 they had yet to find sure signs of the king, despite the fact that the sons of Llywelyn Bren, who knew every inch of South Wales, were among the search party. "Perhaps they have fled the country altogether," muttered Lancaster irritably as he and Zouche and the other leaders sat in a tent that night, cold and miserable. A fierce rain, mixed now and then with sleet, had begun to fall, and the wind blowing through the bare trees completed the dismal picture.

"No, they haven't," said a voice in Welsh-accented English.

Though Zouche's eyes were much more sharp than Lancaster's, he could make out the speaker no more than his companion could. "Who said that?"

A man, dripping wet, pushed his way inside the tent. "Begging your pardon, sirs. You are looking for the king?"

"Yes," said Zouche shortly. By now their search had progressed to the stage where they no longer had to seek out worthless informants, they came to the queen's men on their own accord.

The man stretched out his hand. "Then I've news for you."

"Not until you do this to our satisfaction. Describe them. Use Welsh; some of us here speak it very well."

The man tipped back his head as if to recall them better. "A tall blond man, very well made, with blue eyes. Curly beard. A slight droop to one eyelid. That's the king. Despenser. A good half-head shorter than the king, slight build, dark hair, dark eyes, sharp nose, sharp cheekbones. Short beard. Baldock. Plump little man, balding on top. Five or six others with them. All in mud-splattered clothes, all riding the finest horses money can buy." He grinned. "One of them newly shod. I'm the blacksmith who did it."

Llywelyn Bren's sons were grinning. Lancaster felt his spirits rise. So did Zouche, who handed the man several gold coins. Clinking them in satisfaction, he continued, "They were headed up the road toward Llantrisant."

November 16. The rain and sleet had finally stopped, and Edward could at last see the walls of Llantrisant Castle, perched upon a hill. There they could stay while planning what to do next; there perhaps Hugh could finally be roused from the despondency into which he had sunk since hearing of the death of his father. Hugh might say that all was hopeless now, but he would see. There was hope, always hope...

And then he saw the men, armed men, suddenly appearing in front of him like some horrid phantoms from the Bannock Burn. He wheeled his horse around and saw more armed men behind him. Two hundred men, at least, against eight.

Beside Edward, Hugh sighed sharply. "I love you, Ned," he said quietly. "God keep you in his care."

"I love you, Hugh. God keep you."

The king dismounted and walked toward Henry of Lancaster, holding out his sword in surrender.

At Llantrisant Castle, where the prisoners had all been taken, Lancaster briskly issued orders. He himself would take his first cousin the king to Kenilworth Castle; Henry de Leybourne and Robert de Stanegrave would take Despenser, Baldock, and Simon de Reading, a knight loyal to Despenser, to the queen at Hereford. The other four men would be released. Through them, Lancaster had learned that while at Neath Abbey, the king had had sent records and treasure to Swansea Castle. Zouche was ordered to go there to retrieve them. He was glad for this assignment, for Leybourne and Stanegrave, getting thoroughly drunk in Llantrisant Castle's great hall, seemed to be attempting to outdo each other in devising ways to make Despenser's progress to Hereford as miserable as possible. Zouche, remembering Lady Hastings as she saw her old father's head lifted in the air, had no stomach for such sport. The man's death would be a horrid one enough without such preliminaries.

He was deep in thought when one of his men roused him. "Despenser wants to see you, sir."

"Me?" Zouche doubted that he had ever spoken more than a few words to the king's favorite.

"He asked for you by name, sir."

Zouche shrugged and followed the man to the guardhouse where Despenser, Baldock, and Reading had been taken, the king having been given a comfortable chamber with a fire. Zouche, watching him as he was led there, had thought of the time he'd happened across his young son sleepwalking.

Despenser's cell was unlit, the only light coming from the lantern William himself bore. He sat in a corner wrapped in a blanket. A plate of untouched food sat near him. Zouche stumbled over it in the dark. Irritated, he asked, "Isn't this food good enough for you? It's likely to be the best you'll get from here on."

"Give it to the rats. I've taken my last meal. I only wish it had been a memorable one."

Zouche frowned. "You're planning on starving yourself to death? It won't happen that quickly."

Despenser shrugged. "One does what one can, but it is inefficient, I'll grant you that." He looked at William almost sardonically. "I've treasure hidden in places no one but me knows about. Leave me alone with that sword of yours for a few minutes, and it's yours. You can retrieve it a bit at a time, not too much so as to look suspicious."

"Queen Isabella wants you alive."

"And she mustn't be disappointed, our dear queen. Or what about this proposal? You kill me now, quick and clean. You'd probably enjoy doing it, and you can tell the queen I tried to overpower you."

"Give it up, Despenser. You'll be delivered to the queen alive. I don't need your bribes, and you don't need a mortal sin on your head. You've enough already."

"So what's one more?" As William watched, though, Hugh's bravado seemed to leave him. His tone was almost wistful as he asked, "So you won't put me out of this life, Zouche?"

"No, Despenser. Is that why you wanted to see me?"

"Actually, no. My wife did you a small favor once, Zouche. I'd like you to return it. Don't look so distressed. It's a very small one, and won't get you in trouble with our precious queen."

"I've never met your wife, Despenser. How could she have done me a favor?"

"Did your late wife never confide in you? When she was considering marriage to you, my wife was one of the queen's ladies who encouraged her."

William smiled, remembering now the conversation he had had on his wedding night. It was a sad smile, for his happy marriage had been a short one. Pretty, gentle Alice had died nearly two years before, leaving him with a son, Alan, now nine years old. "That was no small favor, then. So what I can do for her?"

"This." Hampered by his shackles, he was fiddling with a ring on his left hand. "It's for my wife; it was her present to me when she was but a girl, and I'd like her to have it. I'd be thankful if you gave it to her. I don't see much point in asking the queen to do me the honor."

"Where is she?"

"She was staying in the Tower with the king's younger son when we left in October."

William hesitated. "You know what happened in London after you left?"

"Yes, Zouche. A message got through to us. I suppose she and my children are still there; I haven't heard. They're better off with me dead. I know that much."

He pulled the ring off and gazed at it sadly, then dropped it in Zouche's outstretched hand. "With my love. Thank you."

"I've no place to put it for now than on my own hand."

"I understand."

William slid the ring onto a right finger with some distaste, for the ring was still warm from Hugh's hand. He wondered whether Despenser's wife would feel relief or regret at his execution. "What's she like, your wife?"

Despenser smiled wryly. "What are you doing, Zouche, going to market? Can't you wait until they carve me up? She's too good for you." His voice changed. "Too good for me, too." He drew his blanket back around him and settled into his corner. Then he rallied one last time. "Tell her not to marry the first handsome young buck who comes her way, Zouche, will you? A man has his pride."

The day after the king and Hugh were captured, yet another captive, the Earl of Arundel, was brought to the queen at Hereford. Little could be really said against him except that he had acted as one of Thomas of Lancaster's judges, had acquired some of the Mortimers' seized estates, and had married his son to Despenser's oldest daughter, but these facts, particularly the last, were quite adequate for the queen to order that he and two of his men be beheaded straightaway.

While Arundel was being executed, none too efficiently, that seventeenth day of November, John de Gisors, who just hours before had been given the keys of the Tower of London, was walking through his new charge like a proud parent. The White Tower! St. Thomas's Tower! The Wakefield Tower! His step gradually lost its bounce, however, as he neared the Lanthorn Tower. The bishop had been clear that the first task assigned to him had to be carried out immediately. It would not be a difficult one, but it might be unpleasant, depending on the temperament of the female involved.

"Lady Despenser? I am the new constable of the Tower, as perhaps you have heard."

"I have heard."

"And I have orders to take you and your children into safe custody. Safer than you are in now."

"To imprison us, you mean."

"Well, yes."

"So I had thought. Where are we to be housed?"

"In the tower built by the first Edward," said Gisors, referring to what would in later years be known as the Beauchamp Tower. Relieved at her calmness, he added, "They're very comfortable lodgings, considering. You may pack some necessaries for you and your children. I'll wait as you do so."

Eleanor nodded. Despite her apparent composure, she moved as if in a trance, picking up an object and staring at it vacantly before setting it down again. Gladys, meanwhile, scurried in and out of the room with armloads of garments, which she piled up in heaps on the floor until a manservant materialized with a chest, and then another and another. Gisors scowled. "I said some necessaries, not everything she owns."

"My lady has six children here with her," said Gladys coolly. "They must have warm clothing. And where are they to sleep? My lady must have a regular bed. She cannot sleep on a pallet night after night."

"Why not?" said Gisors philosophically. But the woman was a king's granddaughter, after all; perhaps she could not sleep on a pallet night after night. "She can bring beds with her. But we'll leave all the elegant trappings behind, shall we?"

Eleanor in the meantime had left the room. When she returned after a time, she was holding only a cloak that was clearly a man's. Gisors frowned. "Is that your husband's, my lady? All of his chattels will be forfeit to the crown. You can't take that with you."

"I can, and I will. He has had this cloak for as long as we have been married. It's not a very costly one, and I must have something of his to cherish—until he returns."

Was the woman fool enough to think that Hugh would return? Gisors started to say as much, then bit back his comments. It was too much like striking an unarmed opponent. He said, "Very well. Stop at that. Your quarters aren't large enough for your entire wardrobe, or his."

Gladys said, "My lady, I have done packing. Shall I get the children?"

"No." Eleanor had gone white. "I will get them."

In a very long time she returned, carrying a baby and trailed by five children. Christ, there were a lot of them! thought Gisors. Aside from the baby, whose sex Gisors could not determine, there were three girls and two boys, all with the same dark eyes and auburn hair and all showing their mother's eerie composure. Were they not Despenser's offspring, Gisors would have admitted them to be a handsome family. Each carried some belongings with them, including the baby, who clutched a blanket, and all watched Gisors levelly as they came to stand in front of him. "We are ready, sir," said their mother.

"Very well." He glanced at the cluster of servants, many of whom were in or near tears. "Say goodbye to your mistress, if you please."

Eleanor had produced a purse and was pushing coins at each servant in turn. When it came Gladys's turn, however, she shook her head. "No, my lady, I'm staying with you." She looked at the others. "You are young, and I don't blame you for leaving. Neither will my lady. But I'm up in years, and I've served my lady since she was thirteen. I won't leave her now."

"My good woman," said Gisors, "the crown will be paying your lady's expenses, and it won't pay a halfpenny more if you stay with her. There will be less to go around."

"Aye, and I can stand to stint myself if need be."

Eleanor's eyes were filled with tears. She whispered, "I should be telling you to go, Gladys, but I cannot. I am so glad you are staying with me."

"Then that settles it." Gladys patted Eleanor's hand and looked at Gisors. "I packed my own things with the others, my lord, so there is no need to delay further."

"Well, that's something to be thankful for," snapped Gisors.

He conducted the eight of them out of the royal apartments and into the Beauchamp Tower, where they were taken to two connecting rooms, gloomy but not as miserable as they had feared. There were fireplaces in both, and access to a garderobe, and the single window allowed them a truncated view of the Tower grounds. Eleanor roused herself enough to suggest that straws be drawn to determine which room the boys should have and which the females should have. The boys had won the room with the window, but with the smaller fire, when the chests and beds arrived. After all was arranged, Gisors, promising them that supper would be brought in an hour or so, locked them in with a great banging of keys and took his leave. Then the questions began.

"Is Father ever coming back, Mama?"

"Is my doll here?"

"Will we be here long?"

To all of these questions, Eleanor could answer only, "I don't know."

On November 24, a few miles outside Hereford, Hugh lay where they had shoved him the evening before, conscious but with closed eyes. His cell was freezing and the clothing he wore still sodden from yesterday's rain. Had he been asked whether he was cold he would have said yes, but his self-imposed starvation and the fever that was beginning to creep in on him prevented him from caring much.

Footsteps and voices near him alerted him that he was not alone. "Hugh!"

"Dear heart!"

"Rise to meet the glorious morning!"

"Oh, Hugh!"

The day before he had been roused by having a bucket of human waste dumped upon him, and in some still half-curious part of his mind he wondered whether Mortimer's men would excel themselves today. They settled, however, for prodding him in the ribs with a stick. He ignored it as long as he could. Then with the utmost difficulty he pushed himself up upon his elbow and looked at them. "Awake, Hugh? Good. Today is the day you meet your maker."

Hugh formed the simple words with difficulty. "You people said she wanted to kill me in London."

"True, love. But the queen frets that you might not make it there alive. So to Hereford—and to hell—you go today."

So at least his sweet Eleanor would not have to see him die in London, his worst fear. Following the ramblings of his mind, he asked, "My wife. Have you word of her?"

"Your wife the king?"

"My wife. Eleanor."

"Wasn't it she who was lying with the Tower constable the other day?"

"Nah, she doesn't look that high. The guards."

"Two?"

"Both at once. She's a lonely woman, your wife."

"So what else is new?"

Hugh dragged himself to his knees and moved a few feet away. He bowed his head. "Lord, damn me if you will but protect her and our children. Spare them."

He collapsed to the ground and someone kicked his hand. He looked up into the eyes of a young guard, who said gruffly, "Your wife is in the Tower as a prisoner, I heard. That is all I know."

Then the same guard yanked him up so roughly he nearly swooned. "Now move your feet! The queen hasn't all day for the likes of you."

"Wait." Hugh's head was spinning, and he was leaning against the guard, but he managed to force out another question. "My eldest son?"

"Your whelp still holds Caerphilly Castle. Now go on!"

Hugh's mouth twisted into a ghost of a smile as he obeyed the guard.

Leybourne and Stanegrave and their men had made Hugh's journey to Hereford as miserable as Isabella and Mortimer could have wished. Lest any dozing village miss the fine sight of Hugh le Despenser chained to a mangy horse, a drummer and a trumpeter had been put at the head of the procession to announce his arrival well in advance. This was the cue for villagers to throw anything they could find at Hugh, and at Simon de Reading as well. Hardly anyone knew who the latter was, of course, but as he too was in chains, everyone realized that he had to be associated with Hugh, and his presence made the proceedings twice as fun and provided some consolation for those whose aim was too unsure to hit Hugh himself.

But the true festivities started when the troops, trailed by an ever-increasing crowd of citizens eager to see Hugh hang, reached the outskirts of Hereford, where they were met by a contingent of the queen's men coming from the city, led by Jean de Hainault and Thomas Wake. There, to the delight of the crowd, Hugh and Simon were dragged off their horses and stripped naked, then redressed in tunics bearing their coats of arms reversed. With the help of a clerk, whose Latin was needed for the purpose, the words from the Magnificat "He has put down the mighty from their seat and hath exalted the humble" were etched into Hugh's bare shoulders. His chest bore psalm verses beginning, "Why dost thou glory in malice, thou that art mighty in iniquity?" Thus decorated, and wearing a crown of nettles, he was put back on his horse. Then, to the blare of trumpets and drums, accompanied by the howling of the spectators, he was led into the city with Simon de Reading forced to march in front of him bearing his standard reversed. As there were only so many horse droppings that could be found to throw at the captives, the enterprising were selling eggs for that purpose.

Zouche had hoped to miss these proceedings. He had retrieved the records, and the little treasure that could be found, from Swansea, and had delivered his load to the queen two days before. But having made good time to Hereford, he could not leave once the execution had been scheduled. Thus, he was standing in the market square, near the queen, Mortimer, and the Duke of Aquitaine, when Hugh and Simon, so covered in filth that they resembled scarecrows more than men, were brought there for trial.

Isabella, still clad in widow's weeds, wore a look of resignation as William Trussell stepped forth to read the charges against Hugh. Only Mortimer, making no attempt to hide his own satisfaction, saw the sparkle in her eyes.

At what passed for his trial, Hugh's mind wandered from the past to the present, sometimes lucidly, sometimes not. There were many charges against him, some true enough, some with a bit of truth to them, some so patently absurd that it was a wonder Trussell could keep a straight face. Piracy. Returning to England after his banishment. Procuring the death of the saintly Lancaster after imprisoning him on false charges. Executing other men who had fought against the king at Boroughbridge on false charges. Forcing the king to fight the Scots. Abandoning the queen at Tynemouth. (*That* again, Hugh thought.) Making war on the Christian Church. Disinheriting the king by inducing him to grant the earldom of Winchester to his father and the earldom of Carlisle to Harclay. Bribing persons in France to murder the queen and her son... He drifted off into a world where his death was not imminent, and when he was shaken back to the here and now once more, Trussell was still going on, perhaps beginning to bore those assembled a little. Trussell himself must have sensed this, for he sped through the last few charges (leading the king out of his realm to his dishonor and taking with him the treasure of the kingdom and the Great Seal) before he slowed his voice dramatically for what all were anticipating: his sentence. Though no one could have possibly been surprised by it, least of all Hugh himself, there were nonetheless appreciative gasps as Trussell, all but smacking his lips, informed Hugh what was to be done with him.

"Hugh, you have been judged a traitor since you have threatened all the good people of the realm, great and small, rich and poor, and by common assent you are also a thief. As a thief you will hang, and as a traitor you will be drawn and quartered, and your quarters will be sent throughout the realm. And because you prevailed upon our lord the king, and by common assent you returned to the court without warrant, you will be beheaded. And because you were always disloyal and procured discord between our lord the king and our very honorable lady the queen, and between other people of the realm, you will be disemboweled, and then your entrails will be burnt. Go to meet your fate, traitor, tyrant, renegade. Go to receive your own justice, traitor, evil man, criminal!"

At Hereford Castle, to which Hugh was dragged by four horses, a gallows fifty feet high had been erected. "Just for you!" said one of the men who untied him from his hurdle and hauled him toward the gallows. "Ain't we the special one, now?"

Simon de Reading, having been drawn behind the usual two horses, was hung on a smaller gallows. Hugh, propped up between his guards because one of his ankles would not allow him to bear any weight on it, shakily crossed himself and whispered a prayer for Simon's soul.

When he was twelve he had had to have a tooth drawn. His father, always anxious for him, had told him as he lay miserably in the barber's chair, "Get a pleasant picture in your mind, son, and fix it there. It'll take your mind off it as it happens." He'd obeyed, fixing first on his new horse, then, more satisfyingly, on a buxom village maiden he'd long admired, and it had worked, at least to the extent that it'd taken his mind off his tooth until the barber actually yanked it. Eleanor, after the birth of their first son, had told him that her midwife had given her similar advice when her labor pains became intense. "She said, 'Think of something you enjoy doing, and imagine yourself doing it,' so I thought of making love to you. Isn't that terrible? But it helped."

He thought of his wedding night. He was nineteen years old and pulling the sheets off his skittish little bride, chosen for him by the great King Edward himself, and he had been the happiest creature in the world. She was lovely and sweet and all his, and it had not yet occurred to him to want anything more.

He'd been guilty of no greater sin back then than poaching the occasional deer, and if he had died at that time, there would have been no cheering. Perhaps someone might have even wept for him. If he'd just taken life as it came to him his old father would be nodding off in a comfortable chair by a roaring fire now and his wife would be welcoming some pretty heiress as their son Hugh's new bride. His son Edward would be mooning over some wench and the rest of his children would be playing some absurd game. The king would be on his throne, taking the purely disinterested advice that Hugh could have offered him but never did.

He'd truly loved them all, and he'd brought them all to ruin. It was by far his worst sin. Why had not Trussell included that in his thunderings?

He prayed for forgiveness, perhaps audibly enough to be overheard by those surrounding him, for there was scornful laughter. Then a man in black appeared beside him. Of the faces that surrounded him, his was the only one that showed no hatred on it. It showed nothing, in fact; the man was simply following his trade. Hugh hoped he was reasonably good at it; Arundel's executioner, as the queen's men had delighted in informing him, had been a rank amateur who had taken twenty strokes to sever the earl's head. He slid his rings off his fingers and handed them to his executioner. "Go to it," he said tonelessly.

To separate them from the increasingly boisterous crowd, a little stand had been erected near the gallows for the queen and her son and the higher nobility. Still wearing a look of patient, slightly pained endurance, Isabella watched as Despenser, wearing nothing but his crown of nettles, was lifted aloft. Zouche, standing a few feet off with the queen's other leaders, glanced at young Edward's face but could read nothing in it.

After dangling in the air a short time, Hugh was lowered to a platform below the gallows, next to which a good-sized fire had been lit. For a moment, he lay still, much to the crowd's dismay; then, after a few slaps from the executioner, he started to cough and gasp and opened his eyes. The executioner, satisfied that his charge was as awake as he was going to get, nodded to a boy who like a surgeon's apprentice was standing nearby with several knives and an ax. The boy handed over the smallest of the knives, and the executioner bent to his work.

Despenser let out a strangled cry, and the executioner held up Hugh's genitals. Amid the cheers and jests, Isabella's smile was too slight to be detected as they quivered in the air. After dropping them in the fire ("Listen to 'em sizzle!" a spectator shouted happily. "Like bacon!"), the executioner took a larger knife and opened Hugh's abdomen. Hugh moaned and turned his head back and forth, then grew quiet. He was motionless when his heart was plucked out and thrown into the fire.

The boy handed over the ax. "Behold the head of a traitor!"

The crowd shrieked with sheer joy, and men clapped each other on the backs and shoulders as if they had personally caught the king's chamberlain and brought him to justice. As the head, which was to be sent to London, was carefully put aside, Zouche found that he could not watch Hugh's blood-covered body being cut into four pieces. Instead, he stared at the ring on his right hand as he twirled it round and round.

Isabella and Joan of Bar sat in the queen's chambers, Joan's face a distinctly greenish color. Hugh le Despenser had been cut up an hour ago, and somewhere his quarters and head were being parboiled before being sent their five separate ways, but the crowd was still celebrating. "Will that racket never cease?" muttered Isabella. She itched for Mortimer's presence instead of that of Joan, but since they had arrived in England they had forced themselves to be drearily chaste, for appearances' sake. But with Bishop Orleton out of the palace—he had been sent to seize the Great Seal from the king at Kenilworth—surely they could indulge themselves a bit...

"They're bound to run out of ale soon," said Joan listlessly. She watched as Isabella nibbled on a pastry. Joan herself was uncertain whether she would ever have much of an appetite again, although she had contrived to arrange her veil in such a manner that she had not seen a thing. But the pomander she had held to her nose had not done much to disguise the horrid smell, and there had been nothing she could do to keep the man's dying moans from reaching her ears. "You know, we were married on the same day."

"Who, my dear?"

"Despenser and I. He married my cousin Eleanor on the same day I married my detestable husband." She thought of the mass knighting that had taken place a few days before the weddings, and the huge banquet that had accompanied it, and her stomach once again started to churn. "I wonder how she will take his death."

Isabella regarded her friend thoughtfully. "I had not thought of the new widow. She should be told, shouldn't she?" She turned to a servant who was standing discreetly nearby. "Go, man, and fetch me—let me see—William Ogle. He will do nicely."

"I have not heard of any William Ogle," Joan said weakly.

"You wouldn't have; he served in Lady Mortimer's household at Wigmore Castle and served her when she was imprisoned in Hampshire. But he joined Lord Mortimer after he had her released, and he is a good man for my purpose."

"Which is?"

"Delivering a message quickly, of course. Go and lie down, Joan dear. You look ill."

Joan curtseyed and left, heading for the garderobe with all due speed. Her place was soon taken by Ogle. "You can ride fast, man?"

"Very."

"Do you have a good memory?"

"The best."

"You can give a detailed account of what happened today?"

"Certainly."

"I want you to speed to London and tell Hugh le Despenser's widow—she is a prisoner in the Tower—of all that transpired since he was captured. She is a foolish little thing, and may faint. If she does, wake her up. Don't go until she knows all."

"Yes, your grace."

"And, Ogle? There is no need to be delicate with her. She is not such a fine-bred creature that you need mince words." She smiled.

"I won't, your grace."

Isabella turned back to the servant. "Now please go fetch Lord Mortimer for me."

"Yes, your grace."

The queen took another pastry—Bishop Orleton's cook had truly outdone himself on this occasion—and a large sip of wine, deciding that it would be enjoyable to be a little tipsy when Mortimer arrived. He would be wild to take her, she knew, and it would be a wonderful ending to this truly special day.

PART II

▼

NOVEMBER 1326 TO
JUNE 30, 1337

CHAPTER 19

▼

NOVEMBER 1326 TO FEBRUARY 1327

In Eleanor's cell at the Beauchamp Tower, William Ogle frowned. Either the widow was exhibiting extraordinary self-control or she had not cared a whit for the life of her late husband. Either way, he sensed, the queen would be disappointed. He went on, "After they hung him, they thought he was dead, but then he woke up right nicely. Just in time to have his, er—"

Ogle's French did not include the word for "genitals." But Isabella had counseled against delicacy, so Ogle did not search further for euphemisms. "Balls and cock chopped off."

The fat old damsel standing by the widow looked at Ogle as if she would like to chop his own off, but the lady showed no emotion aside from widening her green eyes a fraction. Ogle chuckled silently. It was obvious that even Hugh's wife had detested him. He finished smoothly, "He knew what was happening to them, all right. Then they cut him open, and he moaned and carried on a bit, but I think he was dead or close to it right afterward. Then they took his guts and heart out and cut the head off. Then they quartered him. His head will be coming to London pretty soon, I imagine. The rest of him goes to York, Bristol, Carlisle, and Dover."

"Are you done, sir?"

Ogle considered. He'd told her about the stripping of him, the writing on him, the reversed coat of arms, the crown of nettles, the filth heaped upon him, Simon and the standard, the four horses, the fifty-foot gallows. "I am done."

"Thank you for informing me of this. If you have nothing more to tell me then I will wish you good day."

She closed the door against him as if she was in her own castle instead of in a cell at the Tower. Only when she heard his footsteps receding into the distance did she let Gladys take her into her arms. She was not crying, but she was shivering, and she allowed Gladys to lead her beside the fire and sit her down awhile, murmuring words of comfort. Then she whispered, "Let us tell the children."

"My lady—"

"I can tell them, Gladys. They must hear it from me."

The other room, where the children had been sent upon Ogle's arrival—even he had thought they should be sent away—was unnaturally quiet when she entered it, and there was no need to ask for their attention. She said quietly, "I told you when I heard that your grandfather was dead that we must prepare for the worst, and the worst has happened. Your father is not coming back."

Her daughter Joan let out a little cry, and Edward—the most undemonstrative person Eleanor knew—took his sister's hand. The gesture made Eleanor's tears start to run, but she managed to continue, "He died several days ago, in Hereford. It was quick, I am told"—the lie for the younger children sprang to her lips readily, and was the only sign she had that God was still with her in any way—"and he will soon be in a much better place than here. Let us pray for him."

She knelt and led them in a prayer before they had a chance to ask any questions, but when it came time to rise, she was trembling so badly once again that she could not get off her knees. She looked quizzically at Gladys, who swiftly moved to her side. "Let me put you to bed, my lady."

"There is no need, Gladys. I am fine."

"True, my lady, but you need your rest. Edward, help me."

Together Gladys and Edward raised her and walked her into the next room. "Lie down, my lady."

"Oh, there is no need for that." But Eleanor allowed herself to be helped into bed. "He was lying to me, wasn't he, Gladys? He was only trying to make me unhappy. They could not have treated him so horribly."

"Mother—"

"I know he was lying." Eleanor was trembling even more violently than before, and even her teeth were chattering. "He had to be. Wasn't he, Gladys? Wasn't he?"

"Mother!"

"He was lying, my lady." Gladys turned to Edward, who was whiter than his mother. "Get her some wine."

Edward obeyed. "Drink this, my lady. It will calm you."

"But I am calm. He was only lying." She made no resistance, however, and drained the cup slowly as Gladys removed her headdress and wrapped Hugh's cloak around her. Eleanor slept snuggled within the cloak every night, and she smiled as her hand touched its fur edging. Gladys pulled the bed covers tightly around Eleanor and helped her drink another cup of wine. Gradually, the trembling stopped. "I am so tired, Gladys."

"I know you are, my lady. Go to sleep."

Eleanor turned on her side and closed her eyes. Only when they heard her snore did Edward whisper, "Gladys, has she gone mad?"

"No, Edward. The news has given her a shock, a very bad one, but she will be better after she rests."

"*Please* don't let her be mad."

Gladys looked at the twelve-year-old boy, knowing how badly he himself needed comfort. She put her arm around his shoulders, and he allowed it to rest there a minute or two. "I promise you, Edward, she is not mad."

"He died a traitor's death. Didn't he?"

Edward was too old to be fooled. "Yes." She reached out to hold him, but the boy pulled away, looking numb. She could think of nothing to say but, "It is all over now, Edward. Try not to think about it. Come with me. Your brothers and sisters will be frightened that we have been gone so long."

They were terrified, in fact—four of them sitting huddled together by the fire, one-year-old John having fallen mercifully asleep sometime earlier. Edward took charge of Gilbert, while Gladys saw to the three girls. For a few hours they tried to busy themselves, succeeding to the point where the girls began quarreling and John woke and started crying. Edward was trying in vain to break up the argument, Gilbert was trying to get involved in it, and Gladys was trying to console the baby, when they heard a footstep, and Eleanor entered the room. She was chalk white, but her voice had authority when she said quietly, "All of you. Listen to your brother."

"Yes, Mama."

"Come here, little one." Eleanor took John, who snuggled against her.

"You scared us, Mama," said Nora reproachfully.

"I am sorry, Nora. But I am better now."

Gilbert's lip was trembling. "Is he really dead, Mama?"

"Yes." Eleanor looked at her wedding ring. "He is really dead, my children, and we must be strong." She tried to smile. "Your father would want to see it so. He was proud of all of you always."

"Will they kill us, Mama?" Joan asked.

"No. We are not important to them."

"What about Hugh?"

"I wish I could tell you he is safe, but I cannot. We can only pray for him."

They sat in silence for a while. Then Eleanor said, "Soon it will be time for us to go to bed. Let us talk of the happy times we had with your father, and that is what we will think of when we go to sleep tonight. I will start."

Hugh's head arrived in London several days after Ogle did, making the journey in a jaunty little cart painted especially for it with edifying scriptural verses and the Despenser arms. (The queen's troops had become quite good at drawing the Despenser arms, the queen observed to Mortimer; by the time the brat in Caerphilly was taken, they would be masters.) Most of the staff at the Tower, including the cook assigned to the Despensers, went to London Bridge to see it placed there, and they spent several hours afterward celebrating. It was some two hours past the family's supper time when a guard finally handed them some bread, ale, and milk; no one, it appeared, was quite sober enough to do the cooking yet. Gisors, himself somewhat worse for wear for drink, came up later to apologize. "Well, it's up there," he whispered to Gladys as he turned to go. "Not a pretty sight."

Since Eleanor's captivity, her sense of hearing had sharpened. "*Him*," said Eleanor softly. "Not *it*."

Isabella and all four of her children spent Christmas at Wallingford, joined by Mortimer, whose wife had settled conveniently at Wigmore. Mortimer had seen to it that her household was reestablished properly and had given her more money than usual so that she could replenish her wardrobe and furnish her castle comfortably. These matrimonial duties completed at no cost to Mortimer himself—the royal treasury held a whopping sixty-two thousand pounds, and Isabella saw no reason why she and Mortimer should not help themselves to part of it—he could lie with his royal mistress with a clear conscience and a fat purse.

The treasury aside, Arundel had left money and plate in Chichester Cathedral, and Despenser had left plate in the Tower, that the queen had ordered to be delivered to her. Already she had had a fine time sorting through Arundel's silver cups, delivered to her shortly after the earl's death, and the Bishop of Winchester, who had superintended the moving of Despenser's plate into the queen's wardrobe in London, reported that most of his cups were gold. And more treasure, looted or seized from the estates of the Despensers and Arundel by the queen's supporters or found secreted in monasteries, was appearing every day.

But despite the presence of her lover and the prospect of booty, Christmas at Wallingford was not quite as pleasant as the queen could have wished. All three younger children, once the glow of their reunion with Isabella had worn off, had an irritating habit of asking about their father. Where was he? Was he sad to be away? Why could they not see him? The girls had an even more irritating habit of asking about Lady Hastings. Why had she gone away so suddenly? Was she ill? And John had a truly maddening habit of asking about Lady Despenser. Was she being treated well in the Tower? Was she lonely? Would she be getting out soon? To these questions Isabella parried answers as best she could. The king needed time to himself after his exhausting sojourn in Wales, where he had been dragged shamefully by Hugh le Despenser. Lady Hastings, though sweet and pleasant on the surface, as the daughter of a Very Bad Man was unsuitable to be around the girls, as they would understand someday. And Lady Despenser was a traitor's wife and therefore had to be kept fast, for her own safety and that of the realm.

To her further annoyance, Isabella's marriage had been a subject of episcopal concern. On the day after Despenser's death, the queen (suffering from a slight hangover along with the rest of Hereford) had cast off her mourning robes and appeared in the finest cloth to be found in Paris, but she had not suggested returning to her husband. This, the bishops gathered in Wallingford posited, could be taken the wrong way.

It was Orleton who solved her problem. If the queen returned to her husband, he explained to all and sundry, she would be in the direst physical danger. Why, the king was known to carry a knife in his hose to kill Isabella with, and if this were not available, he had threatened, he would use his bare teeth! The danger had only been increased by the death of Despenser. Edward had loved him immoderately and inordinately, and would naturally want to avenge his death.

Well pleased as she was over this quick thinking on the part of the bishop, Isabella knew that something would have to be done about the king, even if she had a temporary reprieve from having to live with him, and it was a matter that she and Mortimer put their minds to as the New Year approached. But it was not the only matter of business that was taken care of Wallingford that Christmastide.

On January 4, 1327, the queen arrived at Westminster, and on that same day, the Tower's latest constable, Thomas Wake, knocked on Eleanor's door. "My lady, let me have a word with you in private."

Since his arrival, Wake had been reasonably polite to Eleanor, but on this day, his face was ominously kind. Eleanor knew immediately what he had to tell her: her eldest son was captured, or dead. She thought back to the day she had given birth to him, the happy little boy he had been, the joy she would have had in welcoming his bride. "My son is dead," she said quietly.

"No. No one is dead." Wake looked at the parchments he held in his hand and coughed.

"My daughter Isabel? I heard that she and the Countess of Arundel and her boys have been staying with the Earl of Surrey since the Earl of Arundel was executed. Has she been harmed?"

"I know nothing of her. This concerns your three daughters here. They are to go to convents, my lady." He coughed again. "They are to take the veil."

She stared. "You must be mistaken, sir. They are far too young. Margaret is not even four years old!" She went on patiently, "Joan is only ten, Nora seven…"

"Here are the orders themselves, my lady."

She read the orders, identical for each girl, hearing the queen's pleased triumph in every word. "To be admitted and veiled without delay, to remain forever under the order and regular habit of that house, and to cause her to be professed in the same as speedily as possible…"

Forever. She sagged against the wall and dropped the parchments to the floor. From a distance she heard Wake saying awkwardly, "You won't be here forever, my lady. Then you can visit them."

"Yes. I can visit them."

She picked up the parchments and studied them again. Margaret was to go to Watton, Nora to Sempringham, Joan to Shaftesbury. They were issued in the king's name and bore his Great Seal, as did all the orders these days that emanated from the queen and Mortimer. But the king never would have signed such an order. Never in his life had he been unkind to her. She looked at the date: January 1, only a few days after Christmas. So this was how Isabella celebrated the birth of the Lord, that friend of children, by caging hers for life.

She looked at the dagger at Wake's side. With one swift movement she could take it; with another, perhaps, she could put it in her heart. But he would try to stop her, surely, and she was half his size. She would undoubtedly botch it any-way and die slowly, painfully while her children watched. No, dying was too much trouble. And she had the boys to think of—at least until Isabella took them too. "When are they to leave?" She hardly recognized her own voice, so dull was it.

Wake had seen the glance at the dagger, and he put his hand on it. "Tomorrow, my lady."

"Then I must prepare them for their new life now. Excuse me, sir."

Joan was the worst. Margaret and Nora had only vague ideas of what was happening to them; they were being sent to live with nuns, just as they had been sent to live with nurses not long ago. But Joan understood. She said quietly, "But Mama, Papa said I was to get married. He said after the Earl of Kildaire's poor son died that he would find someone else nice for me to marry."

"Things are so much different now, child."

"But why is the king doing this?"

"It is not really the king, it is the queen. The king would never have made you part from me like this. He loved our family. But this is not about the queen, or your papa, Joan, you must remember. You have been blessed and honored to be chosen as a bride of Christ. It is God's will, Joan."

"I don't want to be a bride of Christ. I want to be a real bride. And I *hate* God! First he took Grandfather, and then Papa, and made us prisoners— I *hate* God!"

"Joan! You must not say that."

Joan threw herself on the bed the three girls shared, weeping. Edward, who had taken on almost a paternal air since Hugh's death, came over and patted her on the shoulder.

"Don't worry, sweetheart," he said, in a voice that before it cracked up an octave was so like his father's that Eleanor started. "I hate Him too."

It was mid-morning when the door to her cell finally opened and a familiar face appeared—her cousin Joan of Bar, Countess of Surrey.

As Gladys readied the girls, Eleanor whispered, "How could she, Joan? How could you?"

Joan of Bar said crisply, "Your husband sent Mortimer's daughters to convents, after all."

"As boarders. He did not make nuns of them, Joan. He did not force them to take vows that can never be broken, without fear of damnation."

Joan shrugged. "It is what the queen deems best." Not unkindly, she added, "You must be realistic, Eleanor. They are better off as nuns now. With Hugh's goods and lands forfeit and his name in ruins, they could hardly hope to marry men of any substance."

"Not men of any substance, perhaps. But they might have married decent men of modest means who would be good to them. They might have had children of their own to love."

Joan snorted. "Yes, they might have married such paragons as you speak of. Or they might have married a profligate like I did, or a pervert like the queen did, or a villain like you did. At least there shall be no surprises for them as there were for us." She sighed. "Don't fear, Eleanor. I shall take good care of them on their journey, and I am sure the nuns will too." Joan looked at the three bundled-up little girls and smiled at them. They gazed back at her unsmilingly, three sets of Hugh's brown eyes meeting hers. "I brought them plenty of provisions for the trip."

Eleanor bent and kissed the three of them. "Good-bye, my pets. You know that I cannot leave here now, but someday I will, God willing, and then I shall write and visit you. I love you dearly. Not a day will go by without my thinking of you."

They were filing out in front of Joan of Bar. As the stout countess followed them slowly, still breathing heavily from her climb up the Tower stairs, Eleanor seized her by the shoulder and hissed, "Joan, wait! Please don't let them see Hugh—on the bridge—if you have any kindness in your heart."

Joan sighed. "Do you think I am some sort of monster, Eleanor? I will guard their eyes. In any case, though, they would not know it was their father. He is already unrecognizable. You would not know him yourself."

Boisterous Gilbert was unusually well behaved that day, settling himself to his lessons without the usual protest he thought behooved him. Even John played quietly with the wooden pigs and cows the king had carved for him. As for Edward, he showed none of his usual moodiness. When he saw Eleanor sitting staring into space, he put his arm around her and whispered, "I didn't mean what I said to Joan, Mother. God will protect them," in such a manly fashion that Eleanor, who had thought she could feel nothing now, felt a surge of pride.

Two days before, she had snapped at Margaret when she misplaced her doll for the dozenth time and wanted Eleanor to find it immediately. (How could she lose something in such small quarters? Eleanor had wondered.) Only yesterday morning before Wake came, she had told Nora not to chatter so incessantly. Four days ago, she had told Joan that just because they were prisoners was no reason why things should not be put away neatly. Now she would never search for Margaret's doll again, would never hear Nora's volley of questions again, would never pick up after Joan again.

Did the girls know she loved them? She had tried so hard to be good to them since Hugh died, knowing that they were grieving like herself and were more bewildered at their sudden change of fortune than she. But she had not always succeeded. She had been so weary, so on edge since the news came of Hugh. Would they remember the mother who had tucked them into bed each night with a gentle word and a kiss, even on the nights that she had wanted to do nothing but lie on her bed with Hugh's cloak, draw the curtains around her, and cry in peace? Or would they remember the shrew who had pounced on their every imperfection?

A guard had appeared in their rooms without her noticing and was standing by her. "My lady. Would you like to go to the chapel for a while?"

She nodded numbly and let him conduct her to the Chapel of St. Peter ad Vincula, just a few feet away from the Beauchamp Tower. Several times in December, she had been allowed to go there to pray for Hugh's soul, and she had come out feeling a dim sort of comfort that was better than none at all. But today when she was left there kneeling all by herself, nothing came—no prayers, not even tears. What was the point of praying or crying? If there was a God, he was clearly on the side of Mortimer and Isabella.

She got to her feet and knocked at the door, where her guard waited tactfully on the other side. "You were not here very long, my lady."

"No. My thoughts are not of the sort one wants to be alone with, and there is probably no one to hear my prayers anyway."

The guard, a young man named Tom, looked shocked by this blasphemy. Eleanor added dully, "But thank you for taking me there. It was a change from our cell at any rate."

He led her back to the Beauchamp Tower, and had conducted her through her doorway when he hesitated. "My lady, I would like to bring you something. May I?"

"What? Daughters to replace the ones I have lost?" She recoiled at Tom's hurt look. "I suppose, Tom. What is it?"

"You will see."

Not really caring what he brought back, Eleanor nodded. When Tom returned, Gladys had taken the boys outside, and Eleanor in an attempt to numb her mind through activity was mending one of her sons' shirts—trying to ignore

Nora's smock that had been put in the same basket of items needing repair. Tom was carrying a small sack, which clinked when he set it down. "What?"

Tom opened the sack and pulled out a large gold cup. Eleanor gasped as she saw the Despenser coat of arms on it. "My husband's goods?"

"Or his father's. More are being brought here every day, now that your husband has—um—passed away."

The absurdity of the euphemism in Hugh's particular case almost made Eleanor laugh.

"They're in a storehouse here on the Tower grounds, still to be sorted and valued. Some were taken from the Despenser manors that the queen's men looted after she landed, and some of these came from your husband's wardrobe here. The queen has already ordered your late husband's wardrobe keeper to give her the best ones for her own use."

Eleanor started. "What does she want with my husband's jewels? If they are forfeit to the crown, aren't they to go to the treasury?"

"She wants them because they were your husband's, my lady. She wants to gloat over them."

"The same way she must be gloating over our little girls. As trophies."

"Yes, my lady." He bent down over the sack. "It's not just cups. There's florins here, salt cellars, other jewels—all sorts of beautiful things." He picked up a florin and turned it over and over. "I know nothing can make up for you what happened this morning. I know that what I'm saying doesn't make much sense. But I thought that if you took some of these things for yourself it might give you a little satisfaction at least. At least you would be keeping something from the queen she wanted."

"You are right. It doesn't make much sense." Eleanor picked up another cup, one with no heraldic designs on it. "But it does give me satisfaction. I shall take some." Picking up a florin, she handed it to Tom.

"No, my lady. I would hang."

"You could hang just for doing what you are doing now! Put them back, please."

Tom stopped her as she began to place the cups back into the sack. "I'll take my chances; I know the right time to go and can avoid being seen. Those little girls—it makes me angry. But if you truly wish it, my lady, I will return the treasures from where I got them."

Eleanor smiled grimly. "No. I'll take my chances too."

William la Zouche had spent Christmas with his young son at Ashby-de-la-Zouche. When he arrived in London for Parliament in early January, he cast guilty looks at his right hand, which still bore Hugh le Despenser's ring, and at London Bridge, which now bore Hugh le Despenser's head, but could not bring himself, as one of Hugh le Despenser's captors, to meet Lady Despenser in the Tower of London just yet. Her grief, he argued to himself, would still be too raw. And Zouche believed from Hugh's face when he had pulled off the ring that there would be quite genuine grief. Still, Zouche, not a man given to fancies in general, could not help but fancy that the head on the bridge looked reproachful.

It turned out to be a Parliament not like any other, and there would come a day Zouche wished he had taken no part in it. Whether the king had refused to come, as Bishop Orleton announced, or whether it had never been intended that he come, Zouche never knew, but he was certainly not there. This was a good thing, the bishop announced solemnly, because Edward had threatened to kill the queen with a dagger if he ever saw her. In the general indignation this remark excited, it did not occur to Zouche, or to many others, that the queen had shown herself remarkably able to fend for herself.

"What have we come to when our king will not come to Parliament?" the bishop asked the members mournfully. "Do we want to continue under his rule? Or do we want to be ruled by the king's noble son?" He raised a hand as those assembled began to argue among themselves. "Consider this matter deeply," he said solemnly, "and return with your decision the next morning."

It was Roger Mortimer, who Zouche knew had lent his military expertise to the queen's noble cause, who led off the proceedings the next morning. The great men of the land, he declared, of whom he was merely a humble representative, were united in agreeing that the king should be deposed. The Londoners, he added, had all asked too that the members of Parliament swear an oath of fealty to their cause, which now included deposing the king as well as supporting the queen, her son, and the enemies of the Despensers. As Parliament collectively remembered what had happened to the Despensers and to those unfortunates in disfavor with the Londoners, Thomas Wake, son-in-law to Henry of Lancaster, sprang up. "As far as I am concerned," he shouted, "Edward should no longer reign!"

Bishop Orleton took over. "The Lord tells us, 'A foolish king destroys his people.' Shall we let England be destroyed, good men? Or shall we save her, and ourselves, from certain destruction? For twenty years, since the death of the great first Edward, we have been teetering on its brink! Need I recall the signs the good

Lord our God has sent us? Gaveston, the witch's son? The Bannock Burn? The famine? The wicked Hugh le Despenser? Will we heed them, once and for all, and save our beloved kingdom before it is too late?"

"Save England!" shouted the members. "Away with the king!"

"My head is sick," the Bishop of Winchester said dolefully when the tumult died down. "The head of England is weak, and therefore sick, and the governance of all of England has suffered as a result. The king's evil counselors have preyed on this weakness, and bled England until it has oftentimes seemed there is no cure. But succor has come to her, in the form of a noble boy and his brave, devoted mother. Shall we crown that shining sun of a boy with the shining crown of England, or shall we let the shining crown of England continue to sit on this weak and festering head? You decide!"

"What will it be, sirs?" shouted Wake, arms extended and hands waving as if he were trying to put himself into flight. "What do the people say? Shall the son reign?"

"Yes!" cried Parliament as one.

Archbishop Reynolds, who owed his post to the second Edward, took his turn. "The voice of the people is the voice of God," he said. "After years of oppression, you have spoken your will that the foolish king be deposed and that his son rule in his place, and your will is God's will."

Wake, all but flying now, yelled, "Is this the will of the people? Do the people will that the second Edward be deposed and his son made king in his place?"

"*Fiat! Fiat!* Amen!"

A door swung open and fourteen-year-old Edward, magnificently dressed, came slowly in, followed by the queen, who for Parliament had resumed her black robes, albeit in velvet. Reynolds shouted, "Behold your king!"

The queen was both weeping and smiling, evidently torn between grief that her husband had sunk so low and joy that her son was soaring to the country's rescue. Zouche's own eyes, and those of many others, were streaming tears; it was all Zouche could do to croak out the words to "Glory, Laud, and Honor." Only a few dissenters stood silent, not even humming, and for several days afterward, they would be nursing the bruises they subsequently received at the hands of the watchful Londoners.

With Bishop Orleton to London had come Robert Baldock, formerly the Chancellor of England. As a member of the clergy, after his capture he had been spared the humiliation meted out to Despenser and Simon de Reading, but instead had been allowed to ride inconspicuously from Llantrisant to Hereford with the troops' servants. Once in Hereford, he had been turned over to the bishop to be tried by his fellow men of the Church.

In London, his luck ran out. Bishop Orleton took him to his manor to stay while awaiting trial, but the Londoners, learning of his presence there, prized him out on the pretext that the bishop had no right to keep him out of their own prison. Hence, he was dragged off to Newgate, where by May he would be dead of maltreatment. Though Orleton would later claim to have done nothing to harm him, he had also done nothing to save him.

Edward had no complaints to make of his own jailer, Henry of Lancaster. The king had a set of rooms to himself, comfortable furnishings, warm clothes, blazing fires, good food and wine, and a staff to take care of his needs. He could go for long walks within the castle grounds and was allowed to attend the entertainments by Henry's minstrels. But since he had heard the news of Hugh's execution—and like Eleanor, he had been given all the details—his days had become things to be endured.

They were long days, for he had no visitors to break them up, and expected none. Eleanor, he knew, was a prisoner in the Tower; she could help him no more than he could help her. Still, the memory of her red hair cascading to her bare hips was a pleasant one; memories of her, and his memories of Gaveston and Despenser and Lucy, were all that made life bearable now. Who else was there? Certainly not his children; that his whore of a wife would never allow. Mary, his only sister left in England? The days when she could leave her convent on a whim had ended, he knew, the day he had been captured at Llantrisant. His brothers? Not those faithless knaves. If they ever turned up, he'd refuse to see them.

He was wrong, however, to have expected no visitors, for on January 20, an entire crowd of them came. A delegation, he was told, from Parliament.

A make-believe, play Parliament it would be without him, he thought, but as under the circumstances he could hardly refuse to receive the delegation, he let himself be led into the great hall. He was dressed from head to toe in black. Henry had frowned a bit when Edward insisted on having mourning clothes for Hugh le Despenser, but as Henry himself had donned black for Thomas of Lancaster, a man he had never liked much for all of his dutiful avenging of him, he hadn't belabored the point.

Edward recognized many of the men in the great hall. Orleton, who only eight weeks ago had taken the Great Seal from him. The Bishop of Winchester. The Earl of Surrey. Lancaster, of course. Barons, abbots, priors, justices, monks, knights—who was the knight staring so arrogantly at him?

Sir William Trussell. The man who had pronounced sentence on Hugh and his father. His cruel face was one of the last things they had seen in this world—

Edward's feet slid from under him, and the world went black. "Hugh?" he whispered gratefully as someone took him by the arm. "Hugh, it is you?"

"Cousin, you were faint. This room is too hot, and you ate but little this morning. Do you need to rest awhile first?"

On one side of him was Henry of Lancaster, on the other the Bishop of Winchester. Edward sighed. "No. Have them say whatever they have come to say."

After Edward had been helped into the great hall's chair of state, Orleton was only too glad to proceed. The king, he pronounced dolorously, had been controlled and governed by others who had given him evil counsel. He had given himself up to unseemly works and occupations, neglecting the realm in the process. He had lost the realm of Scotland, and territories in Gascony and Ireland that the first Edward had left in peace. He had destroyed the Holy Church. (Edward, looking at Orleton's rich vestments, thought for his part that the Church, or at least Orleton's share of it, looked quite healthy.) He had also put many great and noble men of the land to a shameful death or imprisoned, exiled, and disinherited them. He had broken his coronation oath. He had stripped the realm and done all that he could do to ruin it. In doing all of these evils he had shown himself incorrigible without hope of amendment. These things were so notorious, Orleton concluded, that they could not be denied.

"But I do deny them."

"It matters not whether you do or not, because the people, as one, have demanded that you resign your rule to your son."

"And if I do not?"

"Then the people will choose someone more suitable, someone more experienced. A grown man, perhaps, not one necessarily of royal blood."

A long silence ensued as all present stared at Edward. Mortimer? Was that whom they had in mind? Madness! His sons, his brothers, his cousin Henry, his nephews all stood closer to the crown than Mortimer; none of them would consent to have that upstart reign over them. There would be civil war. Did he want to subject his sons to that? To risk destroying his royal line? He shook his head, unaware of the tears falling down his face, and said, "I will not see my own son disinherited. If the people are that dissatisfied with me, I will resign the crown to him, and only him."

The stares turned to smiles or at least looks of relief. As Henry of Lancaster ushered the king respectfully out of the room, Edward's sobs began to mix with wild laughter. For the first time in his reign, he had done something that met with the wholehearted approval of the land.

The next day, William Trussell, acting on behalf of the whole realm, renounced homage and allegiance to the king. Thomas le Blount, the king's household steward, broke his staff of office. The royal household was no more.

Edward the Third was crowned on February 1, 1327. Isabella celebrated by granting herself a dower of twenty thousand marks per year—over thirteen thousand pounds. It was nearly triple the generous income she had received before the confiscation of her estates.

"They have appointed a regency council to advise the king. Archbishop Reynolds, Archbishop Melton, the Bishops of Winchester and Hereford—"

"Melton is the only one of them worthy to be called a man of God. But go on, please."

"The Earls of Lancaster, Norfolk, Kent, and Surrey. Thomas Wake. Henry Percy. Oliver Ingham. John de Ros."

"Hugh should have killed him when he had the chance," said Eleanor sourly. "So Mortimer does not have a seat on this council? Then I doubt it will be much of one. Thank you for our dinner."

As the guard left, Eleanor pushed away the food he had brought along with this latest news. Gladys shook her head. Eleanor had eaten little after the death of her husband, less than that after her daughters' removal, and almost nothing after her uncle had given up his crown. "My lady, you cannot go on like this. You must eat."

"I am not hungry."

"I know, my lady. But you must force yourself. You cannot starve your unborn child, after all."

"Child? I am not with child."

"You have not had a monthly course since you have been here, my lady. Your waist is thickening, even as you eat nothing. You must be with child."

"But—"

"You and Hugh were together here before he left. He came to your bed, didn't he?"

Yes, thought Eleanor, he had most certainly come to her bed. She frowned. Lately she *had* felt tired and nauseated, but she had attributed the symptoms to the effects of grief. Might Hugh had left her a last gift?

For the first time since Bishop Stapeldon had died, she felt hope rise within her. Then it faltered. "But Gladys, what if I bear a girl? Will the queen take her as she did the others?"

"How can we know what will happen? But you must have faith, my lady. Surely God would not be so cruel as to bring you this child only to snatch it away."

Eleanor pulled her plate back to her and began nibbling at her food.

That night, she lay in her bed and touched her belly, then the fur on Hugh's cloak. "Thank you, my love," she whispered.

CHAPTER 20

▼

FEBRUARY 1327 TO APRIL 1327

Parliament was still sitting in mid-February when Zouche was ordered to see the king. The lanky fourteen-year-old sat in his chamber, accompanied not by any of the members of his council, but by Mortimer and Isabella. Zouche had scarcely had time to kneel and be ordered to rise before Mortimer started speaking. "Are you ready to undertake another trip to Wales, Zouche?"

"Why?"

"Hugh le Despenser's whelp, that's why. He still holds out in Caerphilly Castle, along with its constable, John Felton, and a hundred men or so. They claim that the former king made them swear on the Host that they would give the castle up to no one but the king, and that they'll hold it until their rightful king comes to claim it. Of course, the boy has an additional incentive to hold out, in light of what happened to Papa and Grandfather."

"Is he accused of any of their crimes?"

Mortimer shrugged. "He's eighteen, old enough to have been involved in them. He's not without courage, I understand; he was a hostage for England after the last Scottish fiasco and never flinched when they took him across the border, so they say. Such a boy is dangerous, particularly now that he has a father and grandfather to avenge. The king wants you to take him and the castle into custody." He grinned and held up a piece of parchment. "The king has issued a pardon to all those in the castle except Despenser, excluding him by name. We'll see how many friends he has after that. If the loyalty his father and grandfather inspired is any indication, the brat will soon be taken."

Isabella was studying her robes with a pained look. "It is a harsh necessity, Lord Zouche, but the family are the enemies of the realm."

William hesitated. Casually, he asked, "Might I ask what is the status of the late Hugh's widow?"

"The redheaded little cat and her mangy kittens are locked up in the Tower for safekeeping," Mortimer said.

Isabella gave a sigh as pained as her look. "She is a granddaughter of the first Edward and must be treated with a certain respect, but it cannot be forgotten that she aided and abetted her husband in his schemes against me. Why, he made my husband appoint the wench as my housekeeper, solely to humiliate me! And the devious woman entered into his scheme wholeheartedly. She must be punished for her misdeeds."

"Lady Despenser is my first cousin," said the new king. So much he had fallen into the background that the adults in the room started when he spoke. Isabella herself appeared to be about to scold her son for his interruption when she recalled just in time that he was the sovereign of England. "She was always respectful to me, and John is fond of her. I'll not have her shut up for life."

"Why, of course not, my lord," said Isabella with a brittle smile. "But this is none of Lord Zouche's concern, is it? He will find this all quite tedious."

"And there are other matters you must attend to this day," added Mortimer.

"I shall prepare to go to Wales straightaway," said Zouche, profiting from the hint.

"Visitor, my lady."

Eleanor started at the small figure in the doorway, half the size of the burly guard standing behind him. "John?"

"I just wanted to see if you were doing all right," said John of Eltham formally. The door closed and with the guard gone, John rushed into the room and hurled himself into her arms. "Lady Despenser, *are* you all right?"

"Of course I am, John. But what a pleasure! What are you doing here? Is the court here?"

"No, still at Westminster. I came here by barge."

"With permission?"

He grinned. "No. I can't stay long or there'll be questions. But I did want to see you."

"You are my first visitor—*our* first visitor."

"I was afraid you would be in chains," he admitted, looking around for any fetters that might be in sight.

Eleanor laughed. "We have not come to that, John, rest your mind easy. See?" She waved her hand around the room. "We have proper beds, and a table to eat off of, and food and ale and—"

"No sweetmeats," muttered Gilbert darkly.

John looked around. Edward, Gilbert, and Eleanor's John had come to stand by their mother, but there was no sign of the Despenser girls. "Lady Eleanor, where are the girls? Aren't they in the Tower?"

"No, John, they are staying in convents. They are—nuns now."

"*Nuns?*"

Edward, who had become fiercely protective of Eleanor in the last few weeks, put himself in front of her. "Drop it, John. You'll upset my mother."

"Edward! Don't be rude. He means no harm." Eleanor managed a smile. "The queen thought it best that they be veiled."

"Oh." John winced. At ten, he was not yet that good at reading faces, but he was good enough to see that Lady Despenser was very, very sad about her girls. He coughed and decided to change the subject. "I wanted to bring you something, Lady Eleanor, but I wasn't sure what. I couldn't bring too much or it would be missed. But I did think you might like these."

He held out a basket full of marzipan animals. Gilbert all but knocked the others down to grab a particularly fat cow, and even Edward's face crinkled into a half-smile as he bit into a pig. "Thank you, John. This is so sweet of you!"

"Sweet to bring sweets?" John smiled. He and Lady Despenser had enjoyed playing with words.

Gilbert in between bites informed John, "Mama is to have another baby."

John's eyes widened. "Really, Lady Despenser?"

Eleanor helped her youngest son with his rooster. "Yes, John, in June I think, please God."

"I wish you didn't have to have it here. I do ask Mama and my brother often to let you out, you know."

"I know you do, John, and I thank you."

John dropped his eyes and said formally, "I am sorry about Lord Despenser, Lady Eleanor. I know you all must miss him."

"We do, John, thank you, but he is in a better place now, and someday we shall be reunited there, please God."

This was not the prognosis of Lord Despenser's fate that John had heard from his mother, but he kept a diplomatic silence, which Eleanor broke by saying, "Tell me, John. Do you hear from your father?"

It was John's turn to look sad. "I haven't seen him. They say he is—not quite right in his mind, that he needs to be away from other people for a while."

Good Lord, could not Isabella even have the decency to let Edward see his children? "I am sure he will be better soon. When he is, and you get to see him, I want you to give him my love. If you can do so in private, of course."

He grinned, a conspirator again. "I will try."

After answering a few inquiries from Eleanor about his pets and his knightly progress, John sighed with regret and rose. "I had best go. I told my brother's bargemen that I wanted to see the menagerie and that then I would go. I don't know when I'll be back, Lady Despenser. I think the court will be going north soon. The Scots."

Eleanor had heard something of this. The very day her cousin Edward was crowned—Eleanor had the greatest difficulty calling the boy the king—the Scots had attacked Norham Castle. Though the raid had failed, there were rumors that future incursions were planned by Robert Bruce. Good, she thought viciously, let Isabella and Mortimer themselves fight the Scots. With luck, they would be sent back south with their tails between their legs...

She stifled these unpatriotic thoughts and hugged John. "I want you to know that your visit today meant everything to me. Thank you."

The queen's cries were echoing through her chamber at Westminster. Lying atop her, Mortimer, whose powers of concentration were such that he could think detachedly even as Isabella's fingernails were tearing into his back during her climax, compared her to his wife with satisfaction. Even after a dozen children, Lady Mortimer was as quiet during lovemaking as she was during mass, and about as lively. It did not occur to her husband that she might have been receptive to his teaching had he taken the same trouble with her as he did with the queen. For Mortimer had certainly taken a great deal of trouble with Isabella.

He reached his own climax and, lying by the queen's side, waited a decent interval before coming to the business at hand. Isabella was most amenable to his ideas after a vigorous bedding, he had discovered; in this, he suspected, she was similar to her husband. "We need to discuss what I spoke of earlier, darling."

"Oh?"

"Your husband."

"What about the fool?"

"There's a plot afoot to free him, led by your husband's old confessor, Thomas Dunheved."

"Oh, a Dominican monk! What a mighty force!" The queen giggled.

"He has a brother, Isabella, named Stephen, and a host of other men, all little more than outlaws. It's not wise to discount them, darling. We need to get Edward in more secure quarters, with more reliable custodians. I've a place in mind: Berkeley Castle, my son-in-law Thomas de Berkeley's home. It's out of the way, and Thomas will keep the late king as secure as I wish. John Maltravers will help him. He's Berkeley's brother-in-law and an old associate of mine."

"I know, darling. I met him in France." Isabella moved her hand to a place of great interest to Mortimer; she seldom liked to make love only once. "Do what you like with him; I find this business tiresome."

"Wait, just one moment. You know that eventually something is going to have to be done about your husband, don't you? He can't stay a captive indefinitely; it's too dangerous for us. One fool after another coming out of the shadows, wanting to restore him to his throne. We are going to have to make some decisions, hard ones."

Isabella laughed and mounted him. "Not tonight."

Contrary to Mortimer's prediction, the garrison at Caerphilly Castle had not abandoned Hugh le Despenser when all but he were offered pardons. Although William la Zouche had applied all of his considerable military skill to the resulting siege, it was ultimately Robert Bruce he had to thank for the castle's surrender, for with the threatened invasion by the Scots, England could not waste four hundred of its foot soldiers in Wales. Another pardon had therefore been issued to all of those in the castle, this time including Hugh le Despenser by name. Near the end of March, he and its constable, John Felton, surrendered to William.

The last of the Hugh le Despensers was an open-faced youth who looked somewhat younger than his eighteen years despite the beginnings of a beard on his chin. Zouche had forewarned him that he would be taken into temporary custody pending further orders of the king, and he made no protest as he was shackled. "So shall I give you the grand tour, Lord Zouche?"

"For now, we'll go to the great hall, while my men look around."

"You'll find it quite a sight. It was one of my father's special projects."

Two squires came racing in. "Lord Zouche! Lord Zouche! You would not believe how much money we have found! Barrels and barrels stuffed full of it."

"There must be thousands of pounds in it," said the other squire.

"Try thirteen thousand belonging to the crown," said Hugh calmly. "And you'll find another thousand belonging to my father." He shrugged. "They had hopes, Lord Zouche. They did have hopes."

Leaving Roger de Northburgh, the Bishop of Coventry and Lichfield, to deal with the treasure, as he had been sent to Caerphilly just for that purpose, William led his prisoner to the great hall. It was a sight, as Hugh had promised. Light from the four huge windows, decorated delicately but elaborately, filled the room and brightened the walls. Even from the other end of the hall, William could feel the heat from the fire that burned in the fireplace between the two pairs of windows. "My father had this hall redone just last year. Nice, isn't it?"

"Beautiful."

"There were to be some murals on the walls, but there wasn't time for them." Hugh's shackles rattled as he pointed to the corbels underneath the great hall's ceiling supports. "See the heads carved there? The king—the real king, that is—and my father. And there's the queen and my mother, though I don't think the mason did my mother justice. She's prettier. I could have done without the queen, but my father was a great one for symmetry." He said in a lower voice, "This was to be my father's showpiece castle, this one and Hanley. I suppose you'll see Hanley sooner or later. He got the best masons, looked over their plans, spent a fortune on these places. My mother was born here, did you know that? She's never seen the work he did here, and I suppose now she never will. He was going to bring her and the younger children here to look and admire, once it was all done. He was so proud of it. And now it's come all to naught. It's the queen's now, and she's welcome to it, damn her soul."

He was standing by one of the windows, and for a minute William thought he was going to attempt to smash his fist through it. Instead, he sank down on the window seat and put his head in his hands. William beckoned to a guard to stand by Hugh and continued on his tour by himself, wandering from tower to tower, gatehouse to gatehouse, looking for a suitable place to lodge the lad and making sure his men were not doing any looting. Finishing his journey where he had started it, he saw that immediately off the great hall were private chambers, one of them brilliantly lit by a large, delicately traceried window and so comfortably furnished that it must have been the former king's. Hugh the younger must have taken the adjoining chamber, just as comfortable but on a more modest scale. No one had disturbed its furnishings, and it had been kept clean and tidy, almost as if in readiness to receive its dead master. William shivered.

And now Despenser's splendid castle would be a prison for his young son. William made his way back to the great hall where Hugh still sat on the window seat. He had regained his composure and appeared to have been in an amicable conversation with the guard. "So where are you going to stow me, Zouche? Plenty of room here, as I was fond of pointing out when I was a child. One of the chambers next door would be rather comfortable, if I had my druthers, but I suppose that's too much to hope for."

"A mite," said William. "There's a room in one of the gatehouses that will serve the purpose nicely, though. There's a window and a fireplace, and you'll be able to get to the chapel nearby if you wish."

He had expected a facetious reply, but Hugh's face softened. "I would like to use the chapel, Lord Zouche. Thank you."

He rose from the window seat, somewhat hampered by his shackles, and stumbled. Zouche reached out to steady him and said, "We'll take these off once you're in your chamber. Why, what is it?"

Hugh had started and was staring at his hand. "Where did you get that ring, Lord Zouche? It looks like—"

"It is your father's, Hugh."

"Why the hell are you wearing it? It was my mother's gift to him, you whoreson! Did you take it off him while he was dead? It was the only way he'd ever give it up! You son of—"

Two of William's men grabbed Hugh, but William shook his head. "Let him go. Hugh, it is not what you think. Your father gave me this ring to give to your mother. It was not taken from him. I swear."

"Then why do you have it? You were at that farce of a Parliament, were you not? The Tower's just down the river from Westminster, in case you've forgotten, and Mother hasn't exactly been moving between her estates these days."

"I should have given it to her long ago, you're right, Hugh. The truth is, I've not wanted to face her yet. As one of your father's captors—"

"She's not what I would call an Amazon, Zouche; she won't tear your throat out. But I suppose I understand what you mean." He shuddered. "When I got the news of my father's death it was bad enough, but then I started thinking of how she would receive it. I can't imagine what it must have been like for her, hearing. Not being able to go to her, that's been the worst part of being here."

"God will comfort her."

"And what will she do without him? He was devoted to her."

One of William's foot soldiers overhearing, snorted. "Not as much as he was to the king, bloody sodomite!"

Hugh went white, and Zouche turned. "Any one who speaks ill of this boy's family in his presence, or mine, shall regret it. Do you understand?"

The men fell silent. Hugh said in a lower voice, "I heard what they said about him and the king. I don't know if it's true. If you've proof, keep it to yourself; I don't care to know." He put his head in his hands for a moment before lifting it and adding, "I heard the charges that were brought against him when he was killed, and I suppose some of them were true too. Maybe more than some. So what I am to do? Pretend he was a stranger to me? I loved him. And he loved me." He smiled faintly. "And he loved my mother. He told me one Twelfth Night—he was half in his cups—that he could still scarcely believe his good luck, having the old king's granddaughter for his bride. His red-haired angel, his little piece of heaven. Perhaps he was further in his cups than half." Hugh sighed. "I talk too much, don't I? My father told me often enough that I did. He didn't mean it unkindly, though, more as a word to the wise. I've missed him." He averted his eyes from William's face. "I hate this place."

William said, "Write a letter to your mother. I'll deliver it to her when I'm in London."

Hugh's face, which could hide nothing, changed in an instant, and he looked as happy as a man in shackles, facing an uncertain future, could possibly look. "You will? I thank you."

"And then I'll deliver the ring, too, I promise."

Hugh smiled. "You'd better. My father's ghost will haunt you if you don't."

For several more days, William stayed at Caerphilly, arranging for his own men to take over its administration and watching as the goods inside were inventoried. The king had not traveled light to Wales, although he had stowed almost all of his worldly goods in one place or another by the time he was caught at Llantrisant. There was armor, of course, and weapons, but there were personal items as well, and William found them unexpectedly touching. Chapel goods, so mass could be celebrated properly. A red retiring robe, decorated with bears. A black cap lined with red velvet and covered with pearled butterflies. Another of white beaver lined with black velvet. As if the king, when his goods in the Tower were packed to be shipped to Caerphilly, had had hopes that more pleasant days were to come.

Before William left for London, he went to take leave of his prisoner. William had made sure that Hugh was comfortably housed, albeit under a heavy guard and with nothing that could be used as a weapon or as a means of escape. Though clearly already growing restless, his captive was determinedly cheerful as he handed over the letter. "It took a while to compose, but then I had the time to pass, didn't I? You've seen those books of letters for clerks to follow? Something for every occasion? I don't think they'd have anything for these circumstances.

Maybe I'll work on that while I'm in here: letters from prisoners to their fellow prisoners." He laughed. "Maybe Mortimer's sons and I could collaborate someday."

On April 3, 1327, Edward, late the king of England, as he was now known, was awoken in the dead of the night, hustled onto a horse, and taken from Kenilworth Castle to Berkeley Castle by his new keepers, Thomas de Berkeley and John Maltravers. Life had taken a grimmer turn, he knew as he approached the castle walls of Berkeley three days later; just how grim he was yet to discover.

For months after the executions of her father and her brother, Lady Hastings was in a grief from which no one and nothing could rouse her. When her councilors had to ask her about the running of her estates, she would say only, "Do what you think best." She would allow her ladies to dress her each morning and undress her at night, but she never went to the great hall to eat with the rest of her household. Her chaplain came and prayed with her; she mouthed the proper words but could have been praying to the Devil himself for all she knew or cared. Her children and their spouses, along with her stepchildren and their spouses, all tried to coax her out of her chamber, but to no avail, and although Bella accepted their visits, she showed no interest in the individual visitors. The Lord himself might have arrived in her chamber, with a company of archangels, and would have got no more than a polite, "Good day to you."

Bella was by nature neither self-pitying nor slothful, and she was disgusted with herself. Each night as she laid her head on her pillow, she vowed that the next day would be different. She would attend a meeting of her council, give alms to the poor, dine with her household, ride her favorite horse, Isolde, who sat in her stall almost as forlorn as Bella herself. Each day she awoke, and she could do nothing but sit at the window and stare out of it, except when she cried.

Had she continued in this manner for much longer, she would likely have followed her menfolk to the grave within the year, for she ate only as much as was needed to keep herself alive and never took in the fresh air. But in April 1327, a messenger, not a liveried household messenger but a mere lad on a spawn-backed horse, brought a letter to her steward, who in turn brought it to her. Bella was about to give him his usual command, to do whatever he thought best, when she looked at the letter more closely. It was not sealed, and the handwriting was not that of a clerk but the scrawl of someone who evidently wrote but seldom. It was from her niece and goddaughter, Isabel Arundel.

Bella read the letter. Isabel was living with the Arundels at Fairford, one of several Despenser manors that at the urging of the Earl of Surrey had been recently awarded to the Countess of Arundel to maintain herself and her boys. Isabel had just given birth to a beautiful boy, but no one wanted her or her son at the Arundel residence, and she had nowhere to go and no money; she'd sold her wedding ring just to pay a local boy to go to her aunt Bella for her. Could Bella help her?

Staring at the letter, Bella recalled things that had been told to her, but to which she had had no reaction at the time. From her Monthermer stepsons, who were friendly with their half-sister Elizabeth de Burgh, who was friendly with the queen, she had heard that her sister-in-law Eleanor and her children were in the Tower. From her sons she had learned that their cousin Hugh was holed up in a besieged Caerphilly Castle. There was nothing Bella could do about Eleanor in the Tower and Hugh in Caerphilly, but, she reflected, she could certainly help her niece. For the first time in months, Bella gave a command. "Pack a few things for me and have Isolde made ready," she said softly. "I am going to Fairford."

Seldom had Bella been angrier than when she saw Isabel Arundel, living with her husband, mother-in-law, and young brothers-in-law on the lands that they had been granted by the king to live on. Grieving for her father and grandfather, frightened for her mother and siblings, she had absolutely no friends in the Arundel household, for the Countess of Arundel and her son alike blamed Hugh le Despenser for the earl's death, and with Hugh out of reach forever, they had turned their hostility on his fourteen-year-old daughter instead. Not that they were openly cruel to her; their acts were those of neglect. When the household had to be reduced, those waiting on Isabel had been the first to go. She had no wet nurse for the healthy boy she had borne, and she had to tend him all by herself—an unheard-of state of affairs in a noble household. Little Edmund had been baptized, but with the bare minimum of ceremony, for his very existence was an affront to Richard, who otherwise could have packed Isabel off to a nunnery without qualms. Most of the Arundels' clothes had been seized with the Arundel goods, but even after the Earl of Surrey's brotherly affection gave the countess money to re-outfit herself and her children, Isabel wore the same gown, inexpertly dyed black, day after day. She who had been daughter to one of the richest men in England had no spending money of her own; she could give no alms, buy nothing pretty for herself or for her baby, purchase no masses for the salvation of her father and grandfather's souls—all things she dearly longed to do. She ate in the great hall with the family, unless Edmund required her attention, but save for that one courtesy she might have been a laundress, for no one spoke to her. Her one friend was her lap dog, which somehow no one had thought to take away from her; had they known that it was Hugh le Despenser himself who had given it to her when it was a puppy, it probably would have been drowned in a well.

Lady Hastings' temper had been renowned in the Despenser family for its mildness, but it took every bit of self-control Bella possessed not to slap the Countess of Arundel or her son when she saw Isabel, wan and thin, sitting alone with her baby and her dog in the garden that had once belonged to her own mother. As politely as she could, she asked the Arundels if she might relieve their burden by having Isabel and Edmund stay with her indefinitely. As the Arundels were only too glad to pack off Hugh le Despenser's daughter and grandson to Hugh le Despenser's sister, Bella sent a servant back to her land with detailed instructions, and in due time he arrived back with Bella's chariot, amply filled with cushions and provisions, and a cheerful nursery maid who had served in Bella's own household.

"Thank you for saving me," said Isabel shyly as the chariot holding her, Edmund, the nursery maid, and the dog lumbered away. "I was so wretched there."

Bella, riding beside the chariot on an impatient Isolde, shook her head, thinking of the months she had spent in her chamber, unable to think of anything but her father's swinging body, her brother's mutilated one. "No, sweet one," she said. "It is I who must thank you for saving me."

"Lady Despenser?"

"I am she." Her soft, sweet voice was so out of key with the expression on her face that Zouche started. "What do you wish with me?"

William could not answer that question honestly, for what he wished at that moment was to take her to bed. She was dressed entirely in black; though in its wearing she had sought to honor dead Hugh she could not have picked a better color to set off her white skin, all the whiter for her months in the Tower, and her curly red hair, rebelliously emerging from underneath the headdress she wore. Her eyes, which had met William's face only for an instant, were green. Her cat-like face with its sprinkling of freckles was not a beautiful one or even a conventionally pretty one, but it could catch at the heart of a man, and it caught William's.

To stop staring at her, he turned his eyes to the children. The boy who he would soon learn was named Edward could have been the young ghost of his father. His resemblance to the late Hugh was even more pronounced when, as now, he was glaring at an intruder. Already he was taller than his mother, whose arm he had taken protectively. The younger boys had chubby, unformed faces but the same dark eyes, though theirs gazed at William with more interest than hostility. Behind them stood an older, rather large lady, her eyes neutral but her lips unsmiling.

Eleanor moved from behind the table where she had been sitting. To his shock, Zouche saw that she was heavily pregnant. He took Eleanor's resisting hand. "I am William la Zouche. I captured your husband and accepted your son's surrender."

The green eyes looked full at him now. "And you are here to gloat or torment me with tales about their suffering. Why trouble yourself, sir? I have heard all. No words can hurt me now."

"No, no, my lady. I bear messages from both of them to you. That is all I came here for." Getting no response, he continued. "Your husband gave me this ring at Llantrisant Castle, where he was taken after he was captured. He asked me to deliver it to you, with his love." William handed it to Eleanor, who took it with a small cry. "That was the only time I spoke with him. I can report to you that your son defended Caerphilly Castle well and bravely. He told you to be of good cheer and that he would soon be reunited with you. He was in good health when I saw him and appeared quite cheerful—under the circumstances. He sent a letter to you through me." He handed the letter to Eleanor, who took it silently and sat at the table to read it, pulling it gently now and again out of the grasp of her inquisitive youngest son.

Having read the letter several times and passed it on to the oldest boy, Eleanor looked up at William. Her eyes and cheeks were wet, but she was smiling. "I am sorry, Lord Zouche, for my rudeness to you. I am gratified for your messages, and it was kind of you to deliver them. Many in your position would not have bothered to come here."

"This has been a difficult time for you." William had no desire to leave the Tower at all. He found a way to gain a little more time. "I shall be returning soon to Caerphilly Castle, where your son will remain for the time being as a prisoner. I should be happy to take a message to him."

"We are well." Eleanor considered for a moment, then brightened and gestured toward the table, which was heaped with books and paper. "Tell him something that will amuse him. To pass the hours here we have been improving ourselves—Edward is teaching Gilbert and me Latin, and he and I are teaching Gladys how to write."

"Fine lot of good it'll do me," said Gladys, "but my lady is right, it does pass the time."

"We tell stories, too, Gladys and Edward and me, each on alternate nights, to entertain ourselves, and Gilbert and John have to vote as to which they liked the best, or at least Gilbert does. Edward usually wins."

Edward glowered at William.

"Next we plan to begin acting our stories out, and I tell the others that if we are let out of here and have nothing else to live upon, we can set ourselves up as a traveling troupe."

"I will be happy to tell your son that you are doing so well."

"Tell him the whole truth," Edward said. He stepped directly in front of William. "Tell him that my mother has nightmares. Screaming nightmares about my father being killed. Tell him that she cries every night about him and my sisters, thinking we don't notice. Tell him that there's a guard here who stares at Mother as if she were in a Southwark stew and that he would have forced himself on her long ago if Gladys and I ever left her alone. Tell him—"

"No!" Eleanor, weeping, leapt up, then wobbled on her feet. "Tell him none of those dreadful things. Don't tell him. Please."

She was near to fainting. William pushed Gladys, who was trying to help, away and with military efficiency helped Eleanor back into her chair. "It is all right, my lady," he said gently. "I shall tell him only what you wish him to hear. Do you understand me? Only what you wish." She nodded and propped her elbows on the table, her head in her hands. William turned to Edward. "Are you happy with yourself? You've upset your mother and scared your little brothers. That's a good day's work for honesty."

"I'm sorry, Mother." Edward awkwardly touched her shoulder. "I get so angry sometimes. I don't know what makes me say things then. I didn't mean to hurt you."

Eleanor nodded. "I know." Her voice was barely a whisper.

"I'll take the boys to the other room and amuse them."

William remained next to Eleanor. "Tell me this guard's name," he said gently. "There is no reason that you should be subjected to such treatment."

Eleanor lifted her head and stared dully at her lap. "His name is Jacob, one of the night guards. He does leer at me, it is true—or did before I became so great with child. He may not be a real threat, but I am more nervous as of late, and Edward sees the worst in everyone now."

"Whether your fears are well founded or not, you should not be in such distress of mind, particularly in your state of health. I am on friendly terms with the constable here. I will talk to him about having the guard's duties assigned elsewhere."

"Thank you." Some color had returned to her face.

"It will please your eldest son to hear how you are making the best of your time here. My own son has some Latin books he no longer uses. I'll have some sent to you. You are likely to advance very quickly, and will have need of some more."

"I fear you overestimate our abilities." Eleanor managed a slight smile. "But I thank you again."

"So you can write, Lady Despenser?"

"Yes. My mother had us girls taught; it was a fancy of hers."

"Then perhaps you would like to have me carry Hugh a letter from all of you. I don't know how long I will be custodian of Caerphilly Castle, or how long he shall be there. But as long as he is in my custody I will be happy to deliver him letters from you when I can."

"He is not forbidden to receive letters?"

"He would probably be if it were known that he was receiving them. But there is no reason why it need be known that I can think of, my lady."

The green eyes sparkled at him. "Then we will write him a fine letter. Thank you, Lord Zouche."

"And now I will be taking my leave." He took Eleanor's hand to kiss it, and this time she did not pull her hand from his. He decided not to risk taking leave of the boys in the next room. "Good-bye, Gladys. Look to your lady here."

"It has been my pride and pleasure to look after my lady since she married the late Hugh," said Gladys loftily. "I'll not stop now."

William smiled and left the room. Before he left the Tower, he went to speak to some clerks who were inventorying and valuing the Despenser treasures stored there, and he wondered what the men would say if William told them that the most priceless of all the treasures was living and breathing in the Beauchamp Tower. Probably, William thought, the men would say William had lost his mind, and William, as stupidly in love as any prentice boy within the city of London, would have no call to disagree.

Several days later, he was back in the Tower, bearing gifts: a chessboard and men for Edward, a top for Gilbert, and a toy horse for John. He had considered bringing something for the ladies, but had rejected the idea as too presumptuous. Now watching the delight with which the younger children received their toys, he wished he had found something, even a thimble, for each of them.

Edward, however, greeted his gift with an expressionless face. He said coolly, "No, thank you."

"Edward!" Eleanor frowned. "It was kind of Lord Zouche to bring you something to amuse yourself with, and you were wishing only the other day that you had thought to bring your chess set with you."

"My *father's* chess set. Not this man's." He scowled. "I'm going to the other room to do my lessons. Though what good they'll ever do me I don't know."

Eleanor flushed as her son left the room as noisily as possible. "I am so sorry, sir. He was not brought up to be so rude."

"I know."

"These past months have been very hard on him. He worshipped his father."

"Boys that age do."

"He has always been quiet, but now he broods and almost never smiles, although he is very good with the younger children and tries to rouse himself with them."

"He is grieving. It is natural."

"He was so different before."

Eleanor seemed on the verge of tears. He changed the subject by saying quietly, "I came to pick up your letter to your son Hugh, Lady Despenser, if it is ready."

"It is ready, and I thank you again." She gave him a folded piece of paper. "I did not seal it, Lord Zouche, because I thought that you might have to read it."

"There is no need."

"Thank you." She got the materials for sealing her letter and began to let the wax drip. "It did Edward good to write his part of the letter, I know. He is fond of his brother. He had wanted desperately for his father to take him with him, but Hugh said he should stay and help take care of me."

"That was sensible of him. He seems a brave boy."

"He has been so much help to me here, although I know he regards himself more as a nursemaid to the younger children than as my protector. But I am boring you with this chatter about my children, Lord Zouche. I am sorry."

"You have not bored me at all, my lady." What would she say if he told her that *he* wanted to be her protector? He took the letter Eleanor offered him reluctantly, for now there was no reason for him to prolong his visit. A thrill of delight ran through him when Eleanor said in her soft, sweet voice, "Perhaps you might stay a while, Lord Zouche? It is a treat, I do confess, to have a visitor."

"I will be happy to stay."

"I wish I could serve refreshments, but my cook has been lazy today."

"I will excuse the impropriety."

"I have been trying to remember, Lord Zouche." William felt a thrill to hear that Eleanor had been thinking about him. "I believe you were married to Alice, the Earl of Warwick's widow?"

"I was, indeed. She was a lovely woman."

"She spoke very highly of you before your marriage, as I recall." Eleanor's smile had a hint of mischief in it. "She was Hugh's aunt by marriage. Warwick was brother to Hugh's mother."

"I respected Warwick." He paused. "For a time."

"So did Hugh, for a time." She shook her head sadly. "I hardly knew him. The Black Dog of Arden, Piers Gaveston called him. And he did bite."

"Yes," William said regretfully. "He did."

Searching for a more cheerful topic of conversation, he noticed a basket full of sewing materials and cloth. "Even in here, you sew? You ladies amaze me."

Eleanor laughed. "Not another infernal altar cloth, thank God!" She displayed a child-sized tunic, then set to work upon it. "There is the baby to come, of course, and the boys are growing apace, so Gladys has taught me to do plain sewing. Yet another means to support myself when I get out of here." She glanced out her window. "Lord Zouche, do you think we shall get out of here?"

"Yes, when time has passed."

"And my oldest son?"

He respected her too much to offer false hope. "It is different with a man, Lady Despenser. There is always the fear that a man might raise an army."

"Isabella managed, did she not? Perhaps you underestimate our sex." She laughed again, then shook her head. "Not with me you don't, Lord Zouche. I don't want power or revenge. I only want to get out of here and live quietly somewhere."

"It is a pity for your sake that your husband did not wish the same."

"You are right. It is a pity. For my sake and for his, Lord Zouche."

He'd gotten her angry, he saw, and it was entirely worth it to see that flash of color that turned her pale cheeks to rose. What had Hugh done to deserve such a lovable, luscious creature? Nothing! he told himself stoutly. He thought of rousing her again, but the prospect of having his visit cut short deterred him. Instead he sat quietly and watched Eleanor as she stitched determinedly, her eyes bent over her work. After a few minutes, she said, "Tell me, Lord Zouche, why did you join Isabella against the king? I don't ask to accuse you or quarrel with you. I only want to know, as you seem a good man."

"My lady, I respect you, so I will give you a truthful answer. I believed, as did many people wiser than myself, that your husband was self-seeking and corrupt and that he shamelessly abused his power to acquire lands to which he had no right. I believed that the king had fallen so deeply under your husband's influence that he was no longer able to govern wisely or fairly. I saw widows and children being punished for real or imagined crimes of their husbands and fathers that were not of their own making—much as, I regret to say, I see that you and yours are being punished for crimes of your husband. I believed that the queen had the best interests of England at heart and that she could set it right."

"And do you still believe she is the one to do it?"

He hesitated. "Our new king is but a youngster yet, but I believe he will prove good and just. Henry of Lancaster, the head of the regency council, is a good man."

"You do not mention Isabella or Mortimer, I notice." Eleanor jabbed her needle through the cloth with satisfaction, then started and touched her belly. "Ouch! This child has no respect for my abilities as a seamstress, Lord Zouche. He or she has been kicking me all morning, but that was a particularly vicious one."

"I have been meaning to ask you if there is something I can do to assist you with—"

Eleanor's mouth twitched upward. "As you cannot make baby clothes or deliver the baby, Lord Zouche, I think not, but I thank you. Thomas Wake has promised to bring a decent midwife here when the time draws near. In any event, Gladys has helped me bring nine children into the world, eight living and one dead, and I daresay she is as good as any midwife now. We will muddle through one way or the other."

William hesitated. "Did your husband know?"

Eleanor shook her head. "It was far too early when he left me. No, Lord Zouche, he never knew."

William said gently, "I would not cause you further pain, my lady, for the world, but your son Edward mentioned your daughters. Where are they?"

Eleanor's voice grew hard. "I have four daughters, Lord Zouche. Isabel is married to the late Earl of Arundel's son. Where he is now and how she fares I have no idea. My other daughters are nuns. Isabella and Mortimer made that choice for them. I try to tell myself that God had some say in it."

"I am sorry, my lady."

"Whatever your motives might have been, Lord Zouche, you serve a vile woman. Don't let yourself forget it."

A door banged and Eleanor composed herself as her sons hastened to the door. "It is time for our walk, Lord Zouche. Since you first visited us, the guards have been much more regular about letting us go to the garden. I have omitted to thank you for that. Will you go outside with us?"

William nodded.

Outside in the garden, Eleanor chased after John, who was headed straight toward a particularly dirty-looking mud puddle, while Edward and Gilbert began to toss a ball around. William caught Gladys as she began to follow her lady. "It is true? The girls were forced into convents? Like Mortimer's daughters?"

"Not like Mortimer's daughters. They were never forced to take the veil. My lady's daughters were. The youngest only a child of three, Lord Zouche."

"Is it true she has nightmares?"

"Almost every night. Since the queen sent a man to tell her all the most vile details of her husband's execution."

William shut his eyes. "That was uncalled for."

"It was cruel and wicked, that's what it was, knowing as the queen did how fond my lady was of her lord. What my lady doesn't know, though, is that she was lucky. If he'd been taken to London as they planned, as the guard told me, she would have had to sit through the whole execution, I don't doubt it for a moment. And that would have driven my lady mad."

"I doubt whether they would have been so cruel."

"They were cruel enough to him, weren't they? No, they would have made my poor lady watch, and as it stands now, she never has a good night's sleep. I know; I share the bed with her every night, and I soothe her when she wakes. The Tower chaplain and the physician here told me that the nightmares would pass with time, but they're no better. Or at least—"

"At least what?"

"Your bringing the ring and the letter from Hugh her son seemed to help. She woke only briefly that night and started, then went back to sleep." Gladys glared at William. "Don't you be speaking of this to my lady, mind you! She prefers not to discuss the matter."

"I won't."

"The worst of it was the night after the girls had been taken away to their convents—three separate ones, mind you, lest they find some comfort in each other's company. My poor lady! She told them that God had chosen them in particular to serve Him and they were to consider themselves honored and blessed. What else could my poor lady say? They finally left, with Joan of Bar their cousin—at least the queen had the decency to send them with her and not just some soldier—and we tried to carry on as normal. But that night my lady was awake every hour, screaming and crying. I thought she'd go mad, I truly did. But the next morning she was as if nothing happened, and that's the way it's been ever since." She looked at Eleanor pulling John away from some rose bushes. "Hugh's all she had for twenty years, poor thing, all she knew. Her mother died not long after she was married, and her menfolk are either dead or shut up or not in a position to be of any help, and her sisters were loyal to their husbands, as she was to hers, not like that French whore parading her paramour before her own son the king while the old king sits God knows where."

Gladys's voice was one that carried. "My good woman, you border on treason."

"Ah, the rope wouldn't hold me. So I'll say what I please. But I'll have done, because I *am* done."

She moved away to rejoin Eleanor.

The day was fine and warm, and from a distance William could see three tradesmen's boys, having delivered their goods, playing a spirited game of tag before they went back to their masters. Thinking of the three little nuns, shut away forever from such amusements, he turned toward the guard, who had once or twice picked up the Despensers' ball when it landed near his feet and thrown it back to the children. "Can you take them to the menagerie?"

"It is not secure, sir—"

"The little ones and the women won't escape, and I'll watch Edward myself." He handed the guard a coin. "No harm will come of it."

The guard shrugged, and William whistled. "Come! Let's go see the lions."

Though the menagerie at the Tower of London was not in those days open to the public, a handful of visitors, mostly rich merchants who supplied goods to the new court and their families, had been allowed in. The approach of the five well-dressed people under guard caused a bit of a sensation, the more so as the knowing began to guess their identity, and for a moment William regretted his idea. Eleanor seemed to shrink within her robes, though Gladys, a large woman, glared with such effect that only the boldest spirits continued to stare. Gilbert and John, however, were oblivious. They ran to the cages, dragging the others along. "Look, Mama! The lion is still here. And the monkeys!" Gilbert turned to beam at William. "Lord Zouche, we went here all the time before Father went away, and then we stopped going. Have you been here before?"

"Several times."

"It's wonderful, isn't it? Look, John, at the monkeys! See the one here? He's picking fleas off the other, to be kind. Do they have names, Lord Zouche?"

"Mortimer and Isabella," offered Edward, so softly that no one could hear him but his mother and William.

Eleanor giggled and said in an equally soft voice, "Our Isabella here is being much too discreet."

"Come now, you two," William said good-naturedly. He raised his voice. "I believe they are called Samson and Delilah, Gilbert."

"Tat!" said John, pointing at the lion.

Gladys glared at the beast. "With you out here, how come there's so many mice in there?"

"We need a cat to chase them," said Gilbert. "Or a dog to scare them off." His chubby face turned wistful for a fleeting moment, but just for long enough to give Zouche an idea.

Thomas Wake shook his head as he looked inside the basket Zouche bore. "And who is going to exercise this creature, Zouche?"

"Gilbert and Edward can. The guards are always stationed nearby; they can bang when they want out to walk him. Come, Wake. They're boys, for God's sake, cooped up here with two women. A dog would help them pass the time, Gilbert in particular. He's but five years old, you know."

"Very well," said Wake. "But don't get your hopes up, Zouche."

"I don't understand you."

"Despenser's little widow, Zouche. She's nice-looking enough, I'll warrant you, and amiable enough, for a traitor's wife at least. But if she gets out of here she'll either have nothing to live upon, in which case you'd be a fool to marry her, or she'll get her lands back, in which case the king will marry her off himself. Or, of course, she might take a vow of chastity. She was fair besotted with that husband of hers, you know. The guards who have taken her to the chapel say that she prays and cries for him there. No, I don't think you stand a chance, Zouche."

"I'm not trying to marry the lady, Wake. I'm just giving her sons a dog to pass the time."

"Oh, of course," said Wake. He was much younger than Zouche, twenty-nine to Zouche's mid-forties, and Zouche was beginning to find him insufferable. With a scowl, he turned on his heel and headed toward the Beauchamp Tower, his basket barking with an indignation that matched his own.

"Have them name it William," Wake called after him as he left. "That way, the little widow won't forget you while you're gone."

CHAPTER 21

▼

JUNE 1327 TO SEPTEMBER 1327

On a rainy afternoon, Edward and Gilbert le Despenser sat glumly in a window seat at the constable's hall at the Tower, while John le Despenser and their puppy bounded about heedlessly, interfering in every way possible with the meal that was being served to the garrison. "Edward, will she die?"

"No," said Edward with a confidence he did not feel. "She had all of us, didn't she?"

"But that was before Papa died," Gilbert said. "And Grandfather."

"It's not *contagious*, Gilbert. Don't you remember when John was born? She did fine."

"But she was hurting when we left, so badly."

"That's what always happens, Gilbert, when a baby is born."

Gilbert considered this for a moment. "Not with me," he said firmly. "I wouldn't have hurt Mama." Before Edward could contradict him, he said, "I wish Hugh were here. Don't you?"

"Yes," said Edward. "I do."

The door swung open and Gladys walked in. She walked slowly, for it had been four hours ago that the boys had been hustled out to the constable's hall, and she had been on her feet the entire time, but as the boys hastened to her they saw she was smiling. "You have a baby sister now," she said. "Elizabeth. Your mama is very tired, but she is well, and she wants you to come and see her as soon as she and the baby are cleaned up a bit."

"Take the brat to London Bridge so that the proud father can have a look, why don't you?" said one of the men in the hall, overhearing, to his mates.

Gladys, forgetful of her aching joints, would have cuffed the man, but his companions, many of whom had become rather protective of the widow and her brood, beat her to it. Edward, always alert to any slight upon his father, had heard the remark too, but for once he did not care. He could feel nothing but gratitude that his mother was not going to die after all.

Eleanor lay behind her bed curtains as Elizabeth suckled her, making her pleasure manifest with much smacking and gulping. Never before had Eleanor nursed one of her own children, and though Lizzie's hunger for the breast kept her up at all hours of the night, her birth and her constant presence had worked more of a healing upon Eleanor than she had ever thought possible. Though she still mourned Hugh, grieved for the loss of her middle daughters, and worried about her two oldest children, the desolation that had settled over her had lifted. No longer did she cry herself to sleep every night, and her dreams—in between night feedings—were no longer something to be feared.

Lizzie ceased smacking and contentedly closed her eyes, which were slowly turning to Hugh's dark shade of brown. After burping and changing and swaddling her, Eleanor placed her in the rough cradle that two of her guards had brought to the Beauchamp Tower in May. From its ungainliness, Eleanor suspected that they had made it themselves, but her heartfelt thanks had been received with embarrassed mutters, as if she had caught the men in some indiscretion.

As her shift was the worse for wear after Lizzie's last resounding burp, she opened a trunk to get a fresh one to sleep in and gazed inside as the candlelight revealed the faint outlines of the array of gold plate and florins concealed beneath the clothing, all taken from the storeroom in the Tower. Before the three girls had been sent away, Eleanor would not even have taken an apple from someone else's tree, and yet now she must have accumulated at least several hundred pounds of stolen treasure, all of it brought to her by the faithful Tom. Now that God had brought her Lizzie, Eleanor longed to restore the goods to their rightful place, even if doing so meant that they would line the queen's own chests. But she did not want to hurt Tom's feelings or to put him to further risk, so she had simply told him that she was afraid that harm would come to him if he did not stop.

She would give the loot to the Church; that was it. Surely the king would see fit to let her leave here someday, and then she would offer up the treasure at holy shrines, bit by bit. God was bound to forgive her then, and the treasure would go to better use than it would be gracing the queen's own groaning tables. This problem solved, she climbed back into her bed and drifted off into a peaceful sleep.

William la Zouche would have stopped in to see the baby and the puppy (which a delighted Gilbert had in fact named Lord Zouche, to the infinite amusement of Thomas Wake), but in June he had joined the court at York, where the English were preparing to do battle with the Scots. Isabella and Mortimer, remembering the great success they had had with Jean de Hainault and his mercenary troops when they invaded England, had bought his assistance again, and York was teeming with homegrown troops and the Hainaulters.

The queen held a splendid dinner to welcome Jean de Hainault, but the English soldiers were not in a welcoming mood. It was one thing for the queen to rely on foreign assistance when she had been desperately trying to save England from the Despensers; it was quite another when there was Scottish booty to be had, and why should good fighting Englishmen be forced to share the spoils with a pack of foreigners? The dinner had scarcely progressed to the second course when a fight broke out between the English soldiers and the Hainaulters, spreading into the city's streets. By the time order was restored by the king and his elders, dozens of men lay dead.

It was a bad start to a miserable affair. Several months before, despite having been ill for some time, Robert Bruce had journeyed to Ulster, which had been in disarray for some years and had edged toward chaos after the death of the Earl of Ulster in 1326. The earl's heir, Eleanor's young nephew William de Burgh, was but fifteen years old and had yet to be knighted. Still in England, with little military or governing experience, he was hardly in a position to take over his Irish lands. With the idea of eventually securing William de Burgh, who was Bruce's nephew as well, as an ally, the Scottish leader had determined to take control of the situation in Ulster himself. He had left his lieutenants, James Douglas, Thomas Randolph, and the second Edward's faithful friend Donald of Mar, to deal with England.

But the presence of Robert Bruce turned out to be quite unnecessary; the lieutenants could humiliate the English all by themselves. The Scots, as usual, had traveled light, slaughtering local cattle when they became hungry and supplementing their diet with oatmeal, which they baked into cakes on the iron plate each man carried with him. The English, as usual, had traveled heavy, their pace slowed by their groaning baggage carts and their lumbering packhorses. Only when the English army, which had set out from York on July 10, had traveled for days without encountering the enemy did the leaders—the Earls of Lancaster, Norfolk, and Kent (officially), Mortimer (unofficially), and the king (when anyone paid any attention to him)—decide to speed up their pace by leaving the baggage train behind. Smoke having been sighted billowing in the distance, they ordered each man to take a loaf of bread with him, strapped to his saddle, in the conviction that where there was smoke, there had to be Scots. No further provisions were deemed necessary, it being certain that the English would defeat the Scots the next day.

Instead, it began raining, and stayed raining for eight days. Those who had had the stomach to choke down their loaves of bread, sodden with rain and the sweat of their horses, were only slightly less hungry than those who had been more finicky. When provisions were sent from Carlisle and Newcastle, they proved barely edible. Horses were dropping dead, and men were shivering with ague. The Scots had long disappeared from sight.

By the end of July, the Scots, full of cattle and oatmeal, were getting rather bored. Having captured a young English squire, they released him so that he could bring the English army to confront them. Finally, on the banks of the River Wear, the English at last faced the Scots—and realized that with the Scots securely stationed on a hill, crossing the river would be madness for the English. Invited by the English to battle them on equal ground, the Scots refused, though not without admiring the heraldic crests on the English knights' helmets, the first they had seen, and puzzling over the peculiar weapons, called "crakys off wer," that the English had brought with them. But the gunpowder that lined the iron buckets was so sodden with rain that no one standing by the River Wear had any inkling of the havoc it would someday wreak.

For several days the armies engaged in minor skirmishes, save at night, when the Scots employed every stratagem they could to keep the English from sleeping. Then, on August 3, the Scots camp grew strangely quiet. The next morning, the English found that they had moved to Stanhope Park, to yet another hill from which arrows could be showered down on the English.

Yet for once it appeared that the Scots were at a disadvantage; they could be surrounded and starved out. But this was not to be. On August 4, as the English camp lay sleeping, men woke to find their tents falling around their heads and spears being poked through the fabric into their bodies. James Douglas had arrived in person with several hundred men.

William la Zouche, hearing the commotion before his own tent could be reached, grabbed his sword and ran toward the direction of the king's pavilion, where Scots were slashing furiously at the ropes. As Zouche and others began to attack their attackers, the king emerged from the tent and had been all but grabbed by the Scots when his chaplain, having picked up a sword from somewhere, flung himself in front of the boy and began frantically striking about him with his weapon. His heroic gesture, fatal to himself, gave Edward's servants time to form an armed circle around the young king while the rest of the English camp, now fully roused, began to drive the Scots away. In minutes they were heading back out into the darkness, leaving behind a field of crumpled tents and dead and dying men.

The next evening, the English were on full alert for another night attack. Instead, while the Scots' campfires burned through the night, every one of Douglas's men rode quietly away toward the Scottish border, their absence undetected by the English until the next morning. With no enemy to fight, Edward and his troops headed back to York, Edward weeping tears of frustration and anger. His own father, he thought, could have hardly done worse.

"There's more bad news," Mortimer said abruptly to the queen when the two of them were finally alone in her chamber there. "The Dunheved brothers prized your fool husband out of Berkeley Castle in July. Though he's back there now, by God, and closely kept."

"He was freed from the castle? Why was I not told?"

"I am telling you now, am I not? We must make a decision, Isabella. Thomas Dunheved is at the bottom of a well, if you are interested, but Stephen Dunheved is still at large, and there will be more such attempts to follow. If not by this gang, then by others. Perhaps even by the Scots. There's your fool husband's old friend Donald of Mar, for one. He could free him, set him up as king again—provided that he dances to Robert Bruce's tune. And then where would *we* be?" He pointed in the direction of the city gate where Hugh le Despenser's left leg was rotting. "With Nephew Hugh, my dear."

"That is impossible! The English people would never accept Edward as their king again. With all of his faults—"

"Men have short memories. So what shall we do with our former king, Isabella? Put him in a more secure castle and hope that he is forgotten eventually? Or take more final action?"

"I will not decide this, Roger!"

He shrugged. "Very well. I suppose it's to be expected that you would have some womanly indecision, some feminine weakness."

"Womanly indecision! Feminine weakness!" Isabella's eyes blazed. "I saved this country from the Despensers, have you forgotten that?"

"Following my advice, have you forgotten that? Without me, today you'd be sitting in your chamber making altar cloths while your precious Edward let Hugh up his bum." He paused. "Or perhaps by now they would have allowed you to join in."

She started to slap him, but he caught her hand. "Admit it, Isabella. It's what you've wanted all along. You're not one for half-measures. You and I took the king off the throne, but that's not good enough, not in this world. Don't you want to do it right? There's only one way, and you know it. And it's the best way. Good for me, good for you, good for your son. Good for your fool husband, even."

"Good for *him*?"

"Certainly. Nothing separating him from Piers Gaveston or Hugh le Despenser then, will there be? A blissful reunion. Oh, we'll be doing him the greatest favor we can do him, my dear."

She began laughing, was still laughing when he carried her to her bed, was still laughing when he stripped her. "Do whatever you want," she gasped as he pushed inside her. "Anything you want. Anything."

His first months at Berkeley Castle had not been so bad. The room he was assigned was small, nothing like the chamber he'd been given at Kenilworth, but tolerable at least. The food was plain, but wholesome and not terribly offensive to a man who had once bought cabbages from a peasant and used them to make soup in his barge, right then and there. Berkeley was gruff, Maltravers gruffer, but his guards were civil enough, and willing to tell him news. He was occasionally allowed to go to the chapel.

Then in July he was freed by Thomas Dunheved and his followers, and then recaptured, and after that everything changed for the worst—but he would not have traded those few summer days of freedom, of hope, for the most comfortable quarters in Kenilworth. On that dreadful day in Kenilworth when he had resigned his crown, he had thought he was utterly alone in the world, or at least that the few who cared for him—his son John, his little girls, his niece Eleanor, his sister Mary—were powerless to help him. On the night when he awoke to find his old confessor, Thomas Dunheved, standing over him, he knew he had been wrong. He did have friends, and surely those who could do nothing else to help him had led them to him with their prayers.

Even when he had been captured by Berkeley's men, now all action and vigor after their prisoner had so embarrassingly escaped from them, his hope had not died. "There are others," Thomas had hissed to him as they were being hustled in opposite directions by their captors. "You'll see, your grace. Be of good cheer. You'll soon be free again."

And he would be, one way or another, even though he was kept more closely than ever before and treated considerably worse than a common prisoner would be. In the last day or so, he had discovered that however cold, hungry, and dirty he was in his cell, he could take his mind anyplace it cared to go. Helping Lucy shear a sheep. Rowing down the Thames with Piers. Hunting with Hugh. Showing Eleanor how one of her birds would sit on his finger. He could retreat there and no one—not sour Berkeley, not cruel Maltravers, not the mean-faced guards who kept him now—could touch him.

He settled back into the window seat where he spent most of his days—his bed was a mere pile of rags on the floor now—and let his mind roam where it would.

Thomas de Berkeley looked through a grill at his prisoner, who huddled in the window seat staring into space. Since the restoration of Edward to Berkeley, Thomas had followed his father-in-law's oral instructions to the letter—a poor cell, poor food, poor ventilation, poor bedding, poor clothing, poor sanitation—and his former king seemed hardly worse for wear physically, although mentally he was clearly losing ground. Oh, he knew where he was and who he was and what he was doing there, most of the time at least, but in the last day or so he had acquired a strange ability to absent himself from whatever was going on about him, something that made him oblivious to the taunts of his guards and Maltravers, who took such relish in his role as jailer that one would think it was he, not Berkeley, who had spent the years after Boroughbridge in a cell instead of quite comfortably in France. "Your grace?" he called through the grill.

Edward blinked and started; being addressed with respect never failed to bring him out of his reverie. "Lord Berkeley," he said, as if being asked to identify him.

"Your grace, the queen has sent you a cloak. Here it is."

He fitted the cloak—a plain woolen affair that would never have touched Edward's shoulders while he was king—through the grill. Edward took it and turned it in his hands. "That is kind of her," he said distantly.

"She has not forgotten you, your grace. She still looks kindly upon you."

"If that was true she would let me see my children, wouldn't she? The whore!"
Edward subsided back into himself as quickly as he had erupted. "It grows chilly
at night now," he said politely. "This will be useful."

"I've a mind to move him back to his old room and make him comfortable
there," Berkeley said to Maltravers later. "All this is for naught. He's growing
worse in the mind each day, poor creature, but no less sturdy."

"Poor creature!" mimicked Maltravers. "I daresay you weren't poor-creaturing
him when he was taking your estate and giving it to Nephew Hugh. And who, by
the way, is 'Nelly'? The guards and I were having a chat with him the other day,
before he became so barmy, reminiscing about Hugh's execution—"

"Good God, Maltravers, why do you keep harping on that with him?"

"And he started crying, which is hard to get him to do these days. 'Poor
Nelly,' he said, again and again until we cuffed him to get him to stop. 'My poor,
sweet Nelly.'"

"That's his niece, you fool, Hugh's widow. They put her in the Tower." Berkeley pushed his cup away and stood. "I'm having a featherbed brought in there,
and giving him some fresh clothing, at least."

"Against Mortimer's orders."

"This is my castle and I'll not be dictated to as to how I treat my prisoner."

"Not your prisoner, the crown's prisoner. And what do you think will happen
if he doesn't die of natural causes? You're doing him no favors, Berkeley. Mortimer will see to it that he goes, one way or the other."

"I'll worry about that when the time comes," said Berkeley.

The Scots had not finished with the English. Having left Stanhope, they
turned their attention to invading Northumberland, this time under the direct
supervision of Robert Bruce himself. The English army, meanwhile, had mostly
disbanded, and the Hainaulters, to whom England owed over forty thousand
pounds for this campaign alone, had been sent back to Hainault. Henry Percy
was left to protect the north as best he could, while the court moved south, from
York to Nottingham to Lincoln. While some districts nearby were able to raise
the money to buy themselves out of a Scottish occupation, Northumberland's
towns were burnt to the ground.

One Scot, however, did not join the others in the north: Donald of Mar, now
the Earl of Mar. With the blessing of his uncle, Robert Bruce, he was in Wales,
stirring up trouble against the new English regime. Roger Mortimer had also
eschewed the north in favor of Wales. He was at Abergavenny when he received a
certain letter.

"According to Lord Mortimer's lieutenant, William of Shalford, men in Wales, South Wales and North Wales alike, are plotting to release the old king," said Sir Thomas Gurney, who along with William Ogle had hurriedly arrived at Berkeley Castle on the evening of September 20. "They are led by Rhys ap Gruff-ydd. Shalford says that if this plot succeeds it could be the undoing of Mortimer." He looked toward the direction of the guardhouse and smiled. "Lords Berkeley and Maltravers, you are to acquaint yourself with the contents of this letter and find a suitable remedy to avoid the peril. Well. It's pretty damned obvious what they have in mind." Gurney passed the letter to Berkeley and Maltravers, who read it silently.

Maltravers laughed when he finished reading, but Berkeley said, "I'll have nothing to do with this, nothing."

"Nothing! The man's been living in your castle since April, except when you let him escape," said Gurney.

"I did not *let* him escape," snapped Berkeley. "I underestimated the determination of his friends, that is all. Be that as it may, I'll still have nothing to do with this." He turned and left the room.

"Well?" said Maltravers. "How?"

"Mortimer says it will have to leave no mark, as people will be expecting to view the body."

"So chopping his head off is out of the question," said Ogle cheerfully. "Well, there's poison."

"We'd have to find someone to make it up for us," objected Gurney.

"Strangulation?"

"Strong as he is? He'd have to be knocked cold, and that would leave a bruise. Bruises around his neck, too."

"Suffocation?"

"I suppose that's the only real choice," admitted Gurney. He shivered and looked at the fire, which was dying. "Can't Berkeley's servants make a decent fire?" He took a poker and began prodding the logs with it. He poked too hard, and he had to pull it out of a log with some difficulty. Then he began laughing.

"Are you daft, man?"

"No," said Gurney, laughing all the harder. "I've an idea. A most fitting idea."

Edward, comfortable and warm on the feather bed Berkeley had so kindly brought him several days before, raised up on his elbow and stared as he heard his cell door being unlocked. He watched as Maltravers, the Gurney fellow who had just arrived at Berkeley, and a number of men he did not know filed in, smiling most peculiarly at him and not bothering to invent any excuse for their being there in the middle of the night. So he had been right; he would soon be free, free with Piers and Hugh and Hugh's dear old father. His favorite sister, Joan. Adam and Lucy. His mother, his stepmother, his father... His mouth almost crinkled into a smile. No, his father probably wouldn't be pleased to see him, under the circumstances.

In the torchlight he could now see that the men were carrying some rather incongruous items. A drinking horn? A table? A cooking spit, glowing red hot? He frowned. Were they going to *feed* him first? But before he could make any inquiries, he was seized and pushed over on his belly and felt the table, legs in the air, being pressed against his back as someone ripped off his drawers. Then the drinking horn was shoved into his body, then the spit through the horn, and Edward's screams were echoing through Berkeley Castle. Just as Thomas de Berkeley, lying in his chamber weeping, thought he could not bear to hear them any longer, they died.

Eleanor's screams that same night of September 21, 1327, woke not only her family, but the guards dozing outside the Beauchamp Tower. Their sleepy fumblings at the door, combined with the howling of Lizzie and John and the barking of the dog, only caused her to scream the harder. It was not until Tom, in the kindliest manner possible, resorted to slapping her briskly across the face that she calmed enough to sit in a chair and sip the wine Gladys carefully gave her. "Another nightmare about Hugh, my lady?"

"No." Eleanor took a shuddering breath and stared at Gladys in bewilderment. "My uncle."

▼

CHAPTER 22

DECEMBER 1327 TO MARCH 1328

Shortly before Christmas, Tom hurried into the Beauchamp Tower, his face alight. "She is here in London, at last!"

"Is she pretty, Tom?" Eleanor asked. "You have an eye for a pretty woman, Tom, I know."

Tom considered the question with the air of authority. "Hard to say, wrapped up as she was, but I thought she was nice-looking. Pleasingly plump, I would describe her as."

Since the news had arrived that fourteen-year-old Philippa of Hainault and her uncle John had landed in Dover, in preparation for her marriage to the fifteen-year-old king, all of London had been abuzz with excitement, a happy excitement for a change, and even Eleanor had caught a bit of the anticipatory mood. It was much more pleasant for all concerned to think of the wedding, which was to take place at York in January, than of the funeral that had taken place at St. Peter's Abbey in Gloucester on December 20. There, Edward, late the king of England, having lain in Berkeley's chapel for a month and by the high altar at the abbey for two months, had at last been interred amid great pomp.

The details of the funeral reached the Tower at about the same time the bride-to-be, her carts groaning with the weight of the gifts presented to her by London's officials, proceeded on to York. The queen, dressed suitably and elegantly in mourning, had spared no expense in burying her husband. Edward's body had been watched and prayed over constantly, before and after being personally escorted to Gloucester by Thomas de Berkeley and his followers. Each side of the hearse bore a gilt lion, wearing a mantle bearing the arms of England, and one of the Four Evangelists. Eight angels holding censers, and for good measure two more lions, stood outside the hearse. Edward was enclosed in his coffin, but a wooden figure of him, draped in cloth of gold and bearing a gilt crown, had been carved to rest upon the hearse. New robes had been provided for the knights in attendance. Roger Mortimer himself had ordered a black tunic (very somber, very expensive) especially for the occasion.

The young king, of course, had attended the funeral, along with his brother and sisters. John of Eltham and the girls, Eleanor thought, must have shed some honest tears for their father. So, perhaps, had Mary, Edward's sister. Eleanor's own sisters, she heard, had also gone to the funeral, though she herself, needless to say, had not been offered the opportunity. It was just as well, she knew, for she had never believed for a moment the official announcement that the former king had suddenly been taken ill. She could not have sat through the hypocritical business without shouting out to accuse the queen and Mortimer of murder, and where would she and her children be then? Better for all concerned that she mourn the king whom she had loved first as a niece, then as a woman, privately in the Chapel of St. Peter ad Vincula.

"What are you planning to do with that thing, anyway?" Mortimer asked the queen.

He was pointing to a small silver casket that Isabella had been given a few days after the funeral by Hugh de Glanville, a clerk who had been overseeing the burial arrangements. Inside the casket was the dead king's heart. "I shall keep it, of course. After all, I asked for it."

"Why, for the love of God?" He grinned. "Oh, I see. As a trophy." Isabella shook her head. "Surely you cannot be mourning this man, can you?"

"No!" Isabella tried to laugh. "God knows I am not. But he was the father of my four children, Roger, and it becomes me to affect some grief for their sake. They do mourn him, you know. The king for one is very upset that he did not see him before he died."

"That ripe-looking Hainaulter girl will get his mind off his father." Roger crossed the room restlessly. "What did the old crone tell you?"

The old crone in question was the woman who had removed the king's heart and embalmed his body. Isabella had asked Glanville to bring her along with the king's heart. "She told me that there were no marks on his body until, of course, she opened his chest and broke his ribs to get at his heart."

"I told you the men had been gentle about it," said Mortimer, who would certainly have had the woman killed had she been more forthcoming with the queen. But she was a woman who understood the value of silence, and Mortimer had quietly rewarded hers very handsomely. "A little poison in his last meal, they said, did the trick."

"I don't wish to hear about it, Roger."

"Very well." He jabbed a finger toward the silver casket. "Best keep that well away from your jewels, my dear, or your poor ladies are likely to get an unpleasant surprise when you ask them to fetch you a brooch."

On January 30, 1328, Edward took Philippa of Hainault as his bride at York Minster. Parliament convened on February 7. Before it was very disagreeable business, at least from the English point of view: the recognition of Scottish independence. With an empty treasury, a fifteen-year-old king, and a populace that had grown less enamored of the queen since the embarrassment on the River Wear and the mysterious death of the notoriously healthy second Edward, Isabella and Mortimer had decided that they could ill afford more fighting. An English embassy, led by the Bishops of Lincoln and Norwich, chief justice Geoffrey le Scrope, Henry Percy, and William la Zouche, was delegated to meet with the Scots in Edinburgh.

William was honored to be given such a delicate task, in such exalted company. But it was another decision made by the king at York toward the end of February, one that was a matter of total indifference to most of the lords there, that filled his thoughts as he headed across the border.

Edward and his council had ordered that Eleanor le Despenser be released from the Tower.

"*Free*? I am free?"

"On sight of this order," said Thomas Wake's deputy constable, waggling it in front of her. "There is a slight hitch, however. You have also been ordered to go to the king. He will be sending an escort."

"Go to him? For what?"

The deputy shrugged. "I suppose he wishes to obtain a pledge of your future good behavior."

"As I had not behaved badly before being put here, that should not be difficult," said Eleanor dryly. She remembered the jewels in her trunks and flushed.

"But where I am to live? I see nothing here about that. My lands are in the crown's hands."

"I imagine that will be discussed with you also. One of the merchants here might be able to let a house to you in the meantime."

Lease a house from one of the queen's supporters? Eleanor frowned. Then she brightened. "My stepfather left my sister-in-law Lady Hastings a life interest in his house in St. Dunstan's in the East. Unless she has leased it out, she would surely let me stay there."

"You could leave the children there with me while you travel to York," suggested Gladys. "Better than dragging them there and back in the cold."

"Yes, and I doubt the king wants to see five Despensers when one will do!" Almost expecting the deputy to stop her, she went for her cloak. "I will go inquire about Lady Hastings' house. She will surely have someone staying there and watching the place. Now, where is St. Dunstan's? It is—" She suddenly turned pale.

Edward said, "I will go with you, Mother. A woman shouldn't be in the streets alone."

"It is not necessary, Edward. I am sure that one of the guards would be allowed to—"

"Please, Mother."

He had remembered, just as Eleanor had, that St. Dunstan's in the East was very close to London Bridge.

Her business at St. Dunstan's was soon and satisfactorily concluded. Lady Hastings, the cheerful-looking servant said, would be only too glad to let Eleanor use her house. Did she want it by evening? Upon being assured that Eleanor could wait a day, he promised to have all in readiness for her the next morning.

They walked on to London Bridge. Eleanor took a breath, then lifted her eyes to the spike on which Hugh's head was impaled, still wearing traces of its crown of nettles. The head was now unrecognizable as any particular man's, but a cloth tied below it bore the Despenser coat of arms. Tears began to run down her face. She was being jostled by persons coming from all directions, and a few people were openly staring at her, but she did not care. She crossed herself and said aloud, "Someday I shall give you a proper burial, my love, and you shall lie under a beautiful monument, for you loved beauty. And there shall be chants said for you, and you will lie in peace. None shall gawk, and our children and I will come and pray for your soul. Someday, my dear. Someday."

Beside her stood a silent Edward. Eleanor turned to look at her son. "Edward? Are you all right?"

He nodded, and Eleanor knew that was all the response she would ever get from him. She took his arm, glad that the press of the crowds around them gave her an excuse to touch him. "Will you take me back now?"

"Yes, Mother."

Together they walked back to the Tower, trailed, unbeknownst to either, by a protective Tom.

The sun was barely up the next morning when Bella's men began moving Eleanor's belongings to her new abode. Tom had been no less active. London swarmed with his relations, and he had found a widowed cousin with a young baby who could act as a wet nurse for Lizzie, a great-aunt who could work as a laundress, and a person of uncertain consanguinity to serve as cook. Her new retainers all proving satisfactory, Eleanor had only to stand back and watch as her goods were loaded into a cart to be sent to St. Dunstan's. As her expenses during her imprisonment had been paid by the crown, and Gladys had managed to hide some money in their trunks when they were taken prisoner, she could give generous presents to the guards who had been kind to her.

She turned to Tom, her partner in felony and the kindest of them all. "Tom, I do not know what the king has in mind for me, but if I have the means, I hope you will join my household when your term here expires. You have been so good to me."

"I'd like that, my lady."

He took her hand, and when he released it she found a shining florin in it. "Tom!" she said half-heartedly.

He shrugged and helped her into the cart that was to take her and the children to Bella's house. Holding a swaddled-up Lizzie, who was staring at the vast space in front of her with bewilderment, she looked around her too at the place that had been a home to her as well as her prison. The Beauchamp Tower, where Lizzie had been born. The Lanthorn Tower, where she and Hugh had spent their last night together. The great hall where she had sat so often by the side of her uncle the king at the high table. Probably she would never see any of these buildings from the inside again, for whatever her new life was to consist of, it would certainly not include the new king's court.

"Lord Zouche! Lord Zooouche! Oh, there you are!"

Gilbert grabbed up the dog and all but sprang into the cart. Whatever concerns Eleanor might have about beginning life anew, they were not shared by her six-year-old son. Settling down beside him, she smiled and ruffled his hair.

Gilbert had been in London only for a short while—one could not really count the Tower grounds as London, he had decided, since all one saw there were boring guards and clerks and the stray merchant—but already he loved it. This very morning, he'd been roused from sleep by a pieman shouting his wares outside, and several peddlers had been to the door. His mind was busy working on a way to evade stuffy Edward and go outside for a walk by himself.

There were, of course, rules he had to follow. He could not wear fine clothing out of doors, not that his clothing was much to boast of these days. If he met a stranger, he had to call himself Gilbert of Gloucester, if anything beyond "Gilbert" was required at all. People would not like him if he gave his father's name, Mama and Edward had told him. Gilbert knew this was true. While baby Elizabeth had been being born, and they had all been taken to stay in the constable's hall of the Tower, he had seen some mean men looking at Edward and saying how much he looked like his whoreson father. Gilbert knew that this was an ugly word. It was just as well that he himself looked nothing like his whoreson father, whatever it meant, and so much like Mama. Edward had heard the men too and had become very angry, but he had said nothing. They had to be good, Edward had told him, or the queen might decide to take them away from Mama, just as she had their sisters.

His family had already created some sensation in the neighborhood, however, for an hour or so after the pieman's departure, there had been a new commotion outside his window. A man had appeared, a knight from the looks of him, bearing the royal standard, and it was his own mother he had come for, to take her to the king! Sir William de Montacute had stayed only long enough to take some refreshment, but he had allowed Gilbert to give his horse some oats and had told him that Lord Zouche was a fine-looking dog. He reminded Gilbert a little bit of his brother Hugh. Every night, Gilbert prayed to God that Hugh would come back. He had been so tall and so kind and so brave, and Gilbert knew the latter for certain, for he had held Caerphilly Castle—Papa's castle—against the wicked queen.

Now that they had been allowed to leave the Tower, perhaps Hugh would be allowed to leave his prison too? He had thought of asking his mother, but it would probably make her sad, and Edward got very angry whenever Gilbert made Mama sad. Not that he ever meant to do so. The queen had done enough of that already, killing Papa and Grandfather and sending his sisters away and shutting Hugh up. Gilbert would have hated the queen, but Mama said it was wrong to hate. But he didn't have to like her. Mama and Edward had said that not liking her was all right.

Edward was calling him, in the man-of-the-house way he had assumed since Papa died. Edward could be irritating, but he could be kind, too, almost like his brother Hugh. After Papa had died—Gilbert thought it must have been in some dreadful but exciting battle—Edward had caught Gilbert crying in the bed they shared, and he hadn't scolded him at all, the way he had when Gilbert had cried when his pony had thrown him just a few months before.

His pony. Might he ever get his pony back? He'd been such a good rider for his age. Papa had told him so. So had Hugh.

Edward himself had arrived in Gilbert's room, with a very dreary-looking book in his hand. Gilbert sighed, then brightened. There would be plenty of time, after all, to explore London now that they were free.

Eleanor had been uneasy when she was told that the king would be sending an escort for her, wondering what sort of man the king—or Mortimer and Isabella—would choose for the task. William de Montacute was an immense relief. He was the son and namesake of the man who had been a good friend to the late king after the Bannock Burn, and that in itself augured well.

Montacute was not particularly talkative, both by nature and by his instinct that Eleanor wished to be left alone with her thoughts as they headed north, over countryside that Eleanor had traveled so many times in state as Hugh le Despenser's wife and the king's niece. From time to time, however, he broke their companionable silence. Did Eleanor know that the French king—the last of Isabella's brothers—had died suddenly on the first of February?

"I did not know that, sir. Who shall take the throne? I know with the French law the way it is, our queen is out of the question." She muttered in her horse's receptive ear, "And a good thing that is."

"His wife is with child, so there may be an heir yet, but he had named Philip of Valois, his cousin, as his successor in the event he had no son."

"Do you think Ed—our king will try to claim the French throne?"

"It's a possibility," said Montacute. "Certainly as a grandson to Charles the Fair he would seem to have more right to it than Philip of Valois."

"Philip of Valois," said Eleanor. "Isn't his sister Queen Philippa's mother?"

"Yes. But the lady Philippa is technically not queen yet, you know. She has not been crowned."

"Not crowned! What are they waiting for?"

Montacute shrugged uncomfortably. "She is but fourteen."

"Why, Isabella was crowned when she was twelve, alongside my uncle and with just as much ceremony! Indeed, I was part of the procession!" Isabella,

Eleanor thought to herself, was evidently not eager to be supplanted by this young girl.

By the third or fourth day of their journey she felt so comfortable with William de Montacute that she could ask him about her uncle's funeral. "I so much wanted to have been there, to tell him goodbye," she said softly after Montacute had praised the music at the service. "But at least now I hope I can visit his grave."

"You will not be alone, Lady Despenser. Many are coming there now, as pilgrims you might say. They started coming in droves after the funeral, even in the dead of winter. The abbot, they say, is thinking of making improvements to the place with all the money they are bringing in."

"The queen and Mortimer do not try to stop the people from coming there?"

"What good would it do them? It would only raise more sus—"

He called to one of his men and began to issue orders about finding a suitable abbey to stay the night. For the rest of their trip, they talked of nothing but trivialities, and when Montacute had occasion to mention the young king, he did so with the utmost respect and warmth. But his slip had told Eleanor that while Montacute might be the king's man, he was certainly not Roger Mortimer's and Queen Isabella's.

The king had been moving south as Eleanor and Montacute moved north. For several days, he stopped at Lincoln, and it was there that Eleanor was taken to see him.

She was surprised when she was conducted to a small but reasonably comfortable chamber in the castle, for she had expected Lincoln to be so full with the king and his followers that she would have to sleep at an inn. It turned out, however, that Isabella and Mortimer, and their retinues, had left court and were not expected to return until some time in April. "It seems that they are spending some time at one of the queen's castles," explained Montacute, his face impassive.

"Together?" Eleanor thought of all the men of the Church who had flocked to the queen's banner. She wondered if they thought now of Lady Mortimer, far away from court and alone in one of the Mortimers' Welsh castles.

"So it appears."

Eleanor could hardly complain about this lovers' retreat, though, for it would be a great deal easier to face the king alone than with his mother and his mother's lover. Having sent in a message through one of Montacute's pages that she would await the king's pleasure, she had nothing to do but to change her travel-worn black dress for a slightly fresher black one and to clean the grime of the road off her face. These tasks being accomplished quickly, she sat and stared at the fire, waiting for the king's summons and thinking of the days when she had been a cherished member of her uncle's court.

The king's pleasure turned out to be an hour or so, but at last a page knocked on her door and led her to the king. Her hope that she might see him alone soon died as she heard her name announced loudly and saw a crowd of courtiers standing near the throne, all with seemingly nothing better to do than to watch her. Lifting her chin, she approached the throne, hearing titters as she did so, and knelt to the boy whom she regarded as little better than a usurper.

"You may rise, Lady Despenser."

A young knight stepped forth and helped her to her feet. "*Merci*," she murmured, and surveyed the king as best she could without looking him full in the face. She had not seen him in two and a half years, when he had not yet turned thirteen, and she felt a stab of pain when she saw how much he had grown to look like his dead father.

"Welcome, cousin. I hope you had an uneventful journey here, and I am glad to see that you reached here safely."

"Thank you, your grace. I had a very kind escort."

"Ah, Montacute," said Edward, his voice suddenly relaxing. Then it abruptly stiffened. "Your late husband was a traitor to the realm. But we, with the aid of our council, have considered the matter of your own status and have deemed it just that you be released from the Tower. You may go wherever you wish in England now. Of course, like any other subject you must gain permission to go abroad, and you may not remarry without our license."

Remarry! The thought was so startling that Eleanor nearly forgot her own prearranged formalities. She recovered herself. "Your grace, I thank you for my freedom. And now, if it pleases your grace, I do have several petitions to place before you."

"We will hear them."

"My eldest son, Hugh, was pardoned a year ago, yet he remains a prisoner. I ask that you show him the same generosity you have shown me and free him. He will serve you loyally, I assure you, if only given a chance."

"It cannot be, Lady Despenser."

His dismissal of her petition was so abrupt that Eleanor forgot all protocol. "Your grace, why not? What crime has he committed? What has he been accused of?"

"He held Caerphilly Castle while your husband beguiled my father into abandoning the realm for Wales."

"He held Caerphilly Castle because his king asked him to. He held it because he was loyal to him. And loyal to his father, your grace. Does not the Lord command us to honor our fathers?"

She had stung the king, she saw. Edward flushed and said curtly, "Go on, Lady Despenser, with your next petition, if you have one."

"I do, your grace. I would ask that you allow me to bury my husband's bones in consecrated ground."

"No, Lady Despenser. His quarters and head must remain on display as an example to all who crave royal power."

"Your grace, I have been told that my husband was stripped naked for the amusement of the crowd, crowned with nettles, pelted with dung, castrated—all before he died a traitor's death. Surely that is example enough?"

Behind her, someone gasped, and the king himself looked uncomfortable. Who in the world had told Lady Despenser so many of the details of her husband's execution? But he said coolly, "Your next petition."

"I ask most humbly that your grace restore my Clare lands. As your grace knows they were mine through my late brother, who died nobly in service to the crown. Without them I shall be dependent entirely on charity, for all that I had of my late husband has forfeited to the crown."

"Don't let the traitor's wife beguile your grace," warned a voice behind her. John Maltravers, the king's new steward and watchdog, had arrived beside them. Eleanor knew that he had been around her uncle when he died, and she shuddered. "She gives a pretty petition, but has she forgotten that her husband used trickery and fraud to deprive her sisters of their share of the inheritance?"

"I do not ask for their share, only for what was originally mine." Eleanor's heart was thumping, but she kept her voice level. "I trust to your grace to do what is right and just."

Edward's formal voice had become a trifle weary. "We shall consider your petition."

"One more, your grace. My young daughters. They have offended no one. Might I visit them in their convents, and be allowed to receive visits from them?"

"We shall consider it." Maltravers coughed a reminder. "And now, Lady Despenser, we must ask you, what do you know of your late husband's assets? There is much that the crown has not been able to recover. It is certain that he must have had money and jewels hidden in many places besides the houses of Bardi and the Peruzzi and the Tower and Caerphilly. Tell us what you know, and we shall be well pleased."

Was this why she had been asked to travel two hundred miles to see the king? "I am sorry, your grace, but I know nothing about those affairs of Hugh's. He kept many matters of business to himself, as men are wont to do." She kept her face calm with difficulty, although save for what she had taken from the Tower, she knew nothing of where anything belonging to Hugh might have been hidden.

"How the creature lies!" said Maltravers.

"Lady Despenser, you must tell us what you know."

"I have told you all that I know," Eleanor said. Had it not been for Maltravers beside her, standing so close to her now that she could feel his breath come and go, she might have confessed to her theft and begged for mercy from the king then and there. She added, "Should I recall something, it will be my duty to let your grace know immediately."

"Please do so," Edward said wearily. He seemed glad to be finished with the issue.

Eleanor was about to ask him for permission to retire when a girl in her mid-teens, dark and plump, came to his side. So unassumingly had she taken her position there, and so flustered was Eleanor, that she did not realize until a moment had passed that she was in the presence of the new queen of England, uncrowned though she might be. She hastily sank to her knees as Edward said, in his easy manner again, "My lady, I present to you my kinswoman, Lady Eleanor le Despenser." Edward rushed over the surname. "She has come to join us from London."

"Where she has lately been a prisoner in the Tower," said Maltravers.

Philippa frowned slightly, but her frown seemed directed more to Maltravers than to Eleanor. "Do you stay at court long, my lady?"

"I think not, your grace." She waited to see if the king would contradict her. "By the king's leave I will depart for London tomorrow morning."

"Then you must at least come to dinner tonight," said Philippa. "There will be a delightful entertainment."

"I thank your grace." She curtsied. As she began to back away, she heard the king's voice, his friendly one. "Cousin."

"Your grace?"

"Don't fret, cousin. You won't be forced to beg your bread."

There being no separate table for the widows of the disgraced, Eleanor found herself seated between two knights, whose faces she dimly recognized but whose names she did not recall. As she had expected, both conversed with the persons on their opposite sides and said nothing to her. She nibbled at her food—the portions at the Tower had been small, and her appetite had shrunk accordingly—with her eyes cast down, raising them only to indicate to a serving man that he could pour her some more wine. She had already taken more than was usual with her, but the events of the last few hours—the shock of being at court again and the stares of the bystanders and the refusal of her petitions and the queries about the jewels—had together been too much for her.

Even had she been bold enough to attempt a conversation with one of her neighbors, and the neighbor had not snubbed her, what would she have spoken of? Sixteen months in the Tower with only her children and a damsel for company did not make for sparkling conversation. Perhaps they should have put her next to one of Mortimer's sons, one of those who had been locked up; one of them would have had something in common with her. She chuckled to herself at this thought, and as she did so she felt a pair of eyes—those on her left side—upon her. Then a pleasant voice said, "Forgive me, Lady Despenser. I have been ignoring you very rudely, but it is only because I don't know what to say to you. I know you have been a prisoner for some time, and I know your circumstances have been very miserable as of late. I have been searching for some innocuous remark I could make to you, and I can find none. So I can only say that I hope you are well as can be expected."

The man who was speaking was probably not quite thirty, and was good-looking enough to almost rival Gaveston—still Eleanor's point of comparison for male handsomeness, and probably that of any other woman who had been at court at that time. Startled to be addressed so forthrightly, though not offended, Eleanor managed with a small smile, "You may start by telling me your name."

The man laughed. "That's fair and reasonable. I am John de Grey of Rotherfield. You won't remember me, my lady, but I occasionally saw you at court when I was a boy. I was a squire there for a time."

"Yes, I remember you now."

"The old king was kind to me. I remember him fondly." John smiled. "And you were kind to me too. You always had some pleasant remark to make to me, not like some great ladies who sought to intimidate me."

"I do not think you would have been easily intimidated."

"True! But ladies tried!" He laughed. "I was always doing something reprehensible at table—feeding my scraps to the dogs, or humming some tune, or speaking to my fellow squires with my mouth full. How I got my ears boxed! I hope I am better behaved today."

"Somewhat."

"Only somewhat?"

"I have been longing for that basket of fruit on your left side all evening, sir."

"My lady!" John immediately passed it to her, and she gratefully accepted it and began nibbling at an apple before she tired of that and reached for the wine again. "Now tell me what you were finding so amusing. I saw you smiling to yourself."

"A silly, idle thought, sir."

"The best kind, sometimes. You must tell it to me."

"I cannot remember it."

He was still coaxing her to tell him when their attention was diverted by the court fool. Eleanor found herself laughing at his antics harder than anyone nearby her, so much so that several censorious glances were sent in the direction of the traitor's widow who was enjoying herself far too much. She did not notice them. When the musicians came in, playing melancholy tunes she knew well, she sang softly to them, unaware of John de Grey's admiring glances at her or his hand on hers. It was only when the music had stopped and she felt her head drifting onto his shoulder that she pulled back from him and said gravely, "Sir, you have let me drink far too much wine."

John de Grey laughed. "You have not had that much at all, my lady, but it is probably more than you have been used to as of late." He smiled at her tenderly. "It is good to see you smiling and laughing as I remembered you. You are delightful company."

"Only when tipsy." Eleanor giggled.

"Nonsense. Shall I visit you when you are quite sober and have you prove it?"

"Indeed, but now you must help me remember where I am sleeping tonight. I can hardly hold my eyes open. Might we leave now?"

"Yes, the queen and king have left already."

"Though it hardly matters when Mortimer and Isabella are gone, does it?"

"My dear lady, you *have* taken a great deal of wine. Even with them gone, I think you must be careful of what you say still. Let me help you to your room."

She obeyed, and he helped her to rise, feeling nearly as giddy with a new idea as she. He had been widowed not very long ago, and though he had grieved sincerely for the loss of his young wife, enough time had passed for him to begin considering various girls of fourteen or fifteen as a second wife, girls who would bring him a respectable dowry and good connections. But Eleanor le Despenser? Though he had seen her audience with the king—it was he who had helped her to her feet—and had admired the proud lift of her chin, the fight she exhibited as she begged for her son, he had also thought of her as plain and rather haggard looking. He had spoken to her only out of pity, the sort of pity he would have felt for a injured horse or dog. Then, under the influence of wine and even more of simple human kindness, her manner had become more animated and her face had lit up, and she no longer seemed plain or worn to him. Instead, he had noticed her sweet voice and her pretty green eyes. She would, he thought, be a most agreeable person to have in his bed, even when sober.

And this lady leaning against him so trustingly was the heiress to a third of the Clare fortune, if the king chose to let her have it back. The fool Hugh le Despenser had destroyed himself with that fortune, but what might a sensible man, one not given to overreaching, do with it? What a chance had almost literally fallen into his arms!

He led Eleanor back to her chamber, the location of which it turned out she did remember after all, holding her more closely than really was necessary for her support as she hummed one of the tunes the musicians had played. It was like having a songbird on his arm, he thought, albeit a sweetly addled one. Walking by the passageway to his own room, he was tempted to coax her into it, but she was not that inebriated or he that unprincipled. Instead, he gently guided her along, noting as he did so that she had a delightful figure. He was struggling with more temptations when she lurched to a halt. "Is this your chamber, my lady?"

"I think so." Eleanor frowned. "They all look alike, though, don't they? Knock and make sure, please, Sir Grey."

She was leaning more heavily against him now, her face turned up to his, her hair coming loose from its headdress. He wanted to take her on the floor, against the wall, anywhere. Instead, John de Grey knocked. A very large female opened the door and surveyed the two of them coolly. Eleanor gasped. "Gladys?"

"Lady Hastings had business in London, so she came to her house soon after you had left it. I left her with the children and hurried here with some of her men so that you could be properly attended." She glared at John de Grey. "And I daresay you are in need of proper attendance."

"Your lady was just a little faint," said John smoothly. "The hall was very hot. Good night, my lady."

"Good night, my lord. Thank you for taking me here." She giggled again. "Without him, I might have ended up in a garderobe, Gladys."

"Is that a fact," Gladys said evenly. "Good night, sir," she said emphatically.

John transferred Eleanor to Gladys's arms and fled.

Gladys bolted the door quickly, as if keeping an invader out, then began to braid Eleanor's hair for bed as Eleanor yawned on a chair. "You seemed to have an agreeable companion, my lady."

"Sir Grey? Yes, he was an amusing young man. He felt impelled by chivalry to be kind to me, I suppose." Eleanor was making an effort to pronounce her words very distinctly even as she slumped lower in the chair. She hummed some more.

"If chivalry means plying you with wine," muttered Gladys. "Sit *up*, my lady."

"He did not ply me with wine, Gladys, and he was very gentlemanly. He took me straight here."

"With his hand on your rump the entire way, I'll wager."

"I did not hear you, Gladys."

"No matter, my lady."

Eleanor opened her eyes the next morning and discovered that the hammering she heard was not coming from her aching head, but from the door. Beside her, Gladys muttered, "If it's your young knight, tell him to go play quietly somewhere and leave you alone."

"He is not that young, Gladys, and I will tell him no such thing. He was a perfect gentleman, I tell you, and I recollect everything he did perfectly well. Yes?"

A youthful voice called from behind the door, "I come from the lady Philippa. She wishes to see you this morning, at your earliest convenience."

"I will be there straightaway. Thank you."

In a half hour, wearing a dress that Gladys had lovingly brushed the night before and with her hair arranged as only Gladys could arrange it, she was kneeling before the queen. She had barely touched her knee to the floor when Philippa bade her to rise again. "I am sorry I did not get a chance to speak with you more yesterday, Lady Despenser. I understand that you are my husband's first cousin. He told me his father had a very deep affection for you."

"And I for him, your grace."

"And he told me someone else was fond of you, too." Philippa rang a bell. "John!"

John of Eltham rushed into the room, beaming. "Lady Despenser! I told you that you would be free, now, didn't I?"

"Indeed you did, John. Is it to you I owe it, then?"

"Not exactly," admitted John. "I pestered my brother the king enough about it, but it was he who insisted that you go free."

"He did?"

"My mother didn't want to let you go, I am afraid, and neither did Lord Mortimer. My mother relies a great deal on Lord Mortimer, you know." Eleanor nodded. "I don't know why; I don't like him much myself. They said you should stay in the Tower for your own misdeeds—something about your spying on my mother and dictating what she could do with her money. But he finally wore them down. He said you were family, after all."

"I am grateful to him, then."

John's face turned somber. "I never did see Papa again, you know. I miss him, Lady Despenser."

"So do I, John. Very, very much."

They both wiped tears from their eyes. John went on, "Philippa—she lets me call her that because we are so close in age—says that you are starting back to London today. I hoped you could stay a while."

"I would like to, John, but my children are there, you know, and now that Lady Hastings has been left with them I feel I must hurry back even faster. Gilbert will have her treating him like a very sultan. You know how she spoiled your sisters."

"Not as much as you did me. Good-bye, Lady Despenser. I'm glad you're out."

He hugged her and left the room. Philippa tactfully let Eleanor stare out at the window for a while. Then she said, "The king has gone hunting this morning. He has not changed his mind about the petitions you put before him yesterday with regard to your son and your husband, and it is not my place to say whether he is wrong or right in doing so. I know so little of these affairs, after all. But he did ask me to give you copies of these."

Eleanor read the letters. They were addressed to the prioresses of Sempringham, Watton, and Shaftesbury, and informed them that the late Hugh le Despenser's daughters were to be allowed to leave the convent for visits with their relations at the prioress's discretion, just as would any other nun not under discipline, and that the girls' relations were to be allowed to visit them provided that they did not interfere with their religious duties. She knelt before the queen. "Your grace, how I can thank you for this?"

"It is the king you must thank, Lady Despenser. But he will be gone awhile, so I will relay your thanks to him."

"Then tell him I thank him from the depths of my heart."

Gladys stared suspiciously at Sempringham priory as their horses approached it. "There are certainly a lot of men around it, my lady."

"The Gilbertine order admits both men and women, Gladys. Sempringham is what they call a double house, but with the nuns and the canons safely divided, of course! It is the only monastic order founded in England, did you know that? St. Gilbert, its founder, came from a wealthy family, but he was crippled and could not take up his duties as a knight—" Eleanor flushed. "I am rambling, aren't I, Gladys? But I am so worried. What if they do not let me in?" Lady Hastings having sent men with Gladys to Lincoln, Eleanor had not needed a royal escort back to London. Now she wished she had the power of the royal banners behind her. What if the prioress had some grudge of her own against Hugh?

After Philippa put the letters in her hand, Eleanor's first impulse had been to go north to see Margaret at Watton in Yorkshire, then south to see Nora at Sempringham and farther south to see Joan at Shaftesbury, but doing so would have kept her from her young children in London for so long that she had determined for now to visit only Sempringham, as it lay between Lincoln and London. "And what if Nora does not know me? What if she wants nothing to do with me?"

"You are too uneasy, my lady."

Eleanor sighed and fidgeted with her reins.

The prioress, however, greeted her courteously. "We are honored by your visit, Lady Despenser. You will be staying overnight, I hope? Then I shall have you shown to your chamber. I think it will suit you. Your sister stayed there while she was—er—boarding with us."

"My daughter?"

The prioress smiled. "I will send her to you shortly."

She was conducted to a pleasant, airy chamber. Gladys had hardly helped her out of her cloak when a light knock sounded on her door and a little girl, dressed as a miniature version of the sister who had just left Eleanor, stepped into the room. "Mama!"

"Nora!"

Clasping Nora to her, she could not say anything more for a few minutes. Finally she managed, "Can you show me around?"

"Yes, Mama." Nora led her from room to room, chattering all of the time. Eleanor, sinking back into her usual role of not getting many words in edgewise while Nora held forth, noted with relief that her eight-year-old daughter was well grown for her age and from the fresh color in her cheeks appeared to be getting outdoor exercise. Though she shared a room with other nuns, she had a bed to herself, piled high with warm coverings, and the sisters she introduced Eleanor to as they moved through the priory spoke to her kindly. "You are not lonely here, my sweet?"

"Oh, no, Mama. Everyone is very friendly, and when Sister Anne's bitch has puppies by Sister Mary's dog, I shall have one of them for my very own. But I have a *particular* friend, Mama, whom you have not seen yet."

Eleanor smiled. Nora's vocabulary had been impressive before she was sent away by the queen, and it was no less so now. She was still smiling as they entered the priory's herb garden, where a tall nun was gathering sprigs of lavender. Then she involuntarily gasped as the nun turned and Nora chirped, "Here she is, Mama. This is Sister Gwenllian!"

The nun was well into her forties, but even under a veil and wimple she was the most beautiful woman Eleanor had ever seen—next to her the queen, up to now England's greatest beauty, would appear almost ordinary. And why should she not be beautiful? She was from a line of beauties: Eleanor her mother, daughter to Simon de Montfort; Eleanor her grandmother, wife to Montfort and sister to Henry III; Isabella of Angouleme, her great-grandmother, wife to King John; Eleanor of Aquitaine, her great-great-grandmother.

Sister Gwenllian seemed used to being gaped at by first acquaintances. She said in a lovely contralto voice, "Your daughter is a sweet child, Lady Despenser, and very intelligent. You must be very proud of her."

"Thank you, your grace. I am."

Nora said cheerfully, "When I came here, I *was* sad, Mama, because I missed you and Papa and all the others. But Sister Gwenllian was kind to me right from the start. When she heard two of the younger sisters saying that Papa was a great sinner she got very angry and told them that we were all sinners and that they should not be unkind. They apologized to me straightaway. People listen to Sister Gwenllian. Did you know, Mama? Sister Gwenllian would be Princess of Wales, if her father had not been killed. Did you know that?"

"Yes, Nora, I did."

Nora looked keenly disappointed, so Eleanor added kindly, "But I had forgotten until you reminded me."

"Isn't the garden pretty, Mama? Sister Gwenllian is in charge of it, although the gardeners do the heavy work, of course. She is teaching me all she knows about herbs, just as the nuns taught her when she was little. I will know all about their properties."

"It is beautiful, Sister Gwenllian. We had herb gardens too, of course, but never as thriving as this."

For a while Eleanor and the two nuns worked in the garden and talked. Sister Gwenllian indeed had a wide knowledge of herbs, and Eleanor made mental notes of much of what she told her. But when Nora had moved off a ways, she asked, "Your grace, I beg your pardon for my impertinence, but do you never get angry that you are here?"

Sister Gwenllian shrugged. "What would I gain by that? In any case, I am not sure that I should have enjoyed my birthright. I might have worn a crown, and then I might have spent all my life guarding against someone taking it from me, or from my husband. Think of our late king. From all I that have heard, his crown brought him no happiness. Perhaps it would have been better if he had been professed as a monk."

"I do not think he would have been the best of monks," said Eleanor dryly, "but I do see your meaning."

"This is a comfortable, respectable life, after all. It is too small a world in some ways, I think, with sometimes too many squabbles over trifles, but at least we are protected from some of the horrors of the larger world. I realized that again when your sister Margaret came here, all anger and bitterness over her first husband's death and her second husband's imprisonment, and when Joan Mortimer came here, all bewilderment, poor thing. And then they left at last, and then in less than eight weeks your little one came here. I thought, will this never end? Must innocents keep paying the price for others' will to power and riches?"

She sighed and jerked at a weed. "You know the new king, Lady Despenser. Is he the man to end this?"

"I don't know. He set me free against his mother's wishes, so I am told, and he—or his good wife, I know not which—paved the way for me to come here. But when I spoke to him the other day it was as if he were reading words that someone else had written for him. I have heard he was not happy to treat with the Scots, and yet men have been sent to do just that. But he is a boy, after all. You may have a chance to decide for yourself soon, for I understood when I left Lincoln that he too was headed for Sempringham on his way south."

"Here? Someone must tell the prior, Lady Despenser. There is nothing we religious dread more than a royal visit. It will set us back for months!" Sister Gwenllian's laugh was bell-like. She added after a moment or two, "But I will take the opportunity to ask him for something for my maintenance, which of course shall add to the comfort of all of us here. It is but fair, don't you think? Ten or twenty pounds per year for the kingdom of Wales?"

"More than fair." Nora, having weeded her allotted area to perfection, began to move in the women's direction. "Sister Gwenllian, I want to thank you so much for your kindness to my daughter."

"There you have nothing to thank me for. Your daughter is a lovable child." Sister Gwenllian started to rise from her weeding with some difficulty, and Eleanor hastened to help her. "Thank you, Lady Despenser. Tell me, what shall you do now that you have been set free? We nuns must gossip, you know, and there was some speculation on the subject after your man told us to expect you. Will you take the veil, do you think?"

"No. I have been blessed with my young sons and a baby daughter—one that Nora does not yet know about, actually. I will care for them—ever supposing that I have the means to do it. The king has not told me of his plans as far as my estates go."

"I shall pray he restores them to you."

"I shall too, and for a better reason than you might think. I have been thinking since I was released, and I should like to be a good lady of the manor, as they say my sister Elizabeth is. I do think my husband wanted to be a good lord, in his heart of hearts, and maybe he might have been if he had lived out his time, but other things got in the way."

Sister Gwenllian said, "Your sister Margaret expounded a great deal on the 'other things' when she was here, I am afraid, but I suppose there was another side to your husband—no, I know there was, because your daughter speaks of him with great love. She has all Sempringham praying for his soul."

Nora had come within hearing range. "We do, Mama, day and night—and for those of others as well, of course. Will you join us when we pray tonight?"

Eleanor pulled her daughter close to her. "Nothing would give me more pleasure."

At St. Dunstan's, she found Elizabeth thriving with her wet nurse, John's vocabulary larger than ever and with a generous helping of English added to his repertoire as well, and Gilbert with such an extensive knowledge of London that he could have drawn a map of the place. Even Edward seemed a little less guarded in his manner. All of them were doubly precious to her after her visit to Sempringham, and she had hugged and kissed each of them, even Edward, three times over when Bella slipped into the room. Eleanor had forgotten how much Bella looked like Hugh, and when she saw Lady Hastings' face, a feminine, gentle version of her brother's, she gave way to her emotions entirely. Lady Hastings herself was greatly moved by the sight of her sister-in-law in her widow's barb, and it was a long time before she had sufficiently recovered her composure to say, "Nelly, dear, you have not seen everyone yet. Come upstairs with me. I have a pleasant surprise for you."

She led Eleanor to a small but comfortable chamber where a girl in her teens sat sewing. "Isabel!" Gladys had told Eleanor in Lincoln that Isabel had gone to visit Lady Hastings, but had not told her that she would be at St. Dunstan's with the rest. She hugged Isabel, then saw the baby sleeping in a tiny bed in a corner of the room. "Then this must be—"

"Edmund, Mama," said Isabel.

Feeling both very joyful and somewhat elderly, Eleanor held her first grandchild.

That night after the rest of the household went to bed, Eleanor and Bella sat by the fire. "Bella, do you think Isabel will return to her husband?"

Bella shook her head. "As far as I know, neither has sent any message to the other since the day I took her from Fairford."

"They never liked each other, not when they were little, not when they were of age to consummate their marriage. We should have let them out of it, his parents and Hugh and me."

"How could you have known, Nelly? Many couples start out disliking each other and grow into love, or at least into mutual affection. I was married to my first husband a full month before I warmed to him."

Eleanor smiled. "For you, Bella, that must have been great dislike indeed!" She looked at her workbasket in a corner, which already contained the beginnings of a smock for Edmund. "But even men who dislike their wives warm to their sons, and Richard seems to want nothing to do with Edmund either, does he? That I do not understand. He is a beautiful little boy."

"He looks at him and sees Hugh, whom he blames for his father's death. I think Richard loved his father very much."

Bella's voice faltered. Eleanor took her sister-in-law's hand. "Bella, I have been rather sheltered in my cocoon, but you have had to face the world all these months. It must have been dreadful for you."

"It was hard, Nelly, but not as bad as it might have been. My stepchildren by Ralph have been good to me, and Aline and I have been able to write to each other and visit. Hugh and Thomas and Margaret have been the best children I could ask for. Even my turncoat son-in-law has been kind to me. He sends me so much venison I expect to grow antlers any day now, and he is good to Margaret, I must admit. Amie has been very good company—I want to look for her a husband, but she will hear nothing of it yet—and I have some of my old friends still. I cannot complain."

"Have you been able to get your father's body for burial?"

Bella ducked her head. "No, Eleanor. I see you were never told. His head is in Winchester still, but his body was cut up and fed to dogs."

Eleanor closed her eyes. "Bella, I am so very sorry. My guards kept that from me."

"My men kept it from me too, until I started to send a petition to the king, in my own dreadful scrawl, and then they had to tell me, which they did very gently." She took a deep breath. "I can talk of it now, which is more than I could before. It was, after all, just his body; it matters not where it is."

"No, Bella." But she felt such an intense rush of hate for Isabella and Mortimer that her body trembled. What would it have cost those two to let Bella and her sister, who had done so little to offend them, give their old father a decent burial?

Bella brushed at her eyes. "But I have a pleasant thing to speak of now. Did you know I have another brother? Well, I do. My father's bastard. His name is Nicholas, and he is but a boy still. We have visited back and forth several times, very quietly, because it would not do to let people know whose son he is, not the way things are now, but I like him a great deal. Papa wanted him to be a monk, and he is agreeable to that, but my sons have taken him falconing, and he enjoyed that immensely."

"I do so want to meet him. Is he like—?"

"Hugh? Not physically, he resembles his mother more than Hugh or my father. He does have Hugh's laugh, though. The rest is too soon to tell. Perhaps now that the weather is so fine he will come to London for a visit. Papa wanted him to be professed at Westminster, so it is good that he should have a look at the place. I suppose you wish to remain in London while you are awaiting word from the king?"

"Yes, I had better. I hope he will make a decision soon, for I have imposed upon your hospitality greatly."

"Nonsense! Though it *is* expensive keeping Gilbert in pies!" She laughed. "He would be as plump as a pig, but he spends so much time sneaking around London that he runs it all off."

"I must get him a tutor before he turns into a savage." Eleanor frowned, for after the presents to her guards, a generous contribution to Sempringham priory, and the expenses of their journey back from Lincoln, her store of cash had dwindled quickly. And there were more expenses besides a tutor. Bella could not be allowed to keep paying Isabel and Edmund's upkeep out of her own purse, and the children could all use some clothes, particularly Edward, who was at an age to be keenly sensitive about looking shabby. And if the king granted her some lands, there would be the expense of traveling to him and the expense of furnishing her household. Except for what she had taken into captivity with her, everything she and Hugh had owned had gone into the hands of the queen and her supporters.

Except for what she had taken from the Tower. Eleanor lay awake much of that night, considering. She had vowed to give the treasure to the Church, and she fully intended to do so. But surely there was no harm in using some of the items as security for a loan in the meantime...

The next day, over the strenuous objections of Bella, who would have given her all that she needed, she packed some of the treasure into a small chest and went to the offices of Benedict de Fulsham, the pepperer who had been present when she had surrendered the Tower. He looked startled when he saw her, as if seeing a ghost from those days of murder and pillage when London had run amok. With the unease Eleanor was quickly growing used to, he stammered, "Lady Despenser? So you are free. I am glad of it."

"Thank you. I have only my freedom for now, but I hope to soon regain some land. In the meantime, I and my family must live. I wish to borrow money from you, sir."

"I do lend sums from time to time, my lady, but only with security. It is a necessity, the more so in these uncertain times."

Did he think she was asking for alms? That she was offering something else to him? With a haughty expression that would have pleased her queenly ancestors and namesakes, Eleanor gestured to Bella's manservant and opened the chest that he sat on a counter for her. "Be assured, sir, that I can do business with you properly. As you can see, I have brought more than adequate security."

Benedict stared in the chest. "Where did you get these, my lady? Surely they are not your husband's property, forfeit to the crown?"

"You forget that I am the granddaughter of a king and the daughter of an earl, sir. My father left me many precious things upon his death, and so did my mother, and I have bought and been given fine things over the years myself. I was allowed to keep these personal items in the Tower with me."

"I beg your pardon," said the pepperer, thoroughly abashed.

Presently, they agreed upon a loan and interest. Only when Eleanor signed the note to Benedict as "Eleanor le Despenser, late the wife of Hugh le Despenser," did her hand tremble.

CHAPTER 23

▼

APRIL 1328 TO JUNE 1328

The king's court, graced again by Mortimer and Isabella, was making its way to Northampton for Parliament when, one April night, Mortimer came to Isabella's room. He undressed and climbed in bed beside her, but his words, as they so often were these days, were ones of business. "I think we should give that Despenser creature her lands back."

"Why on earth should we?"

"The king and his council wish it, for one."

"Bother the council!"

"Lady Despenser is not hated as her husband was, Isabella. She is a grand-daughter of the first Edward, who unlike his son was held in high regard—"

"You needn't remind me of that."

"She is a granddaughter of the first Edward, and there was respect for her brother as well. Many think it unfair that her sisters should have their lands and she have nothing because of the marriage her grandfather made for her."

"Fine, we give the creature back her lands. So what of her husband?"

Mortimer looked at the queen as if she were slightly daft. "Despenser? Could he possibly be more dead?"

"Her next husband, you fool! Do you think the heiress to Glamorgan will remain unmarried? She's only in her thirties. Aside from the land, she's amiable enough, and she's not unattractive, if you like orange cats. Some men do."

"She might take a vow of chastity. I have always heard that she was fond of that wretch Despenser."

"She wasn't fond of him; she adored him. I can't tell you how many times I have sat and listened to a litany of the virtues of Hugh le Despenser! But that doesn't mean that if a man was kind to her and her wretched brats, she wouldn't marry him. Hers is an affectionate nature, and I don't think she is averse to being bedded either." She scowled. "I could smell him on her sometimes when she came to my chamber, fresh from his bed. The slut!"

"Be that as it may, the king wants her to get her lands back, and as we are going to have to cram this Scottish truce down his throat, we ought to give way on this minor matter. After all, she has to get the crown's permission to marry, and after her spell in the Tower, I can't imagine her not getting a license." He laughed. "And what's to stop me from finding a suitable husband for her? She might even do for one of my sons, for a first wife anyway. The wench has probably got some babes left in her, and a young man might appreciate some experience in bed, not to mention Glamorgan. I'll have to think about that."

"Very well. I shall tell Edward to give the order."

Mortimer settled back against the pillows more comfortably. "By the by, what shall we do about the bun in the oven Despenser left behind him?" Thomas Wake had kept quiet about the birth of Elizabeth le Despenser, but Mortimer had a spy or two among the guards, who had been more forthcoming. "Shall we help Hugh's salvation further along by bestowing another of his girls on the Church?"

Isabella started to chew a fingernail, a bad habit she had developed since Edward's death. Mortimer slapped her hand, and she withdrew it from her mouth. Though she had spent many pleasant evenings picturing Lady Despenser's face when her girls were hauled away, the pictures were not so pleasant these days. One of the provisions of the proposed truce with Scotland was that her own daughter Joan, not quite seven, was to marry Robert Bruce's little son. It was a provision the queen could live with, especially as the Scots had promised the English twenty thousand pounds, but she did not look forward to telling the child that she was to go across the border to dwell with the man whom most Englishmen regarded as a mortal enemy. Nor did she look forward to parting from the girl. "Let the woman keep the brat," she said irritably.

From a table a little distance off, William la Zouche and Thomas Wake watched as the royal family and the earls of the land settled themselves at the king's high table after having spent the morning in Parliament. The man who took the place next to the queen, however, was neither royalty nor an earl, but Roger Mortimer, who seemed supremely unaware that he was lacking in either respect. "Getting more above himself every day," muttered Thomas Wake. "Next thing you know, he'll be making himself an earl. Why, he's seated closer to the king than my father-in-law, and he the greatest earl in the land!"

A week before, on May 4, 1328, King Edward had ratified the Treaty of Edinburgh. He had done so with no good grace and no free will. His sullen mood had been caught by his council, most especially the Earl of Lancaster and the earl's son-in-law, Thomas Wake. Not unnoticed either by the council was the fact that its role was increasingly an empty one; on all matters of importance, it was the queen and Mortimer who dictated policy, with scant regard for the opinions of the peers of the realm or for those of the king himself. It was, Wake muttered now, Hugh le Despenser all over again without the sodomy.

Zouche shifted uncomfortably in his seat. Two days before, he had been appointed constable of the Tower of London and justice of the forest south of Trent, both positions recently held by Wake himself, and he knew well that this was a reward for his part in negotiating what was now being called the shameful peace. He himself thought of the peace as nothing shameful at all. It was a necessity, and though men on both sides, including perhaps himself, would lose land by it, it was surely better than more battles, more land laid waste, more men dead.

At the same time, he disliked the way the peace had been foisted on the young king, for even before the king had ratified the treaty, Mortimer and the queen had seen to it that the peace was proclaimed in London as a fait accompli. And he disliked the sight of Roger Mortimer preening in his fine clothes at the high table—since Parliament began he had not been seen twice in the same robes—as much as did Thomas Wake.

"I'm eating elsewhere," announced Wake. "This Mortimer creature spoils my appetite. But who is this? Why Zouche, it's your little widow, your rich little widow now. Out of mourning, too, and looking quite attractive. You'd better move fast, Zouche."

John Maltravers was leading Eleanor le Despenser toward the high table. She was indeed out of mourning, wearing a dark green gown that despite its modesty and relative simplicity displayed her curvaceous figure nicely. Her hair, pinned up about her ears, was so lightly covered by its netting that its red color was visible to all. Her face was expressionless as she neared the queen, but William could guess at the emotions she was feeling as she approached the woman who had left her a widow.

Eleanor, at Northampton to give the king the homage and fealty required so that she could occupy her newly regained lands, had hoped that she might see the king in private, and she had certainly not wished to see his mother. But as she had no choice in either, she took a breath and let Maltravers lead her to the high table.

As she sank to her knees before the queen for what seemed an interminable period of waiting, she quickly took in the sight of her uncle's supplanters. Mortimer she had seen but twice or three times before he was shut in the Tower, but she had no difficulty in identifying him, for he was dressed more splendidly than any of the earls sitting at the high table with him. Isabella had grown only more beautiful since her departure for France years before. She had not put herself in any danger of being outshone by Philippa by dressing as became a dowager queen. Beside her mother-in-law in her elaborately embroidered and bejeweled robes and sparkling jewels, crownless Philippa looked no more than a prosperous merchant's wife.

Just as Eleanor had been kneeling so long so as to border on ridiculousness, Isabella bade her to rise. Then the queen said charmingly, "You are looking well, my lady."

"Thank you, your grace," said Eleanor warily. Under the shelter of her gown, she knocked her knees together to restore some feeling to them.

"A bit thinner than you used to be, perhaps. But of course, you are no longer breeding Despenser's brats on a regular basis." She frowned. "You are not in mourning, Lady Despenser. I trust you have not forgotten your husband."

Evidently it had not occurred to the queen that she herself was not in mourning. Eleanor said coolly, "I wore black for well over a year for my husband, your grace, but I dislike the color, and so did Hugh. It is no sign of disrespect to wear my other robes now, especially this one. It was his favorite."

"How charming."

Mortimer joined the fun. "Have you seen your late husband, Lady Despenser? On London Bridge?"

"I have seen him."

"He adds a certain *je ne sais quoi* to it, does he not? I suppose you have not had an opportunity to view his quarters."

Eleanor could only shake her head.

Mortimer was frowning. "York, Bristol, Dover... Help me, your grace."

"Carlisle," prompted the queen.

"Ah, yes. Carlisle. Thank you, your grace." He smiled. "Now that you are free and wealthy, I suppose you will have the opportunity to make a leisurely tour of them. He certainly gives the lie to the cliché that a man cannot be everywhere at once."

"Stop!"

All eyes turned toward Philippa, who blushed deeply. Her voice was firm, though, as she said, "Lord Mortimer, your remarks are cruel and uncalled for. I will not tolerate them in my presence."

Mortimer smiled indulgently at the king's young bride. "With all respect, my lady, you are unaware of whom I am addressing. This is the relict of your lord's great enemy, the man who played havoc with the kingdom and dishonored your gracious Queen Isabella."

"That may be, your lordship, but I will not have his widow abused for your sport."

Eleanor did not know whether the queen and Mortimer would have ventured into further sallies notwithstanding Philippa's intervention, for just then a trumpet announced the arrival of the king, trailed by a contingent of knights. At the high table, he paused beside the again-kneeling Eleanor. "You have come to swear your homage and fealty to me?"

"Yes, your grace."

"You may do so now."

Eleanor placed her hands between the king's and spoke the required words. The formalities done with, he ordered her to rise, and she thanked him for restoring her lands. He shrugged and asked, "As the Lady of Glamorgan, that is where you are bound, I suppose?"

"Yes. I shall settle first at Cardiff."

"I think you shall find all in order there." Eleanor sensed that the king might have talked more to her were it not for the queen's eyes fixed on them. "Do take our meal with us before you leave. Good luck to you."

She curtsied and let Maltravers lead her to an empty seat, which turned out to be the one Thomas Wake had vacated in such disgust. Zouche, silently thanking the Lord for his luck, assisted her to it. "You are looking well, Lady Despenser."

"And so are you, Lord Zouche. I understand that you were in Scotland for us?" He nodded. "That was a great responsibility, sir. You should be proud of what you and the others achieved."

"Dancing to the Scots' tune was more like it, I fear, but we did the best we could."

"What was it like, seeing the Bruce?"

"He was an impressive figure, even lying sick and sorely disfigured from his skin condition in his bed at Holyrood Abbey where we concluded the treaty. One could see how he could inspire men in battle. And all of his great leaders were there too."

"Even the Douglas?"

"Even he. Odd, for such a warrior, he's rather docile in company. He didn't snatch a single baby and eat him when we were there."

Eleanor laughed. William added, "I did find going there to be interesting, having fought against these people for so long and viewed them as the devil incarnate. I'm glad to have a chance to talk with you now about it, my lady, because the English are so dead set against the treaty, I've felt as if I should keep quiet about it, as if being there were something to be ashamed of."

"Ashamed of! I wish my uncle had concluded such a treaty, and then my brother would have never died, perhaps. But my uncle thought, as did my grandfather, that it was his duty to conquer the Scots, and goodness knows such a treaty would have made him even more hated by the lords than he was."

She sighed. Zouche said, "Do you stay here at court long, my lady?"

"No. My children—and my grandson, Lord Zouche, a fine boy—are at an inn where we stayed the night. If they have not torn the inn up, we will begin traveling to Wales this afternoon. Us and your namesake, Lord Zouche. I am afraid you sadly misjudged that dog's size." She raised her hand to the level where her breasts swelled invitingly under her gown, not knowing the effect this had on the unfortunate Zouche. "He has grown this high."

"Perhaps I can visit him sometime, Lady Despenser."

"I would like that, Lord Zouche."

He offered to refill her wine goblet and she shook her head. "No, Lord Zouche, not after the display I made of myself the last time I was at court. I was bone tired from traveling, and the king refused all my petitions, and Maltravers was so hateful, and I was so miserable, I drank much more than I should have. Sir Grey had to help me to my room."

"Sir Grey?" said Zouche, stopping himself in time before adding, "That puppy?"

"Yes. He was very kind."

William frowned. He hoped that Sir Grey had been chivalrous, but he could hardly ask. Had he not been, he supposed, Gladys would have beaten him to a pulp.

Eleanor looked at the high table. Mortimer was holding forth about something, the queen watching worshipfully, the king scowling, and Philippa heroically stifling a yawn. Whatever Mortimer was speaking of, it was not intended for more than the ears closest to him, for everyone else at the high table was engaged in conversations between themselves. "I believe I can safely leave now, sir, without giving offense?"

"I think so. Allow me to accompany you to your inn."

She nodded and they went out to await their horses. But it was the puppy, six feet tall with startlingly blue eyes, who came into view first. "Lady Despenser! I am pleased to see you again."

"Quite sober this time, Sir Grey."

And quite fetching, thought John de Grey. "Some of my estates are quite close to yours, Lady Despenser. Should you need a loan of anything while you are getting yours established again, my resources are at your disposal."

Zouche, who had been planning to make a very similar offer, was reduced to saying, "And mine too, my lady."

"I shall remember both of your kind offers."

"I suppose you will be setting off for your lands now?"

"Yes. As I was telling Lord Zouche, my children are at the inn here, and they will be quite ready to go, I am sure. And the innkeeper will be ready to see them go, I suspect. Gilbert is as willful as they say his father was at his age, and John and Lizzie and Edmund must explore everything they see."

Zouche scowled as he saw John de Grey happily absorb the information that Eleanor had young children and therefore could be reasonably expected to have more. Grey said cheerfully, "Perhaps I may accompany you to your inn, my lady? I should like your damsel to see that I am not the villain she took me for when I last saw her."

"Of course you may."

The double escort proceeded to the inn, John de Grey making light conversation that made Eleanor laugh, William making no conversation at all. The day being fine, Eleanor's youngest children and their dog were playing outside the inn, watched by their elder brother and sister and by Lady Hastings, Amie de Gaveston, and Gladys. Zouche's gloom lifted for a moment as he saw Lady Hastings, as yet unaware of the knights' approach, throw a ball to Gilbert with no mean aim. Gilbert caught it and then saw William. "Lord Zouche!"

He bounded toward his mother and William, followed by the rather confused-looking dog, who had indeed much grown larger than William had predicted. "Did you hear, Lord Zouche? Mama has all of her land back from the king, and we can live on it anywhere we please now!"

"I did hear, Gilbert, and I am very glad of it."

"And I have my own pony now. And look at Lord Zouche, Lord Zouche! Hasn't he grown? He can fetch now, at least when he feels like it."

It was now William's turn to feel smug as John de Grey looked puzzled. He took advantage of this by hastily dismounting from his horse and then assisting Eleanor off hers. If his hand lingered too long near Eleanor's waist, it was surely the horse's fault.

Eleanor thanked him and introduced the two men to those they did not know. Edward looked at both Zouche and Grey with the utmost of suspicion, but the others greeted them politely. Zouche admired Edmund and Lizzie and reminded Eleanor that the latter had been only a bulge in Eleanor's belly the last time they met, a reference that discomfited Grey even more than the dog had. He was not easily defeated, however, for while William was having his beard pulled by Lizzie, Grey asked Gilbert, who needed no persuasion, to show him his new pony. Soon he was giving Gilbert, whose riding skills were indeed somewhat rusty, various hints, earning him a grateful accolade from his pupil's mother. "I am so glad you told him to use a lighter hand on the reins, Sir Grey. I have been telling him the same, but he will not listen nearly as well to me, though I have been riding since I was walking, almost."

"He would prefer to get his lessons from a knight, I suppose," said Grey amicably.

William, who had been knighted when John de Grey was still in diapers, considered mentioning this but on reflection thought better of it.

It was Lady Hastings, who having had suitors between her three marriages had a better idea of what was passing in the men's minds than did Eleanor herself, who finally called matters to a halt. "Nelly, don't you think we should be leaving now? I believe if we did we could get quite far."

"Yes," said Eleanor. "I am eager to be moving on." She smiled. "When I am settled I hope I shall have the honor of showing each of you hospitality."

Not, William and John each devoutly hoped, when the other man was within a hundred miles of Glamorgan.

Lady Hastings, worrying that some fortune hunter might recognize the Lady of Glamorgan and abduct her, had arranged for her sons, Hugh and Thomas, and her household knights to escort them to Glamorgan. Their presence had the added advantage of giving Edward, who would be fourteen in a few months, some sorely needed male company.

With him occupied with his cousins, and the little ones being tended in their lumbering cart, Eleanor could ask as they rode along, "Bella, did you ever think of marrying again?"

This had been a subject much on Bella's mind, though not with herself as the reference. "I have thought of it, Nelly, but I doubt I will. I miss Ralph too much. In any case, at my age and after Father's execution there are certainly no men begging for the privilege."

"There ought to be, my lady," said Amie warmly. "You are certainly pretty enough still."

Bella tapped her damsel on the cheek affectionately. "So are you, my dear, if you would let me find you a proper match."

"I like it as I am," said Amie.

Bella said gently, "What of you, Nelly? You have been widowed a year and a half now. Do you think of remarrying? It would be no disrespect to Hugh if you did."

"Goodness, no!"

Amie looked slyly at Eleanor. Lady Hastings had sternly bid her to hold her tongue about the subject of Lady Despenser's knights, but as Eleanor had brought up the subject herself…"Lady Despenser, what about Sir Grey and Lord Zouche?"

"What about them, child?"

"I believe they want to marry you."

"Marry me! What nonsense! Lord Zouche has merely been kind to me, no more, for chivalry's sake. That Sir Grey barely knows me."

"He knows full well that you are Lady of Glamorgan," muttered Gladys.

"And you were looking lovely at court today in your green dress," Bella added.

"I told all of you this morning, I wore that dress for Hugh. It was his favorite, and I thought he would like to see me in it when I got my lands back, instead of those drab blacks." Eleanor's indignation mounted. "Really! Cannot a man even talk to me without you three thinking I am about to marry him?"

Isabel, who had been riding beside the cart holding Edmund and his nursemaid, trotted up now. "Isabel! Have I said or done anything that makes you think I wish to remarry?"

"No, Mama," said Isabel loyally. She added, "But I would not be angry if you did, Mama, truly. I know you must be lonely."

Exasperated at her companions' utter insensitivity and thickheadedness, Eleanor made a sound that was very much like an oath and urged her horse into a canter. "Remarry!" she told the palfrey indignantly as she broke away from the other women. "As if it were just a matter of getting a new one of you!"

The palfrey let out what Eleanor thought was a sympathetic neigh.

As they moved west they passed through Stratford-upon-Avon, a pretty but plodding little town that could boast of only one distinction: it was the birthplace of the present Bishop of Winchester. Which, in Eleanor's biased opinion, was hardly something to be proud of.

From this forgettable hamlet they moved to Evesham, where Hugh and Bella's grandfather had been slain so many years before by royal forces that had included Eleanor's own father. He and the many other Montfortian dead had been buried at the nearby Evesham Abbey. Lady Hastings went to visit his tomb by herself and came out weeping. "I could have buried Papa in the abbey close by him, if the queen had let me," she said later as they headed toward Eleanor's manor of Tewkesbury. "It would have pleased him and done her no dishonor."

Their moods lightened, however, as they neared Tewkesbury, where Gilbert, goggle-eyed, made the stunning discovery that the green fields and rolling hills they were riding on belonged to Eleanor. "This is ours, Mama? Ours?"

"Yes, Gilbert, by the grace of God."

Edward said superiorly, "And this is nothing compared to what Mother owns in Wales."

Gilbert could express his feelings only by whistling in disbelief. Smiling at him, Eleanor could not but wish that her husband had been as easily satisfied.

Tewkesbury was the first of Eleanor's manors that she had visited since regaining her land, and when she arrived at the manor house at Tewkesbury, not far from the Abbey of St. Mary the Virgin, she half expected to have to force her way in, the king's order notwithstanding. The keeper, however, handed over the keys to her readily, if sullenly, and she moved into the great hall. Save for some trestle tables, benches, and chairs, and the supplies the keeper and his men had brought in for their own needs, it was bare, though once the walls had been hung with tapestries and the window seats fitted with cushions. They and everything else of any value had had long vanished, seized either by the common looters who had swept through the Despenser estates during the queen's invasion or by the royal looter Isabella herself. Though Eleanor had expected as much, still she could not keep the tears from her eyes when she remembered how welcoming the great hall had once looked. "We shall make it handsome again someday," she said finally. "But what is that commotion outside?"

"Your tenants, Aunt Eleanor," said Hugh de Hastings. "They want to swear their homage and fealty to you."

"And," said Lady Hastings, "I am sure some of them want to take service with you."

The great chair in which the lord of the manor habitually sat had disappeared with the other furnishings, but the small, battered chair sitting in a corner would do. Edward, following Eleanor's gaze toward it, carried it to the dais at the other end of the hall and dusted it with his own sleeve. Then Eleanor took a deep breath, walked across the room, and sat in it. "I am ready for them," she said.

"Hugh did this?"

The Abbot of Tewkesbury nodded as Eleanor walked slowly down the ambulatory that had been built behind the high altar at Tewkesbury Abbey. Off the ambulatory lay a series of chapels: St. Catherine's Chapel, St. Faith's Chapel, St. Dunstan's Chapel, St. Edmund's Chapel, St. Margaret's Chapel, and the finest and largest of all, the Lady Chapel. "He paid for the improvements, my lady, and he had very strong ideas of what all should look like, too."

"I am sure he did," said Eleanor, smiling as she remembered Hugh and his endless letters to John Inge. "I only hope he did not drive all of you mad in the process."

"Close to it," the abbot admitted. "But it was well worth it. Your lord husband was most generous."

"He never told me about these chapels, and they are so beautiful! Simple, yet elegant. Oh, he did tell me he had given the abbey a bit here and a bit there..." Eleanor's voice wandered off. Only three months before his death, Hugh had arranged for the abbey to receive a large donation of land, in exchange for the monks praying for Hugh and Eleanor's good estate during their lives and their souls after their deaths. Could Hugh have foreseen that his soul would soon be in need of such prayers?

The abbot shrugged. "Perhaps he wanted to show you when it was completed, my lady. He always did speak with the greatest respect of your ladyship and your great ancestors. And as you can see, there is still work to be done. We had planned to rebuild the choir, but late events—"

"Yes, I see." Eleanor followed the abbot into the gloomy Norman choir and by the high altar, where her father, her brother, and her sister-in-law were buried. How Hugh would love to see her finish what he had started! "It could be made so much lighter and brighter. The roof could be raised—windows put in—the ceiling painted..."

"Exactly along the lines of what we monks and your lord husband were thinking."

"Then let us continue it, Abbot! It will be a while before I can be as useful as I would like, for I must put my estates in some order, and it will be some time before my revenues begin coming in. But when that happens, what is mine shall be at your disposal."

"I thank you for your generosity."

"And it will be a memorial, also, to my dear husband. It may be the only one he is ever allowed." Eleanor fingered the purse that hung from her waist. It was full of coins, her own and the florins that she had stolen from the Tower. She had planned to dispose of the florins at the next abbey she visited, but this too was a worthy cause. She took a handful of them and gave them to the abbot. "In the meantime, I hope this will help in finishing what has already been started."

The abbot had to stop himself from whistling as he did a quick calculation. "Yes, my lady, it certainly will."

Eleanor's entourage had grown in Tewkesbury. Several men, younger sons from families who had been on good terms with Hugh, had joined her household as knights. The great hall had been crowded with applicants of the humbler sort as well, eager for the benefits of taking service with a great lady, even one tainted by her husband's treason. Her progress through Gloucestershire had not gone unnoticed, then, and when she arrived at St. Peter's Abbey in Gloucestershire, the abbot himself greeted her by name. After making the usual observation that he was glad to see her freed from the Tower—Eleanor had begun to wonder whether criminals received similar congratulations when they got out of jail—the abbot said, "You are here to see the late king, I suppose? Follow me."

He led her near the high altar, where she saw a line of pilgrims patiently waiting their turns to approach the grave. She looked up at the abbot. "I—"

"You wished to be alone with your uncle?"

"Yes, very much." She took a coin out of her purse. "I will not be long. If they could enjoy a good meal in the meantime—"

"I will arrange it."

The pilgrims having dispersed good-naturedly enough, Eleanor approached the grave, marked by nothing but the wooden effigy that had adorned the hearse. "Ned," she whispered, and sank down beside the effigy, weeping. Finally straightening up, she wiped her eyes and put her hand on the effigy's. "Ned—Uncle—I hardly know what to call you now. All I know is that I love you, very much, and it is good to talk with you finally." She smiled. "I should like to talk to Hugh too, you know, but it is harder. If I were to talk to him on the bridge for any length of time, I would be dragged off as a madwoman, or back to the Tower. But perhaps you are together now, so I really am speaking to both of you.

"If I had known for certain when I said goodbye to you in London that I would never see you again, you and Hugh and his father, I would have said so much. But perhaps I would have done no more than make a fool of myself, so it is just as well.

"Have you seen my mother? She was always dear to you, I know. And my stepfather, I miss him so. When I think of how they braved my fearsome grandfather for love, I always take strength by their example.

"I know you were glad to see Adam. Your children here—I think they all grieve for you, but they cannot really show it. I know that is the case with John. Edward, well, I feel so sorry for him sometimes. He will have to defy his mother and Mortimer sooner or later, and then what will happen? But he has his sweet new wife, and she will be a support to him. You would have liked her.

"Ned, I worry about my eldest son so much. I miss my little girls, but I know at least they are safe from harm. But Hugh—he is in Mortimer's hands somewhere. I pray to every saint there is for his safety daily. If you have any power to help him, I know you will.

"Speaking of the saints, I have been hearing that miracles are said to happen at your tomb, that you are another saint yourself. With all due respect, Ned, I cannot believe that; I know you too well. And I do not think that I could love a saint as well as I have loved you.

"Be that as it may, I have kept these good people from you too long, so I will go. But I did not want to pass through Gloucester without reminding you that you are dearer to me than anyone besides Hugh and my children, and that not a day goes by without me praying for you."

She touched her fingers to her lips, then to the effigy's lips, and stood just as the abbot came discreetly into her line of vision. Eleanor opened her purse and handed her remaining florins to him. "Thank you for taking such good care of my uncle's grave, Abbot."

He bowed in thanks. "We were much honored to receive his body for burial. Someday, we hope to have a tomb more suitable for a king."

An elderly woman prayed at the gravesite, then left her offering. From her vantage point, Eleanor could distinctly see a fish tail poking out from beneath the cloth. She pictured such an gift being left at her grandfather's tomb at Westminster and began smiling. "I believe my uncle might be quite happy with his present arrangements."

Though William la Zouche would have liked to have made a trip to Glamorgan after Parliament closed, his presence was required at Hereford, where Mortimer married two of his bevy of daughters to two of his bevy of wards, one of whom, young Thomas de Beauchamp, Earl of Warwick, was Zouche's stepson. From there, Zouche still in tow, the royal party traveled to Ludlow Castle, where Roger was anxious to show off the improvements he had made.

Roger had indeed worked hard on his castle, adding a chapel and decorating the existing rooms lavishly. For most of the guests, however, the real interest lay not in Mortimer's gorgeous tapestries and silver plate, but in watching Mortimer and his lady. At his daughters' wedding in Hereford, Mortimer had for once stood beside his wife and at a respectful distance from the queen. Rather to everyone's disappointment, he continued this good behavior at Ludlow, sitting beside his lady at meals and leading her about at the dance. Only Lady Mortimer and her own attendants knew that he did not come to her bed at night, and if she was perturbed by this, she was too dignified to let it show. The queen, on the other hand, plainly disliked having her paramour's attentions directed toward his lawful wedded spouse, and no matter how lively her time in bed had been the night before, came down to the great hall in the morning with a sour face.

Aside from the sport of watching the adulterous lovers, there was good hunting to be had at Ludlow. William la Zouche, preparing to ride out with the others, was walking out one morning when he was stopped by a guard. "Sir. You are Lord Zouche?" William nodded. "There's a prisoner in here who wants to speak to you, if you would give him a moment of your time."

He led Zouche to a cramped room at the top of a tower. William winced as he saw Hugh le Despenser. He was much thinner than when Zouche had seen him at Caerphilly, and his clothes had worn areas in some spots and plain holes in others. Both his ankles and wrists were shackled, and it was plain from his pallor that no one had taken him outdoors lately. His face brightened, though, when he saw William. "Zouche! So you are here, after all. I'd hoped you were one of Mortimer's houseguests." He beckoned Zouche forward and whispered, "Could you give the man something for his pains? I've nothing, and he's been decent to me."

Zouche pulled out a coin, and Hugh smiled in thanks. "So how was the wedding, Zouche? I was very hurt that I was not invited. A Despenser would have livened things up considerably, I'm sure."

"How long have you been here, Hugh?"

"Mortimer had me moved here from Caerphilly about the time the king died. I suppose he didn't want any of the king's South Welsh allies setting me free."

"Does he treat you well?"

Hugh shrugged. "I've a fire when it's cold, and the food's edible. I'll be getting new robes in midsummer, if I can stomach putting on the Mortimer livery. Actu-

ally, Mortimer's never visited me himself, and I can stand to postpone the pleasure if he can. His lady's come a few times, though. When I was ill in the winter
she brought me one of her herbal remedies, and it fixed me up well." He
frowned. "You won't tell Mother I was ill, will you? It was nothing, just an ague."

"No, Hugh, of course not."

Hugh hobbled toward his window. "So have you seen all of the improvements? They've kept me well entertained, I'll tell you, watching the workmen
come and go. Have you been to his chapel? He had it built to celebrate his getting
out of the Tower, the guards told me. In honor of St. Peter ad Vincula, on whose
feast day he escaped. Not my favorite saint now, I'll warrant you."

"You heard your mother is free?"

"Yes, Lady Mortimer mentioned it. Do you think she'll be allowed to visit?"

"I doubt it," William said honestly. "But I will tell her where you are, and perhaps they will let you read a letter from her, at least. I'm sure she will send some
provisions for you, and I will make sure she knows to send plenty to you so the
guards can have their share."

Hugh laughed. "Maybe the other way around! But the guards aren't a bad lot,
most of them, though with Mortimer here they've been made to shackle me.
Once he moves on they'll probably take these things off and let me take a walk
outside. Lady Mortimer said she'd show her falcons to me once her lord was
gone. She likes falconing, and so do I."

Zouche frowned. Though scruffy in appearance now, Hugh was a handsome
young man, and even Zouche, who had given Mortimer and the queen the benefit of the doubt for a long time, had finally had to acknowledge the affair. If Lady
Mortimer wanted to get her own back…"Hugh—"

"For God's sake, Lord Zouche, don't look so worried! It would be splendid
revenge for me to seduce Lady Mortimer, if that's what you're thinking, but I'm
no knave and she's no whore. She reminds me of my mother, actually."

"Take heed that you keep on thinking of her in that way," Zouche said
sternly.

His tone was more than a little paternal, so much so that Hugh stopped laughing at the thought of seducing Lady Mortimer and looked at him thoughtfully.
"Lord Zouche, have you seen my mother?"

"Yes, when she came to the king to do homage for her lands. She was in good
spirits, and I saw your brothers and baby sister too. And your eldest sister and her
baby, and your aunt Lady Hastings. They all looked quite well."

"Mother too?"

"Yes. Quite well."

Soldier that he was, William could not keep his face expressionless when he spoke of Eleanor, increasing Hugh's suspicions. As the topic was an awkward one, he changed the subject to the Scottish truce, which the guards and Lady Mortimer had told him about. Zouche was also glad to have the subject changed, and the two men talked well into the afternoon. William knew that Hugh would be glad of the companionship, and quite aside from that, he liked the young man. He was well aware that he was missing the hunt, but with Ludlow Castle so crowded with guests, he doubted anyone would notice.

In this he was wrong. That evening after supper, an occasion from which Lady Mortimer had excused herself, the tables were being pushed aside for dancing and music when Zouche, accompanied by his young son, saw Mortimer stomping in his direction. Much wine had been consumed at the high table, from the looks of Roger Mortimer. Even Queen Isabella, Zouche noted with intense disapproval, was giggling tipsily with her ladies. "Sir, my men tell me you have been talking to Despenser's brat today. Is that true?"

"Yes. I was not aware that he was not allowed visitors."

"What did you talk of?"

"I hardly feel the need to report our conversation to you, Lord Mortimer. But you may be assured there was no harm in it. And why is that boy in shackles? And when's the last time he had a good meal? He's the crown's prisoner; he ought to be kept more comfortably than he is."

"Don't tell me how to keep my own prisoner, Zouche." There was an ugly look on Mortimer's face that made Alan la Zouche catch at his father's arm. "I've an idea of what interests you in the whelp, anyway. It's his mother, isn't it? She's a nice-looking piece of flesh, and rich besides. But her marriage is in the crown's hands, Zouche. She'll marry whom the queen and I please, to our advantage. But if you want to poke her in the meantime—"

Zouche turned on his heel and walked away, taking Alan with him. William was no coward. Much as he would have liked to strike Mortimer down, it would accomplish nothing. The man was drunk, and to harm him in his own castle would only be fatal to Zouche himself. If Mortimer's men did not kill him then and there, they would kill him secretly later, as they had the late king. For just as William had been forced to admit to himself that the Queen of England was no better than a whore, something that very day had also forced him to admit that her lover was no better than a murderer. Was it Hugh's thin face and ragged clothes, the shackles that from the looks of his chafed skin had probably been on much longer than the boy admitted? A man who would mistreat a nine-teen-year-old prisoner solely because of the dislike he had borne his father would not hesitate to kill an imprisoned king. Or was it just the expression on the drunken marcher lord's face, the way the queen was staring at him from across the room as if she wanted him to tumble her that very instant? He did not know; all he knew was that the two of them were repulsive to him now.

His squires and his men soon caught up with him. "Pack my things," he said. "We are going to Cardiff."

"I did not expect to see you this soon, Lord Zouche. But I am pleased to, certainly."

"I wanted to tell you about your son before I left for the wedding in Scotland, my lady."

He told her about his meeting with Hugh, omitting the more disquieting parts of the encounter and quoting some of the boy's livelier bon mots. She listened with gratification, and he talked on, knowing as he did so that he could no longer restrain himself from asking what he had so long wanted to ask her. Finally, she said, "I thank you, Lord Zouche, for all that you have done for us. It is good of you to take an interest in my son."

"My lady, I genuinely like your son. I care about what happens to him. But it is you I care for. Deeply."

He pulled her to him and kissed her, and for a blissful moment, as her lips responded to his and his hands traveled down her body, he thought all would be well. But then she pulled back, and he saw she had tears in her eyes. "Lord Zouche!"

She had misunderstood his intentions. He stroked her cheek. "My lady, do not misunderstand me. I wish to marry you. To protect and serve you always."

"No, Lord Zouche. I am fond of you, I do admit, and you have been the best of friends to me at a time when I had no others. But I cannot marry you. It would be a great disservice to Hugh's memory."

He said gently, "My lady, it would not be at all. You are still young. He would not expect you to live the rest of your life single."

"If he had died a natural death, perhaps I would say otherwise. But to replace him, while his poor head still sits atop London Bridge! And by his own captor! No, Lord Zouche, I cannot betray him in that manner."

"Sweet Jesus, Eleanor! You were a faithful wife to him while he lived. You have mourned for him, prayed for him, had prayers said for his soul. You have suffered all of the consequences his greed and vice brought upon your family with as much fortitude as any woman in the land could have shown. It is time to move forward."

"How dare you insult his memory!"

"He was a pirate, an extortionist, and a sodomite to boot. Other than that, I suppose he had some good qualities."

"Leave me immediately!"

"You were too damn good for him, and you know it."

Eleanor walked toward the door of her chamber. "If you won't leave, sir, then I will. I would not have you and your men go out again this night, but I expect the lot of you to be gone tomorrow."

"I'll not trouble you another minute, my lady, or ever again. Good night."

He pushed past her out the door, out of her life.

CHAPTER 24

▼

JULY 1328 TO
FEBRUARY 1329

William la Zouche was in a foul mood as he crossed the border into Scotland, but no one noticed, for the party was a gloomy one in general.

The king had set the tone by refusing to attend the wedding. England was devalued and debased by the match between his little sister and David of Scotland, he had announced in ringing tones, and though he had been powerless to prevent the misalliance, he would be damned if he would promote it by honoring the event with his royal presence. And that was that. His mother and Mortimer had considered hauling him to Scotland by force, but, as Mortimer testily reminded Isabella, the boy was his father's son and might well take a malicious pleasure in destroying the entire peace process with one word. So the king, and his wife, stayed behind.

Isabella knew that this show of independence could not bode well, either for the future of the Scottish peace or the future of the lovers' roles as unofficial rulers of England. She said as much to Mortimer, who had not dignified her concerns with more than a snort. Nor did he have a sympathetic ear to spare for Isabella's quite genuine grief over parting from her little girl. Royal daughters were supposed to be married, he had said crankily, or else what was the use in having them? By the time he remembered that the queen, married herself as a pawn of peace, and most unhappily so, might have some cause to take offense at this remark, it was too late. Isabella had since refused him her bed for several nights in a row.

Mortimer would have liked some distraction in bed, because Henry, the Earl of Lancaster, was proving to be most troublesome. Summoned to Worcester in June, after the festivities at Ludlow Castle had ended, he had refused to discuss a cause that Mortimer hoped the English could rally around: claiming the French crown for the king. Only before Parliament, he said, could such an important issue be determined. Mortimer had agreed to hold a Parliament in York, but Lancaster had left Worcester in as surly a mood as when he had arrived there. Neither he nor his son-in-law Thomas Wake had come to Scotland. There were also rumors that the Londoners, who had done so much to make Isabella's victory over her husband an easy one, were shifting their sympathies to the earl's direction. And even though not one in ten of them would know a Scot from a Welshman, Mortimer thought irritably, the Londoners, having learned that the English had agreed to turn over the Stone of Scone to the Scots, had suddenly developed an intense attachment to the damned rock. They had refused to allow its release from Westminster Abbey even in the face of an order by the king himself.

The bride-to-be, who had just turned seven, was quiet on the journey, despite her mother's efforts to draw her out. She was too little to have the suspicions about her father's death that plagued some of her elders, but she knew that she missed Papa and her dear Lady Hastings. The timely arrival of her pleasant sister-in-law, Philippa, had done much to cheer her, but now she was being married and neither Philippa nor her brother the king was even coming to her wedding. Little Joan could take comfort in nothing but the pretty new gowns that had been made for her.

The rest of the party, many of whom had fought in the Scottish wars since the Bannock Burn, if not earlier, had nothing to do but brood over England's loss. Once England had determined to conquer Scotland; now Scotland had dictated peace on its own terms.

So William la Zouche was by no means alone in his low spirits. One member of the party, however, was rather aggressively cheerful. He was Elizabeth de Burgh's seventeen-year-old son, William, Earl of Ulster, who had been knighted just days before. Ireland had been volatile as long as anyone could remember, and Zouche pitied any Englishman going there, particularly one as young and untried as the new earl. He himself, however, was brimming with optimism. Though he was aware that entering and controlling his lands would be no easy matter, he planned to get the help of his uncle, Robert Bruce himself, in doing so.

Young Burgh was on good terms with his mother, but Zouche was not surprised to hear that Lady de Burgh would remain safely home in England instead of accompanying her son across the Irish Sea. "She is visiting her lands in Wales at the moment," said the earl in passing. "Oh, but she did mention that she might go to Glamorgan to visit my aunt the Lady Despenser sometime."

William, no less in love with Lady Despenser than he had been before he stormed out of her castle, felt as if the young man had stabbed him in the chest.

Soon after arriving in Wales and getting herself tolerably settled in Cardiff Castle, Eleanor had invited each of her sisters to visit her there. Margaret had sent Eleanor's messenger back to Cardiff with a curt refusal, almost to Eleanor's relief, but Elizabeth had promised to stop by when she was in the neighborhood, and made good her promise at about the same time the English crossed into Scotland.

The sisters kissed each other on the cheek graciously in greeting, after which they retreated to Eleanor's private chamber. Eleanor asked about her nephew and nieces and listened, wistfully, as Elizabeth described the preparations and expenses for her son's knighting. How Eleanor would like to see poor Hugh knighted! But at least she could report that Edward was doing well in the tiltyard under the tutelage of one of the household knights, that Gilbert was a splendid horseman, and that John could string together enormously long sentences (even though, to Eleanor's dismay, one of his more modest productions had been, "Where did Lord Zouche go? I liked him, Mama."). She could also show off Lizzie and Edmund and let Elizabeth see what a fine young lady Isabel had grown into.

But soon the topic of children wore itself out, as did the ensuing topics of Scotland (each sister devoutly hoped for peace but had her doubts) and sheep raising (each sister wanted to expand her flocks). There was no choice then but for Eleanor to look at her lap and say softly, "Elizabeth, I know that we have not been the best of friends lately, but I hope we can become close again."

"We never were close, Eleanor."

"No," admitted Eleanor. Margaret and Elizabeth had been the close sisters; it was Eleanor, tagging along behind Gilbert until he was sent to be reared in Queen Margaret's household, who had been the outsider. "But our husbands kept us from ever being so. Perhaps—"

"Our husbands! Eleanor, it was your husband. Not our husbands."

"I know you had your disagreements with him—"

"Disagreements! Eleanor, do you know the half of what he did? He forced me to stay at Barking Abbey for months after my husband died. Months! My children were there with me. We couldn't get out until I agreed to exchange every acre of land I owned in Wales for that Gower of his. Finally, I gave in, and I did get all of my other lands and dower lands back, as agreed. Then your precious husband had me summoned to York at Christmas—this was in 1322—"

"I remember you coming to York. I heard there was a row—"

"A row! Eleanor, when I got there, I had to sign a quitclaim to Usk. Then I was asked to sign another writing saying I would not marry or make grants of my lands without the king's consent. I put up an argument and got some of my councilors imprisoned for my pains. So I left York for Clare Castle. I'd been on the road five days, in the dead of December, when a messenger from our dear uncle caught up with me with a letter telling me that if I did not sign the writing, all of my lands would be seized. So I went back to York and signed it. Well, I at least had Gower now, plus my English lands. And that's when your husband took Gower from me, using that old and ailing William de Braose as a straw man to bring a suit against me, then hand Gower over to your father-in-law. Who then handed it to him."

"Elizabeth, if this is all true—"

"Of course it is true! Have your lawyers look into it. I daresay the present king will be happy to supply you with all the details."

"I did not know about it! I swear to you."

"Oh, I believe you. He kept you in a gilded cage, like these goldfinches of yours here." Elizabeth waved a hand toward the pretty birds scornfully. "Shall I tell you more? He did much the same to Elizabeth Comyn to force her to give up Goodrich Castle. He forced the late Earl of Lancaster's wife, Alice, to give up much of her lands as well. There was Alice de Braose, once her old father, William, died. There was—"

"Stop it! Just stop it!"

The tears were running down her face. Elizabeth waited for her to regain her composure and then said, more kindly, "He has paid the price for all that, Eleanor, and horribly. I would not wish a traitor's death on anyone."

"You don't know the half of what they did to him. Your precious Isabella, to use your phrase, had me told all." Eleanor looked at the bare walls of her chamber. "You talk to me of all the misdeeds of my husband, but what of yours? He owed everything to our uncle—his lands, his prestige, you! He turned against him out of sheer greed. He and Hugh d'Audley and Mortimer and the rest of those blackguards killed our tenants, destroyed our lands, stole our goods—all out of spite. I could take you around and show some of the damage they did to this very castle; even now I am still making repairs. Where was that righteous indignation of yours and Margaret's then?"

"What could we have done?"

"No more than I could have, I suppose. But the wrongs were not all on Hugh's side, and you know it."

Elizabeth said, "I never loved my husband, Eleanor. How could I? The marriage was forced on me by our uncle, barely after I delivered my second husband's child! But I grew to like him well enough; he was pleasant to me and to my children. What more could I ask for? But I've never denied his faults, as you do Hugh's."

"You wrong me there. I have never denied Hugh's faults. I just did not know he had so many. I suppose I should have had my eyes open more. Well, it will be yet another sin on my head, that I did not. And another one still, that I love him none the less."

She sighed and studied Hugh's ring, made to stay on her finger by the liberal application of wax to its band. "These ladies you spoke of. Have they been restored to their lands?"

"Yes, all brought petitions soon after your husband's death, and the queen had the council pay close attention to them. And Elizabeth Comyn, Alice de Braose, and the Countess of Lancaster are all married or remarried now, in fact. Quite happily, I understand, even though the countess's husband is beneath her socially."

"With our mother's history, we can hardly talk, can we?" Eleanor smiled for the first time since Elizabeth had come to her chamber. "I am glad to hear they are doing well."

They were silent for a long time. Then Elizabeth said, "Have you had much company since you were released?"

"Lady Hastings accompanied me as far as Gloucester, but she went back south after that." Bella had not been able to face the prospect of going to Bristol, where the Despenser party had crossed the Severn into Wales. In the city where her father-in-law had been killed, Eleanor had left the others behind and gone to view the quarter of Hugh that hung on Bristol's gates. It was an arm, it turned out, chained in such a manner that it perpetually waved to passersby. She shuddered and continued, "Hugh's other sister plans to visit me soon. And—one other came. That is all, except people who come on business."

"It must be lonely for you. Do you have no lady friends—friends on your social level, I should say?"

"No, as according to you Hugh appears to have taken land from all the ladies I might choose my acquaintance from," Eleanor snapped. Plainly, inviting Elizabeth here had been a mistake. She said proudly, "I am well occupied here, anyway. The children keep me busy, and my estates take up the rest of my time. I need no society."

"You ought to remarry," Elizabeth pronounced.

"You have been widowed far longer than I have, Elizabeth. Why don't you take your own advice?"

"I don't need to," said her sister maddeningly. "I am quite content as I am; in fact, I plan to take a vow of chastity. I have good friends and many interests, and I have rather come to enjoy my independence. I don't want some man telling me how to manage my lands or, worse yet, setting himself against the king and dragging me into the muck with him."

Eleanor made a noise of disgust. "Why is it that every widow I know has no intention of remarrying, but thinks I should do so? Even Lady Hastings suggested as much." She continued in an injured tone, "It is not as if I am a helpless ninny who can't run my estates. I spend hours with my councilors; just ask the poor things! Even the queen, if pressed, would admit I have some administrative talents, I suspect."

"No one doubts your ability, Eleanor. But you and Hugh were married a very long time, and I know you were fond of him, unaccountable as that is to me. You're so used to being married that you would be happier that way, I think."

Somewhat mollified, Eleanor pulled a man's shirt from her workbasket and began sewing on it. "Who is that for?" asked Elizabeth.

"My son Hugh. He is still in prison, you know. Lord Zouche—" Eleanor turned scarlet. "I heard through an acquaintance that he is at Ludlow Castle. I am sending him a hamper."

"Lord Zouche? I know him slightly. He is a good man, everyone says. He has been checking on Hugh? Why, he would make a good husband for you, you know."

"No, he would not."

"Why on earth not?"

"Because he asked me to marry him, and I refused. He left the castle in a fury, and that is the end of the matter." Eleanor stared at the shirt she was sewing, trying to forget the ache of desire she had felt when William la Zouche kissed her. Not since the day she and the king had lay together had she felt so guilty. To be kissing William while her Hugh still rotted in five places... Remarriage would proclaim to the world that she, who had loved him so dearly, had cast him aside without a backward thought. Why could not Elizabeth and Bella see this?

And yet she liked William so much. He was so kind and gentle, so easy to talk to. Now she would never see him again. He had told her so.

She put her hand across her eyes, pretending to be squinting at her needle-work to hide the tears that were once again rolling down her face. Elizabeth saw them and said, mercifully, "I will go to my chamber and lie down a bit. I am a little tried from my journey."

Lady Mortimer poked her head into the cell where Hugh le Despenser, who had not a whit of musical talent, was gamely plucking on a lute. "Ouch, what noise! Your lady mother has sent your October hampers, Hugh."

Hugh smiled as two men lugged his latest gifts up the stairs. Every month since July, Eleanor had been sending her son goods—clothing, bedding, candles, food, wine, a chess set, dice, books, money, and even the lute. As she had taken the precaution of delivering them to Lady Mortimer, there had been no pilfering by the guards, and as Lord Mortimer had not been to Ludlow Castle since June, there had been no one to cavil at the comforts being sent Hugh's way.

Lady Mortimer was dressed in mourning, for two of her four sons had recently died, one in the summer of an illness, the other in the fall of injuries received at a tournament. They were Mortimer's sons too, of course, but just as Lady Mortimer lived as a single woman these days, she had mourned fairly much as a single woman too. Roger Mortimer had Isabella to share his grief with, and he had not had the luxury of grieving much anyway, for he had returned to England from Scotland to find Lancaster more hostile than ever.

Hugh le Despenser was slightly younger than one son and slightly older than the other. It was scarcely to be wondered at, then, that Lady Mortimer found some solace these days in mending his clothing, seeing to it that he was well fed, and generally coddling him. Hugh had responded affectionately to these motherly attentions, and it had thus come about that he and Lady Mortimer spent much time together, though in a completely different manner than that feared by William la Zouche.

After the men left their delivery behind, Hugh sat cross-legged on the floor and motioned Lady Mortimer to the stool she had had brought in for him some weeks before. Together they searched happily through the hampers. "A nice warm cloak, and some shirts for you."

"And here's the cheese from Caerphilly my mother swears by, Lady Mortimer. Take some."

Lady Mortimer obediently took a chunk and nibbled at it. "You shall have to call me 'Countess' soon, Hugh."

"Lord Mortimer is to become an earl?"

"The Earl of March. John, the king's brother, will be the Earl of Cornwall, and Edmund Butler, who married your cousin Eleanor de Bohun last year, is to be the Earl of Ormond."

"The Earl of March? For the entire march of Wales? I have to give him credit for his nerve, Lady Mortimer. My father never aspired to anything more grand than Earl of Gloucester, and he decided not to press his luck when it came down to it."

"My husband is a fool to grant himself such a title," Lady Mortimer said bluntly. "It will only make the Earl of Lancaster angrier at him than he is already. The Londoners, you know, have come to Lancaster's side, as has the Bishop of Winchester. They are saying that my husband and Isabella have squandered the royal treasury, that the queen is sucking the country dry with the huge grants she has given herself, that they have humiliated the king with this Scottish truce, that they have made the king's regency council a mere joke. I am not sure they are wrong, Hugh."

"So you will tell me when I have to start bowing to you?"

"The ceremony will take place during this Parliament meeting in Salisbury. My men tell me that both my husband and the Earl of Lancaster are traveling around with large armies, and that the Archbishop of Canterbury has tried to mediate between them, with no success."

Hugh shook his head ruefully. "Quite a task for our new archbishop, from what you've told me." Walter Reynolds, the second Edward's faithless friend, had died the previous November, just two months after the old king, and had been replaced by Simon de Mepham, an Oxfordian with no political experience who probably wished by now he had stayed at the university. He had been consecrated only a few months before.

"Lancaster won't even come to Parliament."

"Where is the king in all this?"

"Being led around on his leash by the queen and my husband," said Lady Mortimer. "It seemed that he was going to break free for a while, with his refusal to go to the wedding, but he got right back on it again, good as gold. They have convinced him that Lancaster means him harm, and Lancaster hasn't helped matters, with those troops of his. God knows where it will all end." She shook her head and placidly resumed her search through the hampers. "Ah, some combs, which reminds me, Hugh, I must send the barber to you. Your mother would cry if she saw that raggedy beard of yours."

In December, after a brief stay in London intended partly to mollify its citizens and partly to intimidate them, the court lumbered into Gloucester. There the queen studiously avoided visiting her husband's grave, while the Earl of March raised troops to fight Lancaster, who had brought the Earls of Kent and Norfolk to his side. The king, who truly did worry that the Earl of Lancaster might be taking after his bellicose brother, dutifully signed the orders that his mother and Mortimer had the royal clerks prepare.

He frowned, however, at one parchment that contained a familiar name and that was in no way related to the Earl of Lancaster's business. "Hugh le Despenser, my cousin. He is being transferred to Bristol?"

"Yes, your grace," said Mortimer, who in those days was still most polite to his king. "My lady finds the custody of him at Ludlow Castle burdensome, and he has been presuming on her good nature to be allowed privileges he should not have. Bristol Castle will be better for him."

"With Thomas Gurney for his keeper." Edward frowned, trying to remember how the name was familiar to him. One of many knights who had passed through his court, he decided, and signed the order, unaware that he had just placed his kinsman into the hands of one of his father's killers.

"Not the happiest Christmas I've ever spent, Countess. But it's a change of scene, anyhow."

Lady Mortimer, her eyes welling with tears, looked away as Hugh was chained to his horse. Nearly everything that Eleanor had sent to him had been left in his cell, as Mortimer had instructed his men to allow Hugh to take with him only what he could fit in a saddlebag. "It is my fault, Hugh. Roger has his spies here, as everywhere, and one of them must have told them I was friendly with you. I should have been more cautious."

"Don't say that, Countess. I'm nothing but grateful for your kindness." Hugh tried to smile and beckoned her closer. "My lady, you will not suffer for it, will you?"

The Countess of March shook her head. "There is some advantage to having a husband who is the lover of the widowed queen of England. If anything happened to me, he would be accused of my murder, and he knows it. And he would scorn to beat a woman. He will never do anything more than ignore me, and that suits me well now."

"You deserve better, Countess. I hope one day you will be happy."

"And you too, Hugh."

His hostess turned away and went back into the castle, feeling nearly as bereft as she had when she had lost her sons. Hugh rode on, and on, until he and his guards finally arrived in Bristol, where by Mortimer's special instructions he was taken to the city gate. Hugh had expected as much, and he fought back nausea as he stared at what was left of the hand that had held him when he was less than an hour old. "Hello, Father," he said coolly. He turned to his guards, half of whom were snickering, half of whom looked abashed. "Now that you've shown me the sights of Bristol, can we get on to the castle? Gurney can't keep the Yule log burning forever, you know."

Eleanor had decided to spend Christmas at Hanley Castle, and she had determined to make it as merry a one as she could. The great hall, bedecked with greenery, was crowded each night with guests: her councilors and attorneys and their families, the neighboring gentry, priests, canons, and friars, priors and prioresses, her tenants, and a great many poor people. The best musicians to be found in Worcester had been engaged, and Eleanor danced with nearly every male present, including her son Edward, who was surprisingly graceful. He had become rather good-looking, too, and that and his shyness had led several more forward young women from the village to determine to draw him out, which the prettiest of them did, with considerable success, in a loft in the castle stables one night after Edward had overindulged slightly in wassail. As Edward lay entangled with his buxom new friend, his pleasure was marred only by the fact that his brother Hugh was not there to hear about it.

Joan, Nora, and Margaret had all been allowed to visit for Christmas, Eleanor having prudently cultivated the goodwill of their prioresses with ample gifts. Much as Eleanor had longed to see them, she had almost dreaded their visit, worrying that they might sit silent among the festive company like three specters or seethe with jealousy born of the contrast between the luxury of Hanley Castle and their very modest quarters at their convents. But she was pleasantly surprised. The girls chatted nicely with the guests, bickered with each other and their brothers just as they had in the past, made rather catty comments to each other regarding the follies of their various prioresses, and ate the delicious Christmas fare enthusiastically. Even Joan, the most reluctant of the three novices, seemed fairly content. She had some friends close to her own age at Shaftesbury, and in that fashionable convent her prestige as the great-granddaughter of the first Edward had made her a person whose good opinion was to be cultivated.

It would have been a very pleasant Christmas, then, were her son Hugh there, but Eleanor comforted herself with the knowledge that the Countess of March was taking good care of him. Perhaps she might even allow him to join in the festivities at Ludlow. Eleanor had sent him an extra hamper, full of his favorite foods, to make it a cheerful time for him.

There was another person Eleanor would have liked to see at Hanley Castle. Lately, there were nights when she longed for the hands of a man upon her, nights when she lay awake and aching until she touched herself in a place and in a way that she knew well was sinful, so much so that she would not dream of mentioning it to the kindly young chaplain to whom she confessed. On these occasions she usually thought about Hugh, but more and more lately she'd added to her sin by thinking of a living man. For a while she had never put a name to the man who in her mind touched her so lovingly, but one night she had realized with a jolt who he was: William la Zouche.

What if she wrote him and asked him to visit? She had gone so far, indeed, as to write to him in her own awkward hand—for the invitation, neutral and emotionless as it appeared on the surface, was nonetheless not one she wished to dictate to one of her clerks. Probably he would come; after all, he had asked her to marry him. He would come and ask again, and they would marry—and she would feel everlastingly guilty for betraying Hugh. So she had crumpled up the parchment and sent it skittering toward the fire.

Thus, Christmas at Hanley Castle had not included William la Zouche. But as she sat in her great chair the day after Christmas, an unexpected guest arrived, and she saw, to her shock, that the night's celebrations would include John de Grey.

"I can stay only overnight, Lady Despenser. I must rejoin the king shortly. But I heard you were staying at Hanley and wanted to visit while the court was close by."

"I am glad to have you, sir. How goes it with Lancaster?"

"Badly," said John shortly. "It will probably come to war soon."

Eleanor, whose sympathies lay in Lancaster's direction simply because he was not Mortimer, merely nodded.

She placed Grey next to her at the high table, as befit a royal banneret. Grey made the most of this opportunity, and the two of them were talking together easily when a messenger arrived with a letter for Eleanor. Eleanor read the letter, and John saw her face change for an instant. She turned to one of her men standing nearby. "Have my steward reward him for his trouble." Then she went back to her conversation with John.

The rest of the evening passed uneventfully. Eleanor and John danced together, and Eleanor's children coaxed her into singing a few ballads, accompanied by her minstrels. John, leaning back and listening, decided that this was heaven.

The gathering having finally broken up for the evening, John retired to the spacious chamber Eleanor had given him, close to the castle's chapel, and climbed into bed, pondering his course of action. Pleasant as the evening's festivities had been, they had not been conducive to his purpose in coming to Hanley Castle: asking Eleanor to be his wife. He would have to get her alone and speak to her first thing tomorrow...

He started as a noise came from the chapel. An intruder? His young squires, Fulk and Henry, had heard it too, for he saw them begin to rise from their pallets near his bed. "Leave it to me," he told them.

Grabbing his sword, he hastened to the chapel. There was someone in it, all right: the lady of Hanley Castle, huddled crying on the floor. "Lady Despenser?"

"Leave me, sir. Please."

"No, my lady. Something has upset you. What is it?" Then he saw the letter she held in her hand. "The message that arrived tonight?"

Eleanor nodded and tossed it in his direction. It was from the Countess of March, informing Lady Despenser that her son had been removed to Bristol Castle. "I do not understand, my lady."

"The Countess of March was good to my son, Sir Grey. He wrote and told me so himself; she allowed him to send me letters. She is a mother who has lost sons of her own; she treated him well for their sake. Now he is being sent to Bristol where there will be no one to take pity on him. What will happen to him now?"

"You do not know for certain the change will be for the worse," John said helplessly.

"How can it not be, sir? Look here, the countess tells me that he had to leave most of what I have sent him behind, but she will have the goods sent to me for safekeeping. Why would they make him leave all those little comforts behind if they did not intend to keep him harshly? But that is not the worst of it. His custodian will be Thomas Gurney, who Lord Montacute told me was with my dear uncle the king when he died. His murderer, Sir Grey! I know it!"

John had no reply. He sat silently as she cried a little more. Then she lifted her head and said flatly, "I hate him."

"Who?"

"My husband. How could he not have guessed that Hugh would pay the price for his crimes? Yet he went on and on, acquiring all he could, and now our poor son will rot in prison for it. Or perhaps I am wrong; perhaps one day Mortimer will get tired of him and execute him, just as Hugh did Llywelyn Bren. I hate him!"

She all but screamed the last words. John took her into his arms and held her as she sobbed. For the first time, he noticed that she was dressed in her night-clothes, with a cloak thrown over them either for warmth or for modesty or both. Poor creature, after holding in her anguish about Hugh all night for the sake of her guests, she must have gone to bed, then come to the chapel to cry in privacy. When at last she grew quiet, he asked gently, "Shall I take you back to your chamber now?"

"Yes."

It was but a short walk. As they approached the door, Eleanor said, "I have changed my mind. Take me to yours."

"Mine?"

"Must I spell it out? Yours."

If thoughts could have killed, the Earl of Lancaster would have been dead seventy and seven times over the next morning as a very tired John de Grey cursed him who made it necessary to leave Hanley Castle. For if the night before had been at all typical of Hugh le Despenser's married life, no wonder the man had been so insufferably self-satisfied.

He rolled over, looking for Eleanor's tangled red hair and white skin, and found that her side of the bed was empty. Then he saw Eleanor sitting in the window seat, once again in her nightclothes and cloak. "Sir. We need to talk. Outside."

"I am not a whore, Sir Grey. I behaved whorishly last night, but I am not a whore."

"I thought no such thing, Eleanor."

Eleanor wrapped her cloak more tightly around her. Bundled up as she was now, there was not a spot on her body that John had left unexplored the night before. "That is the first thing I wanted to tell you. The second is that I was angry and grieved over my son, and I spoke and acted in haste. I love Hugh. I know he meant no harm to come to us. But he thought he was untouchable."

"Yes. And now let me say my piece, Eleanor. I came here for one reason, and that was to ask you to marry me. We can marry today, if you wish, and when this damned business of Lancaster's is over I shall return and we shall live together as husband and wife."

"I don't know."

"Why not? We got on well enough last night, I think." He smiled. "I know you still mourn your husband, but there is no disrespect to him in remarrying. Many widows in your position would have remarried long before. You like me, don't you?"

"Yes."

"Well, there's much of your problem solved, right there. And think of your children, Eleanor. The little ones could use a man about, and it would be good for your son Edward as well. You said yesterday that he wanted to be knighted when he was older, and if you were married to me he could act as my squire, go to tournaments, mix with some lads of his own degree, get his confidence up. He's a bit isolated here on your lands, you know, and the past years couldn't have been easy on him. And your oldest son might benefit too. I am in favor with the king, and if he had a stepfather who was trusted by the crown—"

"I will consider your offer, Sir Grey. When you come back I will have an answer for you."

"Very well." He turned around and stalked away. Then, as Eleanor watched in astonishment, he headed back to her, smiling. "I have come back, and I want my answer now, Eleanor."

"You cheated!" she protested. But his effrontery made her laugh, and when he led her into the outbuilding by which they were standing, she was still laughing. Only when he kissed her, gently at first and then passionately, did she fall silent.

He pushed the hood of her cloak back. "You are driving me mad. Do you know how much I want to take you right here? You want me just as badly, don't you, sweetheart? You will marry me?"

His hands and mouth were moving everywhere now, and she did not have the slightest desire to call them to a halt as she and John sank down atop the sacks of grain stacked in a corner. "Yes," she whispered, pressing against him, not knowing or caring which question she was answering. "Yes."

Zouche had watched the quarrel between Lancaster and Mortimer from a distance. Disgusted as he was with Mortimer, particularly in his new guise as the Earl of March, he could not bring himself to join Lancaster either. He blustered well, but was there anything underneath that blustering to offer? Zouche was not sure, and so he stayed neutral. Neutrality, in any case, was easy, for William had found that since he had left Cardiff Castle, he did not much care about anything.

It was with little more than indifference, then, that he watched Lancaster's rebellion falter and die. Days after Christmas, the king had announced his intention to march to Leicester, adding that anyone who surrendered to him before January 7 would receive a pardon. On the way, he had sought access to Kenilworth Castle—Lancaster's castle—and had been refused. Led by Mortimer, the royal army had then wreaked havoc on Lancaster's lands that had not been seen since the destruction of the Despensers' lands seven years before.

Lancaster, whose eyesight was now so poor that he could barely see his horse's head, had determined then to face his army against the king's. But then all fell apart. The Earls of Kent and Norfolk, suddenly losing their nerve, deserted the Earl of Lancaster and submitted to the king. Mortimer, hearing this, advanced the royal army to Bedford, where Lancaster was encamped. With his support having dwindled away, Lancaster surrendered his sword to the king.

All for nothing, Zouche reflected as he sat in his chamber at Ashby-de-la-Zouche, where he had gone to spend a very bleak Christmas. Was that not the way of the world? "Come in," he said listlessly as a knock sounded on his door.

His squire was leading in a very large lady, who had reached the time of life when ladies were known only as being of a certain age. Zouche started. "Gladys? Is El— Lady Despenser well?"

Gladys said, "She thinks I have gone on a visit to my family. Lord Zouche, normally I don't meddle in my lady's affairs, or anyone else's. But now it is time to meddle. Here."

She handed him a crumpled piece of parchment, written in the same hand as the letters William had delivered to Hugh le Despenser at Caerphilly Castle. "Lord Zouche. I hope I find you well. I will be at Hanley Castle this Christmastide, and I hope you will honor me there by allowing me to show you hospitality." He stared at it, hearing Eleanor's sweet voice in each line. "What is the meaning of this?"

"My lady wanted to invite you to stay with her, Lord Zouche, but could not get up the courage. I found this lying just by the fire. She never could hit a target, sir."

"What did she think would happen if I came?"

"She thought you would offer again to marry her, and that this time she would say yes." Gladys shook her head. "My lady loves you, Lord Zouche. No, she hasn't told me so, but I've seen the look on her face when I mention your name, and I've been doing it often enough lately just to check. But she had convinced herself that if she remarried, it would be a disservice to her late husband, and there was no getting the idea out of her head. Her parents were as pigheaded a pair as could be, and so was her uncle, and her grandfather, and she is as pigheaded as the whole lot of them put together."

William smiled. "So what do you recommend, Mistress Gladys? Waiting?"

"You can't. She will be married to John de Grey, if you do."

"She loves me and she will marry him? For God's sake, why?"

"She lay with him, sir." Zouche flushed with anger, and Gladys put a hand on his shoulder. "You must understand, Lord Zouche. He arrived at Hanley for a visit, and that same night she heard news, something that upset her against her husband. Grey was there, and she was angry and unhappy and lonely, and he took his opportunity. She told me later, in tears, poor lamb. Oh, he didn't force her, I'll say that much for him. And he's decent and honorable, I'll give him that. So she will marry him, out of guilt and shame, when it's you she loves."

"Has she agreed to marry him?"

"He asked, and she said she would think about it. He spent but one night at Hanley Castle before one of his men came and fetched him back to the king's camp, quickly. He had just enough time to say a quick goodbye before he left. But she expects him to come back after this Lancaster business, and she plans to marry him then."

Zouche, suddenly feeling a good twenty years younger, rang for his squire. "Not if I get to her first."

Eleanor was sitting with her council in the great hall when Zouche arrived at Hanley Castle. Not since the Scots were on his heels at the Bannock Burn had he traveled so quickly. She saw him, and the preoccupied expression on her face changed to one of shock. "Excuse me, gentlemen." She greeted Zouche. "Lord Zouche, I am glad to see you well."

"Might I speak with you privately, my lady?"

She nodded, and they proceeded to the outer room of her chamber in dead silence. When they stood in it, facing each other, William said, "There's only one thing that stands between us marrying, isn't it, Eleanor? Your late husband."

"My lord—"

"Think, Eleanor. Your husband wasn't a fool, by any means. What if he knew what he was doing when he sent me to you? What if he knew that I would find you irresistible? What if he didn't want to leave you all alone in the world? Have you thought of that?"

"No, but—"

"He told me to tell you not to marry the first handsome young buck who asked you. Note the wording there, Eleanor. Handsome. Young. Nothing about not marrying a homely old fellow like myself. Not a thing."

He kissed her, and this time, he met with no resistance. It was William, as a soldier ever alert for sudden noises, who drew back. "Horses. It looks as if John de Grey has arrived."

"William, I—"

"Yes, yes, Gladys told me. It's best that you get out of here. Fortunately, I noticed you have a barge. We'll take it."

"William, my children!"

"I told Gladys to get them on the barge, just in case. Along with a priest. But hurry!"

They were married on the barge as it traveled down the Severn to Cardiff. All of Eleanor's children watched the short, simple ceremony except for Edward, who took a cue from his royal namesake and absented himself from the proceedings. As William kissed his bride, his new stepson sulked on the edge of the barge and tossed bread to the seagulls.

With so many of them on the barge, there was no question of them consummating their marriage or even having a private conversation. But that night when the barge was tied up for the evening, to keep warm they all had to huddle together under their blankets and furs. Eleanor wrapped her arms around her youngest children and snuggled close to William, safe and utterly content as the warmth of their bodies together and the gentle rocking of the barge lulled them all to sleep.

At Cardiff, Gladys hustled the children away, and Eleanor and William at last climbed the stairs to Eleanor's chamber. Wildly as she had coupled with John de Grey less than a month before, she felt strangely shy as she and William sat sipping wine together. Then William took the cup from her and began undressing her from head to toe, so slowly and with so much kissing and fondling of each part of her he unveiled that by the time he'd stripped her bare, she could not stand to have him outside of her a moment longer and climaxed almost as soon as he entered her. He, aroused as she, gasped out her name over and over again into her hair as he spent himself with an intensity he had not felt in years. "Second thoughts, my lady?" he managed finally.

She smiled up at him. "None at all."

There followed a brief confusion occasioned by the fact that both of them, when sharing a bed with their late spouses, had been accustomed to taking the left side. William accommodatingly rolled to the right, and then they could at last hold each other and talk of the future.

"Shall it go hard on us, marrying without the king's license?" asked Eleanor.

William shrugged. "What's done is done, and couldn't have been done better." He held Eleanor tighter. "I suppose there will be a hefty fine to pay."

"Yes, indeed. Hugh's father and sister each—" She stopped, abashed.

William stroked her hair. "I was harsh on Hugh before, my love, and I shouldn't have been. Anyone whom you loved so well had to have good qualities, many of them. Don't think you have to pretend Hugh never existed now that you're my wife. I know you loved him, and you can tell me all about him, provided that you always speak even more highly of me, of course."

She giggled. "And you may tell me all about Alice, provided you don't dwell too much on her blond hair and sapphire blue eyes."

"More like cornflowers, and I have developed a taste for green eyes in the past year or so, anyway."

They dozed awhile. She woke before he did, and lay still next to him, thinking, until he stirred. "William. Do you forgive me? For John?"

"There's nothing to forgive, my love. You weren't mine at the time." He was quiet for a while. "We've all made mistakes, Eleanor, all done things we were ashamed of. I've done worse, I'm sure."

"Ah, you don't know what a wretch I have been!" She rested her head on his chest. "I don't deserve you, William. I should be in the chapel right now, thanking the Lord for my blessings."

"And so we shall thank Him," said William. He kissed the top of her head, began moving his lips farther down. "But can we wait just a little while, my dear?"

In due time they did go to the castle chapel, where they offered prayers of thanksgiving and then prayed for the souls of all they had loved, especially their late spouses. Eleanor took the time to whisper some private words to Hugh. "I'm sorry, dear," she whispered, touching the wedding ring that she had moved to her right hand. "I do still love you; never mind the nonsense I said that other day. But I love my lord Zouche too, and the world must move on. But I shall never forget you or cease to love you, not for one day of my life."

From the chapel they went to the children's rooms, where they found John and Gilbert in a heated dispute over the question of nomenclature. "Shall we call you Lord Zouche or Father?"

"As you prefer, Gilbert."

"We could call him Father William," said John. "And our other father Father Hugh."

"Why would we need to call our father Father Hugh? He's dead."

"We pray for him," said John primly. "So we will pray for Father William and Father Hugh."

"That makes them sound like priests. I shall pray for Father and Lord Zouche."

"And I will pray for Father William and Father Hugh."

"Pray for them however you like," said Eleanor. "As long as you pray for them."

"His way is stupid."

"Your way is stupid!"

They stomped out of the chamber. "Boys," said William contentedly. "And I still have to alert my own." He glanced at Eleanor's little girl, who had clambered onto his lap. "What shall you call me, Lizzie?"

"Papa," said Elizabeth.

On January 26 at Dunstable, where the court had paused on its way to Windsor, Isabella was startled to see one of her son's most amiable knight bannerets storming away. "What on earth ails him, Mortimer?"

"Sir Grey is having marital problems," said Mortimer grimly.

"I thought his wife had been dead for some time."

"He has remarried, darling, or at least he thinks he has. Do you know who his new bride is? Lady Despenser. Say it, madam."

"I told you so, Roger. But what is the matter with him? I suppose he abducted her and she escaped?"

"No, it's even worse than it appears. She seems to have two husbands at the moment. Sir Grey and Lord Zouche. Husband number two abducted her from Hanley Castle and married her, or so Grey thinks anyway. After she pledged herself to marry husband number one. Jesus! I should have known better. Her mother married that baseborn squire of hers, after all, and her sister Elizabeth eloped with that Verdon fellow. Like mother, like daughter."

Isabella had been in high spirits ever since the Earl of Lancaster, looking ten years older than his true age, had knelt in the mud at Bedford and handed his sword to the king. She therefore could not help but snicker at her former lady-in-waiting's marital misadventures, even as the Earl of March continued to scowl. "So, Roger. Now that we have a choice, which husband shall she stay married to?"

"I would prefer neither of them," said Mortimer irritably. "Grey was practically weeping when he came here, like a baby who's had candy snatched out of his hand; that slut's bewitched him. He was all but whistling when we moved toward Bedford that miserable rainy night, and now I know why. And Zouche is no better. Remember that visit he paid to her brat when we were at Ludlow this summer? They're both besotted with her, I'll wager. They'll do what makes her happy, and that's not what I want in the Lord of Glamorgan. If my damned son Geoffrey had done my bidding, she'd have been safely off the marriage market before now. But he insists on a French bride, and one not fifteen years older than he. Stubborn whelp."

"Did either of the men get a royal license to marry her?"

"Lord, no," said the Earl of March. "They're both too lovesick—or landsick—to bother with such niceties, it seems, although Grey did allow that he had been planning to get one after the fact. Gracious of him to consider the king! But that's a blessing, in a way. I can seize the bride's lands now, as a punishment."

"Until husband one or husband two pays the fine for marriage without a license?"

Mortimer smiled. "Until I decide what to do next. I've recently learned some interesting information about our Lady Despenser, you see."

After a few pleasant days at Cardiff, during which William met his new tenants, the newlyweds decided to ride to nearby Caerphilly for a short visit. As the day was a mild one and the children liked the sprawling castle, the entire family came along.

William had not been idle in the days since his elopement with Eleanor. He had sent a respectful message to the king begging his pardon for his hasty marriage and expressing his wish to pay whatever fine the crown demanded, and he had sent for Alan to join him in Wales. Alan had caught up with him in Cardiff, along with a number of his men, but he had not heard anything from the king yet. Probably, he thought to himself cheerfully as the big castle came into view, the Earl of March, into whose pockets the fine would certainly go, was pushing for the largest sum possible.

Only Eleanor's constable and a small staff were at Caerphilly. Eleanor had sent some of her men up ahead of them in advance to warn them of the approach of their large party. She started as she saw horses galloping toward them from the castle. "William! Those are my men! And my constable there, too. Why, what is it?" she called.

"It is the king, my lady. He has sent his men to take all of your lands back into his hands. As a punishment for marrying without license."

"All of them?"

"So the king's men say."

"They must be seizing Cardiff as we speak," said William. "How many men did the king send?"

"A few dozen."

"How are the supplies?"

"Rather sparse, sir. With my lady staying at Hanley—"

"We can besiege it," William said. "I've my men here, and I can pay more. What of my lands? Are they in custody?"

The constable shook his head. "I don't know, sir, but the men mentioned only the lady's lands."

"We must send the women and children to safety somewhere," William said, looking at his son and the Despenser brood. "Wiltshire might be best; I've manors there. If they've been seized I've friends who will take the children in."

"And Hugh's sisters will help too," said Eleanor. "But Caerphilly is just one castle, William! What of my other lands? We must make the king see reason. Perhaps if I went to London personally and prayed for his forgiveness, he would relent. You should come too, William."

But the men, indignant about this royal interference in the Welsh March, were set on besieging the castle. Roger Mortimer was hated in Wales, especially since the second Edward's untimely death, and from the men's excited conversation Eleanor gathered that the local Welsh would happily seize this pretext to take up arms against him. At the same time, it was agreed that she should go to the king. She would travel with the children to Wiltshire, and then go on to London, where the king was said to be heading.

Alan flatly refused to go with the children, preferring to join his father at the siege. To Eleanor's surprise, Edward, who had scarcely said two words, neither of them civil, since their marriage, elected to stay with his stepfather also. "It'll be good experience," he said sullenly. "And I'm too old to go with the others."

"Very well," said Eleanor, kissing him goodbye to the extent he would allow it. She turned to embrace her husband. "I love you," she said, wishing she could stay in his arms forever.

Eleanor was accompanied to London by her former guard Tom, who just recently had joined her household, and his friend Hugh Dalby, who had come with him from the Tower.

William was aware that Eleanor had borrowed money from Benedict de Fulsham, though not of where the security had come from, and before Eleanor had left Wales, she and William had agreed that Eleanor should ask Benedict for another loan. She had been repaying him regularly for the sum she had borrowed of him nearly a year before, and she was certain that he would lend her more. And more would certainly be needed for William to pay the men besieging Caerphilly Castle, and for Eleanor to pay part of the fine the king would no doubt demand as a prelude for restoring her lands. Though as a married woman (Eleanor smiled at the thought), she could not borrow the money in her own right, she had no doubt that Benedict would advance the money to her on William's promise that he would sign the proper documents later. His word was one trusted by everyone.

With this as her purpose, Eleanor went to see Benedict while she considered whether to go straight to the king or to enlist someone, perhaps one of the priors with whom she had been friendly, to intercede with her in case the king was in a stubborn mood. Benedict, who still held Eleanor's golden collateral, was as agreeable as she had hoped. They were finalizing the repayment terms when Benedict, facing the door of his counting house, suddenly went white and stopped mid-sentence. "Sir?" Eleanor asked.

"In the king's name!"

Eleanor whirled and saw Tom and Hugh being wrestled to the wall by a group of armed men. "In God's name, leave them be! What have they done?"

The leader of the men smiled. "Nothing, my lady. It is you who are under arrest."

He was advancing toward her with shackles in his hands. "Arrest! For what? This is an outrage! I will not go with you; you will not take me!" Eleanor threw herself on the man, who was twice her size, and began to kick and claw him.

The leader hesitated; then, losing patience with Eleanor's ineffective but dogged assault, slammed her across the face, so hard that she crumpled to the floor. He shackled her hands and yanked her up, pulling off her veil in order to wipe her bloody nose. "Look at this, mates! Hair as red as a vixen's, and a temper to match. Calmer, my lady?" Eleanor honked a reply of some sort, which the man decided to take as an affirmative answer. "Good. Then let's get on our way to the Tower."

The distance from Benedict de Fulsham's counting house to the Tower was not a long one, but it seemed endless to Eleanor, walking shackled between two guards as the men at the front of the procession cried irritably, "Make way for the king's prisoner! Make way for the king's prisoner!" every few feet. The king's prisoner being a richly dressed lady, with unbound hair falling to her waist, the cries succeeded only in attracting more interest from the bystanders, and that slowed their progress even more.

The king, it turned out, was in residence at the Tower, accompanied by Mortimer and what remained of his council—for Lancaster and Thomas Wake and their followers, though they had not been imprisoned, had been required to execute large monetary recognizances and were not welcome at court. As Eleanor was brought before her sixteen-year-old sovereign, he looked at her dourly. "Lady Despenser," he said, "we are disappointed in you."

"What is the meaning of this, your grace? Why have my men and I been shackled like common criminals and brought before you? Did not my husband offer to pay whatever fine was demanded of him?"

The king was about to reply, but Mortimer broke in. "Which husband, Lady Despenser? It appears you have two, you know."

"Two?"

"Does the name John de Grey mean anything to you, my lady? It ought to. He says you made him a promise of marriage, followed by sexual intercourse, and that as a result you are his legal wife."

Eleanor stepped back from the king. "No! It cannot be. I am married to Lord Zouche. I never promised to marry Sir Grey. Never!"

"Perhaps your memory will become more clear after you have had leisure to reflect," said Mortimer. "And leisure you will have, Lady Despenser, or Grey, or Zouche, for you are the king's prisoner."

"For what reason? For these sham charges of Sir Grey's? For marrying my lord Zouche?"

Mortimer again forestalled the king's answer. "The crown doesn't care who you spread your legs for, my lady. You are under arrest for stealing the king's jewels from the Tower."

CHAPTER 25

▼

MARCH 1329 TO DECEMBER 1329

On a rainy day, William la Zouche sat in the great hall of his manor in Essex, close to London, watching his stepchildren playing in a corner. Were it not for their presence, he might have believed that his marriage to Eleanor had been but a dream, this last month but a nightmare.

The nightmare had begun in February when one of his good friends from the king's court had arrived at Caerphilly Castle, where William's siege was, thanks to an army of enthusiastic Welshmen, well underway. There he had heard that his wife was a prisoner in the Tower, on charges of theft. She along with two of her men had been haled out of the royal presence to cells somewhere, and none of them had been seen or heard from since. In his shock William had barely registered the other piece of news, that John de Grey was claiming Eleanor as his wife.

A warrant for William's own arrest had issued, it turned out, and William, when the king's men came for him a day later, had not resisted, but let himself be escorted to London. There he had begged the king's pardon, offered to give up money and lands, offered himself in place of Eleanor, offered to keep her in custody himself. He'd begged to see her, begged to be allowed to bring her provisions, begged to send a letter to her. All to no avail. He'd only met with stares: the king's blank one, the queen's amused one, Mortimer's cold one. Then he had been allowed to leave. He had been stripped of his positions as constable of the Tower and justice of the forest, but his lands were his to hold still.

There had been nothing to do after that but to go to Wiltshire and gather up Alan and his motherless stepchildren. He'd told the little ones that their mother had had to visit her lands in Ireland and would be staying there indefinitely. What else could he say to them? That their mother, whom he had sworn to cherish and protect, was back in the Tower, utterly alone, and he had not done a thing to save her? He knew that was what Edward believed; he had said as much that miserable day outside Caerphilly Castle when news had arrived of Eleanor's arrest. Accusation after accusation, curse after curse he had hurled until Alan, angry at the insult to his father, had punched him and the boys had gotten into a fistfight so violent that three knights had had to yank them apart. Oddly, the black eyes Edward had given and received had gone a long way toward relieving his anger; he'd been civil, if sullen, ever since, and he and Alan had become friends of sorts. But his stepson's words rang in William's ears nightly. *She was fine until you came, you whoreson. They would have left her in peace but for you. If she dies in prison, you'll be responsible.*

He wrote to her regularly, hoping that some of his letters got through; they were certainly accompanied by large enough bribes. He sent money and gifts of food to her daughters' convents each month, sent provisions to Hugh at Bristol Castle—though he had no way of knowing whether these made it past his guards. He wrote to the king, to the queen, to Mortimer. None of them responded.

Gladys had traveled to the Tower herself, begging to be allowed to keep her lady company, but had been refused. She had then rejoined William in Essex, where together they had pieced out what must have happened with the jewels. Gladys had remembered the trunks full of cups and Tom's comings and goings, the florins jingling in Eleanor's purse. "My lady's honest, Lord Zouche. She must have had a reason."

"I know it, Gladys."

Without Gladys to grieve with, he must have surely have gone mad, for Edward and even Isabel were distant to him, and he had to pretend that all was well in front of his younger stepchildren. With Gladys, he'd had no reason to hide his emotions when she'd handed him an item that had been tossed in with the children's belongings during their hasty trip to Wiltshire: a brush full of bright red hairs.

A servant came to his side. "Sir, you have a guest. The Earl of Kent."

Bleak as William's mood was, it became even bleaker at the thought of a visit from the Earl of Kent. Though the earl himself was amiable enough, his retinue was notorious for its boisterousness and for its high living. A visit from him would leave his larders bare, and there was not a chance in the world the earl would pay for any of it. So not only was he without a wife, he was about to be beggared, he thought, with the black humor that had become his only defense against utter despair.

Still, the earl was the king's uncle, and Eleanor's too, and if he could be persuaded to say a word for Eleanor…"Show him and his mob in," he said gloomily, and tried to look welcoming as he arose to meet his guests.

Only two men, however, walked into the great hall: the Earl of Kent and a knight. So oddly matched were they that William forgot his troubles for the moment and stared, wondering what on earth had brought them here together. The Earl of Kent was tall, handsome, and blond, like his father and his late brother the king, and was only twenty-eight years of age; the knight was barrel-shaped, short, dark, ordinary-looking, and close to sixty. But it was not merely the men's looks that made them such an odd couple. The Earl of Kent had been one of the judges at the Earl of Winchester's trial. The knight, if not the ghost of the Earl of Winchester, was the next best thing: Sir Ingelram Berenger, his close friend.

William beckoned the children to come pay their respects to the visitors. Alan received the guests politely, but Edward managed only a surly greeting for the Earl of Kent. His manner changed abruptly, however, when Berenger was introduced. "Sir Berenger? In the service of my grandfather?"

"Yes, Edward, God assoil his soul."

"Will you help free my mother, for his sake?"

Berenger was about to reply when Gilbert, John, Lizzie, and Edmund ambled over, leading with them William's canine namesake, whom the children had dressed in some of Alan's cast-off robes. "Lord Zouche? What do you think?"

"I think he needs a better tailor, Gilbert, but now you must greet the Earl of Kent and Sir Ingelram Berenger."

Gilbert bowed, and the three younger children managed a reasonable semblance thereof before Isabel and Gladys, who had just heard of the visitors' arrival, paid their own respects to the men and then led the youngsters away. The Earl of Kent smiled. "Are any of those four scamps yours, Lord Zouche?"

"I think of them as mine now, but they are Eleanor's, except for the youngest boy, who is Eleanor's grandchild."

"I've several children. You should see my little one, Joan. Prettiest lass you'll ever see, even though she's but a baby still. Lord Zouche, might we speak with you privately?"

William nodded and was about to lead the men to his chamber when Edward grabbed his arm. "I am coming, too."

"Edward..."

"I am! If it is about my mother—"

William sighed. "I would ask that he be allowed to join us, if you please. If there are any confidences to be had, he will keep them safe, I know."

The earl nodded. "Very well. He is my great-nephew, after all."

Edward did not look particularly pleased at this acknowledgment of their relationship. He stayed close to Berenger as they walked toward Zouche's chamber.

Once servants had brought wine and food, the earl said, "I don't want to inspire false hopes in you or your family, Lord Zouche. My business doesn't involve your wife, but it could benefit her."

Zouche felt his spirits lag again. "So what does it involve, your lordship?"

"My brother Edward."

"The late king," William said confusedly.

"Yes. Lord Zouche, my brother is still alive."

William knocked his wine to the floor. Recovering himself, he said, "Mother of God, man, you went to his funeral!"

"I never saw his corpse. Did you?"

"No—"

"No one from the court did," said the earl. "So who is to say who died in Berkeley Castle?"

"Thomas de Berkeley, for one. The king was laid out for viewing under his supervision, so I've heard."

"But no one viewed him that closely, did they? And how many of those people had seen my brother before that time, except briefly? Any blond man of about the same age and build might have been taken for my brother at a distance."

"So where do you think he is?"

"Corfe Castle," Kent answered promptly. "A friar told me that he is there." Kent had clearly had enough of these tedious details. He leaned forward, tapping an excited finger against his wine goblet. "I am going to set him free, and restore him to the throne. But to do so I must have help, and that is why I am here tonight."

William stole a look at his stepson, sitting next to Berenger, but Edward's dark eyes, like his father's had been, were unreadable. He said hesitantly, "Restore him to the throne, my lord, assuming he is really alive to be restored? With all of his shortcomings—"

"He is my brother," said Kent simply. "I betrayed him in France, when I joined the queen. I betrayed him at Westminster, when I shouted in favor of his son. I'll not betray him again, now that I know he is alive." The earl drained his glass. "It is best that I be on my way, Lord Zouche. You being out of favor with the crown, it won't do for me to be seen much around you. But talk to Sir Berenger here. I will await to hear from him what you choose to do."

He left the room, and soon William from his window saw him galloping away toward London. Only then did he ask, "Sir Berenger. Do you believe the late king is still alive?"

"No. I believe he is dead. Murdered."

"But you have allowed the earl to believe that you think him alive?"

"No. He knows I have my doubts. He knows we all have our doubts—there's several of us he's spoken to, you see. He humors our doubts, waits for the day he can show us his brother alive and well." Berenger poured himself some more wine. "But if this can be used to stir the people against Mortimer and the queen..."

"Who else is he speaking to?"

Berenger smiled. "A wider range of people than you might think. Men like myself who were associated with the Despensers, of course, who never have borne the Earl of March any goodwill. But there's others too, like yourself, who once followed him and now have reason to want him gone. Men who are ready for a change, all of us."

"Lancaster?"

The old knight shook his head. "There were some moves by the Earl of Kent in that direction, but the Earl of Lancaster preferred to take a different path against Mortimer. Now he's got Mortimer's spies on him and couldn't help us if he wanted to."

"The Earl of Kent abandoned the Earl of Lancaster. What makes you think he won't do the same now?"

"Intuition, I guess. He does feel great guilt for leaving his brother to that she-wolf of a queen. And there's always been something rather lackadaisical about the Earl of Kent. Not now. He's taken this to heart." He shrugged. "If I'm wrong, and he betrays us or bungles this business, you don't need me to tell you that we're dead men. I'm willing to take the risk, myself. My world as I knew it ended when they killed the Earl of Winchester." Berenger crossed himself and then touched Edward on the shoulder. "He was like a brother to me."

"What does the Earl of Kent want from us?"

"Money, at the moment. I'm going to raise some on my lands in Cambridge."

William sipped his wine and pondered. Never in his life, he decided, had he heard such a harebrained scheme. The fact that the Earl of Kent, whose accomplishments thus far in life had not exactly been impressive, was at its head and that his accomplice was a man who was highly lucky to have escaped execution along with the Despensers hardly inspired confidence either. Every bit of common sense Zouche possessed warned him off.

But what had common sense done to get Eleanor back? "Tell the earl I'll give all that I can. Starting with monies from my own lands in Cambridge."

Eleanor's first few days of captivity had been relatively busy. After collapsing in a faint in front of the king and his council she had awoken to find herself back in her old quarters in the Beauchamp Tower, with two of Mortimer's men standing over her. Then, and for several days thereafter, they had questioned her. Eleanor had admitted her guilt. Some of the jewels, she had acknowledged, were still in Hanley Castle; the rest had been brought as security to Benedict de Fulsham, who was in no way involved in her felony. She did not know the whereabouts of any goods belonging to Hugh or his father, except for those she had taken from the Tower and the few worthless items that had been left behind on her Clare lands. Her husband, William la Zouche, had known nothing of her actions, nor had Gladys or any of her children. She'd begged, over and over again, to be allowed to see the king and explain. Surely he, or his kindly wife, could understand how grief-stricken and angry she'd been.

How Mortimer had learned of her felony she did not know. Tom, hearing the charge against her as he and Hugh stood shackled nearby, had cried, "No! I did it. Not the lady! Not the lady!" before being dragged away. It was clear, then, that he had not been the one to incriminate her. (She herself, hoping to save him from hanging, had insisted that she had tricked him into believing that the possessions he took were hers by right.) One of Mortimer's spies among the guards, she surmised, had noticed Tom's comings and goings, heard that he had left the Tower for her household, pieced the information together, and told Mortimer. He had held on to his knowledge until it suited his purpose to inform the king. Probably, she supposed, he had planned for her to marry one of his puppets. When she had run off with William, he had sprung the trap laid for her.

No audience with the king had been granted, and Mortimer's men, not daring to use more forceful methods to get the king's first cousin to confess more freely, had at last left her in disgust. Eleanor had then prepared herself to die. Theft was enough for a death sentence, and theft from the crown... Would she burn, the female punishment for treason, or hang? She'd occupied a good deal of her time wondering which Mortimer and the queen would choose for her. Then she'd occupied more time considering whether she should try starving herself, as Ogle had told her Hugh had. Suicide was a mortal sin, but if she ate just enough to stay alive, she might be so weak that she would die quickly.

But the court had left London by late February, and she was still in the Tower, still alive. The saddlebags she had brought on her journey, containing some changes of clothing and some toiletries and other necessities, had been brought to her, as had a proper bed. (She'd had only a pallet when she first arrived.) So it appeared that perhaps she would not die, after all. Was the plan, then, just to let her languish in prison, like her son?

She picked up the rosary that had been in her saddlebags and began to pray. Praying, though apparently quite useless, passed the time.

By midsummer, her guards had warmed up to her and began to tell her news. Philip of Valois, who had become king of France after King Charles's widow had given birth to a mere girl, had been demanding for months that Edward pay homage to him. Though Isabella had icily responded that the son of a king was under no obligation to pay homage to the son of a mere count, England was in no position to stand by such hauteur. The treasury was nearly empty, and the money that had been sent by the Scots pursuant to the treaty had gone straight to the queen's own well-manicured hands. With no money to fight the French, the king, using money loaned by the Italian house of Bardi, sailed to France and did homage on June 6. The very next day, Robert Bruce died in his bed. The heir to the Scottish throne, little Joan's husband David, was but five years old.

On a more personal level, Eleanor learned that Tom and Hugh were still alive, but were in Newgate. Benedict de Fulsham, despite Eleanor's vociferous protests that he had done nothing more than lend money to her, had also been arrested and imprisoned to Windsor Castle, though he had been released on mainprise shortly thereafter. Mortimer probably held a grudge against Benedict; he like many other London merchants had been a supporter of the Earl of Lancaster.

It was about this time when a letter from William finally reached her. William had obviously written the letter with the idea that it would be read by one of Mortimer's men, but despite, or perhaps because of, its bare simplicity it reduced her to tears. Her children were well, he wrote, and had received visits from both their Despenser aunts. All three of the nuns had been allowed to visit in May. All of them longed to see her and prayed for her every day. He himself missed her beyond words and was doing all he could to see her set free.

She tucked the letter under her pillow and slept with it in her hand every night.

William did not tell Eleanor that he and her father-in-law's retainer, Ingelram Berenger, had borrowed five hundred pounds together in March and that they were getting ready to borrow another three hundred pounds in July. Nor did he tell her that the Earl of Kent had gone to Avignon, officially to press for the canonization of the late Earl of Lancaster, unofficially to enlist papal support for the freeing of his brother. From there, he would move on to Paris, where he hoped to get a favorable response from Henry de Beaumont and several other exiles who had fallen out with the Earl of March.

In August, Eleanor was sitting at her window watching the activity outside—almost her sole diversion—when she saw the Earl of March striding across the green toward the Beauchamp Tower. In a few minutes he was standing before her. "I've news for you, my lady. The king and his council have agreed to let you go free, under your supposed husband's supervision. Here is the order."

He held it up, then snatched it away as Eleanor reached for it. "Not so fast, my lady. There are conditions that you must meet before you go free."

"The king's conditions?"

"No. My conditions. They're straightforward enough. You give me Glamorgan, Tewkesbury, and Hanley Castle."

"You cannot bully me into doing that."

"It worked well enough for your late Hugh, did it not? But I'll give him credit for results where it is due, for he labored under a disadvantage that I am not. He was dealing with honorable women of irreproachable character, like your sister Elizabeth. I am dealing with a common felon."

"I am not a felon."

"Just a lady who deals in a spot of felony, eh? Just as Hugh was not a pirate. He would have been proud of you, now that I think of it. The lord pirate and the lady felon. You were a well matched couple, weren't you?"

"If we were well matched, so are you and Isabella. Two adulterers—and two murderers."

Mortimer did not flinch. "Ah, that tiresome rumor about the late king has reached even your ears, I see. There's no truth to it. He died of natural causes, and was viewed by half the clergy in Gloucestershire. Not a mark on him. But we are getting off the topic of your lands, my lady."

"And if I don't give them to you?"

"Then you rot in prison."

Eleanor snorted. "The king won't let me stay here indefinitely. When he and the council find out that I have not been released as planned—"

"Find out from whom? Nothing gets to the king unless it gets to me first. No one sees him whom I don't want him to see. Nothing leaves the council that doesn't go to me or my men. I have the order freeing you, and if you choose not to give me what I want, it'll go straight into the fire."

"The king won't put up with you forever, Mortimer."

"I am the Earl of March. You shall address me as such."

"I shall address you as I please. You are a jumped-up knight who owes all to that whore we must call a queen. I am the daughter of the Earl of Gloucester. I would be Earl of Gloucester myself if I were a man."

"If you were a man, my dear, I would have stabbed you with my sword six times over by now. The lands. Deny them to me, and this order will be destroyed."

"I'll save you the trouble."

The early morning being chilly, a fire had been lit in her room. Eleanor snatched the parchment from Mortimer's hands and threw the pieces into the fire. Behind her, Mortimer grinned. "You're a haughty bitch, aren't you? Your grandfather and father would be proud to see a lady of such spirit. Pity you didn't think first, though. Men."

Four men with vacant faces came into the room, arms crossed. "Well, look alive, you. You've a lady to escort. Don't think of taking your pleasure with her first, though. We're in a hurry."

Eleanor opened her mouth to scream, but before anything had come out, Mortimer had knocked her unconscious with a single blow. He watched coolly as the men tied her, gagged her, and bundled her into a sack. "Mouthy little slut. Make good time, you, in getting her out of London before she wakes up, and kept that gag on her. We don't want her screeching on the way to Devizes Castle."

Although the constable at Devizes Castle in Wiltshire knew the identity of his new prisoner, his underlings did not, and they listened patiently as their new charge, a knight's widow with pretensions to nobility whom the Earl of March had imprisoned for making wild and irrational threats against the crown, demanded that a letter be sent to her first cousin, the King of England himself! Then she launched into a tirade about the inadequacy of her lodgings, which were no more than a tiny cell with a chamber pot in one corner and a pallet in the other. The guards humored her for a while longer. Then they handed her some bread and ale, locked the door, and left her to rant in solitude.

At Wigmore Castle a few weeks later, King Arthur and Queen Guinevere, otherwise known as Mortimer and Isabella, watched as each of two young knights tried his best to unhorse the other. Every knight in England, except for those out of favor with the court, seemed to have come to Wigmore for the Round Table tournament.

The occasion was another double Mortimer wedding, the juvenile bridegrooms in this case being the future Earl of Pembroke, Laurence de Hastings (rescued by the queen in 1326 from the clutches of his earlier betrothed, Nora le Despenser) and Edward, the Earl of Norfolk's heir. The newlyweds sat in the stand next to the Countess of March, whom the Earl of March had graciously had escorted from Ludlow Castle to spend some time with the court.

Between Arthur and Guinevere and the Countess of March sat King Edward and Philippa. Edward watched the proceedings morosely. It was not that he disliked tournaments. In fact, he loved them, unlike his father who had tolerated them while Gaveston was alive and besting all of his opponents but had afterward regarded them with a mixture of boredom and suspicion. The second Edward's enemies had delighted in plotting against him at tournaments, and who wanted to spend the afternoon trying to knock someone off his horse and watching others do the same when one could be galloping through the countryside in the company of a good friend or two, then cooling off with a swim? But his son thought differently. Had this tournament been somewhere else, in someone else's company, he would have been enjoying himself to the utmost. There was the thrill of competition, the danger, the surprise, the satisfaction in seeing an especially well-aimed thrust, the beauty of the horses and their trappings. There were the ladies, dressed in their prettiest gowns and bedecked with favors, the adoring looks sent to and from the stands as the young knights rode out, the charming flirtations—

There was his mother, the Queen of England, playing the whore to the Earl of March. And their adultery became more blatant every day. No longer did the queen and Mortimer stand apart when England's bishops were around; the men of the Church either discreetly ignored the relationship or stayed far away from the court where they did not have to witness it. No longer did they hide their affair from their families. Even the king's younger sister Eleanor had guessed something of it. Only the other day, she had asked him, "Ned, if the Countess of March were to die, do you think Mama would marry the Earl of March?"

Edward's stomach churned.

Beside him, Philippa was talking gamely to the Countess of March. Edward had yet to meet a person whom his young wife could not put at ease, and the countess's mouth was actually curving into a smile as they conversed. Still, what must it feel like for the poor countess to come to court and have to make small talk? What was it like for Mortimer's young daughters to be overshadowed at their own weddings?

He looked moodily at the play-crown Mortimer was wearing. Why hadn't his own wife been crowned yet? His mother said that it was a matter of money, that there would be a ceremony in due time, but the money had been found for this farce easily enough: a thousand pounds had been borrowed from the Bardi. In the crown's name! Mortimer could have easily financed the tournament himself without the Bardis' help, him and Isabella, with all the loot they had raked in from the Despensers and Arundel, with all the lands the queen had been granted by the crown. Meanwhile, his own household was so short of money that his keeper of the wardrobe periodically threatened to resign. What the king needed, he'd said, was an alchemist, not a humble clerk.

In two months he would be seventeen. Too old to be ordered about by Mortimer and his mother. But would Mortimer give way? Edward doubted it. He was enjoying himself far too much to slip quietly into the role of mere trusted advisor. And Isabella would never encourage him to do so. It had been the loneliest day of Edward's life not long ago when he had realized, first, that his mother was the Earl of March's lover and, second, that her feelings for him were such that given the choice between loyalty to the earl and loyalty to her son the king, she would probably choose the earl.

A new pair of knights rode out onto the field, and Edward's spirits lifted a little. William de Montacute, one of the few people in his household he trusted, was next in the lists. William was about to leave on a mission to the papal court in Avignon. What if William could gain a private audience with the Pope, to tell him the state into which England had fallen? Cash-strapped, cowering before the Scots and the French, run by a man who was intent only on self-aggrandizement, its rightful king cast into the shadows? Edward had no clear plan of what to do yet, it was true, but a change would have to come, and he knew that the change would have to be effected by himself. And on that day papal support would be necessary...

He would have to seek out William alone, of course. No chance of simply seeing him alone in his chamber; Mortimer made sure of that. No, where other kings could talk to whom they pleased where they pleased about whatever they pleased, the King of England would have to sneak away to have a private conversation with his friend. But soon, he vowed, his days of sneaking would be over.

"Jail fever!" The constable of Devizes Castle glared at Robert, head of the prison garrison and known to his fellow English speakers merely as Bob. "We've never had jail fever here before."

"Maybe, my lord, but our fine lady started with it five days ago."

"That creature? She is a vastly inconvenient woman."

"She is very ill, my lord, and has been out of her senses the entire time. Indeed, I believe she will die soon."

The constable sighed. Though the Earl of March had given orders for Eleanor to be treated as a common prisoner would be, he also had been emphatic that she not be treated so badly that she died of ill-use. He would not be pleased to have a corpse delivered to him. "We had best try to prevent it. My personal physician shall attend her."

"Yes, my lord."

"And move her to a guest room. I gather she is in no condition to escape."

"She is in no condition to know her name, poor lady." The constable glared at him. "I beg your pardon, my lord. But after the jailors told me of her illness, I saw her myself, and I do find her a pitiful little creature. She must have friends somewhere—she cries out for so many people. William, and a Hugh, and her uncle, and a Gladys, mainly."

The constable snorted. "Hugh, is it? She'll cry out for him for a long time. I suppose I might as well tell you now who she is. What have you heard?"

"The men say she claims to be daughter to the Earl of Gloucester, Gilbert the Red, and granddaughter to the first Edward, but I know that is a delusion of the poor thing's."

"No. She's right. Remember Hugh le Despenser? That's his relict."

Bob stared. "His widow? Here in rags, sick to death?"

"The Wheel of Fortune turns," the constable said philosophically.

"Then, sir, I pity her all the more."

The constable harrumphed. "Then you take charge of her. As for me, I'm hoping the earl will soon take her off our hands. He told me in August that he'd trouble me with her only for a few weeks, and here it is December."

He went off, still grumbling, and after a while a young servant boy came to Bob to tell him that the lady's room was ready. Bob went to the cell where, by his own, entirely unauthorized connivance, Eleanor lay in some comfort on a clean pallet, wearing only a thin, coarse shift donated by Bob's sister but well covered with blankets. The lady's once pretty red hair had been so dirty and matted that after consulting with his sister, Bob had cut it; he hoped she wouldn't mind too much. Eleanor was mumbling to herself but seemed a little calmer than usual. He picked her up, easily as he might a kitten, and smiled at her as she opened her green eyes, dull with fever, and looked at him languidly. "Hugh? Where are you taking me?"

"To a more comfortable room, where you can get better."

"Am I ill?"

"Just tired out, my lady. You need a change of scene."

She was quiet as he carried her some distance away, to a part of the castle so bright with candles and luxurious it might have been a different building altogether. As he neared her new quarters, she whispered, "Hugh?"

"Yes?"

"I'm married to Lord Zouche now. Are you angry?"

Bob set Eleanor on a bed, hung round with curtains, and patted her hand as he relinquished his charge to a woman who had been brought in from the town as a nurse. "No, not at all. You rest and get well."

During the two weeks Eleanor spent in a delirious haze, there were times when anyone who touched her, even the kindly physician, was an enemy, while at others she lay placidly and trustingly as a young child. It was not until a day in mid-December that she awoke from what seemed to have been an endless descent into another world altogether and knew perfectly well who she was. *I am Eleanor de Clare, late the wife of Hugh le Despenser, now the wife of William la Zouche. My first husband still rots for all the world to see; my second husband is somewhere unknown; my children are scattered around the kingdom like so many stones; and where am I now?* She moved her head to the left and felt the warmth of a fire nearby. She touched the covers she lay underneath and felt fine linen and fur. She might have been in her own chamber, except that there was no one around her whom she loved. "Am I still at Devizes?" she asked. "Are you a physician?"

The man she addressed smiled. "Yes to both questions, my lady. You have been very ill indeed, and you are still very weak. But you will recover now."

"Is that to be desired?"

"Your illness has brought you low in spirit as well as in body, I see, but you must not lose hope, my lady. Rest now. Sleep will help you more than anything." He tucked the covers in around her more cozily.

There were questions that Eleanor wanted to ask him, but as she tried to form them, she drifted off. When she awoke hours later, her nurse was there with some soup, which Eleanor slowly ate. Eleanor thanked her when she was done and then, worn out by even this much activity, lay back against the pillows as the events of the last few months came clear in her mind again.

After Mortimer had come to the Beauchamp Tower, she had come to consciousness to find herself bound and gagged, lying in an open sack at the bottom of a jouncing cart with a blanket thrown over her for good measure. When it had grown too dark to travel, she'd been carried into a manor house—belonging to Mortimer or one of his allies, she supposed later—and had been given to understand that she was the earl's prisoner. If she wished to go free, she had only to ask for him and do as he wanted. If not, she would be taken to Devizes Castle, a somewhat neglected royal castle, to stay at the earl's pleasure. Perhaps she would like to see him now? Eleanor, her head aching where it had been hit and her wrists raw from where the rope had bound them, had emphatically declined his company. No Mortimer, she had said coolly, would bully a Clare. Someone would rescue her.

For several more days she had been on the road, always bound and gagged, always with a blanket tossed over her so she would not be visible to passersby. Then she had been brought to Devizes Castle and seen her new quarters. A cold, damp cell, a thin pallet for bedding. In deference to her royal blood, she had been given a chamber pot. Probably her guards had expected her to send for Mortimer then and there, but Eleanor, reminding herself that she was the granddaughter of the first Edward and the daughter of the Earl of Gloucester, refused to give way. Then they left her. Soon she discovered that the castle garrison believed her to be a genteel madwoman with an unspecified grudge against the crown, too indiscreet to be allowed to roam loose and too trifling to be hung. Her desperate attempts to open some sort of communication between herself and the king had met with amused tolerance at first, irritation as the weeks wore on. She was cousin to the king? Of course she was. She was Lady of Glamorgan, her husband a member of Parliament? Certainly. Of course she could write a petition if she pleased; they'd even brought her pen and parchment and watched her write with the amusement of men watching a trained monkey. The letter she had written had gone straight to the fire. The one weapon she might have had at her disposal—bribery—had been taken from her, for every piece of jewelry she had been wearing had been stripped from her by Mortimer's men before she arrived at the castle.

Had she asked for Mortimer, she knew, she could have escaped her ordeal, for it was the one request on her part the guards had been advised to take seriously. But her ill treatment had only strengthened her stubborn will. And so the weeks had dragged on, and on, until her body had sickened and her mind had become so hazy with fever that she could not remember Mortimer's name, much less ask for him. The last coherent thought she could remember having was, *Perhaps I am mad, just as they say.* Of the days after that she recollected nothing.

And now what would happen to her? Was this respite only a temporary one until she was carried downstairs again? Or was there hope?

Eleanor gingerly eased herself out of bed, holding onto the bedpost for support as her legs trembled underneath her. She made her way carefully to a window, which afforded her a fine view of a snow-covered pond, and tugged it open, breathing in the fresh, crisp December air. After the weeks she had spent in the windowless prison cell, just the sight of a brilliant blue sky and the sensation of outside air on her face raised her spirits.

Too weak to stand for long, she inched her way back to the bed and knelt beside it, offering thanks for her deliverance from sickness, not to mention the prison cell. She prayed for the souls of Hugh and his father, for the king and Adam, for her parents and brother, for her stepfather, for Gaveston, for her other family dead. She prayed for her children, particularly Hugh and her three little nuns. Finally she prayed for William, but perhaps she was praying as much for herself now. "Bring me back to him, please," she whispered. "Bring me to him, safe, and let me be a good wife to him. Forgive me, please, for everything. Bring me back."

She climbed back into bed and drew the warm covers around her. In moments she was sleeping deeply.

For several more days she recuperated, mostly sleeping but sometimes sitting curled up in a blanket on the window seat, watching two boys, hindered by their very large dog, valiantly try to build snow castles in imitation of the real castle towering above them. It was early on the third or fourth day of her convalescence that Bob came into her room carrying a bundle. "My lady, do you think you are strong enough to travel?"

"To travel how? I was brought here tied in a wagon. That took no great effort on my part."

Bob shuddered. "You are to travel to Kenilworth Castle, if you are able."

"The Earl of Lancaster's castle?"

"Yes, my lady, but not to him, as I understand it. The Earl of March is there, with the king and his court."

Irrelevantly, Eleanor wondered if the Earl of Lancaster knew his castle had been taken over by the court and, if so, if he minded. Then she remembered the issue at hand. If Mortimer were intending to imprison her in another miserable cell, he would hardly be doing so in such proximity to the king. In any case, she was willing to take the chance. "I can travel."

"Here are some clothes for you sent by the constable's lady."

She opened the bundle from the constable's lady with gratitude, for her own filthy and tattered dress had been burned. The robes that had been brought to her were not new, but they were clean and warm. They were not flattering either, having been made for a taller, heavier woman with evidently quite a different coloring, but at least the bulky material concealed how skinny her body had become, while the headdress hid her shorn hair. She would be presentable enough to appear at Kenilworth without humiliation.

Bob, apologizing over and over again on the way for not believing that she was the Earl of Gloucester's daughter, escorted her. Because of his solicitude for her health, their journey was a slow one, and it was not until the next to the last day of December that Eleanor arrived at Kenilworth Castle, where she was taken straight to Mortimer's private chamber. "I heard that you had been ill, my lady."

"I all but died thanks to you, my lord."

"The Church tells us that illness often brings about repentance. I called you here to see if you have repented yet of stealing the king's jewels and wish to make amends."

"If you are worried about my repentance then you may send for a priest."

"I am more concerned about your life here on earth. I'm here to renew my offer, which you could have accepted at any time while you were at Devizes Castle, you know, simply by asking to see me."

"I would have soon have asked for the devil himself."

"Indeed? Well, despite your intransigence, I am renewing my offer on more favorable terms to you than the first, for you needn't give up your lands to me— you may give them to the crown. Sign them over—in payment of your fine for your felony—and you will be free in a matter of days, and you will receive a pardon."

"Answer me one question, and answer me honestly, or you will rot in hell. Is my son Hugh alive?"

"Yes. He will stay that way if you cooperate."

"On your honor, or what you have left of it?"

"Yes."

"My younger boys will be safe too?"

"Yes."

"I will be brought before the king to sign?" Mortimer nodded. "Then I will sign it."

"I thought you would see reason." Mortimer smiled. "So much so that I brought your jewels, which have been in safekeeping, here for you." He motioned toward a small chest and watched as Eleanor, eyes shimmering, opened it and put William's wedding ring on her left hand and Hugh's wedding ring on her right. "And I also took the liberty of sending for your husband—Lord Zouche, that is. He has been rather the more energetic of your two mates in attempting to recover you, and as your husband he must sign for you."

"William is here?"

"Outside the chamber."

Eleanor wheeled around and rushed out the chamber door. "William! I prayed to be restored to you, and God has answered my prayers!"

William, looking years older than when Eleanor had seen him last, grimaced. "Probably not under the conditions you had hoped for, sweetheart, but I am here." He looked over in the direction of Mortimer, who had followed Eleanor out of the chamber. "Leave me, my lord, alone with my wife for a few minutes."

Mortimer hesitated. Eleanor said, "I've agreed to sign, and I will, you blackguard. Now let me have a moment with my husband!"

She added a multisyllabic epithet in English, learned from her jailors at Devizes Castle, which was much more satisfying than the French they had all been speaking. Mortimer raised an eyebrow. "A wide acquaintance with the people's language has your lady wife, Lord Zouche."

"She is a remarkable woman, Mortimer. Leave us."

Mortimer shrugged and walked away. When they were alone, William held her tightly. "Eleanor. Believe me. If there was another way I could get you free other than agreeing to sign my part of that damn paper, I would have done it."

"I know, William."

"Mortimer grows more arrogant and out of control every day. Someday you will get your land back, though. Trust me."

"I don't care about the land, William. I only want to be with you and my children."

"The man who escorted you, Robert, told me you had been ill. Did they mistreat you?" He frowned as he noticed how little hair there was under her headdress.

She wrapped her arms around William more tightly. "I am very comfortably lodged now."

"Sweet girl, you make the best of it, as you always have. It is one of the first things I loved about you."

Mortimer came into the room. "Ready yet, you lovebirds?"

"Let's get this charade over, Eleanor, so that you can go free." William indicated the parchment Mortimer was holding. "The Earl of March has shown me the indenture. You're doing this of your own good will and without coercion, so the indenture says, despite the fact that you've been locked up for the better part of the year and look as if a strong breeze would blow you away."

"Shall I have it read to you, my lady?" asked Mortimer.

"I can read quite well myself, thank you." Eleanor read the indenture and smiled grimly. "Mortimer, you are quite reasonable after all. I can have my lands back for a mere fifty thousand pounds, payable in one day. May we go to the king now, so I can express my gratitude for your bounty?"

Edward started as his cousin and Lord Zouche entered the room. Eleanor was much thinner than she had been, there was something peculiar about the arrangement of her hair, and her robes were ill-fitting and ill-suited to her complexion. But the Earl of March had told him that she was suffering from deep remorse about her theft, so deep that it had made her ill, and perhaps that explained her odd appearance. "It is our understanding that you wish to surrender Glamorgan, Morganwgg, Tewkesbury, and Hanley Castle, and all manors associated with them, to the crown, in exchange for a full pardon of your misdeeds. Is that correct?"

"Yes, your grace."

Eleanor's voice was much less melodious than it had once been, and this was also disturbing to the king. But he did not give it as much thought as he might have, for his mind was very much engaged elsewhere. A few weeks before, Philippa's physicians had confirmed the young couple's deepest hopes. Philippa was carrying a child. If God was good it would be a boy... He pulled his mind back to the situation before him and said, "Very well, Lady Despenser. We will accept your offer. Sign it, Lord Zouche."

William stepped to a table and signed. Following his signature with her own, Eleanor wondered grimly how many Clares were turning in their graves as she gave away the lands they had held so dear.

They had taken a respectful leave of the king and Philippa—oddly, Isabella was nowhere to be seen—and were entering the great hall to find William's men when William touched Eleanor on the shoulder. "Look there in that window seat, my dear. Is there anyone you recognize?"

"Gladys!" All of the self-control Eleanor had managed over the last nine months gave way when she saw her friend of twenty-three years standing before her. She ran into her arms, sobbing and laughing. William's own eyes misted.

"I've missed you so," she finally managed. Trying to regain control over her emotions, she brushed at her eyes and smiled. "But I think most of all I've missed a warm bath!"

Gladys rearranged Eleanor's headdress, exchanging a look with William as she did so. "You shall have one this very afternoon," she promised.

They were traveling to Ashby-de-la-Zouche. William had planned to put as much distance between Eleanor and the court in one day as he possibly could, but Eleanor's wan looks soon convinced him and Gladys to stop. He had a friend in the neighborhood and knew that he could count on his manor for hospitality. The master and the mistress were not at home, having gone to visit relations for Christmas and not yet returned, but the servants soon had a fire blazing and water heating in the best guest room for Eleanor. William, having been advised that Eleanor would rest after bathing, sipped ale in the great room and played a game of chess with his squire.

He was deep in contemplation of a move when Gladys appeared before him. "My lord," she said, "my lady wants you."

"Is she feeling ill, Gladys? I didn't like her looks when she came in."

"She says only that she wants you."

William hastened to their room. There Eleanor sat in the washtub, glowing from the heat. Her hair, newly washed and rinsed in rose water, hung around her face in tiny ringlets. "You called, sweetheart?"

"Yes." Eleanor smiled up at him. "I need help getting out of the bathtub."

He handed her out of the tub and set her on her feet. "And drying." He took a towel and dried her, missing no spots. "And going to bed." He carried her to the bed, she breathing as heavily as he, and got his clothes off faster than he had since he was a lad of fifteen. Many minutes later, he whispered, "There may be something to bathing every day."

"There may well be," said Eleanor.

They had been lying together contentedly for an hour or so when Eleanor said quietly, "I told you when we married, William, that you did not know what a wretch I was. The king's jewels—"

"You should have bided your time until I became constable of the Tower. Then I could have helped." She did not laugh. "Why did you do it, my love?"

"Revenge against the queen and Mortimer. Not the most satisfactory revenge. Jewels as revenge for Hugh's life? For my children's freedom? But with every gold cup I took in my hand I felt a gloating within me, because I had something the queen wanted and could never have. I enjoyed it, William. And now because of my stupidity Glamorgan is lost to my family forever. What must my ancestors think of me? What must you think of me?"

"Only that I love you very much."

She said wistfully, "Even with my hair cut short, and me so skinny now? I must look like a boy."

He hugged her closer to him. "No, my love. I checked most thoroughly, as you'll recall."

She giggled, and William's heart ached when he heard a sigh of relief behind that giggle. In a different tone, he continued, "I have been trying so hard all these months to get you back. But all the petitions I sent to the king went unanswered. I went to court to beg for you; my men and your men went to court to beg for you. We were turned away."

"You could not get past that hell spawn Mortimer."

"No." He shuddered. "I thought you were in the Tower all these months, comfortable at least. And it turns out that you were at Devizes Castle! Ill and alone. I failed you, my love."

"No, William. I knew all these months that you were somewhere out there, loving me. It gave me hope. It saved my life." She kissed him on the nose. "And now, with God's grace, we shall at last have a life together."

"With God's grace," agreed William. Eleanor yawned, massively, and William laughed for the first time in many a month. "Let's start our new life by getting a good night's sleep, my love."

The next day, they set off for Ashby-de-la-Zouche. William told her on the way about his manor, one of the few lands he held in his own right and not through curtsey of his late wife Alice. "It's large and comfortable, Eleanor, not what you've been used to, of course, but quite prosperous."

"I know I shall like it," she promised.

Eleanor was feeling so much better after her long night's sleep next to William that their journey to Ashby was a quick one. She smiled in delight as they arrived before the manor house. Not for the house, which indeed was large and rambling, but for who stood in front of it—Edward, Gilbert, John, Lizzie, Isabel, and Edmund. "Whoa!" she cried. She jumped from her horse without waiting for assistance and ran toward them, to be embraced by all of them at once.

"Mama, did you miss us in Ireland?"

Eleanor started. Then her eyes filled with tears at the kindly lie that surely must have saved her youngest children from so much misery. "Yes, dreadfully," she assured John. "I will not go away from you again for a long, long time."

CHAPTER 26

▼

FEBRUARY 1330 TO MARCH 1330

On February 18, 1330, the King of England had his way in one particular. Philippa, his wife of two years, was at last crowned. Philippa was five months gone with child, and even Isabella and Mortimer had had to concede that it was faintly scandalous that the woman who was carrying the potential heir to the throne should be not crowned herself. They could comfort themselves with the knowledge that the lands granted to the new queen had not cost them anything: Philippa had been granted Pontefract, Glamorgan, and Morganwgg, the last two owing to Lady Despenser's timely repentance. Queen Isabella had had to give up Pontefract out of her own tremendous dower, but she had been compensated with Tewkesbury and Hanley Castle, thanks to the obliging Eleanor. But every official who administered the queens' lands answered to Roger.

Isabella, watching in Westminster Abbey as her daughter-in-law with her dark hair and purple robe became the Queen of England, thought disdainfully that the girl looked like a very splendid grape. It was not that she had any hard feelings toward Philippa. Philippa treated her with respect, if no real warmth, and even Isabella could find no fault with her as a wife. No, the trouble lay in the ever-burgeoning belly that gave Philippa such a rounded appearance. For that previous December, at Kenilworth Castle, Isabella had given birth, months before her time, to a stillborn boy.

The midwife who had attended her during the birth, and the physician who had attended her afterward, had done all they could, even though Isabella had sensed that both of them thought all had worked out for the best. "I fear after this you will be unable to bear another child," the physician had told her stiffly, and Isabella, exhausted as she was, had longed to slap his face. She had wanted this child, nuisance as he would have been to her and Mortimer and embarrassment that he would have been to the king. And now she would never have another. Unlike those breeding cows the Countess of March and Lady Despenser, who seemed to have had to get only within arm's length of their husbands to conceive. And Philippa with those great hips of hers was probably another such breeder.

She reminded herself that unlike those other two heifers, Philippa was carrying her own grandchild. She could hardly wish her own grandchildren unborn, now, could she? Yet in a small part of her mind, she did. Being a grandmother would put her in the same category as the dried-up Countess of March, whom Roger had cast aside so easily, only occasionally throwing bones like new gowns and jewels. And she knew what power that small being in Philippa's womb could carry, if it was born male and healthy. It was true that since his extended sulk over Scotland, Edward had been rather complaisant with her wishes—so complaisant, Isabella thought sometimes that her son might have a lazy streak like his father. But the dutifulness that was proper in a son was something quite else in a father to a prince of the realm. If Edward had a son, he would have to declare his independence from her and Roger, for his self-respect in front of his son if nothing else. And then what use would Roger have for Isabella?

She thrust the thought from her mind. Edward might have a girl, and Roger was not about to cast her aside. He needed her, even if her color was not as fresh or her hair as shimmering as it had been five years before, even if she could not bear his children. The plan they had been concocting for well over a year now was well proof of that. And when Parliament met at Winchester Castle, overlooked by the grinning skull of the elder Despenser (Isabella smiled at this memory), it would come to its triumphant fruition.

On a March night, William lay awake next to Eleanor. Her covers had slipped down in her sleep, and he admired her naked body in the moonlight. Though she had been shockingly thin after her release from Devizes Castle, the ensuing weeks of good food and outdoor exercise had had their effect, and her curves were coming back. Then the moon disappeared behind the clouds, and he gently tugged the covers over her so she would not be cold. He reached out to fondle her hair. Since it had been cut it had become a bristling, springy mass of curls, pleasant to touch. Now that he had gotten used to her with short hair he thought it resembled a little cap; rather amusing.

But there had been nothing amusing about her appearance that day at Kenilworth Castle. He hadn't recognized her at first; he only hoped she had not noticed. What in God's name had been done to her? Then came a new worry: what damage had been done to her mind? He would love her always, would protect her for the rest of his life, but was the Eleanor he had fallen in love with gone for good? He'd quickly been relieved of that worry, at least, and could only marvel at her resilience.

Only once, clasping her close to him after they'd made love, he had dared to ask, "My love. Did they treat you badly? At Devizes?"

She was silent for so long he thought she must have drifted off. Then she had said, "I don't wish to speak of it. It is in the past and done with. Do you understand?"

"Yes, my love. I understand. Done with."

"Good." She settled against him, and soon he heard her snoring very faintly.

He'd not raised the subject again. But a few days later after their arrival at Ashby-de-la-Zouche, Bob from Devizes Castle had arrived at the gate and asked to be admitted into their household. Eleanor had seconded his request. He had been kind to her, she said. William had instantly complied—if Eleanor had wanted the whole garrison, he would have complied—and, talking with the man a day or so later, he'd learned enough to sicken him. His wife to be carted to Devizes Castle, shut up in a cell, treated as a madwoman—all so that Mortimer could control her lands, with Queen Isabella's connivance. What had happened to the woman who had decried Hugh le Despenser the younger for his treatment of widows?

With Bob's revelation, which had only confirmed his deepest fears, William had placed aside the last of his misgivings about the Earl of Kent's scheme. Mad it might be, but wasn't it madder to sit and wait patiently for the young king to shake off his yolk?

The Earl of Kent, he heard from their go-between, was making progress. The Pope himself had encouraged him to do all he could to deliver his deposed brother from prison. In Paris, Henry de Beaumont had agreed to help. Donald of Mar, the second Edward's devoted friend and now third to the throne of Scotland, would give money and military aid. The Archbishop of York had five thousand pounds, belonging to Hugh le Despenser the younger, to give to the cause. At the coronation of Queen Philippa, Lady Vescy's confessor had pledged his lady's support. The Bishop of London had joined the Earl of Kent.

William still had doubts that the old king was alive, although he wished for Eleanor's sake that it was true. But if all the discontented and the disinherited— some of them who had loved the old king, some of whom had been attached to the Despensers, some of whom had lost their lands through the Scottish truce, some of whom had been oppressed by Isabella and Mortimer, some of whom were simply disgusted with the new regime—could be brought together, Mortimer would fall.

In the meantime, the king had called a Parliament for Winchester, to meet on March 11. Zouche, though reluctant to leave his wife, had decided to obey the summons. It would be a chance to see the Earl of Kent in person, a chance to see who else might be receptive to the plot.

He had not told Eleanor about the Earl of Kent. Though he trusted her absolutely, he was certain that she would urge him to caution, and he was not of a disposition now to heed such urgings. But when Mortimer fell he would take such joy in telling her the news...

Beside him, Eleanor stirred. "William?" she yawned. "Can't you sleep?"

"Supper was a little rich," he said. "Go back to sleep, sweetheart. I'll be asleep soon myself."

Parliament was well attended, the recent coronation of Queen Philippa having lifted the country's sagging morale and brought many of the lords back to court, banners flying and their horses bedecked in their masters' heraldic colors. The Earl of Kent, flanked by his outsize retinue, hissed into Zouche's ear as he passed into Winchester Castle with his much more modest following, "I have seen him at Corfe Castle! Oh, not face to face, but close enough to know his unmistakable physique. All will be in readiness soon."

Having received this communication, William was tempted to turn back to Ashby and Eleanor. He had been deeply honored when he had received his first summons to Parliament some years ago, but since then he had found it to be a rather tedious business for the most part. This Parliament, he thought, would be little different. There were the usual petitions to deal with, none of them controversial, and there was talk about the ongoing problem of the king's French homage, King Philip, after due consideration, having decided that King Edward's homage had been insufficiently far-reaching. To smooth things over, the English were proposing a royal double marriage, between two of Philip's children and Edward's brother and sister. But all of this was still in the negotiation stage and did not take up too much parliamentary time. Most controversial, it seemed, would be the king's demand for taxes on the common people and on the clergy. No lord wanted to go back to his tenants with such news.

On the morning of March 14, William and his fellow peers were in their places, grumbling about the taxes and waiting for the king to arrive, when the Earl of March strode in. "There is a traitor among you," he said. "This morning, the Earl of Kent was arrested for treason."

William's heart stopped.

"Parliament is adjourned today," Mortimer continued. "It will resume this time tomorrow. Then we will try this enemy of the realm."

It was as if the lords were standing in tar. Too stunned to move or speak, they were looking at each other vacantly when the king's sergeant at arms, the only person in the great hall moving at a normal pace it seemed, touched William from behind. "Lord Zouche, you must come with me. You are under arrest for treason yourself."

At Ashby-de-la-Zouche, Eleanor stretched in her bed lazily, knowing that she ought to be attending to her duties as lady of the manor but too comfortably sleepy to will herself to get out of bed. She had, she hoped, an excellent excuse for her lassitude. Her monthly course for January had delayed itself, most obligingly, until after she and William had had several very busy days together. Since then, there had been no bleeding at all, and whatever else the vicissitudes of Eleanor's life were, she had always been able to count on her monthly course, save for when she was with child. What news for William when he came home from Parliament! But such a gift from the Lord required thanks, and Eleanor reluctantly eased herself out of bed and began to dress to attend morning prayers at the manor's tiny chapel.

She had other things to be thankful for as well. Three weeks before, she and William had gone before the King's Bench and received their pardon for their misdeeds—or, more strictly speaking, Eleanor's. At the same time, her men Tom and Hugh Dalby had been released from Newgate and were safely at Ashby with Eleanor. Benedict de Fulsham, still in possession of the stolen goods—Mortimer had not been the least interested in recovering them once Eleanor signed over her lands—remained under mainprise, but the king's men seemed inclined to leave him alone.

Gladys fastened her new gown on her—William had really spent too much on new robes for her after her release, but she had not had the heart to tell him so—and began to arrange her headdress. "The country around here agrees with you, my lady. I have never seen your cheeks bloom so well."

"It is my lord Zouche who agrees with me, Gladys. He is so kind and loving."

A knock sounded at the door. Eleanor looked around and saw her young chaplain, John de Barneby. She smiled. "John, am I that late? I am afraid I have been very derelict this morning. Pray excuse me."

"It is not that, my lady. Some of my lord Zouche's men have come back, after riding all day and night. They say—"

"Lord Zouche? He is well, yes? Tell me!"

John de Barneby gripped her by the shoulder and led her to a stool. "My lady, he has been arrested."

"Arrested," Eleanor repeated slowly.

"For treason, my lady."

The Earl of Kent stared at the letter that the Earl of March was dangling in front of him like a baited fishhook. "Yes," he said dully. "That is my seal. I do not deny it."

"You do not?"

"No."

Mortimer flipped open the letter, written not in a clerkly hand but a feminine one. "'Sir knight, worshipful and dear brother, if you please, I pray heartily that you are of good comfort, for I shall ordain for you that soon you shall come out of prison, and be delivered of that disease in which you find yourself. Your lordship should know that I have the assent of almost all the great lords in England, with all their apparel, that is to say, with armor, and with treasure without number, in order to maintain and help your quarrel so you shall be king again as you were before.'" The Earl of March looked toward the royal coroner, Robert Howel, acting as the judge. "Sir, I told you at the opening of this trial that the Earl of Kent was plotting with many others to impair our lord the king's estate by delivering from prison Sir Edward of Caernarfon, sometime King of England, who was put down from his royalty by common assent by all the lords of England. This letter, sealed by the earl himself, as he has admitted, proves my case. He is a traitor to the realm, and should be adjudged as such."

"And so he shall be," said Robert Howel, nearly as white-faced as the Earl of Kent himself. "The will of this court is that you shall lose both life and limb, and that your heirs shall be disinherited forevermore, save the grace of our lord the king."

There was a faint buzz of relief in Parliament at the sound of those last words. The king would never let his own uncle die for attempting to rescue his own father from captivity. There would be a fine, perhaps, or an exile in France, perhaps a salutary stay in the Tower. Never death.

"The Earl of Kent has confessed more freely," said Roger, waving a paper in front of Queen Isabella. "A veritable shower of names here. Ingelram Berenger, old Despenser's knight. William la Zouche—no news there, of course. William de Cliff. Fulk FitzWarren. Donald, the Earl of Mar. Henry de Beaumont. Isabella de Vescy; I thought she had more sense. The Archbishop of York, even. Traitors, all of them!" Mortimer chuckled. "Kent has promised to walk through Winchester or London, or anywhere it pleases the king, wearing only a shirt, with a rope around his neck, if the king will spare him. I'll give him a rope around his neck, all right."

"And we caught him," Isabella giggled. "We set him up, we showed him that tall peasant who looked so much like my wretched husband at a distance, and he believed it. The fool!" She reached for Mortimer and tried to pull him down on the bed. "We caught him."

"Yes, my dear, we caught him," said Mortimer patiently. Isabella's voice was slurred; could she be drunk this early in the day? She was drinking much more wine than was good for her lately, but this was a new record for her. Besides the sober person's irritation with the tipsy, Mortimer also felt the industrious person's irritation with the slothful, for he himself had spent the morning very efficiently interrogating Kent while Isabella was swilling her Bordeaux. She hadn't even changed out of her dressing gown yet. "Pull yourself together if you can, Isabella. We need to keep your son from showing him any mercy. Thank God that softhearted wife of his is at Woodstock."

"Not until you pay me," said Isabella. She was pouting prettily, but Mortimer also knew how fast her mood could change to one of anger. "The Earl of Kent was—is—will have been—is—my brother-in-law, and he is my first cousin as well, the son of my sweet aunt Margaret! I might ask for mercy on him myself, if you don't pay me. Because we caught him, Roger, and all those other traitors, and it was my idea as much as yours, you know." She giggled again. "It was such a good one, Roger, wasn't it?" She wriggled out of her dressing gown and smiled at him.

"Oh, all right," said Mortimer irritably.

"I will pardon him, I tell you! He's my uncle, damn you! I know he meant me no harm. He only wanted to help his brother, as John would me, I know."

"You must not pardon him," said Isabella impatiently. Her head throbbed from the morning's imbibing, and repeating herself every few minutes to her stubborn son was not helping. "He wanted to dethrone you, not to rescue your father! He was angry because he did not have the power and influence over you that the much wiser Earl of March has."

"He felt guilty because he helped push my father off his throne, and he wanted to make amends. Can't you see that?"

"No! Look at those followers of his. Half of them were Despenser creatures, who were lucky not to be put to death with them."

"Henry de Beaumont, a Despenser creature? He quarreled with them, and you know it. William la Zouche, a Despenser creature? He captured the younger one, for God's sake! He'd still be loyal to us if Mortimer hadn't arrested my cousin Eleanor."

"But he is not loyal to us now, Ned. None of those men are, whatever their reason. They will put you down if given half a chance, and you know it. If you pardon the Earl of Kent, they will take you for nothing more than a fool, and you will be in the same position as your father was, never breathing easily for a moment. You do not want that, Ned, trust me. You do not want to humiliate your wife and children by being a weak king, as you and I were humiliated by your father. Never would you want that." Isabella's lovely blue eyes welled with tears. "Remember why I came to France in the first place! I was so unhappy. And to think that your uncle would have put my husband back on the throne—or himself—perhaps to shut me up for life like Eleanor of Aquitaine!"

"You're no Eleanor of Aquitaine, Mother."

"You must care nothing for me, Ned. Nothing, after I risked so much for your sake."

Edward grunted and moved toward the door. "What shall you do?" demanded his mother, wiping her eyes.

"I don't know."

The Earl of March having read the Earl of Kent's confession to Parliament that Friday afternoon, the Earl of Kent was begging for his life. "Your grace, I meant you no harm. I only wished to free my brother; he was kind to me always. Your father, your grace, lonely and forgotten in Corfe Castle! Spare me, and I will walk through the streets in my shirt, as I said. I will do anything. I will reside abroad, give up my estates, go to prison—anything! Your grace, have mercy on me."

Roger Mortimer glanced down at the beseeching earl. "Your grace, if you have mercy upon this creature you will endanger yourself, endanger your crown, endanger your heir so soon to be born. He can plot aboard, plot in prison, plot without his estates. You will be setting yourself up for your own destruction." In a lower voice, audible only to the queen mother and Edward, he said, "Your grace, do you want to be the king your father was, or your grandfather? Your grandfather would not have given way to pity. He would order this man to be hung, drawn, and quartered straightaway. With him, the good of the realm always took precedent over all else."

Edward drew a breath, and the great hall was so still that everyone there could hear him do so. "I cannot grant your request, my lord. You are guilty of treason, and as you are so close to the crown, your treason is more dangerous than most. You should have shared your suspicions about my father with me instead of plotting against me with men whose loyalty to the realm is uncertain at best. But I will grant you beheading rather than a traitor's death."

The Earl of Kent stood up, looking suddenly so much like his own imposing father that the older men in the room started. "So be the will of God. May He have mercy on your soul, Edward."

"We must act quickly," said Mortimer the next day to the queen mother. "Your son has gone to Woodstock to see his wife, and you know after some pillow talk he'll relent and commute the death sentence." He handed her a paper. "This order to the bailiffs of Winchester will take care of him, if it's signed by you."

Isabella glanced at the paper indifferently. "So he is to die Monday? What if the king comes back before then?"

"Then we'll have to get another order, won't we? But I doubt he'll leave his love nest that early, particularly as the strain here has been so great for him." There was a contemptuous look on the earl's face that few mothers would have borne with.

Isabella merely shrugged and signed the parchment.

Isabella and Mortimer had not forgotten the Earl of Kent's wife and small children, particularly since the unfortunate countess, whose handwriting was more certain than her husband's, had written the letter read in Parliament at Kent's dictation. They were ordered to be taken to Salisbury Castle, sans the countess's jewels, and imprisoned there indefinitely. The jewels were to be sent to the king.

The Countess of Kent was nine months pregnant.

On Monday, March 19, the Earl of Kent stood in the marketplace at Winchester wearing only his shirt. The king was not there, having not yet returned from Woodstock, nor was the dowager queen, who was lying in a drunken stupor behind her rich bed curtains.

Nor, to the Earl of March's chagrin, was the executioner present. Nor the deputy executioner. Nor the butcher, nor anyone who had experience in wielding an ax. None of the knights present would move against a peer of the realm. No one wanted to kill the first Edward's golden-haired youngest son.

The day dragged on. Finally, toward Vespers, a murdering sewer cleaner found at the Marshalsea prison in London, offered a pardon for his life in exchange for taking Edmund of Woodstock's, mounted the scaffold self-consciously and diffidently ordered the earl to put his head on the block. "Here?" he said, raising the ax and looking tentatively at the earl's neck. "Or lower?"

"There," snapped the Earl of March. "Give him time to cross himself; don't you know anything?" He nodded approvingly as the amateur executioner swung the ax and severed the head with one blow. "Get it and hold it up now, man, don't be squeamish. Behold the head of a traitor!" he called.

The crowd only stared, save for those who wept.

CHAPTER 27

▼

APRIL 1330 TO NOVEMBER 1330

"Thank you, your grace, for allowing me to see you alone."

"You need not look around you, Lady Despenser. There are no spies about."

Eleanor, who had indeed been looking around her warily as she entered the king's chamber at Woodstock, blushed. "Your grace, I shall not take up your time needlessly. I am here to ask that you release my husband."

"He is a traitor, Lady Despenser."

"He is not, your grace. I know he had no intention of removing you from the throne."

"How do you know what was in his mind? Were you involved in this scheme too?"

"No. He told me nothing; perhaps he thought I had been in enough trouble with the crown already." Eleanor smiled, but the king continued to stare at her levelly. "But I know my husband. He was loyal to your father, and he has been loyal to you. It was Hugh he opposed when he joined forces with the queen, not my dear uncle. And it was Mortimer he opposed when he joined with the Earl of Kent. Not your grace."

In coming to Woodstock to beg for William, she had counted on two things: that the king was becoming weary of his harness and that he had executed Kent with the greatest of misgivings. What if she were wrong? Of all the men she had known, Eleanor had never met one as difficult to read as this young king. What if he admired Mortimer and had had no compunctions about sending Kent to the block?

Edward said, "I will consider it, my lady, and give you an answer in a day or two."

This being better than nothing, Eleanor thanked him. Then she ventured, "I understand the queen is with child. I hope she is feeling well?"

"Very well."

"I held your grace when you were newborn, you know. It seems strange to think that you will be a father yourself in two months' time."

"It seems strange indeed." Edward smiled. Then his tone changed abruptly. "Tell me, Lady Despenser. Did your husband ever believe the rumor that my father was not dead?"

"I do not know. I never heard it until I heard of William's arrest."

"You were probably the closest person in the world to my father, after Lord Despenser and the Earl of Cornwall. Do you believe the rumor?"

"No, much as I would like to."

"Why not?"

"It is an illogical reason, your grace."

"Women are illogical, they say. Tell me."

She dropped her eyes. "The night I later heard he died, I had a nightmare. About him. I had not had one about him before, and I have never had once since. I knew that he was in dreadful trouble, and I could not help him. I longed to so badly, but I could not move a step to help him. I know, your grace, that it sounds foolish, like witchcraft even. But it is what I dreamed that night."

"It is what I dreamed that night too, Lady Despenser." Edward turned away from Eleanor and looked out at the window to where Queen Philippa and her ladies were strolling, or in the queen's case waddling, in the April sunlight. "Find some mainprisors for your husband and send them to me as soon as you find them. And then he will be free."

"I saw my old charge, Lady Despenser, leaving as I was coming," said William de Montacute a few minutes later. "I suppose she was here about her husband?"

"I said I would release him if she could find mainprisors."

"Mortimer didn't interfere?"

"He and my mother are out with their falcons. I said I'd keep Philippa company here instead of going with them. I'm doing a lot of that lately."

"Fatherhood does have its advantages," said William. "Even prospective fatherhood."

"I should have said no to her, but after she gave up her lands to the crown I felt guilty, even if she did act of her own free will."

"You believe that?"

"Why, the document she signed said so."

"She was coerced into signing it by Mortimer, Edward. After you signed the order to release her from the Tower, she was shut up in Devizes Castle on the sly by him. She'd still be there if she hadn't nearly died and decided to give in to him."

"I didn't know that." He winced.

"Edward. Other than your lady the queen, there is no one in the kingdom more loyal to you than me. I would risk my life for you. You know that."

"Yes."

"Then you will forgive me when I tell you that there is a lot you don't know, and it is high time you knew it. You're like your father in that way, you tend to shut out unpleasant things."

"I do not!"

"Like your mother's adultery?"

"I know she miscarried of Mortimer's bastard child. You needn't rub my nose in it."

"I'm not. But Ned, you knew that they were lovers months, years, after everyone else did. Of course, you were very young when it started. And part of it, of course, is that you're the king. People don't speak freely in front of you. But part of it is that you'd rather not know."

Edward flicked his hand resentfully. "So what else would I rather not know?"

"The Earl of Kent."

"William, he was a traitor. I know that they were highhanded in executing him while I was away. There's not a day I don't feel guilt and sorrow over that. But at least his death shall serve as a lesson for those who try treason in the future."

"A lesson! He was entrapped by Mortimer, Edward. The friar who told him your father was alive was Mortimer's man. So were the men who took Kent to Corfe Castle and showed him someone who at a distance resembled your father. The letter the earl wrote was to a Mortimer creature. His followers—the Archbishop of York and Berenger and Zouche and the rest—were there honestly, but there would have been no conspiracy if it had not been for Mortimer."

Edward stared at William. "Who told you this?"

"People brag, and their servants listen. One of them thought you should know. So he came to me."

"I ordered my uncle executed at Mortimer and Mother's urging for treason they tricked him into committing. I've arrested, or tried to arrest, three dozen others who got dragged into this affair."

"Yes."

"Why? Why did Mortimer do it?"

Montacute shrugged. "He wanted to intimidate his enemies. Putting Henry of Lancaster to death would be too risky, even after his rebellion, because of his allies. One Saint Lancaster is enough, after all. But your uncle was less influential. He was a gullible man, God rest his soul, and he's always felt guilty about joining your mother against your father. Poor Kent was the perfect bait."

"What else, Montacute? What else don't I know?"

William hesitated, wondering if he was not about to go too far. Telling the king what he knew about Lady Despenser and the Earl of Kent was one thing; telling what else he knew was another. Yet without the telling, how else to force the king's hand?

"Your father, Edward. He didn't die of a fever. He was murdered at Mortimer's orders by his men Gurney, Ogle, and Maltravers after there were attempts to free him from Berkeley Castle. Some of the men who helped have been talking, or raving's more like it."

Edward sank down in the window seat. Barely moving his lips, he asked, "How? Poisoned? Smothered? Choked?"

"It is only a rumor, what I have heard. But it is horrid to tell."

"Tell me."

"They wanted to leave no mark, and they didn't trust anyone to make up a poison for them. So they took a cooking spit, heated it, and used it to burn out his insides. Through his fundament."

Edward stumbled toward the fireplace and began vomiting. William held his head until he could retch no more, then helped him to the window seat and put his hand on his shoulder as he wept silently. Finally, he whispered, "I took his crown, William. I might as well say I took his life."

"Mortimer and your mother took his crown, your grace. You acted for the best by accepting it for yourself, because he had so many shortcomings as a ruler. You did not know they would serve him so."

"No." Edward let William wipe his face with a towel from the nearby washbasin. "But did I ever bother myself with his welfare? Did I ever demand to be taken to Kenilworth to see him, or Berkeley? Did I ever write him a letter? The truth was, he'd become an embarrassment to me, with his favorites and his failures, and I was glad to have him out of the way. Out of sight, out of mind."

"You were so young."

"Not so young that I couldn't have at least tried to see him. Why, my brother and sisters asked about him, wanted to visit him! Not me."

"No matter what you did, Edward, they would have killed him anyway."

"Perhaps. But he died believing that I cared naught about what happened to him." Edward looked out toward the garden at Philippa. "If I thought a son of mine would treat me as I did him, I'd wish him dead in the womb right now."

"Do not even think such a horrid thing, Edward."

"A bad son, and a worse king. I've stood by as my father was murdered, stood by as my uncle was murdered—nay, I passed the death sentence on him myself! The people must hold me in contempt, Mortimer's puppet!"

"They don't, Edward. Truly." William looked out the window too. How much more time would they have alone? Probably not much. He quickened his voice. "But they might, someday, if you don't act soon. You spoke about the need to before—"

"I spoke about it before, and then Philippa got with child, and I've been worthless ever since," Edward grimaced. "But how to act? Half the people in my household are spies, I think. It's not that I could raise an army against Mortimer without anyone noticing. And he's got his horde of his with him wherever he goes."

"I haven't a plan either," admitted William. "But now you know fully what Mortimer is capable of, we should start laying the ground for one. Whom do you trust, your grace? I can talk to them."

"My cousin, Edward de Bohun. Robert Ufford. William de Clinton. John Neville." Edward shook his head. "Isn't that pitiful? In all my household, only four besides you that I can name with no hesitation whatsoever."

"That's enough for a start. In the meantime, you must dissemble. If Mortimer wants to give himself more land and titles, let him. Be obliging and passive."

"That won't be hard," Edward said bitterly. "But what of the Earl of Kent's followers? The Archbishop of York, for one, is scheduled for trial soon. He is to come here shortly."

"I would think that Mortimer would have had others executed by now if he's going to. He's out to harass and intimidate the others, and he can do that just as well by keeping some in prison and getting the others' trials dragged out. Killing them all would create more enemies, just as your father created enemies after Boroughbridge. But we must keep a careful eye on what goes on. Now let's go out to Philippa, so Mortimer suspects nothing when he arrives."

Edward nodded and slowly made his way out to the garden, where Philippa and her ladies, along with Montacute's own wife, had ceased their walk and had settled down to work on a tapestry for the royal nursery. Even from a distance, Philippa glowed; pregnancy seemed to be her optimal state. His mother had warned Edward with a hint of malice in her voice that pregnant women were volatile and moody, but Philippa had been more even-tempered than ever. "Why, what on earth is wrong, Edward? You look positively gray."

"I have had a tedious morning," he lied. "Papers."

"Are you sure nothing is wrong, Ned?"

Philippa's phlegmatic personality hid her sharp powers of observation, Edward knew, although Mortimer and the queen had never understood this. "We will talk later," he promised. "I want to go for a walk alone for just a short time."

He did not have far to go, only into a wooded area close to the manor house. There, soon after Edward's younger sister Eleanor had been born at Woodstock, his father had taken him for a ride on the grounds and carved him a whistle, taken from a branch of the tree Edward stood before. He knew it because of the names that had been carved into it: *Edward Rex*. And below it, carved in a much more awkward writing, *Ned*. He could almost feel his own small hand, being guided by a larger one, writing the word. "There," his father had told him, admiring their handiwork. "Now it's our special tree."

His father had loved him. And he had utterly abandoned his father. Not because of any grand principle, but simply because it had been the easiest thing to do at the time. No matter what kind of king he grew into, no matter what kind of man he grew into, he would never be able to erase that item from his conscience. And there was nothing he could do to make amends, nothing that would alter his father's last terrifying moments in Berkeley Castle. The Earl of Kent had thought he had been given the chance to redeem himself, but he had been wrong, cruelly wrong. And Edward had had him killed for believing, irrationally but irresistibly, that he could do so.

The king leaned his head against the tree and wept.

In June, Philippa gave birth to a fine boy, naturally named Edward after his father (or his late grandfather, Eleanor hoped). Eleanor, though by no means on the list of notables immediately notified of the birth, had found out about it fairly quickly, for she and William and the children had gone to spend some time at her manor of Caversham, not far from Woodstock.

Isabella and Mortimer were not fool enough to skimp on ceremonies for the new heir, and by the end of July word had drifted down to Caversham of the young queen's magnificent churching. "Her robe was purple velvet embroidered with golden squirrels, trimmed with miniver and ermine, William. Doesn't that sound beautiful?"

"Actually, my dear, it sounds a little warm for July."

Eleanor took her pillow and swatted William. "She also had a robe of red velvet."

William patted Eleanor's belly, which amply indicated that Eleanor had been correct in the spring when she thought she was with child. "Maybe we can manage a squirrel or two for you at your churching, my dear."

"No." Eleanor smiled and settled back into William's arms; she was lying with her back to his chest, the only way they could embrace without her belly getting in the way. "I don't need new robes, William. Just you there."

"I hope I won't have to stand trial then."

"I pray not."

Eleanor had found no difficulty in assembling mainprisors to stand for William, and though Mortimer had grumbled when she brought them to Woodstock, he had not gone back on the king's word. Since William had been released in April, he and Eleanor had been on tenterhooks, dreading the day when he would have to stand trial, but weeks had gone by without any summons arriving. They were at least luckier than Edward de Monthermer, Eleanor's half-brother, who had been implicated in the Earl of Kent's plot somehow and had been locked up in Windsor Castle since March. Eleanor, learning of his imprisonment, had tried to obtain his release too, as had her sister Elizabeth de Burgh and Edward's stepmother, Lady Hastings, but each of them, even Elizabeth, had received a chilly response. (Eleanor and Elizabeth's sister Margaret d'Audley was in no position to ask the king for favors; her husband had been involved with Lancaster's rebellion.) Ingelmar Berenger was in prison too, as were a handful of others. The rest were either awaiting future court appearances, like the Archbishop of York, or safely across the English Channel.

None of those remaining in England felt safe. Eleanor and William found themselves speaking more guardedly to everyone, except to each other, Gladys, and a few besides. Who knew who might be serving as a spy for Mortimer, waiting for one of them to make the misstep that would put William on the gallows, Eleanor back in prison? So in the Zouche household that summer of 1330, and in many another household, the public talk was of Philippa's churching and of little Edward's magnificent cradle. Not of the Earl of Kent's posthumous son, imprisoned in Salisbury Castle with the rest of his family. Not of the Earl of Kent's lands, granted either to the Earl of March or his followers. Not of rumors that men in Wales and men in France were plotting against Roger Mortimer. Not, certainly, of the keen disappointment that many felt when the risings came to naught. By not taking any action against his enemies that summer, Mortimer had succeeded very well in terrorizing them into inaction.

In September, Eleanor bore William a boy, whom they named after William. That same month, Mortimer summoned a great council to meet in October at Nottingham Castle.

It started with Mortimer booting the nearly blind Henry of Lancaster out of Nottingham Castle, where he had naturally expected to stay. "You should have seen him!" he told Isabella, chuckling, as they lay in bed that night. "He was red with anger. He was trying to fix me with that cold stare of his as he left the castle, being led by his squires, but of course he couldn't see well enough to tell me from his own mother. So he glared at one of his men's horses!"

Isabella did not find this as amusing as she once might have. "Roger, do you truly think he means you harm? After all, he went to France on the king's business, which we sent him on ourselves."

"And probably took the opportunity to meet with some of the whoresons plotting against me there. It's true he's been quiet since he came back to England, and that's what worries me about him. He's been too quiet. In any case, I'm happier with him a league away from the castle, in the town." He slipped his hand under Isabella's pillow and came up with a large ring of keys. "See these? They are the keys to the castle. They're to be with you at all times. Under your pillow at night where I put them."

"It is not just Lancaster you are worried about, then?"

"I'm worried about the whole damn bunch of them," said the earl succinctly. "I don't like those friends of your son, for one thing. Montacute, the son of your husband's old favorite. Your husband's nephew Edward de Bohun—why, he was with your husband until he and Despenser left Neath Abbey! Ralph Stafford, Robert Ufford, William de Clinton, John Neville—they're all too polite to me these days. God, if I could only hang them all!"

"Roger, what about my son?"

Mortimer frowned. He had found the weeks after the Earl of Kent's death, where Isabella alternated between being tipsily maudlin and tipsily lascivious, to be quite tedious, as he had never had much use for tears and had disliked being required to perform on command like a damned stallion. Since the birth of little Edward, though, the queen mother had been temperate, on the whole. Looking at her now, her eyes alert and inquisitive, Mortimer found himself missing their alcoholic glaze. "What of him, my dear?"

"He will be eighteen next month. You cannot really expect him to sit by quietly forever while you and I run the kingdom, you know. Do you want to hang him, too?"

"Of course not," Mortimer lied. "But I put him on the throne, and I expect to be treated well for it. Not to have his band of just-fledged knights plotting against me."

"William de Montacute is a knight banneret. So are Bohun and Ufford and Clinton."

"I am well aware of their standing in the king's household, Isabella. Now let me ask you. Are you with me or against me?"

"With you!" Isabella laid her head on Mortimer's shoulder and gazed up at him with her beautiful eyes. "With you, always. But I am Edward's mother, and he is your king. You must not forget that. You can continue to guide him, if you will only do so tactfully and not anger him. I have seen him look more and more annoyed lately, when your servants eat in the hall besides his and when you remain seated in his presence and walk beside him as his equal. Show some humility with him, as he grows older, and you will go far."

"They are spreading rumors around that I killed your fool husband."

"But you did have him killed," pointed out Isabella.

"Of course, and I'd do it again. But that doesn't mean that I want the whole kingdom to know about it from those meddling puppies." Roger sighed. "I'm fed up with talking about the matter, and I'm tired to boot. I'll deal with Montacute and the rest of the lot tomorrow."

He rolled on his side and began planning, as he always did in those moments before sleeping. Isabella was right: the king was too much of a man to be discounted for long. So what to do about him? He certainly couldn't be deposed like his father, nor was he likely to be willing to let Roger govern in his name, as the second Edward had done with Despenser the younger. For the old king had loved Hugh le Despenser, loved and trusted him, and if there were any two emotions the new king did not feel toward Roger Mortimer, they were love and trust. Two men could not rule England if one was unwilling. One would have to be pushed aside. But how? Roger decided to think the matter over the next time he went hunting. Hunting, he had found, clarified his thoughts.

Hunting. King William Rufus! Shot by an arrow by hunting. To this day, no one knew whether it had been by accident or design.

If the king were to meet with a hunting accident soon, he would be survived by a baby boy. A baby, in whose name Roger could rule for sixteen, seventeen years or more. By the time the baby developed a mind of his own (and with his infant character formed by Roger, how much of a mind of his own would he have?), Roger at sixty would be ready for a well-deserved retirement anyway.

He wouldn't rush things, of course. There was plenty of time to arrange it, time too to make sure the little heir survived the usual illnesses of babyhood intact. But when the right time came, there would be one of his crack Welsh archers, dressed as a common churl. Accidentally shooting toward the king...

Mortimer rolled back over and for the first time in many nights, reached for Isabella with genuine lust. History, he reflected, was full of useful lessons.

Bright and early the next morning, October 19, he summoned the king's friends to him, one by one. But he might as well have been interrogating slugs, for each stood silent before him. All, that is, except for Montacute, the last of the lot. "Plot? I know nothing of a plot," Montacute said. "I have done, and will do, nothing inconsistent with my duty to the king."

Then he turned as sluglike as the rest.

"I'll let them be for now," Mortimer said later to Isabella.

"Why?"

"I've got nothing to use against them. Nothing but hints, here and there. Nothing I can take to Parliament as we did with the Earl of Kent."

Isabella shuddered. Mortimer stared moodily out of the window. The castle sat high and isolated atop a crag, but God only knew what the people in the bustling little town below were hatching. When would he be allowed to rest and simply enjoy his wealth and power? "But we'll have something soon," he said finally. "Give them a day or so, and they'll go the way of stupid Edmund."

After their meeting with Mortimer, William de Montacute and his companions deemed it best to spend the night in the town, not the castle. There being no place large enough to hold all of them, they had gone their separate ways to find lodgings. William having found a tiny room and seen his belongings bestowed there, he went downstairs to eat, hoping that the ale was better than the accommodations.

Since leaving the castle, he had had the sense of being followed, and his suspicions were confirmed when a man plunked himself on the bench beside him. "William Eland," he said. "You've seen me at the castle."

"Right," agreed Montacute warily. The man was in the guard there, he believed.

"Beautiful, isn't she? I've known that castle from a boy, my lord. I know her better than the back of my own hand."

William Eland was not an old man, only a middle-aged one, and Montacute wondered why he was beginning to reminisce in this elderly manner. More than that, he wondered why Eland was making him in particular his victim. And why was he calling the castle *she*, like a damn boat, when it was on as dry land as it could be? But his mother had taught him to be polite to bores, so he said patiently, "It has a fascinating history, I am sure. But—"

"Let me buy you an ale, sir."

Lady Montacute had also taught her son to graciously accept an offer of hospitality, especially when one was strapped for cash, as he so often was. "Thank you."

He sipped his ale and listened to Eland go on and on about Nottingham Castle. She had been built in wood by William the Conqueror, then rebuilt in stone by the second Henry. She had a very impressive complement of garderobes. ("Indeed," Montacute said politely, through clenched teeth.) She had an underground passage to her, almost obscured by brush, that only Eland seemed to know about these days...

Montacute's ale crashed to the floor. "A secret passage?"

Eland nodded and swallowed his ale with relief, grateful that the young knight had finally gotten the point, for Eland had been beginning to find him uncommonly dense. "Shall I show it to you, sir?"

"Is the king no better?"

Pancius de Controne, physician first to the second Edward and now to his son, shook his head lugubriously at the queen mother. "My assistant is leeching him now, your grace, and I have given him physic, but he must be left to rest afterward."

"It is so odd to find him sick, and so suddenly."

"I have always believed this castle was a particularly unhealthy one, your grace."

Master Controne had yet to find a healthy castle in all of England, Isabella knew, and would have much preferred that the court betook itself to stay in his native Lombardy. The physician added, "He complained of feeling unwell last night too, your grace, but thought it was nothing at the time. He should have let me know then. It is best to catch these imbalances of the system at the earliest possible moment." He squinted at Isabella. "You are looking pale yourself, your grace."

"I do not feel poorly."

"Still, I would recommend that you not put yourself at risk."

Isabella nodded and went back to her chamber, where Mortimer and the Bishop of Lincoln, Henry Burghersh, Chancellor of England, were deep in conversation. Hugh de Turplington, the royal steward and an old friend of Roger's, was also there, as were Simon de Bereford, escheator south of the Trent; and Oliver de Ingham, the seneschal of Gascony. Richard de Monmouth, Roger's squire and his cellmate at the Tower of London, was in attendance upon his master. "How fares the king?" asked the bishop politely.

"His physician is having him leeched."

"Just getting those creatures off me always does me a world of good," said the bishop brightly. "So, my lord. About these conspirators."

"We must imprison them," said Mortimer. "They are dangerous to us and to the king, for they fill his head with wild notions. He is impressionable that way, as was his father." Mortimer hesitated. Criticizing the second Edward was always safe with the queen mother around, but comparing the third Edward to him was somewhat risky. "Of course, his youth excuses a great deal. But until he grows more experienced in the ways of the world, these men must be kept out of his way. We must find some excuse to detain them until—"

There was a cry and a crash, and the queen's door flew open. As it did, Richard de Crombek, an usher, fell across the threshold, bleeding to death. Then two dozen young men, brandishing maces and swords, stormed into the chamber.

Isabella would live to be age sixty-two. Not for one day in the next twenty-eight years would she forget those next few minutes. Hugh de Turplington rushing at John Neville and being killed with a single blow from his mace. Richard de Monmouth lashing out frantically with the only weapon he had, a dagger, and being slain with a stab to the heart by Robert Walkfare. Simon de Bereford and Oliver de Ingham being wrestled to the floor and bound with rope. The Bishop of Lincoln fleeing in the direction of the privy. William de Montacute and a companion whose face Isabella could not make out cornering Roger and holding him at sword point. Herself, springing from the chair to which she had seemed frozen and rushing to Mortimer's side, where she recognized Montacute's companion—the king himself. "Fair son!" she screamed. "Have pity on the gentle Mortimer! Do not harm him!"

Edward shoved her away impatiently and she fell to her knees, then slumped to the ground, only half-conscious of the events that were taking place around her. Mortimer, bound and gagged, being dragged away, along with Bereford and Ingham. Men running out of the room, yelling, "In the king's name! Mortimer is the king's prisoner! Surrender, and you shall not be harmed!" The Bishop of Lincoln, dripping filth from his unsuccessful attempt to escape via the privy, being led away politely by two young, half-grinning squires. The king's physician and Edward de Bohun, her nephew by marriage, hauling her to her feet and taking her to the king's own chamber. Her ladies and damsels, who had been huddled in an anteroom crying the whole time, being brought to her. "She is to be taken to Berkhamstead Castle at first light. No harm will come to her or to you. Pack her things for the morrow."

Someone forced some wine down her throat, and her mind began to uncloud. "Roger! Let me see Roger one last time before—"

"You cannot do that, aunt."

"I demand to see him!"

"The king has forbidden it." Bohun's voice was very polite. "And your grace, the king's word is truly the law now. Not yours, never again."

"I wish I had been there, Eleanor. Everyone in town was getting up when the Earl of Lancaster's men rode in, announcing that Mortimer had been taken and the king would henceforth rule on his own. It was sheer pandemonium after that—sheer joy. Men buying each other drinks—it's a wonder there's any ale left in Nottingham. Women throwing flowers at the king's feet when he came out himself to greet the crowds in front of the castle. William Eland showing every child in Nottingham the passage Montacute and his men came through. The Earl of Lancaster throwing his cap in the air like a boy."

"What will happen to Mortimer?"

"The king was for executing him then and there, they say, but Lancaster warned him that he should have a proper trial before Parliament. So a proper trial he will have, at Westminster in November. He's been taken to Leicester, but he'll soon be moved to the Tower to await trial."

"With an adequate guard this time, I hope."

"With a very adequate guard."

"And Isabella?"

"The king has made it known that he will not tolerate anything being said against her. I suppose he believes that what will happen to Mortimer will be punishment enough for her."

"I almost pity her," said Eleanor. "*Almost.*" She shook her head. "And to think that they should have fallen so suddenly. It all seems like a dream still."

"Doesn't it? All those plots, and what did it take to overthrow Mortimer? Two dozen men and a long-forgotten passage. The king playing sick so he could open the doors inside. Everything planned at the last minute." William shook his head too, for he was still as dumbfounded as he had been when he first heard of Mortimer's arrest. Everything could have gone wrong with the plan, yet nothing had gone wrong. "I do have one regret," he confessed.

"What?"

"That I wasn't in that tunnel with them. But it was a young men's operation, and it had to be a small one."

She kissed him. "It matters not who brought it about, only that Mortimer and Isabella have fallen."

"True. But I wish I had been there."

On November 26, the Earl of March shuffled into the hall at Westminster, bound and gagged. There he was charged in front of Parliament with removing the late king from Kenilworth Castle and having him murdered at Berkeley Castle, of appropriating royal power, of causing the death of the Earl of Kent, of enriching himself with royal money and jewels, of putting discord between Isabella and her husband, and a host of other crimes. As had been the case with those who had gone before him—Piers Gaveston, Thomas of Lancaster, the Despensers, the Earl of Kent—he was not allowed to speak in his defense before being sentenced to be hung, the fate of common criminals.

Three days later, William la Zouche, accompanied by Edward le Despenser and Alan, watched at the Tower as Mortimer was led out of his cell. Someone— the king himself? William wondered—had remembered the handsome black tunic Mortimer had worn to the second Edward's funeral, and Mortimer had been made to wear it to his own hanging.

"He should have been made to die a traitor's death," muttered Edward beside him.

"No," said William, thinking of the Countess of March and her children, who by the king's mercy would be spared the sight of Mortimer's head upon London Bridge or one of his quarters on a gate. "He deserves it; you're right. But there's been enough of that."

Edward shrugged and watched as the earl was tied upon a hurdle, on which he would be dragged to Tyburn two miles off. William wished that his stepson, who had gone to Parliament with him as his squire, would stay away from the execution, as had all the other members of the Despenser family. But at sixteen the boy was too old to be ordered about like a child, and though he had been much friendlier to William since the latter's own arrest, he had refused to listen to his stepfather's advice on this particular matter.

At Tyburn, Roger Mortimer, his smart tunic muddy and ripped, limped up the steps to the gallows. To William's surprise, he was given a chance to speak to the crowd. The bystanders tensed: Would he implicate Isabella in his crimes? But he was too much of a man to do that, as William had thought. Nor would he damage her reputation still further by sending a message of love to her from the gallows. Instead, in a flat voice, he requested forgiveness for his sins and asked for compassion on his wife and children. Then he added, "If I regret anything it is the death of the Earl of Kent. He was a decent man whom I entrapped into conspiracy and treason through his fraternal honor."

He fell silent and gazed tight-lipped over the heads of the crowd toward London. Mortimer's tunic was stripped off him, and he was left stark naked as the hangman adjusted the noose.

The silence of the crowd made the sudden sob beside William all the more audible. William turned and saw Edward, ashen-faced and weeping. "Let me get you out of here, Edward."

His stepson allowed himself to be led to a cluster of trees. "What is wrong with me, Lord Zouche? I've thought of seeing him hang for weeks. I've looked forward to it. But when they put the noose on all I could see was—"

"I know. Your father. Come. Sit here."

Edward started sobbing even harder, and William realized that what he was seeing was the self-control of four years finally breaking down. He patted him on his shoulder and said, "Stay here. I will get you when it is over."

He stepped back into the clearing and watched as the dangling figure of the Earl of March twitched. With a hanging, a man's agony could be prolonged for hours if the executioner had been given orders to do so, but this was not the case today. In minutes, the figure grew still.

William walked back to the cluster of trees and gently helped his stepson to his feet. "It's over, Edward. Let's go."

CHAPTER 28

▼

JANUARY 1331 TO
FEBRUARY 1334

"Your grace, *please*. Hugh is no threat to the realm, and you know it. Why, he is your near cousin! Let him go, and I will never trouble you again. I promise."

Edward looked almost tempted after Eleanor's last sentence. But he shook his head. "As I have repeatedly told you, my lady, it cannot be at this time. His case requires further investigation and deliberation."

"Investigation and deliberation? Your grace, he was but eighteen when he was locked up! Locked up because he was loyal to his father, and for no other reason. He has done nothing since. There! Your investigation is done."

Edward sighed. "My lady, your son is fortunate to have such an advocate. But your time for advocacy has done for now. You will want to be going on to Glamorgan shortly, I know."

Days before, upon William and Eleanor's petition before Parliament, the king had signed a document stating that to ease his conscience, he was restoring Glamorgan, Morganwgg, Tewkesbury, and Hanley Castle to Eleanor and William, on the condition that they pay a fine of ten thousand pounds, in installments. Several days later, Parliament had reduced the fine to five thousand pounds. It was the second of Eleanor's petitions that had met with a favorable response, for the previous month, the king had issued an order allowing her to collect Hugh's bones from their five resting places. Already Hugh's head had been removed from London Bridge and borne in dignity to Tewkesbury Abbey.

Only on one subject had the king been intransigent. Eleanor's son Hugh was still a prisoner. All of the Earl of Kent's coconspirators, Zouche among them, had been pardoned. The Earl of Arundel's son had been restored to his father's lands. Mortimer's surviving sons, Edmund and Geoffrey, who had been arrested soon after their father, had been released after a few weeks. The Countess of Kent and her children were free and had also been restored to their lands. Except for John Deveril, who had been one of the men who had tricked the Earl of Kent, and Mortimer's crony Simon de Bereford, all of Mortimer's followers, including a scrubbed-up Bishop of Lincoln, had been released. Even Benedict de Fulsham had been released from his mainprise. Vigorously as Eleanor had reminded the king of these instances of leniency on his part, she had met with no success.

Now, the king having reminded her not so subtly of what she had been given by him, which could certainly be taken away, she said meekly, "Your grace has been very kind to my family and me, and I do not forget it. But—"

"You may visit him, my lady, and write to him. Send him whatever you wish to make him more comfortable. I wish you a safe journey."

"I'll send him supplies, all right! A rope ladder," muttered Eleanor to William as they made their way out of Westminster's great hall.

William was beginning to make a soothing reply when a young knight, followed by his squires, entered the hall. Seeing Eleanor, he bowed deeply. "Good day, Lady Despenser."

"Good day," said Eleanor.

John de Grey of Rotherfield shot William a venomous look and continued into the great hall at Westminster.

Hugh le Despenser watched, open-mouthed, as luxury after luxury was brought into his tiny chamber at Bristol Castle. A bed, with hangings and pillows. A chest that proved to be full of warm, clean clothing. Wine and food. A chess set. Not since he had been in Ludlow Castle had he been showered with so many goods.

Then he heard a light footstep coming up the stairs, and he saw a woman come into the room. The woman whom on his worst days at Bristol Castle he had thought he would never see again. "Mother!"

It was a long time before either Eleanor or Hugh could control their emotions enough to speak coherently. Finally, Eleanor hiccupped and said, "Your brothers and sisters are downstairs, Hugh, but I wanted to see you alone first." She frowned in the direction of the bed, which two of Eleanor's men, studiously ignoring the reunion nearby them, had been assembling, and wiped her eyes. "And I am not sure they could fit in here now. Why, when your bed is set up there will be scarcely room to swing a cat in here!"

"Then I won't swing one," Hugh promised his mother. "I've stayed on excellent terms with the cats here."

Eleanor laughed, then twirled her wedding ring uneasily. "Hugh, I suppose you have heard about Lord Zouche."

"That you remarried? The guards told me, Mother."

"Lord Zouche and I love each other very much, Hugh. He has been a good stepfather to your brothers and sisters and a good husband to me. I meant no disrespect toward your father or to you in marrying him."

"I know, Mother. It is all right. I like Zouche. He was good to me at Caerphilly and Ludlow."

Eleanor sighed with relief. "Then I shall bring everyone in."

Eleanor's middle daughters were at their convents, but the remaining Despensers were numerous enough to make Hugh's room very crowded indeed. Isabel, Edward, and Gilbert, scarcely less moved than their mother had been, embraced their brother for a long time, but John, who did not remember him, and Elizabeth and Edmund Arundel, who had never known him, looked at him as if he were some sort of natural curiosity. William stood back awkwardly until Hugh, catching sight of him, grabbed him and thumped him on the back. "Lord Zouche! So you married Mother."

"Yes, please God."

"Good. She needs someone to keep her out of trouble."

William smiled and embraced Hugh.

Lizzie had retreated behind Eleanor's skirts, where she peeped out occasionally, and disapprovingly, at the scruffy creature Mama said was her oldest brother. John, more forthcoming, said, "There is another one of us, baby William, but he is too little to travel in the cold, Mama said."

Gilbert said cheerfully, "The king has allowed Mama to bury Papa, did you hear, Hugh? Our men have already been to London, Dover, and here to get him. They still have to go to Carlisle and York."

"Gilbert!" hissed Isabel reprovingly.

"Well, they do," said the boy unapologetically. After pestering the servants for some years, he had finally gotten a very edited account of his father's death, and he took a certain pride in the fact that Papa had not been merely beheaded, as anyone's father might be, but quartered as well.

"God, I've missed all of you," said Hugh quietly. Eleanor stole a look at him. Like his father, he'd never had any excess flesh, and nearly two years under Gurney's governance had left him downright bony. He was more subdued than he had ever been, but Eleanor knew from her own much shorter imprisonments that he was probably feeling overwhelmed by the sudden influx of pleasant company. She squeezed his hand, and he smiled at her with something of his old carefree look.

Edward said, "Can't I stay here with him, Mother, until he gets out? If the constable allows it?"

Bristol had a new constable, for Gurney, along with Maltravers and Ogle, had fled from England when Mortimer fell. Gurney's replacement, a relative of William's, had been most gracious to Eleanor. "If he allows it," Eleanor agreed. "And if Hugh wants the company."

"I do," admitted Hugh. "Very much."

"Then that's settled," said Eleanor.

"*I* want to keep him company," protested Gilbert.

"And me," piped up Edmund.

"And me," said John.

Hugh grinned. "Sorry, mates. You'd get bored very quickly, I fear. But when I come home you shall take turns sharing my chamber." He peeked around Eleanor's dress. "Anyone back there?"

"No!" said Lizzie.

For an hour or so more they visited, catching Hugh up on the news. Eleanor was pleased to be able to report that the Countess of March had been well treated by the king and had not lost her own inheritance. Queen Isabella had been brought by the king to Windsor for Christmas and was still staying there. Her outsize dower had been taken from her, but the king had granted her three thousand pounds a year—a perfectly respectable income for a dowager queen.

"Three thousand pounds more than she deserves," said Hugh with rare bitterness. He glanced at William. "Zouche, may I see you alone for a few minutes? We can walk on the castle grounds. I'm allowed. Business," he explained.

William nodded and followed Hugh outside, noticing that he walked with a limp. "Did Gurney do that to you?"

Hugh grimaced. "I was rather free with my speech to him one evening, and he kicked me with his boot in the ankle. It only bothers me when it's damp. Trouble is, of course, in England it's almost always damp."

"Christ!"

"I repaid him in kind. He didn't bother me much after that." He drew his new cloak closer around him. "It's Gurney I wanted to talk to you about. The first few months I was here, he'd bait me. Mainly about my father and the king, telling me what they did with each other and suggesting I shared their tendencies. I don't, by the way; there's days where I could take the laundress here if she wasn't every bit of sixty. Well, anyway, I'd get angry like a fool and insult him; then he'd have a go at me. That's where my ankle came from. It passed the time, at least. Then he went through a spell when he didn't see much of me at all. He had the good burghers of Bristol to fleece in various ways, and that took a lot of his time. Then he started coming again. Drunk, and prone to babbling, without any regard to whom he was babbling to. Toward the end I thought I should be in Holy Orders, he was confessing so much to me. One night, he told me what he did to the king. I suppose his conscience was finally catching up with him. You heard how they killed the king, Lord Zouche? The spit?"

"Yes. There were rumors at Parliament."

"Does Mother know?"

William shook his head. "She knows that he was murdered; she believed that from the start. I don't think she's heard anything more. I've done my best to keep the rumors from her. I suppose she thinks he was poisoned or smothered, and I intend to let her keep on thinking so."

"Thank you, Lord Zouche. That's what I was worried about. She was very fond of him, you see. I couldn't bear to have her know that he died that way."

"Neither could I."

They walked around in companionable silence for a while. Then Hugh said, "I suppose the king will set me free eventually. When he does, I want to go on pilgrimage, as a thanksgiving."

"Where to?"

"Santiago."

"That's where your aunt Aline's gone. She was planning to do it by foot."

Hugh laughed. "My aunt! I'll have to crawl then, to outdo her. My grandfather went there too, you know." He made the sign of the cross. "There are nights I can't sleep, thinking of him being tried here, his last night here in chains. Gurney, always thoughtful, showed me where they kept him. Mortimer certainly picked my accommodations well, didn't he?"

"There's every reason to believe you will be released soon."

"Once I finish with Santiago, Lord Zouche, I may just stay over there. Or Italy."

"In God's name, why?"

Hugh shrugged. "What's for me here? I've no lands, I'm penniless, I'm not even a knight. Ladies won't exactly be clamoring for me as a husband now. I used to be a decent fighter, and I suppose I still could be once I got into practice again. I can hire myself out as a mercenary."

"Hugh, you know full well your mother won't allow you to stay penniless, and I'm sure the king would let her alienate some lands to you. The knighthood will come. So will marriage."

"Yes. But the king has been taught to believe my father was the antichrist. So has all of England. Isabella and Mortimer being gone hasn't changed that. I don't think there'll be any royal favor for the likes of me. I'm better off just starting off on my own somewhere where no one knows about Father." He sighed. "Forgive me, Lord Zouche. I'm feeling sorry for myself. It happens at times."

Zouche said, "The king is still feeling his way, you know. After being led around by his mother and Mortimer for four years, he's uncertain, I think. Once he gets more confident, he'll be more at ease with the idea of setting you free. And he'd be a fool not to want to make an ally of you, not with what you'll inherit someday. Don't give up on England so quickly. Make your trip to Santiago, and then come home. We'd all miss you, for one."

Hugh shrugged noncommittally, but he seemed a bit more cheerful as the men turned back toward the castle, Hugh walking quickly in spite of his limp. William pointed at his ankle and said, "I hope Gurney paid for that dearly."

"Oh, he did, but I'm afraid I might have hampered the search for him a bit. They may be looking for a man with two front teeth. When I finished with him, he had but one."

"Awkward for you, isn't it?" said Eleanor's aunt Mary to William. "I mean, it's not every man who buries his wife's first husband *after* he's become the second husband."

As far as William could tell with her nun's veil and wimple, Mary was a handsome woman of fifty or so, slightly tall for her sex, with strands of graying hair peeking out from beneath her headdress. Unlike her late brother the king, she was naturally gregarious, and after Hugh's funeral mass she had lost no time in trotting her horse up beside that of her niece's new husband. ("New to me, at least. And new to her, almost, considering how long you were kept apart.")

"It was a trifle odd," admitted William. What was oddest, he thought to himself, were the tears that had clouded his own eyes as Hugh's coffin, draped in cloth of gold, was at last lowered into its resting place near Tewkesbury Abbey's high altar. Through Eleanor and the children, he'd come to like the man he'd barely known in life, numerous as his sins were.

"Well, it was a beautiful ceremony," said Mary briskly. "You served him well with that. Pity his eldest son couldn't be here."

"We thought of postponing the funeral until he was released, but not knowing when that would be, we decided to have it now."

"How is he faring?"

"Well. He was a little low in spirits when we saw him, but his brother Edward's been staying with him, which has cheered him up quite a bit, it appears from his letters. And he's had other company besides." William smiled faintly, for he could not tell Mary of the very special visitor he had arranged for Hugh to have periodically. Guinevere, as she had dubbed herself, might not be the Queen of England, but she was certainly the queen of the whores of Bristol. Any man who was not rejuvenated by her golden hair and her inexhaustible inventiveness might as well start building his own tomb.

"There are my fellow sisters, Eleanor's girls. I must see them, poor dears, and compare convents."

"You will stay with us at Tewkesbury manor, though?" He added, "Tomorrow night we can play at dice."

Mary's face lit up. "Ah, Lord Zouche, I see my niece has told you all about me! She never did have luck at dicing. Perhaps you shall be better." She clucked at her horse and moved on.

Eleanor took her aunt's place. Though William had watched her dress that morning and had of course stood beside her in the abbey, he still blinked to see her in her black robes again. He pressed her hand as their horses moved companionably together. "This has been a hard day for you, sweetheart."

"Yes. But at least he is lying in peace and quiet now, away from all those dreadful people gawking at him. And I shall have a lovely tomb built."

Lady Hastings, trailed by her children, their spouses, and a youth Eleanor did not know, joined them. "It is good to see how many people came to pay their respects to Hugh." It was indeed a good-sized gathering: Hugh's relatives, Eleanor's half-brothers Thomas and Edward de Monthermer (*Sir* Thomas and *Sir* Edward now, Eleanor reminded herself), her half-sister Joan (a nun at Amesbury), some of William's own family, retainers and friends of Hugh and his father, Hugh the elder's relatives, William and Eleanor's household and councilors...

Eleanor smiled. "To think that if all of us had been together just four months ago, we would probably have been arrested for plotting. But Bella, where is Amie?"

"With the queen as one of her damsels, isn't that good news? After Mortimer fell, I wrote to the queen and told her who Amie was and asked if she would give her a place in her household. She agreed and Amie has been there for a couple of weeks now. I shall miss her, but I live very quietly now, and she is too pretty and outgoing for that sort of a life. She will meet a good husband at court, I hope." Bella gestured toward the young stranger proudly. "But you have not met Nicholas, my brother."

From his horse, Nicholas nodded at Eleanor in a manner so like that of his father that Eleanor's heart ached for a moment. "I didn't see my brother Hugh more than a few times, Lady Despenser, but I was fond of him."

"And he must have been fond of you, Nicholas. I hope you shall come stay with us for a while soon."

"Is it true that you have plans to renovate the choir of Tewkesbury Abbey?"

This was such an unlooked-for question that Eleanor looked in confusion at her sister-in-law. Bella laughed. "Nicholas's passion is architecture, Nelly. He was staring at the ceiling the whole time mass was being said for poor Hugh, wondering how it could be improved!"

Nicholas blushed. "I meant no disrespect, Lady Despenser, but it has such potential."

"I quite agree with you. Now that things are different the monks will be able to make the improvements they wanted, and I will give them whatever help they require."

Nicholas was still going on excitedly about the abbey when the funeral party arrived at Tewkesbury manor, where a meal had been prepared for the mourners and a large group of poor people. Eleanor, presiding at the high table with William, was half ashamed as chief mourner to be talking so animatedly with those around her, but after running off with William she could hardly call herself an inconsolable widow. Tomorrow, though, she would return to Hugh's grave with its constantly burning candles and spend some time alone with him. She would pray for him and remind him that she would love him forever.

In any case, Eleanor saw as the meal ended and the guests were preparing to go their varying ways, no one else in the room, including those who had loved Hugh dearly, was particularly gloomy either. It had been, after all, so long since Hugh had died, and so long since many of them had seen each other. Edward, who had left his brother for a couple of days to attend the funeral, was chatting with his cousins, looking more relaxed than Eleanor had seen him in years. Mary, who had seldom ventured from Amesbury during the Mortimer reign, was laughing with Hugh's sister and daughters. Ingelram Berenger and William were talking horses. Eleanor could not see precisely what the little ones were up to, but Lord Zouche the dog ambled by licking his lips very complacently.

"My lady?"

In looking around for her youngest children, Eleanor had not noticed the messenger approaching her. She opened the parchment he gave her—nearby, William was opening a similar parchment—and gasped, "Mother of God!"

"Why, what is it?" said Lady Hastings.

"The whoreson!"

"Nelly?"

Eleanor looked at William, who was staring open-mouthed at his own letter. "It is John de Grey. We are being summoned to Canterbury on his petition."

"Sir Grey?" Lady Hastings said, puzzled. "Why?"

"He is claiming me as his wife."

Standing before the official of Canterbury, John de Grey was the model of a wronged husband, bearing his loss with dignity and stoic calm. Eleanor would have felt almost sorry for him had she not been the bride he was claiming.

"As you know, sir, I had many times asked the Bishop of Lincoln to do justice in this matter, but he had curtly refused me, probably out of fear of offending Roger Mortimer. I thank you for granting me this hearing now." Briefly, he looked wistfully at Eleanor with his blue eyes.

"On what grounds do you claim this lady?"

"It is a delicate matter, sir. I apologize to the lady for speaking frankly. When she is home with me as she belongs I shall make amends. On the day after Christmas, I visited Lady Despenser at Hanley Castle. That night, we had sexual relations. It was my intent in coming there from the start to marry the lady, and the next morning, she did agree to marry me in the future. We had sexual relations again."

"A promise to marry in the future, followed by sexual relations. Under canon law that makes you husband and wife, if the lady does not dispute your tale. My lady?"

Eleanor said, "I will not perjure myself and deny that I had sexual relations with Sir Grey. I do deny promising to marry him. There was discussion, but no promise. Lord Zouche is my husband. I married him before a priest, with witnesses."

"Do you have witnesses to prove your story, Sir Grey? If not, there is no point in continuing with this matter."

Eleanor sighed with relief. Then John said, "Yes, sir. I have witnesses. My squire, who saw and heard us in—er—the act. Another squire, who heard me say goodbye to Lady Despenser as my wife."

Eleanor's jaw dropped. Forgetting about the official, she stammered, "My lord, you had us *watched* while—"

"Of course not," said John, smiling at Eleanor indulgently in a husbandly manner. "My squire had come to fetch me urgently—you do remember him doing so, my lady—and he was waiting for the right moment to do so. While he waited, he saw and overheard things he should not have. You may be assured that I cuffed him soundly when I found out."

Eleanor sagged against William's arm. William said, "By God, man, you shall pay for dragging my wife through this."

"She is my wife, Lord Zouche, and nothing hurts me more than her having to be here today. If you cede her to me, as you should as a man of honor, I shall make all up to her, as I have said. She shall be loved and cherished."

"I'll see you damned before you take her from me, you lying dog."

"Gentlemen!" said the official. "Carry on in this manner and I shall have the bishop's men seize you both. You must settle this under the law. From what Sir Grey tells me, he may have a valid case. It is his right to prove it if he can. He may do so before the Bishop of Worchester's court."

"Worcester!" said Eleanor, lifting her head from William's sleeve. "That is Bishop Orleton's bishopric now! He will give me no justice, sir. He hated my first husband and my uncle the king, and he will hate me because of them."

The official shook his head. "As you were taken from Hanley Castle, Worcester it shall be."

"I heard that John de Grey had claimed that I married him. I heard it from Roger Mortimer when I was arrested."

"And then?"

Eleanor shook her head. "I was imprisoned, and then after I got out, my husband was arrested. John de Grey was the furthest thing from my mind. I heard nothing from him until I was summoned to Canterbury. Of course, now that I have my lands back, he has resumed his interest in me. The whoreson!"

Master Geoffrey Preston, the young proctor hired by Eleanor and William to represent them before the official at Worcester, shifted gloomily in his seat. This was about the twentieth time Eleanor had called John de Grey a whoreson in as many minutes.

Fresh from Oxford, Geoffrey could dispute the finest points of canon law for hours upon hours. He could expound upon its development from Roman times. He could back up any point he made with a reference, however obscure. He was prepared, in short, for any argument that might be thrown at him. But he was rather ill-prepared for Eleanor, because living, breathing clients, as opposed to abstractions, were rather new to Master Preston.

His patroness, Lady Elizabeth de Burgh, who had helped place him at Oxford and subsidized his bills, had recommended him to Eleanor. She had told him, "I urged my sister Eleanor to remarry the last time I saw her, but it seems she took my advice a bit too much to heart and got married twice. Do your best for her and Lord Zouche."

Now remembering the great appreciation he had for Lady de Burgh, he rallied and said, "I think you have sufficiently expressed your opinion of Sir Grey, Lady Despenser. Let us move on."

Eleanor, rather grateful that her juvenile proctor was showing some command, nodded.

Master Preston said unhappily, "I suppose I must start with the most delicate question first. Did you have sexual intercourse with Sir Grey?"

"I did."

"And did you promise to marry him beforehand?"

"No. I lay with him at night and on the morning of the next day. He did ask me to marry him that morning. I told him I would have an answer later. He started to make love to me again and I allowed it. There was love-talk going on between us at that time, and I suppose he might have construed something of that as a consent."

Master Preston said hopefully, "Had you been drinking excessively, my lady? If you were incapable of consent..."

"No. Though on the first occasion I met Sir Grey I did have too much wine to drink. But nothing went on between us then. I seem to have the rare gift of acting most stupidly when I am quite sober."

"Are you and Sir Grey related in a prohibited degree of consanguinity?"

"I seem to be related to half of England somehow, but sadly I cannot count Sir Grey among my near relations."

"He was widowed, and you were a widow yourself."

"Yes."

"You had not taken a vow of chastity?"

"No."

Master Preston said gloomily, "So there would be no impediment to your marrying Sir Grey."

"Save that I did not."

"Sir Grey has a witness to your conversation, I understand?"

"Yes, and our lovemaking as well. I was unaware that we were putting on such a show. Assuming, of course, his squire actually heard and saw us."

"I understood from Lady de Burgh that you were imprisoned twice in the Tower. What for?"

"The first time because I was Lord Despenser's loving wife. The second because I was accused of thieving jewels from the Tower during my first imprisonment. And because the Earl of March was unhappy about my marriage to Lord Zouche and wanted my lands."

"Did you take the jewels?"

"Yes."

Master Preston visibly sagged.

"I took them after my youngest three girls—my little Lizzie was not born at the time—were packed off to convents and forced to take the veil, even though the eldest was no more than ten years old. After my husband, whom I loved dearly, had died a cruel death. I took them for spite of that whore of a queen, Isabella."

"My," said Master Preston weakly. He took some notes as he gathered his courage for the next round of questioning. "Speaking of the queen, Lady de Burgh said that you had superintended her household at one time. Is that true? It might help your credibility if it was."

"It is true, but as I have also been accused of being a spy for my husband at the time, I am not sure it would."

"And did you spy on the queen?"

"Not well enough. No, Master Preston, I was being flippant. I could not have spied on her if I wanted to, for she did not trust me. I managed her household affairs, kept her seal, screened her incoming and outgoing correspondence with her knowledge. It was at the king's request, and my husband's. She resented it." Eleanor shook her head. "It doesn't look very good, does it, Master Preston? A thief, a spy, and a whore. And yet when I was young I used to be regarded as quite priggish."

"I know you are none of those things, Lady Despenser."

He sounded a bit dubious, Eleanor thought. And she hadn't even told him about her uncle. That was probably a matter best kept to herself, she reflected.

By July 1331, all of the testimony had been taken down and copied, and Master Preston brought his copy to Caerphilly Castle for Eleanor and William to read. As he spread the parchments out over the table in William and Eleanor's chamber, Eleanor was once again glad that her oldest children were not living with her. Edward was still with Hugh at Bristol, Gilbert was learning knightly skills in the young Earl of Warwick's household, and Isabel was on one of the Arundel manors. After Richard Fitz Alan had received his estates back—it was thought that he would soon have his father's earldom too—Eleanor's attorney had written to him, demanding that Isabel and Edmund be supported in a style befitting their estate. Richard had grudgingly agreed, and now Isabel had a great household of her own. She saw her husband only intermittently. Eleanor missed having all of them at home, but at least there was no chance of them wandering in as Master Preston, translating from the Latin, read the examiner's summation of the testimony to her.

He started with the testimony of John's young squire, Henry. The brat, having been ordered out of John's chamber very peremptorily by his lord the night he brought Eleanor into it, had spent the night dozing in the great hall, where he had gossiped with several of his fellow squires about his lord's probable doings. The next morning, having received an urgent letter for his master, which he later learned was a command to join the king immediately, he had searched for him and had seen him enter a storage area with the lady of the castle. Guessing what his master was up to, and worrying that he might take an interruption ill, but not wanting to delay overmuch in getting his message to him, he had peeked through the door and had seen his master kissing and talking to Lady Despenser. He had heard Sir Grey ask Eleanor if she would marry him, and sundry other questions, and had heard Eleanor mumble "yes" repeatedly. All the while, Sir Grey had been fumbling with his drawers and with Eleanor's skirts, and he and she had lain down on some sacks of grain and known each other carnally. (The least the churl could have done, Eleanor thought sourly, was to have left the sacks out of it.) Henry had then hurried away, so as to make a show of coming back calling his master's name. Sir Grey, looking rather rumpled, had emerged from the building alone, but Henry had seen Eleanor exit later, wrapped in a cloak and with her hair much awry.

Both Henry and Fulk, Sir Grey's second squire, had witnessed Sir Grey say goodbye to Lady Despenser before he hastened off to join the king. Sir Grey had not taken leave of the lady with a great show of affection, probably out of consideration for her privacy in front of her household standing nearby, but he had kissed Eleanor on the cheek in a chivalrous manner and told her that he would be back straightaway. Fulk had heard him whisper, "My sweet wife," to Eleanor as he mounted his horse. Lady Despenser had not murmured any similar marital endearments, but had smiled (rather forcedly, probably out of grief from parting from her new husband) and wished him a safe journey.

What had he whispered? Eleanor thought it had been, "You will soon be my sweet wife."

Gladys, Eleanor's chief witness, had found her lady several hours later, lying sobbing on her bed. Lady Despenser had confessed to her that she had wickedly lain with Sir Grey and that she saw no choice but to marry him if he returned, as he surely would. Nothing Lady Despenser had told Gladys had led her to believe that Eleanor had already agreed to marry Sir Grey; if she did believe such, she would have never assisted her to marry Lord Zouche, for she was a pious woman, and so was her lady. Why, then, had her lady acted so wantonly? She had been grievously upset at the bad news about her son, and in a fury at her late husband, who was quite beyond any other type of punishment, had offered Sir Grey her bed. Yes, her lady did act impulsively and thoughtlessly at times. There was the time she had stolen the crown's jewels...

The rest of Eleanor's witnesses testified to nothing more than that Lady Despenser had married Lord Zouche on a barge, in a ceremony performed by a priest and witnessed by several bargemen as well as Eleanor's own family. Master Preston, having finished reading the testimony to his clients, was going on happily about the arguments he would be making; clearly, he at least was beginning to enjoy himself. A woman consumed by passion was not a rational creature, certainly not one who could consent to the holy sacrament of marriage. And even if Eleanor had been in her right mind, how could it be proven that she had answered "yes" to John's proposal of marriage, when John's own witness testified that several questions had been asked? And could the simple word "yes," if it did indeed correspond to the marriage proposal, be taken as a sufficient consent to marriage? And could the squires be credible as witnesses, being dependent on Sir Grey for their livelihood and for their advancement? And could—

"Master Preston. What if the official simply decides to believe Sir Grey over me because he is a man and I a woman? Because I was Hugh le Despenser's wife and his bishop despised Hugh? He can couch his decision in any lawyer's jargon he wishes, but what if that is what he does?"

Master Preston suddenly wondered whether it was too late to enter his brother-in-law's corn business.

Soon afterward, Master Preston went to argue the case of *Grey v. Zouche* before the official at Worcester. A week after that, Eleanor, William, and John gathered at Worcester Cathedral to hear his decision.

"*In Dei nominee amen. Auditis et intellectis meritis cause matrimonialis,*" said the official sonorously. His face was unreadable. Master Preston had warned them that he would give no basis for his decision, but simply announce it after first going through a stream of form verbiage to get there. Eleanor closed her eyes as more Latin followed. "This court passes sentence in favor of Sir John de Grey."

For an instant, Eleanor hoped she had misunderstood the Latin. Then she heard William gasp beside her. As if in a trance, she stood silent as Master Preston announced that he would appeal to the Pope.

What would happen now? Would William have to take all of his things off of her estates? Would John be expecting to move in that very afternoon? Would all the Zouche banners have to come down from her lands? How would she say goodbye to William? And how in God's name would she explain to her youngest children? "Mama thought she was married to Lord Zouche, you see, but it appears that she was married to Sir Grey. So it is him you must call Papa now…"

She began to laugh. "So many details!" she explained when all eyes turned toward her. "So many damn *details* to consider!" She doubled over with laughter. Then she began to cry at the same time.

It was Gladys who came to her rescue, hustling her out of the room. "Come, my lady," she said, "let's get you out of here."

"Gladys, where am I?"

"An inn in Worcester, my lady. We had an apothecary give you a sleeping potion. Poor creature, you needed it."

"Was I as hysterical as I think?"

"Worse," said Gladys dryly.

"Where is William? Where is that Grey?"

"Lord Zouche is downstairs. Sir Grey is not here. It is not as bad as you think, my lady. Because your proctor appealed, it was ordered that you not have to live with Sir Grey just now, at least until the appeal is over. Even Sir Grey agreed. He saw how badly you took the sentence, that it would be too sudden a change for you. But you may not have conjugal relations with Lord Zouche either, on pain of excommunication."

"Would you send Lord Zouche to me?"

"Yes, my lady."

She stared at the bed curtains until William came in. "William, forgive me. Please."

"There is nothing to forgive. You are my wife and we both know it. We'll fight this. We'll keep on fighting."

"I know in my heart that I never married Sir Grey. But William, I know this too. It would not have mattered to me if I had. I could not have said no to you. When you came back for me I was as happy as I have ever been in my life."

"Me too, my love."

He settled on the bed with her and held her for a time. Then he said, "I did give my oath not to lie with you while this order stands, and I must keep it. I couldn't do it if I were living with you; I'm having a hard time keeping it now. So I shall go to Ashby-de-la-Zouche for a while. You understand the necessity of that?"

"Yes. There is no need to displease God further."

"Gladys said that she would bring William to visit me soon."

William, their newly bastardized child. "I know he will like that, William."

"Then I must leave now. We will soon be united again, Eleanor. Don't fear that, my love."

He kissed her and hastened out the door.

From Worcester, Eleanor went to Hanley Castle. When she dismounted from her horse, she said, "I am going to the quay, Gladys. I want to be alone."

Gladys's voice sharpened, "The quay, my lady?"

Eleanor smiled faintly. "Gladys, I promise you I am not going to drown myself. I have committed enough sins without adding that to the list. I will be back before long."

Reluctantly, Gladys left her, and Eleanor walked slowly to the barge on which William had married her. She sat down in the cabin, in the same spot where the waves had rocked her to sleep as she lay snuggled next to William, and cried until she could cry no more. Then, exhausted, she slept.

"Mother? Mother?"

She opened her eyes and stared around her. "Hugh!"

Hugh's release had been conditioned on his appearing before the king's council at the October Parliament. Twelve mainprisors had been required to guarantee his appearance. ("Twelve! Shows what a desperate character I am," Hugh had told his admiring brothers.) Accordingly, Hugh accompanied William to Parliament and appeared before the king at the appointed day.

The king stared at Hugh after having ordered him to rise. It had been years, Hugh realized, since they'd seen each other, not since Edward, a reedy youth, had departed England for France to do homage to the French king. The first royal words were not encouraging. "Good Lord, man! You are the image of your father."

This was rather a handicap, Hugh thought as he glanced at the members of the council, most of them older men who had disliked his father and grandfather, all of them studying his features now and murmuring in assent. "That would explain the looks I got from your grace's men as I made my way here," he said cheerfully. "Half looked as if they'd seen a ghost and the other half looked as if they'd like to make me one."

The king's mouth twitched upward, but did not remain there. "Our cousin Eleanor has been begging us for some time to set you free. We wish to gratify her, if we can assure ourselves that you will be trustworthy. How far were you involved in your father's wrongdoing?"

"Very little, that I know of. My father did not confide in me, your grace. I suspect he probably wanted to keep me clean of his own sin. I knew he was disliked, of course, and I don't suppose I ever considered him overscrupulous. It wasn't a subject I cared to analyze deeply, and when I had nothing but time to analyze it deeply, it was too late. My father was dead and I was a prisoner, so it seemed like a pointless exercise, not to mention a depressing one."

"What have you been doing with yourself since your release?"

Trying to acquire Gower, Hugh resisted the temptation to say. "I have been staying with my mother."

"As a chaperone?" the king's chancellor said snidely. He was John Stratford, Bishop of Winchester. It was he, Hugh recalled, who had carried the queen's orders putting his mother in the Tower.

"As the heir to her lands, my lord, it is natural that I should help her with them. And as she has been subject to unkind remarks of the sort heard just now, she prefers my company or that of my younger brother when she goes out in public, and I daresay my being with her has been a comfort to her during this trying time for her."

"Yes, I suppose it would be," said Stratford, a little abashed.

"Your grace, I am well aware that my father's and my grandfather's lands were forfeit to the crown. I am not asking for them or for anything else. I am not asking for my grandfather's earldom, or even for a knighthood. I am not asking you for anything, except to be free of all charges against me. It is my wish to be of service to you someday, so that I may earn your trust and perhaps make my family's name less of a hated one. I cannot do any of those things if I am locked up some-where or confined to my mother's lands."

"We are satisfied with what you have told us, although we may have questions later," the king said. "You shall appear before Parliament tomorrow with your mainprisors, and we shall render our decision."

Hugh bowed and backed out of the room. Edward looked at his councilors and sighed. "While we are on the subject of the Despenser family, let us see my troublesome cousin's husband. Bring in Lord Zouche."

"You and Sir Grey both claim to be married to our kinswoman, Lady Despenser. Correct?"

"Yes, your grace."

"That is in the hands of the Church," said Edward, not without relief. "That is where it should be, and that is where it should stay. We have summoned you here because we have received reports that your men are harassing each other."

"I beg your pardon, your grace. But my men cannot help but feel indignant that that blackguard of a knight, who I might add did almost nothing to recover his so-called wife until your grace restored Glamorgan to her, has caused my wife Eleanor so much grief and pain."

"We shall command you both in Parliament to keep the peace between you, on pain of imprisonment. There is an appeal pending in Avignon about this mat-ter?"

"Yes, your grace."

"I hope that shall settle it. If it does not, we will summon both of you to appear before this council later, with the lady, to see if some agreement can be reached. In the meantime, you and your men are to do no violence to each other. You understand us?"

"Yes, your grace," William said.

The next day, Hugh le Despenser with his twelve mainprisors appeared before the king and Parliament and was pardoned for holding Caerphilly Castle against the queen. William was summoned before the same Parliament and ordered to keep the peace with John de Grey, who was served with a writ commanding him to do the same.

Soon after this eventful Parliament for the Despenser family disbanded, the Pope ordered the case of *Grey v. Zouche* to be reheard by Robert de Welles, the prior of Southwark abbey, and William Inge, the archdeacon of Surrey. With the hearing pending, the king summoned William, John, and Eleanor to his council in January 1332.

"I have called you here to see if this matter can be settled," Edward said. "For the best interest of all three of you. I shall be blunt. My cousin Eleanor is a wealthy woman. If she were to grant one of you some of her more valuable lands for life, with a remainder to her heirs—"

John said, "Your grace, it is not the lady's lands I covet. It is the lady, my wife. I tried to recover her before she got her lands back. But there was her imprisonment, and the Bishop of Lincoln's intransigence—"

"I'd take her if she were a beggar," said William.

Eleanor said, "Your grace, I married Lord Zouche with witnesses, before God. My wedding vows cannot be bought and sold in that manner."

The king sighed. "So it's not money, as I hoped? Very well."

"I only wish to have my wife restored to me," said John. "She promised to marry me, and we consummated the promise. Then this smooth-tongued scoundrel came around and took her, by force and fear, I think—"

"He is mistaken!" Eleanor waved her hands frantically. "I did lie with him, your grace, I was foolish. Call me a whore, but do not call me his wife. It was Lord Zouche I married, Lord Zouche I wanted to marry all along. Only I felt so guilty doing so because of Hugh, and when Sir Grey came to visit—"

"You took advantage of her!" said William.

"I! You had a priest with you, ready to do your bidding, didn't you? No waiting, and why? Because you knew that she was my wife, and you were hoping that once you'd snatched her away, I'd graciously forget about her. Bloody hell I will! I'd as soon cut your throat, you villain!"

He reached for his dagger. Before he could draw it halfway, Eleanor shrieked, "No!" and threw herself in front of William. "Don't you dare harm him!"

"Gentlemen!"

One of the king's sergeant-at-arms grabbed John, and another grabbed William. John, as best he could with the burly man holding him, replaced the knife and said, "Lady Despenser, I did not mean to frighten you, please God. I only—"

"Lord Zouche, Sir Grey, you are both in our custody now. We will not tolerate such behavior in front of us and our council." The members of the council, who throughout the proceedings had looked both attentive and highly entertained, nodded disapprovingly. "Take them both to the Tower."

"The *Tower!*" wailed Eleanor.

William got a hand free to grip Eleanor's. "Don't distress yourself, my love. Just the usual family quarters, no doubt."

As the men were led away, William de Montacute rose and walked Eleanor to his seat. "Sit here, my lady. Someone will get your son to take you away from here."

"Thank you, Lord Montacute." She sank down in her seat, finding as she did so that she still had enough spirit to meet John Stratford's disdainful gaze at her with a magnificent stare that made the bishop blink.

"Then the king's sergeants-at-arms arrested both men and took them both to the Tower," Joan of Bar reported to Queen Isabella a few days later at Windsor Castle. She considered it her duty to keep her friend up-to-date on the news from court, even if the dowager queen did not always show an interest in her reports.

"Are they there now?"

"No. Lord Zouche was released on mainprise. Sir Grey was released into the custody of William de Clinton." Too late, Joan remembered that he had been one of Mortimer's captors. "Not exactly close custody, as they are good friends."

"And the silly little cat who started this nonsense? She is not living with one of these men?"

"No. She is under orders not to bed with either of them, on pain of excommunication, poor thing. Not that I think she needs to be told to stay away from Grey, the handsome one who's years younger than she is. It's Zouche, the gray, homely one ten years her senior, whom she's in love with." Joan giggled. "Funny, isn't it? Zouche is the gray one, not Grey."

Isabella snorted and stared out of her window, seeing nothing but the usual view of trees and river. For well over a year now she had lived here, not exactly her son's prisoner but not quite free either. Her quarters were as comfortable as they had ever been; she was served as obsequiously as she could desire; her ladies and damsels humored her every wish. She had musicians to keep her entertained, scribes and illuminators to produce manuscripts of romances for her, chaplains to see to her spiritual needs. Joan of Bar, her dearest friend, frequently visited; so did the Countess of Pembroke. Her children Eleanor and John came too, though their visits were clearly paid out of duty. The king himself came infrequently, but dutifully sent his agents to inquire about her needs.

For months after Mortimer's death, Isabella had been closely supervised; there had been worries, never expressed to her in so many words, that she might try to kill herself. It was true that there were weeks she simply did not recall, so deep had been her anguish. Gradually, the restrictions on her had been lifted, and just the other day Edward had told her (in person for once) that she would soon be able to leave Windsor and live on any of the lands she had been given. He had been rather disappointed at her lukewarm response; clearly, he had expected a bit of gratitude. He was right to expect it, she knew. Another sort of son might have locked her up for life or forced her into a nunnery; a man like her own father might have had her burned at the stake. Instead, Edward had evidently determined to treat her as if Mortimer were but a disease from which she was slowly recovering, one that was better left unmentioned. Sometimes, she thought, she would have preferred harsh treatment; it would be less humiliating than living her life as the prodigal mother of this saintly son. At least it would have given her someone to be angry at, besides herself.

"Enough about that wretched Despenser woman," said Isabella. "What of my daughter Eleanor? Is there any further news about her marriage?"

"No. The king has yet to conclude the agreement with the Count of Guelders. I still think she could do better, your grace. But as the negotiations with France came to nothing…"

"Aragon didn't want her either," said the queen. "Not surprising, I suppose. They could do better for a marriage. I could have, too. Why, I regret the day I came to this miserable, gray little country. I truly do."

Joan was well used to such diatribes. She said placidly, "Shall I summon your musicians, your grace? That always cheers you up."

"Yes. Summon the damn musicians."

When Hugh le Despenser had assisted his mother from the king's council chamber, the king had instructed him to see him a few days hence at Waltham Abbey, where Hugh duly arrived in early February. "We have released your mainprisors from their obligations, Hugh. You are as free as any Englishman now."

"Thank you, your grace."

"As you may know, your lady mother has asked permission to alienate several of her manors to you. To provide an independent living to you until you inherit her lands at her death."

Hugh smiled. His mother gave him ample money for his wants, and he assisted her diligently in her affairs, but at his age it was humiliating to be living off her generosity while his male cousins ran their own estates. He'd not needed to bring up the idea himself; Eleanor had offered.

"And we have refused her request."

Hugh felt slapped across the face. Making an effort to keep his voice low, he said. "I don't understand, your grace. I shall not argue with your will, but I don't understand. We are not asking for anything more than what is in our family already, only for something that would cost the crown nothing and let me live independently like other men of my age and station. But it matters not. A man who's good with a sword can make a welcome for himself anywhere, and it needn't be in England. When my mother's marital problems are settled I shall leave the country, with your grace's permission, and start afresh elsewhere. May I leave your presence now?"

"Your mother needs her revenues right now, Hugh. She has her fine to pay for her theft, and there is the matter of her marriage litigation, which I'm sure is no small expense. And besides, any grant she might make could be invalidated if it turned out that John de Grey was her true husband." He nodded to a clerk, who handed Hugh a paper. "Read this."

Hugh read it. Halfway through he looked up and frowned. "This is a grant of land to me?"

"Yes. The crown is promising you two hundred marks a year in income from lands and rents."

Two hundred marks. A trifle compared to what his father and grandfather had owned. Yet it would allow him to live independently, and he wouldn't have to learn Italian. He swallowed hard. "Thank you, your grace."

"The manors are from Grandfather's estate, Mother—I think for a while they were in the hands of Simon de Bereford, the man who was executed not long after Mortimer. But he doesn't seem to have spent much time on them, so I'm unlikely to have visitations from his ghost in the middle of the night."

"It is kind of the king, indeed," said Eleanor, a little wistfully, for she would have liked to have seen Hugh given Loughborough. But one could not be particular, and it was good to see her son finding some favour with the king at last. "Freeby in Leicestershire and Ashley in Southampton. An interesting combination."

"Yes, when I get tired of being landlocked at Freeby, I can go to Ashley by the sea, and vice versa. And the king said he'd make up the rest of my grant through lands in the Isle of Wight." Hugh glanced at his mother. "Mother, I can lease them out and stay with you if you would prefer."

"No, Hugh. You have been good company these last few months, but I would not chain you to me while this nonsense of Sir Grey's drags on." Eleanor's cheeks burned. She often wondered what her eldest sons must think of her, getting herself entangled between Grey and Zouche as she had, but each, even prim Edward, had maintained a kindly silence about the matter. She brightened. "But I must come with you to inspect your manors. I know you too well, Hugh. As long as the stables are in satisfactory condition, the manor house could be falling down over your ears and you would not notice. You must have proper wall hangings, and fine plate to eat off, and comfortable furnishings for your bed—"

"Surely you don't expect me to choose these things, Mother."

"No, my dear, I will do it for you." Eleanor smiled, anticipating a delightful time buying exactly what she pleased. Unlike her husband Hugh, who especially as he grew rich had been very particular on matters of color and style, her son was quite indifferent to his surroundings, demanding only cleanliness and reasonable comfort. "And I want it to look particularly nice, Hugh, because when you get back from Santiago, I think it will be high time for you to consider marrying."

Hugh was still feeling overwhelmed by the prospect of a trip to the draper's. "Marrying?" he said weakly.

"Why not? You will have the means to keep a wife, and as the future Lord of Glamorgan you're bound to attract a girl of good family and with a good dowry. Especially now as the king has relented toward you."

Hugh himself had his doubts that the name Hugh le Despenser would meet with excitement in the marriage market, but he would not dampen his mother's cheerful mood for anything. "Well, we'll see, Mother. I'm rather fond of being able to pick up and go as I please, though. I might have a hard time adjusting to a wife just yet."

"Perhaps when you've been out of prison for a little longer," Eleanor allowed a little sulkily. She was eager for more grandchildren. "Now, when shall we travel to Freeby?"

At the March Parliament, William was acquitted of wrongdoing in his quarrel with John de Grey. His good fortune seemed complete when, soon afterward, the prior of Southwark and the archdeacon of Surrey adjudged him to be Eleanor's lawful husband. But John de Grey (pardoned of his wrongdoing at the behest of Parliament) promptly appealed, and Eleanor and William were still bound, on pain of excommunication, to refrain from sharing a bed.

Having recently incurred the royal displeasure, William was surprised to hear that he was to be one of the nobles escorting the king's young sister overseas to her marriage. He was even more surprised to learn that his wife was to be part of the wedding party also. "Yes, your wife," the king had told William when he gave the order. "I like John de Grey, Lord Zouche. I believe him to be a brave, loyal knight, and an honest one too. But I believe he's engaging in a bit of wistful thinking as far as this business with my cousin Eleanor is concerned, and it's made him a bit soft in the head. Probably not wise to have you abroad and her in England, even though he's left her alone so far. And in any case, she was one of my sister's sponsors at her christening, and my sister would like her at the wedding. Her old guardian Lady Hastings too."

So in early May of 1332, Eleanor found herself riding up to Dover Castle, where she had greeted her uncle's young bride so many years before, in the company of her fourteen-year-old namesake and cousin. "Do you think I shall be seasick, Lady Despenser? I have never crossed the sea before."

"I don't know, Eleanor. Your father never got seasick, not in the worst storms. Your mother sometimes did, when I traveled with her, but other times she did just fine." Had Isabella been seasick when she crossed the Channel to invade England? Eleanor certainly hoped so.

The girl turned to her former guardian. "What about you, Lady Hastings?"

"It has been so long, I hardly remember. I have not left England since I was married to my second husband. But Nelly is a great sailor, you know. She shall hold both our heads if necessary."

"Kindly take turns." Eleanor smiled and looked at a group of men riding ahead, her husband William and her son Hugh among them. Hugh would accompany them for part of the journey before heading to Santiago. She was relieved to see Hugh chatting with Lord Montacute and Edward de Bohun, for she had dreaded that he might be ostracized by the other men on account of his father. But they for the most part had been cordial to him, all except his uncle Lord Audley, who had greeted Eleanor and her son with barely a pretense at civility. At least his wife, Margaret, was not there to snub them.

"I wish my little sister could be here," said young Eleanor wistfully. She lowered her voice. "I worry about her so in Scotland, now that Edward Balliol has come to England and is claiming the Scottish crown. I have heard tell that he and Henry de Beaumont and those other men who lost lands because of the peace may invade Scotland. But surely the king would not let harm come to her if they did?"

"Of course not," said Bella, soothing her charge as of old.

"But he despised that peace," said Lady Despenser soberly. "Though to my mind it was sensible." The only sensible thing Mortimer and Isabella had ever done, she almost said. "It was entered into against his will, after all, and I do not think he would shirk at an opportunity to renounce it if it came around. I do believe he would protect Joan, of course, but only as his sister, not as the Scottish queen."

They fell silent at this new worry. After Edward Balliol's father, John Balliol, had been deposed by the first Edward, he had spent some years as a captive in England, then some years as a free man in Picardy. It was from there that Henry de Beaumont, who had gotten on the wrong side of the Ordainers, then the wrong side of the second Edward, then on the wrong side of Mortimer, had escorted him to England in 1331. Beaumont, never one to miss a chance for intrigue, had seen the death of Robert Bruce and his succession by a mere child as a God-sent opportunity to recover his Scottish lands, and Balliol to recover the Scottish crown. That previous November, the Scots had crowned their little king and his small bride with all due ceremony, but with the great Bruce dead, there was nervousness among the Scots and a certain anticipation among the English. Had the time come at last for England to redeem herself?

"What are you ladies talking of?"

Hugh le Despenser and William la Zouche had allowed their horses to slow down so that the ladies were astride them. Eleanor smiled at her son and her husband. "Scotland."

"Just what we men were speaking of! We should all ride together." Hugh chuckled and let his horse go even slower, so that he rode along with his aunt Bella while William and Eleanor pricked their mounts forward. When they were a safe distance from the others, William took Eleanor's hand, the most intimate touch they dared these days. "Sweet wife."

"My dear husband."

"Tonight we shall be housed at Dover Castle. Will you meet me later?"

"William—" For all she longed to lie with him as his wife again, she dreaded excommunication.

He gripped her hand more tightly. "Don't worry, my love. We'll be suitably chaperoned."

That evening, Eleanor brushed the bride-to-be's hair until it shone, arranged it in a single thick braid, saw her to her bed, and then lay on her trundle bed until her royal charge and the other ladies and damsels fell asleep. Then she threw on a cloak and with the aid of a torch made her way outside the castle.

William was already there, alone despite his promise of a chaperone, unless one counted some of the guards wandering by from time to time. "Let's go to the shore, my love."

They walked hand in hand, listening to the waves beating against the shore, until there were no other human beings in sight. Then, without any planning on the part of either, they turned to each other and kissed, not ceasing until they were both out of breath. "William. I long to lie with you so much. But the Pope said—"

"I know, love. I know. I promised a chaperone, and I've a right proper bitch of one."

It was not like William to be crude in this matter. Eleanor was puzzling over this when he whistled, and a large dog bustled over to them. "See, my love? Our chaperone. You sit here, my lady, our chaperone sits here"—the dog settled on her haunches between William and Eleanor—"and all shall be quite proper. Lay a hand on me without my consent, my lady, and Betsy here shall have you on the ground begging for mercy."

Eleanor giggled. "Should we be challenged, William, her testimony will hardly be of much worth to us before the judge."

"One wag of the tail for 'they lay together,' two wags for 'they did not'? Well, it's about as intelligent as that damn squire of Grey's, and just as believable. So. Now that we are suitably chaperoned, we'll sit and talk with the highest decorum. What shall we discuss? Scotland?"

"What else can married people who cannot bed together discuss?" She giggled again, then quieted. "It is a concern to me, William. Do you think we will be at war with the Scots again? I dread it."

"Yes. It saddens me, for I took pride in the peace, hated as it was. But I can understand the king's feelings. It was pressed on him, and England never really benefited, not with Isabella and Mortimer appropriating all of the twenty thousand pounds given by Bruce for themselves. And I can tell you, too, that the young men are hot for war. They're eager to prove themselves, to restore England's reputation and win some glory. And your son Hugh is as hot as any of them."

"To restore our family's reputation, I suppose."

"Yes. He gets on with his fellow men, as you could see coming here, but there's still a distance between him and them, and it'll be there until he fights his way clear of it. A pity, but that's the way men are."

"Yes." She sat awhile in silence, absently patting Betsy. "I know the king meant in having you escort Eleanor to show his high regard for you, and I suppose in having me along he might have also meant to show that I still had a place in his family, that I was no longer simply a disgraced traitor's wife of dubious virtue to boot. That was kind of him. But it will be so hard to watch that wedding, thinking of us, William."

"Yes. There's not a day that goes by that I don't ache to have you in my arms."

"I pray daily that it does not happen, but I have thought what I would do if the Pope were to declare me John de Grey's wife. I had thought that I might run away with you, but I could not defy God in that manner. Do you understand?"

"Yes."

"But I could not live with John de Grey, knowing that my heart was in your keeping. I would take the veil instead. I would go to live with Nora and Sister Gwenllian at Sempringham, and they would teach me patience. It would be hard, but it would be best for all concerned."

He could do nothing but take her hand and squeeze it. For a while longer they sat together, watching the waves crash and break. Finally, William said, "I've always had my will made before I crossed the seas; I'm a man who prefers dry land. I revised it before I left on this expedition. I have asked that I be laid to rest in Tewkesbury Abbey, my sweet. Near the ancestors of my beloved wife Eleanor."

"Where I wish to be buried."

"Yes. They might keep us apart in life, my love. They'll never keep us apart in death. Don't worry, my love. I would do nothing to hurry it on; I fear God's wrath as you do. But there would never be another woman for me if you were taken away, not ever."

She pressed his hand as Betsy, napping, yelped triumphantly in her sleep. William laughed. "Catching a hare, no doubt. Come, my love. Let's go to the chapel and pray that this talk of convents and burials is for naught and that we may have some years together yet."

The Pope, as before, did not make a final decision in *Grey v. Zouche* himself, but sent it to be reheard by the Canon of Salisbury, who found in favor of Zouche. John grimly appealed again. Before the case could be reheard by the Pope's latest delegates (the Bishop of London, the Canon of London, and the Canon of Wells), the Canon of Salisbury ordered John to pay costs to William and Eleanor. In May 1333, the Pope ordered the Bishop of Coventry to hear the case.

Eleanor was not as distressed as she might have been by this delay, for she had other worries. Edward Balliol had invaded Scotland the previous August. He had met with success at Dupplin Moor, where, to Eleanor's regret, her uncle's faithful friend Donald of Mar, who had been appointed regent for the young Scottish king, had been killed. But in December, the Scots had driven the invaders out. In January, despite the reluctance of Parliament, the English king had begun to raise troops. By the time the Pope's decision reached Eleanor, that late spring of 1333, the English were besieging Berwick. With them were her sons Hugh and Edward, her stepson Alan, her half-brothers, her first husband's nephews, and her old charge John of Eltham, and she worried about them all. Her concern extended itself even to John de Grey, for though she did not want to be his wife, she did not want to gain her freedom by becoming his widow. Daily, remembering Gilbert and Adam, she prayed for the safety of all of them.

Then, one warm day in late July, she woke to the sound of the church bells in Cardiff ringing. "What on earth is that about?" she asked Gladys as her old damsel entered her chamber.

"Victory, my lady. The English have defeated the Scots at a place called Halidon Hill."

By August, her sons had come home, bearing booty and making a point of calling each other "Sir Hugh" and "Sir Edward." Soon afterward came the trip to Roger de Northburgh, Bishop of Coventry, a man who had served her uncle, Isabella and Mortimer, and the present king in a variety of capacities and who had gotten through unscathed; it was he who had accompanied William inside Caerphilly Castle when young Hugh had surrendered it. To the bishop John, Eleanor, and William told their stories, by now without blushing or rancor, for they had been told so often. The witnesses were examined again; the proctors argued again. Then at last, in early 1334, the three parties stood before the bishop and waited for his sentence.

"I give sentence in favor of William la Zouche."

As he had three times before, John de Grey whispered to his proctor. This time, however, he shook his head as he spoke. The proctor lifted his head. "My client wishes Lady Despenser and Lord Zouche to know that he will not appeal. He accepts the finding of this court and relinquishes all claim to Lady Despenser."

Eleanor held the table to keep herself from falling. She listened as the bishop said some concluding words, without comprehending any of them. Then they were free to go.

She walked over to John de Grey, who had not lifted his eyes from the table before him, and touched his hand. "Sir Grey, I wish to apologize to you. I never meant to mislead or hurt you in any way, but I did, and I am humbly sorry."

"I know, my lady."

"You must marry a pretty young woman who can give you children. I hope you will do so soon, and prosper. I wish you well, Sir Grey."

She pecked him on the cheek. John smiled sadly and looked at William. "May I, Lord Zouche?" William nodded, and John returned the peck. "Take care of her, Lord Zouche."

He walked out of the bishop's chambers, and then Eleanor and William were alone. For a while they stood holding each other in silence. Then they walked hand in hand, oblivious to all around them, out of the bishop's palace and to William's lodgings at a nearby inn. "At last, my sweet," he whispered as they lay down together, "we're together forevermore."

"Forevermore," Eleanor echoed.

CHAPTER 29

▼

DECEMBER 1334 TO
JUNE 1337

In December 1334, Eleanor and William rode to Shaftesbury Abbey, where they were greeted by Sister Joan le Despenser. But the greeting between Eleanor and Joan was a short one, for it was Lady Hastings Eleanor had come to see. "Is she better, Joan?" Eleanor asked hopefully.

"No, Mama. She is much worse. Her children and Aunt Aline are already here. I will take you to her room."

Bella was asleep when Eleanor came softly into the room, where Bella's sister and children sat on a bench that had been carried there for their convenience. She bent over Bella and kissed her cheek.

Three months before, Gladys, Eleanor's mainstay for so long, had fallen ill. Eleanor would hear of no one nursing her but herself. For weeks they had switched places, Gladys lying in Eleanor's great bed, Eleanor sleeping on a trundle bed, until Eleanor had woken in the middle of the night to find Gladys still and cold, having died in her sleep. She had thought, as she watched as Gladys at her damsel's own request was buried in the Lady Chapel at Tewkesbury, that she would never stop crying. And then the news had arrived that an ailing Lady Hastings had decided to be nursed at Shaftesbury Abbey.

"Nelly? Is that really you?"

"Yes, Bella."

Bella smiled. "I was afraid you would not come—in time that is. The priest has shriven me already."

Eleanor sat on the bed and took Bella's cold hand, shocked at the change in her sister-in-law's appearance she could detect under the layers of blankets that covered her. Always petite, she was now little more than bones, and the thick dark hair that Eleanor knew had been Bella's secret pride had lost all of its glisten. She did not trust herself to speak, so she simply stroked the hand until Bella herself finally spoke again, in such a low voice that Eleanor had to lean over to hear her. "It is odd, Nelly, but I am really quite content to die. There are so many I love whom I hope I shall see. My husbands. My son Thomas. Papa and my mother. My little sister Margaret. My brothers. And yet there are so many others I love here on earth. My son Hugh and my daughter and their children. Nicholas. Aline. And you. I will miss you so much, Nelly."

"And I you, Bella. We have known each other since we were mere girls, and been through such strange times together."

"I remember when you married Hugh, how pretty you were in your green gown. But I was jealous, my dear, because the great King Edward was at Hugh's wedding, and had not come to mine. And I did not think I would like you much, because you were the daughter of such a great earl. I thought you would treat me as an inferior. So I was not happy at first when Hugh married you."

"Why Bella, I never would have known it."

"I kept it to myself."

Eleanor laughed. "Bella, if that is the best you can do for a deathbed confession, you will be in heaven straightaway."

"Oh, I have worse. I lay with Ralph twice before we were married."

"Only twice, dear? Lord Monthermer could have charmed a nun away from her vows, Bella. It is only fortunate that he never got my aunt Mary alone."

"Did Joan tell you I took vows two days before?"

Eleanor glanced at Bella's left hand and saw that she wore the ring of a nun. "No, she did not."

"It was something I had long thought of doing, since about the time Papa and Hugh died. But I was too selfish; I wanted to be with my children and their children. But now I have done so, and I am very happy." She smiled, and Eleanor thought she was about to drift off when she added, "But I am not the most married nun in Shaftesbury, it seems. One of the older nuns had four husbands!" Eleanor laughed, and Bella sighed. "I loved all my husbands, Nelly—even my first, though I was but a girl when he died. What shall happen if we all meet in heaven? I tried to ask the priest, but he only muttered something in Latin."

Eleanor sometimes wondered this herself about Hugh and William. She told Bella what she had often told herself. "Worry not, Bella dear. God will work it all out."

Bella smiled faintly, and Eleanor saw that she was fast losing strength and life. She helped Bella settle more comfortably against the pillows and, seeing her shiver, put the blankets around her more snugly. Then she kissed her sister-in-law on the forehead and stood up, hoping that Bella could not see the tears streaming down her face. "I am going to leave you with your children now, my sweet. I will come again when you have rested a bit."

She took herself outside and waited, William's arm around her, for the inevitable news to come out of Bella's chamber. Very soon, it did. Lady Hastings, a weeping sister said, had lost consciousness and slipped away painlessly, surrounded by at least some of those she had loved. And that, thought Eleanor, was the very least her sister-in-law had deserved.

It had been a mistake, Edward le Despenser realized, to set out from Essendine in Rutland with the sky looking so gloomy. But it was, after all, January, when gloomy skies could be expected, and having been a landowner for only two months, he still took a boyish delight in riding between the manors that had reverted to him in November.

"They're mine?" he had said in disbelief when Hugh told him that the life tenant had died. "They're not forfeit?"

"Father arranged for you to have the reversion when you were but a babe, Edward, and he actually appears to have done it legally. Father did have a lapse or two in the direction of morality now and then." He chuckled. "Mostly then. Did you ever hear of his schemes to raise money for the crown by forcing people to buy bad wine? I hope they at least got good and soused off of it." Edward frowned; he had not developed Hugh's peculiar sense of humor about their father. "So you'll have lands now in Bedfordshire, Buckinghamshire, Wiltshire, Rutland, Northamptonshire, and Lincolnshire, little brother. When shall I visit you?"

There had been, of course, the king to do fealty to. Edward had seen the king fleetingly after Halidon Hill, when he had been knighted along with a number of other men who had been spoken well of by their commanders or who had come to the king's own notice. But he'd not had to speak to him at the time, and so his fealty had not gone particularly well. Oh, he hadn't disgraced himself—he told himself morosely that this would take a lot of doing for a Despenser anyway—but he had gone through the ceremony as though sleepwalking. When the king allowed him to stand and tried to engage him in small talk, he had answered in polite monosyllables, conscious that he probably appeared a bumpkin. In fact, he'd been wondering the entire time, *Did your grace see my father die? Did you enjoy it as much as the others?*

Hugh had gone with him for moral support. As they rode south, for the king was at Newcastle, Edward asked, "Hugh, don't you ever get angry at them? Our father, for getting you in prison all that time? Mortimer and Isabella?"

Hugh looked at his horse, resplendent in Despenser trappings. The king after some hemming and hawing had allowed Hugh to bear the family arms—a display that never failed to attract stares, which Hugh coolly ignored. "What would that accomplish? I loved Father. He's dead. I hated Mortimer. He's dead too. Shall I go to their graves and kick at them?"

"Piss over Mortimer's is what I would do. But that bitch Isabella is still alive. Alive and thriving. I'd like to kill her."

"Don't; it'd be a pleasure to have one generation of Despensers with their heads intact." Hugh saw his younger brother shiver and touched him on the shoulder. In a different tone of voice, a tender one, he said, "Edward, don't get yourself caught up in an endless cycle of hate. It'll waste you. You're young, good-looking, bright, and prosperous. Do the one thing Isabella didn't want any of us to do. Enjoy your life."

And he was trying his best to do so. But at this moment, he was soaking wet, and the rain was beginning to turn to sleet.

He turned to the squire closest to him—now that he had manors in six counties he had a suitable number of retainers, and he was still not used to their constant presence—and asked, "Where are we?"

"Near Groby, sir. The Ferrers family lives there. Perhaps we should seek shelter there."

Edward did a brief review of his father's known misdeeds and concluded that the Ferrers family did not figure into any of them. But Henry de Ferrers was his aunt Elizabeth de Burgh's son-in-law, and there was that Gower and Usk business he had heard tell of...

The sleet was coming down in pellets, and his horse was shivering. That settled the matter, for Edward was fond of his horses and could not stand to see them uncomfortable. "All right. Let's head to Groby and get you a dry stall and some nice oats."

The squire looked confused but turned in the direction of Groby.

Lady Elizabeth de Burgh had known trouble lately; her cocksure son, William, had been murdered in Ireland in 1333, by his own men. Since then she had become especially close to her daughter Isabella and to her sensible son-in-law, Henry, whom she was visiting on the day when Edward le Despenser came calling at Groby. Elizabeth was sitting in the spacious chamber allotted for her, working on a tapestry for her young grandson's nursery, when Henry poked his head in. "There's a drowned rat in the great hall who claims to be your nephew. Are you up to one of your Despenser relations? Edward le Despenser, to be precise."

"Come now, Henry. I've met Edward several times. He's not like his father, he's very quiet and sweet-natured."

"Oh, I suppose. But if you could see him!" He chuckled. "He's soaked to the skin, and then some. And you're right about him being quiet. I gave my poor sister the impossible task of entertaining him while my man looked out for him some dry clothes. I think he said four words to her, and three of them were his name, if you count the 'le.'"

"Anne is entertaining him?"

"Well, she will be once he has had his bath. Unless he bolts first."

Elizabeth said thoughtfully, "Leave them alone for a while, why don't you?"

"Mother de Burgh?"

"Don't you see? You were talking only yesterday about a husband for Anne. Why not the Despenser lad? They're not so far apart in age, he bears a good character which is no mean feat considering from whose loins he sprang, and he's handsome, as you'll find when he's not dripping wet. And I understand he's just come into a very pretty collection of estates."

"But you can't stop Anne from talking when she gets going, and you can hardly seem to start him talking."

"So? Some couples get on splendidly that way. And Anne is a beautiful girl. If the boy won't exert himself a little for her, he's hopeless or half-blind. Come. Sit down and let's play a game of chess and let's see how they get on. The sleet grows worse than ever. He won't be leaving any time soon."

Edward was of two minds as he took his bath, half longing to hurry so he could again see the goddess he had met on his arrival, half longing to linger so that he did not have to think of something to say to her. At last the memory of her golden ringlets, soft blue eyes, and cherry lips won out, and he allowed his man to dress him (another innovation he was having difficulty getting used to) in his borrowed robes, ignoring the squire's half smile. He bowed as he reentered the great hall. "My lady."

"You look quite comfortable now. That must have been a horrid storm."

"Yes."

"Do you live in Leicestershire, Sir Despenser?"

"No. I am passing through from Essendine." Edward thought a moment before coming out with the immortal words, "Have you ever been there, my lady?"

"No. I barely ever get out of Groby. Henry is so lucky. He goes to Parliament, and he will be going back to Scotland shortly, I think, to hold Berwick securely for the king. You know, I have never even seen the king. Have you, Sir Despenser?"

"Yes."

"Oh, how could I be so stupid? You must have seen a great deal of him when you were younger. Your father—"

She clapped her hand across her mouth. "I am so sorry, Sir Despenser."

"It matters not, my lady," said Edward in a gallant tone he did not know he could muster. "Most people shy away from mentioning my father. It's good to have him in the conversation early."

"I was a little girl, you know, when all that happened. It must have been hor- rid for you."

"Someday I would like to tell you about it—when I get better acquainted with you."

"When you get better acquainted with me, sir?"

"That is—if you would like that." He waited for her to recoil with disgust.

She looked at him solemnly. "I would, Sir Despenser."

"Quietly, Henry, quietly. This is how your hopelessly shy knight is barely get- ting on with your sister."

Henry followed his wife and his mother-in-law to the great hall, which was being set up for dinner. In a window seat, oblivious to all around them, sat Edward and Anne, talking and as close together as a couple could be without being seated on each other's lap. As Elizabeth, Isabella, and Henry watched, Edward tentatively put his hands on Anne's shoulders and drew her in for a kiss. It was a long one, evidently highly satisfactory to both parties, and it was followed up quickly by another that showed no sign of stopping in the near future.

"Time to throw some cold water over those two," said Henry. "Sir Despenser?"

Edward turned, looking less flustered than annoyed at being interrupted. "Lord Ferrers," he said. "I would like your permission to marry your sister."

"Yes, I had hoped things were going in that direction," said Henry dryly. "Come to my chamber, sir, and let us talk."

They were married on April 20, 1335, at Groby. Their bedding ceremony was restrained, as Edward had hoped. With his bride's parents dead, the tone was set by Henry, who was a protective brother, and his mother and stepfather, who knew well his bashfulness. Eleanor had helped Anne undress for the evening and, Anne told him later, was most kind, whispering as she tucked the covers round her, "Don't worry, my dear. Edward is the kindest man in the world. You will be happy with him."

Zouche made a friendly toast that could not have offended the oldest lady there, and Hugh, though taking the brother's prerogative of some bawdiness, was so charming that even Edward laughed. He could not resist adding, "A lot about marriage you know, my bachelor brother."

"Then you shall teach me," said Hugh cheerfully.

Edward was a romantic, and it grieved him as he lay with his new wife that he would not come to her pure, as she was coming to him. He took some consolation, however, in the fact that he had not had a woman since the day he had met her.

She was so lovely undressed that he was almost afraid to touch her, but he got over this soon enough, and he put his superior experience to good use in making it a pleasant night for her as well. When all was done and she lay in the crook of his arm, she murmured, "Edward, you have made me so happy, and I love you so much."

Tears stung his eyes. "Anne, I never thought to hear anyone say that to me."

"Why not? You're sweet and handsome and loving."

"My father and grandfather, the men I loved above all others, were hung as traitors. My brother was clapped into prison, three of my sisters were forced to take the veil, my mother and us other children were sent to the Tower. Then my mother was sent back and almost died. For years I hated everyone—or feared them, I don't know which. I thought we were cursed. And now I see that I have been blessed."

"I will do my best to make you happy after all that you have suffered."

"You can't." He drew her into another kiss. "You've already done that, my love."

Coming out of Anne's chamber at Essendine Castle eleven months later, in March 1336, Eleanor collided with her son. "Edward! Why aren't you downstairs?"

"She cried out, Mother! She is in pain, I know!"

"Of course she is in pain, Edward. She is having a baby." Eleanor took her son's arm and managed to steer him in the direction of the great hall. "But you are only making yourself miserable by standing here listening at the door, and she would be upset too if she knew you were here." She looked around for William, who was supposed to have been minding Edward. "Where is your stepfather?"

"I begged him to go for a physician just in case. Mother, what if she dies?"

"Edward, everything is going perfectly normally."

"But what if something happens?"

Eleanor almost caught her son's worry. He was deeply in love with Anne, she knew; what would become of the most vulnerable of her sons if something did happen to his wife? "Edward, I will not lie and say there is no danger. There always is, you know that. But everything has gone well so far. She is not overtired, she is dilating nicely, and she has the best midwife for miles around. And she has me! I helped with your aunt Bella's children, and your aunt Margaret d'Audley's first child, and others besides. Why, I helped with the king himself! And his brother and sisters. She is being taken very good care of, I promise you. But first babies are slow. Your brother Hugh was no quicker than this, and I bore ten healthy babes!"

"But Anne is so small!"

"Small, but not delicate. She is very healthy."

William came in and looked apologetically at Eleanor. "The physician will come as soon as he can, Edward." He did not add that the physician had said he knew far less about babies than the midwife.

"Shouldn't you be going back there, Mother?"

"I came only to tell you Anne was doing fine," said Eleanor patiently. She looked outside. It might help if some imaginary errand were invented for Edward, but if Edward tried to sit a horse in his present state of mind he would probably break his neck. "Sit by the fire, Edward, and have some wine. It will relax you, perhaps."

"All the wine in Bordeaux couldn't do that," William whispered in her ear sympathetically.

It was dark when Eleanor entered the hall again. Edward had been up since the middle of the previous night, when Anne had felt her first contractions, and he had finally dozed off in front of the fire. She touched him on the face. "Come see your son, my dear."

"Son?"

"He is a fine boy, and Anne is doing well. Come with me."

Edward followed her dazedly. Edward's imprisonment in the Tower with his newborn sister Elizabeth had given him baby-minding skills rare in males, but he was out of practice, and after embracing Anne he took his new son with a mixture of such extreme caution and wonderment that the competent but gruff midwife smiled. "I would like to name him Edward, love," said Anne. "After you and after the late king."

"Edward it shall be," said the new father. He stared transfixedly at the sturdy boy, whom his king would one day name a Knight of the Garter.

Eleanor had not seen Edward wear such a blindingly happy smile in his life, not even on his wedding day. "Let us leave them alone," she said softly.

William found the lump soon after Twelfth Night. He had been making love to Eleanor when his hand, caressing her right breast, felt something hard and unyielding in it, not the softness underneath silkiness to which he was accustomed. Startled, he touched it again, and then had his attention distracted, most successfully, by Eleanor. For the time being he forgot about it, but when they snuggled together afterward, he said, "My dear. I felt—"

"I asked the midwife. She said that many women of my age get them, and they are usually quite harmless."

"Ah."

Eleanor was grateful when she heard him snoring a few minutes later. She herself had noticed the lump months ago, while bathing, and she was certain it was getting larger. The midwife had frowned when she heard of this. And Eleanor's own mother had complained of such a lump in the months before she had died, aged only thirty-five. All this would distress William, as would hearing that the lump was sometimes quite painful. So she would not tell him these things unless he asked, and she hoped he would not. Men, after all, knew precious little about women's workings and were not enthralled with hearing about them.

And in any case, *she* could not possibly be dying. She felt quite well, save for the occasional pain. And how could God let her leave her young children? John was only eleven, Lizzie not yet ten, William only six.

But the Lord had taken her old charge, John of Eltham, only the autumn before; the young man, only twenty, had died of a fever, in Scotland. And on the last day of February, He took Eleanor's husband.

Eleanor had thought little of it when William caught a bad cold. Since his last Scottish excursion in the summer and fall of 1335, he had been prone to chills in winter, and usually some rest in bed, combined with soup and an herbal remedy Eleanor had learned from Sister Gwenllian at her last visit to Sempringham, put him on the mend quickly. But this time was different. She was sleeping soundly next to William on the third night of his illness when he croaked, "My love."

Eleanor turned to her husband and touched his arm. He was burning with fever. "William! Good God!" Her scream brought William's squires in the adjoining room to their feet. "Get him a physician!"

But there was nothing the physician, or Eleanor, or even the local wise woman whom she called in as a last resort could do. For days William drifted in and out of consciousness, sometimes speaking coherently, sometimes speaking deliriously, always breathing with the greatest difficulty. Eleanor sat clinging to his hand, hoping to pull him back to health from sheer force of love. But on February 28, he came to himself after a long period of delirium only to say, "My love. I named you my executrix in my will a while back. There's no need to change that, is there?"

"No, William."

"And you will bury me at Tewkesbury? In the Lady Chapel?"

"Yes, William."

"Maybe in a tomb not quite so elaborate as Hugh's…"

Hugh's tomb contained dozens of niches, the largest for intricately carved figures of Christ and the Apostles, the smaller ones for figures of various saints. The figures surrounded a recess in which Hugh's armor-clad effigy stared rather complacently upward. William had not let Eleanor hear of his opinion that Hugh needed all of the saintly intercession on his tomb he could get, but Eleanor had somehow guessed it. She half smiled. "All right, William. But surely it is too early to worry about these things—"

"I should like to make my confession now, my love."

The children—Alan, hers, and little William—had all been summoned home, and when William had been shriven she led them into his chamber. The Despenser children hung back a little as the Zouche children and Eleanor went to the head of the bed, but William said weakly, with a smile, "All of you. I want to say good-bye to all of you."

One by one, each of the children went to William's right side as Eleanor wept quietly on his left. William managed a few words for each. When all had done, he lifted his right hand with an effort and patted Eleanor on the cheek. "Don't cry, my love."

"I can't help it, William. I love you so much."

"Is your lute nearby?"

Startled out of her tears, Eleanor replied, "I suppose so."

"Have someone fetch it, and play and sing to me as I sleep. It will make me happier than anything I know, to hear your sweet voice."

Hugh left the room and returned with the lute, which he placed into Eleanor's hands. Obediently she played and sang love song after love song, her voice quavering at first, then gaining strength. She started to sing a song she had not sang in years. It had been one of her husband Hugh's favorites; strangely, it had been Isabella's and her uncle's too. How odd! She faltered, started singing it again, never taking her eyes off William. He had been smiling all along, first with his eyes open, then with them shut, and now she saw that he was asleep. She let her voice trail off and leaned over to put her cheek next to his. "My love?" she whispered. "Oh, my love!"

How long she sat there weeping over his body, she never knew, but the room was dark when she let Hugh help her to her feet. "Come, Mother," he said gently, a husky edge to his voice. "You must rest now."

The king had called Parliament for that March—William had been summoned—and as word got out at Westminster of William's death, the condolence letters began to arrive at Hanley Castle, where Eleanor had gone to stay. Dressed in the black robes she had worn to Hugh's funeral, she listened listlessly at first as a clerk read the letters to her and her eldest son. Then she frowned as he began to read one bearing a particularly impressive seal. "The Countess of *Gloucester*?"

"That is aunt Margaret, Mother. The king created Hugh d'Audley Earl of Gloucester at Parliament. He created six earls—William de Montacute is the Earl of Salisbury, William de Clinton is Earl of Northampton—"

"Earl of Gloucester! Why, Hugh d'Audley was nothing but a traitor to my uncle, who loved him so dearly that he married him to Margaret, and what has he done for the present king to be made Earl of Gloucester? My father's and my brother's title to be given to that upstart, who has no Clare blood! When you—"

Hugh said, "I know what you are thinking, Mother, that I am your father's eldest grandson and should have been given the earldom, but that will never be, Mother. Not with Father's history."

"But you have served the king loyally! Every bit as loyally as that Audley creature! And Edward has been so stingy with you—only those little manors of yours, and those not even for you to hold in fee. Just because you are Hugh le Despenser's son!"

She fumed a little longer. Hugh, though he himself had been chagrined to hear of Audley's earldom, consoled himself with the thought that the news had at least temporarily roused his mother from her grief over William. "I suppose that is solely why Margaret wrote to me, to show off her new title. Countess of Gloucester!" She muttered under her breath, "Bitch!"

Perhaps she was too roused. "All right, Mother. What's the next one say?"

"From Lord Thomas de Berkeley. His condolences on your loss, et cetera. Oh, my lady, and he wishes to see you next week. He knows your grief is fresh, and will only trouble you for an hour or so. He and his wife."

William la Zouche had served on commissions with Lord Berkeley over the past few years, and the two men had gotten on well enough, but their wives, Hugh le Despenser's widow and the Earl of March's daughter, had never met. Eleanor shrugged. "Tell him he may come at his earliest convenience. I am not leaving here anytime soon."

The Berkeleys arrived two days later, accompanied by their seven-year-old son, Maurice, who stood fidgeting between his parents as they expressed their condolences once more to her. John had gone to be a squire in the Earl of Warwick's household, where Gilbert still was, but Elizabeth and little William were still at home with Eleanor, and they joined her in greeting the Berkeleys. "Elizabeth, William, perhaps you can show Master Berkeley the new puppies while we talk."

"Yes, Mama."

Elizabeth led the boys away. Lady Berkeley said nervously, "She is a pretty child, and your youngest looks like a fine boy too."

Would Hugh or Edward have believed that one day she would be sitting in her chamber with Edward's jailer and Mortimer's daughter, politely chattering about their children? Perhaps they would have found it amusing. But it was time for her to admire Maurice. "Your son is well grown for his age, my lady, and quite well behaved. Many lads would have recoiled from a girl!"

"I would have been sorry to have seen him do so," said Lord Berkeley, with a gesture as if getting to the point. "The truth is, my lady, it is your daughter we have come about. We would like to see our son marry her."

"Marry?"

"It's a suitable match, don't you think? There's a little age difference, but it won't matter much once they're in their late teens. And Maurice is a bit old for his age."

"It is not the age difference, or your son, Lord Berkeley. It is—my uncle Edward. I loved my uncle, Lord Berkeley. I loved him more than any man besides my husbands and my sons. And he died in your care. He was murdered. I know that you have been acquitted in Parliament of blame, but how could you not have known what was meant?"

Margaret de Berkeley was staring at her feet. Thomas said, "Lady Despenser, all three of us have been prisoners at one time or another, if you count my wife's being confined to Shoreditch Priory as imprisonment, as I certainly do. Those were hellish times for all of us. I've done things to be ashamed of; perhaps you have too." Eleanor thought of the jewels and John de Grey, and flinched. "I've told of my role in your uncle's death to my confessor, and I've been doing penance for it."

"And marrying into the Despenser family is part of it?"

"As matter of fact, it would be, if you allow it. Think of it: the children of this marriage would have Roger Mortimer for a great-grandfather and Hugh le Despenser for a grandfather."

"I can think of no one who would dislike to hear that more than my husband and Roger Mortimer," said Eleanor dryly.

"My daughter, Joan, is to marry Thomas de Haudlo. We obtained the papal dispensation on the ground that I sided with the Earl of March and he sided with your husband and father-in-law and that the marriage would promote the peace."

"You are serious about this, aren't you?"

"After all, my lady, you married the man who captured your husband and besieged your son. And I believe that your mourn him deeply."

"I do, Lord Berkeley. As I mourned my first husband too, and my uncle." She paused, thinking of her son Hugh, who appeared destined by his father's misdeeds to be a perpetual outsider in England no matter how valiantly he served the king. "But I would like to see peace between our family and others, and I am willing to consider your proposal."

"Only to consider?"

"As my heir it should be up to my son Hugh to have a say in this marriage, to decide what alliances he wishes to make. He is in Glamorgan on my business and will not be back for some time. But I will write him and ask his consent. I believe that he will give it, Lord Berkeley. He does value good relations with others, and he wishes to live in the past no more than I do."

"Then I shall look forward to hearing from him," said Thomas de Berkeley.

Eleanor walked with the Berkeleys to the stables, where the canine Lord Zouche's daughter had given birth to four of the most peculiar-looking puppies Eleanor had seen. Young Berkeley had been well brought up, she noted with approval, for he thanked his young host and hostess as he prepared to go. "Master Berkeley, if your parents agree, you can take one of the puppies. They are weaned."

"Really?" He beamed at her.

"I make no warranties about the size it will grow to, Lord Berkeley," Eleanor cautioned as his son picked up the wiggling dog.

Lord Berkeley snorted, but made no resistance as his son prepared to take his prize home.

Hugh gave a provisional consent to the marriage, writing that he wanted to speak to Lord Berkeley in person. Which would not be soon, he added, because the king had asked him to come to Westminster.

He arrived at Hanley Castle in early May. It was late, and he came straight to Eleanor's chamber, to find his mother huddled before the fire. Probably having one of her sad spells about his stepfather, he surmised. "Mother? I've good news. The king has given me more land! Rotherfield in Sussex, and two manors in Devon, and the reversion of five manors besides that. Plus a thousand acres of wood and some knights' fees and some advowsons. And the fee of the manors I hold now. Lands that Father held."

"That is good."

"I know it's not the earldom of Gloucester, Mother, but it's something, isn't it? It hurt me too, to see it go to Audley. But I don't feel quite so excluded now. Why, the king even asked me if I've thought of taking a wife!" Hugh laughed. "I told him that asking that was your prerogative."

"Yes," agreed Eleanor. She put her head in her hands and began to weep.

"Mother! I don't understand. I thought you would be happy."

"I am."

"Then—"

Eleanor shook her head. "I am sorry, Hugh. It is just that I am in such pain tonight." She lifted her head, and Hugh saw with a shock that she had aged by years since he had last seen her scarce a month before. "So, so much pain, Hugh. I am dying, my dear."

She had bad days, medium days, and good days after that. On bad days, she lay in bed dosed with sleeping aids and was aware of nothing that went on around her. On her medium days, she could sit up in her chamber for a few hours before going back to bed. On her good days, Hugh or one of her men would carry her to her garden, where she would sit most of the day and be read or played to, or simply listen to the idle chatter of her damsels. They were the daughters of two prosperous local merchants and did not seem to be capable of a serious thought, but they were good company and attended her carefully.

On her best day, Hugh took her, Lizzie, and William for a ride on Eleanor's barge. "I know you like the water," he said simply when Eleanor, tears choking her, tried to thank him. "I wish I could get you to the sea but this will have to do."

"It is plenty, Hugh."

As Lizzie and William pestered the bargemen, Hugh settled Eleanor on a pile of cushions with a basket of provisions nearby, although Eleanor's sense of taste had deserted her recently and one food she ate was as good as another. "You are so kind, Hugh. You should really make some woman happy by marrying her."

Hugh grinned. On his mother's good days, she invariably nagged him about his unconscionable failure to marry. He humored her, which annoyed her, which cheered up both of them immensely. "Who could I find who would match you, Mother?"

Eleanor snorted. "You've used that excuse before."

She sat back and watched the Severn as the barge moved slowly down it, eating and drinking a little as she did to keep Hugh happy. "I know it is not that you dislike women, Hugh. I'm quite sure you wench about. When I visited you at Freeby unexpectedly that time your chamber reeked of cheap scent."

"Nothing gets past you, does it, Mother?"

"Very little," she said smugly. "Do you have a bastard?"

"No woman has presented me with a little replica of myself, so I suppose not."

"Well, that's something. But why waste yourself on whores when you could be married to a sweet young woman who would give you heirs? I don't understand."

He could not tell her that he did not want to marry until he was satisfied that his bride could carry the name of Hugh le Despenser without shame; it would hurt her too much. "One of these days. Now, Mother, tell me about the abbey again, so I will know what to tell the abbot."

Eleanor brightened; her remodeling at Tewkesbury could always get her off the subject of Hugh's bachelorhood. "I have decided on the windows. The east window should have Christ and the Virgin and the Apostles and the Archangel, with the Last Judgment. The south and north ones should have the prophets and King Solomon. And—I am not sure if the abbot will care for this—in the farthest windows to the north and south, my Clare ancestors who have been benefactors of the abbey. And Hugh and William. Do you think he would allow it? They would be looking quite respectfully on; not trying to usurp the holy men." She giggled. "Not even your dear father would be that bold."

"I am sure he will—the abbot, that is."

"I want you to make sure it all is completed."

"I will, Mother."

Lizzie and William drifted back over, and Eleanor put an arm around each of them. Hugh, she knew, had given himself the unhappy task of telling her two youngest children, both of whom were still mourning her husband William, that she was soon to die. They snuggled close to her as the four of them traded family anecdotes back and forth. Then Eleanor grew weary of sitting, and Hugh took her to the cabin where he had had a bed made up for her. When he came back, William had gone back to bother the bargemen again, but Lizzie was sitting where he had left her. "Mama says that I will be going to the prioress of Wix soon, for more education. And she said that my aunt Elizabeth de Burgh has invited me to stay with her for a while."

"Has she? That must have pleased Mother. It has made her sad not to be on better terms with our aunts."

"They were not friends for a long time, were they, Hugh?"

"No, they were not, but it was not really their doing. It was their husbands'. Mostly our father's, I am afraid."

"Was our father a bad man, Hugh? I have heard people say so."

Hugh sighed. "He did some very bad things to get land and money, but he had his good points too. He was clever and witty and loving to us and Mother. He could be generous when it suited him, and he was faithful to his king to the end." He shook his head. "It's hard for you because you never knew him. You'll hear all of the bad, and you won't be able to attest to any of the good. But trust me when I say there was good in him; more good than you'll ever hear."

"Do you ever wish you didn't carry his name, Hugh?"

"Lord, yes! Every single morning I woke up in prison I wished my name was George the baker's son. Once I was free I even thought of running off to Italy, just to get clear of the past. But instead I decided to stay and make what I could of my name, and we must all do the same. We will be a proud family again." He laughed. "And now I will stop speechifying."

He did. Elizabeth lay back, looking thoughtful. She was by far the best-looking member of the family, in Hugh's opinion. Her serious dark eyes were relieved by very long eyelashes, and her hair, curly like her mother's and dark like her father's, fell in a thick mass to her shoulders. "Hugh? Is it true I am to marry little Maurice de Berkeley?"

"Yes, when you are a little older. It will be a couple of years before you go to live with the Berkeleys; they have agreed to that." He patted Lizzie's head. "Sweetheart, I know it is a little daunting, but your mother and I think it will be a good match for you. And for both our families as well."

"I understand. But I am still a little afraid, Hugh."

Hugh started. How much had she heard of what had happened in Berkeley Castle? William la Zouche, bless the man, had kept Eleanor from hearing the details all these years, but had some dolt been gossiping around his little sister? "Afraid of what, Lizzie?"

"Maurice is still a little boy. He will throw frogs at me, I know, and wave spiders in my face. I hate things like that."

Hugh grinned with relief. "Rest easy, Lizzie. He will be a model of good behavior by the time you go to live with him, and if he comes near you with a spider, I will get an annulment for you. Settled?"

Lizzie smiled. "Settled."

The barge was turning back toward Hanley Castle. As he had promised, Hugh went to wake his mother so that she could see the sun set on the river. "Lizzie, William, isn't this pretty?"

"Yes, Mama."

"The king would have me on his royal barge and we would watch the sunset together. Quite a few times."

Neither Lizzie nor William had to ask their mother which king she meant; these days when she spoke of the king, it was always her uncle. William said, "He must have liked you very much, Mama."

"He did, William. And I him."

She smiled, and none of her children caught the glint of mischief in her smile. "He was very dear to me, and very kind."

"But not kinder than Papa!"

"No, William dear. Not kinder than your papa. Did you know that he and I were married upon this very barge?"

William did, but he enjoyed hearing the (considerably redacted) story again. Lizzie, who had regarded Lord Zouche as her father in all but name, also liked hearing the story of her mother's second marriage. For the rest of the way back to

Hanley they talked of Lord Zouche, and then Hugh told them some amusing stories about his own father, Lord Despenser. The four were in good spirits when the barge moored. ""Thank you, Hugh," Eleanor said as her son helped her off it. "It was a perfect day."

That was the last time Eleanor left her chamber. Several days before, Hugh had quietly sent for his other brothers and sisters, and soon they arrived at Hanley Castle, Joan, Nora, and Margaret escorted from the convents by some of his mother's men, Edward and Anne (pregnant again) with their baby and men, the Countess of Arundel and Edmund with *their* men, Gilbert and John in their Warwick livery. On the last day of June, all of them gathered around Eleanor's bed.

Eleanor had been drifting in and out of sleep all morning, and after a long doze she opened her eyes wide and stared around her. "Hugh?" she called in a worried tone. She smiled with relief as he stepped forward, unabashedly weeping, and kissed her cheek. "You should—"

Her voice was very faint, and Hugh saw out of the corner of his eye that a priest was pushing toward the bed with the Sacrament. But he continued to bend over his mother as she struggled to speak. "You should get married," she said finally, for the last time in her life. "It is an incomparable adventure."

Afterword

Eleanor's son Hugh le Despenser married Elizabeth, a widowed daughter of the Earl of Salisbury, sometime before April 1341, when a dispensation was obtained allowing them to remain married. He played a notable part in Edward III's French wars, particularly at the battle of Crécy, where he led the English forces across the Somme. He died in 1349, possibly a victim of that year's plague, without children. His widow remarried but elected to be buried beside him in Tewkesbury Abbey, where their canopied tomb (often confused with that of Hugh's father) can be seen today.

Edward le Despenser died in battle in France in 1342, survived by his wife and four sons. The youngest son, Henry, had a rather controversial career as the "Fighting Bishop of Norwich" and led an ill-starred crusade, although he spent most of his time performing more conventional bishopric duties and died in the midst of performing a church service. The eldest son, Edward, inherited his uncle Hugh's estates. He was created a Knight of the Garter by Edward III, fought in France and Italy, and was lavishly praised by the chronicler Jean Froissart as a gallant knight without whom no feast was complete. His chantry chapel, topped by a figure of Edward kneeling in prayer, is also at Tewkesbury Abbey.

Gilbert le Despenser died in 1381, having apparently had a wife and son who predeceased him. He served as a knight in Edward III's household.

John le Despenser was murdered in 1366, for reasons that do not appear in the records. His murderers were hung. He might be the John le Despenser who was granted an annuity in 1363, apparently at Queen Philippa's behest. This suggests he might have been connected with her household at some point.

Richard Fitz Alan, Earl of Arundel, annulled his marriage to Isabel le Despenser in 1344, rather belatedly, on the highly dubious ground that the couple had been forced by blows to cohabit. He promptly married his mistress, a widowed daughter of Henry, Earl of Lancaster. Isabel le Despenser, who was provided with some estates by her former husband, was alive in 1355; it is unknown whether she remarried or when she died. Edmund Arundel was bastardized by the annulment, which he fought unsuccessfully, but was able to attain knighthood and marry a daughter of the Earl of Salisbury, Sybil, by whom he had several daughters. Perhaps his bastardization benefited him in the long run; his younger half-brother inherited what became the massive Arundel fortune and the accompanying earldom, ran afoul of Richard II, and was beheaded.

Margaret le Despenser died in 1337; her aunt Elizabeth de Burgh sent items to be used in her burial. Eleanor le Despenser was living in Sempringham in 1351, when the crown ordered that she receive an allowance. Joan le Despenser died at Shaftesbury Abbey in 1384.

Elizabeth le Despenser married young Maurice de Berkeley in 1338, spending some time at Wix priory and with Elizabeth de Burgh before joining the Berkeley family. She bore her husband a number of children before his death, after which she married Sir Maurice Wyth, whom she also outlived. She died in 1389.

William la Zouche, Eleanor's son by her second husband, became a monk at Glastonbury. He was alive in 1381, when the abbot there was granted money during William's life.

Alan la Zouche, William la Zouche's son by his first wife, died in 1346, several months after fighting as a banneret at Crécy.

Among many other good works, Elizabeth de Burgh founded Clare Hall at Cambridge University. She died in 1360, leaving behind a set of household records that have been invaluable to researchers. Margaret d'Audley died in 1342.

Amie de Gaveston, Piers Gaveston's natural daughter, married John de Driby, a royal yeoman, having been granted some lands for life by Queen Philippa.

Nicholas de Litlyngton became abbot of Westminster Abbey, the famous Jerusalem Chamber of which was built for him. With a bequest from his predecessor, he resumed construction of the abbey's nave, the work on which was still ongoing when he died in 1386.

Roger Mortimer's widow, Joan, never remarried. She died at age seventy in 1356, having lived to see her grandson, another Roger Mortimer, become the second Earl of March and a Knight of the Garter.

John de Grey's luck improved after his unsuccessful attempt to claim Eleanor as his wife. He was a founding member of the Order of the Garter and served for a considerable time as Edward III's steward. He remarried, fathering two sons by his second wife, and died in 1359.

Princess Gwenllian died at Sempringham in June 1337, several weeks before Eleanor. She was age fifty-four and had been in the convent since infancy. In 1993 a memorial was erected to her memory near the site of Sempringham; it is now tended by the Princess Gwenllian Society.

Mary, Edward II's sister the nun, died in 1332. She was buried at Amesbury.

Edward III and Philippa produced a dozen children during Edward's lengthy, mostly popular reign. Their eldest son, Edward, later known as the Black Prince, was renowned for his military prowess. He married Joan, daughter of the Earl of Kent executed by Roger Mortimer, and predeceased his father. The prince's only surviving son, Richard, succeeded Edward III as king. Richard II's reign was as ill-starred as Edward II's and ended similarly, with Richard II deposed and dying in captivity. One of Richard II's unsuccessful endeavors was an attempt to canonize his great-grandfather Edward II. It fell flat, as did the efforts throughout the fourteenth century to canonize Thomas, Earl of Lancaster.

Isabella died in 1358. She was neither her son's prisoner, a nun, nor a madwoman as is frequently reported even today, but lived a comfortable, conventional existence as dowager queen, traveling between her estates, receiving visits from relatives and friends, going on pilgrimages, and giving to charity. Joan of Bar and the Countess of Pembroke visited her in her last days. She was buried in the Church of the Friars Minor in London, a fashionable resting place that Isabella had patronized and that was also the burial place of her aunt Margaret, Edward I's second wife. Isabella was buried in her wedding garments, apparently preserved for that purpose. Construction of her splendid tomb, long since destroyed, was overseen by a woman artisan. Edward II's heart was placed inside the tomb.

Isabella's daughter Joan, Queen of Scotland, lived an unsatisfactory life with her philandering husband and eventually chose to live in England alone. She was with her mother during the last months of Isabella's life and was buried near her in 1362. Eleanor, Countess of Guelders, was widowed in 1343. Impoverished for a time by her feuding sons, she retired to Deventer Abbey, which she had founded during her marriage. She was engaged in establishing another religious house when she died in 1355. She was probably buried at Deventer.

Thomas Gurney was captured in Naples by a royal agent but died, probably of natural causes, as he was being transported to England. William Ogle (or Ockley) was never found. John Maltravers ended up in Flanders, where he eventually regained Edward III's favor.

The characters in this book are mainly real men and women, though Eleanor's midwife Janet, Eleanor's named jailors, Eleanor's French admirer Jean, John de Grey's squires Fulk and Henry, and Master Geoffrey Preston are fictional. Gladys is based on a damsel of Eleanor's named Joan, whose name I changed as a concession to reader sanity.

Readers accustomed to thinking of Piers Gaveston and Edward II as gay icons may have been surprised to learn that both men fathered out-of-wedlock children. Their existence is established by documentary evidence, though nothing is known about their mothers and very little about the children themselves. Amie does not appear in records until 1331, when she is noted as being one of Queen Philippa's damsels. Adam appears in the records only in 1322, when he was being outfitted for the Scottish war; as F. D. Blackley pointed out, the fact that he was mentioned as being in the care of a master at the time suggests that he was still in his teens. Lucy, therefore, has an invented name and background, as does Amie's unnamed mother.

Nicholas de Litlyngton has been identified by historians, notably Barbara Harvey and Chris Given-Wilson, as likely being an illegitimate member of the Despenser family, and he certainly used a differenced version of the Despenser arms. He called his parents "Hugh and Joan," leading Given-Wilson to suggest that he was a son of Hugh le Despenser the younger. There seemed no good reason to me why he could not instead be a son of Hugh le Despenser the elder, Hugh the younger being more than busy elsewhere.

Allegations of a sexual relationship between Edward II and Eleanor le Despenser are contained in a contemporary Hainaulter chronicle and have been given some credence by Roy Martin Haines, Edward II's recent scholarly biographer. Whether there is truth to them is unknown, and probably unknowable, but records indicate that Eleanor's relationship with the king, whatever its nature, was a close one that predated Edward's relationship with Eleanor's husband. Novelists have often discovered their characters taking on minds of their own as their work progresses; in this case, I left the decision whether to bed together to the king and Eleanor, who finally found it impossible to resist temptation.

Most historians believe that the relationships of Edward II with Piers Gaveston and Hugh le Despenser were homosexual in nature, although Pierre Chaplais has argued that Gaveston and the king were not lovers but adoptive brothers. The evidence as to Edward II's sexuality rests mainly on contemporary innuendo, some of it quite ambiguous, and the reported manner of his death. Froissart, however, stated explicitly that the genitals of Hugh le Despenser were severed because he was a heretic and a sodomite. As Froissart was friendly with

Hugh's grandson Edward le Despenser, it seems unlikely that he would have made such a statement lightly. Whatever the nature of Edward II's relationships with his favorites, they were extraordinarily close and proved to be severable only by death.

The procedural steps of the marriage controversy between Eleanor, William la Zouche, and John de Grey are sketched in the *Calendar of Entries in the Papal Registers Relating to Great Britain and Ireland*, but little is known of the basis for John de Grey's allegations. I therefore invented a scenario that seemed plausible in light of canon law at the time. (Much as I would have liked to write a court-room battle of the sort familiar in domestic cases today, medieval marriage litigation was a rather staid proceeding, with most testimony taken in private by examiners and no opportunity for stinging cross-examination.)

In a petition brought after Mortimer's execution, Eleanor claimed that she had been imprisoned in the Tower of London, and later Devizes Castle, despite the order of the king's council that she be released, and that Mortimer told her that she would not be released until she gave up her lands. She also stated that she feared for her life if she did not agree to his demands. The king's rapid granting of her petition to have her lands restored ("to ease the king's conscience" as he himself put it) is strong evidence that he believed her allegations. I have invented the details of her removal to Devizes Castle and her treatment there, but by 1329 Roger Mortimer, drunk with power, was probably quite capable of the actions I have ascribed to him. In his speech at the scaffold, he did confess to the entrapment of the hapless Earl of Kent.

After Mortimer's fall, William la Zouche told the king that much of the treasure removed from the Tower by Eleanor had come into the hands of Benedict de Fulsham. This suggests that Eleanor admitted to stealing the jewels, but again the details of how and when she obtained them are unknown, necessitating invention on my part. Benedict de Fulsham is known to have lent money to a number of people, so it seems likely that the jewels came to him as security for a loan. He, and a Thomas of Tyverton and a Hugh Dalby, the latter two associated with Eleanor, all were arrested, seemingly in connection with Eleanor's theft.

Maud de Clare, Gilbert's widow, did claim to be pregnant for three years, leading the king's council to advise Hugh le Despenser the younger that he should have obtained a writ to have her belly inspected. Whether she suffered from a physical or a psychological condition that caused a false pregnancy, whether she had a real pregnancy that ended badly, or whether she was simply lying is unknown.

Froissart, though not always reliable, reported that Queen Isabella became pregnant by Roger Mortimer. Ian Mortimer, the latter's biographer, has discussed the possibility of such a pregnancy and found it likely. If a child did result from the relationship, he or she has been lost to history.

There is no record of Hugh le Despenser engaging in piracy before his exile, but as his brief career as a pirate was a successful one, it seemed fair enough to allow him the opportunity to gain some practice at it in his youth.

The exact birthdates of Eleanor's ten surviving children are unknown, or at least have yet to be unearthed, but they can be narrowed by records of land grants, marriage agreements, papal dispensations, and the like. The dates I give for their births here, while never deliberately inconsistent with this documentary evidence, are for the most part my own approximations. There is no evidence supporting a posthumous birth for Elizabeth le Despenser in the Tower, but an *in utero* status in January 1327 seemed the most likely explanation for her having escaped the forced veiling of her older sisters. Evidence that Eleanor bore a fifth son who died young can be found in Thomas Stapleton, "A Brief Summary of the Wardrobe Accounts of the Tenth, Eleventh, and Fourteenth Years of King Edward the Second" in the 1836 volume of the journal *Archaeologia*. There the king is stated to have given Hugh le Despenser a cloth of gold for his son; this appears in conjunction with gifts of fine cloth to others that are explicitly stated as being for burial purposes.

In the nineteenth century, what has become known as the "Fieschi letter" was discovered. The letter, supposedly written by a papal notary to Edward III, details the escape of Edward II from Berkeley Castle and his eventual life as a hermit in Italy. The letter and the ensuing debate about the possibility of Edward II's survival has attracted keen interest from historians. Most (along with myself) still believe that Edward II did die in Berkeley Castle (though perhaps not by the horrific means of a red-hot spit), but Paul Doherty and Ian Mortimer have each recently argued with great vigor the case for Edward II's survival.

Caerphilly Castle, where Eleanor was born and where her son Hugh was besieged by her second husband, still stands in Wales. It had become somewhat of a white elephant and was allowed to deteriorate until the nineteenth century, when restoration began. It is now maintained by Welsh Historic Monuments. The great hall that Hugh le Despenser the younger renovated can be hired out for functions, including weddings—a splendid piece of irony given that one of the chief charges against the executed Hugh was that of coming between the king and the queen.

Much of Tewkesbury Abbey escaped destruction during the Dissolution of the Monasteries, though the Lady Chapel, where William la Zouche was buried, was pulled down. Fortunately, Zouche's tomb was one of the few survivals from the Lady Chapel and was moved to nearby Forthampton Court. Eleanor's burial place in Tewkesbury is unrecorded. Hugh le Despenser the younger's tomb with its statues of saints and apostles attracted the disapproval of the Puritans, who stripped it of those ornaments. Minus them and Hugh's effigy, it remains at Tewkesbury. At some point, Abbot John Coles' slab was placed in the space where Hugh's effigy had rested; this odd arrangement still exists.

Edward II was eventually given a canopied tomb at Gloucester Abbey, now Gloucester Cathedral, though it is unclear whether Edward III or the abbey itself funded it. The king's alabaster effigy is beautiful and marvelously detailed.

In one respect, Edward II and Hugh le Despenser triumphed over their enemies—architecturally. The work Hugh and his descendants commissioned at Tewkesbury Abbey is considered a fine example of the Decorated style and can still be seen today, as can the stained glass evidently paid for by Eleanor, including figures of Eleanor's ancestors, brother, and husbands. The nude, kneeling woman watching the Last Judgment in Tewkesbury's east window may be a representation of Eleanor herself. Meanwhile, the offerings accruing from Edward II's burial at Gloucester Abbey enabled the monks there to remodel it extensively, making the abbey a splendid example of the Perpendicular style of architecture. By contrast, nothing remains of Isabella's and Mortimer's tombs or of the buildings that contained them. Isabella's tomb and its neighbors were sold during the Dissolution, and the church in which the queen rested was destroyed in the Great Fire. Mortimer's burial place is uncertain, but Wigmore Abbey, where the regicide was likely buried, was among the many dismantled by another ruthless man with a troubled marital history, Henry VIII.

Apex, North Carolina
June 2005

978-0-595-35959-2
0-595-35959-0